THE 21ST CODEX

The First Realm

DAVID SUMNER

authorHOUSE®

Eccl 7:20

For there is not a just man upon earth, that doeth good, and sinneth not.

Prepare to be enlightened.

AuthorHouse™ UK Ltd.
500 Avebury Boulevard
Central Milton Keynes, MK9 2BE
www.authorhouse.co.uk
Phone: 08001974150

First published by AuthorHouse 03/11/2010

ISBN: 978-1-4490-6217-0 (sc)

Cover photograph and image on page 5, by David Sumner.

Book Cover design by David Sumner.

Back cover photograph of David Sumner by David Batten

This book is printed on acid-free paper.

Acknowledgements:

I thought the easiest thing to do would be to write it as and when people helped me. I apologise in advance if I have forgotten anyone, since so many people did give insight into writing this novel.

Nathan Scott, for sending me down this road in the first bloody place. Ten years on, and I am truly grateful. Secondly, whenever I was not sure, I could reply on Nathan to rip the story to pieces, sending me in a completely different direction.

Roger Underdown, for being my first proof-reader. The one that got it first; and boy, didn't he pay for that. Thank you.

Sean, who had continually encouraged me along the road.

Bill, Sean's father, the most well read man I have ever met. With similar interests, I found his direction in which books I should read or not, invaluable.

A most important thank you goes to my lovely friends **Sue, Sas, Naomi** and ***Lisa*** for believing that I could do this, at a point, when no one else did. And a BIG thank you to

Clare Tanner, for inadvertently pushing me to finish Book One. Not only did she proofread it, but also, our regular lunchtime chats, assisted in the fourth draft and fifth and… helping me with decisions.

Sophie Johnson, for making sure everything was right.

Becks – my cat, who sat on lap when I was trying to work, sneezed when I was trying to concentrate and woke me up when I was too tired. He died (aged 15 ½) at 15.05hrs on the 3rd November 2004 and I deeply miss his interruptions.

Davinia, formerly at Pollinger Ltd for her knowledgeable guidance and enthusiasm.

Thank you to my **Mother**, for being my mother and all the things that that entails with having an adult teenager.

Thank you to my **Dad** for many things and also coming up with the idea for the book cover. A simple idea that was not as easy to execute.

There is one last thank you. To an *angel*; a young lady that I have yet to be formally introduced. Her image is listed under the name Iinnad on my wall, and if it were not for her face, during the hardest of times, I would not have got through this. *I thank you.*

Tradition

Halfway down the road on my journey to finishing this book, my sister and brother-in-law, Michele and Ian asked me if I could be godfather to their first born, Sally. Considering the topic of this project and where my research had taken me, I was surprised to say the least, but gladly accepted.

My gift to Sally was not of silver or cutlery, but something old and something new. A new teddy bear like the one I received from my godfather, and an old sawdust filled monkey.

The monkey belonged to my mother, I acquired it or stolen it, when I was a kid. On passing the monkey to Sally I had started something, a family tradition. My mother was the first born of her generation in our family, as I was of the first born of mine and Sally, of hers.

Traditions are not created in the present, but inadvertently created in the past and kept alive in the present. It would be nice if Sally was to continue it. By pure chance, the toy happened to be a primate, from whence man came.

Keeping tradition alive.

In doing so creates a sense of being apart of something. It is most comforting to be on the inside looking out, than on the outside looking in.

Now, Open Your Eyes

While researching for this book in Carcassonne (September 2001), I was wandering the cobbled streets when I came across the Cathedral of St Vincent. I admired the stonework, as one does with cathedrals, but I decided that the characters would not visit this place. Then I noticed something. The Cathedral of St Vincent was built in the late 13th Century, a Christian place of worship. The upper windows, however, appeared within the framework the Star of David. Over the south entrance was stonework of a floral design of three or four petals per flower.

I ask only that you look beyond the flowers.

Introduction

The Codex

Codex is the name given to a manuscript, which in layman's terms has pages like a book. This distinguishes it from the much older written form of a scroll. Since scrolls were not easy to store, the codex became a much more popular method for the written form around the beginning of the fourth century AD.

There are codices, which are much older, since the book format was invented during the Roman Empire. The Roman's stopped using papyrus scrolls when the Egyptians put a tax on papyrus. At first animal skins were used instead, but they could not be made into scrolls, so pages were made and tied together.

The Council of Nicaea

In AD 325, the heads of the Church from across the known world formed a Council in the town of Nicaea, modern day Turkey, to formulate a system by which Christians could worship in a unified manner.

All the books from the known Bible and others were put forward for debate over whether or not they were suitable in following the doctrine of the Church.

Some of the votes were very close, but at the end of the day a decision had been made. The books, which were voted for, now form the Christian Bible, as we know it today. Those, which were not past, became known as Apocryphal Books.

However, even at the time of the Council of Nicaea, many books had been lost, only to resurface centuries later. With titles like

'The Gospel of Thomas, Lost Gospel of Mary, The Secret Gospel of Mark; The Books of Adam and Eve; Gospel of Truth; The Book of Judas; The Book of Enoch and the Book of Noah; these lost books tell the world a different story.

The Book of Noah

There is no known copy of The Book of Noah in existence. However, there are references to and views on The Book of Noah, written by monks in the early 5th century. These writings include quotes from The Book of Noah, but this is as much as we have. There is no question that the book did exist. Natural disasters such as fires, floods and, in southern Europe, possibly earthquakes have made sure that these valuable books are no longer with us. Man, with his love for conflict and conquest, his destruction of life, structures, property and historical knowledge has as much to do with the demise of such works as nature.

The Book of Enoch

In Ethiopia the Book of Enoch is still used today, accepted as a part of their faith. This book has been known to have existed for a very long time, but as these manuscripts grew old and decayed they were copied by hand, a new. The old copy was stored away and the new took its place. A direct descendant of Robert the Bruce of Scotland retrieved several such books. They now reside at Oxford University, Librairie Nationale de Paris and the Museum of Amsterdam.

It is a very religious book, which has several parallels with the Bible, and speaks chapters with regards to the angels of heaven. However, in the Bible Enoch only appears as the name of an individual and the name of a city and yet there is a whole book dedicated to him. For a being who had prophesised so much; why?

According to the Old Testament Enoch was the son of Cain and father to Irad.

[Gen 4:17 And Cain knew his wife; and she conceived, and bare Enoch: and he builded a city, and called the name of the city, after the name of his son, Enoch.]

[Gen 5:24 And Enoch walked with God: and he was not; for God took him.]

[Jude 1:14 And Enoch also, the seventh from Adam, prophesied of these, saying, Behold, the Lord cometh with ten thousands of his saints,]

Gabriel – Archangel

The name Gabriel appears in the Bible four times; twice in Daniel (Old Testament) and twice in Luke Chapter 1 (New Testament), when he speaks to the Virgin Mary. The Archangel also appeared to the Prophet Mohammad and recited the Holy Qur'an of Islam. Enoch wrote much about the angels and of their relationships that it would not be a surprise if he had written other books on the subject, since lost in time.

Alas, there is no written record of The Book of Gabriel in existence; it may never have existed.

Translated extract from The 21st Codex 'The Book of Gabriel'

The colour of the sky in the middle of the day is what maketh a happy dream. The magnificent sight before the eyes brings a smile to the face of the beholder. All art content. This is what awaits those who walk on Sagun the Third Realm, a place of happiness and joy where worry and anger are forgotten. It is a paradise fit for angels, cherubim and seraphim. But beneath, lies a different world, a dark world unbeknown to those above.

In the midday sun, on the first day of the second cycle, the angle of the light enters the crystals of the Temple of Icea to be broken into an array of colour, like sunbeams in the rain. This only happens but once a year. And to stand in the rays of colour is one moment in time that would never be forgotten, even for an angelic in the heavens.

The Temple of Icea was said to have been built, when even the angels were young, by two lovers destined to be apart. Their tribes would not alloweth them a fruitful relationship, nor even friendly contact. Iceen would leave his tribe at night and place poles in the ground near the edge of the plain. Eayah would awake before sunrise to see the shadows created by the poles from her window and read the message from her distant lover.

Every night Iceen would leave a message and through his instructions they began to dig the foundations for a monument dedicated to their love and existence. And every morning before her tribe awoke; Eayah would gather crystal that layeth in abundance about the plain. When the foundations hath been completed Iceen began to build his labour of love. In the seven years it took him to build the monument; he never laid eyes on his dear love Eayah.

Eayah gathered the crystals and Iceen cut them and put them in place. Believing it to be magic, neither of the tribes dared to watch the monument being constructed in case the powers that be became angry. It was such a beautiful building and all who saw it grow wanted to see it finished.

The tribes knew when it was finished for a plaque was placed by the entrance to the structure with letters ICEA, the first two symbols of the names of these lovers.

The following day both tribes arrived at the site of this beautiful building. It was the first day of the second cycle and neither tribes members had seen its wonder in the midday sun. The tribes stood in awe at the crystal walls and arches, but inside Iceen and Eayah met for the first time in seven years.

In each others arms Iceen and Eayah stood waiting. For outside the tribes had put aside their differences for the moment, until they entered the great crystal arch. The sight of the two lovers from different tribes was too much. In the anger that followed and the violence that ensued Eayah lay mortally wounded by one of her own tribesmen as she tried to protect Iceen. Iceen was also wounded and in pain picked Eayah up in his arms as the midday sun reached that all important angle. The colour has been seen ever since, at the same time every day since, it was seen for the first time by the members of the two tribes.

In the arms of Iceen, Eayah died. For the one being in all his existence, that was meant to see this beautiful moment, had died before she hath the chance. The amazing light struck at the hearts of the tribesmen and they put down their weapons of war. Out of sight of the tribesmen, Iceen carried Eayah through the light beams and out into the daylight. There he rested a moment, the blood seeping from his wounds. With all his strength, he then rose up and looked down at the blood stained crystal, before carrying Eayah into the great plain and away from the two tribes and the building they hath built.

It was not until the colours began to fade did the tribesmen notice that Iceen and Eayah hath gone. A blood trail was followed from the crystal entrance into the great plain, but it ended many days walk from anywhere. That was the last that was ever seen of Iceen and Eayah.

The tribesmen hath both wanted the building that hath been left and so it was agreed that they would share in its beauty and remember the two lovers that built it. But above anything else, remember why. Because of one simple word, love.

Some saith Iceen and Eayah were taken by the angels; others saith that Iceen still carries Eayah across the great plain until the day there is no reason for hatred. The rays from the sun have been broken more times than there art blades of grass on the great plain since that day and still it is a amazing sight and the blood stained crystal at the entrance can still be seen. Rose quartz, they call it. This is the story, as I tell it to ye now; The story of the Temple of Icea.

PROLOGUE

The First Realm.

65th Sunrise – 1st Cycle (26th May) 7436 BC

The sun rose in a vain attempt to warm the surface of the wet new world. Only this morning was to prove a little harder due to the dense cloud cover. Through the reinforced glass window of the deployment bay of the drop-ship Pestilence, Gabriel could feel the first rays touch his face, the only warmth within the craft that hovered high above the saturated rain clouds. Whenever he had the chance, Gabriel would watch the sunrise. There was an importance that he could not fathom, a reason why the beams of warmth meant so much. He sat, in the deep windowsill his back against the panel, and glanced over at the other members of his tower as they prepared for the mission ahead. They had been at war for so long that each mission had blended into the next. Only now things had changed. This mission would be different, for Gabriel had never set foot on this Realm.

The primary rule of the soulcarrier's realm was not to interfere. Gabriel knew the rule, but not the reason why the mission had been given the go ahead or why he had been put in charge. Surrounded by old friends and trusted warriors whom he had fought along side for eons, he still felt alone. He missed his love, Bethany; a casualty of this war. With every new day, the Archangel would think of his lost mate.

Maybe that was why he watched the sun rise? In his hand he held an old rusty key rubbing the rough edges with his thumb. He tightly closed his fingers around it when one of his colleagues approached.

'Are you playing with that lucky charm again?' inquired Jesuel, Gabriel's Second in Command.

Gabriel opened his hand and stretched the cord that the key was attached to as they both stared at it.

'[illegible],' Gabriel answered in his smooth tongue.

'This is the First Realm Gabriel, Island of the Mighty. Speak their tongue.'

'I guess it is, Jesuel,' he repeated in a soft voice.

'You still wear the cord.'

'It's traditional Jesuel. I used to use it to measure, *all things*,' Gabriel replied as he tugged at it. 'I wear one, as do you.'

Jesuel faintly smiled. 'Although I do not carry a key on mine.'

'No… No you don't.'

Time stood still for the close warriors as the two of them watched the golden yellow ball of fire creep into the sky, enhancing the view of the dark saturated clouds.

'Have you ever wondered if we're wrong?' Gabriel pondered. 'That, maybe...'

'No!' declared Jesuel sharply. 'You are destined to become the Guardian of this Realm. It is only fitting that you should be chosen to lead this mission.'

'You place far too much on prophesy, my old friend.'

'But Guardian of this Realm you will be.'

'The Guardian of a Realm I have yet to set foot on. The Guardian of a people we will *not* conquer.'

'It is not our place to conquer.'

'If we're not here to conquer or control, lead or advise, then why are we here?'

The side of Jesuel's mouth raised. 'We are Watchers. We following orders? Now put your lucky charm away. You are beginning to act like your existence depends on it.'

'Who says it doesn't?'

The view outside became obscured as the transport descended into the rain clouds. The vapour condensed into rivulets on Gabriel's window and then made their erratic course downward. The Archangel's finger attempted to follow the route of a single droplet down the glass. In vain, he failed. The droplet outwitted the angelic finger. He tried again *and* again, but he failed.

'Even the simplest of actions can be difficult to predict,' Jesuel quietly pointed out. 'I am talking about the rain drop, not you,' he jested.

'Why is that Jesuel?' Gabriel asked pronouncing every syllable.

'Only He knows.'

***

The rain fell relentlessly, allowing little shelter under tree or rock. Seeping through every crack in nature, the moisture managed to envelop everything.

Why did it always rain when the strangers came? thought the wise old scribe, huddled under the only substantial shelter he could find. With his clothes drenched and his matted grey hair clinging to his face as the water ran down the cracks in his ageing skin, Enoch tried his hardest, to keep his manuscript dry. What possessed this tired old man to keep writing? Why write, when no one around him could read?

Five thousand years before a reed was used on a clay tablet, Enoch would use a stick of charcoal on a piece of cattle hide. Enoch was certainly a man before his time, but so were the strangers visiting and watching his world. It was no coincidence that they were here at this time, for this was fate, a part of Enoch's destiny unbeknown to him. For this wise old scribe was a Seer, a man of visions, who wrote of what, had been, of what was, but more importantly of what was to be. He had stories to tell of wondrous deeds and great battles, but he was not the sort to the scare the little children with his tales. He muttered as he wrote and what he spoke was repeated. His stories *would* be told to others in distant lands, passed from generation to generation around campfires, until mankind had caught up with the old scribe, and had learnt to read and write. Then, and only then, would the stories truly survive.

For many seasons Enoch had sat in his shelter and observed, the Watchers; giants of strength and speed, being's of learning and great skill, as they wandered amongst the people of his world. He had been told that millennia before, God's warriors had broken from the ranks and two thirds of them had left the Heavens. Fallen from grace, they spread their betrayal throughout the other six realms. Only the wet realm, as it had become known, was forbidden. As the war spread, the battle lines became less defined and clandestine operations became more commonplace. They had been fighting each other for a thousand millennia and now before Enoch's eyes, the battle was being played out on his world: the world that the angelic officially called The First Realm. The old man continued to scribble his charcoal words within the confines of his rock refuge. The rain told him the Watchers were near, but he had yet to see any. They would come. They always did.

***

The towering figure of Michael; Archangel, the right hand of God, stood silently in the centre of the control room. From first glance, the low level of light did not seem to help the situation in the communication control room of the drop-ship Pestilence, but Michael felt that it helped his warriors concentrate on the job at hand. The noise and bustle added to the claustrophobic atmosphere as the *eyes* of the operatives prepared to deploy.

'We are up and running,' called Unael. 'Communications are clear.'

'All clear skyward,' informed Wormwood. 'Raab, Elermir, Tansar and Tutrusa'i ready on line?'

All the *eyes*, acknowledged they were ready with clear lines of communication. For every individual on the ground during an operation, there was a counterpart monitoring their every move. However, Gabriel's *eyes,* was not at her post. The rest of the control room awaited the drop and the arrival of their missing team member. Michael grew impatient with the missing cog in the wheel. He knew her way and the distant feelings she showed for her counterpart. The Archangel tolerated her lack of discipline, knowing that some of the worst of angelic made the best warriors.

Trained as a leader of many, Michael had led the largest known force of angelic ever recorded. His stature equalled his reputation and his army accepted their orders with respect and without question. His light grey shoulder length hair was the only identifiable feature in the darkened control room, full of uniformed angelic wearing the garments of life from the Lord of Spirits. Standing almost majestically in the centre of the control room, he closed his eyes in thought, attempting to shut out the outside world.

It was the calm before the storm.

***

In the deployment bay, Gabriel and his tower were ready for the drop. All communications had been verified with Iinnad, his *eyes*, before she disappeared. Gabriel, like Michael, knew Iinnad would not let him down. Even so, this was not the time to vanish. Now, was when he needed her and she was not there. *Why does she do this?* The concern began to show on the angelic's face. Tension and apprehension filled the bay and Iinnad's lack of presence was not helping the situation.

***

The signal that told Michael the storm had started came from an excited shriek from Gabriel's *eyes*. Michael raised his eyelids, his eyes widened, the eyes that had seen so much, to gaze upon an angelic that had chosen female form. She was a young looking energetic brunette with her hair neatly tied back to show her high prominent cheekbones. A small tufted of hair had fallen loose and rested on her forehead as she jumped to face Michael. Her dark eyebrows evenly curved over her captivatingly large brown eyes showed her beauty as her smile stretched across her pale complexion. Her long neck and square shoulders complement her slender frame that was beguilingly obscured by her tunic. Oblivious to her own beauty and her effect on those around her, Iinnad turned swiftly and darted towards to her station. If ever there was a true image of an angel, Iinnad had picked the perfect form.

'Iinnad!' Michael snapped. 'I am not going to ask what you were doing?'

'Good! Because then I don't have to tell you.'

'You could volunteer the information?'

'*Why* Michael? When has an Archangel volunteered information? I follow your example. You're a good teacher.'

'The worst soldier's,' he muttered to himself.

'We are blue! Ready to deploy!' Iinnad burst.

'What is our altitude?' asked Michael.

'Just above the lower cloud cover,' Iinnad responded. 'No one will see us!'

But Michael's attention had already moved to the doorway of the control room. There, in silhouette, stood another Archangel, his back to the doorframe, creating the perfect overpowering profile. His eyes were closed as he listened to the commotion within the nerve centre of the drop-ship. Perfectly still, he waited to be noticed.

'I am taking a risk here, Uriel!' Michael said speaking directly at the silhouette.

The profile's eyes opened. Uriel, instigator of the operation had been noticed. 'I know,' came his soft toned reply and then he was gone.

Spinning on the chair, back to her control station, Iinnad placed a finger over a light on her panel.

'Gabriel!' she called. 'Brace yourself.'

There was a clicking sound over the speaker.

'Thank you Iinnad,' came that soft reply of Uriel's voice and then silence.

Gabriel and Uriel had never seen eye to eye and to make matters worse, this was Gabriel's mission, but Uriel's directive. Both professional in their designated positions, they would ignore their differences and push on with the mission at hand. Iinnad however, disproved of Archangel and made no attempt to hide the fact. She turned back to Michael, looking for an answer to Uriel's behaviour. 'He cut me off.'

Michael's tone changed to that of his station, addressing the entire drop-ship.

'This is not going to be easy although I wish it will be so,' he announced. 'For some, there may not be a return trip, but my presence and that of Uriel should be enough to emphasise the importance of what has to be done here this day.'

'And Gabriel!' Iinnad butted in.

Michael gave Iinnad a stern glance. Realising she was right, he ignored the comment. 'Thank you, now let us get to it.'

The control room returned to its motion and noise.

'Three Archangels on one drop-ship,' Iinnad mumbled to herself. 'Only one of them is to risk his essence, and high almighty forgets to even mention he's here.'

'I hear you,' Michael acknowledged. 'An error on my part, but this is not the time.'

'It never is!' Iinnad huffed.

Michael ground his teeth. *Another time,* he thought, turning to another station. 'Wormwood! Are the other drop-ships in position?' he inquired.

Iinnad popped her head up from her monitors. *Other drop-ships?* She pressed the button connecting her link to Gabriel, but said nothing.

'Yes, Michael,' Wormwood confirmed. 'All drop-ships standing by.'

'And their altitude?'

'They are presently all lower than us. They have better cloud cover. I'm also picking something else up.'

'A ship?'

'No, Michael,' Wormwood stammered. 'It's a comet.'

'Then it does not concern us. Continue with the mission analysis.'

Iinnad glanced over to Wormwood. He lowered one hand below his console out of sight of the others and then proceeded to count in fingers. The beautiful angelic nodded to confirm she had received and understood the message.

Iinnad was a little surprised that she was only given the primary six numbers. There was no need for the finer coordinates. The comet was huge. Its present path would take it passed the First Realm's solitary moon and off into the vastness of space. Michael was right. It need not concern the mission. That wasn't to stop Iinnad from checking. Once satisfied, she got back to the task in hand.

***

In the deployment bay, Gabriel was still seated on the windowsill staring down at the clouds. The circular disk in the centre of the transparent crystal floor was vacant. His colleagues were assembled and prepared to deploy, occupying their disks, six of the fifty-two alcoves in the panelling of the circular bay. Their tunics, with braid tassels around the neckline, had the ability to change their own brightness, for now they were dark in colour, sleeveless with metallic body armour front and back. The scale-like appearance of the body armour between the shoulder blades was to allow access for their wings. On their left forearm, each wore a brace weapon that fired a spinning blade capable of detonating on impact. The brace also incorporated a telescopic shield, which, when activated, extended to two-thirds the length of their body. The shield also carried the colour of their tower, white, the tower of Pestilence. All the angelic carried a sword that retained the memory of its own existence since the day it was forged. Gabriel's tower all wore them across their backs, whereas the other personnel of Pestilence sheathed them on their waist belt. The belt was plain and simple, as were the trousers, loose for agility and the boots, knee length and made of fine thin lightweight material. Ancient weapons, mighty weapons, elegant weapons for an elegant warrior. Communication came in the form of an earpiece, which was only just visible. Gabriel was still in link with Iinnad. He now knew of the other towers and the comet. Information *had* been withheld, but it was too late to question why. Doing so now could put doubt into the heads of his tower. He glanced over at Uriel in a vain attempt to read his mind. *What else was he hiding? What was so important about the target?*

Uriel stood with his back to the wall and his left hand up by his head still holding the com-link switched off, the other on the hilt of his sword.

'This will not easy,' he announced. 'The atmospheric conditions may effect communications.'

'[illegible]?' blurted out Serael. '[illegible]!'

Uriel ignored the angelic warrior.

Jesuel raised his eyebrows at Gabriel. The Archangel understood what his old friend had implied.

'This is the First Realm,' Gabriel declared as he slipped off the windowsill. 'We are to land on the Island of the Mighty. Speak their tongue!'

'Why don't you just say the rain may effect communications?' Serael repeated the question in a stubborn tone. 'It's raining!'

'Stay on the mission,' continued Uriel. 'Acquire the target!'

Ubaviel shook his head and glanced over to Gmial, smiled and mimed Uriel's words. He turned back to Uriel. 'Are you implying we *will* loose our *eyes*?' he questioned.

'I am saying, stay on the mission, whatever happens.'

'[illegible]?' Serael pitched in an attempt to get a rise out of Uriel.

'Serael!' Gabriel snapped. 'Watch your tongue!'

'Gabriel, I apologise. You've proven yourself in battle. I respect you for that and your rank, and I am grateful that I was chosen for this mission. He,' Serael pointed at Uriel. 'He has proved nothing. He was favoured from upon High and …'

'Know your place, Serael!' Gabriel interrupted. 'I know it's only nerves.'

The angelic lowered his head, but kept one eye on Uriel. The other members of the team stayed silent. Like Serael, Korniel and Phul both kept their heads down. Neither cared much for the hierarchy of the angelic council either. Serael was correct in what he had said; Gabriel *was* the exception to the rule. He behaved like one of the warriors of the tower, but then Gabriel used to be one of them and they knew he would never forget that. The last thing that Gabriel's tower wished for was a new commander. They all responded immediately to Gabriel's orders. His control was through respect, not rank and not the way the Council would have liked, the difference between being given the power and earning it.

'Any questions?' Uriel inquired.

'I have one,' Gmial piped up. 'Phul, as *supreme* Lord of Waters, why does it rain on every bloody realm we visit except Sagun?'

The angelic laughed.

Phul didn't want the attention. 'Because it doesn't have a moon,' he sulked.

'Gmial you forget, Phul is also Lord of the Powers of the Moon,' added Jesuel.

'Just trying to lighten the mood.'

'At my expense,' Phul chipped in.

'Always Phul, always.'

'How come you get so many powers?' Serael inquired sarcastically.

'Anyway, it did rain on the Third Realm of Sagun,' Phul said ignoring Serael and correcting Gmial.

'I know, but not like the wet realm,' Gmial replied.

'The First Realm's moon is very powerful,' Phul explained pompously. 'That could explain why there is more rain.'

'Or more of us?' Ubaviel said expressing concern. 'The more of us, the more it rains.' He shrugged his shoulders. 'I'm just saying…'

'It could be strong gravity,' inserted Serael. 'Will that effect us in any other way?'

Uriel shook his head. 'I doubt it.'

Serael shook his head shocked that Uriel had acknowledged what he had said. The shock was short lived as the lights in the deployment bay dimmed slightly.

'Heads up!' the disliked Archangel snapped.

Gabriel still said nothing. Their target was still unknown to him, or what he was to do on acquiring it. That order was to be given once it had been acquired. Nothing about the mission appeared to fit. *Why had Uriel requested such a force?* All four towers were being called upon for one target, the approaching comet, the strong gravity of the solitary moon; nothing felt right. Michael had already dismissed several of these factors. However, Gabriel's mind was fresh to the possibilities. The Archangel lost his concentration when he heard his name being called over the drone of the engines.

'Gabriel! GABRIEL! I know I am right!' Uriel shouted.

He slowly lifted up his head and walked towards the Archangel. In a soft, but stern voice he replied. 'We're not supposed to interfere!'

Gabriel then turned his back on Uriel, not even awaiting a response and positioned himself in the centre of the bay as he watched the clouds pass below. Serael's concerned eyes darted from angelic to angelic. Something unnerved him.

'Question!' he raised a finger.

Gabriel lifted his chin.

'We're not opening?' gasped Serael.

'No we're not,' laughed Gmial. 'Come on Serael, you've done it before.'

'*Yeah!*' he said out of breath. 'But, not from this height.'

'Once you're comfortable with your descent; transform,' Gabriel said reassuringly nodding his head.

'Before you hit the ground,' Phul added with a chuckle.

Gabriel gave the tower a stern glance, since Uriel was still amongst them. They withheld their laughter, with difficulty.

'Keep your wings behind you,' Jesuel instructed. 'Then spread them slowly.'

Serael nodded.

'It's a walk in Eden,' Phul piped up with confidence.

'Spread as late as you can, drop quickly,' Gabriel ordered. 'We'll be on the ground in moments rather than later. I have a feeling time is not on our side.'

'Gabriel is right!' Uriel stated, to the surprise of the others.

'Standby!' Gabriel snapped.

'Let's do this!' Ubaviel blurted out.

The lights changed to an eerie blue. Uriel stared at the Archangel in the centre of the bay and to his dismay realised… 'You have link to coms!'

Gabriel replied with a smirk.

'You have link to coms!' Uriel's eyes wide.

'Don't hold information from me again, Uriel.' With a glint in his eye and the look of acknowledgement from the other tower members, he pressed a clasp on his armour. The disk in the floor became a hole and Gabriel dropped through into the clouds below. Korniel then vanished. Serael, the third warrior, nervously disappeared. The fourth, Ubaviel dropped out of the bay followed by Gmial. Phul was next. Jesuel looked puzzled.

He called to Uriel. 'You have two ears, you had better listen! Gabriel is right! We should not interfere,'

'Destiny awaits, Jesuel!' he replied over the deafening drone.

'For all of us?'

For the first time, there was doubt in Uriel's mind; it seeped through to his face.

Open Your Eyes.

I

The First Realm.

02.00hrs Friday 13th July AD 2001 Eastern Standard Time EST

A shooting star passed overhead in the night sky; traveling on a journey that might end in a million years or tomorrow, who knew? It passed behind the rain clouds as they gathered over the US capital city below. As the first drops fell from the clouds, a young couple took refuge in an alleyway just off the main street. In the shadows, with the rattling corrugated iron above them, they kissed, out of sight from the world. A cat joined them as the drainpipes creaked, the safety of its window ledge now wet and cold. The young lovers didn't mind sharing their space, they didn't even notice, immersed in each other. In a break, to catch her breath, the elegant dark skinned girl from Atlanta spotted another shooting star.

'Make a wish,' she ordered her secret lover.

'I wish my father wasn't such a bastard and let me see you,' he replied in a very strong English accent. 'I wish that we could live somewhere different. Anywhere!'

'Make a wish, only one; and keep it a secret. It doesn't work otherwise… and what do you mean somewhere different? It's only been six and half months.'

'All this sneaking around; it feels like two years.'

She jokingly jabbed him in the ribs. In response, he just held her a little more tightly. Another shooting star appeared.

'Sean, look!' spinning her boyfriend around to face the star. '*Now* make a wish,' she whispered.

'It's bright isn't it?' he replied.

'*Make a wish*!'

The star reduced in speed through the rain washed skyline. Instead of disappearing behind the clouds it was still visible as it approached the capital. Down and down it came, as though it were guiding itself. This was no star. The bright ball of white light descended vertically, so slowly that it appeared to hover. The couple ignored the cascade of water from the sky and stepped out into the centre of the alleyway to watch the light settle some two hundred yards away. On touching the ground, the light began to lose its brightness, becoming just an ember of what it once was. Then it slowly moved down the length of the alleyway towards the couple.

'That wasn't my wish,' he expressed.

'That isn't a shooting star,' she added.

Transfixed by the light, even though it was still fading, the young lovers didn't move. They could not; something was holding them there. Within the bright sphere they could see the shape of a person, a woman. However, the woman was not in the light. The light was emanating from her. Every aspect of her body glowed from her fingernails to each hair follicle. She shimmered with luminescence. Sean stared without blinking; his field of vision was trained on the woman's curves as he followed them up and down her body. At the end of the day, he was male and she was a bare woman. Then he stated the obvious, only one word.

'Naked.'

His girlfriend grabbed his hand and took one-step back tugging Sean's arm to follow. He didn't respond. The light had now completely gone and before them stood a naked, mature, but elegant woman. Sean was transfixed by her true blue eyes and jet-black hair. She stood there in the rain as though it were completely natural, in an alleyway at two in the morning. This was strange even for D.C. Sean's girlfriend took one brave step forward if only to calm her fear and try to understand why she would be frightened. She tried to speak, but the words blurted out in a slight stutter.

'Hi, my name is Naomi, can we help you?' she politely asked, not even knowing why.

Sheet lightning flashed through the heavens, but it was too far away to hear the thunder. Clear droplets of water glistened in the streetlight as they ran off the naked woman's hair following the contours of her body to the ground. Occasionally, they would take a wrong turn and end up at her finger tips then drip from her unusually long nails into the shallow river that was forming in the alley.

In the blink of an eye she moved. Without warning, quick, silent and extremely violent, her right hand rose, her fingertips making contact with Sean's windpipe as her fingernails, protruding further and made contact with his spine. Naomi turned to flee. The razor sharp talons from her attackers other hand cut her skin neatly around the waist just below her cropped top. She couldn't run. The jabbing pain in the back of her neck prevented it. She tried to look down, but couldn't. She didn't want to be the next victim. As the pain in her neck increased; she noticed that her feet were now not even touching the ground. The naked woman threw Naomi against the nearest building. She then turned her attention to Sean, his blood soaked clothes looked black in the streetlight. Drawing her hand down through his body the naked woman ripped Sean apart, tossing him to the ground like discarded clothing. Attempting to focus, Naomi staggered to her feet bleeding from the waist. The strike from one nail down her front cut her chest and released the clasps on her undergarments. She could not fight back; she could barely stand. Naomi felt herself being spun around to face the building, and then a hand touched her neck again sending a shiver down her spine. Only this time, it slid down her back removing the clothes and the buttons on her shirt. She tried to grab it, but was too slow. With straight fingers the naked woman punched her twice in the back, propelling her against the brick wall and into the nearby dustbins. Each punch left a bleeding wound of five holes where the nails had incised her flesh. In her underwear and petticoat, Naomi lay in the rain near death. Her blood dripped from the attacker's nails and was diluted by the rain. Stepping over her victims, the woman wrote a message in their blood on the wall under the shelter. It was a simple message, albeit in a script very few could read.

When she had finished she stepped back into the alleyway, tilted her head slightly allowing the shower to wash her face and to view her artwork.

‘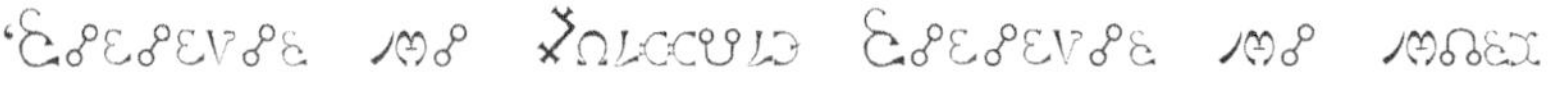 ,’ she read to herself, the crimson symbols that she had written. '[illegible].'

The murderer then picked up Naomi's soaked clothes and stepped into the skirt. She straightened the blouse to conceal the minor bloodstain, and looked down at her bare feet. The woman shrugged her shoulders, smiled to herself and then peered up and down the length of the alleyway. There was no movement from any of the nearby windows. Her actions had gone unnoticed since her victims had made little noise. She briefly crouched with her palms face down and dipped her hands in her victim's blood. Ignoring the bodies she walked down the alley into the shadows towards the main street of the city and let out a high-pitched blood-curdling scream. Then she was gone.

***

02.36hrs Friday 13th July AD 2001 EST

The crowd roared with laughter in the tiny bar, just off Capital Hill, in the early hours. The U.S. capital was quiet that night, except for the early deliveries and a solitary dustcart that passed the noise that overflowed from the partygoer's regular haunt. Doug, the landlord, had arranged a lock in for his prize customers.

'Everybody should celebrate their last days of freedom,' he shouted.

The private function comprised of agents from the most secretive *known* government agency, the NSA (National Security Agency). It was a time for the agile and alert men to relax and be merry. Rarely did these secret men interact socially in such a large group, but then it was a stag party for one of the younger new recruits. The traditional stripper had already removed the groom's trousers and dignity, to the point of never possessing shame again and that left only one thing. Drink. The muscular men pushed and bustled, joked and laughed, as they fought for the barman's attention. With one exception, sitting at the far end of the bar was a lean black gentleman in a smart grey suit, his tie slightly loose and his hair so short that he appeared bald. The forty-one year old finished his bottle of Beck's beer, placed it on the damp counter, stained with years of spillage, then he slid it through the alcohol and parked it next to the other empty. He picked up the two white bottle caps, eyed the logos, to check they were his and placed them in his pocket.

'Hey Cole!' cried the lucky man who was the centre of attention.

The drunk staggered over to the quiet agent.

'Congratulations Nick!' clearly spoke the seated man.

Nick stood to attention with a drunken smile on his face and gave Cole a sharp nod, completely throwing him off balance, the bar jumped to the rescue. Now supported, Nick stood up once again and faced the seated agent.

Cole smiled; he knew what was coming.

'I always wanted to ask, now I'm drunk I don't care! Why do you keep the caps?' Nick sang almost in rhythm.

'Everyone has a habit, I guess this one's mine.'

'What d'you do with'em?'

'I have an ice bucket in the kitchen.'

'And when the bucket's full?' laughed Nick.

'Buy another bucket.'

'You, my friend,' claimed the drunk slapping Cole's back. 'And the weirdest agent in the NSA that I have pleasured... have had the pleasure of being trained by.'

Still laughing, he lost his balance again and dropped his glass. His teacher was off the chair before Nick could blink. He steadied the merry man and placed his glass back in his hand.

'He caught my drink!' the groom announced. 'You see that? You got the fastest reflex... reflexes I ever seen too... seen. You know what I mean?'

'Nick, I've got to make a move. I already have a wife to go home to. Good luck tomorrow, she's a lucky girl and you're a lucky guy. Enjoy the rest of the night.'

'Thanks man!'

Eric, the best man, joined the two agents.

'Hi Cole,' Eric interrupted. 'Can I take him off your hands?'

'I'd appreciate that, I have to make a move,' Cole straightened his jacket. 'I'll see you tomorrow.'

Eric helped Nick to rejoin the crowd as the men waved Cole out of the bar and into the cool night air. In the street, the muffled sounds from the bar became faint as the agent walked around the block to his car. He double-checked the two bottle caps in his pocket. He had eaten well that night and with only two beers he would be safe to drive. The last thing he wanted was to find a cab at this early hour. The rain had already made its presence known; now only a fine spray, the water-cooled his face as he crossed the car park. In the night, only his footsteps could be heard, then silence as he stopped by the Ford salon.

Suddenly his chest vibrated and the two-tone bleep from his pocket broke the silence. He had been paged.

'Jesus!' he jumped as he read the message. 'You've gotta be kidding. She's going to kill me.'

The agent got out of the drizzle and started the engine. He took out his mobile phone and noticed the time, 02:43hrs. He could not phone his wife now and tell her work had just called. Instead he called the office. It had been a long time since he had been bleeped like this. Garrett, his boss must have a serious problem to call at this hour.

***

03.03hrs Friday 13th July AD 2001 EST

The police forensic team were working as fast as possible to avoid the loss of any evidence. Rain was their worst enemy. The loss of evidence was their worst nightmare. Agent Cole sat in his car, sheltered, out of their way and watched.

'Leave the police to do their job,' he murmured to himself. 'Don't get involved unless you have too. So why am I here?'

He bit his top lip as he viewed the scene of panic. Uniformed officers struggled with sheets of polythene to protect vital areas of evidence from the elements as the investigators crouched beneath collecting as many clues as possible. All the crime scene investigators could do was salvage the few remains and pray that they had retrieved everything that the downpour had not taken. The camera's flashgun would help capture what might have been lost. The bulb popped, illuminating the horror. The agent sat back in his seat, he could see the whole crime scene as he patiently waited for the photographs to be taken that would eventually end up in his file along with the other elements of the case. As he watched, he could also hear on the police radio. His I.D. lay next to the radio, open for all to see, he was happy to sit and wait. At least he was out of the rain. Cole didn't want the job. This was not a job for the NSA; the case fell within the jurisdiction of the police and the FBI. To the experienced agent, his presence and the situation was a joke. *Why had he been called?* He could not fathom it.

An adaptor was plugged into the cigarette lighter. The duel connecter split the power line, one to his mobile phone, which lay on the passenger seat, wired to the slim black laptop computer also connected to the lighter. The portable technology's hard drive hummed as it downloaded Cole's e-mails. He was not one of the techno generation, but in this day and age it had been forced upon him. He could not deny that it helped, although it did confuse him from time to time. The police photographer's camera was a high-resolution digital, which within minutes would have the images traveling the airwaves and wires of the government agencies. In turn, the horrific pictures would arrive on Cole's screen.

Yet another plastic covered peaked capped police officer wandered over to his car. The officer spotted the I.D. on the dashboard. Cole would read the man's lips.

'Agent Richard Lawton Cole, NSA,' he muttered before waving him away. *Only doing his job,* he thought. *Maybe they thought the murderer had come back to watch the crime scene. Sometimes they do, but very few would put up with this rain especially at 03:30 in the morning.*

Thanks to the rain, Cole was not holding out much hope of the local police or FBI finding anything. Not immediately, at any rate. The downpour had already dashed their chances of that. The ambulance had left with the girl a few minutes earlier, the sirens blaring. Luckily the photographer spotted she was still alive. That said much! If she survived, she could at least identify her attackers. If Cole were to be positive, Garrett would be in luck. Hopefully for Cole, it would help him in apprehending the killer. For the politicians, it would help answer questions that would avoid a possible scandal. Cole guessed it possible that in the panic to gather evidence, nobody noticed one of the victims was still alive, albeit, barely. Before the ambulance left, the paramedics twice had to jump start her heart.

Cole could have been negative, but it wasn't in his nature. It would be easy to say: 'wait for the police to find something'. The only evidence that had survived the rain thus far was the writing on the wall. That was the key. Cole knew there was a reason behind it. To crack the mysterious writing in blood would reveal much. *The killer wanted to be caught. Wasn't that what all criminologists said? Find the connection between the boy's father and the writing, and it's home to bed. So why was Cole put on this case? Was it solely because of the politics of the situation?* His success rate at solving the bizarre occult cases and, obviously being an agent of the NSA meant there was security. All of these questions raced through his head, but he could not find an answer that gave him peace of mind. He knew he had a reputation at the agency of successfully solving every case assigned. His open mindedness had assisted him in laterally thinking his way out of dried up leads in the past. Although, a blind eye had been turned to the fact that some of the files sat on the shelf for quite a while. He always pursued them to their conclusion and on paper that looked good. He also believed in total secrecy when on a case for obvious reasons, at least until it was closed, and sometimes even then.

'Bloody politics!' Cole mumbled to himself in the quiet of his car.

He had never been into politics; in fact Cole's problem was that he could not be subtle, even when he tried. The political side of the case lay with Sean Grayson the only son of the British Ambassador to the United States. The political bombshell was the barely alive colored girlfriend or prostitute, considering the state of dress, or your perspective. Cole didn't acknowledge the latter; he was near perfect for the job.

The agent accepted from the outset that the girl was most likely the girlfriend with a disapproving father on either, or both sides. *Why else would a rich white boy be down a back alley with a colored girl?* This was Cole thinking positively. He was also in a mixed marriage himself and had been down that road himself.

He had been the black college drop out who was about to join the army when he met and fell in love with a rich white girl. She was about to start university and the world was at her feet. Seeing her was easy once she had a room in halls at university, but in the summer months things were different. Her father still did not know, as they sneaked out of her house for some time together. Then there was the getting caught fiasco: he shuddered at the memory. Although, things did work out, eventually. The proof lay in a recent photo of a pregnant white woman on the flip side of his I.D. Rebecca, once his partner within the agency, now his wife, lying in an empty bed every night knowing exactly what Cole was up to, because she'd been there. He knew he was being used like a puppet.

'We'll get our best men on the job Mr. Ambassador,' he spoke to himself. He held a little self-satisfaction in that thought. The agency would not have called him out knowing Rebecca was seven months pregnant unless it was genuinely important.

The flashgun was off again. Pop. Pop. Pop. *Give it a break,* thought Cole. The strobe reflecting on the wet surfaces was just as bad, on his tired eyes, as when the photographer had been facing him. The rain began to pound the ground crashing on the Ford like steel ball bearings being poured out of a bucket. Cole closed his eyes and tried to rest just for a while. The thumping rain and the flashing light through his eyelids turned his thoughts of Rebecca to memories of a time when things were not so pleasant, before he was recruited into the NSA.

***

Iraq – 01.15hrs 04th February AD 1991 (Local Time)

Greenwich Mean Time (GMT) +4

Stuck in a wadi, behind enemy lines during operation Desert Storm, Captain Cole was alone. Alone, except for the corpses of his entire unit that were scattered around him. They had reached the extraction point, he was certain of it. The GPS (Global Positioning System) couldn't be wrong, but there was no pick-up. During the long wait, they had been discovered and what started as a basic contact turned into an all out firefight. Darkness had been their ally, until the

Iraqi soldiers brought in reinforcements to scour the area. The American Special Operations Unit had tried to avoid contact with the enemy, but things were getting desperate. In their last contact, the unit had inflicted some heavy casualties on the regular Iraqi troops and now the enemy had turned to a different strategy. The Iraqi artillery had begun shelling the area before the advance of their troops, not knowing the numbers they were up against. One man! His saving grace was an air strike, which had so far held the Iraqi troops at bay. It was only by chance that the pilot had seen the enemy movement on the ground and was still carrying ordinance back from an abortive mission elsewhere on the map. The plane had now gone and Captain Cole was alone, once again.

From behind him, over the ridge of the wadi, clambered a soldier. Dressed in black and of European appearance, he raised his weapon and pointed it at Cole. Cole had already raised his. Neither was ready to fire, neither wanted to alert the Iraqi soldiers as to their exact location. Three more soldiers in dark dress joined the first. The last man over the ridge laughed and waved into the sky at the artillery barrage and then down at Cole's men. His expression changed.

'And we thought we started all this,' he jested.

'You're English?' stated Cole, surprised.

'And you're not!' replied the soldier.

The first soldier stepped forward facing up to Cole.

'What are you doing two hundred and fifty-five miles behind enemy lines?'

'Waiting for evac!' Cole replied. 'And you?'

The third soldier, a half-caste in appearance who could clearly be mistaken for an Iraqi, was peering out over the wadi. He looked down the slope to Cole.

'You give information too freely,' he stated with a perfect English accent. 'Lucky for you, we're not your enemy.'

Spotlights appeared in the night sky. Anti-aircraft artillery opened up almost simultaneously. Overhead the powerful engines of the USAF rescue helicopter could be heard and another air strike that would silence the anti-aircraft artillery. Captain Cole's pick up had arrived.

'Your ride?' shouted the leading soldier. 'Marines! We are leaving!'

Over the ridge went the first three soldiers. The fourth gave a quick joke of a salute and shook his head.

'We're not Marines!' he said. 'He's just a Cameron fan.'

Cole tried to laugh, but he didn't get the joke.

'We were *never* here!' the mystery soldier added as he joined his comrades in the barrage lit night.

'I wish I wasn't,' Cole replied in a whisper, but the soldier had already vanished over the dunes.

A light armored shell landed nearby. The explosion knocked Cole to the ground. He was in pain and found it difficult to breathe. The spray of sand struck his face, so he held his breath. Only when the sand settled, did he gasped for air.

'God! Please get me out of this alive!' he shouted to himself.

His voice was drowned by the noise of the rotor blades and the sand being blasted in every direction. The Captain lay there very still, with the sound beating in his ears. He had noticed he was bleeding from the blast that knocked him to the ground. Something hit his boot. No, something *kicked* his boot. He opened his eyes.

'We gotta live one!' screamed an American voice shining a flashlight in his face.

***

Washington DC – 03.58hrs Friday 13th July AD 2001 EST

Through the window a flashlight glared into his eyes, imprinting the circular white on his retina. He could hardly see out of the car as the rainwater flooded his blurred vision.

'And get that out of my face!' he shouted to the police officer outside.

The officer lowered his flashlight and tipped his cap. The rain was falling harder than ever now. He moved his head slowly around and his neck clicked.

'Sorry Sir!' the officer called. 'I have been told to inform you that the language guy is here. A specialist in...' Motioning that he didn't have a clue. 'He's all yours Sir!'

Cole nodded slowly and sat up straight in his seat.

'I didn't request a language specialist in anything,' he howled.

He clicked his neck from side to side again and stretched a little. Through the windscreen he could barely see the well-dressed gentleman crouched and staring at the writing on the wall. He seemed oblivious to anything around him including the deluge. Oblivious to everything except the body of Sean Grayson. Cole watched the man as he scribbled in his notebook and searched around the crime scene. *What is he looking for? There's nothing left. The writing was on the wall.* Not finding anything, the man turned his attention back to it.

'Come on, for God's sake! Clouds can only hold so much,' Cole said to himself, preparing for the moment he would step out into the wet. He looked down at the laptop and rubbed his finger across the mouse pad. The computer awoke from its standby mode and the screen illuminated the interior of the car. Cole had five e-mails, all of which related to the case.

The first was from Rebecca, the important one: Garrett woke me. Tried to phone but your mobile must be plugged into the computer. I'm ok. Get home as soon as you can. Love you Becks xx

The second was also from Rebecca: If you need my help call me. Don't forget your phone. Love you Becks xx

'I love you too,' Cole whispered.

The third was from Garrett: COLE. THE FBI HAVE ALREADY Got images of the writing . sent it to every agency. universities – museums – Langley recognizes bits, but not sure. fbi has found some one who cann help. There picking him now. Talk to him.

'Use the spell check Garrett,' the agent said as though his boss could hear. 'I thought I was bad?'

The fourth e-mail was from the FBI: Agent Cole, The style of glyphs are extremely rare. We have sent out the images, since we are at a loss. Assistance has been offered, but many sources are also at a lost. Every specialist in the field of the occult and ancient studies has recommended one man to us. He has lectured at universities all over the world. We understand that you have been instructed to be involved with this case and therefore I would recommend talking with him. I shouldn't have to tell you to tread lightly, (with information), since he is an outsider, but luckily he was in town. He has also agreed to visit the scene and I would like to take this...

'La la la,' Cole added. 'Give it to the FBI, you guy's don't hang about. What happened to inter-agency one-upmanship? This is an important case, a career breaker.'

The fifth e-mail must have taken ages to download. It consisted of all the crime scene photographs that Cole had just witnessed being taken.

'Now that's impressive! You can't knock new technology!'

Agent Cole switched off the computer and placed it in the glove compartment, along with the power adapter and put the mobile in his pocket, checking the time before he did so. 04.05hrs. He had been in Iraq for about forty minutes. Too long.

Within that time, the crime scene had been washed clean. The police had as much as they were going to get. All that remained was the bloodstained glyphs on the brick wall under the corrugated shelter.

Cole stepped up beside the crouched man. The expert, breathing through his nostrils, took a long deep breath on the damp night air, but took no notice of Cole as he concentrated on the glyphs scrawled across the faded brick wall. A flash went off to their left. Cole raised his hand to shield his eyes; the expert had not noticed it, deep in deliberations.

'I think you've done enough, don't you?' Cole asked the photographer as he flipped open his I.D. enforcing his suggestion.

'Yes Sir!'

'And I think somebody should remove the Ambassador's son before someone gets their butt kicked!' Cole added to the nearby police officer. The agent calmly turned his attention back to the crouched man. 'Sorry about the urgency,' Cole apologized slowly. 'The FBI didn't want to miss anything in the rain and when they heard you were in town, well we didn't want to miss the opportunity.'

'That is fine,' said the man in a familiar voice. 'I understand. The situation was explained to me and I offered to come here.'

'At four in the morning? You offered?'

Cole noticed the photographer move away from the two men, attempting in vain to protect his equipment from the shower. He motioned to the coroner's assistant who stepped forward and swiftly prepared to move the body of Sean Grayson. Behind the police line there was very little in the way of the crowd, which would normally appear at the scene of a murder. Four o'clock in the morning and the driving rain had put a stop to that. The media still pushed and shoved for a clear shot of the crime scene with their respective anchormen and women giving the camera their all. And behind all of the bustle and mayhem appeared a polished black Jaguar with diplomatic number plates. The Ambassador had arrived.

The specialist, still crouched, his back to the scene, watched using peripheral vision as Sean's body was placed in a black body bag and laid on the gurney. Fingers crossed, Cole waited impatiently for the body to be removed. He knew that the Ambassador would stop to view his son and hopefully *not* come over to talk or demand. This political puppet situation was the price of his success in the agency whether he liked it or not. His expression changed to that of a slight smile as the Ambassador stopped by the gurney and asked to see his son. Within moments of a nod of confirmation, Cole's smile had gone. The Ambassador headed straight towards him with the Chief of Police in tow and a representative of the FBI. Police Chief Rosier was an elegant looking woman in a trouser suit. The dark colors blended with her hair and her face harsh, almost striking was definitely displeased. Before Cole could say anything the Ambassador had started his unusual line of questioning.

'Do you carry a gun officer?'

'Agent!' replied Cole.

'FBI?'

'NSA,' corrected Cole.

The Ambassador calmed down a little, realizing that the authorities had already taken the trouble of putting some of their best people on the case. The Ambassador started again.

'I never always saw eye to eye with my son, but then, how many fathers do?'

'I'm sorry for your loss,' Cole replied not knowing what else to say.

'This probably isn't very diplomatic of me, but do you carry a firearm, Agent of the National Security Agency?'

Cole opened both sides of his jacket to reveal a pair of shoulder holsters housing a Berretta 9mm automatic pistol in each. The Ambassador looked surprised by the amount of firepower carried by one individual, but not as surprised as the Police Chief or the FBI, who both thought it excessive to an extreme.

'Does that amount of firepower mean you miss a lot?' asked the Ambassador sarcastically in a stern voice.

The FBI agent smirked.

'No Sir!' replied Cole. 'I hit twice as much.'

Chief Rosier stepped forward as Cole closed and buttoned his jacket. She leant over to whisper in the Ambassador's ear. The Ambassador lowered his head and the Police Chief stepped back. Only his eyes rose to meet Cole's.

'You find the man that murdered my son and you use that firepower,' ordered the Ambassador as he tapped Cole's jacket. 'You use that firepower and you fucking kill him!'

With his demand made, the Ambassador spun on his heel and marched back towards the car, the police clearing a path to avoid a clash with the media. Just visible through the open door of the vehicle was Sean's deeply distraught mother. Angry parents demanding retribution, in Cole's opinion, but showing no concern whatsoever for Sean's girlfriend.

If it were possible, the rain fell even harder. Cole stood with Chief Rosier as the Ambassador's entourage left. She cleared her nose and throat, and turned to the specialist as he stood up. Her raised finger of authority pointed in his direction.

'I… I know you were brought in by him,' she stated referring to the FBI agent standing behind her. 'But I want to know whatever you find.' The finger then turned to Cole. 'As for the Ambassador, he's stressed and angry, you understand?' she explained, trying to clear her nose in the rain. 'I hear you're good. I don't want you to take the Ambassador's instructions literally. Are we clear?'

Cole held his tongue. Once Chief Rosier was satisfied her demand for the information and her instructions were clearly understood she left the two men standing in the rain. The majority of the media circus had followed the Ambassador. The few that had remained finally left with Rosier and the FBI. The alleyway became quiet, what you would expect for that time in the morning, all that could be heard was the noise of the storm as the rain pelted the cars and corrugated shelter. The two faced each other eye to eye, but specialist's attention was elsewhere. They both knew they would be working together in one form or another. Cole got in first.

'The name's Cole.'

The specialist stared through the agent.

'The name's Cole!' he repeated, hoping to get a response the second time.

'Gabriel!' he snapped out of his trance.

'Are you with us?'

'Yes, Agent Cole,' Gabriel answered slowly as he focused.

'Gabriel? As in Archangel?'

'Exactly,' Gabriel replied, hiding a smile, but not the truth.

'I'm sorry you had to see all this,' Cole broadly spoke as he motioned to the blood washed alleyway.

'I have seen worse.'

'Only combat's worse,' Cole added.

Iinnad's voice screamed at him from a distant memory. 'Gabe, fly out! We'll cover you. Evac was going to be a hover anyway.'

***

The First Realm. 65th Sunrise – 1st Cycle (26th May) 7436 BC

'Iinnad! Land Pestilence now! Do you here me?'

Gabriel looked over to Jesuel. 'No it wasn't,' he shouted into his link. 'It was a pick up. We can't fly out! You have to land! Get me the *hell* off this realm!'

Gabriel felt a hand grab him over his shoulder and pull him hard to the ground. Trying hard to keep hold of Enoch as he crashed into the mud, Gabriel realised it was Serael as his finger pointed back the way they had come.

'Hostiles!' he screamed.

Before Gabriel could turn to see, the rain in front of his eyes vaporised into a streak of light as it entered Serael's left side. He dropped his sword. Gabriel took his hand, trying to pull him to cover as a second, then a third bolt of light hit him. Serael died there and then, falling back into the mud. Jesuel repeatedly fired his brace from his vantage point in the direction that the deadly bolts had come from.

***

From the forest, several bolts of light singed leaves as they left the trees. The first, clipped Gabriel's wing. The second released its energy into a panel beneath a window on Pestilence as it landed. It just missed Phul's head as he ducked into the doorway. He immediately spun around to return fire as fast as he possibly could. Enoch began to climb the metal steps. The third blast hit Ubaviel in the centre of the chest as he covered the old man's ascent. The angelic took the full impact of the blast, falling backward pushing the primitive into the steps. He then crashed forward into the sodden sand of the estuary, followed by the soulcarrier. Dead, Enoch knew that the Watcher had given his life for his. It saddened the old man, but gave him the strength to survive; otherwise all the death would be in vain. Gabriel saw Ubaviel fall. His motionless body lay in the dark sand obscured slightly by the spray of the downdraft of Pestilence's engines.

***

Washington DC – 04.21hrs Friday 13th July AD 2001 EST

Very quietly Gabriel agreed. 'Yes, only combat is worse.'

He turned back to the bloodstained wall and stepped forward before crouching down again to finish up his notes. Cole stepped up beside him under the shelter, hands in pockets, trying to salvage the last vestiges of warmth as he glanced between the wall and Gabriel's notepad.

'You Okay?' Cole inquired after the pale Gabriel.

'I am fine. Thank you.'

'I never used to think about it,' Cole prompted. 'But now, with a kid on the way, I wonder why we kill at all.'

'I think about it all the time,' muttered Gabriel as he concentrated on his scribbles.

'I can provide you with photos.'

'I prefer to sketch. I remember more this way, thank you.'

'So tell me! Is it writing?'

'Yes.'

'You know the language? Because the people at my end don't.'

'I know the language.'

'What's it say?'

'Now, there lies the problem,' uttered Gabriel as he closed his notepad and stood up facing the agent. 'To see a language written does not mean you can read it.'

'The FBI spoke to several specialists from numerous museums and universities. They all offered to help. Ancient Studies at Langley even they got stuck.'

'All of this and so quickly,' Gabriel replied.

'Computers… and the fact that a diplomat's son died makes the top of the case pile. It may be a coincidence, but everyone the FBI spoke to mentioned you, and that you happened to be in the country, eastern seaboard to boot.'

'Are you the sort of man that believes in coincidences Mr. Cole?'

Cole glared at the specialist. '*Agent* Cole! Do you know the language?'

'This is probably the most ancient of languages. It is angelic script. And I would need my books to complete the text.'

'Angelic script? As in, angels with wings and feathers?'

Gabriel gave an awkward smile, not quite sure what to say. He was not going to lie, but he could not tell the truth either.

'The angels that work for God?' Cole unknowingly rescued him.

'Yes, angels that work for God.'

'But what can you make out?'

'The symbols are angelic like I said. However, the words they form are not.'

'Langley got that far,' the agent bluffed. 'They identified a couple of the symbols, but that's it.'

'Ancient Kurdish, possibly...?'

'Northern Iraq?'

'Or southern Turkey, take your pick. I did say *ancient* Kurdish, possibly… Akkadian? In layman's terms, what you see is a puzzle,' Gabriel explained. 'It would be the equivalent of say, using Roman characters as the symbols, but instead of the words being in Latin, they are in French or German or both.'

'So the symbols, these *characters* are in angelic script, but the words are ancient… whatever… and you're not quite sure what?' Cole confirmed just to make sure he understood.

'Exactly,' Gabriel nodded.

'Who'd know this stuff?'

'Apart from myself?' he paused in thought. 'Possibly a few university professors and a group… you do not want to know about.'

'What! What are you talking about?'

Gabriel kept quiet.

'What are you talking about?' Cole repeated louder.

'Nothing,' the angelic said as he lowered his head.

'You saying you know who did this? Because if you are I…'

'No!' Gabriel stated calmly, but firm. 'I do not know who did this. What I do know, is that this is a message and I will *need* to refer to my books for the answer. That is what is important right now.'

'Agreed! I've had a few cases dealing with the occult…'

'This is *not* the occult, this is angelic script,' Gabriel quiet spoke. 'It has been a long time since I read it, let alone wrote it.'

'A little rusty huh?'

'You learn a subject at school; twenty years on you are asked a question on it or something along those lines. Yes, a little rusty.'

'You learnt angelic script at school?' asked Cole sounding a little confused.

'You miss the point,' Gabriel responded, as he turned his back on him.

Cole wiped the smile from his face and became more serious when he realized that Gabriel didn't have a sense of humor. It was time to be professional.

'Can you read symbols?' he asked. 'Yes or no?'

'Yes I can, or should I say most of them.'

'But the problem is you can't read the words?'

'Correct! But then, this text is not that simple.'

'That doesn't matter! First things first, you translate the symbols and we'll worry about the words later.'

A police officer broke the conversation as he splashed his way through the alleyway and ducked the yellow police line tape to interrupt them. He handed Cole a piece of notepaper; with the frayed edges at the top, he read it. He nodded in acceptance. The uniformed man left as fast as he arrived. Cole turned to Gabriel.

'You have a car?' he questioned.

'No!'

'Then you're with me. This might interest you.'

'But I have not finished here,' protested Gabriel. 'Plus, I do need to see the survivor at some point.'

'Why? You're just a university lecturer, what can she tell you?' Cole blurted out as he marched off in the direction of his car. 'You coming?'

He took out his mobile phone and began to dial. He tried again and then again. The rain had drenched his pocket and his only connection with his wife.

'I need you with me!' he shouted back to Gabriel.

The angelic reluctantly followed the agent into the shower. Cole gave up on his mobile phone, which was now completely saturated. He stuffed it deep into his jacket pocket in frustration.

'Do you have a phone?'

'No?' Gabriel questioningly replied.

Cole looked up and down the length of the alley.

'Stay here!'

He ran off down the alleyway about sixty yards to the edge of the main street where clearly visible, but badly lit was a public phone. Gabriel stood by the Ford and watched the soulcarrier, as angelic always had. From where he stood, he saw Cole attempt to open the door, whereupon the human froze. Quite motionless Cole stared into the phone booth. Gathering that something was wrong, Gabriel called for a police officer and ran to join the frozen agent. Richard Lawton Cole stood amongst the shards of shattered glass where the door had once been. He was still. Gabriel conscious of his speed, slowed as he approached the scene, now even visible to his eyes. Two police officers followed, along with a member of the crime scene investigative team and the photographer, who had just finished packing their equipment away. The strip light flickered in the roof of the phone booth. The strobe effect was enough to reveal the horror that lay before them. The crime scene had diverted the attention of the police. Cole hid his frustration at the number of elements that were being over looked in the investigation even though it had just begun. He stared inside the phone booth that resembled a mini abattoir, the blood still wet, with little evidence disturbed by the shower. Scattered on the floor were nickels, dimes and quarters from the broken catch tray, which flickered in the flashing light. The killer had made a call. *Why would the killer make a call?*

II

The First Realm. 04.41hrs Friday 13th July AD 2001 EST

The heating was full on assisting both driver and passenger to slowly dried out. As the car sped along the road every five hundred yards or so Cole reached over, checked his mobile shook his head and placed it back on the dashboard heater. Neither individual had said anything for more than ten minutes. Cole put the car through a sharp left turn at the next junction, which made Gabriel grab the passenger door for support. The agent's wallet slid the length of the dashboard, knocked the window and landed in Gabriel's lap.

'Sorry about that,' apologized Cole.

The passenger was silent as he opened Cole's I.D. and flipped the leather wallet to the reverse where he noticed the photograph of Rebecca. Gabriel tilted his head slightly to view the picture before he placed it back on the dashboard. It was not a stunning shot, but more of a graduation style picture of a very attractive woman. She had short blonde hair with piecing green eyes, a round face and a happy smile that showed all her teeth. Rebecca was definitely a catch. Gabriel glanced over at the madman behind the wheel and laughed though his nose shaking his head. Breathing in through his nose, he stopped. He slowly turned to face Cole again.

'What?'

Gabriel's ears were switched off.

'What?' the question got louder.

'I am sorry,' he came to. 'The photograph; friend, partner or wife?' Gabriel asked.

'All the above,' came the short reply.

'Pretty *and* pregnant.'

'Yeah she is,' Cole smiled. 'How did you know she was pregnant?'

'You give information too freely,' Gabriel remarked.

The hairs on the back of Cole's neck rose. He braked hard and brought the car to a stop at the next junction and momentary looked over at his passenger. *You give information too freely.* The words raced through his head. He had heard that line ten years previously. He stared at Gabriel's features, then back at the road. He didn't recognize him, he was not one of the men he met in the Iraqi desert, he was certain of it. *Was it just a coincidence?* Frustrated, he tried the mobile again. The audio bleep told him that his precious from of communication had revived itself; finally it had dried out.

'Yes!' he harked triumphantly.

'Is everything alright?' Gabriel inquired.

Cole impatiently dialed the number, instead of indexing the memory and waited for the tone, ignoring his passenger. The receiver answered almost immediately.

'Hi sweetie... ... need a favor,' he charmed. 'The payphone nearest the crime scene... no ... there was only one. No… on the main street. Sorry, did I wake you?'

Even Gabriel heard the reply.

'Sorry,' Cole begged. 'You OK? There was only one payphone.'

Cole quickly looked over at Gabriel for confirmation of what he had just said. Gabriel slowly nodded in response. There was only one payphone.

'I need a list of the last, say 15 calls made... as fast as you can. Thanks sweetie... and I'm really sorry I woke you. See you soon.'

Cole hung up and placed the phone back on the heater. He placed his hands back on the wheel, his eyes were fixed on the road and without even looking at Gabriel, he continued.

'She's still at the agency, behind a desk, albeit at home and seven months pregnant. And that's all you gonna get out of me!'

'I did not say anything,' Gabriel whispered.

'No! But you would have. You thought it,' Cole declared as he put the car into drive and pulled away again. 'Why call my wife? Why not call the office? Now you know!'

Gabriel smiled to himself, quite content. Agent Cole had given him enough information to draw a picture; enough to show a weakness, in the form of his wife; enough to allow Gabriel to make a decision on whether he liked the agent or not.

Was this Agent Cole's investigative training coming into play? thought the angelic. *Make the individual feel comfortable; present yourself in a likeable formula and then it is up to the recipient to reveal something about himself.*

Gabriel chose not to reveal anything, much to the disapproval of the Agent. Agent Richard Lawton Cole was renowned throughout the agency for his extreme lack of diplomatic skills. His only concern was the mission or case at hand. He had given Gabriel his best shot. That impression had been received – but rejected, although in the politest of manners. Gabriel kept one's counsel. The NSA agent's frustration was revealed in his driving much to the angelic's concern.

Cole decelerated and took another right turn. As he drove into a large residential street; ahead of them was the now familiar site and sounds of yet another crime scene. Peering faces appeared at every available window of each house on both sides of the street. Many of the local residents had braved the weather and stood shoulder to shoulder with the camera crews along the police line.

***

04.57hrs Friday 13th July AD 2001 EST.

The Ford pulled up on the opposite side of the street to the media circus. The crowd, held back by the perimeter tape and several uniformed officers jostled for a glimpse of the mayhem that awaited the agent and his newfound friend, inside the large detached house. The crowd was larger this time, mostly residents woken by the noise, waiting for news of their neighbor's fate. The police were saying nothing. The engine died, but Cole did not open the door. Gabriel waited patiently for the pending question.

'Weren't you *ever* going to ask me where we were going?' asked Cole.

'I thought you would tell me in your own good time,' speculated Gabriel. 'Or the location would reveal itself on arrival, as it has.'

Amazed at Gabriel's lack of basic human curiosity, Cole shook his head in disbelief. He regained his concentration and opened the door, stopping for a moment one foot firmly on the road. He ignored the rain as it bounced off the door's interior and his polished shoe.

'The location would reveal itself,' he said to himself.

Cole then pulled his foot back into the car and slammed the door. He knew this egghead could help. Whether it would be before or after Cole completely lost his mind having to deal with the total lack of curiosity that this individual had, was another matter. Gabriel had given nothing away and Cole had run out of diplomatic tact.

'You're not going to ask, are you?' questioned Cole.

Gabriel's eyes rolled around their sockets, viewing the car's interior and resting firmly in the direction of the frustrated agent.

'Ask what?'

'Why we are here!'

Through the steamed glass and hard rain the angelic peered. The bright lights of the ambulances in contrast to the dark shell of the coroner's car were visible, surrounded by the uniformed officers.

'Another murder!' he sighed. 'Friends or relatives?'

Cole had already decided not to answer. Another murder, more questions and being the political puppet was definitely going to take its toll. On top of it all, having to play mind games with an egghead was making matters worse. Cole pulled the hood out of the back of his jacket and looked up through the windscreen at the rain.

'At least the evidence won't get washed away,' he muttered as he stepped out into the downpour.

Gabriel followed suit as Cole straightened his hood and closed the car door.

'You said you wanted to see the girl, why?' he shouted over the noise of the heavy drops as they hammered on the car roof.

The angelic kept his eyes on the house and watched the humans as they darted up and down the steps, from the picket gate by the pavement to the front door. He walked around the car to join his new partner, but past him and crossed the street. Gabriel looked back at Cole and almost as though he could read his mind, his face saddened as he turned to look at the crime scene.

'Family members?' Gabriel questioned.

'All of them!' was Cole's reply, his tone low. 'Now why the girl?'

Gabriel couldn't answer. He tried his hardest to hide his feelings and ran across the grass verge to the police line. The NSA I.D. allowed them access to the porch at the top of the steps, out of the wet. Now both were watchers. Gabriel not only observed the soulcarriers around him and the mayhem within, but paid special attention to the agent he apparently was being partnered with. Cole observed the doorframe and the surrounding features. There were marks on the solid wooden door around the lock, implying a forced entry. On the right side of the door was an artistic homemade ceramic plaque with the number 1244 entwined with a red snake. Gabriel noticed it as well as he shook the droplets from his coat.

'Are you up for this?' Cole asked showing concern that he was about to bring a civilian into a fresh crime scene. 'Just don't touch anything.'

'There is something else about the writing,' admitted Gabriel changing the subject and trying to show that he was willing to help. 'The style is unique.'

'How unique?'

Gabriel showed a blank expression to the question.

'Unique,' he said by syllable trying to avoid sounding patronizing.

'You're saying one guy did this? No you're not! One could have copied it?' suggested Cole.

'Yes, I think someone did copy it. Writing that old very rarely survives in its original form,' Gabriel divulged the obvious. 'The *style* is unique. My speciality is ancient writings, I take it, that is why I was brought in?'

'The style, you mean like a graffiti artist's tag or someone's handwriting? You're saying we could trace it to one person?'

'Possibly.'

The change in conversation had caused Cole to lose concentration, so he stopped just inside the hall by the front door to listen, before he proceeded. The forensic investigators were already at work, their flashlights slowly moving across the crime scene. Their trained eyes focused only on the circle of light that revealed the horror. The agent and angelic stood, their backs to the wall, either side of the hall as officers passed between them. In the hallway sheets of polythene covered every square inch of the blood soaked carpet. Footsteps made a crisp sound followed by a squelch as the blood created patterns around the officer's shoes.

'You were brought in because we haven't a clue,' emphasized Cole. 'Even the FBI admitted that.'

'There is writing in the house, is there not?'

'So they tell me!' Cole replied. 'At least we're out of the rain.'

The agent's comment brought a forced grin to Gabriel's face.

The Chevalier residence; was a typically large suburban townhouse in a quiet residential area of West D.C. There was nothing out of the ordinary in the early morning light; the picket fence had not been painted for a couple of years; there were a few weeds growing through the cracks in the concrete steps and a tile was missing from the porch. It did not let in the rain, so it had not been fixed. It was an ordinary house until that early July morning.

Cole held his arm to stop the traffic in the hallway.

'What time was this called in?' he asked the first to stop.

'I think it was 03.45hrs. I've been here for about an hour and several units had already arrived,' said the officer.

'Thank you.' Cole removed his arm.

The ambient morning light diminished, as the two carefully stepped further into the building. The first impression was that of a house with no lights. Flashlight beams filled the lounge directly in front of them. *Something* had blown the entire fuse box. The green wallpaper of the hallway appeared black in the lowlight, the red carpet beneath the polythene only showed the crimson footprints. It was the illuminated pulse of the photographer's flashgun that revealed the truth, for the second time that morning. Shouts and howls could still be heard from the locals outside. A sergeant passed by to check out the disturbance.

'Yes!' jubilantly called an officer from under the stairs. 'Fuse box fixed and power back on! And God said let there be light.'

Gabriel had heard that phrase before and as before, the light revealed the devastation. The old TV flickered into life at the end of the hall. Then silence, total uninterrupted quiet. Cole shielded his eyes, giving them a chance to become accustomed to the brightness. Others shielded them from the sight. The fluorescent lights in the kitchen unveiled a bloodbath and the stained carpet in the hallway. The red tacky substance of horror that covered every surface was now stomach churningly visible. The victim's handprints had smeared their blood over every imaginable item. In the casting light from the kitchen a police officer handed out a few of light bulbs, to the forensic team who were still working by flashlight, just in case they needed them.

'Get photos of every bulb that's broken before we replace 'em,' shouted one of the forensic team as the bulbs changed hands.

The stairway lit up, then the dining room and finally the living room, each telling their own story. Seasoned officers were speechless as they stared at the carnage. Several hurried from the building. One hadn't eaten, but his stomach said otherwise.

'This wasn't murder,' uttered an officer, his hand over his mouth. 'This was war.' He followed the others to the fresh air.

Gabriel caught the comment. He said nothing, but the voice inside his head agreed. Every family member killed showed signs of not just a struggle, but inflicting heavy wounds on their attackers. They had literally fought for their lives *and* lost. A broken table and chair used in defense. Shards of glass from the fish tank stuck in the living room wall, told the tale of a failed attack. Every possible household item had been used in a vane attempt by the victims to defend themselves.

'Can we get the coroner in here?' bellowed a forensic officer from the living room. 'We need to process!'

Together, Cole and Gabriel stepped further into the blood and gore. *May be it would have been better if the rain had washed the evidence away. Nobody should have to witness this,* thought the agent as he entered the human abattoir formerly known as the living room.

'You ok?' he asked Gabriel with genuine concern.

Gabriel nodded. But then the glyphs on the living room wall caught his attention. His mouth dropped open. The ancient writing was on every wall and still dripping off the ceiling. It was the only room in the house to possess the satanic artwork. Entering the room, Gabriel was visibly distressed. A police officer with a stronger stomach than his own offered him the only intact chair.

'The chair's clean,' stated one of the forensic team as he handed Cole a pair of thin transparent rubber gloves. 'Be careful.'

Very slowly Gabriel sat down with his back to the wall facing the fireplace on the other side of the room. He closed his eyes.

How could this happen? This was not his field, why was he here? Why did he offer to come? each question repeated itself in his head. *He would have to reference his books to come up with the answers that the agent wanted on the spot.* He stared intensely at the glyphs; the blood, still wet, slowly trying to make it's way down the wallpaper.

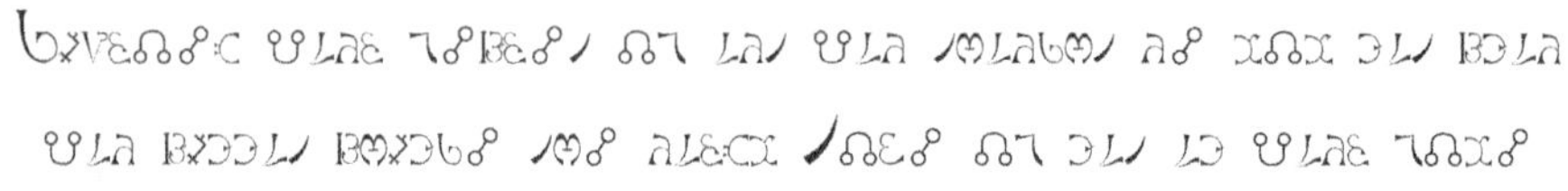

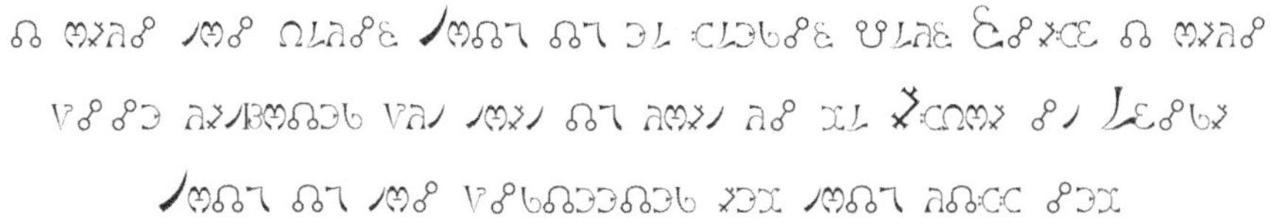

The Archangel recognized several of the glyphs, but their meaning escaped him. Frustrated, he looked up to the symbols on the ceiling.

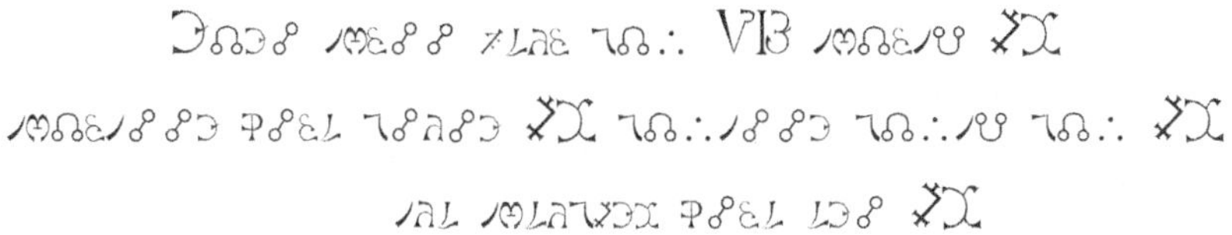

Unfortunately, he saw what everyone else in the room saw, artwork or writing in the style of that of a child, only it was written in human blood. Gabriel could feel the eyes of the police officers watching him, waiting for him to give them the answer. He had an answer, but it was one he could not reveal. The crimes were related to him and his race; the emphasis of the investigation did appear to be heading straight at him; why else would the writing be here? Gabriel would have to find the connection between the crime scene's writings, the couple in the alleyway and the family. There were three elements that connected the crimes. One, obviously, the glyphs. Two, the brutality of the murders. And three, all the victims in the house had the same ethnic appearance to the girl in the alleyway.

The journey had taken about half an hour to get to the residential district. In that time three separate forensic teams had done an incredible job gathering as much data as was physically possible. The removal of the bodies was high on the agenda considering the temperatures that the city would reach in the height of the summer heat wave. The rain in the last few hours had even caught the weathermen off guard.

The head of the forensic team stepped up to Cole. 'Head Forensic Investigator Wood.'

'Officer Wood,' Cole nodded. 'Agent Cole!'

'I'm not sure why the NSA is here, but I thought I'd show you this,' he held up a family portrait. 'The Chevalier family.'

Cole's eyes lowered to view their cheesy smiles for the camera. In a fraction of a second, the photographer had captured a moment in time that would keep the Chevalier family's memory alive.

'The daughter's missing,' added the officer Wood.

The victims were from the *girlfriend's* family. If she was to survive, what would she come back too? Gabriel opened his eyes and glanced over to his left, to Cole. He was still in the doorway now studying the blood, his finger following the damage, trying to understand the pattern of events; the picture frame still in his other hand. A smartly dressed detective approached him as the forensic officer went about his business.

'You're NSA?' he asked.

'Everybody appears to know that.'

'Detective Ashby, officer in charge. 'He with you?' the detective motioned to Gabriel still seated.

'Yes he is,' Cole replied. 'Is there a problem?'

'No, as long as he doesn't touch anything.'

'What 'ave you got?'

Detective Ashby read from his notes.

'Preliminary view of the crime scene reveals the entire family are dead; the mother, father, one son and two daughters; aged between twenty-three and seventeen. The third daughter is in the I.C.U. she is your Jane Doe.'

'I've the family portrait,' Cole raised the picture. 'Just found out.'

'*Naomi* Chevalier, a friend of hers worked at the hospital and identified her on arrival. The motive is unknown; nothing stolen; money in wallets and pockets. The family jewelry is upstairs and no initial or obvious signs of sexual assault on any of the victims. And all secondary wounds appear defensive.'

The detective finished with a snap of his notebook, a sigh and then bit his top lip. There was a long pause.

'Welcome to my hell!' he continued. 'Make sure he doesn't touch anything. We don't bring civilians into crime scenes, you're aware of that! He's your responsibility.'

'Thanks. He won't touch anything. I understand and thanks for the update.'

The detective walked back into the hallway, he snapped his fingers on remembering something and turned back to Cole.

'Oh yeah!' he added. 'There was no forced entry and the front and back doors were still locked. The only damage to the windows was internal and that appears to be due to the struggle. You work that one out!'

'The front door did show signs of a forced entry,' Cole pointed out.

'Observant,' the detective commended. '*We* had to get in after neighbors reported screams.'

Cole walked over to join Gabriel who had listened to everything, but had not taken his eyes of the writing on the wall. Aware that Cole was beside him, Gabriel continued to stare at the angelic puzzle. The agent obscured his view with the picture.

'She was a pretty girl,' Cole commented.

'A pretty family and *she* is still alive,' Gabriel remarked gently lowering the picture with his open hand. 'Something *was* stolen.'

'I was just told that theft doesn't appear to be the motive.'

'Their lives were stolen; their innocence *was* stolen; their souls were stolen and two pictures which were on the wall over in the corner.'

Cole and the forensic team spun around to examine the corner. Blood had been splattered around the room. Arterial spray covered the cream wallpaper on all four walls. When everyone was dead, the killer had removed the two picture frames, leaving a clear outline in its place. Officer Wood stepped forward with his hand raised, to keep the agent back. Without touching anything, the investigator leant over the back of the broken chair and peered into the corner of the room below the outlines.

'Whatever they were, they didn't fall off the wall,' he assured.

'They're not there?' Cole inquired.

'Nope!'

'You missed it,' whispered Cole.

'Hidden in plain sight. An easy mistake, but then again, there is a lot of evidence to gather,' Gabriel pointed out. 'I doubt it would have been missed.'

'Thank you,' Wood appreciated. 'Agent, your partner's right. We have only just got here, so I would appreciate it… if let us process the scene first.'

'I'm sorry, you're right,' Cole admitted.

The agent looked around the living room at the debris on the floor. He stopped at a blood-covered shoebox lying on its side by the door. The contents of postcards lay scattered at his feet. He crouched to take a closer look at the pictures. The coagulating blood splatter had covered many of them forcing the agent to struggle to make out the images.

'Have you photographed these?' he asked pointing at the floor.

Wood glanced over at the photographer who shook his head.

'Not yet!' replied the investigator. 'I would appreciate…'

'No problem! I'll wait! I was just asking.'

The agent tilted his head from side to side in an attempt to gain a better view. Only one postcard was spatter free; that of a sprawling medieval castle upon a hilltop in the bright summer sun. It's battlements; square with round turrets, some with slate roofs and all in pristine condition. In the foreground was a fortified walkway leading down to an old arched stone bridge that ran through the valley below. In bright red, boarded in yellow was the name 'Carc…' the rest of the name was obscured by another card. Cole took out his pen.

'Agent!' called the investigator. 'I said *we* hadn't processed that yet!'

Cole raised his hands in surrender and stood up.

'Agent Cole, I need to see the girl, Naomi,' Gabriel requested as he climbed out of the chair believing they had out-stayed their welcome.

Cole immediately had that frustrated looked in his eye. He walked straight out of the living room and down the hallway heading for fresh air. Too many people were standing on the porch. So he popped his head around the dining-room door, looking for privacy, but failed. He settled on the kitchen. It was also a bloodbath, but it was empty. The harsh truth was that Cole switched off his senses for a moment. Gabriel followed. Cole closed the door behind Gabriel and began his interrogation. He was running out time. Too many people were dead and if he didn't get the answers, he felt it would be his responsibility if more died.

'You know who did this!' he stated sharply.

'No, I do not,' replied a very calm Gabriel.

'But you have an idea, right?'

Gabriel nodded in agreement. 'I cannot lie to you.'

Cole brought up his finger of authority and poked Gabriel in the chest with it, pushing Gabriel up against a freestanding cupboard, which moved from the force.

'I've asked this question and have yet to get an answer. Why do you want to see the girl? My advice to you would be to answer the question this time, because I've had enough. I've had enough, okay?'

'What was written looked familiar,' admitted Gabriel. 'But I cannot remember. Believe me, I wish I could.'

'You told me you could read the symbols, but not the words.'

'In the alleyway, I could. Here I cannot,' Gabriel added. 'The style and the handwriting *is* unique; copied from an ancient manuscript I think. But I *need* to check my books.'

'And the girl?'

'I believe she is the key.'

'No!' answered Cole. 'She's the witness! She won't tell us anything when she discovers her life is being threatened. When she finds out that her entire family has been wiped out, she'll decide to have amnesia. The *key* is in the writing, not the girl.'

'Listen to yourself, Agent Cole. The killer did not kill her family to keep her quiet, you know that. The killer attacked her first. I think the killer's target was the whole family and so do you. Sean Grayson was just in the wrong place at the wrong time. You believe, as I do, that they were lovers.'

'*That* is for me to decide. If she *was* the target, then how is it she's still alive?'

'The police missed it, maybe the killer did to?' suggested Gabriel trying to calm situation. 'Very few can write this well, let alone with style.'

Cole shook his head with anger and frustration. The egghead was now attempting to solve his case. The agent began to pace the kitchen as the friction between them increased again.

'I need your help,' asked Gabriel. 'You are right that I have an idea of what we are dealing with. But *you* have no idea what. I thought, that maybe the girl might say something that would jog my memory. It is not just in the writing or in its style, but also who wrote it.'

'The killer wrote it!'

'That is not what I meant.'

'Then tell me! I've seen my share of weird shit. I've been with the NSA for almost ten years. You see things and you learn to forget about them, classified things, but I've *never* seen anything like this.'

Gabriel attempted to get back to the subject. 'I have my notes. The photographs will be helpful and a number to contact you would be appreciated. I *will* help you solve this. I do not like to see the things that I have seen tonight, the same as you. We *are* on the same side.'

Cole began to calm down and took a sodden business card out of his top jacket pocket, which he then handed to Gabriel without eye contact.

'You are here for the diplomat's son,' Gabriel continued. 'You are not here because of the girl.'

'That's right!'

'Her life and that of her family mean nothing to you?'

'I didn't say that!' jabbed Cole. 'They were just not my priority, *now* they are. As you said, the boy was in the wrong place at the wrong time. But I'm still here, because this killer needs to be caught.'

Gabriel nodded in agreement and understanding.

'The Ambassador wants answers.'

'He also wants you to kill the killer.'

'Unfortunately for the Ambassador, his wish, I may not be able to grant. I am governed by the same laws as you.'

Gabriel smirked at the comment, then walked passed his unwilling partner and opened the kitchen door. He stepped into the hallway and turned to see if Cole had calmed down, but instead, noticed the cupboard he had been pushed against. Its door was closed. On the blood stained wall behind, where it had stood, he could see a large black greasy substance only made visible by the cupboards dislodgment.

'The point of entry was behind you,' Gabriel stated calmly. 'Good luck with your investigation. I *will* call you when I have some information.'

Confused, Cole threw his head over his shoulder. All he saw was the black mark on the wall behind the freestanding cupboard. He put his rubber gloves on to avoid leaving fingerprints and gently moved the cupboard aside. He could clearly see that the back had a large human sized hole smashed into it. Almost, on instinct, he reached in and opened the cupboard door from the inside. On closer inspection, the flimsy catch had been forced. There were no shelves inside and very few utensils. The contents lay on the floor around his feet. In his mind, he had the impression of someone climbing through the cupboard and pushing its contents out into the kitchen. Why hadn't the cupboard toppled over? He shook his head in disbelief. The agent then turned his attention back to the black slimy substance on the wall. Its size matched, almost perfectly, the size of the hole in the rear of the cupboard. He pushed his index finger into the slime and watched in amazement as his finger sank, up to the second joint, *into* the wall. He jabbed at the wall a second time. Again, his finger sank up to the second joint and then hit something solid. Cole removed his finger and took his gloves off. He turned them inside out and put them in his pocket. As he turned around he found Detective Ashby standing in the doorway, observing his every move.

'Your office called,' informed the Detective. 'Your mobile didn't answer… That's interesting, what you found? My boys might have missed that.'

'Missed what?'

'The mark on the wall.'

'Your boys would have found it, I guarantee you,' Cole reassured the detective. 'With the amount of points being missed on this case, I think everyone is watching with keener eyes.'

'Yeah, we heard about the daughter in the alley.'

'From the marks on the wall and the hole in the back, it gives the impression someone tried to climb through the cupboard,' Cole suggested, back on subject.

'Point of entry?' questioned Detective Ashby.

'Why not? This is a weird case.'

'If they can walk through walls Mr. Mulder,' smiled the detective. 'But if they could, why not a cupboard? Ha!'

The detective continued to laugh off his comment as he left the kitchen and began giving orders to the officers in the adjacent room. Detective Ashby was right; it *was* interesting. It also did not make sense. In fact, it was impossible. Cole shook his head and wiped the cupboard from his mind for a moment and headed for the front door, he was forever leaving his phone in the car.

'Mind the blood!' shouted an officer.

'Shit!'

In his rush for the door, Cole had kicked up the polythene sheets and now had blood on his shoes. He took out a tissue and crouched to wipe them clean. In front of him, under the hallway bureau was a glint of light. He reached out and with his clean glove picked up, what at first looked like a gold coin, but turned out to be a pendant of some kind.

'You alright back there?' called out Detective Ashby.

'Just cleaning my shoes!'

The detective's response was more laughter. Not very fitting considering the scene. Cole stood up sharply and left the building. The pendant wrapped in the glove safely in his jacket.

In all the years with the agency, he had never taken any evidence from the scene of a crime and he couldn't say what had compelled him to do so this time. He stood in the rain once again, checking the pendant was firmly in his pocket. The sun was slowly climbing into the sky and the heavy shower had reduced to a drizzle. Cole was ready for the office phone call. He had to try and get out of the habit of leaving the mobile in the car, even if it did make him lose his concentration from time to time. He had given up trying to shelter from the wet, it didn't matter how much he tried to stay dry, it was no use. He was already soaked through to the skin as he watched the crowd in the early daylight hours. In the corner of his eye, he spotted Gabriel talking to one of the spectators. The tall man was in his forties, lean with slightly grey hair and casually dressed. Cole mentally backtracked through the night's events to find a recollection of him. Nothing sprang to mind.

A squelch in the mud beside him drew his attention to a police officer standing in the flowerbed, filming the crowd with a video camera. With the advent of this new technology, it was now standard practice these days to film everyone just on the off chance of catching the killer returning to the scene.

'Could you get the two guys talking,' requested Cole.

'The one who was with you?' asked the cameramen.

'Yeah!'

The cameramen did as he was asked, but then his attention was diverted to a commotion around the side of the house. The cameraman was requested. The agent followed him around to two uniformed officers arguing over a black scorpion about five inches long that had crawled out of the undergrowth.

'That shouldn't be here!' the first officer claimed pointing at the creature.

'It must have escaped from the house,' Cole surmised.

The cameraman briefly captured it of video and then returned to the front of the house. The two officers seemed surprised that the agent remained.

'Something wrong?' Cole asked.

'You're interested in this?' replied the first officer.

'It does seem strange, and anything to do with this case interests me. Now, you said it doesn't belong here. Why?'

'You're the agent with the NSA?' the officer asked somewhat distracted.

'Why?' Cole repeated.

'I'm no expert, but I think it's a European scorpion.'

'You know more than I do; *that* makes you the expert. Why d'you think its European?'

'I guess I watch too much Animal Planet. It shouldn't be here. It maybe Mediterranean? I don't know. What I do know is that it shouldn't be here.'

'It's been a very hot summer?' Cole suggested.

'Yeah, but I don't see any camels.'

'Point taken. *Before* you hit it with the stick… which direction was it going?' the agent inquired sarcastically.

'From behind the bushes by the wall,' point the second officer. 'Across the path away from the house. D'you want me to bag it?'

Cole nodded as he proceeded to pull the bush aside, doing his utmost to avoid dirtying his soaked clothes. The foliage had been moved before and fell aside easily to reveal a muddy flowerbed surprisingly completely void of weeds. Cole's fleeting look over at the unpainted picket fence and the weed-ridden garden left another bizarre question unanswered.

'Your flashlight?' asked the agent as he bent down to inspect the earth.

The officers directed their light at Cole and the flowerbed as he searched for footprints. The rippled circle of light revealed a set of bare-foot prints in the soft earth.

'No shoes?' the agent quietly said to himself. 'We'll need some casts made of these.'

'I'll get someone round to see to…' the officer paused as the flashlight beam slowly made its way up the side of the house. 'What the hell is that?' gasped the first officer.

Cole stared at the darkness. He had missed the huge black patch, in the shadow of the bush, against the wall. Illuminated by the flashlights, everyone could clearly see the thick black slimy substance on the brick, almost as though it were painted. The agent stood very close to the slimed brickwork. He attempted to smell it, but picked up nothing in the light drizzle. The rain ran off it as though it were water resistant. He then took a step back and snapped a small branch, about two feet long, off the displaced bush. He poked the black patch with the stick and found it to have the same texture as the patch inside the house. He let go; the piece of wood stayed put, protruding from the wall.

'Would you believe that?' gasped the first officer.

'Yeah, I would. Hold onto that scorpion.'

The two officers immediately looked down at their feet. There was no scorpion in sight. The second officer turned pale and left without an excuse.

'I'm sorry Sir, I thought it was dead,' answered the other.

'Shit!'

'We're gonna have to report this?'

'Yes you are,' agreed Cole. 'I'm sure Detective Ashby will be interested.'

'And the scorpion?'

'It's gone, don't waste your time. Tell me!' Cole paused. 'What room do you think's on the other side of this wall?'

'The kitchen?' the officer answered.

***

The NSA agent made himself as comfortable as possible in his wet clothes with his earpiece wedged firmly in his ear, ready to take the office call. The heat had not entirely escaped when he opened the car door; Cole was comfortable, watching Gabriel and the mystery man in his wing mirror. The phone rang; Cole jumped.

'Cole here!'

'About bloody time,' stropped Rebecca. 'Do you know how many times I've called?'

Cole didn't answer. He quickly checked the phone and read the screen; 11 missed calls. He bit his tongue as he tried to think of a good excuse. It was the best coarse of action when Rebecca was in a mood.

'I thought it was Garrett.'

'Is that the best excuse you got? You can talk to your boss when I've finished with you,' continued Rebecca, she knew her husband too well. 'Or you can leave the phone in the car like you usually do.'

'Becks! Come on! Why are you in a mood? I'm sorry I forgot the phone.'

'I worry! D'you know what time it is? It's not just the phone! I'm here; you're not! Plus I'm envious.'

'What?'

Cole adjusted the wing mirror to find the mystery man and Gabriel. It *was* 05:37hrs in the morning and his wife had nothing to be envious about. Cole knew this was another one of her little rants.

'Listen up my sexy man! You wanted the callbox numbers. I checked the last ten and gave up. Only three are relevant. Those three calls were made at the suggested time of the incident. 02:04hrs and 02:06hrs. One was to Paris, a central exchange relayed to a mobile. Can't trace it. And the other was to Carcassonne. The Carcassonne number was rung twice, probably cut-off. International calls, payphone to payphone is very unusual, not hard to arrange if you have the change… and very traceable.'

'Stop!' Cole instructed. 'Carc… what?'

'Carcassonne!'

'Carcassonne spelt with a 'C'?

'Yes, why?'

'I knew the postcards were European. They had that look.'

'What postcards?'

'In the house, a postcard with a castle on it.'

'Carcassonne is famous for its medieval fortified town.'

'*How* d'you know that?'

'I have a degree in *history*. There's an obvious connection.'

'A silly mistake or somebody wants to be caught.'

'The latter; it gives that impression,' Rebecca added. 'Especially going to the trouble with all those coins.'

'They didn't. They'd broken the phone…'

'And used the coins,' Rebecca continued. 'Some of this case has no leads. Other areas lead us in a straight line. All leads so far have a French connection.'

'That's why you're envious,' realized Cole.

'Yes.'

'But I'm not going to France because of a phone call and a postcard. Did you find anything about the girl?'

'I had started to check out the Ambassadors son, but then I got the info about the house and that suggests that the girl was the target and...'

'I know!' interrupted Richard. 'So you know about the family?'

'Naomi Chevalier, clean as a whistle. No record; good grades and that goes for all of them; the *whole* family. No criminal records; no parking tickets; good reputation; they pay their bills, their taxes and keep completely out of trouble... until now.'

'Typical! Church once a week?' Richard jested.

'No record of religion here.'

'Not religious or no record?'

'No record! But that doesn't mean anything.'

'We have something here and something there and that's it.'

'Every little piece of something means something,' Rebecca added her piece of philosophy. 'Even *nothing* means *something*.'

'Thank you, darling.'

'Richard! Are you alright?'

'Yeah. So all we have is a witness in the I. C. U.' He took a breather filling his cheeks with air and then blowing loudly. 'I hope she pulls through,' prayed Cole softly.

'And come back to what?'

'Nothing.'

'As they say, from nothing everything is created. Come home soon darling we miss you,' begged Rebecca. 'I'm going back to bed for a couple of hours, so no more information, plus you need a break.'

'Okay sweetie and tomorrow…'

'Today!'

'*Later*! Could you dig anything you have on this language guy, Gabriel?'

'Isn't he helpful?' Rebecca inquired.

'Yes and no.'

'Does he have a surname?'

'No!'

'What d'you mean, no?'

'The more questions you ask, the less straight answers you get.'

'So *arrest* his ass!' his wife raised her voice.

'I really don't think that would work with this guy. There's something about him.'

Rebecca laughed down the phone. 'Sounds like you have your hands full? I'll do it later, okay.'

'Thank you. Good night my sweet.'

'Good morning,' Rebecca replied sarcastically.

Richard Lawton Cole rested his elbow on the steering wheel, his chin on his thumb and kissed his index finger deep in thought, still watching Gabriel. He switched off the phone and then beeped the car horn to get the egghead's attention. Suddenly realizing what he had just done, especially in a residential area at that time in the morning, he sank down into his seat out of sight. Hidden from view, the agent didn't see the mystery man disappear through the growing crowd. Gabriel appeared at the passenger window holding a file. He tapped on the window as Cole sat up to let him in. Gabriel glanced over at the house one last before getting out of the rain, but froze.

'You specialize in ancient writings?' verified Cole. 'You can age writing by its style?'

Gabriel ignored the agent; his eyes fixed on one of the police officers who had just picked up what looked like a child's small dinky toy from the flowerbed. Then the officer shook the brightly colored plastic thing next to his ear. Gabriel could hear the rattle from where he stood. The angelic slowly began to cross the street quickening his pace as he reached the middle. Cole climbed from the car and followed.

'Gabriel!' Cole shouted.

The concerned lecturer stopped in his tracks as the agent caught up with him.

'What's wrong?'

'I have a bad feeling,' Gabriel replied his eyes fixed on the toy.

'What?'

'The officer with the toy.'

'Yeah! It's a toy!'

'A child's toy in the garden of a house full of teenagers?'

Cole's facial expression changed to match Gabriel's; that of concern; the egghead had a point. The officer opened the lid and emptied the contents into the palm of his hand. Gabriel only caught a glimpse. The tiny silver cylindrical object disappeared from view within the wet clenched fist of the policeman.

'Cherubs!' Gabriel announced.

The egghead suddenly jumped forward, but stopped. He could not show his speed. He could not show his knowledge. He sharply turned to the agent.

'Tell the officer to throw it!' Gabriel demanded in an agitated voice. 'Tell him!'

'Why?'

'TELL HIM!'

'Officer!' Cole raised a hand. 'Officer! That toy…'

'NO! The silver thing!'

'The SILVER THING in your hand… THROW IT… NOW!'

'Too late!' Gabriel snapped as he grabbed the agent and pulled him to the ground.

Cole fell back; Gabriel obscuring his view of the explosion that followed. The shockwave vibrated though his lungs. That experience he had felt before. The noise followed a split second later and then the screams. It was Iraq all over again, only with rain. He lay there for a moment, the water in his face; he looked up over his shoes to where the officer had stood. As the smoke cleared Cole could see the officer was gone; as was the porch; the corner of the house and the lives of several local residents. A nearby tree's leaves were still burning, but rain would beat the firemen to it. Several tiles fell from roof, embedding themselves in what remained of the soft scorched lawn. Above, in the semi-lit sky, was the remains of a fireball as it burnt itself out. The officers that were still standing instantly became medics with a few bystanders assisting. Panic was beginning to fill the air. Cole slowly turned to Gabriel who lay on the road beside him.

'How did you know?' he whispered. 'How the fuck did you know?'

'I have seen that type of weapon before.'

'Really! I haven't! What the hell was that?'

Gabriel did not answer.

'You've seen that type of writing before. A lot of this… *you've* seen before… haven't you?'

'A long time ago.'

'I was in the Gulf and I've not seen stuff blow like that,' Cole explained as he got to his feet. 'I know what explosives blow like. The Gulf was ten years ago. *That's* a long time ago.'

Gabriel jumped to his feet and surveyed the mayhem. 'I think we should leave.'

'*You think* we should leave?'

'There is nothing we can do here. The damage is done,' the egghead admitted as he walked back to the car.

'Who the hell are you?' Cole demanded as he caught up with the know it all. 'You say you specialize in ancient writings?'

'*Yes*, and their relationship to cultures.'

'What about weapons?'

'What about them?'

'What do you know about weaponry?'

'What you know!'

'You knew what that was,' Cole pointed to the hole in the lawn. 'I didn't!'

'I had seen it once before. The metal reacts with water. I do not know any more than that.'

'And the writing? So how ancient is angelic script?'

'As old as the angels.'

'Right!' bellowed Cole a little frustrated at the answer. 'So how common is the script?'

Gabriel got into the car trying to keep the conversation away from the recent events, but knowing that Cole would obviously not leave it alone. Cole joined him.

'You didn't answer my question. How common is the script?'

'Many have heard of the script. There are people who know of true angelic script, but very few. And even less could construct a sentence.'

'Let alone with *style*,' Cole answered, finishing Gabriel's sentence.

'Am I now the suspect?' asked the egghead.

Cole ignored the question and continued with his interrogation. 'Can you?'

'Can I?'

'Construct a sentence?'

'No! Not now. But as I said before, it has been a while.'

'So help me out here Gabriel!' pleaded Cole and then paused for what seemed like an age. 'Cherubs! I'm talking to a guy called Gabriel about angelic script.'

'It was the first question you asked.'

'Funny, I didn't notice. *Look*, we asked you, as a professor on this stuff, to help. I take it that your knowledge has helped the police on cases before. But you know more than you're willing to admit.'

'We could have driven off and we would have missed this. I tried to stop that explosion. Time was not on my side. If it was not raining, no one would have been hurt.'

'…or killed!'

'Or killed,' Gabriel lowered his voice. 'I thought I could stop it. I was wrong.'

'Why did you call them, Cherubs?'

'A friend of mine once used them. He called them Cherubs. I do not know what they are called. I do not know what they are, but as I said… *they* react with water.'

'Well, they have a name now… Cherubs. So who else would know this stuff? You're friend?'

'My friend died in combat,' Gabriel paused to see Cole's reaction. He got the response he wanted. 'I *will* tell you this. There are characters in this world, you would not want to meet or have any dealings with.'

'*Obviously*!' joked Cole. 'These *characters* kill innocent people.'

'Let me work on the translation.'

'I will, but first, what do you know about the family?'

'I do not know *anything* about the family,' Gabriel insisted. 'Chevalier means 'Knight' in French, as in suits of armor. Other than that, I know nothing.'

'French,' Cole mumbled to himself. 'And you know the bad ass characters that killed the Chevalier family.'

'I did not say I know them. I said I know *of* them,' stated Gabriel firmly. 'What is the French connection?'

'A movie with Gene Hackman,' Cole replied, being as evasive as Gabriel.

'Nothing I have seen relates to France, ancient or modern,' Gabriel explained ignoring his comment. 'Why do you say France?'

'I don't know! Maybe the family,' Cole changed the subject. 'You knew that guy in the crowd?'

'Yes!' answered Gabriel as he placed the file hard on his lap, making a slapping sound. 'Mr. Cole, I have not lied to you! I have however, withheld information, because you are not ready for it. I cannot remember all the text that I have seen this morning. I believe it is a quote or quotes from an apocryphal book. Which one, I do not know. I clearly recognize the large symbols, but they are no relation to the text.'

'Why an apoc… ryphal book?'

'Because this style of text is not used in common usage with the bible.'

'You're saying this is all religious? That's interesting, since the Chevalier's have no record of religion on file.'

Gabriel was silent. He opened his notepad and pointed at a symbol on one of the pages. It looked familiar. Cole thought he recognized it to be one of the symbols from the alleyway.

 'This basically represents the letter 'O'.'

Cole watched carefully attempting to memorize the symbol. Gabriel turned the damp page to reveal two more symbols; copies of the ones seen on the wall in the Chevalier's home. 

'This one,' Gabriel pointed.  'Represents the letter 'Y' and the other one,  the letter 'L'. O. Y. L. means nothing to me and I doubt that it means anything to the NSA, its computers or its experts. My own personal conclusion is that this was to get an individual's attention and guide them in a particular direction. Satisfied so far?'

Cole calmed down and nodded his head. The egghead was right about one thing; the NSA would not have a clue what the letters meant. He motioned to Gabriel to flick through his notepad so as Cole see all the symbols again. The angelic did as was requested.

'Stop!' shouted Cole making Gabriel jump. 'On the ceiling in the house, those two symbols were in groups, two or three times. They were also larger than the others. Does that mean anything to you?'

'It was four times, and I am not sure what it means. The first symbol represents the letter 'A'. The second represents the letter 'N'.' Gabriel paused in thought. 'No,' he said slowly correcting himself. 'The second symbol is the letter 'D' I think.'

'A D,' Cole stated. 'Anno Domini, it's Roman. That means the writing on the ceiling are dates. Yes?'

Gabriel nodded very slowly. 'They could be. They could very well be.'

The agent was now getting into the swing of it and snatched the notepad from Gabriel. He thumbed the pages as fast as he could, then stopped.

Cole tapped the pad with his finger.

'You think the first letter is 'A'? The next large letter *is* 'O'. What is 'A' and 'O'? In all your ancient writings, ignoring angelic script for a minute... What is 'A' and 'O' in ancient *anything*?'

'It is Greek... Alpha et Omega. The beginning and the end,' Gabriel whispered, surprised at the agents ability to grasp the symbols so quickly.

'The symbols are angelic which you can't remember,' Cole ranted. 'But, the words from all forms of ancient text, Greek, Roman, Akkadian or Iraqi, whatever!'

'I need my books!' Gabriel blurted out.

Cole threw the pad into Gabriel's lap and started the engine.

'I'll drop you off. I need to get some sleep. Shit! I'm going to miss the wedding.'

'What wedding?

'Nothing.'

'A wedding is not nothing.'

'A colleague. His... I'll drop you off,' Cole gave up explaining.

'What about the wedding?'

'He'll understand.'

Gabriel flicked back though the pad with the new information.

'Something is still missing,' he pondered as the car sped through the wet streets. 'Could you drop me off at the hospital?'

Gabriel did not stop scanning through his notes. He shook his head in disappointment at not finding what he was looking for.

'Apart from a French name, nothing suggests a connection with France.'

'Yeah, but three calls to France from the payphone in the alley does,' Cole butted in. 'Maybe the girl knows the connection? What do you think?'

'Mr. Cole, please don't ask me any more questions because I have no more answers,' the angelic replied. 'You have a determination about you. You want to resolve this, and so do I. Help me and I promise I will do whatever I can to help you.'

'Okay, I'll drop you at the hospital and then I've got to sleep… I hate being used like a puppet, so I'm gonna finish this.'

Gabriel smiled at his new partner. 'A puppet?'

'Yeah, being used; pulling strings.'

'I know that feeling.'

'I usually hate eggheads. But you, I don't know yet.'

'So I am awaiting sentence?'

'You could put it like that,' replied Cole, a little laughter in his voice. 'You did save my bacon back there; and I admit you tried to save the officer. The jury's out. Look! I have a personal question to ask…'

'Then ask.'

'Are you a religious man? I only ask because of the script, now Cherubs and your name, Gabriel, it must run in the family?'

The angelic smiled at the comment, but said nothing.

'It was personal. You don't have to answer.'

'You could say it runs in the family,' Gabriel smirked.

'Do you believe in God?'

'Do *I* believe in God?'

'Do you believe there is a God?' Cole was determined to get an answer out of Gabriel, other than another question.

'Do *I* believe there *is* a God?'

'*Will* you stop repeating what I say,' snapped Cole.

'Yes, there is a God.'

'There *is* a God! So you are a religious man?'

'I would not say I was a religious man.'

Cole sighed in disappointment at yet another cryptic reply. 'Why d'you have to be so bloody confusing? This investigation appears to delve into ancient history and religion, both of which I know very little about. I should really bring my wife and mother in on this.'

'Why?'

'Rebecca studied ancient history at university before joining the agency and my mother is a devout Catholic. I think they are more qualified than me.'

'But you have the open mind, do you not?' Gabriel inquired.

'Yeah!'

'Right now, that is the most important thing to have. Be open to the possibilities. Listen, watch and learn and keep that mind open.'

'Thank you,' Cole appreciated the compliment.

'You do not have many friends do you Agent Cole?'

'I get the impression, neither do you.'

III

The First Realm. 06.45hrs Friday 13th July AD 2001 EST

Gabriel sniffed the air. Hospitals around the world always have that clinical smell; well, most do. But this hospital, as clean as any other, had another scent. He knew that scent; a living breathing scent he had smelt it a million times. An odor that could be picked up by any angelic; even a fallen one. It was not quite the same as that of an angelic, but it possessed similar traits. As Gabriel walk the corridors, following his nose, the blanks began to fill. The writing was a message; the message was aimed at an individual. Only, that individual was *him*. Who could read what was written? Who would understand the connection between the writing and the victims? The murders were pointless in themselves; only they highlighted the point than Gabriel now understood. Somebody, out there; somebody on the First Realm wanted him. They wanted him and his secret made public. He understood the message. It was a warning.

***

Gabriel found himself standing in the doorway of the I.C.U. (Intensive Care Unit). The odor that brought him there was close. He sensed the presence of being, more than there should be, hidden beneath the skin, running through someone's veins. He had already felt it once that day. It was not a coincidence. Gabriel had not sensed the presence of being for decades and now in Washington DC, he experienced it twice in one day. Someone in the US capital knew he was present.

'Friend or family?' asked the doctor, breaking Gabriel's train of thought.

'A friend, *of* the family,' replied Gabriel with a start.

'I'm sorry, only family members are allowed to visit the I.C.U. and not at this hour,' informed the doctor. 'Who is it you wanted to see?'

'Naomi Chevalier. Her family are… dead, I am probably all she has right now.'

'I'm sure you're mistaken, a friend of hers works here, we have all her details.'

'Her family all died tonight.'

'The police… said it was an isolated incident,' the doctor look stunned.

'Not anymore.'

'It's not much to come back to, is it?'

'Everyone appears to say that. Is she going to survive?' asked Gabriel.

'She has a willpower stronger than steel. She won't quit! Most people would have died from that amount of blood loss. If I wasn't a doctor, I'd call it a miracle.'

'You just did,' Gabriel emphasized quietly in the noisy corridor.

The doctor acknowledged the comment with a slight cynical expression and left Gabriel standing there in the doorway, patiently waiting for permission to enter. There was nobody to stop him, but he waited all the same. An orderly passed by. A blonde female nurse; her actions, a striking resemblance to someone from his past, was flirting with a couple of doctors in the staff room. One of them glanced through the open door in Gabriel's direction, but resumed to watching the flirtatious nurse. She had caught Gabriel's eye, but now her appearance had reverted to that of any other blonde woman in a crowd. Gabriel waited. The familiar sounding bell that lifts make made Gabriel turn around. The corridor was filling with armed uniformed police officers. The angelic backed away from the entrance to the I.C.U. and slowly moved down the adjacent corridor, coming to a halt by the coffee machine. He read the notice, 'Out of Sugar'. The police took up positions near the entrance to the I.C.U. The commotion began to erupt as the doctors argued with the stubborn officers. Gabriel continued to back down the corridor to the stairwell.

'We won't be in your way. It's for the safety of your patient!' bellowed the officer across the hospital floor in an attempt to get his point across.

***

07.17hrs Friday 13th July AD 2001 EST

The angelic retreated to the quiet safety of his rented accommodation. If he had been fast enough or asserted himself in the right manner; he could have seen Naomi Chevalier. He could have confirmed his suspicions. He had sensed the presence of being, but that was not enough. Gabriel needed to be sure it was her. Agent Cole would have walked in, but Gabriel followed the rules, as best he could. Gabriel's patience lost him another opportunity. For eternity Gabriel had followed the rules and on the one occasion that he didn't, he paid for it and still was. The memory of that fateful day was still strong in the back of his mind, and evident in his mind as he tossed and turned on his bed, restless. The flirting nurse was a reminder of that. There was, also, standing in the corner of his open plan apartment, a partially finished wooden carving that appeared abandoned. The two worn carving chisels, well and truly stuck, stabbed into the wood, hardened with age. An age, that mankind could not comprehend, an age before empires and civilizations. Over the centuries, its shape slowly had taken the form of an ancient temple. The building with high spires fighting to be revealed from the trunk oak; another element from Gabriel's past. Modern day carbon 14 dating techniques on the carving would disclose his secret. Luckily, no one would ever consider it. For now his secret was safe.

His writing table was by the window. On the left, a selection of pens and pencils in a peanut butter jar; on the right, a neat stack of books; The Apocryphal books of the Bible, ancient languages among others, none less than two hundred years old. Outside, the city was starting to wake. *Why would anyone want him now? Now, after all this time, what could be so important? What was he missing? Cherubs.*

***

The First Realm. 65th Sunrise – 1st Cycle (26th May) 7436 BC

Beneath the foliage of the most dense of forests, out of view, lay the fallen, followers of Sataniel, also aware of Gabriel's target, probably more aware than he was. The downpour already heavy, increased. Visibility was down to a few paces due to the array of tree trunks, undergrowth and uneven terrain.

Gabriel nodded to Jesuel to continue. He did so, but cautiously listening. The water ran off his nose as he shook his head at Gabriel. He couldn't hear anything. The deluge that crashed into the undergrowth drowned not only the vegetation, but also the sounds of the forest.

***

Over the ridge, the trees had thinned out to a clearing with a wooden structure at the eastern end. Gabriel scanned the perimeter, but there was no one to be seen. *Why weren't we dropped here?* Jesuel had gone to ground and was covering the rest of the tower as they climbed the small but steep ridge. Gabriel cautiously approached the outcrop of rock to the north. Under the overhang, Enoch had taken shelter. He sat on a polished stone speaking the words as he drew them on loose damp pages. His clothes, a full-length garment of heavy weave, tied with twine around his waist, were as sodden as the nature around him. Gabriel could not believe what he saw. Jesuel brought up the rear, but with still no sign of any hostiles, he was now becoming very weary.

'Seven Mountains of Fire Falling from the Sky,' claimed the old scribe as he wrote. 'The stars of heaven fell unto the earth, as a fruit tree untimely casts its fruit in a mighty wind.' He paused and looked up at

Gabriel, then back to his book. 'And when the heavens parted, every mountain and every island were moved out of their places.'

The angelic military unit stood, ankle deep in mud, in disbelief, soaked, cold and breathless in front of the old scribe. Disbelief was the only expression any of them could muster. Their target was a soulcarrier, a *human*, despised by the angelic for being favoured above all others.

Why risk angelic life on a being of the First Realm? What was so important that the Council of the Seventh Heaven would even risk setting foot on the First Realm, blatantly ignoring the first rule of not to interfere. The questions flashed through Gabriel's head. Then he stated the obvious. 'He's a soulcarrier!'

'What were you expecting?' asked Jesuel. 'This is the First Realm.'

'I never really thought about it until now.'

'Do we take it with us?' spluttered Korniel over his should, his back to Gabriel, as he watched the tree line. 'Or do we kill it?'

'Gmial!'

'Yes Gabriel! You want me to kill it?'

'This mission is an extraction!'

Without warning, a flash of sheet lightning filled the sky. As the clearing became illuminated the angelic immediately froze.

'One Archangel! Two Archangel!' Ubaviel counted.

The thunderclap that followed shook the ground beneath their bodies.

'Hell! That was close!' he continued. 'Barakiel must be about.'

Gabriel thought of his close friend, Barakiel, the Angel of Chance and the Lightning of God. 'We are the only one's on the ground, right?' he questioned.

Ubaviel opened his mouth to answer, but stayed quiet. Then an interruption came out of that solemn moment, in the rain. A crackle of a voice in their ears broke the silence. Uriel's voice came over loud and clear.

'The target is right in front of you!'

'Iinnad we're running silent,' reminded Gabriel.

'Is Enoch OK? I need to speak with him!' Uriel broadcasted.

Gabriel could not believe that an angelic of Uriel's calibre would be stupid enough to mention the name of their target on an open com-link.

'Iinnad! Explain *running silent* to Uriel,' ordered Gabriel, the damage already done. 'And land that bloody thing. I want to get out of here.'

'Hostiles!' screamed the reply.

Out of every muddy ditch and rut, from behind every bush and tree, the fallen came. The first fallen to capture Enoch alive would get some form of reward or promotion; it was their way. Falling from grace leaves the spirit of the Lord in the heavens. The physical appearance was the same, however, their clothes begin to fade, pride becomes a trait, injuries took time to heal leaving scars. Above all, they lost the gift of flight, having only the ability to glide. None of the changes made them stupid. They knew that the human must have been tagged, but the fallen needed to be sure.

'Gabe! Gabe!' shouted Iinnad. 'Get outa there!'

Acting on Iinnad's warning, the entire tower went to ground, backs to the rock, as Enoch continued to write, oblivious to the angelic's actions. The Watchers had never hurt one of his people before. Through the shower, Jesuel's observant eyes caught the fallen approach from behind a fallen tree.

'Incoming!' he shouted.

Streaks of bright light burst across the shelter and vaporised the rain on exit. This was heavy weaponry for the fallen to be carrying around in the rain and the angelic tower had no form of defence against it. Gabriel slammed the manuscript closed much to the annoyance of Enoch who was still writing. He then roughly bound it in leather and took hold of the old man's arm. As the rain vaporised around them, the tower returned fire. Gabriel, without thought, dragged Enoch into the rain and the battle zone. He jolted the old man from side to side, avoiding the enemy fire.

'Can we kill it and get outta here?' Gmial eagerly asked.

'The target is to be kept alive,' Gabriel replied.

'South!' screamed Iinnad over the com. 'South of the clearing, through the trees! There's a footpath towards the sea!'

'To the sea?' Serael shouted.

'Evac on the beach of the estuary,' Iinnad corrected herself.

'No! Evac here!' Gabriel replied.

'Gabe! I've been instructed south. Head south!'

With Enoch in tow, they could not fly. Their only option *was* to run. The forearm brace weapon was having little effect in there present conditions. It fired a blade at high speed, which was capable of bouncing off hard surfaces to cause maximum damage. Mud, water and very few rocks meant the brace were no use at all. What the angelic needed now was firepower and lots of it. There was nothing the tower could do but head for the wooden structure and the southern tree line beyond. The presence of the large numbers of fallen did explain one thing, the hard rain, but that didn't seem to matter now. If anything, it aided in their escape, for the visibility to be poor meant that the pursuit would be difficult.

Suddenly, out of nowhere a mass of brace weapon fire filled the area with light. It came from the west. The figures of the fallen dived for whatever cover they could find. The tables had turned. It was time to run.

Gmial handed Enoch to Jesuel as they headed across the clearing.

'Iinnad!' called Gabriel. 'Tell Michael, thanks for the back up.'

Just as Gabriel's tower reached the southern tree line, Serael was killed. For Pestilence to land the Concentrated Electrified Light weapons, CEL, needed to be silenced. The drop-ships were designed to take hits, but sustained firepower, especially as accurate as those being fired was too accurate for comfort and Serael's death was evidence of that.

'Unidentified! Stand down!' shouted Michael, over the com-link.

'Pestilence control!' came a jovial voice. 'Pestilence control! Barakiel here! We've Gabriel in our sights, presently giving cover fire.'

Minimum risk to all the angelic would have been Michael's priority in saving the life of the soulcarrier. Now, even that had gone wrong.

‘Barakiel! This is Michael!’

‘Michael!’ dropping the jovial. ‘How are you?’

‘Do not engage! I repeat! Barakiel do not engage!’

‘What!’ Barakiel screamed. ‘You haven’t seen what’s flying down here!’

‘We are on our way! Stand down and get back to your own ship.’

‘Negative!’ replied Barakiel. ‘Gabriel’s up to his neck! Whose idea was this anyway? Uriel’s?’

‘LAND THAT BLOODY THING!’ screamed Gabriel.

Drenched, the angelic moved through the dense undergrowth, in and out of water filled ditches until they found the path.

‘Found the footpath,’ Gmial announced.

‘That’s a stream!’ Phul disagreed.

One part of their training had always been to stay off worn paths. On the other hand, Phul was right, it was a stream. The downpour was flowing towards a river.

‘The path you’re on, follow it. South!’ Iinnad instructed. ‘And Gabe, I don’t think the link interference is to do with the rain. Just get outta there!’

***

Finally, from the ground Pestilence could clearly be seen coming through the clouds. The roar of the engines increased as it attempted to hover with its gun turrets vaporising the rain and scorching the earth. With the element of surprise on his side, Barakiel had managed to reduce the numbers of the enemy by enough for a possible safe extraction.

The jovial Barakiel made it to Gabriel's position. In effort to greet Enoch, uncharacteristically he stopped. Spinning back to Gabriel, he switched off his link.

'He's a soulcarrier! We risked our necks for a soulcarrier?'

'No!' Gabriel replied slapping Barakiel's shoulder. 'We did. You disobeyed orders.'

Barakiel shook his head and looked through the trees. He could see movement. The enemy had begun to regroup and were to close in.

Gabriel signalled for his tower to cover Jesuel and Enoch, while he prepared to cover the rear with Barakiel.

'This stinks,' launched Barakiel. 'Who's idea was this anyway?'

'Uriel's,' replied Gabriel.

'I knew it! Didn't I say Uriel?'

Barakiel took out his sword and flipped the cap off the end of the hilt to open a small-concealed compartment. He tilted the tip of the blade into the air to allow the contents to fall into his hand.

'I have to be quick with these,' he explained. 'Find me a target Gabe cause these little Cherubs don't like water!'

Barakiel gently shook his sword and five silver cubes the size of a pebble dropped into his hand. They began to sizzle and steam on contact with the rain in his palm.

'A target Gabe!'

Gabriel motioned to the ever-increasing numbers of figures that emerged in the undergrowth to his left. Barakiel had already stood his sword in the wet earth and shared the shinny metal cubes into both hands and began to throw them at the figures. Replacing the cap on his hilt, Barakiel took Gabriel's arm and pulled him away from the direction he had thrown the cubes.

'What's supposed to happen?' the Archangel asked.

'Like I said, they don't like water.'

'What?'

Barakiel began to drag his friend from the battle zone. Gabriel was hesitant, more curious of what was about to happen, than make a quick exit. Then it happened. All five cubes exploded within a moment of each other, exerting an immense amount of energy for their size. The shockwave knocked the two angelic to the ground. Sliding over the mud, Gabriel almost let go of his sword. A fraction of a moment later the searing heat from the flames caught them. The tree canopy was engulfed with the bright colourful display of destruction at least twenty paces deep. All that remained within the mayhem; were dark figures on fire. The two friends wet and muddied picked themselves up. Above them, the fireball rose into the grey sky changing the colour of the clouds and reflecting off the surfaces of Pestilence.

'Wow! That worked better than I thought,' Barakiel jumped. 'We gotta go!'

'What in God's name was that?' screamed Michael over the link.

'Barakiel?' answered Iinnad.

The Angel of Chance laughed as the balls of flame dispersed into the rain. On the ground the foliage was still on fire. Through the yellow orange flickers of the firewall came the occasional indiscriminate beam of CEL weapons fire in a vain hope of finding a target.

The remainder of both towers had already disappeared into the trees. Nothing was said between the two old friends. The flames obscured the fallen's view. Nevertheless, the amount of energy beams that ripped through the trees to the south of the clearing put the fear of hell into the fleeing towers. Luckily, the dense woodland was beginning to protect the hunted. The scorching light was finding trees before it found one of them. The thundering rain struck the foliage and the falling trees, their trunks shattered by energy beams, was deafening to the acute hearing of the angelic. *So much for a covert operation.* Barakiel looked back over his shoulder to Gabriel who was signalling to his tower to keep moving. Enoch was as confused as he was old. He may have been a primitive, but he understood that this was a battle and for some reason, he was the prize.

'Is he *really* that important?' Barakiel screamed to Gabriel over the explosions.

'Uriel and Michael seem to think so,' replied the Archangel.

'You're about to engage more hostiles, so keep heading south,' blurted Iinnad. 'And that's the good news. The bad news is that the Damocles has confirmed the comet is coming our way... Fast!'

'Catch up Iinnad! Work with me. We *are* heading south!'

'We are landing in front of you by the water's edge. See you in five.'

'Five what?' Barakiel broadcasted as he reduced speed.

'Barakiel, it's time to go!' shouted Gabriel.

'I'm your cover brother,' came the faint reply.

Gabriel's tower pushed forward, ignoring the cuts inflicted from the brambles and branches. Assisted by Jesuel, Enoch staggered out of the forest and into the clear of the river estuary, his thick weaved clothes entangled with twigs and thorns. The old man slowed even more as his feet sunk into the silt of the riverbank. The soft mud of the forest had been pleasant in comparison. In front of them, the clouds began to move and twist in an unnatural manner, instead of several layers drifting at different speeds; they started to form a dense plume that funnelled down in a spiral towards the ground. The tip of the spray radiated a mini rainbow of colour refracted in the vapour as it caught the sun trying to break through cloud cover. Hidden within its grey moist mass was Pestilence. Its front, two massive vertical lift afterburners bellowing out columns of flames onto the beach as the sides of the burners, acting as mechanical feet, extended out for touch down, surrounded by spray and steam. As the majority of the debris cleared leaving only spray, the drop-ship appeared, its cockpit window lights visible through the dust like a giant face.

Enoch's eyes were wide open. *How was he to write this down?* The old man did not complain.

'We are running out of time!' interrupted Michael on the com-link. 'Barakiel, I want to see a tactical withdrawal. Gabriel! Make sure he does!'

Barakiel glanced over to his own tower then, staring Gabriel right in the eyes, he smiled. He was never one for taking orders, but that didn't mean he was all bad.

'I'm not the Angel of Chance for nothing!' he shouted over the roar of Pestilence's engines as it settled on the beach. 'Get out of here! I'll cover you.'

'And you?'

'You get the primitive back to the ship, then cover me. Now go!'

The eye contact between the two old friends was all they needed. Gabriel left Barakiel by the mounds of grass that lined the silt beach and entered the downdraft of dust and spray. Protecting the primitive was Gabriel's primary objective. Jesuel moved as quickly as was angelically possible, pulling Enoch through the wind and rain, as they aimed for the shelter of the bay doors.

On Gabriel's order Gmial and Korniel instantly took flight. Flying up and out of the downdraft, they positioned themselves for cover fire. Jesuel, in one swift movement, removed his brace and threw it into the air. The rotating brace reached its pinnacle and then began to fall back to earth only to slip onto Korniel's other arm. He locked it, now with two brace, he began to fire at the tree trucks so that the blades would detonate. A blur of fallen figures filtered through the trees into the marsh grass. Korniel and Gmial continued to find targets. At the sight of these two beings, saviours in flight, Enoch stumbled. The remnants of Barakiel's tower took pop shots at the fallen as they awaited their leader in the long grass. Additional support for the beleaguered towers came from the drop-ships lower gun turrets. The barrage did not stop the enemy's advance. Seven to one, ten to one, as every moment passed the odds multiplied. Both towers *had* to leave. Jesuel plucked the primitive from the riverbank and dragged him to the relative safety of the bay doorway, but as he climbed, Ubaviel was hit. Barakiel's tower faced up to the overwhelming numbers of the fallen. The Angel of Chance's time to play the odds was at hand. To win or to lose had not entered his head. Barakiel just smiled to himself; wiped the water from his eyes, as he left his friend and took his tower towards the advancing hunters.

Through the swirling dust Gabriel could also see Barakiel and the remainder of his tower attempting to take flight. Another bolt of light caused more death as Tabaet, from Barakiel's tower, dropped to his knees then over onto his side by the edge of the forest. The increased roar of the engines told Gabriel their transport was leaving. He stared straight ahead at the side entrance to the bay; it was now moving, slowly rising. Enoch forcefully climbed to his feet, his precious book still tucked under his right arm. Jesuel attempted to assist him up into the bay as Pestilence continued to rise. As though he were summoned, Uriel appeared in the doorway. His bloody nose was clearly visible though the debris as his outstretched hand greeted Enoch. The old man grabbed his friend's hand with his left and then with both allowing the bound manuscript to fall back towards the First Realm. Jesuel made a snatch for it. He briefly grasped the book, but his fingers slipped across the wet leather binding. The wrapping became loose and the manuscript was gone. He then pulled himself into the bay. Once safe, he turned to offer Gabriel a helping hand, but he wasn't there. His Commander had decided to assist Barakiel since Enoch, was out of harm's way.

'Standby! Full burn!' came over the com-link.

The down draft from Pestilence increased creating a gale that blew against Gabriel's back. He stopped in his tracks half way between the transport and the trees. The Archangel gradually looked up at Pestilence as it rose into the grey debris filled sky. He could just see Jesuel in the doorway shaking his head. The burners of Pestilence had blasted four massive holes in the riverbank as it left the surface. Now, filling with water, Gabriel struggled for the marsh grass and a more stable footing.

'Your orders Gabriel,' came Michael's voice in his ear.

'I'm sorry Barakiel,' Gabriel said to himself as his wings opened.

He turned to face the down draft. Instantly, the wind filled his wings and lifted the saddened angelic high over his beleaguered friend. Gabriel did not look down. He kept his eyes focused on the bay doors and Jesuel. He could not look down.

'Barakiel!' called Michael over the link. 'You are on your own!'

'What?' Barakiel screamed. 'Gabriel!' the Angel of Chance's scream became nothing more than a faint cry. 'Don't leave me! Gabe!'

Still taking heavy fire, Pestilence unrelentingly, climbed into the dark morning sky. The fallen had completely overrun Barakiel, Balberith, Asbeel and Lauviah. There was nothing Gabriel could do for Barakiel without Michael's support and he had no intention of giving it.

Landing in the doorway, Gabriel ignored Jesuel and Uriel as he turned to check on his flying support. Members of *his* tower were still in the line of fire.

'Gmial! Korniel!' he snapped into his link. 'Our job is done here!'

Both the winged angelic continued to rain fire down on the fallen in a futile attempt to aid their four abandoned saviours.

'That's an order!' Gabriel reminded them.

Gmial hopelessly fired a couple of shots into the trees and then banked towards the transport and safety. Korniel in anger released every blade he had in both brace. The colossal rate of fire forced the angelic higher into the sky, only for him to drop and swoop into Pestilence's belly. He touched base and swung around on the frame handle into the bay before Gmial. His partner was a little slower, but managed to reach safety. Just inside and glad to be in one piece, Gmial took a moment to catch his breath. From the dust cloud below one last energy beam rose like a flaming sword from the realm's surface. Gabriel caught it in the corner of his eye and shoved Gmial out of the way as the beam entered the bay, putting a second clear scorched hole in the Archangel's wing. With the last tower member aboard, the door closed. Gabriel showed no concern for his own injury as he checked each surviving member of his tower. Jesuel without his brace sat on the crystal floor staring at his bare arm. He was interrupted, by a very grateful, Korniel, who handed back the weapon. Jesuel looked up and shook his head.

'I will never wear them again,' he said quietly.

'For what it's worth, thank you,' Korniel said as he left Jesuel to his thoughts.

The transport soared into the sky. Gabriel sat opposite Jesuel on the translucent floor and looked down at the coastline and the river estuary where they had left their brothers in arms. He had fought alongside each and every one of them, and now they were gone. Again, Gabriel had survived. In his mind, it was as though he had wanted a different outcome. Serael had saved his life. Ubaviel made him laugh. Not one of them would be forgotten; not even the Tower of War, Douis, Islesen, Lauviah, Tabaet, Asbeel, Balberith and his dear old friend Barakiel. No one spoke. Their introduction to the First Realm was over.

IV

The First Realm. 07.25hrs Friday 13th July AD 2001 EST

Even with the curtains drawn, there was enough light in the early hours of that summer day, to creep into the hallway, without Cole having to switch the light on. As he sneaked into his apartment the boards creaked. Cole had accepted that Rebecca was now the boss of the house, while pregnant at least, and asleep; this was not the time to wake her. He passed the open door to the living room, took off his jacket and threw it through the doorway, over the nearest dining chair, as he had a done a hundred times before. It missed the chair and hit the polished floor, as it had done a hundred times before. He winced as his mobile made a loud thud. He crept into the bedroom. The bedside lamp came on; he covered his eyes, in both shame and from the light. With his night vision shot, he stumbled.

'You missed the chair!' Rebecca stated, tiredness in her voice. 'Jacket still on the floor is it?'

'I didn't want to wake you!'

'Fat chance!'

Cole stripped to his boxers and attempted to join his pregnant wife.

'Teeth!' she barked.

Cole froze one leg off the floor.

'And while you're at it, your jacket as well.'

Slowly he reversed and walked out of the bedroom backwards to the bemusement of his loving spouse. Once out of sight of the Master of the House, he darted into the living room to deal with the jacket and remembered to put his mobile phone on charge. Something else he was always forgetting. Within seconds his mouth was full of mint with a stick of plastic bristles protruding from his face. Staring at himself, unshaven in the bathroom mirror, he could not help but smile. He was home, he was happy and the evil of the early morning had been left at the front door. The bottle caps were in the bucket on top of the kitchen cupboard. Everything was as it should be. With the light now off in the bedroom, and his eyes not accustomed to the dark once again, he fumbled his way into bed and snuggled up to his very understanding partner for life, if only for a couple of hours.

'Do the letter's O.L.Y. mean anything to you,' asked Cole breaking the silence.

'At the door! Leave it at the door!'

Cole didn't bother to mention that he was almost blown up that morning.

***

France – 11.30hrs Friday 13th July AD 2001 GMT +1

Over three and half thousand miles away in Paris, the sun had been up and the French capital had been busy for several hours. Through the narrow full-length window of an executive office of one of the many swish architectural masterpieces of the twentieth century, unbeknown to Gabriel, stood his nemesis. The Guardian of the First Realm was unaware of the presence of the fallen on the wet realm. It had been so long since they clashed that it had slipped Gabriel's mind that some might still reside. Abbadon preferred it that way.

From the outskirts, his three-storey office building rose above the surrounding properties. It overlooking the aged city to the southwest, sprawled over the low land severed by the River Seine. The building, with blackened windows circling each floor and resting on sandstone blocks gave an oriental appearance, complemented by the short grass lawns at the front and a large mass of pampas grass by the footpath leading to the entrance. A solitary Japanese pine stood in the open lawn to the east of the entrance, with a water garden to the side of the main complex gave a pristine image of peace and tranquillity. This was the European headquarters of Apolyon Incorporated, Abbadon's company. Just as misleading by appearance, the building's foundations, hidden by the modern façade, held an evil secret. Abbadon's company had a history stretching back through the centuries. As the Managing Director had always said, 'If you're going to live for eternity, then you have no excuse not to live well.'

Abbadon was one of the great angelic that fell from grace and took many of the daughters of men as his wives. The dark angelic was Chief of the Demonic of the Underworld Hierarchy. Once, he had resided on Sagun, the Third Realm. However, since his removal, he had taken a liking to the wet Realm and his only ambition was to rule it for himself. In the Underworld, he was second, only to Sataniel and Death was his equal. Sataniel was the left hand of God, the greatest of them all to fall from grace. However, Sataniel was not on the First Realm. Therefore, it was for Abbadon to rule. This was *his* realm.

The steel tipped stiletto heel struck the polished marble floor of the corridor outside the MD’s office as it left the confines of the lift. Taking long strides the skin-tight leather clad woman marched down the walkway between the offices towards the mahogany double doors of the Managing Director’s office. In the reception area opposite, carpet replaced the marble floor and the footsteps quietened. The true blue eyes and the black shoulder length hair made her instantly recognisable. She ignored the receptionist; nor did she await an invite, opening both doors to the office. The elegant woman stopped in the doorway, turned to the objecting secretary at the desk and with her blue eyes, glared the point as if to say, ‘I have the right!’ The objecting woman sat back down as the leather-clad female closed the doors behind her.

‘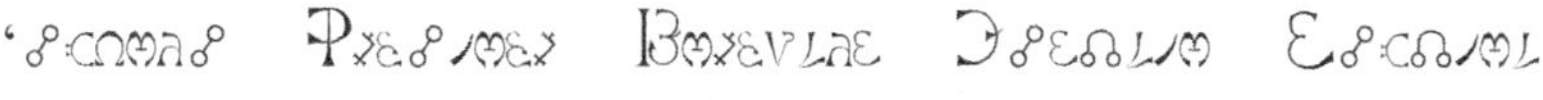 ,’ chanted the woman in leather. ‘Chemiath Aroura Maridon Elison Marmiadon Seption Hesaboutha Ennouna.’

The executive office of the MD of Apolyon Inc was oval in shape and dark, very dark. The grey carpet and the black silk walls sucked the light out of the room. Around the walls at waist height were pages from a manuscript, encased in an illuminated reinforced display. The display was broken by two sets of mahogany double doors; one set at its narrowest point, by the reception and the other to the right on its length leading to the boardroom. At the opposite end from the boardroom was a large black leather in-laid desk and chair. A chessboard had been placed carefully on the furthest corner and on the nearest corner another chequered board game with black and white counters. In the middle of the office were seven disfigured life-size statues, aged bronze in colour, assuming painfully twisted positions. In the corner behind the desk, on a pedestal, stood the statue of an equally painfully twisted bird with very few feathers. The only other source of light was three full-length windows on the outward facing wall. Silhouetted in the window closest to the desk stood a beast. He was a massive bulk of a figure that could have easily been working out in the gym for at least fifty years. Only the large jagged ears and the extended bony tentacles protruding from his back showed that this was no human. Like a silver lining the sun shone off the scales that lined his physique. The contrasting light highlighted the scars that cover his body, the signs of a warrior that had seen too many wars. The silhouette turned from the window into the centre of the office and disappeared. Standing before the woman, was a 6½-foot gentle giant with a round face, which cracked when he smiled giving him an elderly, but not that elderly, and learned appearance.

In a quiet unruffled voice, he spoke 'How are you Lilith?'

She smiled in response. It was rare for her Master to bother with small talk.

'So tell me,' Abbadon continued sitting on the front of his desk. 'Was the trip successful?'

'I'd say so,' she smirked. 'Although… it depends on your point of view, what with… *death* and all…'

With that, she unzipped the top of her leather outfit. With the absences of a bra and unabashed by nudity, she revealed more than a human female would have. Her right-hand retrieved a metal canister and handed it to Abbadon, and then swiftly zipped herself back up. He took the tube; the metal warmed by her skin, and opened it very gently removing the contents. He stood up and walked over to the window to view the pages. This gentle giant's figure became that of a beast once more in one blended movement. Uncharacteristically, the beast, in silhouette carefully unrolled the two pages in the light, glistening razor teeth revealed his smile.

'Only two?' he asked.

'It's all they had!'

The dark angelic examined the pages for authenticity and then took a moment to read them. He took his time, going over the sections again and again if need be. Then he marched across the office to a gap in the display casing. His hand disappeared under the rim and several audio-bleeping tones could be quietly heard. There was a hiss as the air pressure changed and the lids over the gap in the display opened.

'Behold, he came with ten thousand of his warriors, to execute judgement upon them, and destroy the wicked, and reprove all the carnal for everything which the sinful and ungodly had done…' Abbadon read, then switched to the other page. 'And drew nigh to a spacious habitation built also with stones of crystal. Its walls too, as well as pavement, were formed with stones of crystal, and crystal likewise was the ground. Its roof had the appearance of agitated stars and flashes of lightning; and among them were cherubim of fire in a stormy sky.'

Lilith frowned as she listened to Abbadon's words. 'The Temple of Icea… how could anyone *here* know?'

'A flame burned around its walls; and its portal blazed with fire. When I entered into this dwelling, it was hot as fire and cold as ice. No trace of delight or of life was there. Terror overwhelmed me, and a fearful shaking seized me.'

'The Temple of Icea was destroyed,' Lilith interrupted a second time.

'The events have already passed,' the Dark Prince whispered, slightly disappointed. 'At least your efforts will help to complete the manuscript, if nothing else.'

'I wasn't to know,' Lilith responded. 'I'm sorry.'

'No matter… So, did he receive the message?' Abbadon asked as he carefully placed the two pages into the display and closed the lid.

'Most definitely!'

'Did he *read* the message?'

'I'm informed that he read all the messages, but not completely understood I fear.'

'HA!' burst Abbadon. 'You fear nothing Lilith and that will be your undoing.'

'Only a figure of speech my Lord. Am I to understand you're saying… you fear Gabriel?' Lilith asked hesitantly.

'Fear? No! Wary of? …Yes! I have good reason to be… and you're not?'

'No.'

'Your undoing.'

Turning back to Lilith and deep in thought over what he had just said, Abbadon was contemplating his next move. He moved gracefully to the corner of his desk. The gentle man re-emerged.

'I'll give him a little time; a day maybe. And then...'

Abbadon stopped to think, but was distracted by the chessboard on the desk. Lilith began to grow impatient awaiting the end of the sentence and her next set of instructions. Abbadon moved a chess piece. His eyes still trained on the board. He had made his decision.

'Do you fancy another trip?' Not waiting for an answer. 'In fact, I'll come with you, I don't want things… to get too *messy*.'

'Why not just kill him?'

'I just said; I don't want things to get too messy. Anyway, could you kill him?'

'No problem!'

Abbadon walked across the office to the window and shook his finger.

'There you go again with that lack of fear,' he answered. 'Because he destroyed me once; made me look a fool, I want to *destroy* him and to do that, you don't just kill. You do everything you can to ruin them and *then* and *only then*, do you let them know it was you.'

Abbadon glided over to the fossilised bird on the stone pedestal and stroked its featherless back.

'You let them know it was you,' he repeated quietly.

'It's just a game, isn't it?'

'This is no game Lilith! This is revenge, but even revenge can be enjoyable and remember it as thou it were yesterday.'

***

The Third Realm. 18,009 years ago

Sagun, the Third Realm, where a war had waged for over two centuries; causing the deaths of so many angelic on both sides and with the destruction of so much, to such an extent that even the climate began to change. Nature had become an unwilling participant in the battle between good and evil. Defenceless and with nothing more to lose, the barren wasteland was now fighting back. The Great Plain left no shelter from the sun. At night, the icy cold winds penetrated their armour touching the hearts of the angelic.

A scrawny half starved bird with few feathers managed to fly low across the Great Plain. On the dusty ground, the military might of an angelic division, watched in amazement that the little creature could sustain flight. It came to rest, perched high above on a burnt crystal column of the ruins of the Temple of Icea.

***

Bethany awoke with a start. Gabriel, Iinnad and Jesuel were already awake, leaning against the crystal temple awaiting the arrival of the sun, which had just begun to peak through the gaps in the jagged horizon on the near side of the Great Plain. The sunlight warmed the surface of the crystal. The bird had watched the army that night.

'I'm gonna shoot that damn bird!' shouted Barakiel making everyone jump.

'Thought you were asleep?' Iinnad questioned.

'I *was*!'

'We need to get moving,' Gabriel informed Jesuel.

'I thought you always watched the sunrise?' Jesuel asked.

'Not today.'

'And if it were to be your last?'

'It won't be my last.'

'And if it is mine?' Bethany whispered giving Gabriel a tight embrace.

Gabriel submitted and sat back down his eyes fixed on the eastern horizon. On every realm, the sun had risen in the East. Bethany sat behind him and wrapped her arms around Gabriel's waist, her chin rested on his shoulder. Iinnad stood with Jesuel and Barakiel as they watched the sun climb. Slowly the sky changed colour and its rays hit the temple as it cleared the mountain range, its light being refracted once again, as it had done every morning since the temple's creation.

There was still no word from the Sword of Damocles. It appeared that Gabriel *was* to lead the angelic army into battle. He had been chosen by his fellow warriors to command and command he would. He surveyed the encampment and allowed his eyes to follow the course of the footpath from the circle of stones past the temple and into the foothills of the Malam Grigori Mountains. The angelic army was on the move once again.

Gabriel, with his closest friends by his side at the front of the column, led the army, following the path through the foothills. Slowly, they gained altitude and as they did so, the climb became more difficult.

'Gabe!' Barakiel called out. 'Are you sure about this?' 'The path is safe. The fallen's only advantage is in defence.'

'That's it?' Barakiel inquired now behind him.

'That's it.' Gabriel said staring into Barakiel's eyes. 'Can you sense them?'

'No!'

'So why are you worried? You'll sense them when we reach the caves.'

A head of the column, Iinnad raised an arm. 'I sense something!' she butted in, scanning the ridge. 'I'll take point, someone cover me.'

'Barakiel, Phul, Gmial, Asbeel and Tabaet!' Gabriel snapped. 'Back her up before she does something crazy!'

***

On that fateful day, evil sat at the entrance to the Caves of Enlightenment. A price had to be paid for the enlightenment that was offered in the dark damp tombs within the Malam Grigori Mountains. The caves held many secrets, but it was not enlightenment that Gabriel sought. The being that lurked in the shadows was the reason he had to enter. This was Sataniel's world, Amente, the Underworld. To most forms of life it was known as hell. It was said that, 'Sataniel stood at its gates.' The statement was not entirely accurate. Abbadon, one of Sataniel's princes and trusted second, stood watch over the entrance. It was Abbadon's army that the angelic had been battling on the Third Realm and it was Abbadon that Gabriel wanted.

***

By mid-afternoon, Iinnad, still on point had arrived at the Col of Descent that was situated in a dip at the head of the present valley gorge they had climbed. The Col of Descent was topped with shale and led down into the next gorge of green and rock towards the Caves of Enlightenment. She gazed back down the path in awe at the angelic might that she was leading and couldn't help but smile at that thought. The view of the mountains and valleys, rocks and warriors was spellbinding. Gmial and Phul followed, slipping on the shale as they ascended to join her. Barakiel, with Asbeel and Tabaet raced to catch up.

'What did you stop for?' he asked.

'Look,' she motioned with her head.

'It's hell,' replied Barakiel missing the point.

'It's beautiful,' Iinnad explained.

'It's also hell!'

The column of warrior's halted as Gabriel, Jesuel, and Bethany joined the scouting party. The nine of them stood in a line and gazed down into the next valley. The shale broke into very short dry grass, littered with white chalk boulders. The grey path cut through the grass and lead straight towards a horse-shoe shaped ridge with its opening on the far side.

'Shall we spread out?' Iinnad asked. 'We don't have to follow the path any more. We could work our way around and attack from all sides.'

'I will have a look,' Gabriel replied as he slowly negotiated the shale. 'Wait for me. The caves should be in that crescent shaped ridge,' he pointed. 'When I signal, fly in and evenly spread out around the edge to the cliff's edge.'

'What cliff edge?' Barakiel asked.

'Understood,' replied Jesuel forcefully. 'Barakiel, the caves are at the base of a cliff face. There has to be a cliff. Tell the tower commanders.'

The moment he had given the word, the entire angelic force began to arm their brace weapons and then transform. The sound of rushing wind gently filled the valley as the warrior's of God stretched their wings.

'Do you want me to come with you?' Bethany called after Gabriel.

Gabriel shook his head. 'Make sure the column fly through the Col and follow the path, just to be safe.'

The remaining angelic stood on the Col of Descent and watched their leader carefully walk down the path across the sandstone shelf, fractured by the weather of many cold wet nights in the distant past. Nervously, Gabriel edged his way to the crest of the slope and stared downward. The ridge dropped sharply for several paces and then an extremely steep grassy slope funnelled into a scar in the earth that was the top of the cliffs, less than fifty paces apart. The path led straight down towards the top of the scar, joined by a stream, which sprung from the rock, half way down. A single tree marked the source of the water as it tumbled over the rocky trail into the gorge. With the entrance to the caves still obscured by the cliff face, Gabriel gave the signal. Jesuel relayed it to the tower commanders, who in turn took flight and swooped over the Col, followed by the angelic army. Gabriel's closest friends joined him by a stream that turned into a cascade about sixteen paces from the floor of the gorge. The air was cool and moist; moss grew on the sheltered rocks as the group rested from the sun, still alert to the possible dangers.

'I will go alone,' Gabriel announced.

'No!' Bethany objected. 'I'm coming with you.'

'I must do this alone,' Gabriel stressed, kissing her cheek.

Bethany looked to Jesuel for support.

'Gabriel!' his old friend called. 'You are not to enter the caves. Those are the orders. Discover the caves and destroy them.'

'They are caves Jesuel, you can only destroy them from within.'

'Then we all go,' Barakiel stepped forward, occasionally glancing skyward searching for the scrawny bird that was still following them.

'I agree,' added Phul.

'Anyway, you can't the break the rules alone,' Tabaet supported.

'Thank you, but I will go alone.'

High above, Gabriel's army stood watching and waiting. They were out in the open on the steep grass rock littered slopes. Their wings were still open, awaiting the signal to attack. Gabriel stood on the edge where the slopes broke away to reveal a vertical drop of seventy paces, eroded by the stream at the bottom.

'Inform Damocles of the location and prepare for a bombardment, but wait until I say,' Gabriel ordered. 'A bombardment will only drive the fallen deeper into the ground. We need to flush them out.'

‘And how are you gonna do that?’ Iinnad inquired.

‘I have no idea,’ Gabriel smiled as he began to climb down the waterfall.

The base of the scar was flat and only thirty paces wide. It was scattered with loose rocks and the stream had found a hundred routes out of the gorge. The vertical rock face and the steep slopes above completely blocked out the sun. The warrior of light stood alone, ankle deep in water, in the gloom facing the entrance to enlightenment. He smiled with confidence, winked at Bethany and looked up high above to his army, proud of each and every one of them.

‘A leader will lead by example,’ he muttered to himself, repeating a line Michael had once told him. ‘…and so must I.’

With that in mind he stepped even closer to the opening in the rock face. One more pace and Gabriel would enter the darkness. He paused before he took the final step. The dimly lit cavern impaired the angelic’s vision. Within, Gabriel could hear the heavy breathing of a four-legged beast.

‘You have entered the Caves,’ announced Mithra. ‘You have entered of your own free will. Are you prepared to be judged?’

‘I was expecting to see you with a lion’s head Mithra,’ Gabriel replied recognising the fallen angelic. ‘I’m not here to be judged. I’m looking for Abbadon.’

‘First you must rest and then be judged,’ Mithra said as he approached.

‘You never did listen,’ Gabriel replied as he punched the Judge of Souls.

The bulky being crashed into the dust grabbing the hilt of his sword as he did so. His long hair like a mane covered his face as he drew the blade from beneath his grubby crimson cloak.

'You did not hear me!' retorted Mithra.

'You did not hear me, Mithra!'

Gabriel continued through his motion, kicking the steel from Mithra's hand and holding his own blade to his neck. The judge sarcastically smiled, wiping his hair from his brow with his now free hand.

'Hello Gabriel,' he panted.

'From high, they wish the angelic that have fallen to repent. Since you will not, this may be your new role for eternity. I hope you enjoy it. Now tell me, where's Abbadon?'

Mithra motioned down one of the passages deep into the labyrinth of Amente. Gabriel removed his sword from the fallen's neck.

'That wasn't so hard was it?'

'Somebody must be judged.'

'I won't be here long enough,' advised Gabriel.

'There is more to all of this than you realise. I wouldn't take another step.'

'You're giving me advice, Mithra?'

A booming voice blasted from the shadows. 'I'd listen to him!'

Gabriel knew who had spoken, but he could not yet see Abbadon, the Destroyer.

'I wouldn't take another step either,' the Dark Prince advised.

'You hide from me?' Gabriel questioned.

'Did you hear what I said?'

'I heard you, Abbadon,' Gabriel answered with familiarity in his voice.

From the shadows stepped the Destroyer, the majestic beast of the Underworld. Not a silhouette, but a demon incarnate. His hooves scraped the stone floor as he walked and in the dim light the Dark Prince's eyes glowed a faint red, occasionally blinking in the darkness of his face.

'Allow your eyes to adjust to the dark,' Abbadon instructed. 'Wait on the threshold. Beyond… and any creature here, can and *has* the right to kill you.'

'Why tell me?'

'Don't you want enlightenment? Don't you want the knowledge that comes with wisdom?'

'I came for you, Abbadon!' cautioned Gabriel.

'Everyone comes here eventually,' howled the Dark Lord. 'Everyone; whether they like it or not.'

'For enlightenment?'

'To be judged,' Abbadon answered. 'Punishment has always been an instrument of leaning. Personally, I don't see any problem with it. Be nice and realms fall to pieces and civilisations crumble. Discipline is what they lack. Here we judge… *and* we punish.'

'As you are to be judged,' Gabriel responded. 'My army has destroyed you. The Third Realm is ours!'

'Sagun is yours? *Your* army has destroyed me, has it? Who are you talking to?' Abbadon stepped closer. 'I am Seraphim; you're merely angel. Destroyed am I?'

Gabriel's eyes had become accustomed to the low level of light and he could now see his nemesis. He did not want to show any sign of fear forcing himself to control the tone of his voice. The embers of the three fires at the back of the entrance flared up, to reveal the silhouette of Mithra as he stood and returned to his seat.

With the help of the fires and torches, Gabriel could now make out additional movement within the cave. Crouched and twisted, they were the minions of Sataniel, squatting in every corner, watching and waiting, like the angelic army above. Gabriel composed himself. With his minions here, *where was Sataniel?*

Abbadon benefited two-fold by allowing Gabriel to adjust to the light. He was trying to show Sataniel's minions that he had what it took to lead, and also attempted to give Gabriel a false sense of security. Gabriel had forced Abbadon into a corner without even knowing it. For within the caves Sataniel lurked. Being in the presence of Sataniel was not something that he had anticipated. Maybe Sataniel was the reason Gabriel was instructed not to enter? Deep down, Gabriel knew he had to confront Abbadon and this, only this, should have been at the forefront of his mind. This battle was to be of strategy as well as strength. Entering the caves would open Gabriel's eyes to the evil that lurked within himself. If Gabriel were to succeed and kill Abbadon, then the prophecy would not be fulfilled. It had taken until now for Gabriel to realise why he had been ordered not to enter the caves. Now, it was too late.

He mentally prepared himself for the onslaught of evil and quickly glanced over his shoulder to his friends, but the rock face kept them from view. He carefully stepped over the threshold. Suddenly, a wide-eyed minion with wrinkly grey skin leapt from the ledge it was perched on and raising its arm high, a short blade in hand, it attacked. Gabriel's sword was already drawn. A few drops of blood fell on Gabriel's arm as the creature collapsed into the dust, cut in two by Abbadon's sword. Gabriel turned his blade to ward off Abbadon, but the beast took no notice. He turned towards the minions and flexed his muscles in the light of the flaming corpse. In response, the minions concealed themselves in every crevice. They had got the message.

'If any *one* of these creatures kills you, they get promotion.'

'And you?'

'Including me!' Abbadon gloated spinning round and in the same motion bringing his sword down hard on Gabriel.

Only Gabriel's speed in deflecting the blow avoided injury. The force of the strike knocked him to the ground. Rolling out of the way to avoid a second attack, Gabriel sprung back to his feet. As the swords clashed, Abbadon blocked the entrance, pushing Gabriel back. The angelic met every blow stepping further into the caves.

'How do *you* get promoted?' Gabriel panted with each blow.

Abbadon answered with another strike. 'Prize or a promotion?'

'But you said promotion, Abbadon,' Gabriel pushed.

'I lied,' Abbadon grinned. 'There is one position higher than me and it's taken.'

'But you want it?'

Again, the Destroyer answered the question with his sword. Neither angelic nor fallen was better than the other. And so the battle waged on, the clash of metal echoing down the tunnels. Even when the two warriors paused, you could still hear the sounds of battle. He realised, even though partly willing, he had been led further into Amente. The tunnels, illuminated by flickering torch flame had an uncomfortably warm feel about them. Now he stood in the heart of the Malam Grigori Mountains, a circular cavern with tunnels of all sizes radiating out in all directions. In the centre was a pit, a bottomless pit, the abyss. This was the heart of Abbadon's world. The Dark Lord rested for a moment allowing the point of his sword to dig into the rust coloured dusty ground as he leant on it. He knew the angelic had not the energy to attack. Gabriel stepped back to view his surroundings and to catch a breath before Abbadon resumed the violence once more. Gabriel realised he should have destroyed the mountain. But it was too late to think of what should have been. As he quickly surveyed the cavern, Gabriel could hear the shadows whisper, the unseen minions muttering to each other. Somewhere close by was their king; their Lord. Gabriel had got his breath back and was ready to take the upper hand, he turned to Abbadon, but he was alone.

***

Bethany climbed down the waterfall. The water causing her white linen tunic stuck to her skin. She thought she had heard her mate call, but she wasn't sure. The angelic army waited on the slopes as Bethany approached the entrance to the caves. She would not venture inside, it was too dangerous, but she drew her sword all the same.

'Bethany!' came that familiar voice from within the caves entrance. 'Bethany! I have done it!'

Bethany stepped closer to the entrance, still cautious. Gmial and Phul transformed and took flight, gliding down the cascade to give her support. She glanced up, waiting for their arrival. Feeling a sharp jolt in her arm, she dropped her sword as a demonic dragged her towards the caves. Brace weapon fire hit the ground, illuminating the threshold and the ugly faces of her captors. Gmial and Phul were too late. They touched down and rushed to the entrance. There was no sign of her. The two angelic remained motionless at the edge of the darkness. Their orders were to not enter, under any circumstances.

'Jesuel! What do we do?' shouted Gmial.

'NOTHING! We wait!'

***

Gabriel circled the abyss. He had become lost in the labyrinth that resembled the darkness of the hell he had heard of. He could fight his way out, but alas, he didn't know which direction to take. All he could do was wait in the silence for Abbadon's return. He knew he was being watched from every crack that held a shadow. A short drop below him, within the abyss was a set of gates, closed, the key still in the lock. He crouched down at the edge, cautious and wary of his surroundings, listening for anything which might creep up behind. Without climbing onto the gates, which were below the level of the cave floor, Gabriel would not be able to retrieve the key. Surveying the cavern again, he spotted an old spear, he saw earlier. It could have been there for a thousand lifetimes waiting for Gabriel's use. He took the spear and still wary, leant over the edge of the abyss in an attempt to retrieve the key.

'I wouldn't do that if I were you,' burst Abbadon. 'It doesn't belong to you.'

Startled, Gabriel dropped the spear on the gates, the noise echoing around the evil chamber. The angelic was on his feet; sword drawn and ready once again for anything. Abbadon laughed, his echo chasing his voice down the tunnels of the world beneath. Hands up, he gestured; no weapons. Two minions entered the cave with Bethany in tow. Gabriel sniffed the air to check the scent of the captive. His nemesis had his mate. The angelic of light was not ready for anything. If Gabriel had a strategy it now had to change. This was no longer about him. Somehow, Gabriel had to find a way of getting Bethany back to the surface and that was no small feat. Abbadon confidently stepped forward, his weapon sheathed.

'It's very simple,' he hinted. 'You have a choice, either you jump into the pit or I throw her in. It couldn't be easier.'

Bethany couldn't struggle; the minions had too tight a grip. Her white tunic, already dry, reflected a warm glow, flickering from the light of the flaming torches around the walls of the chamber. Her blonde hair captured the colour of the fire and in that warm mood, a chilling thought; Gabriel knew his existence could end. From a military point of view, Gabriel knew he stood more of a chance at survival. He knew Abbadon wouldn't keep his word. From a personal point of view he was willing to give up his existence to save Bethany. He could not comprehend the thought of not having Bethany by his side for eternity. However, each thought contradicted the next.

'I want you in the pit!' Abbadon demanded. 'You destroy half my army. You come down here thinking you… *you* can beat me, on *my* ground.'

'I didn't come here for enlightenment,' Gabriel highlighted.

'I don't care about enlightenment; I want you in the pit!'

'If I enter, I will have enlightenment.'

'Is that what your stories tell you? Pity… Now, you have no choice; so jump!'

Abbadon snatched Bethany, to the surprise of both Gabriel and the minions. She began to struggle and attempted to charge her brace, but she was unable to aim it at her assailant. Gabriel raised his arm to fire his brace.

'That won't work here,' laughed Abbadon and threw Bethany into the abyss.

'Bethany!' screamed Gabriel not even bothering to fire.

As she fell, below the level of the floor, the gates parted in the centre and swung open, gravity assisted them in crashing against the sides of the bottomless pit. The spear lodged itself between a metal hinge and the earth wall. Protruding out across the entrance, Bethany landed directly on it, holding on, to gain balance and control before swinging her body over to one of the gates. Abbadon's sword was free of its sheath, but so was Gabriel's. His eyes red and his head full of hatred, Gabriel cut Abbadon across the waist before his nemesis had even struck a blow. The swing of Gabriel's blade was still in motion, continuing its path through the first of the two minions. The creature fell to the ground in flames; squealing in pain. Fire, the natural form of cleansing works in nature as with the fallen. Standing tall, Gabriel was more than willing to cleanse Abbadon. Bethany didn't know Gabriel *could* cross the entrance of the abyss. They had both heard the stories, but they were inaccurate. She began to change form, struggling to hold onto the gates as her wings opened. In her given form, she now had the strength to survive and side with her mate to battle the Destroyer. Out of the shadows, on the other side of the abyss, Sataniel's minions appeared. Without thought, Gabriel instinctively fired his brace in their direction. The continual release of blades hit most of their targets and if not, ricocheted off the walls and eventually found a target somewhere in the chamber. Gabriel realising he had been tricked, lowered his brace. The dead continued to burn.

'So I lied,' admitted Abbadon. 'Who's the fool?'

The few minions that were left ceased to advance, parting to make way for their Master. This was becoming an eventful day. Gabriel had never met Sataniel either. He appeared in a pleasant form, no demonic features or wings. His grin was caught by the firelight. If ever looks could be deceiving…

'What were you expecting?' he asked Gabriel with his cheeky smile. 'The devil? Well here I am.' He opened his arms to embrace.

'Never trust the devil; never make a deal with the devil. Just something I've always been told,' Gabriel responded. 'He smiles and you stare, but behind you the blades are out.'

Acting on that, Gabriel spun around, his sword at shoulder height. The heads of two minions drop to the dusty floor as their bodies burst into flames. Out of the corner of his eye, Gabriel could see Abbadon back away. An elegant fallen female tended his wound. Her true blue eyes visible in contrast next to her master's red glare. He could only see her outline, but *why would someone with such grace be in such a place?*

'Elphue Zarethra Nemioth Charboum Melitho,' she muttered as she attended to her master. 'Mephnounos Thraboutha Chemiath Marmiadon Aroura Maridon Elison.'

Gabriel ignored her chanting and stepped-up to the edge of the abyss and looked down at Bethany, fully transformed, she climbed the gates as though it were a ladder. Training his eyes back to Sataniel, Gabriel noticed that he was watching Bethany also.

'She can't leave!' stated Sataniel. 'She passed the entrance and the gates opened. They will close when they have received.'

'When they've received what?' Gabriel demanded to know.

'You! Me,' motioning to Bethany. 'Her!'

'But, Bethany can get out?'

'If only existence was so simple,' Sataniel replied.

Gabriel glanced down at his brace, but left his arm by his side, a gesture of trust. Slowly, step-by-step, he walked around to Sataniel's side of the abyss. The devil waited, only his minions moved, most of them backing away from the vengeful angelic. Now Gabriel was in a position to play the Devil's game. Sataniel calmly took his eyes off Gabriel and looked down at his sword. The angelic sheathed his weapon and switched off his brace. There was nothing else he could do to lure Sataniel into a false sense of security. Gabriel had already made up his mind.

'I am surprised that your loyal army has not come down here to save you,' Sataniel articulated. 'They follow you and then they wait; strange!'

'My warriors follow orders,' advised the angelic. 'They were told not to enter and that means they won't. Ruined your plans?'

'No!' disregarded Sataniel. 'At least you didn't follow those same orders.'

'I have my reason.'

'It's not worked out the way you planned, has it?'

Gabriel didn't answer.

'Abbadon! Take Gabriel's image and order his warriors to enter,' ordered Sataniel, without taking his eyes off his prey. 'Get as many of them as you can to cross the threshold.'

'I wouldn't do that Abbadon,' cautioned Gabriel returning the favour of warning his nemesis. 'They'll kill you, the moment they pick up your scent.'

Abbadon stepped out of the shadows a little confused at the fact that Gabriel was correct, especially with his wound, which would make his scent stronger. He cautiously glanced over to Sataniel to verify his instructions.

'You have your instructions,' snapped Sataniel. 'I will not repeat them.'

Abbadon nodded slowly in his Master's direction and disappeared up one of the tunnels followed by the elegant female. Sataniel gave Gabriel a knowing smile.

'I could have those orders changed before he reaches the surface,' he suggested motioning with his head to the demonic bird perched on a nearby ledge. It was the same scrawny bird that Barakiel had wanted to shoot. 'Abbadon still has a lot to learn, but then, so do you. It's a pity.'

'I think not.'

With those words, Gabriel firmly grabbed hold of Sataniel and pulled him back to the edge of the abyss. The forward motion was faster and more forceful than he was expecting. As Sataniel's centre of balance moved in Gabriel's favour, he began to panic. A few minions, looking for promotion, stepped forward to save their master as Gabriel began to lose his balance over the rim of the abyss.

'Bethany!' he shouted. 'Use your brace!'

Bethany fired one shot and a minion fell from the struggling angelic. She fired again, but then changed her aim and fired at the ground. The ground on the perimeter of the abyss gave way and Sataniel, Gabriel and one of the minions toppled over the edge. Bethany locked her arm into the gates, and with the other out-stretched, she reached for her mate. Gabriel made contact with her, but still struggling to free himself of Sataniel broke free and fell to the lowest part of the gate, just managing to hold on. The gates began to close. Turning his head quickly, from side-to-side, Gabriel looked for Sataniel. On the other half of the gate, Sataniel was climbing fast, with his minions waiting at the rim to pull him to safety. Gabriel re-charged his brace as he climbed and once clear of the edge of the gate, accurately fired. The blade burst into the ground exploding just below where the minions stood, causing them to fall onto their Master; taking him with them into the bottomless pit. The gates were still closing and Sataniel was now desperately scrambling to climb on top before they incarcerated him. To give him strength he began to change form, but he was out of time. As his fingernails became claws, he scratched at the rusty framework, cutting into the metal and the wooden surround. It was no use; he looked up through the grid at his jailer, standing above him as the gates lock shut. A rustic clang of certainty sealed the Supreme Lord of Darkness in the Bottomless Pit. Gabriel darted across the framework to the lock and grasped the key in both hands. Putting his hand through the grid of the gate, Sataniel attempted to stop Gabriel from turning the key. A quiet, but clearly defined hum could be heard as the gate began to shimmer a pale blue. The illumination changed the entire appearance of the cavern. Sataniel's loyal army of minions began to flee with the apparent lack of shadow to dwell in. Sataniel, still hanging from the lattice beneath Gabriel's feet began to laugh.

'And I still win,' he gloated. 'You turn the key and you hold me here for a thousand years. I congratulate you.'

'And you still win?' Gabriel inquired.

'You can leave, Gabriel,' the Devil instructed, then motioning to Bethany. 'But she cannot. These are the Caves of Enlightenment. As I said you have a lot to learn.'

The talons beneath Gabriel's feet let go and Sataniel fell into the abyss.

'Watch all and let Abbadon know all,' called out Sataniel from the darkness.

Confused, Gabriel looked down into the abyss and then around the cavern trying to understand the meaning of what Sataniel had said. The demonic bird leapt from its perch and swooped low passing Gabriel and up one of the many tunnels before the angelic could release a blade. It had followed its Master's instructions and had watched. For a moment, deep in the heart of the underworld there was a sense of peace.

'I should have let Barakiel kill that bird,' Gabriel remarked disappointedly.

'You weren't to know,' encouraged Bethany brushing the dust from his face.

The warrior lovingly embraced his mate and then climbed out of the pit. Turning he offered Bethany a hand, she shook her head, taking heed of what Sataniel had said. Gabriel searched the cavern for movement, but it was empty. Reassuring Bethany with a smile he reached down to take her hand.

'For eternity,' she pondered, breaking the silence and taking her mate's hand.

Gabriel pulled his love from the abyss. The shimmering blue of the solid lattice began to intensify as Bethany crossed the rim. As strong as she was, still in her changed form, blood began to seep from her back. The light intensified still further, until the membrane of her extended wings became transparent; the bone structure and veins visible through the outstretched appendages. The taut skin that connected each and every joint rapidly began to age. The moisture was unexplainably draining from her wings; drying the skin to the point of cracking, allowing the blood to flow. Finally, only the skeletal wing remained calcified; the weight of the bones pulling at Bethany's back until they broke away into the pit, shattering on the gates below. Pure panic covered Gabriel's face as Bethany fell into his arms. He held her tightly as her back profusely bled from the partially cauterised wounds.

She looked into his eyes, 'For eternity,' she repeated.

The hazy emanating light subsided until it disappeared altogether taking Bethany with it. Mystified, Gabriel stood alone;

Bethany had lost her wings. Now, she was gone, literally. Sataniel had taken Bethany from him. He peered over the rim of the abyss, but saw nothing. In the light of the flaming torches his hands were black with Bethany's blood.

'I will see you in a thousand years,' Sataniel called out from the depths.

'NEVER!' Gabriel demanded. 'Not even in a thousand years.'

The angelic leapt back into the pit; landing on the lock and in one swift move removed the key, placing it in his tunic. Suddenly, from the depths, Sataniel appeared beneath his feet. He tilted his head to one side to get a better view of his jailer.

'You killed Bethany,' accused Gabriel.

'Bethany's not dead,' Sataniel calmly answered. 'She is here with me. Release me and you release your mate.'

'If Bethany's not dead, then I will see her again.'

'Not for a thousand years. Apparently, the stories you were told are not entirely accurate. Someone's withholding information from you all, Gabriel,' Sataniel suggested. 'I wonder why? The key you possess will not open the lock until that time has lapsed. Do not lose it. My existence in your hands.'

'Until I have proof that Bethany is with you, I will never give up this key. If she is with you; touch her and I'll kill you.'

'You have my word,' Sataniel replied.

'Your word?'

'I wouldn't lie to you, Gabriel.'

'You want me to make a deal?'

'Gabriel, never make a deal with the Devil! You know that?' Sataniel taunted.

The jailer ignored his prisoner, picking up the spear; he climbed out of the pit.

'Bird!' Sataniel shouted. 'Seek out Abbadon and tell him all.'

The demonic bird flapped its damaged wings as it lifted itself into the air. The scrawny thing had never left. Gabriel, with the anger once more in his veins; his eyes red with hatred, threw the spear at the bird. He missed; the shaft embedded itself with considerable force several feet into soft earth wall.

'Gabriel!' screamed Sataniel. 'Incline your ears to my mouth Gabriel! My words are sayings of old; darkness in your world of light, Gabriel!'

With real purpose, the bird flew as fast as it could up the tunnels to the surface. Gabriel matched its speed, but couldn't gain on the scrawny creature's head start. As he raged through Amente, Gabriel charged his brace and drew his sword; no warning was made for the burning minions he left in his path. The last thing each minion saw before they burst into flame was a blur of anger passing by. Gabriel didn't count the number of fires he left in his wake in pursuit of the bird on a mission.

As the warrior of light approached the threshold, he transformed. Passing Mithra and exiting the caves at speed, there was no sign of Abbadon. His wings caught the air and took him straight up out of the scar to meet is awaiting army. Hovering above the angelic force, in an updraft that had pushed its way into the gorge, Gabriel waited for his friends to join him.

'What happened to Bethany?' Iinnad demanded.

Gabriel's glazed eyes gave her the answer she didn't want.

'Take flight and destroy that place,' Gabriel ordered. 'OPEN FIRE!'

Explosive brace weapon fire rained down on the valley floor and the entrance to the caves. The crumbling rock of the cliff face fell away to reveal a honeycomb of tunnels within the mountain. The angelic army took flight. At the rear, the portable CEL weapons were brought up and joined the onslaught in destroying the home of the fallen. The sky became dark as the beating wings blocked out the sun, circling the Malam Grigori Mountains. A hole in the middle was left clear for the Damocles to enforce its authority on the fallen. The energy bolts from the heavens cut through the sky, ripping into the rock, the grass ignited and the boulders cracked under the heat. As the debris flew into the air, the angelic rose to avoid the destruction.

Over the ridge, a dust cloud could be seen rising up from the valley floor. Like the wind blowing holes in the clouds in the sky, gaps appeared in the dust to reveal the mass of minions and demonic fleeing the Underworld. There was also an escape craft, larger than an angelic drop-ship. Being larger would also mean that it carried a transgression point that would allow Abbadon to travel to another realm. They could not allow Abbadon to evade capture.

***

Gabriel and Jesuel dropped through a clearing in the dust. From their position they could make out a path, made by the parting minions, which led to the evacuation craft. The Tower of Pestilence followed Gabriel down, firing indiscriminately at the hordes below. Every shot made a kill due to the density of their targets. At the foot of the mountain, a bulk of a creature coated in scales, chased by a slender female swiftly ran along the clear path towards the craft.

'ABBADON!' pointed Gabriel with his brace arm and fired an explosive blade.

His entire tower opened up as explosive blades rained down on the Destroyer. Every blade hit a target, but not the intended one, for Abbadon's demonic and Sataniel's minions created a shield, so that he could escape. One by one they died to protect their Prince and the female. The fallen Angelic of Destruction struggled through the flaming corpses, until finally he successfully reached the craft, its thrusters burning and a scrawny bird swiftly glided into view. It shot through the steel doors as they shut and the blasts of dust rushed from beneath the crafts engines filling the valley as it rose.

***

The First Realm.

France – 11.41hrs Friday 13th July AD 2001 GMT +1

Abbadon stepped away from the window and stroked the head of the scrawny bird. He quietly chuckled to himself.

'My Lord?' Lilith queried.

'A naïve angel beat me…' Abbadon pondered. 'Gabriel never realised that Amente could never be taken. It belongs to the Underworld. He just weakened it. I wonder if he ever understood why he was not to enter the Caves of Enlightenment? There has always been a heaven; there will always be a hell. Gabriel paid a heavy price for his enlightenment.' The Destroyer smiled. 'Revenge will be sweet.'

'As long as I get to kill soulcarriers, I don't really care,' Lilith grinned.

V

The First Realm.

Washington DC - 11.45hrs Friday 13th July AD 2001 EST

A thud at the front door awoke Gabriel with a start. Three hours ago he closed his eyes for a moment to be rudely woken by his landlady leaving his morning paper, late. Very slowly, he stood up taking the TV control from the arm of the chair, turned it on to catch the day's news as he crossed the apartment to the front door. The TV sprung to life and as the picture became clear the sound came through.

He sniffed the air and his face brightened as he opened the door to retrieve the news. An old woman with a hard face and a mean scowl confronted her tenant.

'You need not have waited for me,' Gabriel informed her.

'You slept in your clothes again?' she asked. 'I'm a good landlady Mr Gabriel. I wanted to make sure you were still alive, that's all.'

The tenant nodded his head frantically hoping it would the end the conversation.

'Lots of bad people out there, you know?' she continued. 'I just...'

'Thank you Mrs Kingsley,' Gabriel butted in as he waved the paper and uncharacteristically closed the door behind him before she could finish her sentence.

The angelic didn't like to be so blunt with his landlady, but he knew that he would be standing there until dusk, if he didn't walk away. He had spent so many days conversing with her that he knew the outcome; the world was in the state it was because of him, or whoever else she collared to talk to. If she had her way things would be better.

The volume on the TV increased on its own as the old set sometimes did. It was the local news channel with pictures and reports from the alleyway and the Chevalier home. Gabriel threw the newspaper into the chair and then in one clean move he removed his shirt. Glad that he had left his shirt on when he answered the door, since it would be difficult to explain the two twelve inch scars resembling a 'V' sign on his back, but then, Gabriel would have difficulty explaining a lot of things in his life.

He entered the cramped kitchen; put the kettle on and stuffed a couple of slices of bread in the toaster, then for no apparent reason he ran back into the lounge to the telephone. As he reached it, it began to ring and the insightful angelic answered it.

'Successful?' Gabriel asked. 'Have you an address? …is everyone OK? I have my reasons Henry, but for now you will have to trust me… I know you do.'

Taking a pen from the peanut butter jar, he wrote the address down in the notepad. The toast popped and Gabriel headed back to the kitchen to finish breakfast.

He then returned to his desk and prepared to refresh his memory in angelic script. To make space he placed two of the larger books on the floor next to his carving.

'[illegible],' he fluently spoke to himself; the line he had repeated for centuries. If only he could clearly remember his mother tongue. 'For eternity.'

The steam from his mug of coffee began to condensate on the window. He smiled as he tried to predict the route of one of the droplets. Memories.

VI

The First Realm.

Washington DC – 12.25hrs Friday 13th July AD 2001 EST

The summer had returned to the US capital city. For several weeks the temperatures had soared into the low hundreds; some of the highest readings on record. The night of the murders was the exception to the rule. Less than ten hours later and the city was back struggling with the heat. Convenience stores were ordered to issue bottled water and fire hydrants were switched on throughout the streets.

Cole couldn't sleep as he roasted in bed. Rebecca was awake and at work in the living room, sifting through the information on the computer linked to the office network at Fort Mead, several miles outside the city. Although Richard had woken his wife several times during the night, she had managed to get enough hours' shuteye, to start before he arose.

The future father stumbled into the lounge, his dressing gown barely covering him. He wrapped his arms around Rebecca, kissing her on the top of the head as she continued to stare at the screen. Cole kissed her again. He could see her smile in the reflection of the monitor. He kissed her a third time, and then began to work his way down the side of her face. Finally, in response, she looked away from the screen and kissed her husband.

'Now, are you going to make me breakfast?' she asked.

'You haven't eaten?'

'No.'

'Okay, what would you like?'

'Surprise me! I have work to do.'

Richard headed for the kitchen and checked the fridge. He removed the milk and put the kettle on. The doorbell rang.

'I'll get it!' he shouted believing he would be saved from making the wrong decision about breakfast.

On his doorstep stood a gentleman with several years on Cole. He had a round face and thin grey hair and he was commanding in stature in his smart dark suit. Bob Garrett was also Cole's immediate superior in the chain of command at the NSA. His smile cracked his face as he raised his hand holding a green folder.

'You gonna invite me in?' he asked in that tone where you're not quite sure whether he was joking or not. 'Coffee! Black! …but you know that!'

Cole said nothing and headed back to the kitchen. The smartly dressed man closed the door behind him and followed the dressing gown down the hallway. He popped his head around the corner into the living room.

'Morning Rebecca!'

'Morning Bob, is that for me?' she inquired about the folder.

He handed the green package to her out stretched hand and continued into the kitchen. The kettle had just boiled and the toaster was now on.

'Tea or coffee?' Cole yawned.

'You're not awake Richard, are you? COFFEE, BLACK! I'm a coffee man, always have been and always will be.'

Richard made Rebecca's cup of tea and then her toast. After making his delivery he returned to make the coffees. Instinctively placing the two mugs in the microwave and setting the timer.

'Bad night?' Bob started.

'I've had better. I take it from the suit you went to the wedding?'

'She a beautiful girl and Nick's a *very* lucky guy.'

'I was shattered. I'm sorry.'

'Nick'll understand.'

'He's a good kid. It's good to start them young, don't you think?'

'I agree with you,' Garrett replied. 'When they get to your age they can move on. I guess you're the exception to the rule. You started late, but you still have the speed.'

Ping! The coffees were done.

'What is that supposed to mean? I'm too old for this? Take me off the job!'

'I can't… thank you,' Garrett took his coffee. 'I understand that you accepted a personal request from the Ambassador.'

'It was nothing… just hot air…'

'…You stay in there and talk behind my back!' Rebecca bellowed from the computer. 'I prefer to work alone.'

'I think we better…'

'Yeah! My wife has a temper when she's fat.'

The men laughed as they strolled into the living room. Rebecca greeted them with a sarcastic smile, which rapidly turned to a scowl.

'I heard that!'

Both men stopped laughing and sat down to hear what Rebecca had to say.

'Where d'you want me to start?'

'You're the boss!' Richard admitted.

Rebecca glanced over at Garrett.

'We're not at the office. So… you're the boss,' Garrett admitted lowering his head to meet the rim of his steaming mug.

'Well, visitor Garrett, Sir! This is what I have. Oh I would like to add that… there was a request for an inter-agency link on this information. Did you make that call?'

'No that came from above.'

'Fair enough! All relevant information has been passed on to all the other agencies. Now! Let's start with the alleyway,' Rebecca continued. 'We have no fingerprints; that avenue is a complete dead end. There were none in the Chevalier home either, but I'll come to that in a minute. Thanks to the sudden appearance of the rain last night there is very little evidence to speak of at all. But before you say anything, that was expected.'

Both men simultaneously sipped their coffee.

'I wish you wouldn't do that!' Rebecca broke her flow referring to their loud sips. 'The victim; Sean Grayson, was *dating* Naomi Chevalier. The Ambassador doesn't seem to accept that; reminds me of someone else I know. The young Grayson died instantly by one direct strike to the throat by what appeared to be a multiple pointed object.

This cut his windpipe, but what killed him was the upward thrust that severed his spinal cord below the third vertebrae. Now it gets weird. The coroner's answer and this is the preliminary report – is that it was done by a hand with long nails or a Freddy Kruger glove. Due to the curve of the wounds, I would go with the nails.'

'What?' Richard blurted out.

'Possibly a female hand,' Rebecca added.

'But with an upward thrust that would make her very short or she lifted him off the ground.'

'Correct! The gap in the wound indicates that he was lifted.'

'I've seen some of this report,' admitted Garrett. 'But that strength means we're looking for a guy, no offence, a woman can't be that strong.'

'A female bodybuilder could have done it?' Rebecca replied. 'Point two: All subsequent injuries are after the fact. The first strike killed him. He didn't know what hit him other than the fact that he was facing his attacker.'

'What about the girl?' Garrett asked.

'Naomi!' Rebecca stressed. 'After or during the attack her heart stopped.'

'She had a heart attack?' Richard questioned. 'How d'you know?'

'Doctors have ways of testing for that sort of thing. That could explain why they thought she was dead at the scene? Her injuries were inflicted by the same source.'

'The hand!' Richard added.

'We're already concluded that we are looking for one perpetrator,' Garrett announced. 'So have any of the other agencies come up with anything?'

'Just what I'm giving you. Now the writing; we have a problem with this.'

'Don't I know it,' Richard jibed.

'Something you want to tell me?' Garrett asked.

'Gabriel! There's something about him. He knows things that he won't tell you, I feel it. No… I know it.'

'Has he been helpful?'

'Yeah, sort of. Sort of? Don't get me wrong – he's on our side. There's just something… I can't put my finger on it.'

'Gabriel,' Rebecca snapped. 'Gabriel has appeared at universities all over the country and in Europe. He mainly works abroad.'

'So why's he here?' Richard asked.

'He had been lecturing in DC. In fact, he's been lecturing up and down the eastern seaboard. No one knows his last name or if Gabriel *is* his last name.'

'I told you there was something about him.'

'And there's more,' Rebecca smiled. 'If you need to get in touch with him there is a number that everybody apparently knows in London. *But*… the people that have that number have never heard of him. The FBI did a background check and asked Scotland Yard to check it out. That info came in about twenty minutes ago… It's morning over there.'

'It's morning here!' Richard pointed out.

'*Midday* darling! He did, however, leave a message on your answer phone,' Rebecca continued her reading from the computer. 'Ancient Studies at Langley are trying to decipher the symbols now they know where to look. Also knowing that the words are from multiple languages was a stroke of genius. Next! As I told you this morning about the phone box; we have nothing else other than the Paris number and the town of Carcassonne. The NSA computer banks networked with the Bureau of Census found a branch of the Chevalier family immigrated to France in the 1920's. Don't ask; I don't know why? People *do* leave the US.'

'And they reside in Carcassonne,' Garrett surmised watching the husband and wife team. They had always worked well together.

'Yes,' agreed Rebecca.

'What about the house?' Richard was eager to know everything. 'The kitchen wall?'

'The black stains on the kitchen wall and the outer side have drawn a blank.'

'They weren't stains, they were sticky.'

'The report says nothing about them being sticky, it was just a stain or a mark.'

'Then why did I mention it first, my sweetie?'

'*Because* you requested that Detective Ashby be informed of all the weird stuff. He was around the side of the house when the explosion happened. …and thank you for telling me! Where were you when it went off?'

'With Gabriel,' Cole replied with the truth, but limited with it.

'You're saying you saw nothing?' Garrett asked.

'Nothing! A police officer picked up *something*. It was booby-trapped. Gabriel pulled me out of the way of the blast.'

'And you left?' Garrett pushed. 'Why did you leave?'

'There was nothing I could do,' Cole replied turning to his wife. 'Really! There was nothing I could do. Can we stick with what we've got. What about the scorpion?'

'There's no information on the scorpion and there were no fingerprints, other than those of the victims. The only alien fingerprints were smudged and ID couldn't be made. The footprint was just that... a footprint. It's useless unless we can find a match. *All* victims died in a struggle. Lastly; we have the blood. Hundreds of samples were taken and quickly check with blood type. DNA will follow, but that takes time. As for blood type; all samples so far match the victims. Therefore, at present we can only assume that the attacker or attackers were not injured. At the end of the day, there is less information from the house than the alley. And that is it!'

'Luckily for us, the explosion didn't effect the crime scene,' Garrett added. 'It just created a second one; and you my friend... are off to France,' Garrett slapped Cole on the back.

'Now you know why I'm jealous,' Richard's wife glared.

'Has anyone spoken to the girl?' Richard asked ignoring his wife's comment.

'She's still in I.C.U. but recovering remarkably quickly. She won't talk,' Garrett explained. 'She has a police guard, but that seems to be making things worse. The FBI said they would talk to her. I was thinking that maybe you, Rebecca... maybe you could talk to her? She might open up.'

'Gabriel kept on about wanting to talk to her. He wouldn't leave it alone. I said he could. He has a way of getting under your skin. Maybe he can get something out of her?'

'I'll give Gabriel access,' granted Garrett. 'But we'll watch him. Considering the situation, I think we're gathering the information like lightning. The Ambassador will be pleased.'

'The Ambassador only wants a name,' Richard pointed out. 'He wants nothing more, other than me to kill who killed his son.'

'You're kidding,' Rebecca expressed concern.

'Nope!'

Garrett stood up and put his empty cup on the coffee table.

'I thought you said it was hot air?' Garrett added straightening his jacket as he marched to the hallway.

'Rebecca!' he announced. 'Thank you!'

The smiling blonde accepted his thanks with a nod. Richard rose to let his boss out.

'There is a plane to Paris at 17.30hrs. The ticket will be in your name. That gives you just under five hours. I'll see you at the airport.'

Cole nodded. Then sudden something flashed through his mind.

'The other guy!'

'What other guy?' Rebecca turned back to the computer.

'Do you have the police footage of the Chevalier house? I mean of the crowd. Do you have the footage of the crowd?' Richard urged.

'Yes I do, well, I don't! I have stills from the video footage. Almost everybody in the crowd were residents. The few that weren't worked in the area or were media.'

'Was Gabriel there?'

Garrett had already stopped in the hall. 'Gabriel was there, talking to a man that the FBI can't identify. Although, they did pick him up on airport security, leaving the country. He caught a flight to *France*.'

'France?'

'I'll be making a move,' Garrett said. 'I'll get the office to pull the passenger manifest and find out who he is. Saying that, the FBI probably already have it. I'll ask them first. At least it will look like we're keeping them in the loop.'

Cole saw Garrett to the door. He then returned to his resourceful wife who was carefully maneuvering her belly out from the desk.

'I need to lie down,' she stated.

Cole rushed to her aid.

'I'm fine, it's what happens when you're pregnant. You're useless at packing and I can't help you. You've got four hours to pack. You need to be at the airport for check in. And by the way, one word notes in your notepad is not a record of events.'

'I was in a hurry,' Cole said as he helped Rebecca to the sofa.

'Have I told you that I love you.'

'Not today you haven't!'

They kissed a gentle kiss.

***

13.15hrs Friday 13th July AD 2001 EST

When the lift doors opened, Gabriel stepped out into the corridor and boldly walked towards the I.C.U. As he approached the entrance he noticed that the police had gone. Looking concerned for Naomi's well-being, the doctor that he had spoken to earlier approached him to calm his nerves.

'You're Naomi's friend of the family, aren't you?' asked the doctor.

'She is out of I.C.U. already?' asked Gabriel.

'Yes! Amazingly,' replied the doctor. 'We moved her to another area, the police were getting in the way when we had an emergency, but she's still under observation. And I do have some good news, I take it you're Gabriel?'

'Yes, I am. Will she recover?'

'Oh yes! No doubt about that, 100 percent. She's definitely a fighter.'

'May I see her?' asked Gabriel.

'That's the bit of good news. The police have been told to let you through.'

***

In Naomi's private room, Gabriel had that uncomfortable feeling of someone watching his every move. The police officers outside the door were taking it in shifts. The uneasy feeling came from the police officer slumped on the chair in the corner of the room. There were so many things that Gabriel wanted to say, but couldn't. So much he needed to be explained, but he dare not say. Naomi lay on her side staring out of the window. The room had no TV; the police didn't want her to know about her family just yet. Gabriel stood by the bed with his back to the door. Naomi had seen him enter her jail, but not recognizing him, chose to stare out of the window. Her beauty reminding Gabriel of an Egyptian he had once seen.

'You're not a doctor? You don't look as if you're in law enforcement. So you're the friend of the family are you?' Naomi asked.

'Yes,' Gabriel replied.

'I don't ever remember seeing you round the house.'

The police officer's ears pricked up and he stirred in his chair on hearing Naomi's comment as his crossed arms opened and he rested his hand on his side arm. Gabriel motioned to him to calm down and that everything was okay.

'You've made a remarkable recovery.'

'So the doctor's tell me… so you are?'

'I am Gabriel, I knew your father,' he replied, hoping to get a response.

'Why are you talking in the past tense?' she asked. 'Had a bust up did you?'

'Why do you not have a television in the room?'

'The cops won't let me have one. I answered your question, now you answer mine.'

The uniformed officer jumped to his feet, his hand still poised ready to grab his revolver. The purpose of which, even he was not sure.

'I'm under instructions to make sure the victim doesn't find out what happened to…' barked the officer.

'What happened to what?' interrupted Gabriel.

'Yeah! What?' snapped Naomi as she sat up in bed looking at Gabriel for the first time. 'You spoke about my dad in the past tense?'

'You were not told because everyone thought it might effect your recovery,' Gabriel said quietly. 'I am sorry.'

The police officer, instead, took out his radio and pointed it at Gabriel. Gabriel raised his hands slowly. *How ironic,* he thought. *All the times he had followed orders and done as he was told and not been so bold or forward and now, when he makes a conscious decision to be forceful and pushy with information, no less, a police officer threatens him for opening his mouth.*

'Sean is dead,' Gabriel broke the news as calmly as was possible. 'I take it, you were not told?'

Naomi settled back down a little.

'I thought as much. The cops hadn't said anything and no one mentioned his name so… I don't know. I had a feeling he had died… back in the alley.'

Naomi lay back down and pulled the blankets up over her shoulders. The police officer lowered his radio and then placed his hand on Gabriel's shoulder.

'Don't push it teacher,' he cautioned. 'For a moment I thought you were someone else. Now you're just here to break the rules.'

Gabriel stared right into his eyes as the police officer froze. Standing there in the hospital room with his arm up, his fingers cupped where Gabriel's shoulder used to be. He didn't even blink. Gabriel walked around the bed and sat down next to Naomi.

'I am sorry,' he sympathized as he placed his hand on her shoulder. 'I have something else I need to tell you, about your family.'

Naomi looked round to see the police officers response to Gabriel's comment. Still motionless, the human stood there. Confused, Naomi turned back to Gabriel for an explanation.

'What are you? Why did he call you teacher? And another thing; are you why I have police protection?'

'What am I? A friend. Teacher? I lecture in ancient languages. As for your last question; the answer is no,' he replied calmly. 'I think the man that attacked you, is responsible for the attack on your home.'

'My home?' questioned Naomi. 'Firstly, it was a woman that attacked us, and… who… are they… everybody's okay… right?'

'I am sorry,' Gabriel said shaking his head very slowly. 'I am so very sorry.'

'Everyone?' she asked in a broken voice, close to tears.

Gabriel nodded without a word. He could feel her pain and her anger, but as Naomi's anger grew her pain diminished. *How could any human take that information in so calmly?* Naomi looked back at the statue in the centre of the room.

'What are you?' she repeated. 'And why are you here?'

'Your guardian angel?' he replied questioningly.

'You're doing a fine job aren't you?' she jibbed, laughing to herself.

'I wish I could have stopped this. At least you are alive and your wounds will heal. You have to believe that some good will come from all of this.'

'Don't preach to me, if you knew my father at all, you'd know we're not the religious type.'

'I am sorry,' said Gabriel. 'I meant, at least you are…'

'..alive. I got it. Was that your doing? Is that why I'm still here? Is that why I'm the one that was left behind?'

'Not exactly. I do not have all the answers,' Gabriel paused before getting up off the bed. 'I have to go. For your own safety keep one of these with you,' tapping on the police officer's head, '...at all times. I will see you soon, trust me.'

'Trust you? I don't even know you! You walk in here; you tell me my family's dead and then you leave! Where are you going? You can't leave me!'

'I have to Naomi. I have to go to France for a few days. Carcassonne.'

'Why?'

'To find the woman that killed your family.'

'You believe me?' Naomi questioned, shocked that someone would believe her story. 'You think you're gonna find her in the south of France?'

'Yes,' Gabriel replied softly. 'It is an old city, with as much mystique as it has beauty.'

'You're selling flights there? Or are you looking for my relatives?'

'I said I was an old friend of your fathers. Can you trust me?'

'You know who killed my family, don't you? You know who that woman was?' asked Naomi. 'You have a clever way of not answering questions Gabriel.'

'I have an idea who killed your family and if I am right, it will be safer for you here,' the angelic admitted.

'Because I'm out of the way?' questioned Naomi.

'I will not lie to you. The answer to your question is yes. Now, you said relatives?' Gabriel inquired. 'Do you have relatives in Carcassonne?'

'My father always said we had distant family there. I never met them,' Naomi replied as she calmed down a little. 'I don't know who they are. We got postcards from them every now and again.'

'Distant family?'

'Yeah! Distant.'

'How distant?'

'Four thousand fucking miles!' she jumped. 'I don't know!'

'Then help me.'

'How?'

Gabriel stepped closer to the girl in the bed and very gently placed his hand over her eyes. Naomi lent back removing his hand with hers. A look of concern flashed across her face, but Gabriel responded with a smile and replaced his hand. This time she did not stop him. He closed his eyes. Naomi murmured in discomfort for a moment and fell back on to the bed, her head sinking into the pillow.

'Crap!' she barked.

Gabriel was astounded that she was still conscious. He had seen through her eyes. He had the information that he needed. He knew who he was after, but not the reason why.

'Crap!' Naomi repeated. 'What the hell did you do to me?'

'I saw what you saw; what you have seen, only though your eyes.'

'I don't know what you are… but you have to protect me from her,' Naomi panted still a little out of breath. 'Why can't I stay with you? I know what she looks like.'

'So do I. I will find them and I will be in touch. I promise. Now I must leave.'

'Then leave!'

The Archangel rose and walked to the door.

'Gabriel!' Naomi called out. 'I'm sorry. Thank you for telling me... about my family. No one else would.'

Gabriel left Naomi alone with the statue. As the door closed under its own weight the police officer came to. Not quite sure that something did or didn't happen he checked his weapon was okay, sat back down and smiled at Naomi as if everything was okay. Naomi just sat there and tried to come to terms with what had been said and what she had just seen.

'I don't believe this,' she said quietly and lay back down.

She closed her tearful eyes and tried to sleep. She sniffed the air, but the blatant sniff became a sniffle.

***

16.55hrs Friday 13th July AD 2001 EST

Cole sat nervously in the airport departure lounge, tapping his foot as he waited for his flights announcement. The agent passed the time watching the people around him, each in their own world. There was an elderly man with a long face, wire steel rimmed glasses, thin hair and a naturally sad expression sitting opposite. He sat quietly making no sudden movements ignoring his complaining wife.

'I've had a look and I can't find anything,' she complained. 'Can you have a look?'

The man shook his head slowly, but didn't answer. His khaki coat flapped as he brought his hand down quickly to his lap. His mannerisms and body language made it blatantly obvious that he had no interest in what his wife was saying.

'Looks like I'll have to find a book on my own,' she continued, wandering off.

The man glanced from right to left and then down to his watch. Cole found himself doing the same. In complete contrast the even older man sitting next to the first now had Cole's complete attention. The newspaper he had been decimating lay about his blue PVC chair. His polished head had a white rim of hair around the base. Cole wasn't sure whether he wore glasses. He held them in his hand and then would place them on his head for a moment, just a moment and then whip them off again. Every minute or two he would check his coat pockets as though he was missing something. The dark green corduroy trousers were too short for his legs and as he crossed them the tops of his dark blue socks revealed bright white skin. He hadn't seen the sun in a long time. Cole continued to observe. Below the glasses was a large nose flanked by saggy cheeks, a sign of his age. But it is never easy to guess one's age. With his glasses on, he had that permanently pissed off and confused appearance. He picked up a sheet of newspaper from the floor; held it up and read a line. No, not even a line; the paper was down and fidgety man was now peering over the heads of the other passengers in the lounge in search of someone. He turned back to the paper, read another line; stopped and looked down at the mess on the floor. He dropped the sheet he was holding and selected another sheet from beneath his chair. Another line was read and the sheet hit the floor once again.

Cole checked the time as the fidgety fellow checked his watch. An announcement on the speaker system was made for a pair of sunglasses that had been left by the security area, would the owner collect. The old man jumped to his feet and scanned the passenger lounge for anyone heading in the direction of the barrier. He sat down again as sharply as he had stood, disappointed. Cole could clearly see no wedding ring; he smiled to himself at the thought of this man waiting at the altar. She never showed.

'Are you staring at me?' the man accused in a foreign accent. 'Are you looking at me?'

'Me? No!' Cole lied.

The man got back out of the plastic padded chair and darted off. The fidgety man had finally gone leaving the debris of the paper behind. The quiet gentleman with the nagging wife had also left, Cole hadn't even noticed. Cautiously, Cole had a look around the lounge and cafe area; Rebecca came into view followed by Garrett. Although he was past the passport barrier his wife and boss had the security clearance to avoid all that. A little comfort from his wife before the long flight would not go amiss. The pregnant woman waddled over and greeted her agent husband with a kiss, gently pulling him towards her.

'Sorry there was a queue in the ladies. Look who I found.'

'How are you holding out?' Garrett asked.

'Fine, just watching people.'

'As always,' Garrett replied. 'Seen anyone interesting?'

Fidget men was back picking up his paper in a vain attempt to reassemble it into some sort order. He sat back down and began again the already observed routine.

'Yeah, him,' Cole motioned with his head.

Garrett sat down a couple of seats away from the couple and took over Cole's observation of the bizarre behavior of the character opposite. Cole could now have a moment with his wife. Rebecca held Cole's hand for comfort. Out of the corner of his eye, he noticed a stewardess quickly walk across the lounge to Mr. Fidget Man.

'Excuse me, Mr. Ridefort?' she inquired.

'Oui,' he replied in French. 'Yes.'

'We've been looking all over for you. I don't know how you ended up here,' the stewardess apologized. 'This is the departure lounge, you should have been out by arrivals.'

'Yes,' he replied. 'I have… only just come to this country.'

'Would you like to come with me?'

Mr. Fidgety Man aka Mr. Ridefort left the lounge with the stewardess leaving Garrett to his own devices. He slammed his hands together and stood up. Garrett was one of those men that you would notice in a crowd, if *he* wanted you to; a distinguished looking gentleman with a secret. Garrett knew more than most about almost everything. A man of knowledge and in the business of intelligence, knowledge was power. Garrett had the power, but he also had the experience of when to exert it and when not to. With those qualities in his particular field, he was well respected the world over; even when most of the world did not know it.

'I've never known Rebecca to be so mad with me, just over a trip to Europe,' interrupted Garrett, his dominating voice bellowed through the departure lounge. 'For Rebecca's sake, since I'm paying, I don't want you to enjoy yourself. Do you hear me Cole?'

Garrett started to laugh at his own little joke. Rebecca hid her amusement since she knew how much Cole hated flying. Cole attempted to laugh with the others, but couldn't for the life of him find the funny side.

'I promise I won't enjoy myself.'

'Right! Now down to business. We received the passenger manifest with passport images,' Garrett declared. 'The man in question is English, well Scottish; Henry Sinclair son of Sir William Sinclair. Talk about throwing a spanner in the works. With the evidence pointing at a woman I have no idea where Mr. Sinclair fits in. So while you're in Europe, see what you can find out. Interpol have also confirmed two families in the Carcassonne area with the surname Chevalier, but having checked back through their records, they hadn't found any family connection. I've asked them to keep a discreet eye on them until you can talk with them.'

'So!' Rebecca interrupted. 'We could be sightseeing after all.'

She dug into her handbag and pulled out a small box and opened the lid. Garrett leaned forward to view the gift. Cole looked up at him and smiled.

'It's my travel chess set,' divulged Cole in jest. 'Not a gun!'

'I was just being inquisitive, it's a part of the job.'

'It's only if you're not busy dear,' his wife suggested.

'I have a feeling I'll be busy. This killer *wants* to be caught,' Cole replied. 'The only problem with that is that it doesn't mean she wants to be stopped.'

'You'll stop her!' ordered Garrett. 'I don't want Interpol beating us to it; BUT I *don't...* want to see another bloodbath either. A feather in our cap would be a nice one over Interpol, but you *ask* for help if you need it! Now, you have a long journey so get some sleep or *something* and I'll talk to you when you get there. Oh! Before I forget.'

Garrett pulled a small sealed envelope out of his suit and handed it to Cole.

'This is for Soames, our man in France. Well, we have several, but he's the guy you'll be dealing with' Garrett added. 'He's a good man, seven languages and years of experience in the diplomatic section. He's not to up to date in your line of work, but you should find him useful. You could learn a thing or two from him. You know; help you with those diplomatic skills you never had. He'll arrange your firepower, but don't go shooting up the locals. Remember, in Europe they have a different way of doing things. Europeans always have.'

Cole understood. Stay on your best behavior so that the boss doesn't have to use any favors that he has built up over the years to bail you out. He got the message. The hard earned favors are valuable and operatives are... well, operatives.

Garrett gave Rebecca a quick glance to say 'he's all yours' and left the departure lounge. Rebecca squeezed Cole's hand tightly.

'Perhaps some reading material for you to calm your nerves,' she said. 'The apocryphal books of the new testament are a little hard going, so I picked up a little book about them. It might help.'

'Why this?'

'The script is angelic, the book might give you a little insight. I studied history remember, you didn't. So read up.'

The announcement for Cole's flight was heard over the speaker system. The agent slowly climbed out of his chair and gave his wife a loving hug and a long kiss. Rebecca gave her husband a cheesy grin and a kiss on the cheek. She also gave him the green folder to refresh his memory during the flight.

'I'm not going to wait, I'll see you soon.'

'I tried to get hold of Gabriel,' Richard stated. 'The message was just a thank you for letting him see Naomi. If he gets in touch, tell him where I am. There is definitely something about that guy.'

Rebecca nodded and left the departure lounge so that her husband could gather his own thoughts and overcome his fears on his own before boarding the plane. It was only a psychological thing and he knew it. He had been on many planes, only he very rarely landed in one.

***

17.28hrs Friday 13th July AD 2001 EST

Mrs. Kingsley sat on the bottom step of the stairs watching the tenant that had listened to her idle chatter for several months. Gabriel signed the paperwork for the large package that the man from UPS had struggled to put in his van. The man, in his brown uniform left, as Gabriel addressed his landlady.

'I have paid up till the end of the month and you can keep the deposit,' he said.

‘I’ll keep the room just in case you are coming back,’ she replied hopefully.

‘Thank you, but that will not be necessary Mrs. Kingsley. I have been here too long. I have neglected my duties else where.’

‘The past, young man, catches up with everyone.’

Gabriel smiled as the elderly woman jumped up to give him a goodbye hug. He was surprised by the amount of affection she showed towards him.

‘I will hold the room till the end of the next month just in case you change your mind.’

‘I have to return to Washington for a day or two. If I do, I will pop around for tea, I promise.’

Gabriel kissed the lonely woman on her wrinkled cheek then exited the building down the steps and into the street. As he walked up the street he glanced over his shoulder to see Mrs. Kingsley waving goodbye. He returned the wave and turned the corner into a side alley. Saddened, he transformed.

***

02.36hrs Saturday 14th July AD 2001 Greenwich Mean Time

High above the earth’s surface where the hot and cold streams of air circle the globe, invisible to man’s eye was where Cole had to control his nerves. To assist in its speed and for economic reasons, Cole’s jetliner traveled in one such stream of air at 34,000 feet. This was the sort of information Cole preferred to forget about, one of the reasons he didn’t like flying. Sitting cramped in his seat, next to the aisle, Cole made the best of what was, for him, a bad journey. His makeshift table folded down from the backrest in front, was cluttered with papers and Rebecca's reference book. All those around him had their headphones and were quietly watching the in-flight movie. The old lady, in the seat next to him, smiled when she saw the titles, 'The Apocryphal and the Bible'. Cole flicked through the pages.

'Jesus!' he said to himself. 'That makes him about six hundred years old.'

The smile disappeared from the old lady's face as she repositioned her headphones and concentrated on the movie, trying to mind her own business. Cole's only distraction came in the form of a pair of beautiful legs, which stopped by his seat. Following the contours up to a pretty stewardess with a welcoming smile holding a sheet of paper.

'I have a fax for you Mr. Cole,' she said. 'From your office.'

Cole caught the subject header as the stewardess placed it on his table.

'The point of entry. Yes, thank you,' Cole responded eager to read the report. 'Thank you very much.'

'Forensics did another test on the stain. Thank you Bob!' he waffled to himself. 'Silvery black greasy stuff hardened. Now solid. The wall was already re-hardening.'

Cole's eyes dropped to the bottom of the page to read the conclusion. Then staring into space for a moment amazed at the lack of positive thinking that the boys back at the lab had, he took a deep breath and then sighed.

'Inconclusive!' he read. 'No forced point of entry and therefore the victims must have known the attacker. You idiots!'

There was a scribbled note at the bottom from Rebecca, which read 'I never found Gabriel, but he saw Naomi. I will visit her. I love you. Becks.'

Gabriel was nowhere to be found. The mystery man, Sinclair, was in France. All connections with the case were pointing to France. And now Cole was on his way to France. He had no back up and temporarily, no weapon. Great! Cole had a feeling this was the sort of case that could change your life. The problem was that he was happy with his life.

VII

The First Realm.

Near Carcassonne – 18.16hrs Saturday 14th July AD 2001 GMT +1

Gabriel followed in the same jet streams that crossed the Atlantic Ocean. As he approached the coast of Europe he could see the clouds forming over the land. The darker shades of grey holding the water that would feed the rivers and streams as they had done since the beginning of creation. The grey mass formed swiftly as he glided into French air space and headed southeast towards the southern region of the Languedoc, north of the Pyrenees Mountains that formed the natural border between France and Spain. In the low plains to the north of the foothills lay Carcassonne.

Gabriel landed in a clearing shaded by trees several kilometres up stream of the town on the east bank of the River Aude. He sat under a tree and rested after the long and physically demanding trip. The Archangel looked up at the sky, the clouds trying their best to shake the moisture from within. On the other side of the river was the main road, D118, that ran south towards Limoux following the route of the river up the valley. A eighteen wheeled lorry roared up the road carrying its load of farm machinery, from the roadside small rocks fell away, loosened by the noise and the vibration of the passing vehicle. Several of the stones reached the base of the valley splashing into the water, the spray creating little circles across the slowly moving surface. The circles became more frequent as the clouds succeeded in their mission and it began to rain. The Guardian of the First Realm rested.

***

The First Realm.

The Levant. 10th Hour – 15th Márhéshwan Hebrew Year 4009

(16.00hrs 9th October AD 9)

Gabriel had flown around the landmasses of the world in an attempt to pick Jesuel's essence and join up with his old friend. It was to the east of the Sea of Chinnereth near the tiny village of Nazareth that he sensed what he had been searching for. He landed in the dusty sand by a stream beneath an olive tree. There was a small boy sitting on the bank throwing stones at the water.

'Don't do that!' Gabriel ordered. 'It might cause the stream to change course and then where would we be?'

'Gabriel!' the boy beamed; glad to see him. 'Where in the hell have you been? I have been waiting for ages.'

Gabriel looked at the hillside of loose rubble, then back at the boy.

'You've been throwing stones all this time and you built that?' he joked.

'You would not know if I had.'

'So *you* did change the course of this stream!' Gabriel responded, still trying to come to terms with Jesuel's new appearance.

'This realm has changed. Its people have changed. They believe in one God. Therefore, I have one question for you Gabriel, what have you been up to?'

'What have you been up to?' Gabriel asked staring at the boy.

'Watching, which is less than I can say about you,' replied Jesuel with concern in his voice. 'Have you any idea what you have done?'

'What? I've been looking for you. Why? What have I done?'

'I left you in Egypt where you were going to watch and learn their customs. But you went and did a little more than that.'

'I did?' Gabriel replied, confused. 'You left because you believe it was wrong to worship the underworld. You were right. I arrived in Thebes when the old Pharaoh died. Amente worship was everywhere. I spoke to the young Pharaoh. He thought I was their god Horus…'

'So you did reveal yourself?' Jesuel interrupted.

'Yes – and I spoke about his belief in the gods.'

'You had one conversation with Pharaoh and that changed the world.'

'But you said that worshipping the dead was wrong. Everywhere I go mankind is doing it. In central Merica, the Olmec were also doing it. How could one conversation change the world?'

'Because that conversation was with Pharaoh. If that conversation were with a trader or a farmer then it probably would not have amounted to much,' he waved his boyish hands. 'But you had to choose, Pharaoh.'

'I don't understand,' Gabriel admitted. 'Maybe I've been away too long.'

'Did you not stay around to find out what would happen? Did you not think that what you said would change things?'

'No. I hoped it would do some good, but I didn't think more than that. I came looking for you. I did see Iinnad. The Council had questions about Enoch and his book. Remember him and the mission that went wrong?'

'I remember. I remember dropping that book,' Jesuel gave a slight nasal laugh. 'The mission… was a success. Yes, angelic died, but Enoch was extracted and walks with the Lord. So… you came looking for me and… it has taken you 1350 years to find me. You were not looking very hard, were you?'

'No, not really.'

'Gabriel, your actions have consequences!'

'My actions have put mankind on the right course,' Gabriel argued. 'Jesuel, I agree with you. I do not think that man should believe in many gods.'

'But it is not your place to change the way people think.'

'I thought our meeting would be more enjoyable than this,' Gabriel pointed out changing the subject, since he had never liked arguing with Jesuel because he always lost.

'Gabriel, you have two ears, so you had better listen. You spoke to Pharaoh; he changed the religion in his land because of *you*. No one understands why he did it, but he did. The Jews in his lands, the workers and the labourers followed a similar faith. Some say, that was already their faith and they left Egypt and came here to Canaan, Israel, Judea and Samaria.'

'I thought the Romans ruled this land?'

'They rule the land, but they do not control the mind of its people.'

'How long have you been here?' Gabriel asked.

'Several generations. The communities and tribes here believe that a messiah will come and save them.'

'And you're waiting to meet this individual?'

'Can you think of anything better to do? This is a new realm. Its people are growing again, just as Uriel had said they would.'

'Jesuel, I am sorry that I spoke to Pharaoh. I thought I was doing the right thing. I can't undo what is done. And Iinnad says hello, by the way.'

Jesuel laughed. 'How is she?'

'Fine!'

'Still beautiful?'

'Yes!'

'Why have you not…'

'Bethany!' Gabriel snapped. 'Change the subject!'

Under the olive tree the angelic and the boy sat, looking in opposite directions. They did not speak as they both threw stones into the stream trying to change its course. The sun slowly dropped down behind the dry outline of the mountains in the distance.

'Jesus!' called a young lady, not even twenty years. 'Where are you?'

The boy raised his head.

'What?' Gabriel inquired.

'That is me.'

'You are Jesus?'

'I was sitting here waiting for you, when a little boy came to collect water for the evening meal. He slipped and fell. The villagers say he was born under a star. The villagers also say that it is a sign, that he has been chosen for great things.'

'Jesuel, nothing good will come of this,' Gabriel urged.

'You told *me* we cannot interfere. You already have. So, I brought the boy back,' Jesuel explained. 'I found him a good family in the House of Levi and took his form.'

'And what now?'

'I am Jesus,' replied Jesuel. 'I will return with the water and give it to my mother.'

Gabriel shook his head. 'And you say *I* interfere?'

'I will be this little boy until the day he dies.'

'He did die!'

'Until the day *I* die,' Jesuel corrected himself.

'Until the day *you* die! Do you really want to do this?'

'Gabriel, if I, as an angelic am going to learn about man, then what better way to learn than to become one. I have lived a thousand life times; this is but one life. I am surprised that you have not done the same.'

Jesuel picked up the full pale of water and began to walk up the slight slope of the footpath to the brow of the small hill near the edge of the village. Jesuel had just broken the rule of resurrection. Then he had taken the form of a boy to experience *life* as a soulcarrier. Jesuel had complained about how Gabriel had altered mankind's course, mankind's evolution. That was rich!

***

After Sunset – 13 Nisan Hebrew Year 4030 (19.00hrs 2nd April AD 30)

Gabriel stood in the dark on the balcony of a mud brick town house in the centre of Jerusalem. Little had changed in the last twenty or so years since he had last seen his friend. Inside the house there was laughter and cheers as the supper continued into the evening; none of those inside knew of Gabriel's presence. The angelic sipped the water from his clay cup and waited. Jesuel however, sensed his presence and stepped out onto the tiles for a breath of fresh air. He left the light and the din behind him as he leant over the wall and looked down into the dark narrow street below.

'They say you're the Son of God,' Gabriel spoke.

'I have never said that,' Jesuel calmly replied as though he expected the question. 'I have denied it every time. I have told them I am a Son of Man.'

'But you *are* the Son of God!'

'So are you,' Jesuel replied, with a snigger.

'Yes, I know, but I'm not the one on trial.'

'Neither am I!'

'Word in the temples is that you brought someone back from the dead,' Gabriel was stern in his voice. 'Now, what if you did? Then you deserve all you're gonna get. As I understand it, you've upset a lot of people. The priests aren't happy with you. Their guards are looking for you as we speak. I think it's time to leave.'

'Then they will find me.'

'They'll hang you.'

'Then I shall die,' Jesuel calmly replied.

'Why?'

'They listen to me.'

'They don't listen to you, Jesuel. A few here and there maybe… you may draw a crowd every now and again, but the majority listen to the priests; and they're displeased with you. You're the Son of God!'

'I just told you, that I have never claimed that,' Jesuel demanded.

'Even so… Do not interfere. Those are the rules.'

'What did *you* do? *You* started this!'

'Jesuel, you were the one who was uneasy about all the gods; all that Amente worship. You were so uneasy that you left. I stayed and watched those people. I spoke to *one* man and yes he changed the world. You have spoken to *thousands* of people. They love you. But they also listen to the priests and what will your death prove?'

'They will learn.'

'Heaven won't help you,' Gabriel stated. 'You brought a man back to life for Hell's sake. You brought that boy back to life. What were you thinking?'

'I was thinking about the boy. How is he?'

'I don't know! You found a good family. The problem as I see it, is that you brought a second man back from the dead. On top of that, Amente is not going to be pleased. If I had brought Amenophis back from the dead when he died – the whole world, well *this* half would believe, but I didn't. Why? Because I knew that I would be seriously interfering with the course of mankind… There's no point lecturing you…'

'... seriously interfering with the course of mankind?' Jesuel repeated Gabriel's line. 'What did you do? You had a conversation. Did you reveal your wings?'

'What's that got to do with it? What have you shown them? Water to wine!'

'I gave them what no eye has seen, what no ear has heard, what no hand has touched, what has not arisen in the human heart, but I did not reveal my wings. Gabriel, I ask you again, did you reveal your wings?'

'I did it because of what you said.'

'Thank you, you blame me?'

'I'm not blaming you, I accept the blame and I have learnt from it. If I was to pass the blame, then no one is blamed and no one learns anything.'

Jesuel smiled. 'That is a good train of thought, where did you learn that?'

'The Far East about five hundred years ago; I travelled a bit.'

'How are they doing in the far east?'

'Following a different philosophy... The priests men will find you,' Gabriel got back to the matter at hand. 'The priests and elders will have questions.'

One of Jesuel's followers rolled out of the supper with a large clay vessel. He carefully found the steps and head down into the dark of the street below to the water fountain.

'Questions are only words and words will not kill me.'

'Will your followers die with you?' Gabriel asked.

'You know they will not. Why do you think this life, *my* life is in danger?'

'I was trying to make a point,' Gabriel explained. 'Word is, the priests really aren't happy. When man can't explain something, it is shut out *or* shut up. You won't go quietly. That leaves only one answer.'

'Gabriel, the priests will not kill me.'

'Jesus!' called Thomas from the top of the steps. 'Come back inside and enjoy the rest of supper. We are running low on wine.'

He tapped the side of the vessel as he carried it back indoors. The noise increased as Thomas returned to the supper.

'Thomas is a good man. Unfortunately he writes down everything I say.'

'Another Enoch?'

'No, Thomas records what he sees and hears. His writing will help those who will never know.'

'Know what?'

'The Pharisees and the scholars have taken the keys of knowledge and have hidden them. They have not entered nor have they allowed those who want to enter to do so. As for mankind, they must be as sly as snakes and as simple as doves if they are to learn the hidden secrets. I must return to my people.'

'Jesuel, we have stood side by side for hundreds of thousands of these soulcarriers years. You have been with these people for a mere thirty; what makes them *your* people?'

'I will teach those that are willing to listen. The thirteen souls within that room listen.'

'Thirteen? I thought there were twelve.'

'I have twelve disciples who are willing to listen and learn; but Mary listens also. Those who seek should not stop seeking until they find. When they find, they will be disturbed. When they are disturbed, they will marvel, and will reign over all.'

'You are willing to teach the women of this Realm to seek and marvel?'

'You revealed yourself to Nefertiti. Why? Women give life, but men are willing to take it. Yes, I am willing to teach women. Mary sees with different eyes. My disciples see more through *her* eyes. You could learn from this.'

'I could *learn* from what?'

'One day… you will see. I hope that one day you will see what I see. Not everything is black and white, Gabriel. Know what is in front of your face, and what is hidden from you will be disclosed to you. For there is nothing hidden that will not be revealed. And there is nothing buried that will not be raised.'

'Jesuel, you obviously know more than you are letting on; so just tell me!'

'I believe, I have cast fire upon the world, and look, I am guarding it until it blazes.'

'You might be here when it begins to blaze; and anyway, I think Abbadon started that fire,' Gabriel suggested. 'But fire or no fire *I'm* still going to be here.'

'This heaven will pass away, and the one above it will pass away.'

'Jesuel, now Bethany has gone I am not whole. Gabriel explained in a vein attempt to be as cryptic as his friend, not quite understanding the path of the conversation. 'You know what is to come, so what do you want from me?'

And Jesuel replied. 'Perhaps people think that I have come to spread peace upon the world. They do not know that I have come to cast conflicts upon the earth: fire, sword, war. I only meant to do good, but I fear that my words will be twisted and man will fight man. When I have gone Gabriel; show them. Give them what no eye has seen…'

'…what no ear has heard, what no hand has touched, and what has not arisen in the human heart. I will,' Gabriel promised. 'I will… Your friends are waiting; I'll see you later,' Gabriel said as he tapped Jesuel on the arm.

The loose grip of his cup let vessel of wine over the edge of the wall. It fell almost in slow motion until it hit the street below, the clay shards flying across the stone as the wine like blood in the moonlight came to rest in patches in the street. Both angelic looked up and then at each other. Neither spoke for loss of words.

'Take my cup,' Gabriel offered. 'It's only water.'

Jesuel shook Gabriel's hand and took the cup. At the doorway of the balcony Jesuel stopped for a moment; one last look at his dear old friend. Gabriel nodded his friend inside, but Jesuel did not move.

'Anyone here with two good ears had better listen! The soulcarrier's of this Realm are like little children living in a field that is not theirs. When the owners of the field come, they will say, 'Give us back our field.' The owner's are wrong Gabriel; this is their field. It has always been their field. Do not let them take it from them.'

He left his old friend yet again to join *his* people. Gabriel was becoming used to being alone on the First Realm.

In the house the supper came to a sombre end as one of the disciples left the building in a hurry, visibly distressed. Gabriel watched from afar as Jesuel led several of those that remained to a nearby olive grove. The Archangel could hear Jesuel ask his followers to wait for him as he went further into the olive trees to pray alone. However, when he returned, they had fallen asleep. Gabriel chuckled to himself as Jesuel woke them and complained. Jesuel left them once again, but as he returned a second time he was met by a multitude of the priest's guards.

From the balcony of the empty house Gabriel watched as one of his followers stepped forward from the crowd of armed men and embraced his old friend. With swords and staves held high, the priest's men took Jesuel away leaving his followers shocked beneath the trees.

Gabriel stayed in the empty house waiting for a signal from his fellow angelic. It would have only taken Jesuel a moment to signal and Gabriel would have come to the rescue. However, the signal never came. Jesuel had chosen his fate. Gabriel knew as Jesuel did, that Heaven would not help him. Jesuel was stubborn, he always had been. Gabriel also knew that his friend would not answer the priest's questions. He knew that the angelic would allow the holy men to pursue their course of action. What he did not know was that the priests, elders and scribes, frustrated with Jesuel's lack of co-operation had handed him over to the Roman authorities for punishment, since they could not. Their rules of faith forbade it. Jesuel's fate now lay with the governor of the province.

On that terrible day the side streets of Jerusalem were deserted. The crowds like sheep had begun to assemble in the main square of Gabbatha. Even before the cockerel had announced the new morning; Jesuel had been falsely accused by the priests of the Temple. After sunrise the priests had sent Jesuel before Pilate, the Roman governor of the province. He in turn, not sure as what he should do, had sent him to King Herod who gloated the alleged King of the Jews and gave him a glorious robe and then returned the angelic back to the governor. Pilate realised that in recent years on the first morning of the Jewish festival of Passover, the governor had freed one of the criminals held within the garrison's prison. He ordered the known murderer Barnabas and Jesuel to be offered to the multitude that had gathered in the main square; the people of Jerusalem would decide. Urged on by the priests of the Temple, the crowd called for Barnabas to be freed. Jesuel's fate was sealed.

He had been betrayed by one of his followers; the life of an angelic for thirty pieces of silver.

***

5th Hour - 14 Nisan Hebrew Year 4030 (11.00hrs 3rd April AD 30)

Gabriel stood on the balcony overlooking the quiet city. The cheers of the baying crowd could be heard in the distance, lining the streets through the town to a place outside the city gates known as the Place of a Skull, Golgotha. The Archangel felt someone was watching him. From the house ambled two sorrow-looking individuals.

'You're not joining the party?' Gabriel sarcastically inquired.

'There is nothing to be joyful of when our master is to be executed for what he believes,' said the first man.

'And you are?'

'Bartholomew,' the man replied. 'And this is Philip. The man they are to crucify is our master.'

'He is no one's master,' Gabriel replied as he sipped the wine from his cup. 'And I advise you not to speak so loudly. If the wrong person were to hear, you may be joining him.'

The murmur of the crowd in the distance fell silent. The only sound that could be heard over the city was that of faint tapping. With each tap the three on the balcony winced with the thought of pain.

Bartholomew tried to ignore the thought. 'Who are you?' he asked. 'We have not seen you before.'

'Someone who came to see an old friend, but I fear I am too late.'

The three leant on the wall of the balcony, even at that hour, each with a cup of wine in hand and attempted to bury their sorrows. A barking dog broke the quiet in a side street, and then stillness.

'When man crucifies one of his own, the residents of hell know that one that is evil is coming,' Gabriel began to explain, as the light began fade.

The sky grew darker as it formed into heavy storm filled clouds and the wind picked up. The main concentration of clouds was over Golgotha were it started to rain.

'Crucifixion is a form of punishment for evil men,' Gabriel articulately spoke. 'The fallen are dispatched to watch over the released soul as it travels to hell, where it will spend all eternity.'

'But, what of an innocent man? What is to become of his soul? What happens when Hell makes a mistake?' Bartholomew questioned.

'Then someone will be in for a hell of a surprise,' Gabriel grinned.

'How can you smile?' Philip asked.

'Because I know more than you. Because I know that death is not the end. Because I know that someone is in for a hell of a surprise.'

Gabriel knew what was to happen to Jesuel. He knew that it was Jesuel's chosen fate. From the balcony, Gabriel could see the demonic arrive. The people of the city were afraid as darkness fell early that day. As the point of death drew closer, the fallen filled the skies. Unlike man, Gabriel could see the wings of the fallen blocking out the sun. He felt uneasy at the numbers, hoping they would not sense him. The rain would help.

'You can't see them,' Gabriel explained. 'But when an angelic or a fallen opens his wings the sun fails to pass through. When the sky is full of fallen, as it is now, the sun is blocked. The air cools, creating the clouds and then it rains.'

'And I once said, can any good thing come out of Nazareth?'

'Did you? Can some good come from this Bartholomew?' Gabriel asked. 'I know not.'

'I promise you he will not be forgotten. I will write this all down,' promised the disciple. 'So the closer Jesus is to death, the more fallen will arrive from hell to take his soul?'

'Basically, yes.'

The wings of the multitude of the fallen had almost completely blotted out the sun when Jesus died and the three souls were taken back to Sagun, Amente. The sky did not change since the ninth hour was upon them. Gabriel knew the perils that faced his old friend. As for Gabriel, he could not help his comrade in arms. All he do was remember his words.

VIII

The First Realm.

France – 11.45hrs Saturday 14th July AD 2001 GMT +1

Carcassonne is only inhabited medieval walled city in Europe. The city that was as majestic in size, as it was in beauty; had stood in one form or another for over two thousand four hundred years. The Celts of the 4th century BC named the town Carcasso, but it was the Romans that first designated it a city. However, the turrets around its walls that towered over the River Aude had only been there for some eight hundred years. To the north was the Canal du Midi that was designed in the 17th century to connect the Atlantic Ocean with the Mediterranean Sea. The large number of hotels highlighted the fact that this was a tourist trap for foreigners and the French alike.

Abbadon and Lilith stood on the corner of one of the flat roofed apartment blocks in Carcassonne's modern city, admiring the view of the old city on the hill, south east of their position, less than a mile away. Between the old and the new was the shallow and fast flowing river.

The fallen gazed into the narrow streets at the tourists and locals as they unsuspectingly went about their business. What were the fallen to bring to this beautiful city? If nothing else, blood and fear; of which the old city had much in its long history.

'Look at all the little people,' Abbadon said. 'What do they know?'

'Do we care?' emphasised Lilith.

'Oh, we should do.'

'Why?' Lilith asked curiously. 'We're not Gabriel!'

Abbadon started to smile. It was a lovely day; the clouds had started to form, but no rain, as yet. After surveying the city he turned to his accomplice.

'The best laid plans can still have a flaw. Especially, when soulcarriers are involved. They have that… *unpredictability* about them. As for this place… I haven't been to this beautiful city in about; what, seven hundred years,' he reminisced. 'Those were the days. Back then… I miss it. Well, even I can only take so much. So what shall it be?'

'Can we visit the relatives?' suggested Lilith impatiently.

'You can,' Abbadon gave permission. 'You seem to enjoy it more than I.'

'Are you sure?' Lilith wanted to be certain about her Master's instructions.

As strong as she was, she didn't want to get on the wrong side of Abbadon. He gave the reassuring glance she needed and with that she walked to the back of the building, peered over the edge, then stepped off, and out of sight.

'Gabriel, time is running out my dear enema,' Abbadon laughed to himself. 'Ha. It's not like it used to be.'

Abbadon stood there, motionless, timeless, as he watched the sun arc across the southern French sky. His shadow stretched out across the rooftop as the day drew on. Abbadon had waited a long time to take his revenge.

***

23.57hrs Saturday 14th July AD 2001 GMT+1

Carcassonne didn't have the largest police force in France and staking out the two families without causing alarm, just to help the Americans, on the word of their intelligence was not the best way to start good diplomatic relations. In recent years, American intelligence had failed its own government, people and army on more than one occasion. Garrett would never release all information unless it was absolutely necessary. However, with a police force you were potentially going to liaise with, Garrett went along with Cole's request anyway, even though he knew he didn't have much time. Time was definitely not on Cole's side, with a seven-hour flight from Washington to Paris, then catching the Airbus to Carcassonne. Typical European travel meant Cole had a seven-hour wait in Paris, which he could ill afford. He decided to take the TGV high-speed train to Toulouse and then hire a car and drive to Carcassonne. He would be in Carcassonne before his flight left Paris. Cole was happy with his plan. His time in transit was put to good use, sleeping a little to adjust to the time difference and reading up on the information Rebecca had given him. His plan was sound and Cole was positive about reaching Carcassonne at a reasonable hour. He would arrive to a fully informed police force with all the co-operation that he required. With his lack of French, the American still managed to hire a car and it was an easy journey. Cole made good time thanks to the well signposted route. His only regret was in the waste of 35 francs on the road map that he never used.

Agent Cole arrived late in the town. The streets were empty and wet, but with a light summer night breeze. The drizzle left that fresh pine smell in the air as the American struggled to follow the poorly lit signs through the streets to the city centre. The problem was that the town was basically laid out in three sections, La Cite Médiévale, the walled city overlooking the town. Then there was the sprawling suburb that surrounded the town centre, which Cole had just negotiated.

'Gare SNCF,' Cole read the sign and turned right towards the station.

Before reaching the station, he parked the car beneath a large beech tree where Cole stretched his legs. He then wandered through the public garden and wound his way between the water features towards the information booth; its closed pine shutters inconveniently preventing him from viewing the town map. However, opposite was the Grand Hotel Terminus, with its restaurant, a large red and white rowing boat parked on the pavement and a display case with a faded map. Cole stared through the glass.

'You are here,' he self-proclaimed. 'And the police station is?'

Cole pressed his finger hard against the glass, covering the discoloured red square that *was* the station. He found the canal and looked right up the street, passed the traffic lights and into the pedestrianised tiny street of the town's centre. The cast iron street lamps with white spheres a loft dotted their way long his route.

'When in Rome, a stroll will do you good,' Cole recommended. 'Nice night for a wok!' he joked.

The agent, with a holdall on his shoulder, walked along the enclosed Rue Georges Clemenceau towards the police station. The paved streets narrowed, then without warning, appeared a square on his right, Place Carnot, half the size of a football pitch, paved and raised by three steps all the way around. The top of the steps were lined with trees and in the centre surrounded by neglected tables and chairs from the multitude of closed cafés, was a large round water fountain, the bronzed fish at the front spraying water into the light rain. Just beyond, still heading south, was a very small crossroads, a chemist on each of three corners and on the fourth, facing him, was the police station. He had made it. The Carcassonne coat of arms, a simple two-turret castle with a portcullis open, was carved onto a stone shield over to the right of the doorway. The shield on the left was that a lamb holding a lance, The Paschal Lamb surrounded by fleur de lis. It was an emblem Cole thought he had seen recently, but he couldn't remember. Through the glass, Cole could see the reception area was empty and dimly lit. He tried the door. To his surprise it was open. He approached the reception desk to ring the old brass bell and get some service. The crystal clear ring echoed through the empty halls of polished marble. The place didn't appear to be a police station, but Cole rang the bell again anyway.

'Good evening, bonsoir,' called a sleepy voice from around the corner.

Cole peered around the edge of the reception down the corridor to a bench with a smartly dressed man clambering off it. The man hadn't noticed that Cole could see him as he straightened his suit and brushed his hair with his hand. Rubbing his eyes he looked up and saw Cole staring at him.

'Hello,' he said startled. 'You must be Cole?'

'And I take it, you must be Soames?' the agent replied.

'Yes.'

Soames held out his hand to greet the fellow countryman. Cole handed him the sealed envelope that Garrett gave him.

'Oh,' was Soames' only response.

'Sorry,' replied Cole realising his rudeness.

They shook hands. Once formalities over, Soames eagerly ripped open the envelope and read it. His eyes nearly popped out as he glanced up to meet Cole's eyes in disbelief. The shopping list of ballistics was more than he was expecting.

'Bloody hell!' he blurted. 'This *shouldn't* be a problem, but following French law would *probably* be a better course of action. I can't do this right now,' checking his watch with a yawn.

'We could have a situation,' Cole began to explain. 'And in the event, I'll need to be prepared. How long will it take you to get me a weapon?'

'Oh, I don't know.'

Soames smiled, though not knowing the situation, understood what Cole was getting at. He tucked the request into his jacket pocket. Then removed an automatic pistol from his shoulder holster and gave it to Cole. It looked brand new.

'Never even used it, *except* on the range,' he divulged. 'I want it back mind.'

Soames was clearly starting to wake up now. He glanced past Cole and around the police station, then up at the ceiling. Listening, he realised something was wrong.

'Where is everyone?' he asked.

He didn't wait for Cole's answer, instead he quickly headed around to the front reception and leant over the desk and grabbed the radio. He switched it on and patiently listened to the chatter. Cole had no idea what was being said, but from the expression on Soames' face, it told him that he was too late.

'It sounds like they got your family,' Soames whispered switching off the radio. 'I take it you have a car?'

'Yeah, but I parked by the train station.'

'Why? You could have used the Commissariat car park.'

'I know that now,' Cole admitted as he headed for the door. 'Don't *you* have a car?'

'Yes, but a stone shot the radiator,' Soames replied as he marched out of the building. 'It's in the shop being repaired.'

Their pace quickened without a word spoken. By the time they had reached the square, both men had broken into a gentle jog as they headed for Cole's tiny Citroen.

As Soames climbed into the car he froze. He stared across the car park and water feature to a row of houses. Deep in thought, he took a piece of paper out of his pocket and read it.

'Promenade du Canal! It's at the second address,' he stated.

'How d'you know?'

'Because that house,' he pointed, 'is the first address. D'you see any police?'

***

The car sped off into the night with Cole behind the wheel and Soames shouting directions. They turned into an avenue lined with blocks of flats, concrete 1960s style, which led towards the river.

'This is the second address,' Soames announced.

The wide street was quiet and empty; the first address was the wrong one. The second hadn't a police car in sight either.

'Crap!' Soames piped up as he grabbed the radio in a panic.

Cole stopped the car and then turned to Soames. Something was very wrong. Either his aid had got the addresses wrong or there was another Chevalier family that had been missed. Soames listened to the chatter on the radio and then joined in.

'Je vous Soames,' he said in perfect French. 'Emplacement s'il vous plait?'

'Six Rue du Grand Puits, La Cite Médiévale,' the radio blurted out.

Soames didn't write it down.

'End of the street turn left,' he snapped.

Cole obeyed, but then he suddenly halted.

'It's one way!' Cole pointed out.

'It's also one o'clock in the morning! GO!'

Cole drove the wrong way up the one-way street to the main road then crossed the Pont Neuf bridge.

'C'est un massacre!' blurted out the radio.

Even Cole with his lack of French understood that.

'Where am I going?'

'Right! Left! Then left again! Then first right!'

Cole immediately swung right and exited the main road following the instructions. The car accelerated up an incline through the quiet street and into the trees with the battlements of the medieval city on their right.

'STOP!' Soames screamed.

Cole did as he was told, skidding to a halt in the dust beside a police car and a children's merry-go-round beneath a canopy of trees. He didn't bother to park the car. Before the engine had silenced, Soames was already out. Cole joined him trying to guess which way next. He couldn't hear anything.

'I think you should stay here,' Soames said as he turned back to Cole. 'I get the impression from the radio chatter, that the police are a bit pissed with you.'

Soames slammed the car door. He didn't wait for Cole to answer as he disappeared behind the brightly coloured horses of the merry-go-round. He was about to pursue, when he noticed several Gendarmes watching him, muttering amongst themselves. Cole stayed put and watched the police go about their business. This was becoming a regular thing. There *were* only two Chevalier families in Carcassonne. Cole didn't understand. Rebecca wouldn't have made a mistake like that. The French police would have double-checked the American information anyway, not out of a lack of trust, but more as a matter of course.

Cole decided to follow Soames regardless, but then his holdall started to vibrate on the back seat. He struggled over the seat and unzipped the pocket to find his mobile phone. The lucky dip was successful and with a childish smile, Cole pulled his phone from the bag.

'Hello,' Cole panted.

'Cole?' inquired Garrett. 'Is that you?'

'Yeah,' he replied. 'The phone does work in Europe.'

'What the hell is going on over there?' screamed Garrett.

'What? I haven't done *anything*! I've only just got here!'

'The French have already been in touch. Looks like someone screwed up? Where are you, at this moment?'

'Sitting in the car. Soames has gone to the house.'

'What the bloody hell are you doin' in the car?'

'I was trying to be diplomatic,' answered Cole. 'Diplomacy takes time and I tried to add the personal touch. We were late sir! The bad guys beat us to it.'

'You're not a bloody diplomat,' stormed Garrett. 'You've a job to do, so do it.'

'The French police were watching both houses, but a third house was hit.'

'I'm aware of that! How many bought it?' asked Garrett. 'The French say they have corpses, but they didn't say how many.'

'I don't have that info yet. So I don't know,' Cole replied calmly. 'I don't think I'll get access, but all I need is the photos of the writing and the egghead's help.'

'Your Gabriel guy?'

'Yeah.'

'Nobody can find him and he hasn't contacted Rebecca,' informed Garrett. 'He did visit the victim though. Now she won't say anything. He's left his digs and his landlady isn't talking. She thinks he's wonderful. I don't trust him. I agree with you; he knows something.'

'I'll deal with Gabriel when I get back,' Cole pondered. 'There is one thing you can do for me. Find out who this family was.'

'The Rossal family,' replied Garrett immediately. 'Interestingly, we dug up a little on this family. It's a medieval name, but the family in Carcassonne is the only known family. Interestingly, the Chevalier family here is in same boat. No family tree, just a family line. Only one child in every generation has a family, hence a family line.'

'Which has now stopped!' finished Cole. 'Someone is trying to wipe out this family; which means we still have a chance of catching them. Unless everybody's dead? So what's the connection?'

'I don't know. I say, leave it to Interpol,' Garrett hinted. 'We've done what we can. We can't help them. Let the French have it.'

'But it's not finished,' stated Cole. 'We have Naomi!'

'*Let* the French have it!'

'No! I want this man, woman… whatever! Give me ten days!' demanded Cole. 'The Ambassador wanted me to finish this. This is a political situation whether we like it or not.'

'You'd be lucky if I give you a week. I'll give you two days,' ordered Garrett.

'Five,' haggled Cole.

'Five days and no more bodies. Any bodies and you're on the first flight back!'

'Plus support!' added Cole.

The line went dead and Cole put the phone in his jacket pocket. He looked out of the car window at the figures milling around in the dark. The bodies here weren't his fault. He had only just arrived. *Why was Garrett so annoyed?*

From the car park strolled a man in the direction of the city gate. As he stepped under the streetlight the agent recognised him. It was Gabriel's friend, the man in the crowd from the Chevalier crime scene, in Washington D.C.

'Son of a bitch,' Cole blurted. 'It's the Brit!'

Cole slid down in his seat, making sure he wasn't seen and watched the mystery man as he eyed the police wandering about. Cole waited until the Sinclair had entered the drawbridge, before he opened the car door. The agent then rushed after the shadow, ignoring his interpreter's advice.

'Henry Sinclair!' Cole said to himself remembering the man's name from the file. 'What are you doing here?'

He followed his target over the tiny drawbridge, not wide enough for a car, and stopped. Even in the moonlight the American could view the beauty of the tiny cobbled street with its closed miniature shop fronts. The man was several metres ahead up the steep street at the first minuscule crossroad. To avoid the uneven cobbles, Cole walked up the central drainage channel that was smooth but slippery and turned right still following the stranger. Ahead and still ascending, red and blue flashing lights were reflecting off the walls in the narrow lane as it veered to the left.

'How the hell did they get a car up here?' Cole muttered to himself.

Henry entered the crowd. Cole kept his distance finding a dark porch for cover and watched the house; number six Rue Grand Puîtes. The tiny lane levelled off and had opened up slightly joining several other tiny cobbled streets. Beyond was a well, partially obscured by locals that had filled the square, eager for peek. Three police bikes had been tied with crime scene tape to keep the observers back. That answered one of his questions; police bikes, not cars. Their lights continued to flash much to the annoyance of everyone. From his private spot, Cole couldn't see the front door, hidden from view by the corner of a guesthouse. From the darkness, the hunter watched his prey. If Cole had been more forthcoming with his information he probably would have already had access to the crime scene. This was a minor setback, but most definitely an error on his part. As far as he was concerned, Garrett had given the French authorities all the information that was available. They didn't need to know about the massacre in D.C., but in hindsight, maybe it should have been mentioned. From the expressions on the faces of those that left the building, he knew the tale that was to be told from the evidence held within. His presence was not required and it was unlikely that there was anything else he could learn. Being honest with himself, he knew that his presence would probably cause more problems than necessary. The photos of the writing on the walls would be quite sufficient; assuming there was writing at all. In the shadows, Cole waited for Soames to emerge and in the meantime, he would observe Gabriel's mystery man, Henry.

***

High above the crowded street and harsh shadows was the angelic that Cole had become acquainted with. Gabriel was perched on the edge of the eastern most buttress of Chateau Comtal, looking down upon the street, watching his newly formed ally. His carefully trained eyes could see through the darkness, helping him to study Cole as he in turn overlooked the crime scene from his hiding place.

'Why cannot man open his eyes?' Gabriel asked himself. 'You watch each other while I watch you.'

'And we watch you!'

Gabriel spun around, startled to find himself not alone. Lilith was standing on the near side turret watching him, watching Cole, watching Henry. He was speechless. He recognised the elegant woman, but sensed something was wrong. Gabriel, as always, tried to stay very calm.

'Have we met?' Gabriel asked.

'I think I'd remember. I'm Lilith!'

'Black suits you, so does the leather.'

'Thank you! White was never really my colour. I'm glad I got rid of it thousands of years ago,' she replied. 'Sorry about the family. Abby said they were friends of yours.'

'And he would kill you too, if you called him that to his face,' Gabriel warned trying to ignore the comment, knowing he was face to face with the murderer. 'I do not know any Chevalier in France.'

'Chevalier?' questioned Lilith. 'There are no dead *Chevalier* down there.'

Gabriel was now concerned, since he did not understand where Lilith was going with her riddles. His mind was racing through every possibility. The Chevalier in America had the *presence* of being. He had sensed it in Naomi. However, the Chevalier in America had changed their name. That was why he did not know who they were, until he met the soul survivor. Then it became apparent.

'You killed the Rossal family?' said Gabriel with a shaky tone. 'Why?'

'Orders!' Lilith sharply replied. 'You know what they are, don't you?'

'Abbadon is here?'

'Don't underestimate Abbadon,' Lilith cautioned. 'He is far superior then you, *but* I think he's tired of killing. He is Lord, while you are one of seven. Maybe not even that.'

Gabriel shook his head in disagreement. Trying very hard to hide his feelings. Gabriel was still in a state of shock and confused.

'Why have you done this mother?' he asked calmly.

'You have been around humans too long,' Lilith replied. 'I never thought of you, as one for sarcasm. Your *mother* is probably doing her duty as always. You know how it is? Following orders, there's that word again!'

Lilith quietly laughed to herself. She could see the confusion on Gabriel's face and realised he was still in the dark, metaphorically as well as literally. The fact that Gabriel might be completely alone on the First Realm was starting to sink in.

'Let me spell it out for you,' said Lilith harshly. 'Your *mother*, Sophia, fooled us all, even Abbadon. How she passed herself as me, I have no idea.'

'You are alike, visually I mean.'

'She's now gone back. On this realm, it is only you. We *will* crush you.'

'I have a few tricks up my sleeve,' Gabriel bluffed with a smile.

Lilith shook her head in disagreement and walked up to the edge of the Chateau. She stepped onto the ledge, and gaining some height over Gabriel, looked down at him.

'Tricks are only forms of illusion,' she clarified. 'You're gonna need more than that boy!'

With the insult made, Lilith stepped off the ledge and dropped into the dark. Gabriel didn't even bother to check to see if she had gone. He turned back to watch Cole and the crime scene below. Beneath his calm features was a racing mind of panic. He had neglected some of the duties that he had imposed upon himself. It was now time to bring everything up to date, before it was too late.

***

Upon one of the highest vantage points in the medieval city, the spire of the Basilique Saint-Nazaire, stood Abbadon the Destroyer. He could see Gabriel and smell his fear. His game of chess was being played out nicely. Each pawn was playing its part; each soulcarrier was dying. Abbadon sniffed the night air.

'Little does the watcher know, he is being watched,' Abbadon said to himself.

***

Soames staggered from the house appearing quite distressed. Even from a distance, Cole could see that Soames was shaken by what he had seen. He remembered the feelings that he had had less than 48 hours previous in the Chevalier's home. Even hardened by war, it was never something you could become accustomed to, and Soames didn't seem the sort of person that had been hardened by anything. The smartly dressed liaison officer slowly walked passed the crowd and down the street unknowingly in Cole's direction. Cole slowly stepped out of the shadows and approached the tired liaison. He stopped when he noticed the agent was not where he was supposed to be. Disappointment and anger could easily be read across his face as he searched the vicinity for any other surprises.

'One fucking phone call could have stopped this!' burst Soames uncontrollably. 'One *fucking* phone call!'

'No it wouldn't,' replied Cole quietly shaking his head. 'We had no idea that there was a connection between the Chevalier family and that of the Rossal. We still don't know what the connection is.'

'You want the killer found?' stated Soames. 'Well, I've got news for you, he's on our territory now, so get in fucking line!'

'I need photos of the writing on the wall,' requested Cole. 'The writing in blood. That's all I need.'

Soames stared straight into Cole's eyes, the anger welling up inside.

'You knew! You know what we're dealing with?' he stated, his body shaking. 'One fucking phone call!'

'So there is writing. Look… I don't know what we're dealing with,' admitted Cole. 'I *do* know that they're playing with us and that the writing is the clue.'

'Monsieur Soames,' called a police officer from the entrance of the house. 'Monsieur Soames!'

The liaison left Cole in the middle of the street and ran back up to the house. The police officer led him inside. Cole stood in the middle of the cobbles and patiently waited. Soames reappeared and motioned to him, to come into the house.

'Agent Cole!' he shouted. 'You're with me!'

***

The crime scene went silent when Cole entered the tiny house. Six bodies from three generations lay about his feet. The outsider tried to ignore them and scanned the walls looking for the symbols, searching for the clues. The police photographer had taken a selection of photographs of the glyphs in blood with a Polaroid and handed them to Soames. He flicked through them as though he was shuffling cards and then passed them to Cole.

'You have what you want,' he said bluntly. 'You have no reason to be here now. I suggest you leave. I'll try and calm the situation with the authorities here.'

Cole gratefully accepted the Polaroids and the fact that he was not wanted. He stepped over the body of a young male and noticed a gold chain that had been ripped from his neck and thrown to the ground, without saying a word he briskly walked out of the house. The agent calmed himself as he re-entered the street, brushing passed the potted palm tree by the door and took a deep breath trying to relax. In the corner of his field of vision he could see Gabriel's mystery man, but his attention was not on the crime scene, but somewhere else down the street. Taking on a tired posture, Cole walked back towards the porch, but was stopped by a rushed Soames who had some information bursting to come out.

'The killer didn't get them all!' panted Soames. 'He missed the eldest son.'

Cole pushed Soames out of the streetlight and into the shadows in front of a brown garage door that separated the two streets just east of the guesthouse.

'His name's Sébastien. He's twenty-six years old, five foot eight with black hair, brown eyes and broad build.'

'You mean him?' Cole motioned with his eyes to a young man walking up the side street to their right. 'Is that him?'

'Oh shit!' Soames panicked.

Sébastien clearly saw that the police were at his home. Being the first-born he was also aware, probably more so than Cole, of the danger. The NSA men made no sudden movements and waited for Sébastien to come to them. However, Sébastien had no immediate plans of going anywhere near the house. Suddenly, out of the crowd stepped Henry Sinclair.

'Sébastien!' he shouted in a friendly manner.

The soul survivor didn't recognise the stranger in the dark and out of self-preservation, turned and ran. Sinclair was in pursuit before Cole could react.

'Stop!' shouted Cole. 'We need...' his tone changed. 'What's the use?'

The experienced agent, for a moment in two minds as to what to do, turned to Soames who was already starting to run down the street towards him. The street, if you could call it that, was only five feet wide and dropped off the citadel. Its cobbles were slippery due to the moss and the rain that had begun to fall. Even with Cole's speed and fitness Soames managed to keep ahead. He was wearing the right shoes. Cole, however, continued to slip. The two men chased Sébastien and Henry down the alley that re-joined the Rue du Grand Puîtes at its end. At the mini crossroads, Sébastien turned right, heading away from the drawbridge and ascended the slope. He had lived in the old city all his life and knew the layout like the back of his hand. Unfortunately, his hard leather footsteps on the cobbled street helped keep the pursuers on the right track. Soames followed, but Cole paused at the crossroads.

Less than fifteen meters away the street opened up at a junction with a bronze sculpture of the city in the middle. Soames stopped to catch his breath. Sébastien had hair-pinned back on himself and came back into Cole's view up the street in front of him.

'Get some back up!' Cole shouted to Soames who leant against the bronze city.

He took out the radio raising it to speak. Out of the corner of Cole's eye a shadow moved behind Soames as a jabbing pain shot though the back of the translator's neck preventing him from speech. An eight-inch dart had severed his spinal cord, cut through his voice box and stopped abruptly, when it pierced the radio. Soames collapsed on the ground, dead, the blade still embedded in his neck with the radio skewered on the point. Cole glanced over his shoulder before he left the crossroads, only to see Soames lying by the mini city. He stopped in his tracks. A police officer appeared under a streetlamp and started to shout.

'Une autre! Nous avons une autre cadavre!'

Lights in the residential houses began to come on, curious as to what had caused the commotion. Cole couldn't wait. He had to continue the pursuit leaving the screaming policeman and the body of Soames. No more bodies or it's on the first flight home, Garrett had said. But the killer was here!

As the rain began to increase, the American ran up the slight slope of the street, until he came to a square packed with tables and chairs and several large trees in the centre. Each table had a collapsed sunshade protruding from it making visibility difficult. The Place Marcou was flanked on three sides with cafés and restaurants. To Cole's left was a low lying wall, in the middle a gap with a wrought iron gate and an iron cross over it. Beyond, up the three steps was a small square grassy area with a monument in the centre, several evergreens protected it from the rain and beyond that; the derelict eastern wall of the ancient city.

'Sébastien!' Cole shouted out. 'I hope you speak English?'

Cole didn't know what else to say. He didn't speak French so he was hoping.

'The Chevalier's in Washington DC are dead! I came here to help you.'

Sébastien stood up from behind the low wall where he had been lying in the wet. He brushed himself down and faced the American. Cole meandered his way towards the Frenchman.

As he reached the wrought iron-gate Sébastien screamed in pain. A woman's hand with sharp nails, razor sharp nails cut upward through his chest and as a final stroke, cut his throat. Sébastien fell over the wall into the cobbled square. It had been several centuries since the streets had seen that quantity of blood. Lilith stepped forward into the light. The agent drew his weapon, Soames' weapon, and aimed. Suddenly, out of the shadows, with incredible speed appeared another figure in the form of a beautiful blonde her long hair matted by the rain; her tunic clinging to her skin. The appearance of the outsider surprised Cole, but was a shock to Lilith.

'Iinnad!' she huffed. 'Died your hair?'

Iinnad said nothing and gave Cole a stern glance as he lowered his weapon. Lilith sniffed the air and then having a change of heart, stepped back melting into the shadows. This was not the time or the place. The blonde angelic approached Sébastien's body and crouched down to tend to him. She noticed the pendant around his neck and then closed Sébastien's eyes for him. The tender moment was abruptly interrupted by Sinclair. He charged into the square from the opposite side, gun in hand, and ran straight up to Iinnad, ignoring Cole completely.

'Ne touché pas!' he demanded. 'The police are coming!'

'Il n'y a rien que je puis faire,' Iinnad quietly replied.

Iinnad looked up at Henry and noticed the pendant around his neck was the same as the one on the body in front of her. She then motioned to the shadows behind her. The look of concentration flashed across her face as her mind changed from French to English.

'She went that way,' Iinnad instructed quietly. 'She's in the shadows!'

'She?' inquired Henry.

Henry carefully crouched beside Iinnad with the gun still pointing in her direction. He looked into the innocent eyes and then down at Sébastien's body. All he could see was sorrow. His mind turned to that of the shadows on the other side of the grassy square, and his weapon followed his train of thought. The sound of heavy footsteps could be heard by Iinnad's delicate ear.

'People are coming!' she pointed out keeping her voice down so that Cole could not hear. 'The shadows,' she whispered.

Henry stood up, aiming his weapon into the shadow behind Iinnad. He was motionless. He couldn't see Lilith, but for some reason he trusted the beauty with the brown round eyes.

'Am I a fucking statue?' Cole barked.

In a blur, Iinnad made herself scarce as Cole approached. People do not move that fast. He could not get that out of his mind. The agent then stopped by the body of Sébastien and tried to focus on the corpse. The first thing he noticed on the body was the gold glint around his neck. It was the same as the 'coin' that was still in his pocket. Cole cautiously bent down and snatched the pendant from Sébastien's neck. As he did so, he carefully listened for footsteps, for his prey, for anything. Considering the violence of the night, the city was quiet. Then Cole slowly approached Henry, gun in hand still aimed at the shadows in the corner of the square. Cole slowly raised Soames' weapon and pointed it directly at Henry's head.

'Don't you bloody move!' he said very slowly.

'I don't have the time for this,' Henry called back over his shoulder.

He gave Cole a quick glance and realising that there was an automatic pistol being pointed at him, he tried to explain. 'The killer is in the shadows. Have you any idea what you are dealing with Agent Cole of the NSA?'

'Put the gun down!'

'You want Sébastien's killer to get away?'

'Put the gun down!' Cole repeated.

Henry lowered his head as if to give up, but instead turned and re-aimed, pointing his gun directly at the agent. This was not what Cole had in mind.

'C'est dingue!' Iinnad interrupted as she walked into the light from the opposite direction that she left.

Cole, caught completely off guard, spun around changing the direction of his aim and pointed his weapon straight at her. Cole jokingly put her hands in the air with a big grin.

Henry's footsteps distracted Cole as he looked around, but it was too late. His target had already gone; there was no sight or sound of him. Cole lowered his weapon in disappointment, but then he remembered that the blonde was still there and he raised it again.

'This is becoming one hell of a night,' he said, weapon still trained on Cole.

'I would have said, interesting,' she replied.

'You speak English?'

'Yes!' Cole replied. 'And you stopped me getting my man.'

Cole looked up the side street nearest to where Henry had stood. She stretched for the sky.

'I've watched TV,' she admitted. 'This is how they do it.'

Then Cole let her hands drop to her side, turned away and began to walk towards the side street that Henry had disappeared up.

'I don't believe this,' Cole said to himself.

'You don't?'

Cole continued to walk. Frustrated, he motioned to point his weapon even harder in her direction. He glanced in the direction of the sounds of the local police, but he had to focus on the mysterious woman and forget about Soames for a moment.

'Wait lady!' he shouted. 'You can't walk away, I'm the one with the gun.'

Cole had never been in this situation. He knew he couldn't shoot her, but what else could he do? This young and attractive woman, who just happened to be wearing the most revealing clothing, was taking no notice of his authority in any way what so ever. She showed no sign of concern as she continued to walk away and Cole found himself unwillingly following her. He glanced over his shoulder at the shadows of the eastern wall, but saw nothing. He had no choice. He was compelled to follow.

'Are you French?' he asked.

'What makes you think that?'

'Are you with Interpol?' he questioned.

'Dressed like this?' she motioned to her attire. 'Not a smart agent, are you?'

'Then tell me,' Cole pleaded.

'No, and no more questions.'

Cole hadn't realised it yet, but they were no longer in the square, but in a side street headed down hill towards another yet, larger square. Cole continued to walk as Cole followed.

'I need to know what I have here,' requested Cole. 'You stopped me catching a killer.'

'I'm Cole.'

'Why were you after him?'

'Why were you?' she replied sharply.

'He's a killer.'

'I know,' Cole agreed. 'You can see it in his eyes. But he kills only those that really deserved it, a bit like you. I see it in your eyes too.'

As she approached the Basilique Saint-Nazaire, Cole ignored her stalker and entered the open street to the south of the old city. Embarrassed, Cole put the weapon away. Above on the spire, Abbadon watched. Cole's presence was unexpected and definitely unwanted. She was here to see Cole, so why was she with the American? Cole could sense something; she knew she was being watched. With Lilith on the First Realm, Abbadon had to be close. She casually wiped the thought from her mind for the time being. She had no fear of Abbadon. He would have softened up from centuries on the First Realm. Cole on the other hand, had been in conflict after conflict. She was toned, sharp and quick.

Cole exited the old city via the Porte d'Aude and quickened her pace down the cobbles past the Eglise and over the old stone arched bridge of the Port Vieux, into Carcassonne's modern town. Cole trailed behind, but kept his distance. He didn't know why. It was obvious that she knew he was still there; but how long had she been watching him? She knew he was an agent. Soames had called him Agent Cole before he entered the house, as had Henry.

***

Back in the tiny square a policeman had found the body of Sébastien. As he began to radio it in he caught the glimpse of a disfigured shadow sitting on the nearby over-grown steps of the battlements. From another side street appeared another disfigured shadow. The hairs on the back of the policeman's neck rose and the jitters had set in. Out of the dark casually strolled Lilith in black leather with her razor sharp nails still coated in blood. The policeman wisely chose to back away. A few steps at first and then he turned and ran. Lilith smiled at the sight of the fleeing male. Her smile was wiped from her face when she picked up a scent on the breeze. Gabriel!

He fired up his brace weapon. From his high vantage point, he launched a blade at a shadow and then made sure he had easy access to his sword beneath his coat. The demonic received the sharp metal in the centre of his forehead before igniting. The Archangel closed his red eyes and concentrated on the transformation that he had been so accustomed to in the past. With the pain gone, Gabriel stood on the edge of the rooftop looking down into the tiny square. With his wings outstretched and his brace fully charged, he effortlessly stepped off the building and glided down to land in the middle of the grassy square, several feet from Abbadon.

The other demonic began to dart from side to side through the tables and chairs as it drew closer to the angelic. Gabriel raised his brace weapon again and lined it up with the corner of his eye to his right. With confidence he headed straight for Lilith. As the demonic tauntingly darted across his line of sight, Gabriel clenched his fist. The blade released a familiar hum as the demonic's head toppled from its shoulders and the second corpse burst into flames.

'Truce!' called Lilith as she raised her hands in an open gesture.

'Truce?' questioned Gabriel. 'You deserve what *he* got.'

Lilith began to back away from Sébastien's body, since Gabriel was still headed in her direction. Two more demonic appeared and came to Lilith's aid. Even with her back up she looked concerned. Gabriel was fully transformed and far more powerful than she presently was.

'Thank god for bodyguards,' she joked as she backed away.

'Do not even go there!' Gabriel said in a hardened voice.

The first of the two demonic drew his blade and attempted to strike. Gabriel fired his brace twice. The first was at the ground between them and the second at head height. The first blade ricocheted off the cobbled square and up towards his attacker, who jumped to avoid it, only to be met in the chest by the second blade. The second attacker stood his ground. Gabriel fired the brace again, only this time in the direction of the tables.

'Stop!' bellowed the silhouette sitting on the steps.

It had been an age since Gabriel had heard Abbadon's voice. The *fallen* didn't move. Gabriel lowered his arm. The single blade had already ricocheted of a wall and harmlessly landed in the shadows. If there were any more demonic, none would cross Abbadon's order.

'That's very unlike you,' said Abbadon. 'Instant violence.'

'What do you want Abbadon?' demanded Gabriel.

'Your attention, Gabriel.'

'Is that what all this is about?' the Archangel asked. 'Why could you not sniff me out and give me a call?'

'Cute,' Abbadon smiled. 'Because I'm also trying to make a point. I want this Realm! You took the third one from me, but this one's mine.'

'I'm stronger than you think,' bluffed Gabriel.

'I believe you are,' whispered Abbadon. 'That's why I'm not attempting anything right now.'

'Stop playing, Abbadon.'

'Ah, you got me,' Abbadon replied. 'You're right, I do want to make it enjoyable. I also want to have fun. We live here, but everything is far too serious. Don't you think? Why can't we just enjoy being alive? I *also* want this realm.'

'Well then, I will give you this,' answered Gabriel. 'I am full of surprises.'

Lilith began to snigger at Gabriel's comment.

'You're full of surprises,' repeated Abbadon as he shook his head. 'No you're not Gabriel. I know everything about you.'

Suddenly and unexpectedly, that fear was back. *Was this a part of his game?* Abbadon climbed down from the stone steps and joined

Lilith amongst the chairs. The Destroyer didn't look back, but continued to walk away. Lilith gave Gabriel a childish wave and followed her master. They both turned their backs on him. His transition was complete. They could not have beaten him for he was too strong, and yet, they *still* turned their backs on him.

'Say hello to Iinnad for me,' shouted Abbadon from the shadows.

The master and his servant left Gabriel in the tiny square, the fires of the dead demonic, still burning. Iinnad was banned from the First Realm, as were most, if not all angelic. Gabriel knew it and so did she. The mixed up angelic switched off his brace. The alarm had been raised by the petrified police officer and reinforcements were coming. Gabriel glanced over at the body of Sébastien and slowly shook his head.

'I am sorry,' he paused, feeling out breath for no apparent reason. 'I am sorry for everything.'

With several beats of his wings, he lifted himself over the eastern ramparts and gently landed in the cemetery on the other side of the trench beneath the battlements. He closed his wings, tired and confused.

'Say hello to Iinnad,' he copied Abbadon's voice.

Landing amongst the gravestones, Gabriel had avoided the police. None of them had seen him, so it was safe for him to re-enter the medieval city. Only this time he would pay no attention to the commotion and head for his hotel.

***

Iinnad peered over her shoulder to see if Cole was still there. Unlikely, that he wouldn't have been, but she checked all the same. It was still raining as she kept a fast pace through the town. Not tiring, she had made a point of pushing, to see what the human would do. Cole was not quite out of breath, but after thirteen hours of travel, the amount of exercise he had exerted that evening was a shock to the system: as was the jet lag. He wasn't as fit as he used to be, but he had an inner strength that had helped him in the past. He continued to follow. Although married, and faithful to his wife, Cole could still admire the beauty in the blonde woman called Iinnad. The clothes that clung to her wet body barely covered her. They were made of a white Hessian material in the style of a tunic with a loose fit. *'Well, hey, there's nothing wrong in admiring beauty.'* Plus she was fit, and moved well, presenting herself with elegance and an overpowering amount of confidence. The American was intrigued, almost captivated.

Iinnad practically walked back to the Information booth. Within a few metres of it, she turned right into a side road off from the canal and stopped in front of the Hotel Eclipse. It was a cheap 120 francs a night, no star hotel. It also happened to be the hotel that Cole had been booked into, but he didn't know that yet.

'We've walked and not talked for about fifteen minutes now,' Cole claimed. 'And I still know nothing about you.'

'I said no questions,' replied Iinnad. 'This is your hotel.'

'But I haven't booked in,' admitted Cole a little surprised.

'Someone did. Goodbye Mr Cole.'

'Richard, my friends call me Richard.'

The agent stood in front of the hotel as Iinnad sniffed the night air. She paused for a moment, turned her head and sniffed the air in a different direction.

'I'm not your friend,' she said with a large cheesy grin on her face and then she briskly walked off towards the canal once again.

Cole stood there… captivated by her arrogance, her beauty and her blatant disregard for danger or authority, even though he knew in the present situation he had no authority in France whatsoever. *Maybe she knew that? Maybe she didn't? Or maybe she just didn't care?* Cole had a weird feeling it was the latter. Iinnad was still in view and Cole had to act quickly. To his surprise, the door was open for that hour. He ran into the reception and struck the bell on the desk. Impatiently he tapped his nails on the hard wood, leaning over every couple of taps to make sure the blonde was still in view. Cole struck the bell again. And again. A tired unshaved man in a woman's dressing gown appeared through the beaded flytrap of the back door. He didn't smile.

'Merde! J'ai oublie de fermer la porte de devant. La femme voudrait me tuer si elle savait!'

'Richard Lawton Cole!' announced the American before the man could ask a question. 'Am I booked in here?'

'Oui Monsieur Cole,' he yawned.

Cole placed his passport on the desk. The man forced his eyes open to read it. Then handed Cole his keys. From under the counter he removed a large book.

'Chambre… Room 16. The keys; one front door and for your room. I have messages also...'

Cole had already left the hotel and was running down the street towards the canal. Within a matter of seconds, he caught sight of Iinnad who was still briskly walking through the drizzle. He was careful to keep his distance. Hastily, he took his mobile phone from his jacket pocket and dialled Rebecca. It didn't take long for her to answer.

'Hi beautiful,' he said. 'How are you? I need you to run a check for me. The name is Iinnad; no surname and check all agencies... yes, just like Gabriel! I don't know how to spell it. Five foot eight inches, slim and blonde.' Cole laughed. 'Yeah, my type. Present location Carcassonne... …Yes I'm fine… I got here ok. I got two more bodies though, so can you keep this quiet for now? I don't need Garrett on my back right now. Yeah... OK.'

Cole was still walking briskly, but stopped on the corner of the street opposite the Canal du Midi. He watched Iinnad stand at the waters edge.

'Yes,' he spoke into the phone. 'I love you too.'

Cole put the phone away and concentrated on watching the captivating Iinnad. She had left the lights of the café front behind and headed down stream, along the towpath, into the dark of the low arched railway bridge. At the waters edge she stopped and sniffed the air again. Her tunic was no longer translucent, just skin tight. She was on the right scent. She was not the only one in the shadows. Lilith stood in the blackness beneath the masonry out of Cole's view. Iinnad walked over to greet her.

'How are you, Lilith?' she casually asked. 'I didn't the get the chance to say hello properly, earlier.'

'Funny,' was Lilith's sarcastic reply.

With no complications, Lilith toyed with the idea of fighting Iinnad. She carefully began to position herself to strike. Iinnad was not stupid and well versed in nearly all forms of combat for many millennia. She slowly moved to position herself in response to Lilith's moves. Abbadon stepped from behind his servant and gently tapped her on the shoulder. Lilith down and relaxed a little. Abbadon wanted to talk, not fight.

'Iinnad, what are you doing here?' he inquired.

'I smelt something bad,' she replied as she smiled at his pet.

Lilith stepped forward regardless of her master's instructions. Her nails were fully extended and she flexed her muscles, squared her shoulders and clicked her neck from side to side in order to loosen up.

'I have no problem about fighting you Lilith, so come on,' Iinnad beckoned. 'Give it your best shot. I want to see if you *really do* have what it takes to take me.'

Abbadon firmly placed his hand on Lilith's shoulder and stopped her from moving to intercept. He pulled her back and took centre stage.

'Why are you here, Iinnad?' he asked again.

'I am the bearer of news.'

'For who?' said Lilith staring straight at Iinnad.

Lilith wanted to prove she could beat her. Iinnad had a reputation for being insolent with regards to the Archangels, pointing out their errors. Not that the Archangels ever made mistakes, but rumour had it that if they did, Iinnad would be the first, and perhaps the only one to highlight the fact. The fallen had much information on

Iinnad. An angelic after their own heart, they were amazed that she had managed to avoid falling from grace.

'For *whom*?' Iinnad corrected. 'Now there's a silly question. She's pretty Abbadon, I have to admit, but also *dumb*.'

Lilith jumped forward and was met by Abbadon's arm across her chest. She leant against his arm as he forcibly pushed her back into the shadow.

'Lilith!' he warned. '*Our* fight is not with Iinnad.'

'*Our* fight? That's fair enough Abbadon.'

'Stay away Iinnad,' the beast replied. 'This is not your fight.'

Just like her character, Iinnad boldly stood up to Abbadon, face to face. She gave a little laugh to herself and stared into the Destroyer's eyes.

'Nervous?' she asked.

Abbadon held her shoulders and pushed her back to arms length.

'I won't fight you Abbadon. You have my word, but I will complete my reason for being here. Try and stop me and I will take back my word. Are we clear?'

'I have your word?' Abbadon confirmed.

'I have never broken my word. Stop me in my mission and I *will* fight you. Attack me and I *will* fight you. Any attempt on my existence… and I *will* fight you. It's that simple. Are we clear?'

Iinnad glanced over at Lilith and smiled. She turned on a heel and marched away along the side of the canal. Lilith started to move in for the kill before she could get too far, but again, Abbadon stopped her, only this time more forcibly than before.

'Let her go!' he breathed into Lilith's face.

'Next time she's mine,' claimed the angry servant under her breath.

'Lilith my dear, next time… she'll kill you.'

Abbadon stepped into the darkness under the bridge leaving Lilith to watch Iinnad walk away. The angelic warrior didn't even look back. Lilith accepted that there would be another time and followed Abbadon into the night.

Even in shadows, Cole was able to see everything from his vantage point. However, he did not hear everything that was said. As Iinnad swiftly paced away in the rain, Cole watched as he moved out into the open.

'No one is that confident without reason,' he said to himself. Who are people? What are these people? You're definitely not agency of any kind. Cole, what are you getting yourself into?'

He stood by the canal, hands in pockets, as Iinnad made her way back towards him. She passed by as she strolled along the footpath.

'Goodnight Richard,' she said quietly without even looking in his direction.

Like a child about to have a tantrum, Cole frustratingly approached the waters edge. The impression was that he would have jumped in, but instead, finding the pendant in his pocket, he took it out and threw it at the water. It spiralled to the bottom with the chain trailing behind. Realising what he had just done he stared into the black pools pelted by the rain.

'Shit! Shit! Shit! Damn! Damn! Damn!'

His mobile phone rang, bringing Cole back to the adult world.

'Hi Becks, what have you got for me?' he asked.

He listened to what Rebecca had to say and then hung up. Rebecca had found nothing on any Iinnad. The name was quite unique. The quiet summer night was shattered by a crack of thunder and the rain began to increase. Already wet, Cole stood by the canal as he watched the droplets making rings on the surface. It was one of the wettest July's he had ever known. Staring into the slow moving waters he could still see a glint from the pendant at the bottom. Cole was in a world of his own. Completely out of his depth and not quiet sure which way to turn. He was wet and none the wiser. *'Where was she going? Was Gabriel here?'* The hotel and sleep could wait. He had that feeling that he was becoming a puppet once again; only this time he didn't know who was pulling the strings. For the time being, he would follow the elegant blonde.

IX

The First Realm.

Carcassonne – 03.01hrs Saturday 15th July AD 2001 GMT+1

Gabriel relaxed on his hotel bed, his eyes closed, with his arms by his side. He lay perfectly still. He would not have admitted it to anyone, but the transformations had taken a lot out of him, as had the flight from the States. It had been a long time since Gabriel had transformed and it reminded him that there was more, than just his duties that he had neglected. He took a deep breath, in through his nose and out of his mouth, naturally smelling the air as he did so. He winced when he picked up a scent, and opened his eyes. The silence of the room was broken by a knock at the door.

'The door is open,' he spoke to the ceiling.

The door swung wide and Gabriel's *eyes* entered the room, closing the door behind her. Gabriel closed his eyes again and proceeded to breath in through his nose.

'Were you followed?' he asked.

The comment caught Iinnad off guard. She looked around the tidy room with an expression of surprise on her face. She was sarcastically shocked. *Had someone followed her into the room?* Silently she stepped into the centre of the floor.

'Iinnad, were you followed?' Gabriel repeated.

'Yeah!' she replied sharply. 'Right to the bloody door! Is that all I get? Were you followed? How about… How are you? Or… Iinnad, how long has it been? 200, 400 years? A thousand years? More like three and half thousand years?'

Gabriel opened his eyes and looked over at Iinnad. She ran towards the bed and dived onto it, but he was up and standing beside it before she landed and bounced on the springs. The bubbly blonde rolled over and lay on her side to look up at the Archangel.

'You never were any good in bed,' she joked in a pissed off way.

'This is not funny Iinnad.'

'It was only a joke.'

'I was referring to your being here,' Gabriel replied.

'Don't you need my help?' she asked pouting.

'Do they know you are here?' he asked ignoring her facial expression.

'Who?' Iinnad motioned up. 'Them? Or…'

'Abbadon,' Gabriel interrupted. 'He took the pleasure of letting me know.'

'Sorry.'

'Is that it Iinnad? Sorry?'

'No! Actually, there is one other thing.'

Her train of thought was distracted for a moment as she sniffed the air. The both of them turn to face the door.

'He just won't quit!' Iinnad complained as she got off the bed. 'When are we going to get some quality time?'

Gabriel interrupted the knock at the door and called to the person in the corridor to come in. Cole entered and immediately faced off to Gabriel. There was movement in the corner of his eye, turning to get a better view, he saw Iinnad standing there.

'What the hell, are you doing here?' he blurted, almost spitting at Gabriel.

Iinnad moved towards the agent. Instinctively, he drew his weapon.

'You do not need that,' Gabriel said.

'Who the fuck's the blonde?' replied Cole.

'How macho!' Iinnad responded.

'Her name is Iinnad,' Gabriel answered. 'We used to work together.'

'Ha!' Iinnad said in a huff. 'He didn't believe me.'

'Cole, please put the gun away,' Gabriel asked. 'Iinnad is an old colleague.'

'Bloody hell!' blasted Iinnad. 'Now I'm reduced to a colleague.'

Cole lowered his pistol, since there was obviously more to all of this. He closed the door and moved to the opposite side of the room to the blonde.

'Does he know?' Iinnad asked Gabriel.

'Know what?' asked Cole.

'Nothing,' said Gabriel.

'What am I missing here?' demanded Cole.

'Nothing!' repeated Gabriel.

There was silence in the room for a moment. Gabriel was right; Cole knew nothing. He had already come to the conclusion that he was out of his depth, but he was always eager to learn, and from his experiences, he could learn fast. He gave a sigh and put away the automatic. While his hand was still under his jacket, he pulled out the Polaroid's and threw them down on the coffee table in the middle of the room.

'I don't know why I'm even showing you these,' he said. 'But maybe...'

'These are from the Rossal house?' Gabriel butted in, moving straight to the table and sitting down to view the images.

'Yeah,' Cole slowly replied. 'My liaison got them for me, just before someone stuck a spike through his neck.'

'I am sorry,' Gabriel shuffled through the pictures.

He started to place the Polaroid's on the table in a pattern to see if he could make anything of it. He rearranged the Polaroid's again.

'The letter 'N' and 'P',' he said to himself as Cole and Iinnad moved closer to view the images on the table.

'What is this, remedial?' asked Iinnad, still jovial.

Gabriel ignored the comment as he continued to study the symbols. Cole sat down next to Gabriel. However, he spent more time watching Iinnad than the table.

'I think this is more of the New Testament apocryphal book,' Gabriel pondered.

'You mentioned that before,' said Cole. 'As in the Bible, but not in the Bible?'

'I've read that,' Iinnad smiled. 'Not much in it about us, well, you're mentioned a couple times.'

Iinnad jokingly gave Gabriel a friendly comrade style hug with one arm. She then proceeded to sit down in the chair opposite the two and began to study the Polaroid's from where she sat, upside-down.

'Iinnad please!' Gabriel warned impatiently. He turned to Cole. 'You have been reading up on the subject?'

'A little,' Cole replied sheepishly. 'On the flight over here. But I didn't get it all. In fact, I didn't get any of it.'

'OK… very basic Christian and Bible history in six easy sentences,' Gabriel began attempting to straighten Cole's confusion. 'One, Adam and Eve...'

'You're going to start at the beginning?' asked Cole.

'I said six sentences,' responded Gabriel. 'One, Adam and Eve, Abraham, Moses, Jesus, the cross and everything gets written down, creating a series of books.'

Cole nodded in agreement. *'That was fair enough,'* he thought.

'Two,' continued Gabriel. 'At the Council of Nicaea, in the fourth century it was decided that a unified version of the Bible would be required. Three, the bishops and the church leaders voted on which books, that were available at the time, would be entered into the final version of the Bible.'

'That's simple enough.'

'Yeah, even I get that,' Iinnad added.

'Not really, some of the votes were very close,' answered Gabriel.

'Four!' jokingly screamed Iinnad breaking Cole's concentration.

Gabriel glared at his colleague, who wiped the smile from her face.

'Four,' stated Gabriel. 'The books that were chosen became the Bible as we know it today and the others became the apocryphal books. Five, some people of the world use the apocryphal books as a part of their religion and the Holy Roman Church deemed them heretics. And six, to control the situation, the church banned education, learning etc and the world fell into the dark ages, which it eventually climbed out of.'

'So some people see the apocryphal books as a form of secret knowledge?' suggested Cole. 'Is that factual knowledge?'

'In a way, yes they are esoteric,' replied Gabriel with a smile. 'But now most of the books have been translated from their original text. Computers and the Internet have made these ancient text readily available to Joe public, hence the vast interest in the subject matter. It will not be long before we have novels and movies.'

'But the text is not in its original form?' Cole inquired. 'Hence the reason for the difficulty in reading this script.'

'It takes some doing,' Gabriel replied as he realised Cole had caught on.

'Yeah! Right!' Iinnad butted in. 'Actually it's a language. Gabriel's just forgotten it. And that was more than six sentences.'

'I am a bit rusty,' Gabriel defended himself.

'Rusty? Gabriel you're practically seized up.'

Cole raised his hands between the two angelic, in an attempt to calm things down. He didn't want to be caught in the middle of a domestic.

'Iinnad, are you saying you can read this?' Cole asked calmly.

'Dah!' she replied. 'Is the Pope...'

'Jewish,' Cole interrupted.

The expression on Iinnad's face was that of a small child, who hadn't done their homework and was being questioned in front of the class. She didn't say anything, but Cole could read the answer in her eyes. *'How could she not know?'* The angelic brushed off the question as though it didn't matter, but it did matter. Cole was learning more about the two than they realised.

She smiled the smile of an innocent girl. That innocence that they have before the corruption begins. This beautiful female form knew so much and yet at times appeared so naive. She sat slumped over the coffee table, elbows on knees, opening her legs then slapping her knees together, repeating the action over and over. Cole, ever the gentleman, focused on the table, making a conscious effort to avoid viewing her inner thigh.

'Iinnad! Do you mind?' Gabriel barked.

'What?'

Iinnad slapped her knees together and kept them there. Gabriel threw the remaining Polaroids at her, stood up and walked over to the balcony windows. He was more annoyed with himself than with Iinnad. She had always been like this, it was in her nature and he loved her for it, though he would never admit it. He knew Iinnad could read the script, this was yet another one of those duties he had neglected for so many years. Iinnad studied the pictures, tilting her head from side to side in an attempt to read them, without touching any.

'How long have you been here?' Cole asked.

Iinnad perked up, like a deer grazing in the forest when it hears the hunter. She glanced at Gabriel not quite sure how to answer the question.

'How long have you been in Carcassonne, Iinnad?' Gabriel clarified.

'A couple of days,' she barked. 'One day... Well... Last night.' She cleared her throat, 'about six hours?'

'Are you sure?' Cole questioned.

'Six hours!'

'So, in six hours, how come you know more than me?'

'Guesswork!'

'Guesswork?' Cole questioned. 'You're kidding?'

Iinnad stared at the photos ignoring the agent's comments. 'None of this makes any sense,' she stated. 'Do you want me to read it?'

'Please,' Gabriel calmed down. 'There is a file on the bedside table which has the other symbols in it.'

Cole fetched the file, returning, he placed the rest of the images next to the existing ones. Iinnad fanned out all the photos and placed them in rows correcting their direction when necessary.

'Do they have an order they're supposed to go in?' she asked.

Gabriel shook his head while still looking out of the window at the night's sky.

'Only the order the photos were taken in,' Cole added. 'But we know from the early symbols, that this is a puzzle.'

'This is easy,' claimed Iinnad. 'First the symbols.'

Cole was already prepared with notepad and pen at the ready. Maybe this beauty really did know the stuff and was a colleague of Gabriel's.

'O... Y... L...' Iinnad read. 'The second lot are N... P... A.... and the third lot are O... I... That's strange...'

'What is?' Gabriel asked.

'The last two symbols,' Iinnad replied curiously. 'A little n... and a little c... They're so small that they're not a part of the main text.'

'As in Inc?' asked Cole showing Iinnad his notepad.

She looked down at the notepad and agreed. She didn't know what the abbreviation meant.

'I'd say Abbadon is having a bigger game with you than you think Gabe,' Iinnad suggested. 'This is all too… …too tidy. I don't like it.'

'Abbadon?' queried Cole.

'Gabe?' Iinnad urged. 'Doesn't he know, *anything*?'

'Would someone care to enlighten me into what the fuck is going on?' Cole demanded. 'Because these letters mean nothing to me.'

'Apolyon Inc,' Iinnad pointed out obviously. 'What is Inc?'

'Incorporated,' replied Cole. 'It's a company of some description.'

'A company of what? I don't know about any company, but Apolyon is the name of Abbadon's old ship. You remember Gabe? The one he lost near Icea.'

Cole was beginning to lose his trust in Gabriel again. It had now come to the forefront of his mind, as had how Gabriel managed to get to Carcassonne so quickly.

'You knew all of this?' Cole pleaded.

'I know Abbadon,' Gabriel replied. 'I know he lost a ship near Icea and I know he is after me. I did not *know* that Abbadon was behind this. I had my suspicions.'

'This wouldn't happen to be the big guy that Iinnad was talking to down by the canal would it?' Cole asked.

Iinnad buried her head in her hands. Gabriel's disdain for what he had just heard was evident. Gabriel thought Iinnad should not even be on the First Realm and now she had been seen with Abbadon.

'What were you doing with Abbadon?' the Archangel politely asked.

'Confronting him from what I could see,' Cole divulged.

'You're really not helping!' Iinnad snapped at Cole.

Gabriel opened the balcony windows and went outside. He definitely needed the fresh air on this humid summer night. Cole joined him as they both looked out over the drenched rooftops of the medieval city.

'You're an egghead,' Cole explained calmly, but also in a polite manner. 'You read ancient text and stuff. What does this nutter want with you?'

'Gabriel, an egghead!' shouted Iinnad from inside the room. 'I like that.'

'People are dying to bring you out of your books? Is that what this is about?'

Gabriel did not reply. He slowly looked at Cole and then he turned away again, staring out over the city, deep in thought.

'What makes you think you could beat a mass murderer like this, Abbadon? Look at you! No offence, but this Abbadon's built like a brick shit house.'

Gabriel turned back to face Cole. Iinnad was still in the room sitting at the coffee table. She mimed the words as Gabriel said them.

'Have a little faith.' Gabriel watched Iinnad play with the photos. 'Look at her, Agent Cole. When she was with Abbadon, did he fear her?' Not waiting for an answer. 'I take it Lilith was there? Did Lilith fear her? Look at her. How could anyone fear her? Now look at me… What do you see?'

Cole didn't answer; instead he ambled back into the room and the coffee table.

'Did you hear that?' he asked Iinnad.

Iinnad glanced up. 'Have a little faith? All the time,' she replied, purposely trying to confuse him. 'Why do they fear me? Because they should!'

Cole sat down in the chair in the corner of the room.

'Time to rest,' Iinnad observed.

Cole fell asleep. The art of suggestion can be a powerful tool.

X

The First Realm.

Carcassonne – 05.10hrs 17th July AD 2001 GMT+1

In contrast to the medieval surroundings, the metallic telephone box was a blot on the landscape. It only managed to blend in after dark. Henry inserted his phone card and began to dial. It didn't take long for the fourteen-digit number to be entered and the tone on the other end began to ring.

Henry had been in contact with Gabriel for some time, ever since the angelic had started to lecture ancient languages at a select few East Coast universities. He knew what Gabriel was. From birth, his life had already been set out for him. In one form or another he was to serve the angelic. Well, that was the way Henry saw it. What Henry did not initially realise was that serving the angelic, in turn, meant he was serving mankind. This was something that he, and the entire organisation that he was part of, had missed, all except possibly Henry's father, leader of their secret organisation. Through Henry's father, the organisation had begun to understand their true purpose in the world and since working with Gabriel; Henry had been shown what his father had achieved. However, unbeknown to Henry, he was also Gabriel's only saving grace, from his neglected duties. The soulcarrier had contact to the organisation through him; the organisation that Gabriel had helped to create.

Henry spoke the languages and knew the layout for the battle ahead. More importantly than anything, unknown to him and every member of the organisation, he possessed, an essence, the presence of being. All the members of the organisation knew they had a gift for speed and agility, but how they processed it was alien to them. The essence was a scent that the angelic or fallen could sense. In the case of the fallen, they could hunt. This essence, when honed and forged, served many purposes.

Some religions or belief systems have a train of thought that relates to the inner power of a human being. The Chinese call it Chi and some Middle Eastern countries call it Chakra. To others it may be known only as the seven levels of power. However, in modern time and to science fiction fans it is jokingly called the Force; but it was more than that. The people of the First Realm, over the centuries had learnt to harness this inner strength, but in most cases, once discovering a level of power they had concentrated on it, nurturing it and therefore had failed to explore or to discover if there were more. With the essence that ran through Henry's veins and his training from childhood, he and the members of the organisation had managed to harness all seven, in one degree or another. To these unique people, this ability was believed to be the next step in the evolutionary ladder. How wrong could they have possibly been? The essence, the presence of being, doesn't grow on trees; it was not a natural form of evolution. It was something quite unique; passed on through generations. It was in their *blood.* They *were* of a bloodline of something far greater. At the other end of the line was the answer. As was Henry's phone call.

'Aston! It's Henry… Sinclair. I'm in Carcassonne, but I'll be leaving tomorrow. I should be back in a couple of days... No, things are not going according to plan. I don't even know what the plan is... Have you found anything on this family yet? Okay …Say hello to dad for me. …I've got a bit of a surprise coming his way.'

'Your coming here will be surprise enough,' Aston said loud enough to be heard down the street.

'I'll see you in a couple of days,' Henry replied hanging up the phone.

Henry wasn't looking forward to going home, since he wasn't looking forward to seeing his father. It had been a long time. His slight American accent emphasised that. But working directly with Gabriel would hopefully put the whole prospective of going home in a better light. On the other hand, Henry knew how stubborn his father could be. His treatment within the organisation was probably as harsh as was seen fit, considering his father sat at the head of it. Henry's work had also taken him away from his son who he missed dearly, but he knew that his father would have looked after him and trained him well. Henry leant against the side of the phone box as he thought about his family, the loss of his wife seven years ago to a heart defect, and of his growing boy. *Snap to it,* he thought. *Henry Sinclair you have a job to do. Get some sleep.* He left the phone box and disappeared into the dawn. He returned to his hotel room and bed.

His thoughts didn't leave him, turning to the uncontrollable agent preventing him from getting the sleep he required. Gabriel would have to deal with this man. Little did Henry know, that Gabriel's plan was to leave the fate of Agent Cole in his hands. Henry's immediate problem was something more trivial, he could not sleep. There was something at the back of his mind, but what?

'Get a coffee,' he thought.

'I don't want a coffee,' he told himself.

Nevertheless, Henry found himself getting up, quickly dressing and leaving his hotel to find a café that was open.

***

Carcassonne 05.37hrs 17th July AD 2001 GMT+1

Gabriel sat at the end of his bed staring out of the window, watching the array of colours disappear as the sunrise ended and daylight arrived. It was one of those things he tried to do as often as he could. Wherever he was around the world, one thing was always certain, the sun would always rise. It brought back faint memories of a time he was not quite sure about, before he lost his soul. Images would flash through his mind, scenes from someone's life, that he was certain were not his own. As the sun rose, it glistened on the morning dew like crystal, creating rainbows with images he could not understand. Gabriel had been on the First Realm for over 3500 years and in that time he had seen many sunrises and learnt the ways of mankind, and more importantly had grown to care for them, the soulcarriers, which like all angelic he had once despised. Every decision he made determined who would live or who would die; every action taken would change the lives of so many people. This was the responsibility he had undertaken, but not in the role of Guardian of the First Realm.

Iinnad sat at the coffee table still moving Polaroids around to create different images and patterns attempting to create an overall picture using the individual segments. She hadn't slept either. As she made notes she knew there was a pattern and Abbadon was playing his game again. The television was still on the news channel with the volume barely on, though Iinnad could hear it perfectly. In the corner of the room slumped in an armchair was the NSA agent, silent and in a world of dreams.

'How could you forget your native tongue?' Iinnad asked without taking her eyes off the table. 'I won't tell anyone, but come on!'

'It has been a while. I lost track of time,' replied Gabriel.

'You needed to forget?' Iinnad inquired.

'No,' said Gabriel thoughtfully. 'To forgive... myself possibly?'

Iinnad stopped what she was doing and looked over her shoulder at Gabriel. He was still watching what was left of the sunrise. She always liked Gabriel more than she would admit, but his love for Bethany was too strong even though she was gone. Iinnad had dyed her hair Bethany's colour, but Gabriel hadn't even noticed. Secretly she felt a fool. Maybe it was never meant to be?

'So it still feels like yesterday?' she quietly asked.

The memories of that heartbreaking day came flooding back. Gabriel could not forget or forgive as he turned to Iinnad, a tear in his eye.

'I saw Abbadon last night,' he admitted quietly. 'As close as you and I, now.'

'Abbadon's showing his hand.'

'He would never do that, not until he had won,' replied Gabriel.

'Then why did he show himself to you?'

'To protect Lilith? I do not know,' Gabriel shook his head.

'On the plain of Icea we had a simple battle plan. In fact, it was so simple that Michael explained it to the eyes unit using a board game...' she moved another image on the table. 'Abbadon lost his ship and the battle – Not before the fallen destroyed the Temple.'

'And then lost Sagun,' Gabriel added. 'The point being?'

'I didn't mean to bring it up... but the point being that life is really quite simple,' she turned to Gabriel again. 'We just make it complicated.'

'Abbadon wants me,' Gabriel stated. 'I am losing my people... and I cannot stop it.'

'Yeah! And he is taking a bit of you at a time. So what have you been doing for the last… few thousand years? And please don't say wasting time.'

'Trying to save a realm from self-destruction,' Gabriel stated confidently.

'Ha! You make it sound so melodramatic. Why do you *even* care? I wanted to lead an army *once*. You did, I never will. No one ever listens to me. Has a soulcarrier ever listened to you? Have they ever done your bidding? They would never do mine.'

'They are not at my beck and call, Iinnad,' Gabriel replied calmly. 'Bidding… I have not heard that phrase in a long time. Soulcarriers make their own decisions.'

'Which will be their downfall,' Iinnad said harshly as she raised her voice. 'Are you going to stop the killings? Or disappear for a few hundred years and show up again when it's all forgotten?'

Cole awoke to Iinnad's voice.

'We're gonna stop the killings,' Cole joined in, opening his eyes, '…and not in a hundred years!'

The angelic turned to the slumped agent and then back to each other.

'There is nothing for me to do here now,' Gabriel announced changing the subject. 'I have got to go to London.'

'Why?' Cole asked stretching as he sat up in his chair, seeing how wide he could make his mouth.

'The Rossal's were my family,' Gabriel replied.

Cole jumped to his feet in response to Gabriel's comment. He was back on the same train of thought that he was on when he fell asleep.

'I had their background checked out,' he admitted. 'You weren't listed. In fact, you're not listed *anywhere*. Which brings me back to you lady!' He stared straight at Iinnad. 'You're not listed anywhere either.'

'That! I can explain,' she began. 'You won't believe me, but I *can* explain.'

'You're not with any organisation,' Cole stated.

'Well I am. It's just... that *you* don't have them listed,' she looked at the ceiling. 'Well… you might do?'

'Lady, we're the NSA,' Cole said forcefully.

Iinnad looked confused for a moment then attempted to laugh it off. 'Is that big then? I'm supposed to know what that is, right?' she grinned.

'Are you telling me you've never heard of the NSA?'

Iinnad did not answer, rushing through her most recent memories, she tried to remember if she had seen anything on TV, but she hadn't. Iinnad then glanced over in Gabriel's direction for some support. He gave her none.

'Where are you from?' asked a puzzled Cole.

'Ah! Like I said, you wouldn't believe me.'

Gabriel snatched his holdall from the end of the bed and proceeded to the bathroom, leaving the two in a staring contest over the subject of the NSA and Iinnad's origin. In the bathroom, he cleared his belongings. It was time to leave.

'I am going to London,' Gabriel repeated as he re-entered the bedroom.

'You said that,' Iinnad replied, always jovial, she jumping to her feet. 'I'll come with you.'

'Iinnad!' snapped Gabriel as he lost his patience. 'You should not even be here. The answer is no! There are things I need to do.'

'What? Boy things?'

Not getting a response, Iinnad turned to Cole. 'Did I ever tell you, how much I hate males as a species?'

'You don't like men?' Cole looked surprised or was it disappointment, or intrigue? That would make her the most beautiful lesbian he had ever seen.

'You weren't listening,' she said as she turned to Gabriel. 'Gabe, I thought this human was supposed to be intelligent?'

'Human? *Human*?'

'Iinnad!' Gabriel snapped again. 'Do not start!'

'Start what?' her innocent voice peaked.

'Playing games,' Gabriel answered as he began to stuff the few clothes he had, into the holdall.

'Abbadon does,' Iinnad pointed out calming her tone.

'That does not mean you should,' Gabriel spoke with his lecturer's voice.

'I'm having great difficulty following you here,' Cole opened up. 'But there is one thing I know when it comes to winning. Play them at their own game, but harder.'

Cole had caught Gabriel's attention and he stopped packing. 'Your point?'

'They kill one of yours,' Cole stated. 'You take two of theirs. Don't put them in jail. They'll only get out and do it again.'

'I can see why you are not in the police force,' Gabriel resumed packing.

'My father was NSA, it's in the blood.'

'Yes it is,' Iinnad jabbed in.

Gabriel glared at her.

'WHAT?' her hands up in submission.

'You learnt a lot from him?' Gabriel inquired.

'Not a thing. He died before I was born.'

Gabriel was tight-lipped, but slowed down with the packing as he thought about the situation. Can history repeat itself over and over? The 'son of a widow' was what legends were made of. King Arthur was the first to spring to mind, but the American was not King Arthur.

'Eye for an eye policy, I can live with that,' Iinnad interrupted.

'But that is wrong,' Gabriel stressed.

'When it comes to organised crime, hit them where it hurts,' Cole demanded. 'It doesn't appear in the press that way, but *they* get the message.'

'Do all government agencies operate the same way yours does?' Gabriel asked sarcastically.

'They can't,' replied Cole. 'We have a few political advantages. We also use several military ones.'

'Gabe,' Iinnad whispered very gently. 'You're gonna need an army to stop Abbadon... and I don't think the council will approve it.'

'The council?' questioned Cole.

'Hypothetical question for you,' Iinnad raised her pitch, as she changed the subject and turned to Cole. 'If you could live for say… a thousand years. What would you do?'

Iinnad faced up to Cole for his answer and then something in the back of her mind clicked, why she was on the First Realm. For Cole, the answer was simple.

'I'd see the world,' he replied.

'Then what?' Gabriel asked.

Cole looked surprised. 'What you mean, 'then what'?'

'You would see the world, and then...?'

'You have a thousand years,' Iinnad reminded Cole.

'If I *knew* I had a thousand years,' Cole emphasised. 'Then I suppose… I could do anything. I've got all the time I need.'

'So has Abbadon,' Gabriel expressed softly as he walked to the door and opened it. 'I need some air. Excuse me.'

'The greatest game of strategy, is that of life,' Iinnad stated calling after Gabriel who had stopped in the corridor.

'Yes, but Abbadon cheats,' Gabriel reminded her.

'How's that?' Cole asked.

'How long has he been alive?' Gabriel asked.

Cole laughed. 'Everybody has to die sooner or later. Everyone and everything, there are no exceptions.'

Cole's comment put a smile Iinnad's face and Gabriel could see she was impressed. He closed the door behind him and walked straight out of the hotel. Iinnad looked behind her and saw that Gabriel had left his holdall. He would be back.

'So tell me,' Iinnad asked. 'What is the NSA? It doesn't ring a bell with me.'

'I now have a hundred questions. Firstly, how old is Abbadon?'

'Well! Let's start with one answer. What is the NSA?'

XI

The First Realm.

Carcassonne 06.22hrs 17th July AD 2001 GMT+1

The small café was almost full with locals as well as few tourists fighting for the hot croissants and coffee that made up the typical European breakfast. The light summer rain didn't help, forcing more of the patrons to take shelter and steal the seats. Henry sat at his tiny table opposite an empty chair in the centre of the café. He considered the fact that he had tried to sleep, except something told him to go to a café. He did not have to wait long. Gabriel swiftly walked through the labyrinth of tables and chairs having already spotted Henry and weaved his way over to the only remaining space. Henry stood to greet him and instinctively bowed his head slightly in respect. In response, Gabriel held out his hand and firmly grabbing Henry's. He shook it and sat down. Before Henry could say anything, Gabriel was distracted by the overheated argument between the father and daughter of the establishment, which started in the kitchen, but had now drifted out to the bar.

'Que veut tu dire?' blurted the elder man. 'Tu veut partir aux Etats Unis?'

'C'est ces que je veut faire,' replied the waitress.

'Nous avons soutenu ton séjour au université et maintenant tu veut être au paire en Amérique? Pour quoi? Qu'est que ne vaut pas avec le café?' the father asked raising his voice even higher.

'Oh, laisse la porter,' her mother supported her daughter. 'Si c'a ne marche pas elle peut toujours revenir.'

'Reviens pour m'aider?' moaned her father. 'Yvette, nous n'avons pas gaspille notre argent pour une vacance.'

'Ce n'est pas une vacance!' Yvette stubbornly replied. 'Je travaillerai comme une nourrice et peut-être.'

'Mais L' Etats Unis est dangereux!' her father pointed out ignoring his daughter's explanation. 'Mannequins? Nais l'Amérique est dangereuse!'

'Mère!'

'Yvette peut se débrouiller,' her mother added.

'Mais que passé t'il avec mon café?' the father objected.

'C'est ton café! Je suis plus que ça!' Yvette sharply answered leaving to wait the tables.

Although speaking fluent French, the angelic, Henry and the patrons of the café learnt the intimacies of the daughter's desire to be a nanny abroad paying her way with some modelling. It conflicted with her father's wishes of sticking with the family business. Her mother stopped the argument with that knowing glance that all mothers have.

As the quarrel ceased, all heads turned back to their respective tables and the general level of conversation rose again. Flustered, the petite blonde straightened her white blouse, adjusted the little enamelled badge on her collar and then placed two cups of coffee on a tray and re-entered the mêlée of tables. She approached Henry and proceeded to place the coffees on the table.

'Nous n' avons pas encore commande,' Henry stated in fluent French as he caught a glimpse of the badge. It was circular with a white background and old styled yellow cross in the middle. He thought it unusual that she was wearing it, but he gave it no more thought.

'Pardon!' replied Yvette. 'I have the wrong table. I come back.'

'We have not ordered?' Gabriel repeated, to Henry. 'Your French is good.'

The two watched the waitress leave and turned back to each other.

'I see you got my message,' Gabriel began.

'Message?' Henry responded. 'A little voice in my head said 'go get a coffee,' so I did.'

'Yes, would have been sufficient.'

'My lord… Gabriel,' Henry began correcting himself immediately. 'I haven't had the chance to thank you for asking me to serve you.'

'Just call me Gabriel, and you are not serving me. You are *helping* me. Have you been in touch with London?'

'Yes, last night and again this morning for an update,' replied Henry. 'The situation has been approached as a standard operation, but my father doesn't know that I'm the field agent *or* that you are involved. You've got me running around like a bloody idiot. I'm also being monitored by *certain* governmental agencies.'

'Agent Cole and his contacts have not been as helpful as I would have liked,' Gabriel explained. 'The information is not as forthcoming as I would have hoped, but I believe this is because they genuinely do not know anything. That is an error on my part. Also… as much as I try, Agent Cole does not trust me. I hope that will change, but it will not be my doing. And there is something else. Agent Cole never appears to be phased by the things I say, but we will see. Now, what did you find out about the Rossals and the Chevaliers?'

'The American Chevaliers aren't *even* family,' Henry stressed with disgust. 'Unless they changed their name generations ago.'

'They did,' Gabriel confirmed. 'Their real name is Rossal.'

'But the Rossals all died. Their line was wiped out hundreds of years ago,' Henry replied. 'They never even made it to Scotland.'

Gabriel just smiled at Henry. He did not have the time to explain or wish to change his view of history after having had the importance of the truth emphasised since he was a boy.

'What will amaze London,' Henry continued. '…is the fact that the Chevalier's in America changed their name from Rossal. Can you believe it? Everyone loves to have a bit of heritage, a bit of history with their name, but to change your name and lose that history, to lose that *identity*. God! Have you any idea of the significance of the name Rossal?' Henry inquired with excitement. 'As far as London can make out, there was only one family line that stopped, but there was really two. Can you believe that?'

'I am only too aware of the importance in the name,' Gabriel replied quietly as he looked up to greet the arrival of the pretty blonde once again.

'Qu' est-ce que vous prenez?' the waitress prepared to take Henry's ordered.

'Deux petite déjeuner s'il vous plait,' Henry replied.

Gabriel politely waved down the offer and the waitress noticed

Gabriel's gesture and crossed out the second breakfast as she turned back to Henry.

'One full breakfast,' Henry corrected. 'And deux cafés. Merci!'

The waitress nodded and left the two to continue their conversation.

'Abbadon is out to get me,' Gabriel informed Henry. 'It was he, or at least his orders that saw to the demise of the Rossal family line.'

'Killing bloodline just to get at you?' Henry inquired nervously. 'Then... we are all at risk aren't we?'

'Possibly?'

'*Possibly*?' Henry leant across the table to emphasise his point. 'Then *use* us!'

'No, this is not what you have been trained for, and I do not think Abbadon knows about you yet. The organisation should be used when the time is right.'

Sitting bolt upright in his chair, Henry's tone changed to that of a force not to be messed with.

'My father disagrees with you,' he came clean. 'There is the vague possibility of a coincidence, but my father doesn't believe in coincidences and the murders in America took place on Friday the 13th July.'

'I know,' Gabriel retorted attempting to understand. 'I was there, and so were you.'

'Look at the date Gabriel,' Henry stated, the tone of his voice didn't waver.

'July 13th 2001?' inquired Gabriel.

'Gabriel, this is Europe. Look at the numbers the way you

would if you were in London, not America.'

'The 13th of July,' Gabriel said quietly. 'The 13th day of the seventh month... 1307 Friday.'

'Unlucky for some,' Henry claimed. 'Now do you see why my father disagrees with you? Abbadon doesn't just know about the Rossal family. He knows about all the families.'

Both knew the significance of the date and the importance of the situation.

'I saw Abbadon last night,' Gabriel replied in a very solemn mood. 'He told me, he knew everything about me. I said I had a few surprises and he said I did not.'

'Abbadon was right. You don't! He knows about us, so what do we do?'

'What is your father doing about it?' Gabriel inquired hoping to find some common ground with which to approach Sinclair senior.

'My father has been searching for Abbadon all his life. He knows he is out there and what he is. He once told me that an angelic told him all about the battles of the past when he was a wee boy. I thought it was a bedtime story, but it was you. He is the only reason the organisation has held together. He is the only one who truly believes. Some laugh at him and some just do as they're told. Very few believe in you any more.'

'This is not going to be easy, is it?' Gabriel whispered. 'I know I have neglected my duties and in some cases I do have reasons, but I must rectify what I have failed to do. Do you think your father will accept me?'

'I think he would be *pissed* at you! *Pissed* at you for leaving. As for the others… *seeing is believing*.'

'And that goes for you too,' Gabriel suggested. 'I have done nothing that would suggest who or what I am.'

'My father believes,' Henry replied. 'And as much as I don't see eye to eye with him, that still means something to me. Plus… being around you, I have found certain things don't always add up. For a start, it always bloody rains. I don't have a problem with the rain; I'm Scottish! This is the south of France, mid-summer, you're here and it's still bloody raining!'

Both of them laughed off the comment as the waitress arrived with Henry's breakfast and Gabriel's coffee. The angelic paid the young waitress and included a tip, before she left the table putting the money in her pocket.

'I have a question,' requested Henry. 'Who was the blonde girl?'

Gabriel glanced over to the waitress. 'Daughter of the owner of the café.'

'That's the first joke you have ever made with me and it wasn't a good one.'

Gabriel smiled and sipped his steaming cup. 'Iinnad? She used to be my *eyes*, but that was a long time ago. The answer to your next question is yes.'

'She's angelic?' Henry inquired curiously.

'Yes!' Gabriel grinned at his prophecy. 'But, fortunately she will not be around long. She has… *trouble* blending in.'

'Are you referring to the outfit?' Henry asked with a grin. 'I can't see a problem with it. It's revealing; it draws a lot of attention. I can understand you not wanting her around.'

'It is her traditional dress and that is why she wears it, she is stubborn.'

'Gabriel, I'm *not* complaining,' Henry replied. 'She looks... But you're right, she does stand out in a crowd.'

They sat quietly for a moment sipping their morning drink.

'I have a favour to ask before you go back to London,' Gabriel urged changing the subject. 'Something to give to your father. I want you to go to Paris and gather any first-hand information you can about a company called Apolyon Inc. Their headquarters are based there and it looks like Abbadon has moved in.'

'No he hasn't,' Henry corrected. 'If the dates mean anything, he never left.'

'And you know this?'

'No, it's just a hunch.'

'Can you do that for me?' Gabriel asked as he stood up from the table.

Henry nodded but didn't get up. He realised after repeated requests not to treat Gabriel like a lord. The angelic gave Henry a tiny salute as he left the café and entered the light summer rain.

'Merci!' the waitress called after Gabriel as she returned to the table to collect his cup.

There was no cup, just Henry with his breakfast. She put her hand into her pocket and counted the money, she shook her head and returned back to the bar. Something wasn't right, but she didn't know what.

Henry sat there eating his croissants and sipping his coffee with a smile on his face. This was one of those unexplained things that just seemed to happen whenever the angelic was around. Maybe it was time for Gabriel to visit London. The sceptics in the organisation would be in no doubt if Gabriel proved who he was. The only problem that Henry could foresee was that Gabriel did not seem to be the sort of being who would want to prove anything.

A local had finished his breakfast and climbed out of his seat gently knocking Henry in the process causing him to spill a little of his coffee.

'Pardon, Monsieur,' apologised the elderly gentleman as he hobbled over to the payphone under the stairs. He placed five francs in the machine and began to dial. The person on the other end connected the elderly gentleman through to Abbadon's office.

The fallen were the angelic that fell from the grace of God in the first war of the angels and they were limited in their numbers to 133,306,668. The servants of the fallen were the demonic, humans with a streak of evil within them that had been turned to serve. As for the number of demonic; that was anybody's guess. Abbadon had turned countless numbers; from the young to the old, all over the First Realm. They were his spies; his ears to the ground in every town.

Henry had not noticed as he finished his breakfast.

***

Carcassonne 06.49hrs 17th July AD 2001 GMT+1

Gabriel strolled into the reception of his hotel to find Cole trying to explain to the receptionist that he was only visiting a friend in one of the rooms. He had his holdall on his shoulder and a file under his arm and was becoming frustrated by his lack of knowledge of the French language and the lady's refusal to help. Gabriel approached the desk and smiled at the receptionist, putting his hand on Cole's shoulder and in his fluent French explained they were friends. The receptionist looked a little embarrassed and allowed Cole and Gabriel to go back up to the room. The agent was pleased that the situation was resolved so quickly, but he didn't quite understand the receptionist's embarrassment.

'I told her we were good friends,' Gabriel divulged with a smile. 'I get the impression she thought we were homosexual.'

Cole's smile turned to an expression of horror. One, the homosexual angle had not crossed his mind and two; the egghead had a sense of humour. This was not going to be a good day. In fact it was turning out to be a pretty bad week.

Gabriel opened the bedroom door to find Iinnad lying on the bed. The Polaroids had been rearranged on the table to create an additional image, that of a winged demon with the number 1307 beneath it. Cole closed the door, dropped his bag on the floor and threw his file into his sleeping chair and walked over to the coffee table.

'Anybody could have walked through that door,' he said as he looked in Iinnad's direction. 'It wasn't even locked.'

'You haven't washed,' she replied without taking her eyes off the lines she was following on the ceiling. 'Did everybody do what they had to do?'

'Got the laptop from the car,' Cole replied. 'And the rest of my paperwork.'

'I think so,' Gabriel replied quietly.

'What is the significance of 1307?' Cole inquired as he stared at the coffee table. 'Is it a date?'

'Yes, several,' Gabriel replied, confusing the agent. 'Is there anything that you might have missed, possibly even relating to older cases at the NSA which might help us here? We are shooting in the dark. Abbadon has been around a long time.'

Iinnad impatiently jumped off the bed and walked straight across the room to Cole. 'Close your eyes,' she requested.

'What?'

'Close your eyes!' she demanded and placed her hand gently over them as he did so. 'Relax!'

Cole nervously did as he was asked and Iinnad closed her eyes and concentrated on the task in hand. Within a few seconds, Iinnad opened her eyes again and took her hand away from the agent's face. His eyes were still closed as he collapsed to the floor.

'Thank you,' Gabriel said sarcastically. 'There are certain things you just *do not do* on the First Realm, and *that,*' pointing at the past out agent on the floor. '…is one of them.'

'How long was it going to take for him to remember?' Iinnad asked as she motioned to the body on the floor. 'We don't need him, I now know everything he knows. They had a couple of cases under investigation a few years ago. Something to do with buying up small manufacturing firms, but that was it. Nothing important. And I now know what the NSA is,' she added with a smirk. 'Well, he told me.'

Iinnad walked over to the bed and dived onto it purposely bouncing on the springs like a little child yet again. Gabriel attended to

Cole, picking him up and putting him in the nearest chair. He opened his eyes to see Gabriel staring back at him. The initial shock was overcome quickly.

'Iinnad, you've changed,' he said jokingly as he touched Gabriel face. 'What just happened?'

Gabriel initially resisted, but gave up and bluntly answered. 'Iinnad read your mind. I am sorry.'

'So how do I read hers,' Cole replied taking it calmly in his stride. 'What's your story Iinnad?'

'Me? Oh, nobody wants to know about me.'

'Why not?' Cole provoked. 'You're fast, you're knowledgeable and you back the egghead.'

Iinnad was stumped for a moment as she tried fathom out what Cole was getting at. Once she had understood the comment she rejoined the conversation.

'Gabriel's not an egghead. We used to work together. I was his *eyes*,' she responded. 'Eyes! When an operative is on an operation there is some one to provide back up information, layout, support and the like to make sure they come home safely. That was my job. Each operative had their own personal eyes watching over them. I was Gabriel's.'

Gabriel was standing by the window looking out in an attempt to see over the ramparts of the city. With Gabriel in the corner of his eye, Cole cautiously leant forward towards Iinnad.

'Do you fancy Gabriel?' he quietly asked.

'I was just his *eyes*,' she replied sharply. 'As I said, a part of Gabriel's unit. That's all. I watched over him.'

'One on one,' emphasised Cole.

'Yeah,' Iinnad replied.

'The technique is a new one on me. That would take a lot of man power.'

'It's an old technique and a long story...'

The conversation was interrupted by Cole's mobile phone.

'... and your phone is ringing,' Iinnad stated the obvious.

Cole was oblivious to the phone as he was intrigued by everything that Iinnad had said. He franticly dived into his jacket pockets to find it before it stopped. The thought that it would not stop until he had it did not register.

'Yeah!' he shouted, out of breath. 'I'm here... No, I never booked in, I got a little side tracked. Oh, you heard about that... No, I didn't get around to picking up my messages... Yes I will call in every four hours... Do the authorities know I had nothing to do with those murders?' his tone dropped. '…I have two days... but what about the authorities? …I have two days. Yes, I will call in every four hours. Thank you.'

Cole hung up the phone and put it back in his pocket, resting his hand there for a moment. He took a deep breath and then straightened his jacket.

'I have got to go,' he announced. 'It looks like I am going to London as well. I have to report to the British Ambassador and then it is back to the US. Nice chat, I'll see you around.'

'That's it?' Iinnad questioned. 'But it's not over. Haven't you learnt anything?'

'I got the idea,' Cole replied sarcastically. 'You read minds, live forever and can probably fly. You're fast and smart and you have your own little war going on, and it has *nothing* to do with me. I have an open mind and I have a boss chasing me. Every body's going to London, so I'll find what I'm looking for there. I have a long drive and a shitty train journey ahead of me. I also have to write this one up. So… have fun.'

Cole picked up his file and holdall and then checked the room for anything he might have missed. After a quick double check he opened the door and left the room. Gabriel did not say a word. He did not even take his eyes off the ramparts.

'You can't just let him go,' Iinnad demanded.

Cole's head popped around the edge of the door. 'You avoided the question; do you fancy him?' He then closed the door before she could reply.

Gabriel smiled and checked the window was locked before he picked up the images off the coffee table and placed them in his holdall.

'It is time I went to London,' he informed Iinnad. 'And time you went back.'

'I came here for a reason, Gabriel. I have something to tell you.'

'Well, you have taken your time about it, so it cannot be that important.'

'I got distracted,' she snapped as she fell back into one of the chairs. 'Sorry!'

'So what have you to tell me?'

'Time on the different realms travels at different speeds,' Iinnad began.

'Believe me, I know. It has got me in enough trouble as it is,' he interrupted.

'Let me finish,' Iinnad moaned quietly. 'Over a thousand years have passed on the Third Realm. The force field, on the gate of the Abyss, has spent all its power. The key can now open them.'

'So why are you telling me?' Gabriel cautiously responded.

'The Council knows that a key can open the gate and release Sataniel,' Iinnad explained. 'They want to know if you remember what happened to it?'

'They know about the key?'

'Yeah.'

'It took them a while,' Gabriel smiled.

The Archangel sat down in the chair opposite Iinnad and took a deep breath. He tugged at his trousers and revealed a small chord that was tied around his waist, just below his belt, on it was the ancient key.

'This key,' he asked Iinnad. 'I think it is safe.'

Iinnad's eyes lit up. She was amazed that Gabriel was actually carrying the key that was keeping Sataniel at bay from the Seven Realms of Heaven, down his trousers.

'May I?' she asked.

'You want my trousers?' he joked.

'Humour really doesn't suit you,' she replied. 'You're an egghead remember?'

'I still have the key,' Gabriel said as he put it away and tucked in his shirt.

'The Council want it,' Iinnad demanded. 'That's why I'm here.'

'To collect the key or to tell me to give it to the Council?' Gabriel asked.

'Do you think they would trust me with that?'

'And then you are to do what?' asked Gabriel.

'Leave!' Iinnad piped up as she dropped her head to stare at the floor. 'I can't help you fight Abbadon. I gave him my word that I wouldn't. There is more to all of this. So what aren't you telling me?'

'Nothing,' Gabriel replied. 'Why is it always the Council that are making the decisions?'

'*You're asking me*,' Iinnad blurted. 'Who am I? You're the ranking Archangel. What are you going to do?'

'I will try and talk to Him,' Gabriel answered softly. 'But He does not answer.'

'I haven't spoken to Him in ages. I wouldn't worry about it.'

'But we used to talk all the time.'

'What aren't you telling me Gabriel?' Iinnad repeated.

'I told you. Nothing!'

Iinnad darted across the room with incredible speed, straight at Gabriel, knocking him over the back of his chair and onto the floor. He slid across the polished wooden floor with Iinnad on top of him and stopped when he hit the wall. The beautiful angelic, forcibly placed her hand over Gabriel's eyes and closed hers. Gabriel struggled to push her off, but couldn't, she was far too strong. Abbadon was right to fear Iinnad. She had been in combat situations ever since the Third Realm. Gabriel had grown weaker and lost his edge. His only saving grace when matched against Abbadon was that he too had not seen any combat and had grown weaker. However, Iinnad was faster and stronger than she had ever been. The Council had transferred her to the Second Realm for the 10,000-year war. She was the perfect warrior of God and she knew it.

She opened her eyes and took a quick deep breath, then released Gabriel, removing her hand and rolling off him onto the floor.

'The first rule of the First Realm,' she said out of breath. 'Don't interfere... Boy! You broke that one!'

Gabriel sat up, speechless.

'Was there… at any point in the last three thousand years where you just left them to get on with it?' she asked.

Gabriel scratched the top of his head like Stan Laurel and pulled a face. 'Not really.'

'Why?'

'Stupid question, you just read my mind,' he sniffed.

'I know why, but do you?' she hinted.

'Do you like the soulcarriers?' Gabriel inquired. 'Do you care what happens to them? Because I do, I admit I never used to, but now, I do. I have asked for help, but He does not hear me. The Council will not help because deep down most angelic agreed with Sataniel. *We* should have been chosen. Those that spoke out were kicked out and the smart ones kept their mouths shout. No angelic is going to die for a soulcarrier. Not again. The last one to do that was Barakiel. So I train them, a select few.'

'The ones with the pendant,' Iinnad stressed. 'The ones with the essence of the presence of being. Does the Council know who they are?'

'No and they must not find out either,' Gabriel declared. 'I am leaving Carcassonne, are you coming?'

'I'm your *eyes*; that was a stupid question too. This is not how soulcarriers are to evolve Gabriel.'

'Do not blame me. The essence was not my doing.'

'Then whose?'

'I have an idea.'

'That's why I couldn't read it,' Iinnad jabbed jumping to her feet, brushing herself down and offering a hand to Gabriel. 'You've never spoken it or written it down. That's clever.'

'So when do you have to go back?' Gabriel took her hand.

'A few days ago,' Iinnad replied with a cheeky grin. 'But there's something I need to do first. Can I meet you in London?'

'What are you going to do Iinnad?'

'Something. There's something else. You haven't asked me about the line at the bottom of the images. I thought I'd mention it since you can't read.'

'Are you going to tell me,' Gabriel urged.

'Whoever finds the interpretation of these sayings will not experience death. The problem is that, like Richard said, everybody dies. But you and I know that death isn't the end, so why that phrase?'

Gabriel took a deep breath through his noise. 'It is a line from a lost gospel.'

'A book of the bible?'

'No, it was never a book of the bible, because it was *lost*,' Gabriel insisted. 'Now, can I read your mind?'

'Why? Need to learn to read? The answer is no! And if you try, I'll stop you. Now, I need to go.'

'What are you going to do Iinnad?' Gabriel repeated as he collected his holdall.

'I'm on your side Gabriel. Trust your *eyes*!'

XII

The First Realm.

The Levant (AD 1096 – AD 1189)

During the early 1030s the Seldjuk Turks had begun to expand their territory in several directions, including Syria. With their increase in power and land, the emperor of Byzantium asked Pope Urban II for help against the Turks. In Clermont, central France, on the 27th November 1095 Pope Urban II called for a Crusade to help the Byzantines and to free the city of Jerusalem from the Muslims. In the autumn of 1096 those that chose to wear the cross gathered in Constantinople and after several changes in leadership the First Crusade was underway. After several more setbacks, the Crusaders seized Jerusalem on the 15th July 1099. Pope Urban II died fourteen days later without ever knowing of the Crusaders had succeeded.

Fighting continued throughout the region for many years, since several major towns were by-passed in the pursuit of Jerusalem. The Christians took Acre in 1104 and Tripoli, Beirut and Saida in 1110. Once the entire coastline was under Christian control pilgrims began to travel to the Holy City. However, it was not an easy journey since pockets of Muslims and thieves lined the route.

The Order of the Poor Knights of Christ and the Temple of Solomon was founded in 1118 by nine French knights, Hugues de

Payens, Geoffrey de St Omer, Payen de Montdidier, Archambault de St Aignan, Andre de Montbard, Godefroy Bisol, Rossal and Gondemare. Although, variations in names appear, the ninth knight's name never appeared within the pages of history. Their mission was to protect the route and Christians on their pilgrimage to the Holy Land. King Baudoin II, (commonly referred to as Baldwin), granted the knights lodgings in the Temple of Solomon's stables and hence the name. The nine knights took vows of poverty, chastity and obedience, in the presence of the Patriarch of Jerusalem.

Bernard de Clairvaux was a supporter of the Order and wrote a letter to the Pope recounting their deeds and their commitment to God. In 1128, the Templars, as they had become known received a Rule of Order laid down by the new Pope. New members flocked from all over the Christian world to join the Order. Although, mainly from France and England the members already held the position of knight; relinquishing their wealth to the Order, whether it be land or gold.

Over the coming decades, the Order was to grow and become the most powerful military Order in the Christian world, answering only to the Pope himself. They would not even answer to an individual king, since they were the maker and breaker of kings.

***

Towards the end of the ill-fated Second Crusade AD 1149, the young Gérard de Ridefort found himself in an awkward situation. As second son he would inherit little on the death of his father, so seeking fortune, choose to stay in the Holy Land when all the French forces returned to Europe. He aligned himself with Count Raymond III of Tripoli and served him as best he could in the hope that when the next fief was available by marriage he would have security in old age.

However, in 1180, when Lucia of Botron, sole heiress after the death of her father, William Dorel, became available, Raymond gave Lady Lucia to a wealth merchant from Pisa for her weight in gold. It was a hefty amount by all accounts.

Gérard de Ridefort had nothing left except hatred and revenge for the Count and in disgust joined the Order of the Knights Templar. Within five years his meteoric rise through the ranks put him in the incredible position as the tenth Grand Master of the most powerful military Order of the day. He had heard the stories that each new Grand Master would be met by a messenger and shortly after taking his appointment; Gabriel appeared to the knight and wished him well in his new position.

However, to Gérard de Ridefort's surprise, enforcing his belief that in some way he was blessed, a short while later a second messenger appeared to him.

***

Sunset – The Levant 12th December AD 1185

Abbadon sat on the stone window ledge of Ridefort's quarters waiting for the knight to notice his presence. Ridefort finished his evening prayers and turned to his bed catching a glimpse of a silhouette in the corner of his eye. He flicked his body around to face the Dark Prince.

'Qui es tu au nom de dieu?' he spluttered.

The temptation to kill the Grand Master on the spot, just for being one of Gabriel's chosen men was overpowering. Restraint was the only thing on Abbadon's mind as he tried his best to be civil. It was only then, that the Destroyer realised the Grand Master had asked a question. Who was he?

'A messenger!' Abbadon replied in English with a smile.

Ridefort frowned as he tried to understand the answer. 'Liiike… Gabriel?' he replied; only Gabriel spoke French when they had met.

'Oui,' the Destroyer lied, although not *entirely*.

'What can I do for you my Lord?' Ridefort bowed beginning to realise that he could speak the foreign tongue.

Abbadon produced an old page of text from a manuscript and showed it to the Grand Master. It meant nothing to Gérard; he could barely speak English let alone read or write in *any* language. It was the clerics that were given that task. Abbadon already knew this. As for the text, it was in angelic script and Ridefort had unwittingly played into Abbadon's hand.

'This is a page of prophecy, prophétie,' explained the fallen angelic. 'It tells of a leader; *a dirigeant, vous…* that would be you! A leader that has been betrayed *a dirigeant trahir,* by a man he served and trusted. A man who seeks revenge, *se venger sur,* for the way he has been treated and how he will gain his revenge through his death.'

'Oui, moi Lord.'

'This,' Abbadon shook the page, choosing to speak slowly, knowing that Ridefort's English was poor. He had all the time in the world to learn the language, but had never bothered. 'This,' he shook the page again. '…tells of a great battle that you will enter *and* survive. The Saracen army know your face and you will not be harmed under pain of death. You will lead your army into battle and… win or lose you will survive.'

'And… I do this… for you… my Lord?' questioned the knight.

'You will do this because I will give you something worth more than gold. I will give you life eternal, *vie éternel*; a deal to be struck between you and I. I promise you, that if you do this, you will live to serve again. Not here, not now, but I will give you eternal life to serve in the future when all of this is forgotten. *Vous éternel vie, comprendre?*'

'What… must I do… my Lord?'

'Be a brave knight and fight with honour. I ask nothing more. Will you join me in an agreement to that fact?' Abbadon rose and held out his hand.

'Oui my Lord,' Gérard replied shaking the Destroyer's firm grip confident that he had grasped the conversation as well. He then knelt and kissed Abbadon's hand.

'Then I bid you farewell and remember our agreement.'

Abbadon left the Grand Master to his thoughts as he climbed through the window and leapt into the night. Gérard pondered his fate. He was truly blessed. But why had Gabriel not spoken to him? He also realised he must find one of the clerics that spoke English and learn the language before his next encounter.

'I will survive,' Gérard de Ridefort spoke quietly to himself. 'Je survivrai.'

***

The Levant – May AD 1187

In the first few days of May the knights of the military Orders were escorting several dignitaries on an official mission of peace. Gérard who led the Templars himself received word that a scouting party of Muslims were in the area. He was also informed that Raymond had an accord with Saladin, the Muslin leader, with regards to the scouting party. The force was large in number and Gérard remembering his promise believed this to be the battle that was to be waged. If fact, the force was so large that the Grand Master called for additional knights from the nearby garrisons of Caco and Nazareth to join the Christian army. The Grand Master of the Hospitaliers and even his own Marshal, James de Mailly were in favour of leaving the scouting party be, but Gérard demanded they attack. Believing all around him were cowards he sent out a party to find the exact whereabouts of the Muslim force. The news they brought on their return was not good. Near the Springs of Cresson, the enemy were found totalling over five thousand strong. With his accusations of cowardice and fear, the Grand Master of the Knights Templar led a mounted charge against the Saracen that outnumbered his one hundred and twenty-three knights by fifty-seven to one. In the fierce mêlée, Christian and Muslin swords clashed, limbs were severed, and heads did roll. Only three Templar managed to flee with their lives. The aged Gérard was one of those that survived the battle as the messenger had foreseen. The Grand Master of the Hospitaliers and James de Mailly fell in the massacre. However, Count Raymond was still alive. With his eagerness for battle and his hatred of the Muslims being greater than that of Count Raymond, Gérard had forgotten that the man was not present. That would never happen again. The slaughter at Cresson would not go unpaid. Saracen blood would flow in return for the loss of so many good men.

Incursion followed incursion by the Muslims over the next few weeks. Therefore, it was decided by the unpopular Guy of Lusignan; the recently crowned King, by his wife Queen Sybilla, to stand and fight the Muslims in one battle to finish the quarrel of ownership of the Levant once and for all. King Guy's decision may have been grand, although it was encouraged by Ridefort, who had at Guy's coronation the second key to the royal strong box. Still indebted to Gérard for his actions that day, he agreed to the Templar Knight's request. A call to arms by every able-bodied man was raised throughout the Holy Land and a force of twenty-three thousand strong gathered at the Springs of Saffuriya. The Christian army would have water and grazing for the horses, while they formed a strategy to deal with the Muslin leader.

Unfortunately, news came that Saladin had attacked the city of Tiberius, Count Raymond's home city. The city had fallen, but not the castle, which held Raymond's family captive within its walls. To leave the safety of the springs would be foolhardy, but Gérard demanded, yet again that there was cowardice within his presence and that the force should push forward across the desert plain. The distance was but fifteen miles. However with harsh land, rocky features and dry water holes, the force struggled in the summer heat.

The march was slow over the undulating terrain and made harder by the constant hail of arrows from the Muslim scouts that had been sent to slow their progress even further. Finally, by the evening the thirst ridden Christian army had to stop. They set up camp near the village of Lubiyaon, on a plateau overlooking the village of Hattin. Behind them were a pair of hills known as the Horns of Hattin, and from their elevated position Gérard could make out the lantern light in the city of Tiberius and the sunset glimmer on the Sea of Galilee.

'This, truly is the Holy Land,' he said to himself admiring the view.

***

The Levant – 3rd hour after sunset 3rd July AD 1187

The campfire was small, giving off little warmth in the cold desert. Gérard de Ridefort sat alone. The knight of little wealth joined the order to gain prestige and notoriety; he had succeeded. For him, joining was a mixed blessing. The women he wished for did not return his affections. If knightly status meant nothing in this day and age then what would? Revenge was still on his mind. The world had changed; only wealth mattered. For the Grand Master, one mistake in battle, a misjudgement that had cost the lives of so many men was in the past. Retribution was at hand. One strike of his sword in the wrong direction and Count Raymond would fall. Ridefort solemnly prodded the embers with the tip of his vengeful sword. The flames struggled in the wind clinging to the few dry branches that had been found in the sand. Gérard de Ridefort *was* Grand Master of the Knights Templar. He had followed the rules of poverty and chastity for many so years there was no returning to his old life. The only thing that remained was his hatred of the enemy and of the Count of Tripoli, Raymond.

The solitary knight sat by his fire in front of his tent, the black and white beausant standard flapped in the chilling night breeze as it crossed the dry plateau. In the Royal tent, nearby, was the True Cross, the most holy of relics that had been carried by the Templars into every great battle. It was the symbol of Christianity that had kept all the Orders bound in belief. The wood that Jesus Christ and had been nailed upon must never fall to the enemy. There were many things on Gérard's mind.

He rubbed his sore throat, parched and yearning water after the long day's march. Gérard, like the other 23,000 strong force prayed for rain. But it was summer in the Levant and the streams and village watering holes were dry. The only water for miles around was at the base of the plateau beside the enemy encampment.

Several foot soldiers, maddened by thirst and unable to sleep sneaked down to the stream, only to be captured and swiftly beheaded. It was a high price to pay for a vessel of water.

The tall unmistakable shape of Abbadon stepped into the circle of light emanating from the fire. He sat down opposite the Grand Master.

'Revenge is a good thing,' Abbadon began. 'It keeps the mind focused. You will have your revenge. Tomorrow Raymond of Tripoli will die.'

'As will I,' Gérard solemnly replied.

'Saladin and his men know you. No harm will come to you. We had an agreement. Did we not?'

Gérard de Ridefort slowly nodded.

'Well then! You have nothing to fear, nothing to lose.'

‘If what I have done is right, then why do I feel sorrow?’

‘Even medicine tastes sour in the mouth,’ replied the Destroyer.

‘I wish Gabriel were here,’ Gérard quietly spoke.

‘Gabriel? Gabriel is busy. He is Guardian of this Realm. He can’t always be by your side.’

‘When I was first appointed Grand Master, he introduced himself to me. He told me of the wonders of the heavens and the history of man. In all those stories, he never mentioned you.’

‘I am just the messenger, one of many. I myself have only met Gabriel the one-time and that was a long time ago. He’s probably forgotten my name,’ Abbadon laughed himself. ‘As for you; you will survive.’

The Destroyer stood up and the entered darkness, leaving the Grand Master to his thoughts and thirst. The night was quiet again. There were murmurs within the camp; the occasional knocking of metal in the wind was faint as the Christian army awaited the rise of the scorching sun.

***

The Levant – 1st hour 4th July AD 1187

As the sun peeked over the hills, the one thousand knights and twenty thousand foot soldiers prepared for battle. A faint smell of burning filled the air. Saladin had other plans. Knowing that the Christian army was desperate for water he opted to set the scrub-brush that covered the slopes of the plateau ablaze. The wind was in the Muslim’s favour as the black clouds of choking smoke gathered and swept through the Crusader's camp. Watery eyed, with dry throats the knights driven by rage, instinctively attacked their agitator. Down the slopes rode the Christian warrior's out-numbered twenty-to-one. The foot soldiers were in quick pursuit. As the mounted force reached the Muslim line, Saladin gave the word for his forces to break their lines and allow the tiny attacking force through. The momentum of battle could not halt their charge and as the last of the soldiers entered the trap, the Muslims closed the net on the Christian army. Several of the mounted knights continued to ride and forced their way through the rear lines of the enemy. To return to the main body of the army would mean certain death and so they fled. Gérard rose to his feet only to catch a glimpse of Raymond's standard fleeing the battlefield in the direction of the city of Tiberius. He had nothing to lose; even revenge had been taken from him. He took up his sword and joined the remainder of the soldiers that ran down the slope and through the burning brush, to their certain death.

His age reduced his speed so he stopped for a dry breath. From the east he noticed Saladin's horsemen had entered the encampment. Below him, near the village of Hattin, the Christian's fate was sealed as the Muslim army encircled Gérard's knights. With blades drawn and the net so tight that not even a cat would escape, Christian heads began to roll, until they surrendered.

From the Grand Master's position, the edge of the plateau obscured the camp. Only King Guy's tent and standard could be seen, but that too fell. His King would live, Saladin would make sure of it. Nevertheless, the knight's heart sank, for beneath the canvas lay the True Cross. The Templar had protected it for over one hundred and fifty years and now under his command, it was in the hands of Saladin.

***

Abbadon sat upon one of the Horns of Hattin with a grin. Gabriel would be pleased he sarcastically thought. The Dark Prince knew what Saladin would offer the knights a choice; renounce their faith or accept a life of slavery. He also knew their response. Never!

In the quiet desert, without complaint they awaited death in the name of their God. Of the two hundred and thirty surviving Templars; each and every one bowed their head in silence as their necks received a scimitar.

Even in death the Muslim's honoured and respected their enemy and their unwavered belief. Knowing this, many foot soldiers willingly stepped forward claiming to be Templar Knights and accepted death rather than a life of slavery. All but a handful of heads rolled in the evening sun of the 4th of July 1187. Only Guy of Lusignan King of Jerusalem, Count Reginald de Chatillon, Humphrey de Toron and the Grand Master Gérard de Ridefort were spared.

The sandy plains beneath the Horns of Hattin ran red with Christian blood as the survivors stood parched in Saladin's tent. Still armed, the men had no will to fight and to what end? The guards would have dropped them in an instant and then been executed themselves for killing their king's prisoners without permission.

Saladin then appeared before his captors, his hands washed of the blood of war, and sat on the cushions facing the men. Two servants brought food and water, placing the refreshments on a low table beside their victorious leader who had yet to speak. The knights could smell the fresh cool vessel that could quench their thirst. Their tired eyes gave away their desire, for nothing but hot air had passed their lips since late morning the previous day.

Saladin lent over the table, his gold inlaid garments hung from his arm as he poured a gourd of iced water and passed it to the defeated King of Jerusalem. Guy eagerly accepted it and began to gulp the refreshing liquid, trying not to spill a valuable drop. Reginald cursed the enemy under his breath as he impatiently waited his fill. Once King Guy had quenched his thirst he passed the gourd to Reginald. Saladin rose sharply, knocking the water to the ground before it touched the Count's lips. His fate was set. The leader of the Muslims had heard Reginald's mutterings, but the Count repeated his curse out loud all the same. Before he had finished his sentence, Saladin's blade had been drawn and Reginald went numb. He stared up at his headless body, his limbs and torso crashing to hit the sand by his severed head. Gérard de Ridefort stood calm as he awaited death. Guy did not act like the king that he was supposed to be, but trembled with fear.

'Kings do not kill kings,' announced Saladin as he refilled the gourd. 'You will be safe as my guest until the ransom is paid,' he jested.

Saladin then graciously handed the water to Gérard, who accepted it politely and drank. He was spared as the mysterious being had told him. It was Muslim tradition that if you were granted food or drink in the presence of the king then your life was spared. A sip of water; a simple gesture that had saved his life.

***

Within eight weeks Ridefort's freedom was secured in return for the surrender of the majestic Templar castle of Gaza. Shortly after, King Guy was freed and the two men immediately prepared for revenge, once again. In their absence, the city of Acre had surrendered, so the King and Gérard marched north.

Since all the knights had been killed at the Horns of Hattin, many of the Templar castles in the Levant were left undefended. One by one the castles, forts and towns fell as Saladin swept through Outremer like the raging scrub-brush fire he had started.

On his release, the Grand Master had given his word to discontinue hostilities against the Muslims. However, in his eyes, his word was not valid to a Saracen.

***

The Levant – 6th Hour 4th October AD 1189

As the sun reached its zenith, Saladin's relief force entered the theatre of battle to the cheers of the town's folk of the Port of Acre. Gérard's ambitious plan to retake the city from Saladin was to fail. In the short battle and hail of arrows that followed, Gérard, swinging his sword wildly, quickly became surrounded. Refusing to leave the field of battle the Grand Master was physically disarmed and dragged to Saladin's tent. Once again he stood before the King of the Muslims. The Saracen held a gourd before him, as he had before, only this time he did not allow the Grand Master to drink.

'Give me a reason why I should let you live?' Saladin asked.

'I am but a humble knight. Noble… but humble. Kill me, if that is what you wish,' the Grand Master replied, his shoulder square, his back straight.

'Noble? When I last released you, you vowed never to war against Islam and yet...' the Muslim raised a finger to the roof of his tent. 'Yet you chose to fight before the next new moon, and… and you continue to fight, besieging my people for *two* years. You are not noble!'

Abbadon stepped from behind the coloured drapes and squinted at the captured knight. He gave a little nasal laugh.

'Hello Gérard,' he calmly said. 'Do you remember our agreement?'

'Our agreement is void. My entire army died that day. Thousands have died since. There is no agreement!'

'But you lived,' Abbadon reminded the tired warrior.

'Take him!' Saladin ordered staring at the ground. 'You have what you want. It has cost many lives.'

'I have what I want,' Abbadon agreed. 'You have your Holy Land. Gérard... you get to live. That is what you wanted.'

'At what cost?' Gérard added.

With Gérard's chilling words Saladin glanced up at the Christian. Their eyes met. Only now had both men realised who they had been dealing with. Only now had they realised that the price in blood had been too high a price to pay. The Muslim turned away as Abbadon took Gérard by the arm.

'What do you want with me?' Gérard asked.

Abbadon did not answer. His only request of Saladin was to

spare Gérard de Ridefort and that, he had done.

'History will say that you died in this tent,' Saladin called after Ridefort. 'History is a lie!'

On the 4th October AD 1189, Gérard de Ridefort, tenth Grand Master of the Knights Templar, disappeared from Saladin's tent as he did from history, leaving the Levant in ruin, the Templar in disarray and the Holy Land, lost to the Muslim army.

'Your move Gabriel!'

XIII

The First Realm.

Carcassonne 08.15hrs 17th July AD 2001 GMT+1

The shutters were open, permitting some light into the small room. The oval handle in the centre of the window protruding between two sheets of lace that constituted a curtain. The pipe work to the radiator was not concealed. On the contrary, the gloss white pipes dropped from the ceiling, highlighted by the dark green patterned wallpaper. The radiator itself was gloss white, it didn't want to be missed. The wardrobe was a dark wooden stand-alone hunk of furniture over seven feet tall with two side panels and a large mirror that twisted on the handle in the centre. It was completely out of place with the rest of the room. Out of place was how Cole was feeling. He tried to concentrate on the events that had occurred the night before and on the conversation he had had less than an hour earlier. *'Large wardrobes don't die,'* he thought. *'They live out their days in one or two star French hotels.'* The agent couldn't focus; his mind was racing. The American sat down on the edge of the bed.

'Why do all beds in France squeak when you move on them?' he asked himself. 'Too much use, I guess. Now there's a thought.'

He took out his laptop and placed it on the bed beside him. He then plugged in the mobile phone and passed the time reading his two messages while the computer downloaded his encrypted e-mails from his extremely irate boss. 'No more bodies' he had said and one of the victims was one of their own. The messages meant nothing now. The first was to meet the local police chief. The second was from Soames letting him know where he was. With Soames's experience in the Diplomatic Corps and fluent in seven languages, he would be extremely difficult to replace. Cole turned his attention back to the computer and read the titles of the e-mails, a selection of autopsy and crime scene reports. He had too many questions and too few answers. None of the e-mails were from Rebecca. Therefore none of the information really mattered. *Were Gabriel and Iinnad pulling his leg?* He didn't think so. *Then what if Abbadon was for real? What if they believed he had been alive all this time?* He juggled a few of the ideas around in his head and slowly, bit by bit, he realised that if he took Gabriel and Iinnad at face value many of the questions could be answered. He engaged the word processor on his laptop; rested it on his lap and stared at the blank screen searching for the first line of his report.

'The X-Files!' he chuckled to himself. 'Episode one! One three zero seven.'

He slammed the lid of the laptop shut. He had no idea how he was to write this one up. In detail, he retraced the events leading up to Soames's death and could not comprehend, from who or where the blade came. He felt completely at a loss, a puppet dancing on strings, only somebody was cutting one every now and again. Eventually he would fall.

Gently, he reopened the laptop and logged onto the Internet, he accessed a search engine for historical data. He typed in the date 1307 and pressed enter. It took a minute before a flood of information appeared on the screen. At a quick glance, Cole could see in the year 1307, all the juicy bits of history were being made in France. As he scrolled through the pages of text he noted one of the significant dates that appeared; taking out his pen and notepad he wrote down 'Friday 13th October, 1307'.

'Friday the 13th,' Cole read what he had written. 'The DC murders were on Friday the 13th of July. July the seventh month; this Abbadon *is* playing a game.'

The Agent then clicked on the link to reveal a page of text. He read aloud.

'The demise of The Holy Order of Knights, correction, the Poor Knights of the Temple of Solomon of Jerusalem, better known as the Knights Templar. Jacques de Molay, Grand Master meets Pope Clement V in an attempt to avoid an amalgamation of the two great Holy Orders, the Knights Templar and the Knights Hospitaliers of St John. Politics, politics, politics! And money.'

The symbols, red crosses of different designs, on each side of the text caught the agent's eye. He scrolled down the page further.

'King Philip the Fair of France devalues the currency to such an extent that the country was on the brink of bankruptcy. He needs funds and the Templar have the money. Told you it was money,' he chuckled to himself. 'He owes them money himself. So why not steal it all? Why not take their lands too?' Cole kept questioning the text. 'King Philip sends out secret orders for the apprehension and detention of all members of the Knights Templar for crimes… that were too horrible to contemplate, and a detestable disgrace, these people were to be set apart from all humanity. What the hell does that mean?' Being in law enforcement, Cole read the line again. This time he put his own take on it. 'I am going to arrest you for something so terrible, I can't tell you,' he said. The agent re-focused on the screen. 'The sealed orders were sent out to every sheriff whose town or village housed property belonging to the Templar. Efficient!' Cole shook his head in disbelief. 'Some 15,000 knights, sergeants, and clerks from the territories that were governed by King Philip, were arrested on the morning of Friday the 13th. Unlucky for some. No Knights Templar resisted arrest. However…' Cole licked his lips with anticipation. 'This is the bit! It was reported that some Templar, including Gérard de Vil… the Preceptor of France, had escaped arrest and that 18 ships of the Templar fleet had escaped capture when they set sail from the port of La Rochelle that very morning. Three of the ships sailed south… and sought refuge under the protection of the King of Portugal. The others sailed north to the distant safety of Scotland and the clan of St Clair. Saint Clair?' Cole stopped for a moment. 'Or is that Sinclair?' he questioned. 'And then what?' Cole continued to read aloud. 'Molay and Charney awaited the King's soldiers, to be arrested in Paris. So why didn't you run? The King had already taken the wealth from the Jews and the Lombard's. So why didn't you run? All the Knights denied the charges against them. Only under torture by the Inquisition did some of them change their minds. Many were burnt at the stake.' Cole rubbed the dryness from his mouth. 'They sacrificed themselves. Why? What were you hiding?'

He scrolled the page again.

'Papal Bull is issued by the Pope. It stated that all Christian kings should arrest the Templar on the same charges and accusations as Philip and confiscate their property. *However*, the King of Portugal, owing so much to the Knights Templar and not believing in the charges, suggested that they changed their name to the Knights of Christ. He then confiscated all the property belonging to the Knights Templar and handed it over to the Knights of Christ. Smart! So some of them are still around.'

The American's history lesson was almost over.

'As for the fifteen ships that sailed north, fourteen arrived in Scotland where Robert the Bruce was in the midst of fighting the English. Robert the Bruce had already been ex-communicated by the Pope and took no notice of the Papal Bull, sparing the lives and property of the Scottish Knights Templar and of those that had sought refuge within his country.' His eye's skipped a line. 'To further save their existence the few remaining Knights went underground, forming a secret society, which would keep hold of the knowledge that was so precious.' Cole slowly scrolled back up the screen checking that he hadn't missed anything. Satisfied, he closed the laptop.

'OK! What happened to the eighteenth ship?' he raised his voice, expecting an answer from anywhere. 'And Gabriel, what have you got to do with all of this?'

XIV

The Seventh Realm.

26th Sunrise 2nd Cycle (AD 2001 First Realm Time)

Iinnad stood alone in the brightness of the Grand Hallway. She was surprised at the lack of activity. Far away in the distance were the great doors to the Celestial Court. She walked in the opposite direction. As she approached the Chamber of the Luminaries, a few angelic appeared. Iinnad made herself scarce. If the Council knew she had returned they would revoke her permission to travel and therefore she would not be able to return to the First Realm. At the door to the Chamber of the Luminaries Iinnad spotted Sophia speaking with Phul. That was a piece of luck. The coast was clear, so from behind a white marble pillar, Iinnad surprised the two.

'How can you be surprised Phul? I'm not here!' Iinnad explained.

'No, your not!' Sophia emphasised. 'Why are you here?'

'Sophia, I need to speak with you.'

'I think that means I should leave?' Phul suggested. 'You're getting a bad reputation, Iinnad.'

'Phul I need to speak to Sophia about Gabriel.'

'[illegible],' Phul replied and left, he would not say a word.

'No you haven't seen me, Phul. Thank you.'

Iinnad led Sophia into the empty Chamber of the Luminaries. The Mother of the Angels closed the doors behind her. Resting her hands on the handles she paused and waited for what Iinnad had to say. Iinnad knew that she had to grab Sophia's attention. In Iinnad's eyes, Sophia had never appeared to like her and she was only there because Gabriel trusted her and spoken so highly of her.

'Gabriel's out-numbered,' Iinnad stated. 'Abbadon is after him. He has no support and there are questions I need answered. Will you help me?'

Sophia did not move. Impatiently Iinnad marched to her side and placed her hand over hers.

'Will you help me?'

Sophia let go of the door and moved to the centre of the chamber so that no eavesdroppers at the door could hear them. The Mother of the Angels held the young angelic's hands.

'I will help Gabriel.'

'But not me?'

'Iinnad, you are wild. You cause so much anger amongst the hierarchy. I cannot be seen to stand by you. Do you understand?'

'I don't *care* if you can't be seen to stand by me. No one stands by me. I'm getting used to that. One being won't make a difference; I just want to help Gabriel survive Abbadon's attack, when it comes.'

'You care for the soulcarriers?'

'No, why should I?' Iinnad responded sharply. 'They're primitive!'

'Your harsh exterior hides a soft side Iinnad. I see it.'

'I don't *have* a soft side!'

Sophia shook Iinnad's hands. '*You care*! Everyone sees it. It is seen through your passion. You have a passion for the innocent; *whoever* they are. You stand up to the Council *because* of your passion. You care nothing for yourself. On that alone; I will help.'

'Why didn't you just say yes? I don't have much time!'

'Because you need to understand why,' Sophia replied. 'Now!' Sophia shook her arms again. 'You have questions?'

'Yeah! What is so important about the book that… that primitive wrote?'

'Enoch is a wise man. He has written much in his time here. He wrote much when he was on the First Realm. The codex, *that book*, that Uriel speaks of is a book of prophecy. It is a history of the First Realm.'

'I thought it was Gabriel's history?'

Sophia shook her head in a pleasing manner. 'Where do you get your information from?'

'Am I wrong?'

'No. The codex that Uriel seeks is a history of the First Realm and its Guardian, Gabriel. It covers thousands of years from the beginning to the end. We only know this from the pieces of information that Enoch can remember; and that I fear is not much.'

'Why?'

'Enoch is a seer, an oracle if you choose. However, he can only see through the words he writes. Uriel knows that now, but he did not know that when he was taken from the First Realm. The codex was lost and so were the stories.'

'But some of these stories are known by the soulcarriers.'

'I did not know that.'

'Yes you did,' Iinnad replied a little confused at Sophia's answer.

Iinnad broke free from Sophia and rechecked the chamber for anyone that may be listening. 'What about the key?'

'The key that locked Sataniel in the Bottomless Pit? The key to the Abyss.'

'Yes, I know what it is, but how did the Council know?'

'Iinnad… there are some questions that I cannot answer.'

Disappointed, Iinnad marched away from Sophia and flung her arms in the air; then slapped her sides.

'I saw Lilith on the First Realm. She looked just like you; down to the blue eyes. You pretend to be Lilith and spy for the Council, don't you?' Iinnad deduced. 'Why can't you answer my questions – is that because… is the answer… is the answer,' Iinnad's voice wavered as a tear rolled down her cheek. 'Why are there so many secrets?'

Sophia responded with a glare. She was in no position to answer, but it was no use and she knew Iinnad would tell no one.

'How can you stand being around evil like that?' Iinnad inquired.

'It is necessary. I am the image of Lilith and she is the image of me.'

'When I saw Lilith, it threw me. For a moment I lost my edge. I *don't like* to lose my edge. Losing my edge means I could lose all together. I *don't like* losing, but I knew it was Lilith.'

'How did you know?'

'She cold bloodedly killed a primitive. You wouldn't do that!'

'Was Abbadon present?'

'No, I don't think so,' Iinnad replied.

'Then you are correct. I would not have.'

'You're saying you could have?' Iinnad stressed.

'I am saying that I would have done what was necessary.'

'I couldn't,' Iinnad admitted.

'This war is going to get dirtier as time passes. Soulcarrier and angelic alike will do whatever it takes to win. You may fight, but not like angelic. You *will* do this to win!'

'I don't believe that!'

'Iinnad, you have grown. You are beginning to believe in the soulcarriers, as Gabriel does.'

'They're primitives! I don't see what Gabriel sees in them!'

'But you will not stand by and watch them die.'

'I will if I have to!'

'I do not believe you will, Iinnad. The Council *will*, but you will not! Stand by Gabriel as you always have. He needs you. The soulcarriers need you. You have a strength that Gabriel has lost.'

'What about the Council?' Iinnad inquired.

'What about the Council? When did you ever care for Council?'

'That's true!' Iinnad declared with a smile as she wiped her face dry.

'Iinnad! You have always done what you believe to be right. Stand by your judgement and *I* will answer to the Council.'

'On my behalf?'

'Now go, before someone sees you and remember, do what you believe is right.'

XV

The First Realm.

Washington DC – 13.15hrs 17th July AD 2001 EST

The freshly cut lawn on capital hill had that sweet smell of summer about it. The sun was out and it gave the impression of being a lovely day in the city after such a surprisingly large amount of rain for one night a few days previous. On a bench overlooking the building that held the US Congress, sat a man in his late-fifties. He stared out over the capital in wonder at practically everything he could see, from the cars and bikes to the distant skyscrapers, even the clothes that the passers-by were wearing. He placed a pair of sunglasses over his eyes and then removed them again, only to replace them once more. He took in the sun as though he had not seen it or felt its warmth in a long time. A man with dark swept back hair approached. The hard leather of his cowboy boots caught the old man's attention, as he walked up the tarmac path towards the bench. He was casually dressed, but smart with a waistcoat and a broad grin, which was not always a good thing if you knew the gentleman's character. He stopped in front of the seated man placing him in his shadow with the sun like a halo, outlining his head.

'May I sit down?' he asked in a husky southern accent.

'As you wish,' replied the grey-haired gentleman, in a French accent.

‘As you wish,’ repeated the southerner. ‘Be careful what you wish for, it might just come true.’

The two men faced each other eye to eye.

‘You are Monsieur Kell?’ inquired the older man.

‘Yes,’ the southerner replied. ‘Just call me Kell.’

‘Gérard de Ridefort, I take it?’

‘This is not quite what you expected, is it?’

‘Non!’

‘Sitting here, halfway around the world 800 years after you made a deal.’

‘I will stand by my word,’ Gérard stated. ‘As a matter of honor!’

‘Honor? Now there’s an interesting word; and you’ll stand by it. I’m sure you will,’ replied Kell with a smirk. ‘You’re a long way from home Gérard de Ridefort.’

‘It makes no difference to me. I have no home.’

‘I’ve seen it all before and I will probably see it all again,’ Kell admitted. ‘What you mortals don’t understand is that what you want is what you get, but you’re not that smart. You made a deal with the devil; well, one of his princes. It’s as simple as that.’

‘It was just that… a deal,’ Gérard emphasized. ‘Which, I might add, he went back on.’

‘A deal is like any agreement. It’s binding and… the agreement *is* to the letter.’

Kell paused for a moment. The old man lowered his head almost in humiliation. To be illiterate in his time was commonplace, but as he suspected from the tone of Kell's voice and what he had seen, times had changed.

'You betrayed your own side for 30 pieces of silver,' Kell continued. 'In the history books you were seen as misjudging a situation, *actually*… several situations. You made mistakes, your orders were followed and those actions caused the Holy Military Orders to lose the Levant.'

'I was not to know who I was dealing with.'

'And it all started with *you* at the Springs of Cresson.'

'I'm sorry.'

'Why?' blurted Kell. 'From our point of view you're to be praised. You did well. Above all else, no one would ever expect or suspect that there was outside interference and *that* is the most important thing of all.'

Kell gave the old man a pat on the back.

'You should be proud of what you've done, not ashamed of the fact that you betrayed those that wouldn't listen to you. Look at the advances that have been made in the direction that man has taken...' Kell waved his hand out to show off the city.

'And the people that have died?'

'People die, that's what they do! I can't help that. I can't stop that. Mortals die; they always have and they always will.' Kell's tone changed. 'Are you trying to tell me that you feel guilty? That you have sorrow in your heart for what you've done?'

'I didn't say that.'

'It was 800 years ago and your heart is now as dark as the innermost Caves of Enlightenment. I don't want to hear your pity, you've been sent here to do a job. *I* have been sent here to assist you and to make sure you don't balls it up.'

'I know I have a job to do, but that doesn't mean I have to like it.'

'You were the Grand Master of the Holy Order of the Poor Knights of the Temple of Solomon in Jerusalem, and now you're in *Washington* DC. A city larger than anything you have ever seen before, in what used to be called the New World, and *even that* was before your time. Times change buddy!'

'All Abbadon told me, was that this was quite simple, and that for security I would have to wait until I was here before I would know my mission,' explained the old man attempting to get back to the business in hand.

'You are to be a courier service. There is a package that requires shipment to Europe and it will be your responsibility to ensure that it reaches its destination,' instructed Kell. 'Abbadon was right; it is quite simple.'

The old man stood up and took a deep breath and surveyed the modern buildings of the new city in which he stood. He turned and looked at the seated Kell and beamed.

'I never expected the world to change so much,' said the old knight. 'All I wanted was for the war to end and for my army to have the opportunity to go home.'

'That war did end. It took another hundred years, mind you. As for your army, well, they all died.'

'I will be remembered as a traitor to those that believed,' Gérard admitted calmly. 'Those that remember.'

'No,' Kell lied. 'You *were* remembered as a man that misjudged a few awkward situations. Those that would have recognized you as a traitor died 800 years ago.'

'Maybe you're right,' replied the knight. 'And I have a job to do, so where do I find this package and how many men do I need?'

***

Washington DC – 17.45hrs 17th July AD 2001 EST

The police officer sat in his chair and with a glazed look in his eyes stared across the room at Naomi who sat on the side of the bed looking out the window. There was only another fifteen minutes until the end of his shift, but every second felt like a minute and every minute felt like an hour. The officer struggled to keep his lids from closing. Naomi, however, was wide-awake, alert. She had questions, but no answers. Gabriel said she was safe and that she should stay put until he sent for her. In the back of her mind Naomi knew she could trust him, but could she trust the policemen with her protection? A bird flew past the hospital window, brown in color; Naomi didn't know what it was called. On a gust of wind against the hospital building, it rose in the up draft, soaring high into the sky without even beating its wings. Naomi smiled to herself, and with a little laugh tried to imagine Gabriel sprouting feathers. The police officer stirred in his seat catching Naomi's attention. Sitting on the side of the bed she could see, over the police officer's shoulder, a small black circular mark that began to appear on the wall. The circle grew larger and then larger still. It did not increase in size smoothly like the ripples on a pond, but in spurts and jumps like someone had stamped a mark on the wall in at next room. Naomi stood up and walked to the end of the bed. The officer didn't move.

'How can you sleep with your eyes open Officer Jenkins?' she said to herself reading his nametag.

Now scared, the patient kicked the officer's foot and he awoke with a start. Jumping to his feet he was about to scream at the young lady when he could see the fear in her eyes. He closed his mouth without saying a word and turned around to see the black mark on the wall that was now almost three foot wide and still growing. As Naomi moved towards the door, the police officer picked up the spare chair by the bed and prodded the wall with it. Two legs of the chair sunk into the soft surface and as the policeman attempted to pull the chair out his hands slipped free. Jenkins stepped back to protect Naomi from the ever-growing black mass with the chair still protruding from it like a piece of modern art. The officer drew his firearm as Naomi opened the door to see the other police officer calmly standing on guard outside, oblivious to everything within her room. The officer in the corridor glanced over his shoulder at Naomi and gave her a welcoming grin. She didn't smile back and his expression change as he realized there was a problem.

'Hanmore!' called Jenkins. 'Get in here!'

Hanmore drew his weapon and push the door wide open before entering. He just caught sight of the chair protruding from the wall before it broke into pieces that sprayed over the tiled floor. Naomi leapt out into the bustling corridor of doctors, nurses and patients. She realized she was still wearing the standard issue hospital gown and although with ties at the back, she was naked beneath. Dressed in so little, she still blended in. Nobody in the corridor had yet noticed the commotion in her room. Through the doorway she could see the bedside cabinet, which contained her clothes. She took a deep breath as she peered around the door; one of the officers fired. She screamed with surprise and jumped back out into the corridor. Startled and confused, patients and staff alike began to panic and run in all directions. Another shot rang out and then another. For a split-second, Naomi closed her eyes and concentrated on calming herself. She knew the situation was weird and let's face it; a couple of days before she had been talking to an angel or *something* that could freeze time. Naomi opened her eyes and focused on her clothes in the cabinet. Another shot went off and then a scream. Such a terrifying scream that Naomi froze in her tracks as did most of the people in the corridor. In front of her, the clean tiles were suddenly awash with blood; her bed sheets, the walls and her bedside cabinet all turned a bright crimson in the sunlight. The door slammed shut inches from her face.

'No time for clothes!' she said to herself, searching of an exit.

In all the mayhem of screaming patients and worried staff, she saw an elderly gentleman with grey hair calmly walking towards her. He was tall, square shouldered, confident and battle scarred. She had never met Gérard de Ridefort, but there was something cold about his eyes. The decision had been made for the direction she was to take, even though the exit sign was just over Ridefort's head. Instinctively, she chose the other way. Naomi ran down the corridor, frantically searching for another exit sign. She turned left at the first junction she came to in an attempt to get out of sight before making her escape from the building. A calmness and commonsense had come into play in a situation that she had never been in. Maybe she had picked it up from watching too much television as a child, or was it the pre-emptive thoughts that had been rushing through her mind ever since Gabriel's visit? She didn't know, nor did she have the time to think about it. At the end of the corridor on the left was the children's ward, but to the right was the fire exit: the stairs that would take her out of the hospital. It was obvious that she would try to escape. She kicked the cross bar of the emergency doors as hard as she could causing them to swing wide-open. The alarm sounded. Then she checked the corridor and could not yet see her pursuer, so she entered the children's ward and closed the door behind her. Considering the commotion outside, the children seemed very calm until the power went out. The emergency lighting kicked in as did the kids screams. On the ward the few nurses that were still present, attempted to calm their little patients. Naomi bent down behind the door and peered through the small round reinforced window into the corridor. All she could see were the emergency doors slowly close with the help of their hydraulic arms.

'What happened to the lights?' came a little voice from the bed to her right.

Naomi ducked down behind the door and looked over to a little boy who sat bolt up right in his bed. This kid was not going to stay quiet she thought.

'Sssssh!' Naomi instinctively responded.

The little boy said nothing and stared straight at her as he spun the wheels on the red toy car he was holding. She peered back through the window to see a grotesque looking creature with what could only be described as scales on his torso, pointed ears and red eyes, push open the emergency doors just as they were about to close. For a moment, Naomi realized that what she could see was not possible, but for some bizarre reason she accepted it without question. *If angels exist; why not demons?* And then to make matters worse, a second demon came into view. With torn rags for clothes it had a row of spikes protruding out of its back from its neck to the base of its spine and it had *claws*. *Why don't they look after their nails?* was the only thing that came to Naomi's mind. Her fear seemed to have gone.

'I can see your butt,' announced the little voice from the bed.

'Sssssh!' Naomi whispered ducking down behind the door. 'That's because I haven't got anything on, but neither have you!'

'Success,' thought Naomi as the little boy bit his lip. However, innocence had reminded her that she was vulnerable. Out of the corner of her eye, Naomi saw a wooden baseball bat by the little boy's bed.

'Can I borrow that?' she quietly asked pointing at the newly found weapon.

The little boy frantically nodded, but said nothing. The near naked young lady picked up the baseball bat and returned to the door. She held it tightly in her hand as she turned back to the window and came face-to-face with the old knight peering through the glass.

'Shit!'

The ward door swung open, knocking Naomi to the floor. Two demonic entered and were met by a hail of screams from the children. They approached Naomi with their claws out and their teeth on show, but it made no difference to Naomi. She had nowhere to turn, nowhere to run. Her first thought was the children, but they did not want the children. They wanted her. Through the subdued light, Ridefort caught a glimpse of a six-inch metal red Ferrari, as it flew through the air and hit the spiked demon hard on the shoulder. In an instant, the demonic spun around in an attempt to catch little devil that threw it. Naomi had a chance and took it; raising the baseball bat high she brought it down on the demon's back as hard as she could. The demonic fell to the ground pulling Naomi off-balance as she attempted to retrieve the bat. It had lodged itself quite securely on one of the demonic's spikes and when he rolled over to see who hit him she lost her grip and her only weapon of defense.

'Get up you idiot,' ordered the scaly demonic as his palm faced the floor.

The spiked demonic climbed to his feet; baseball bat still attached and grabbed Naomi's arm. If they were to go to so much trouble to capture her then they obviously wanted her alive. The scaly demonic's hand began to shimmer and a black circle began to appear on the floor between beds. Gérard de Ridefort stepped back to check that the corridor was clear of staff, but it was filling with police.

The spiked demonic increased the pressure of his grip on Naomi's arm; there was no way she could escape without losing a limb. The creature dragged his captive over to the ward's main door to where Ridefort was standing.

'Small and colorful, producing much chaos, like children,' spoke the demonic.

Naomi noticed the old man did not understand, but she did. The demonic hit the tiny plate of glass surrounded by its red housing. The glass broke and the button was pressed. The fire alarms began to ring;

instant commotion filled the corridor outside.

As the black mass on the floor grew larger Naomi was pushed towards it. The alarms rang in the children's ward, but the patients were silent as all those present watched in amazement as the scaly demonic stepped onto the blackness and slipped through the floor. The spiked one jerked at Naomi's arm tugging her in to the slime. She lost her footing as the demonic let go of her arm and she too, disappeared down. Gérard de Ridefort followed.

'What about my bat?' the small boy called out.

The last demonic straightened his back and tried to remove the baseball bat from his spike. It was committed to remain firm. He edged to the rim of the circle and glared at the boy, his eyes glazed red, before he stepped through the floor.

'What about my bat?'

XVI

The First Realm.

Heathrow London 19.55hrs Monday 16th July AD 2001 GMT

The NSA agent 424890 ID lay face up on the table in front of the captured Cole. He patiently sat, hands handcuffed behind the back of his chair. The room was sparse, square and clinically clean. There wasn't even a scuffmark on the polished linoleum. To Cole's left, in the corner, stood a uniformed police officer with a bullet-proof vest and a H&K MP 5 sub-machine gun resting on his chest. Cole had never seen an armed British policeman before. It was a shock to the system that the first one he saw carried a machine gun. But then, this was Heathrow airport and times change. England was still having trouble with terrorism in the form of the IRA (Irish Revolutionary Army), so he should have expected it. The American people were used to gun crime on their streets; England didn't have that problem, they had terrorists. *It's what you're used to.* With that it mind, it also didn't help matters walking through a metal detector concealing a firearm, hence the handcuffs, NSA or not. Cole had gone quietly, he wasn't in any hurry and the police were only doing their job. He was the one who had screwed up, again. He did remember that hand guns in any form were illegal in England. Unfortunately, it was the metal detector that reminded him. The door opened.

'Well Mr Cole!' bellowed a truly English accent. 'For someone in our profession you do an incredible job of cutting against the grain.'

The suited officer walked around the table, the metal in his heels clicked each time they hit the shiny floor. Then he slammed Soames' firearm on the table. The noise echoed in the tiny cell. As he removed his hand, it slipped across the surface and came to rest next to Cole's ID.

'Explain yourself!'

Cole said nothing and allowed his eyes to follow the reflection of the strip light across the table from end to end. He could hear the bustle of the airport outside the room, the door had yet to be closed. He slowly turned his head towards the limey.

'I forgot about the piece,' he admitted motioning with his eyes to the Beretta.

'That's it? You forgot!'

Cole had been honest and they weren't buying it. The Englishman leant forward and using both hands placed the ID and the Beretta in his jacket pocket.

'Someone wants to talk to you!' he announced. 'Stand up and I'll...'

Cole instantly stood, knocking the chair to floor. He then placed the handcuffs on the table and adjusted his jacket to the amazement of the two men present. Cole noticed the uniformed officer very slowly move his right index finger to the safety switch on his weapon.

'How did you do that?' asked the Englishman, starting at the handcuffs.

'Someone wants to see me,' asked Cole ignoring the question.

'How the hell did you do that?'

The suited officer led the two men out of the office and down the corridor towards the VIP reception area. The MP5 occasionally nudged Cole in the back, reminding him that the armed officer was still there. As the corridor widened and the VIP lounge became apparent, Cole recognised the face of Ambassador Grayson.

'Oh shit!' Cole muttered to himself.

'Up to your neck in it,' added his escort, whispering over his shoulder.

In an attempt to avoid eye contact with the Ambassador, Cole turned away. As he passed the passage to his left, which led to the main terminal, he could see the tide of passengers of the many delayed flights littered about the floor and doorways. There was little movement in the terminal except for one man, a man he recognised, Henry Sinclair. The agent slowed his pace, but was nudged again by the MP5.

'Hey! Do you mind?' Cole warned and stopped.

The armed man was about to push Cole too far when the suit intervened. The two officers switched roles and Cole continued, his eyes front staring at the back of the armed officer's head. He looked over the man's shoulder to the Ambassador, catching his eye and then looking down to the holstered sidearm in front of him.

'I can't stay,' the agent said to himself loudly.

'Back to the US I hope,' was the Inquisitor's reply.

Reading Cole's body language the Ambassador was already aware that something was wrong and he left his entourage and headed straight towards him. The Ambassador raised his hand in a futile attempt to stop what was about to happen.

'I gotta go!'

'Not yet. Not until I'm told or until I say so,' was the response from behind in addition to the firm grip on Cole's right shoulder.

The uniformed officer began to turn, also sensing something was wrong, but it was too late. In one swift and premeditated move, Cole engaged both men. The agent pushed the armed man sharply, unclipping the holster with his palm and removing the Browning 9 mm automatic as the officer fell forward. Cole's sudden jolt pulled his Inquisitor closer and passed his right leg. Retracting his arm, weapon in hand, Cole's elbow met his captor square in the chest. As he stepped back to regain his balance he tripped over the agent's extended leg. Cole was gone before his victims had reached the floor. The Ambassador just stood over the two defeated men shaking his head.

'I was told he was the best,' he said quietly to those on the floor. 'I just wasn't told, at what.'

***

Knights Templar HQ (The Castle)20.04hrs Monday 16th July AD 2001 GMT

The divide between old and new was quite evident within the Command and Control room. One could only describe the C&C as massive; some two hundred and fifty feet long and seventy-five feet wide, with its marble columns, stone and English oak floor, the style was by no means modern. The ceiling was covered by row after row of three-feet by four-feet rectangular sections, each section containing a carefully illustrated shield, a coat of arms. To complete the artistry, in the centre was an ornate circular compass dial of ancient design, surrounded by the star constellations of the zodiac highlighted in gold on a rich dark blue background. Running the length of the room on either side, suspended halfway up, some twenty-feet from the ceiling was a railed walkway giving access to the numerous control panels, which were situated above the glass-covered bookshelves that were now filled with digital data. The marble surround of the room protected the banks of communication equipment and columns of memory storage. Row after row of desks and control stations littered the floor, their cables covering the backs of every desk.

Busily working at their stations in a vain attempt to capture every available scratch of radio traffic, the team of dedicated operators frantically rushed about their business. Audio speakers occasionally jump to life with the sound of static, as switches were flicked and dials were turned as the energetic team tirelessly attempted to gain some comprehension of what was happening. Their superior; an elderly man, calmly walked between the rows of workstations.

'We have an armed black man!' came the voice over the speaker. 'I repeat! We have an armed black man!'

'We have him,' came the reply from a different voice on the speaker.

'This is Heathrow traffic! This is Heathrow traffic!' broadcast a commanding voice. 'Give me a location!'

'Terminal 3, we're in Terminal 3!'

'Confirm the man is armed!'

'Confirmed and in pursuit,' replied an officer's voice.

The elderly gentleman in the C&C stood by the workstation

with his hand resting on a loudspeaker. His fingers gently tapped a rhythm as the entire room listened to the chase unfold. The gentleman, in his tweed suit, had the respect of his team due to his years of experience in both his profession and his secret life. The workstation operator motioned to the elderly man that he could intervene. A gentle shake of the head and a slight wave of his fingers was enough for the young operator to stand down, and wait.

'Heathrow traffic are unaware of Mr Cole's position,' he explained in a calm and collect manner. 'I wonder if any of them are aware of who he is?'

'Sir! You wish to test Mr Cole?' questioned a female operator.

'Let's just see what Mr Cole is up to,' he replied. 'Can we put the Airport and station cameras on the main screen?'

At the far end of the C&C, the entire wall was a bank of video screens of varying sizes. The largest, in the centre, took up a third of the wall. The images varied from what looked like power grids to TV news stations, from weather satellites to the stock exchange. Everything that could be monitored was being monitored. The centre screen flickered into life as multiple images of Heathrow's Terminal 3 and the London Underground system came to view.

'What are you chasing Mr Cole?' the elderly gentleman asked himself.

***

Heathrow – 20.07hrs Monday 16th July AD 2001 GMT

Henry reached the bottom of the stone steps and within a few strides disappeared out of sight as he took a left turn. Cole was close behind, but when he turned the corner, into the walkway leading to the Underground, Henry had gained a tremendous distance. The agent ran down the centre of the walkway as fast as he could, only gaining a few yards on an old lady with a suitcase trolley. At the other end of the walkway, Henry left the moving floor and darted between the passengers queuing for tickets to the Underground. The American didn't know the tunnel system beneath the airport. Henry was definitely on his own turf. Armed police officers joined the pursuit from a different direction and chased the agent down to the platforms and an awaiting train. The continuous bleeping tone told the agent that the doors were about to close. At last, some luck. He jumped on board.

From the train, Cole could see the police franticly trying to radio for back up as the train pulled out of the station. He knew it wouldn't be as easy as that. The police would try to keep the train moving, until they could set up a secure station with enough armed police to control the situation. Commonsense dictated that Cole had to find his quarry before the train stopped. He also had to lose the weapon. The American checked the carriage he was on, but there was no sign of Henry. The thought had dawned on him that his prey might not even be on board. However, over confidence sprung to mind in the fact that Henry knew London. That would mean that he would not have wasted time reaching his destination. He proceeded to walk the length of the train. Carriage by carriage, Cole visually checked every passenger until he came to a locked door, which separated the next carriage. In any normal situation, one would just wait for the train to stop and using the platform, bypass the obstacle. The problem being that when the train stopped there would probably be armed police awaiting him.

'We apologise for the inconvenience to your journey,' came the voice of the driver over the speaker. 'But we are unable to stop the train at this time due to an emergency that has occurred on several of the platforms. Our next stop will be Barons Court. There is no cause for alarm and we are sorry for any inconvenience caused.'

Cole sat down. There was nothing he could, but wait. He loosened the automatic until it gently dropped onto the seat under the cover of his jacket and then he tucked it down into the folds of material, out of sight. Nobody noticed what the agent had done; the carriage was now full of nervous passengers each in their own world. Twenty minutes later and Cole was still patiently sitting and watching the stations go by. '*Boston Manor, where do these names come from? Barons Court.*'

***

The train had been decelerating for sometime, but as the driver applied the brakes more heavily all the passengers lulled forward with the momentum. The train stopped. The station was lined with armed police officers. The doors of the tube carriages stayed shut, causing more paranoia in the passengers. The doors were opened, one car at a time, and the people were asked to leave. Complaints from businessmen and misunderstood tourists were ignored as the passengers were herded out.

'If you have missed your station,' came an announcement. 'Could you cross the footbridge to the west bound platform and join the next available train. Thank you!'

Cole waited. Sinclair had to be here, somewhere. The next car was opened and the people spilled out. A black youth was stopped by the police and questioned. Out of the corner of his eye, Cole carefully watched the situation. After a quick search and a minor protest by the lad, he was allowed on his way. An African gentleman was asked to step aside. He politely agreed and again was questioned and frisked. Again, he was allowed to leave. Cole now knew the police were only looking for him. He tilted his head back and gave a large sigh as he stared at the handrail for inspiration. Cole was not the only one on the train to notice who the police were questioning. All the ethnic minorities on board were getting agitated. The doors to Cole's carriage opened and the passengers began to file out. Three smartly dressed black gentlemen stood up. The agent could only describe them as bankers. They had that look. They shut their briefcases and left the car. One of them left a newspaper behind. Cole casually picked it up and joined the gentlemen on the platform. The police politely asked the coloured gentlemen to one side. Each in turn, the men were searched. Cole raised his hands, to be frisked. As he looked up at the newspaper, he shook his head in disbelief; he couldn't believe his luck, it was The Financial Times. He briefly read the small print.

'How much d'ya lose?' the officer asked misinterpreting his motions.

Cole played on the officer's mistake. 'I didn't lose, but I didn't win either,' Cole calmly replied changing his accent. 'If I had bought before they had amalgamated,' pulling one word out of the headline. 'I could have won.'

'In your business, isn't that a loss?' asked the policeman.

'Yeah, I guess so,' replied Cole depressingly playing the part.

'WHAT!' screamed a policeman from the other end of the platform.

All attention was on the officer with the radio. The man held the microphone tightly and stretched the wire until the plug popped out of the radio. He was about to throw it onto the tracks when a second officer asked the first to calm down.

'Stand down!' came the crackled voice over all the radios.

The police openly stepped back away from the passengers they were questioning and began to apologise for the inconvenience. Cole looked surprised. He could not understand, why the sudden change of heart. One of the radios came to life.

'I thought we were looking for a black American?' asked a confused officer.

'We've let everybody else go,' came the reply.

'They know who they want, they'll pick him up,' crackled the radio.

'Will all remaining passengers please board the train. Thank you. We are sorry for any inconvenience,' was the final announcement.

Cole re-boarded the train and sat down right next to the Browning automatic. *This situation doesn't make sense. The police know who I am. The Ambassador would have informed everybody. Who had the power or the connections to call off a search on such a scale just like that?*

***

London – 20.41hrs Monday 16th July AD 2001 GMT

Behind the ornate closed doors, out of public view, within the exquisite buildings, which house the gentleman's clubs of London that litter the city; the historically rich men of the United Kingdom socialised. In the drawing-room of one such club, Gordon's Gentlemen's Club (GGC) surrounded by teak covered walls and red leather studied armchairs sat a group of six elderly gentleman reminiscing on the old days, when life was hard and when life was fun. They compared then to now and how soft society had become; how lazy the youth of today had grown into a society fixed around one box in the living room of every household.

'The youth of today wouldn't appreciate this,' stated one of the gentlemen as he drew on his pipe. 'There is nothing, even in this room, that they would care for.'

'I don't know my dear Count,' replied the strong voice of the Scotsman from behind a high backed chair. 'We have firearms and swords on the walls. Violence has always grabbed the attention of the young.'

The hard polished wooden floor didn't hide the approach of the waiter, in his dinner suit with white gloves holding a silver tray. He crossed the drawing room and approached the high backed chair, bending down to allow the occupant to read the card.

'Sir William,' the waiter announced.

'Just read it to me,' snapped the Scotsman. 'Just read it!'

'You have a phone call Sir William.'

'I'm not here!'

'Very good Sir,' replied the waiter as he began to leave.

Halfway across the polished floor, the waiter stopped; concerned that he had not fulfilled his mission. He returned, tentatively, to the Scotsman. Sir William jumped out of his chair. He stood tall and proud, with dinner jacket and bow tie and Highland dress from the waist down. His white hair and matching beard showed his years, but he was a strong man with a keen eye and those eyes stared straight at the waiter, piercing to the back of his skull.

'What is it boy!' he snapped. 'Can't I have a brandy in peace?'

The elderly group began to chatter amongst themselves. One of them stood up to join Sir William.

'I'll take the phone call,' he said.

'No you bloody won't Hugh!' snapped Sir William; then he turned back to the waiter. 'Did they say what it was about?'

'It's about your son, Sir William,' replied the waiter.

'I don't have a son,' replied the Scotsman as he turned away and sat back down, picking up his brandy glass swirling the contents around.

'I'll take it,' said Hugh rushing across the polished floor as fast as his old legs would carry him.

Sir William calmly carried on, as though they had not even had an interruption.

'Well…' announced the Count of Savoy. 'Nice weather we're having.'

'Oh please!' Sir William barked. 'Don't dance around on my account.'

The gentlemen that remained knew the friction between father and son and thought it wise to stay quiet. They had known Sir William since childhood and generations of his family had sat in the chairs of the drawing room for hundreds years. He was proud of his traditions and he was proud of his family, all of them that is, except Henry, the one that left the fold.

'William,' called Hugh from the doorway. 'We have a situation that you are going to need to attend to.'

'Is he dead?'

'No! Henry's fine.'

'Good!'

'So you do care about your son?' the Count of Savoy pointed out, raising his empty glass to get the waiter's attention. 'Sir William cares.'

'My dear Count. If you had a son like mine, you'd act the way I do!'

Sir William finished his brandy and climbed back out of his chair. He nodded to the elderly gentlemen still seated and bade them good evening. Then he briskly left the drawing room to join Hugh in the corridor outside.

***

London Underground – 21.21hrs Monday 16th July AD 2001 GMT

The train pulled out of the next station down the line. Cole read the station sign - Gloucester Road. He had lost his prey. He was in the middle of London and had nowhere to turn. He remembered back to when he was a boy and people used to stare at him; the little black boy of a single mother in an affluent suburb of D.C. He had always tried to ignore it, but people always stare at you when you are different. Back then, having no father made you different. All those eyes, hundreds of eyes watching everything you do, every move you make. He was an alien in a foreign land and he felt the eyes on him once again. Hyde Park Corner. Cole's mother had always said that someone watched over him. Cole didn't think that anymore. In the Gulf War, Cole had been alone, but somehow he had made it. When he thought he was going to die he managed to survive. Leicester Square. Even in a crowd you can feel alone, no one to talk to, no one to hear what you have to say. Holborn. Then out of nowhere someone stands in front of you; someone that you have been searching for; Henry Sinclair, albeit, separated by a pane of glass. Cole darted from his seat and managed to get his arm between the closing doors. They retracted and the agent was free to continue his pursuit. With a broad grin, Cole leapt onto the platform and drew his weapon.

'Freeze!' he screamed. 'Don't fucking move!'

Henry recognised the voice and stayed perfectly still. The train moved away and the surrounding tourists disappeared in screams. The two men were alone on the enamel-tiled platform, motionless. Henry took a couple steps forward, still with his hands aloft, he positioned himself in plain view of one of the many security cameras. Cole, not yet aware of them, followed matching Henry's steps one on one.

'I was speaking English,' Cole calmly stated. 'Don't move!'

***

KT Castle – 21.28hrs Monday 16th July AD 2001 GMT

On the main screen, in the C&C, the tweed-suited gentleman watched the situation unfold. In his mind he was trying to read the situation, but couldn't. Agent Cole should know what sort of a situation he was in.

'A bit of luck on his part, don't you think Sir Geoffrey?' questioned the young operator. 'Or with a little help?'

'His luck won't hold out.'

'It won't, if I can help it,' bellowed a strong Scottish voice.

The entire room jumped to the sound of Sir William's voice from the back of the hall. Sir Geoffrey casually glanced over his shoulder to his old friend while the younger operators attempted to look busy.

'You run a sloppy ship Sir Geoffrey,' Sir William stated as loudly as he could giving him a quick wink. 'A sloppy ship! You hear me?'

'Then it is God I thank for not being at sea,' he replied with a smile.

Not a head was raised in the room. No one dared meet Sir William eye to eye. At the opposite end of the room from the main screen, the floor was slightly raised and made of stone. The rear wall was also stone and covered in engravings positioned between two great pillars giving the impression that it was a doorway, a stone door that could not be opened by any mortal man. In front of it, stood five wooden high-backed chairs, the wood blackened with age. In the centre of each chair's back was a Coat of Arms, each different. Sir William stepped up to the central chair and took his place as the head of the organisation; the Grand Master of the Holy Order of the Poor Knights of the Temple of Solomon of Jerusalem, the Knights Templar.

'What does one do with a loose cannon and a runaway son?' questioned Sir Geoffrey. 'An American agent and a member of the Order.'

'The loose cannon is NSA?' Sir William asked. 'What have you got on him?'

There was no reply from anyone at any of the workstations.

'Well!' Sir William snapped. 'Do you want me to sit here all night?'

'Don't hound them William,' Hugh asked quietly. 'Let them do their job.'

'French CRS don't like him,' stated one of the female operators. 'The NSA brass put up with him, because he has a 100 percent success rate. At present he has pissed off, just about everybody.'

'And Henry?' inquired Hugh.

'I don't want him in the castle,' Sir William responded sharply.

'You can't do that,' argued one of the Knight Commanders. 'He is bloodline. You can't turn him away.'

'Then bring them in!' replied Sir William. 'Bring them *both* in. And make sure we have no outside interference. Mr Cole has been making quite a noise. He will show up on everybody's radar.'

XVII

The First Realm.

Kingsway – London – 21.32hrs Monday 16th July AD 2001 GMT

Two red, armed response, police cars screamed north up the wide road, their lights flashing. They screeched to a halt outside Holborn Tube Station. The three passengers of each car scrambled out, each officer carrying a machine gun. The six men, two in uniform, the other four in plain clothes except for police baseball caps, dashed straight into the station, down the stairs and jumped the ticket barriers.

Very few people had remained in the station since the alarm had been raised making the job for the police that much easier. The station security operator viewing the monitors had alerted the police the moment he saw Cole confront Henry.

***

Down on the platform, Cole was still waiting for answers. It didn't appear that he was going to get any. Behind him was the exit and he could hear the heavy footsteps of the approaching police.

'It won't be long,' he said to Henry.

In the blink of an eye, Henry moved. Cole instinctively fired a shot. The bullet cracked the tiles on the station wall. Everyone within the Underground heard the echo; that distinctive crack of gunfire.

'Shit!' Cole screamed, his echo repeated down through the tunnels.

Henry had gone; disappeared down an interconnecting passageway to the other platform. By the time Cole had got there, Henry was about to exit to the other tube line, in the opposite direction to the advancing police. Cole gave chase once again. This time, angry and running on adrenaline, for he was now being closely pursued by a well-trained armed posse of police. He had broken British law and disobeyed orders. The agency wouldn't help him. For now, he was on his own. Using all his senses, listening for footsteps, Cole was barely managing to keep up with Henry, let alone gain ground. But then, around the next corner the American ran straight into the back of his stationary prey. The agent crashed to the ground, taking Henry with him. In the collision, he dropped his automatic pistol, watching it bounce off the curved porcelain wall before hitting the ground. In front of them both were five well-armed men, weapons trained on the two on the tiled floor. One of the men, swiftly stepped forward, bent at the knees.

'Identify!' the man called out. 'Identify!'

Henry said nothing.

'Cole. NSA'.

'NSA?' questioned the armed man.

As Henry and Cole lay on the floor not moving from their position, the weapons that were trained on them raised sharply to counter another threat. Cole looked over his shoulder to see another group of well-armed individuals, male and female this time. Their uniforms were black Kevlar body armour, similar to the first five, but on their right shoulder sleeve was a large embodied patch, a coat of arms. The patch, he did not recognise. On their left shoulder sleeve were, what looked like, small flags; the Union Flag, a white cross on blue and the French flag. Curiously, no sign of the word – police.

'Anyone here, American?' he asked.

Both armed units ignored the *foreigner*; their weapons trained on each other. The expressions on the gunman's faces told Cole the two groups hated each other. Then stupidly or bravely, even he wasn't sure which. Cole decided to intervene and stood up between the two lines of machine guns. He raised his hands in a motion to lower their weapons. Every individual ignored him. For a second, he felt very unimportant. He knew he had entered something new; a world that he knew nothing about, a war that his agency probably knew nothing about. However, events appeared to be getting worse.

'Henry!' greeted the leader of the second group of men.

'Troy!' Henry responded getting up and stepping behind the line of the men and women. 'Thanks!'

'I get the impression that neither side here are police?' Cole stated. 'Now, I've already been told today, that it is illegal to carry firearms in this country.'

'He with you?' asked the leader of the first unit ignoring Cole completely.

'We have orders, with regards to him,' replied Troy. 'He's not your concern.'

'What orders?' interrupted Cole.

The police could now be heard closing in on Cole's little shin-dig with his new found friends. Cole faced up to the second unit as they lowered their weapons.

'That's more like it,' he responded as he turned around to see if the first unit had done the same.

They had gone; disappeared without a trace. Silent and swift. They had left just as they had appeared. Cole spun back to the second unit, but they had also gone. So had Henry.

'Fuck it,' he quietly said to himself. 'I'm screwed!'

The agent snatched his gun and noticed that someone had lost their pendent. It was just like the one he had thrown in the canal in Carcassonne. He picked it up.

'FREEZE!' screamed a police officer. 'Do not move!'

Cole froze.

'I am NSA.'

'Do exactly what I tell you,' said the police officer in a perfectly clear voice. 'If not, you'll be DOA. Slowly! I repeat slowly! Place your hands above your head and look at me!'

Cole did as he was instructed. He knew he had messed up again.

'Now! Slowly get down on the ground! Spread your legs and your arms out! DO NOT make any sudden moves!'

Cole did as he was told.

XVIII

The First Realm.

London – 22.08hrs Monday 16th July AD 2001 GMT

'Time does not pass for those that live for eternity. As daylight fades and the creatures of the night come to life, the sunset reminds those that have lived since the beginning of time that another day has passed. This is the way of things. This has always been the way of things.'

'Shut up Gabriel!' Iinnad complained. 'That's just depressing.'

'Keep your voice down!'

'What?' replied Iinnad, ignoring the request. 'Who's gonna hear me? In fact, *where* are we anyway?'

Gabriel sat at the blackened oak table with his back to the complaining angelic. He continued to read aloud.

'They say that action speaks louder than words. Then let there be action. We cannot sit idle and watch time pass as day turns to night, over and over. Mankind has to learn; to learn one has to look with both eyes and listen with both ears for us to move forward. As the time draws closer for mankind to take that action, we see chaos all around. This chaos becomes clear in our eyes. When the mind is clear and focused, we see what has always been there, hidden in plain sight.'

'Enoch wrote that, didn't he?'

'Yes, he did. Among other things.'

Iinnad slowly walked clockwise around the small stone room, her hands out as though brushing long blades of grass in a field. Her fingertips gently touched the ancient trinkets, scrolls and manuscripts, leaving furrows in the dust. The room had a slight echo due to the large stone blocks that made up the floor, walls and ceiling. The main door was on the largest of the uneven walls and large enough to allow an angelic entrance, even fully transformed. *Their* entrance, if you could call it such, had no door *per se*, but for a ledge, which extended out into the darkness of a wide shaft. The shaft was also stone lined with the roof about twenty feet above. The base of the shaft was filled with water, thirty feet below the ledge and twenty feet deep. Iinnad sat down on the only other chair in the room and stared at Gabriel as he continued to make notes by candlelight.

'How long are we going to wait?' Iinnad asked.

'Abbadon will not be long.'

'I don't care about Abbadon,' she replied taking a deep breath and blowing a cloud of dust in Gabriel's direction. 'Abbadon is not my problem.'

He stopped writing and gently put his ink pen down. The chair creaked as he turned to face Iinnad. Resting his elbows on the arms, he stared at her.

'Why are you so impatient?' Gabriel asked. 'We rushed here, I agree, there was just cause. Now we are here. Nobody has died, so we wait.'

'For someone to die?'

'No.'

'But you're not waiting for Abbadon, you're waiting for the soulcarriers; and to be honest, we could have waited in a better place than this.'

Iinnad surveyed the dusty time capsule. The Archangel got up out of his chair and crossed the room to the opposite wall made up of a single block of stone, and placed his ear to it.

'What now?' Iinnad called.

'Sssshhhh!' Gabriel replied. 'Behind this stone lies the heart of an army that I once founded several hundred years ago, and this room is at the centre of that heart. I had it built this way so I had easy and instant access to my warriors without being seen by the lower ranks. That should answer your question, as to where we are.'

'I know that, I saw it in your mind, but if they are all going to die for you; why can't they all see you?'

'I hope none of them die for me. Die for this realm maybe, but not for me.'

'And easy access?' Iinnad interrupted. 'That water was *disgusting*.'

'It is called the Thames,' Gabriel explained with laughter. 'And it used to be a lot worse. A demonic will not survive that distance underwater.'

'I realise that, but the fallen can.'

'But the fallen can only glide, *not* fly, hence the shaft. For its time it was the best I could do.'

'Not bad,' Iinnad nodded. 'Not bad.'

The molten wax had dripped from its ledge onto the table. The monstrous sculpture of rippled layers, each a slightly different shade of colour, created from the hundreds of depleted candles, began to move under the heat of the flame.

'Why not use electricity?' Iinnad asked, staring at the flame.

'You sound like Cole.'

'It's a valid question.'

'The last time I was here, it had yet to be invented,' Gabriel replied. 'I tell a lie. I was briefly here to collect some things during the war.'

'And I thought it was one of your traditions. Apart from your research, it's nice to see that there is nothing from *our* time,' Iinnad said making a point of the fact that Gabriel should move on.

'We should not forget our past.'

'Says he, who has forgotten his own tongue,' came the sarcastic reply.

'I admit I have neglected my duties, which I am presently rectifying. This is partly due to Abbadon's interference, but more so, there is very little time left. Time - which you and I have taken for granted for so long, is running out.'

'No it's not.'

'On this Realm it is.'

Iinnad got out of her chair and stepped out onto the ledge again. She looked down into the darkness trying to make out the waters surface.

'Is it to do with the key?' she inquired.

For several seconds Gabriel said nothing; caught off guard by the question.

'No,' he replied calmly. 'The key has nothing to do with this realm.'

Gabriel watched Iinnad carefully for a response. There wasn't one. He began to unbutton his shirt, revealing the small piece of metal that kept Sataniel at bay.

'I have had this key for thousands of years. Believe it or not, sometimes, I forget what it opens. I have even misplaced it a couple of times.'

Iinnad glanced over her shoulder in shock at Gabriel's comment. 'You can't misplace something that important.'

'Maybe it would be better that way,' Gabriel continued. 'Lost, never to be found, never to be used.'

'But it's not lost,' Iinnad injected. 'You have it.'

'Maybe it would be safer if you had it, Iinnad?' Gabriel suggested as he held the rusting item in the palm of his hand.

'Keep it!' she ordered. 'You give it to the Council.'

'But I might lose it in the mean time,' Gabriel added with a grin.

'In all these years, you haven't lost it yet,' Iinnad stated. 'On the other hand you can give it to the soulcarriers on the other side of that wall.'

'The destiny of the First Realm is in the hands of a chosen few. The destiny of Sataniel in this hand.'

'And nobody has a clue.'

Gabriel's smile disappeared with Iinnad's snide remark. It was not easy to explain certain points to soulcarriers. The problem was that man either did not believe or took every word as gospel. After Gabriel's conversation with Jesuel, he had been very careful about who he revealed himself to. He had taught the Knights Templar of old to drop hints and ideas so that mankind would find the answers for themselves and believe the truth more willingly. With this in mind, Gabriel had to do the same again. Those on the other side of the wall possessed the presence of being, but they were still soulcarriers, and for a soulcarrier, seeing was believing.

'What are you going to do Gabriel? Open that stone wall, with your wings out and shout *I'm back*? Or are you going to sit here and read and write?'

Gabriel didn't answer.

'You could at least use a computer or *something*. You remind me of Enoch.'

'The handwritten form is slower,' Gabriel replied. 'And in that time you can revise what you wish to write. Yes, it takes time, but in this form I make less mistakes.'

'Coming from an angelic that has made so many,' Iinnad snipped.

'We shall wait, it will not be long.'

XIX

The First Realm.

London – 22.19hrs Monday 16th July AD 2001 GMT

Within Holborn Police Station, Cole surveyed yet another interrogation room. It was apparent that it was not as clean and well kept as the one at Heathrow. He sat at the table with his hands in front of him, handcuffed, staring into the mirror on the wall. The interrogating officer had no time for Cole.

'You have no statement to make?' asked the officer smartly dress in a grey suit, his I.D. hanging from his breast pocket. 'Nothing to say at all?'

'I bet a months salary Ambassador Grayson is watching me right now,' Cole replied. 'And if he's not, he'll get a copy of the video tape.'

'You're in a world of shit,' the officer claimed. 'But not that much shit.'

Cole was thrown by the statement. 'So, I'm not that important after all?'

The officer gave a nasal laugh. 'Armed and on holiday?'

'I'm on a case. I'm NSA.'

'I know you're NSA! And you *were* on a case. The US Embassy has already been in touch. You *were* to meet with Ambassador Grayson.'

'I don't have to answer your questions,' Cole stubbornly replied.

'Someone by the name of Garrett says you will and just to let you know – the Fifth Amendment or whatever is, doesn't apply here.'

Cole collected his thoughts. Quickly, he decided it would better to give his interrogator something. He didn't want to leave the British in the dark the way the French had been. He turned slightly towards the two tape recorders on the near wall.

'I had a suspect,' he started.

'And you know this suspect?'

'No! I saw him… … I saw him in DC. That's Washington.'

'I know the capital of the United States, Agent Cole.'

'He was also in Carcassonne, in…'

'… Southern France. I am not stupid Mr Cole.'

'Well I didn't know where it was, but I'm not stupid either.'

'A fair point,' the officer calmed down as he gave a passing glance into the mirror. 'So that gives you the right, to chase him from Heathrow to the city on the Underground brandishing a firearm, does it?'

'Everywhere I have been, someone has died! Everywhere I have been, I've seen this man; from DC to Carcassonne… and now here. *Somehow* this man's involved.'

'So are you!'

'What?' replied Cole sharply, questioning the statement.

'You said it yourself, everywhere you have been someone has died. Who is going to die here in London, Mr Cole?'

'You've got to be fucking kidding?'

'Do you have anything other than a trail of bodies?'

Cole didn't answer the question.

'Look at it from our point of view,' asked the officer leaning on the desk. 'In a way, you are in law enforcement. Do you see our situation? What are we to think?'

Cole understood, but he still said nothing.

The questioning officer shook his head at the mirror. Cole rocked his head side to side, clicking his neck. He could wait. How much more trouble could he possibly get into? The door opened and an elderly man in a tweed suit entered the room, his hands behind his back concealing something.

'Sir Geoffrey!' the officer quickly responded. 'I didn't know… this interested you?'

'I'll take over from here Detective Brent,' said Sir Geoffrey. 'I would appreciate it, if you could give us a minute. I need to have a chat with our friend.'

The Detective left the room, closing the door behind him. The elderly gentleman raised his right hand above the level of the desk and placed Cole's Beretta and ID on the table. He then approached the tape recorders and turned them both off.

'You're like one of those package holidays aren't you?' Cole said in jovial mode. 'I travel from 'A' to 'B' without a care in the world. And then, you make sure all my belongings get there before I do. I left them at the airport.'

'That's not very funny Mr Cole.'

'Have you got my bag? I left that at the airport too.'

The gentleman's left hand threw the bag down onto the desk. Cole had to smile.

'So, who are you?' Cole calmly asked.

'I *was* the Deputy Chief of Police,' answered the old man. 'I still have a lot of clout, which could be your saving grace.'

'And what do you want with me?'

'Hypothetically, as a police officer, nothing,' replied Sir Geoffrey. 'In another capacity, a lot things.'

'You say you *were* Deputy Chief of Police?'

'Now I'm not!'

Cole raised his handcuffed hands in gesture. Sir Geoffrey walked back to the door and gave it one sharp knock. It opened. He glanced over his shoulder.

'Agent Cole, I understand you can get out of those *quite* easy. Now get out of this station!'

***

22.29hrs Monday 16th July AD 2001 GMT

The City of London is the City on the Meridian, for the whole world the start of time. London was all you would expect of a capital city and once, for many decades, the most important City on the First Realm. However, those with the ability of flight brought the rain. The presence of the angelic and the fallen had formed the clouds. The large droplets crashed down on the bonnets and roofs of passing vehicles.

The pavements of the crowded city streets were empty. Every shop entrance was filled with people trying to avoid the downpour, with strangers rubbing shoulders with strangers just to stay dry. No one was prepared, not an umbrella in sight.

It was now late evening and even the nightlife had stayed indoors. Cole stood in the arched entrance of the police station and viewed the drenched street. He admired a group of young ladies as they crossed the glistening tarmac, their blouses wet through and clinging to their skin revealing their underwear.

'Too much of that and I could go blind,' he smiled and chuckled to himself. 'Or maybe I'll get arrested.'

He then thought of Rebecca, and maybe, he would just receive a black eye. He shook his head at the thought. The soaked ladies were met by a male friend, just as wet, his shirt transparent revealing the seams of its pockets and their contents.

Parked directly opposite, on the other side of the street, was a polished new Aston Martin with the shadow of a man sitting in the rear. The driver's door opened and a buxom brunette in a chauffeur's uniform stepped out into the downpour. Her peaked cap shielded her face from the water and the streetlight.

'Mr Cole!' she called. 'Mr Cole! If you don't mind?'

The chauffeur motioned to the agent to climb into the rear of the vehicle. Cautiously, the foreigner scanned the length and breadth of the street. There were very few people to be seen and those that were, were taking no notice. He stepped out into the rain. The chauffeur patiently waited for him and as he approached the car, he still could not make out the figure on the back seat. The ringlets of water running down the windowpane distorted the image too much. As Cole reached the car, the chauffeur, by now, almost soaked through, opened the rear door. The American bent down and wiped the water from his eyes to see Henry patiently waiting for him in the dry. The agent stood upright and turned to the chauffeur, staring into her dark brown eyes.

'You've got to be kidding?' he asked.

'Please Mr Cole,' she replied taking his bag and then whispered. 'I'm soaked.'

With an apology to the chauffeur, Cole briefly shook his clothes and climbed into the back of the car, whereon, the young lady closed the door and briskly jumped back into the driver's seat. For a moment, Henry ignored Cole and leant forward to whisper some directions to his wet driver. She removed her cap and carefully placed Cole's bag on the passenger seat, then started the engine. Henry sat back in his seat and mentally prepared himself as he turned to face the American.

'Who the hell are you?' Cole blurted out before Henry could say a word.

Henry had originally prepared a statement of explanation, but due to Cole's outburst it would be better to allow the evidence to reveal itself. Henry surmised that the agent was a man of little faith. Seeing was believing; and so Henry would have to show Cole who and what he was; then and only then, with his fingers tightly crossed, would Cole understand. The Aston Martin smoothly wound its way through the streets towards its destination.

'Who the hell are you?' Cole repeated.

'My name is Henry Sinclair and I'm not your enemy Agent Cole.'

'I saw you in D.C. I saw you in Carcassonne and now you're here.'

'So are you,' Henry said stating the obvious. 'As the police suggested, there are several individuals who can be placed in the vicinity of each crime. Does that make me the criminal?' Cole said nothing. Henry had already captured Cole's attention. *How did he know what the police had suggested; let alone which police station he was being held at?* And when these questions surfaced, there was another question, deep at the back of his mind. *How could anyone, obviously older than himself invade him so easily?* However, his first question was obvious.

'Where are you taking me?' he asked. 'Or is this to be more cat and mouse?'

'When you were with Special Forces, you were trained to observe,' Henry replied. 'My advice… observe!'

The American made himself comfortable in his leather seat and out of the window, watched the wet world passed by. He didn't aimlessly gaze out of the magnified windowpane, but took note of every street and corner the Aston Martin took on its route. The chauffeur only took the honeycomb of side streets; row after row of eroding bricks and mortar. The agent got the impression that they had not travelled far, just in circles, when finally the car pulled up under the canopy to the entrance of a small, but elegant hotel. From the architecture and the bustle of the streets, he concluded he was still in the heart of the city.

'Beats a police cell!' Cole said to himself as the footman opened his door. 'Do I have a reservation here?'

The three of them exited the vehicle and as Cole walked around the back of the car to join Henry, he noticed the chauffeur was following them, carrying his bag. She noticed the agent's inquisitive glare.

'I need a change of clothes,' she explained. 'The car will be looked after.'

She handed him his holdall and disappeared off to her left through a doorway marked concierge. Cole, now walking backwards into the hotel, keeping his eye on the Aston Martin, saw her replacement appear and drive it into the night. He spun around to admire the grandeur of the reception. In front of him, opposite the entrance, was the reception desk with a large carved stone disk five feet in diameter hanging on the wall behind. The elevators were to his right and the majestic marble staircase to the left. Henry received a nod of recognition from the receptionist as he passed on his way to the lifts. As Cole watched him, he took a key card from his jacket pocket and placed it in the lift control. The doors opened and Henry signalled the NSA agent to join him.

'Nothing ventured nothing gained,' he muttered under his breath.

***

The two men, apprehensive for different reasons, stood side-by-side in the enclosed space of the elevator as it continued downward. Henry had not seen his father since his wife died and was not too eager for the inevitable moment. The consolation was that he had an opportunity to see his son, but even that had mixed blessings. The discoloration in the layers of stone and brick were visible through the glass window of the door as the elevator continued hell-ward. *To an archaeologist,* thought Cole, *each layer of the earth's surface represented an event, a year, a lifetime or an age.* Whichever it may have been, it encompassed the past, stage by stage going back into man's history. The elevator was taking Cole back in time. This was no New Order for Internet conspiracy theorists; this was old, very old. So how was it that the NSA, answerable to but a few, with an unknown budget and countless facilities at its disposal, didn't know of these people? Agent Cole didn't get handed every unusual case, but an organisation like the NSA would have had its rumours. Somewhere down the line an individual would have squealed; even if only canteen whispers. Then suddenly the big question hit him. *Why was he being shown all of this? Why him?* He felt his damp jacket pocket; Soames' automatic was still there. Cole knew that Henry knew about the conversation in the police station, which meant he must have known that he was still armed. It could be overconfidence. But then, what if Cole was only a little bug in the middle of the proverbial anthill; they would have little to worry about.

The elevator stopped. Through the glass, Cole could see another reception area. On the wall opposite, above the aged marble staircase was a plaque.

Cole read the words aloud. 'As Above, So Below.'

Henry said nothing and opened the elevator door stepping out. He was grinning to himself at the fact that the agent was beginning to see. Cole cautiously followed, curiously scrutinising everything. The reception area had exactly the same layout of the hotel above, except for a large circular stone tablet, larger than the one above, about ten feet in diameter, suspended on the wall behind the reception des. The grotesque markings, recognised even by a layman, were of Mayan origin. A middle-aged man in smart dress stood below the Mayan calendar and with Henry, patiently waited for Cole as he slowly tiptoed about the reception, staring at the walls as one would in a curiosity shop. Henry wondered if the outsider was beginning to understand.

'As above, so below,' Cole repeated. 'This place mirrors the hotel topside.'

'Everything around you is as you see it,' explained Henry. 'But everything you see can have a dual purpose or meaning. *You* have to learn to decide which has purpose and which has meaning.'

The agent noticed that the man behind the desk nodded in agreement.

'Just when I thought I'd got it,' Cole said disappointedly. 'This disk,' he pointed. '…is Mayan?' Cole pointed up. 'The disk upstairs is different. It's small with a different design. It's not Mayan.'

Henry and the receptionist both smiled.

'No, it's not Mayan,' Henry emphasised. 'It's Aztec. They are different, but the same.'

'Henry's the best teacher I ever had,' the receptionist added.

Cole turned back to Henry. He was totally out of his depth, having trouble taking it all in. He was missing his wife. Rebecca's degree in ancient history would have helped to understand Henry's cryptic lines.

'You've noticed that both receptions are the same,' Henry said. 'But why?'

Henry then walked away down one of the corridors not even waiting for an answer. He knew that Cole wouldn't have one. He was right; he hadn't a clue. The teacher stopped just inside the corridor and waited for the student to catch up. The moment he did however, Cole stopped again. The corridor, to the left, was lined with small flags hanging from the ceiling. On the walls, were display cases, rows of them, filled with clocks, very old clocks.

'What's with clocks?' Cole asked.

'Timepieces,' Henry corrected.

'All I see are clocks.'

'That is an hour glass,' Henry replied as he pointed at one of the nearby displays, 'not a clock. Timepieces; every possible type imaginable. Every hourglass from every age, to watches for your pocket and wrist; we have sand and water clocks, pendulum, quartzes crystal and obviously digital ones; you name it, we have it. We even have an Atomic clock, although it's not as accurate as the NIST F-1 in Boulder, Colorado Laboratories; but we have one all the same. '

'Have you got a sundial down here?'

'We have sundials and candle clocks, what type?'

'I don't need a tour, but I have ask… why?' Cole said defeated. 'This is like one mad collection or… a museum, so why here? Or am I *missing* the *other* purpose?'

Henry smiled. Cole realised he had got something right, but what? Next time, he would reduce his options. He was starting to understand how to deal with this man. He could see why Gabriel worked with him. The agent's expression changed to that of a beleaguered man and Henry was forthcoming.

'A museum as such,' Henry explained. 'Most of what is here now, are replicas. The originals are kept in another... museum, our museum. If you have seen it in a museum and there are two in existence, then we have the other. If there is only one, then the one you saw was probably a fake and the original ended here, somewhere.'

'The museum's around the world are full of fakes?'

'No not at all, listen!'

'So every original timepiece is here?'

'Everything is here,' Henry proclaimed. 'Not necessarily on display.'

'You said, somewhere?' Cole was now confused again.

He followed Henry down the corridor of time. At the next intersection Cole stopped again. The intersecting corridor was lined with more display cases and the little flags still filled the ceiling.

'Coinage, money, every form of currency going, and gone.'

'And all the fakes are in the world's museums?' Cole snapped sarcastically.

'Luckily, no,' replied Henry. 'Unlike clocks, it's always easier to find more than one coin or note.'

'And everything is here.'

'From a dime minted the year you were born to a penny minted the year I was. As you said, a museum. And the flags you keep looking at; each is a shield or standard which represents every individual member who was of noble birth who joined the Order during the Crusades and since.'

'Wait a minute! Who you are people? And what do you mean, the Crusades?'

'You know, take up the cross, let's go kick Muslim butt. And then get our butts kicked.'

'How long has this place been here?' Cole inquired.

'Not as long as the Crusades,' Henry answered. 'Come on, there is someone you need to meet.'

Henry led the outsider to the end of the corridor, dropped a few steps that opened out a little at yet another junction and a wooden boarded floor. Cole stamped his heel hard on the oak panels.

'What's under here, the water of life?' asked Cole.

'A stream.'

'An underground stream?'

Henry gave a very broad grin. 'Yes, that's exactly what this is. It flows, like some of the knowledge you now possess, hidden from the people of the world, like the stream flows unbeknown to those above. We just boarded it up for safety.'

'So it's symbolic?' Cole questioned sarcastically.

'Don't you see? This is the essence of what we are. Father to son, mother to daughter; the knowledge continually flows.'

'We pass on what we've learnt,' Cole added.

Henry's grin informed Cole he had got something right. Everything around him held a secret meaning, something symbolic. The problem he had was that he did not think the way Rebecca did.

Down another set of steps and in front of them was a large re-enforced metal blast door with a keypad and a palm scanner. Henry placed his hand on it as the beam of light travelled up and then back down across the panel's surface. He then punched in his code on the keypad and smiled, like a child, at the camera above. Cole stood a few paces behind Henry, on the yellow safety line, as the blast door began to rise.

'What is this, NORAD?' he asked.

'We are blessed with 10-inch deep blast doors at every entrance. However, our security isn't as strong as NORAD, but it's sufficient,' Henry replied. 'Our best form of security is concealment.

'It works. I don't think the NSA even knows you exist, who ever you are.'

'The NSA is not a problem for us.'

The door came to a halt inches above Henry's head. Unveiled behind was a small underground platform with a train, four carriages in length, parked there. On entering the platform the blast door closed behind them.

'Is that to keep people out or keep them in?'

'Out!' replied Henry. 'The cars are old as you can see…'

'You're telling me!'

'But they are well maintained, fast and efficient.'

'Why not just buy new rolling stock?' Cole inquired as he viewed the carriages they passed until the two men reached the front car.

'To buy new stock without owning a railway line would draw unwanted attention; don't you think?'

'I guess a little digging and any agency could pick it up.'

'A rich train spotter could acquire one of these for scrap or the price of transport and shipping. That way nobody knows.'

'From what I've already seen, I would have thought with your contacts, getting new cars would have been easy?'

'When you're not working, do you buy a newspaper?'

'Yeah, what's that got to do with anything? And how did you know I don't buy one when I am working?'

'Why buy a paper when you read the one at work? You can afford to buy one every day, but don't. It's a question of money?'

'Or convenience!' Cole added.

'Do you drive or walk to the paper shop on your day off?' Henry continued.

'Back to the paper! I walk!'

'Why not drive? Why not have it delivered?'

'I don't get one delivered because… I don't always get one. And I walk because… I walk!'

'Wouldn't driving be easier?' Henry questioned.

'Yeah, but it's not necessary.'

'We have contacts, but we only use them when… …it's *necessary.*'

'Why didn't you just say that?'

'The more you learn by example, the less pointless the questions you'll ask. You are going to meet people that when they ask a question; they want an answer not an essay. When we are being social, idol banter is a given. When we are working, they will listen when it is necessary. Some of your questions will fall on deaf ears.'

The two men stepped onto the wooden ribbed floor of the nostalgic carriage and closed the door. Cole sat down, gazing down the length of the empty car, that old feeling that can stir forgotten memories took the agent back to his childhood.

'This reminds me of the subway cars in New York when I was a boy.'

'I thought you had always lived in DC?' Henry questioned, nodding to the only piece of modern technology on board, the security camera.

'I have,' Cole replied to the question late. 'I spent an Easter holiday in New York with my aunt. My father died the year I was born.'

The train began to move.

XX

The First Realm.

23.26hrs Monday 16th July AD 2001 GMT

Iinnad was bored. She sat on the ledge, her legs dangling over the water. Her earplugs were in, but the volume even Gabriel could hear. Frustrated, he forced his hand to his free ear and the other against the stone and listened. It was no use.

'Iinnad!' Gabriel barked. 'Turn that…'

The beauty swung her legs to the music from her personal stereo and bobbed her head from side to side as the electronic melody filled the air. She began to sing; badly.

'First… Tell me I am crazy… and I'm wasting time with yooouuuu. You'll never be MINE!'

Gabriel darted across the floor. 'Iinnad!' His hand clipped one of the headphones. 'I am trying to listen!'

'… just be gooood to me! So was I!'

Suddenly the floor began to vibrate. The ripples on the water could be seen by the candlelight. For a split second the two angelic stared at each other, then Gabriel rushed at the stone wall. He thumped at the stone.

He had to transform to gather his strength to move the stone. The Archangel turned to Iinnad; she was already on her feet and as she beat her wings in the confines of the small room the candle flames died.

'Out of my way moron!' she demanded from the dark.

Gabriel jumped aside as her footsteps marched towards the stone. The angelic raised her hands, but didn't stop. Gabriel could just see her slender frame strike the wall as a crash of broken tiles was heard over her music. The gap widened and both angelic were blinded by fluorescent light. Iinnad entered the bright dust cloud that had formed and appeared puzzled. She turned back to Gabriel.

'I think you seriously fucked up!'

'Iinnad, your language is unnecessary and I…'

Gabriel stopped. As the dust settled he could see the tiled walls of the tube station. The Archangel wandered out onto the platform; he glanced down as he kicked a broken tile into the sump that the track lay. He was astonished at what he was looking at. He studied the length of the platform trying to fathom what had changed.

'You may be right?' he said slowly.

'It's the Underground!' Iinnad stated the obvious. 'What were you expecting? We are *under* ground!'

'This should not be here.'

'D'you want me to help you move it?' Iinnad joked.

'This should not be here!' Gabriel raised his voice in anger.

Iinnad had never in all the years seen Gabriel like this. She stepped away from her favourite Archangel and viewed the tiny tube station. With Gabriel this way, she thought her humour would have to wait.

Calmly she spoke. 'When was the last time you were here, Gabriel?'

'I told you! Centuries ago!'

'The tunnel only goes one way,' Iinnad pointed out. 'Maybe this isn't a part of the Underground, but something else?

'This was once a great hall. This was the heart of…'

'… of the army you created?'

Iinnad wandered down to the blast door and tapped it. The echo filled the station. She tapped the cold steel again.

'Do not do that, some may hear!'

'Gabriel! This door would even stop me. As for hearing us? They can already see us!' Iinnad pointed at one of several security cameras that lined the platform.

'Get back in the room!' Gabriel snapped. 'Wait until I call for you!'

'Are you serious?'

Gabriel began to transform. 'Yes! Light a candle; read the books and learn!'

'Read the books? I read your mind, I know everything!'

'Get in the room and listen to your music!' Gabriel enforced. 'You can tell me where you got the Walkman later.'

'Is that what it's called?'

'Get in the room!'

Under protest Iinnad regressed back to her human form and did as she was told. Gabriel now fully transformed and with his strength closed the stone door behind her.

'What happened, William?' he said to himself.

With one beat of his wings Gabriel's feet left the tiled floor. He tilted forward and flew down the platform drifting over the rails and disappeared into the tunnel.

***

23.31hrs Monday 16th July AD 2001 GMT

Henry intensely watched Cole. 'How did he die? Your father.'

Cole glared at Henry standing in the aisle.

'I'm sorry I didn't think,' Henry added.

'That's ok. I don't know how he died. Unnatural causes. I think that's how most agents die.'

Cole paused. The agent stared out of the window at his reflection in the dark.

'You maintain the rolling stock with an old look about it. What about the line?'

'The original tunnel is lined with reinforced steel casing. The outer layer is made up of decayed brickwork.'

'Why? If it has no purpose.'

'Who says? Building contractors, London Underground tunnel extensions, you name it, when they come across a new tunnel, not on the maps the media jump on board. But…' Henry raised a finger. 'When they find a lost sewage tunnel or something; they first contact the records office, which is where we step in.'

'Contacts when necessary?'

'Something like that.'

The train stopped, shortly followed by a thud on the shell of the carriage from the rear. Then there was jolt to the side, uncharacteristic for a train. It gave the impression the carriage had been hit from the side and was being moved.

Cole stood up. 'That was quick.'

'We're not there yet.'

Henry sat down and the American joined him.

'The tunnel appears derelict,' Henry continued. 'It also has a dead end. Several massive hydraulic cylinders are presently moving us to another tunnel that will take us directly to the main base of operations. That way we can never be followed if the old base is breached.'

The side motion ceased and the subway car continued its journey at a much faster pace. Before Cole had even got comfortable, the fluorescent lighting of a very modern tube station illuminated the inside of the carriage. As the train came to a halt the doors opened and Henry, already on his feet, stepped out. Cole delicately followed.

The second station was nothing like the first. The shine of the marble floor stretched over seventy feet to the seven long steps that lined the portico. Behind the Romanesque columns was a semicircle of seven large open doorways. Imbedded in the floor of the semicircle was a mosaic of a compass, which pointed true north, although Cole did not know it at the time. In the centre of that was a red cross, its tips spread out in a traditional medieval style. Cole marvelled at the sight. The whole station could house twenty times the number of people than the older one, but as Cole looked around it was just as empty. Footsteps down one of the corridors caught both men's attention as two groups of five Orientals; five men in the first group and two women and three men in the second; entered the station followed by, presumably a member of the complex. The visitors glared at the two men as they passed. The five men were dressed in grey suits, businesslike in appearance, but carrying harsh faces. The men and women of the second group were all attractive, with short black hair, the women with harsh but dark complementary make-up; their clothes smart and elegant, but in contrast; leather and silk; the colours in black and red. They passed by the new arrivals almost in slow motion, but with no emotion and silent before boarding the train. The agent glanced over his should to watch the carriage leave, but saw Gabriel in human form standing there. Cole checked to see if the man that had accompanied the visitors was still about but he wasn't, obviously taking the guests back to the hotel.

'Hello Henry.'

'Gabriel!'

'Hello Richard.'

'How the hell did you get here?'

'He probably flew,' Henry jibbed as he mounted the steps; walked to the centre of the compass and faced them. 'Welcome to the headquarters of the Knights Templar,' he announced.

'I don't believe this,' Cole muttered.

'Don't believe what?' Henry inquired.

'Triads?' Cole motioned with his head to the departing train. 'Triads and Yakuza; great!'

'We don't deal with criminal organisations,' Henry enforced.

'They look like Triads… and Yakuza.'

'Looks can be deceiving. I thought you would have learnt that by now? Our organisation only has one goal.'

'Which is?' Cole snapped.

'We believe that people should find answers for themselves rather than be told. That way people believe more from what they learn than what is forced upon them.'

'Seeing is believing?'

'Yes!' Gabriel added.

'This complex is new to you Gabriel,' Henry turned to the angelic. 'So, you're both in the same boat. My grandfather chose to covertly move the headquarters here when he realised that the *museum* was becoming too big.' Henry began to walk down one of the marble corridors. The tourists followed. 'Originally it was just going to be a storeroom as such, but during the digging the workmen came across some caves which meant the complex became vast – we call it The Castle. It was then decided to move more than just artefacts here. My father made the decision to relocate the entire HQ. It was also his idea to keep the hotel and the underground complex in London as operational as possible. That way no one would suspect and the enemy would believe that we might be a little over confident. Gabriel, I take it, you've seen the hotel?'

'No… I came in via another route, but I am aware that time has passed me by.'

'I have a question,' Cole stopped as his echo continued down the passage. 'Actually, I have two. Firstly where the hell is everybody? This place looks like it could house thousands, but so far I've only seen one. Secondly, if those people weren't Triads, then who were they?'

Henry smiled. 'We have the man power, and as for the Orientals… that's none of your concern.'

'How do I know they're not a criminal element?'

'Because…' Gabriel slapped his shoulder and continued walking. '…Henry said so.'

Henry joined Gabriel as they left the American standing in the corridor.

'You coming?' the Templar asked.

Cole obliged. 'Henry I've just figured it out,' he called out. 'The only way I'm going to learn is when I say the right thing, you smile like a Cheshire cat.'

The Templar grinned and led the American and the angelic into the unknown. Within the heart of the Castle Cole could only guess as to how far underground he was. As the corridor widened Henry led the two strangers around a bend to the right and into the grand hall that made up the Command and Control room of the Knights Templar. Gabriel held back, disappearing from view, as Henry led Cole into the heart of the machine. Within feet of entering the C&C, the agent had managed to gain the attention of all those within. He stood in front of the main video screen with every station operator watching his every move. At the opposite end of the hall sat Sir William Sinclair, Henry's father. Quiet fell upon the room like a blanket as everyone waited for the Grand Master to speak.

Cole got in first. 'What? Never seen a black man before?' he broadcast.

The agent briefly stared at each face that was focussed on him, until he came across a black glare.

'I stand corrected,' Cole said to himself, somewhat embarrassed.

'It's not the colour, it's the continent,' Henry spoke directly into Cole's ear.

A blank expression appeared on the American's face as he turned to Henry.

'What the hell are you doing here?' echoed the strong Scottish accent around the hall. 'I could have been at the club, but I got called away because of *you*.'

The American lowered his head, not quite sure how to take this new face. Everybody he had met so far on his trip seemed to be a character of extreme in one form or another. *'Play the situation with caution until backed into a corner,'* he thought.

'He's referring to *me*,' Henry whispered.

The agent straightened his back and stood bold when he realised it was not he who was at fault. Henry didn't reply to his father's question. He knew it would make no difference as to what he said. His father was *always* right.

'Nothing to say?' echoed Sir William. 'All this time and not even a *hello dad.* And what about the American standing tall like a peacock! Have you...'

'Will one of you people here shut this silly old bastard up!' Cole interrupted addressing the room. 'I've had a really bad couple of days…'

Sir William stood up sharply. All those on their feet turned to face Cole and those seated stood immediately, in unison. All eyes were focused on the American. *Maybe he should have followed his thoughts?*

'Well!' Sir William broke the tension. 'No manners, typically American!'

'Likewise for a Scot,' Cole quickly replied with a smirk.

Sir William was used to the unexpected, but Cole's comment caught him by surprise. He paused for a moment as he monitored the room for some verbal ammunition. Cole began to approach the elderly man as he walked down the centre aisle with Henry in tow. The only sound was their footsteps chased by their echo.

'Agent Richard Lawton Cole NSA,' introduced Henry. 'My father, Sir William James Sinclair, Grand Master. He is...'

'I know what a Grand Master is,' Cole interrupted. 'I play chess.'

'No manners or respect,' Sir William added with a stern stare. 'So *you* are the idiot that's been running around, making a complete fool of himself. Is this your usual method of investigation, Agent Cole? Or, have you left the best bit till last?'

'Why are you so pissed?' Cole asked. 'I never saw any of your people out there... until today.'

'You wouldn't have! We've been too busy digging you out of the shit,' Sir William replied. 'If you had waited five minutes at the airport you could have walked away. Instead, *we* had to distract the police. *We* had to falsify paperwork so that you could walk away from a *police* station. Do you have any idea how difficult that is?'

Cole noticed the gentleman in the tweed suit walk across the hall and join Sir William on the steps by his *own* chair. The two elderly men stood there with their small aged smiles that only old men seem to be able to do.

'Even your own agency is not willing to help you,' Sir Geoffrey added. 'That puts you in our favour. Not that we particularly wish it. You offer us very little and we don't want the body count to rise.'

'I didn't kill anybody!' Cole started to explain. 'It was a woman...'

Sir William's expression changed. Cole had his attention. It was not until this point, that everything Cole had said, Sir William already knew. Now this was information he did not know. Cole had to play this very close to the chest.

'A woman?' Sir William inquired.

'Yeah! You know… with breasts.'

'It wasn't a large bulk of a man?' Sir William suggested.

'No. A woman, yeh high,' Cole said holding his hand out, palm flat to the floor, at his eye level. 'A real looker too… and fit. Nothing like Abbadon.'

Sir William's eyes lit up. The American knew he dealt a good hand. These people, these Knights Templar knew far more than he did. Not only that, but they could provide him with the information that Gabriel appeared to be withholding.

'You know him?' Sir Geoffrey asked.

'I've seen him, wouldn't want to know him,' replied Cole as he tried to bluff his confidence building exercise a little further. 'Obviously, not a friend of yours.'

'And *you* saw Abbadon, where exactly?' Sir William asked.

'Carcassonne,' replied the agent. 'In Southern France.'

'I know where it is,' replied Sir William sharply shaking his head.

'Everybody knows where it is, except me,' Cole chipped in glancing around the hall. 'So, who is Abbadon?'

'You've seen him; you know what he looks like; but you don't know who he is?' asked one of the operators, as though Cole was stupid. 'This is unbelievable…'

Cole faced up to the operator. He was half-caste in appearance with a broad beam, his white teeth on show. Cole's face was overflowing with confidence. Yet he recognised the voice. He also recognised the face, but he couldn't place it.

'Have we met?' he asked quietly.

'Yes we have Captain,' replied the operator. 'I was a lot younger then.'

'Mr Cole,' interrupted Sir William. 'I see you have crossed our path before.'

'It appears that way.'

The tension in the C&C began to subside and slowly one by one the operators began to return to their stations. The very low volume background chatter was reminiscent of Agent Cole's own working environment to the extent that the similarities were uncanny.

'I know that you can learn from us,' Sir William continued. 'There is a slight possibility, that we can learn from you.'

Cole glanced around the hall again. He took in all he could see; the make and model numbers of the terminals; operation stations; the programs that ran on the monitors and screens.

'I doubt it,' replied the impressed agent. 'You seem to have everything you need. The programmes you're using are the same ones we have. You're also using French Spot Imagery. You must have a KH 11 satellite up there, or something similar.'

'No, nothing of the sort,' replied Sir Geoffrey.

'Then how does all this work?' Cole questioned. 'You've even got programmes running on your monitors, which were designed for the KH 11. They don't work with anything else. So if you don't have one, why the programmes?'

'We use yours,' replied the operator with a slight laugh. 'If we put our own satellite up, everybody would know. And we can't have that, can we?'

'Concealment Mr Cole,' Sir William said as he loudly clapped his hands. 'Back to it ladies and gentlemen! Aston!'

The half-caste turned to acknowledge Sir William in military fashion, sharp, abrupt and precise.

'Aston, could you deal with Mr Cole. Rule 102 and 138 through to 40. We will talk later. As for my son...'

'I thought you'd forgotten,' Henry blurted out.

'I have,' replied Sir William sharply as he turned on the ball of his foot and left the hall.

'Henry, your quarters are dusty, but they've not been touched,' informed Sir Geoffrey. 'As you may already be aware, your codes have not been changed either.'

'Thank you Sir Geoffrey,' Henry acknowledged. 'It's nice to see you again. I wasn't expecting to.'

'And I you, Henry,' he replied. 'I'm just visiting. I'm an old man, past his time.' He then hobbled off following his old friend.

'Do I get a code?' Cole joked.

Nobody answered. Nobody had his poor sense of humour.

At which point, Henry leant on Cole's shoulder. 'You are in,' he whispered. 'As Gabriel requested. They don't trust you yet; so don't push it. Go with the flow and do as you are told. Your life is not in danger here. So, I'll see you later.'

With that, Henry vacated the room via another of the many exits. As he did so, his eyes roamed the hall as though he was searching for something or someone.

'Follow me,' Aston instructed.

The outsider did as he was told without question or complaint. As Henry had said, 'he was in', but who was Gabriel to request that he'd be in anyway? Who were these people? Obviously Knights Templar, but they were burnt at the stake or tortured by other means seven hundred years ago.

***

00.12hrs Tuesday 17th July AD 2001 GMT

Sir William sat at his desk in his private quarters. They had an aged appearance to them with the walls lined in blocks of limestone. He stared at the stone in front of him, studying the cracks and each grain that made up each block. The door was open; the corridor outside was new and polished, but Sir William had wished for his quarters to remind him of the Order's past, hence the appearance. However, it was the immediate past that concerned him. Henry entered and closed the door to give father and son some privacy. Henry also knew how vocal his father could get and he didn't want the entire Order to hear their conversation. The old man looked over his shoulder as the door closed, then back at the stone wall. Henry said nothing and patiently waited for his father to make the first move. Henry had patience; it was one of his redeeming features; standing, waiting and watching.

'So, you want me to start?' said his father. 'You were a good teacher once. Anybody can show someone how to do things; how to learn things. But you made them *want* to learn... And you don't get that everyday. You taught everyone the rules, you even reminded me of a few. Didn't you once tell me that 'you have two ears and one mouth, use them in that ratio'?'

'K'ung Fu-tzu said that,' Henry elaborated. 'Confucius... in Latin.'

'There you go again. Teaching me.'

'I don't mean to teach. I don't mean to correct. I know what's right and I know what's wrong and I like to show people the difference between the two.'

'And you do *every* time.'

'Is there to be a truce between us?' Henry asked.

'I'm talking to you, aren't I?' replied Sir William without turning around. 'I could have had you kicked out of the Castle, but I didn't.'

'No you couldn't,' Henry confidently replied.

'Yes I bloody could!' snapped Sir William, raising his voice as he jumped out of chair to face his son. 'Yes I bloody could! And do you know why? Because I'm the Grand Master! *My* decisions, not *your* actions, will determine the future of the Order.'

Sir William stared into his son's eyes in an attempt to get his point across. Henry bowed his head and admired the floor. How right he was to close the door.

'Every man and every woman,' continued Sir William, 'has their duty to perform within the Order, once they are enlightened. Tradition has always dictated that the age of enlightenment be twenty-one.'

'I know.'

'What else do you know? Did you know, that in the last 40 odd years, you are the only member of the Order who has not seen military service within her Majesty's army? Every member has managed to persuade, in one form another, their offspring to take their exams at 'A' level; leave school at 18 for three years military service. Every member that is, except me. How do you think that looks? By the age of 21, they have all the training and education they need for the Order. There is no harm in starting university at 21. Is there? Especially when you have the support of the Order. I'm referring to financial support… God only knows, students need it in this day and age.'

'I wanted to learn. I wanted to teach.'

'And then you went and met Alice. The only good thing to come out of that was my grandson. Who, I might add, is the only reason I did let you in.'

'I'll thank him when I see him; if he wants to see me. You forget I was also happy with Alice,' whispered Henry. 'But that doesn't matter does it?'

'No. This is a *military* Order and *you*… you ran away from your duty… your training. You ran away to learn *what*? You got married because you got a girl pregnant...'

'I came back!'

'You came back when Alice died and you couldn't even look after your son. You came back to tell everyone everything that you felt they needed to know. But you wouldn't accept the training yourself.'

'I'm not a soldier,' Henry claimed.

'You were *born* to be. But no! You ran away, again. And now, here you are. How many years has it been?'

Henry waited for his father to answer the question for him. A second of silence was stretched to a minute.

'Six years,' continued the senior man. 'What could you possibly do to further the Order's mission for six years on your own?'

'I'm surprised you didn't have me followed.'

'Don't flatter yourself,' Sir William huffed. 'I wouldn't waste the man-power. Each person has their place within the machine, and so do you.'

'But I told you, I'm not a soldier.'

'And yet, you managed to evade the NSA,' Sir William said in a raised voice. 'So don't bloody tell me you're not a soldier. You were born to it, remember?'

Henry walked across the small room to the untouched candle on the desk. He lit it and switched the table lamp off. Henry then returned to where he stood, by the door.

'Apart from pissing off the NSA, FBI and God only knows what other agencies in the U.S.; are you going to tell me what you've been doing on your one man crusade?

'I wasn't alone.'

'Not alone?'

There was a moment of silence as Sir William thought. 'Not that bloody American? Not him?'

'Gabriel is here.'

Sir William was stumped as he took in what his son had just said. The angelic that he had seen as a child was back. He had revealed himself to his son as he did to him all those years before.

'In London?' he asked calmly.

'Not exactly. He was in London.'

'And you know this, how?'

'When I saw him.'

'Why you?'

'He sensed me. I was walking down a street in New York and this man...'

'He's *no* man!'

'Well, he looked like one and he came up to me and asked me my name. I told him and he asked me if my father was James or William. I told him and you know what he said?' Henry paused for the answer that never came. 'He said, he remembered you. He said that he'd met you, only once, when you were a boy. He had been to an important meeting in Scotland and when he left the house, he saw a small boy...'

'Fall off a wall that I was climbing,' interrupted Sir William. 'He told me I reminded him of a close friend. He also said he'd come back, but he never did.'

'Well, he's here now,' said Henry. 'He might not be *in* London at this present moment, but he *was* in Carcassonne as well.'

'Let's say, I believe you. Does this mean that Gabriel has met

Agent Cole?'

'Yes, Gabriel is working with Agent Cole. Gabriel was brought in by the NSA, to help them with the murder of the Rossal family, in Washington D.C. They don't know what he is. I don't think the agent is aware of what he's in the middle of either.'

'Is *he* aware of what Gabriel is?' Sir William asked, attempting to keep up a hardened front. 'The Rossal's… so that's how Aston came by the information.'

'I think Agent Cole is more concerned about staying out of trouble to even consider that Gabriel is an angel,' Henry replied, ignoring his father's thought aloud. 'There is something about Agent Cole…'

'Yeah, he's a bloody American.'

'No… there's more. Gabriel likes this man. I don't know why, but I do know that there is more to this. I think we should keep him around.'

'You think *we* should keep him around?' Sir William snapped. 'I've just given him food and lodgings because you brought him here. Of course we're going to keep him around! I don't want that idiot out of my sight!'

'He's not an idiot. He's just out of his depth.'

'We'll see.'

Henry studied the floor. 'I will see you tomorrow, I need some rest. Do I still get my quarters?'

'Yes, Sir Geoffrey told you you did.'

'Just checking. I'll speak to James tomorrow. Goodnight.'

'Goodnight Henry.'

Henry pondered for a moment; waiting for some form of fatherly physical contact, but decided against it and opened the door. Stepping into the corridor, his father called after him.

'Henry! Have you told me everything?'

'No, I left a few things out, but you wouldn't believe anyway. Goodnight dad.'

Sir William smiled at the comment. 'So Agent Cole doesn't even know what Gabriel is? That's interesting,' the Grand Master told his shadow in the candlelight.

XXI

The First Realm.

KT Castle – 00.29hrs Tuesday 17th July AD 2001 GMT

Aston Benoit – Commander of the House, could trace his family back to Southern France at the height of Templar power in Europe around AD 1198. He was proud of his ties with the Order and had always excelled in every aspect that was put before him. Even his name said as much; Benoit – the blessed ones. Although he was young, only thirty-four years, he had the respect of many around him for his honesty and devotion to those within the Order and its goals. His father had been the Seneschal, until his untimely death in a helicopter accident five years previous. With that in mind, Aston had something in common with Cole, the element of living up to his father's reputation. Aston had no need to prove anything in the eyes of the Order, but in his, it was another matter.

The Templar Knight marched down one of the many corridors and turned at the next intersection. The American followed, trying his best to remember the route and gain an understanding of his surroundings. Unfortunately, every turn looked the same and he failed abysmally. He was in, but he was in so deep he could not see the surface. All he could do was hold his breath and wait until it was time to come up for air.

'What is Rule 102?' echoed Cole's voice down the corridor to Aston. 'In fact, what about 138, 139 and 140?'

'The Papal Rule,' Aston answered.

Cole was none the wiser as the two men stopped in the corridor by the entrance to the dormitory of six bunk beds. The bottom bunks were laid out with identical bedding, the top contained all the individual's personal equipment, again neatly and identically laid out.

'Yours is the furthest from the door,' Aston informed the visitor.

'And the Rules?'

'The traditional Rule of 138, 139 and 140, relate to the equipment and utensils that you require to exist within the Castle and that you would need in battle. Rule 138 is a list of weapons and clothing.'

'I have practically no clothes,' Cole admitted. 'I wasn't expecting to be here that long.'

'The Drapier will arrange for additional garments, if you require them,' Aston answered. 'Rule 139 relates to your bedding; 140 to the utensils you require to live.'

'*Utensils* I require, to live?'

'You need a spoon to eat cereal, don't you?'

'And I get all of this, in return for what?' Cole asked.

'You're American, therefore, your philosophy in the land of the free is that nothing is *free*. Everybody wants something for something. Welcome to Europe!'

'So this is free? I don't have to pay for anything?'

'That is up to the Grand Master,' Aston replied. 'Any of your spare belongings can go in the bedside cabinet. Everything that you need, you will find on the top bunk. My advice to you would be to familiarise yourself with the equipment that you have been given and the method in which they are laid out. Everyone is equal here Mr Cole.'

'And Rule 102?'

'Rule 102; the Marshal requires your weapon. It doesn't belong to you and therefore it should be handed over,' Aston replied holding out his hand politely.

'I thought you'd forgotten,' Cole spoke quietly as he placed Soames' automatic in the hands of the Templar. 'I take it I'm supposed to rest now?'

'It's late, I will see you in the morning.'

Aston left the agent alone in the dormitory to sort through his things. Cole looked around the room and noticed how tidy everything was. He opened his bedside cabinet and stuffed his holdall into it forcing the door shut. He lay down on his bed, rested his head on the pillow, and stared at the wooden slats under the bunk above. *A double bed would be nice,* he thought. Rebecca, although pregnant, would be a nice comfort by his side. Right now though, Cole had to play things very carefully. If this Order knew so much about him, then they knew he was married. He checked his mobile phone, but the battery was dead. *It would not be too much difficulty on their part in allowing him to talk to his wife? Saying that, would they let him leave the castle? Probably, but the chances were that the police would pick him up the moment he left the hotel.* Cole had given the American Embassy officials the slip too many times and Garrett would have been brought in for questioning by *his* superiors. As Henry had said, Cole would be safe here. So here was where Cole was going to stay.

***

KT Castle – 03.10hrs Tuesday 17th July AD 2001 GMT

How many days does it take to get over jet-lag? Cole thought. He hadn't slept for long. The door to the dormitory was open, he couldn't remember if he closed it. It made no difference; the corridor was quiet, unfortunately he was just restless. The offer had been made by Sir William to look around; *maybe he should do just that?* On the other hand, fresh air would be good, but a bathroom would be better. *Where were the toilets?* The agent got up; subconsciously found himself checking the neatness of his bunk before entering the corridor. He turned right; it made very little difference for he had no idea where he was.

Museums had never really interested Cole. As for mankind's past, Cole felt that he was 'Mister Average'. To catch a programme on the Discovery Channel or read an article that caught his eye was as far as his interest took him. But as Cole walked corridor after corridor he found a different type of attraction. These weren't museum displays the agent was looking at; these were mementos, mementos of mankind's existence. Several personnel within the Castle had passed him; and yet, only he was staring at the display cases. The others had become accustomed to them, as would any individual to a painting in their own living room. There was something else, a commonality amongst the collections. They were total. There were no individual items; from the very first to the very latest, whether it be a copy or the original; one version or another was present. A simple question sprung to mind. *Why?* The other point that had crossed Cole's mind was that he had seen no weapons. There were clocks, medals, plates and cups, and jewellery, even Faberge eggs, but not one knife, bullet or firearm. *It was time for some fresh air,* thought Cole. The agent asked the next person he came across the way to the train platform. He had already found some stairs that led to another level and more displays. In his brief travels he had also come across the mess halls and some of the recreation rooms, but he would need a map to find them again. He marvelled at the size of the place and for every step he took it would add another question to his ever-growing list that he was building in his head. The entire Castle was a working museum; a labyrinth that housed departments of science, research and development, astrophysics, intelligence and surveillance, an armoury, the living quarters and a hospital. Finally, he found the station where a carriage had just arrived. The doors opened and several smartly dress men and women crossed the floor, heading for the living quarters. One man stopped, the receptionist. It must have been a shift change, not realising how long he had spent wandering.

'Can I help you?' he asked.

'I wanted to go top side,' Cole demanded.

'Certainly, the car is returning to the hotel,' the man pointed.

'Thank you,' replied Cole realising his initial rudeness with embarrassment.

Just before entering the train, he stopped, anticipating a challenge of some kind.

'Do I need a card or password?' he asked in a more relaxed

manner.

'You're the NSA guy?'

'Yes, Richard Lawton Cole,' he said his hand outstretched.

The receptionist shook his hand. 'Allen, I'm Allen Greenwood.'

'Does that mean I don't get a card?'

'Not at all, you'll get a swipe card eventually.'

'But, can I go outside?'

'You must think you're a prisoner here?' Allen surmised.

'Yeah, I was told…' Cole hinted. 'Well, not exactly. Listen, if I wanted a secure line to say, phone my wife, could you do that?'

'I couldn't. Not un-traceable, not from here. Communications could.'

'I don't need un-traceable,' Cole stressed. 'I want to talk to my wife.'

'Within the Castle, you *want* un-traceable. But since you're going out. On the corner of the hotel building at the back by the soup kitchen is a telephone box. A red telephone box, you can't miss it, there aren't that many left.'

'Soup kitchens?'

'For the needy; the poor. It's been a tradition since the beginning of the Order.'

'By the soup kitchens... a red phone box? Got it!'

'Dial 550055 followed by your number in full. If anyone tries to trace it, they'll get a lingerie shop on the Edgware Road. The call won't cost you either.'

'Thank you.'

'It was put in years ago, but most people use mobiles now.'

'I know,' said Cole. 'But my batteries are dead and I don't want to be found just yet. Sir William offered me a trusting hand I feel I should return the gesture.'

Cole entered the car feeling a lot less apprehensive about his present situation. *It's all about mind games.* His last comment, he hoped, would be relayed back to Sir William, in turn giving him more access to the Castle. He was right. Allen changed direction, heading for the C&C the moment the train doors closed.

***

KT Hotel – 06.55hrs Tuesday 17th July AD 2001 GMT

The foyer was just what one would expect, at the break of day. The occasional customer and deliveries would come and go, oblivious to the goings on below. The concierge was signing for a large parcel. The innocent brown paper was just as misleading as the hotel.

At the back of the hotel was the soup kitchen for the city's homeless, just as Allen had described. On the corner stood the instantly recognisable old-style red phone box. Cole pulled at the heavy cast-iron door and entered the usual unpleasant odours associated with British phone boxes. He chose to wipe the receiver with a tissue before dialling home. The agent hated to be cryptic with Rebecca, but since he knew the call would be recorded, he didn't want to lie to the agency. With a pregnant wife, the delay in answering was expected.

'Hi darling, it's me,' Cole said in a raised voice. 'I'm in London.'

'I know. Garrett had his butt kicked over your little stunt at the airport,' she replied, not impressed. 'Upstairs has told him, to leave you to the British authorities. The only thing that seems to have impressed them here is that the Ambassador likes your determination and the fact that you just walked out of a police station armed. The British really don't like that sort of thing.'

'You heard about that?' Cole quietly answered.

'The entire intelligence community has heard about it. I just want to know how you did it.'

'I'll tell you, but not now.'

'Listen to me Richard. The US Embassy is not going to help you...'

'How far have they got on the trace?' Cole interrupted.

'Very close,' Rebecca replied. 'North London I think.'

'I'm sorry about all this. I miss you. I only phoned to see how you were bearing up.'

'I'm fine; worried about you, that's all.'

The line became muffled; plus the passing traffic on Cole's end didn't help.

'I'm not going to lie to my husband!' Rebecca screamed.

'Cole! This is Garrett! Now you listen to me!'

'You located me yet?' Cole asked ignoring the statement.

'We have,' Garrett declared. 'Just wait where you are and we'll pick you up. No authorities, just our people. Too many people are dead and we need to know what you know.'

'And I thought I was the criminal. I haven't shot anyone yet.'

'You're not a criminal. I know that; so don't run,' Garrett confirmed.

'Robert, I have no intention of running. You might not think I'm a criminal, but there are a lot of people who do. I'm just being careful.'

'Careful? Soames is dead!'

'Soames was a good man and he'll be impossible to replace. I know that,' Cole emphasised in agreement. 'The same woman killed Sean Grayson.'

'You know this? How?'

'I was there, I saw it,' the agent admitted.

'Richard, we've known each other for God knows how long. I know that you're doing your job, as you see it. I also know that upstairs wants you out of the picture, but the Ambassador wants you to stay. Unfortunately, the Ambassador doesn't work for the NSA, so you're off the case. Things are happening that just don't add up. Word is that when they send in a team to check out something new, chances are your name pops up.'

'Ask me anything,' the agent calmly said. 'I won't lie to you.'

'Where is the language guy? Gabriel doesn't appear on any of our computers.'

'I left him in Carcassonne, but he turned up here.'

'And you failed to mention to me that he was there.'

'I spoke to you before I knew he was here.'

'You know that thing in you hand? It's called a phone,' Garrett screamed.

'Tell my wife that I miss her and that I have a lot to tell her.'

'You can do that when you see her. You will be on the next flight home.'

'Why do you say that?' Cole asked.

'Because the police are there!'

'The police? Robert, you said this would be dealt in-house. What makes you think I'm in North London? Tell my Rebecca I have a lot to tell her,' Cole cryptically stated as he proceeded to hang-up.

From inside his glass and iron cubicle, the agent was protected from the elements. This was British weather in the summer. The agent scanned the street with his limited view before leaving the stinking shelter. Paranoia had started to creep in. Trained in subversive combat by stealth, one thing was very apparent to the agent as he walked the wet streets. Passing traffic was noisier in the rain, concealing the sound of any approaching enemy. The loudest noise his ears picked up was the raindrops hitting the hood of his jacket. He removed the hood. *Rather be wet than dead, but then, if these creatures can move at the speeds that he had witnessed, he would be dead anyway.* He raised his hood once more, concealment. Then changed his mind again.

'Hell with it,' he said to himself. 'I might have a fighting chance.'

Paranoia had set in. With his head down, the American briskly walked back towards the safety of the hotel, out of view of the security cameras that littered London. Cole, observant as ever, spotted a man in the doorway of a closed sports shop on the opposite side of the road. He was following his every move, but the hood of his raincoat hid his features. Cole stopped. Out of the corner of his eye, he could see the man's head stop turning. The individual pulled his hood from his head.

'Asshole!' Cole muttered to himself as he ran across the road to face the man. 'Hello Gabriel. Welcome to London.'

'How was your introduction to the Order?' he calmly asked.

'You planned that?'

'I asked Henry to take you in, yes! However, you cannot tell anyone.'

'I'm aware of that.'

'I will walk you back,' Gabriel said stepping from his shelter. 'Did you speak to your wife?'

'Yes, and Garrett; my boss. I'm off the case and they're looking for *you*. I'm supposed to go home, but I haven't finished here yet.'

'That is your choice.'

'I have questions,' Cole began. 'Why me? Why show me all this?'

'You were the investigating officer and…' Gabriel paused.

'… and what?'

Gabriel was staring at a blonde girl opening up the window grate on a shop several paces ahead. She was slim and her hair shone in the morning sun that poked its way through the gaps in the rain clouds.

'The girl catches your attention, but you don't see Iinnad; interesting,' Cole pointed out. 'You were saying?'

'Sorry… I was saying, that I felt there was something different about you. I felt you could handle the situation. If you cannot, then tell me and I will arrange for you to return home on the condition that you speak of none of this.'

'I'm staying. I have a killer to find.'

'Then I will see you soon,' Gabriel quickly spoke, as he began to cross the road.

'Wait! Why didn't you show yourself to the Templar?'

'Neglected duties; the Templar are not ready for me,' Gabriel shouted back. 'Henry is smoothing the way. I might add that you are not helping. See you soon.'

Gabriel left Cole to return to the hotel and back to the Templar.

XXII

The First Realm.

Apolyon HQ – Paris 08.44hrs Tuesday 17th July AD 2001 GMT+1

Gérard de Ridefort was a proud man. A little too proud some would say.

As Grand Master of the Knights Templar, Gérard was revered in the Levant, respected by kings. All his misfortunes of his former life were flooding his head, but that was in the past. However, on this occasion he had followed his instructions to the letter, even if he had trouble reading it.

The past Grand Master bowed his head in the presence of the Dark Lord, Abbadon. The elderly man stood in the light from the window, with the distorted statues in his peripheral vision, in a hope that he would not become one again. It was said that it reminded his superior of Amente. Gérard had been prevented from going there, so was therefore ignorant of the significance of his surroundings.

'The girl is in the boardroom,' he informed Abbadon.

'Awake?'

'Yes my Lord, for some time now.'

'So, you managed the task without too much trouble my old Grand Master?'

Gérard frowned at the comment to his past. He still regretted his deal and passed each day awaiting a way out. It was not going to be today.

'I take it Kell was helpful?'

'Yes my Lord. He provided the breathing bottle, for the plane ride back,' Gérard replied impressed with the smoothness of the operation. 'He also made her sleep, with a needle, like 'Sleeping Beauty'.'

'You've been reading?'

'Books for children. I never learnt in my former life, but now, I have to.'

'Show me the girl.'

Abbadon walked the length of his office, straight up to the boardroom doors. He gently opened them and entered. Naomi stood by the window, the morning sun brightening her clothes revealing the cut all the way down her back. She ignored the beast, staying put with the boardroom table between them both.

'Welcome to France.'

Naomi calmly turned to face her captor.

'So you're the fucker that sentenced my family to death?' completely out of character. 'I understand you're Abbadon.'

The tone and phrasing of the question caught Abbadon by surprise. He thought the girl would be a walk over, fearful and easy to manipulate. He was wrong. She was overflowing with hatred, similar to her kidnapper. In Abbadon's eyes, the only difference between them was that Gérard de Ridefort knew his place.

'Yes,' was the only word to reach Abbadon's lips.

He took a deep breath and walked around the table meeting the petite girl halfway. She faced up to the monster inches from his face.

'Now this is where I make a mental note that at some point in the near future, I will fucking kill you.'

Abbadon did not flinch, but then neither did Naomi.

'Such beautiful skin and a lovely neck. I could snap your spine like that,' he said as he flicked his fingers.

'So why don't you?' she replied tilting her head and brushing aside her hair.

'Don't push it little girl.'

'Push what? You killed my family; I have nothing to live for. If you wanted me dead you wouldn't have gone to the trouble of dragging me all the way over here, to France, of all places. St. Lucia would've been nice.'

'You over-estimate your importance. You're not that important to me.'

'So kill me,' Naomi demanded and then shook her head. 'But you don't want to kill me, do you?'

'I don't *need* to kill you,' Abbadon carefully replied. 'You're to be used as a weapon if need be. If not, then I'll kill you. Is that fair?'

'And I thought you would have me as bait?'

'*I am the bait*. You are required to create instability.'

'You don't think you can beat him?' Naomi deduced. 'You need an edge.'

'He may have friends.'

'And if he doesn't, you'll use me anyway.'

'I want to fight Gabriel one to one.'

'Something to prove, have we?'

Abbadon, although beginning to lose his patience with the assertive young lady, stood his ground. Naomi was right about one thing; she had nothing to lose. That on its own was going to make her difficult. However, there was something else.

'For someone of your kind, in this situation, you seem to take this all well within your stride.'

'Someone of my kind? You mean human? I like Sci-Fi, which means I have an open mind, and I'm not *stupid.* And…'

Naomi walked around the boardroom table and through the double doors into the darkness of the adjoining office. Abbadon didn't follow her, but stood facing the windows smiling in anticipation of the reaction he was about to get.

'SHIT! Is this what it's all about?'

The beast continued to smile until he heard the sounds of a struggle behind him. Gérard, at his age, was having great difficultly holding Naomi down on the floor.

'She tried to break the display my Lord,' he said out of breath.

'Tried? Yes! Failed? Most certainly,' Abbadon smirked. 'Now you see, I already have what I wanted. You're not important.'

Naomi gave up the fight and hammered the floor with her fist. She hadn't the strength to remove the old man that sat on her.

'You killed my family for two pages of some fucking book?' she screamed.

'No, I had your family killed to get Gabriel's attention. Does that make you feel better? We knew Gabriel was stateside, we just didn't know where. The time was right, and I hadn't the time to sniff him out. We hadn't seen him in 700 years, so I wasn't sure what he would look like. I wasn't to know he hadn't even grown a goatee.'

'So he really is an angel?'

'You're fighting Gabriel?' Gérard asked quite surprised. '*The* Gabriel?'

'Oh yes, as Grand Master you would have met him. He always made a point of meeting each new head of the Order. Funny,' Abbadon paused for a moment. 'Gabriel really doesn't think I know and yet I know everything about him.'

The towering man beamed to himself thinking back to the conversation he had in Carcassonne. 'I have a few tricks up my sleeve,' said Gabriel inside the beast's head.

'Are you saying the pages were a bonus?' Naomi questioned. 'Nothing more?'

'A bonus. Nothing more,' Abbadon repeated as he squatted down beside the squashed girl. 'You see, these pages,' he continued pointing to the circling display. 'Are from the Book of Gabriel. The history of his life *and* it is said his death.'

'Gabriel's been around a while. That makes it a pretty big book.'

'Originally written almost twelve thousand years ago. As far as I'm aware, what you see here is the earliest known copy.'

'If it was written thousands of years ago then there has to be a load of prophesy in it?' Naomi said struggling to get her words out with Gérard still on her back.

'Only the latter pages. When I have completed my collection, I could publish it just to cause havoc in the religious community. I don't think the Roman Catholic Church would approve. In fact, I don't think any church would approve.'

'So why do it if it would draw attention to you?'

'Why not? You think I care for the soulcarriers?' Abbadon gasped.

'What?'

'You! *Humans*!'

'Yeah, you do. You're fallen aren't you?'

'Yes I am,' Abbadon said proudly.

'You fell from grace because God gave us souls. You felt you deserved them.'

'Not just a pretty face and beautiful skin.'

'I hadn't finished,' Naomi continued. 'You not only fell from grace, you also fell for human females. Angels and humans are a no no. Aren't they?'

'Like I said, not just a pretty face.'

'Give me the chance and I'll destroy this book solely because it means that much to you.'

'What a silly reason. Why do you tell me everything you want to do knowing that you never will? Gérard will get you better clothes, the funeral attire has served its purpose. As for escape? You can't, but you'll probably try. If you do, I'll tear your feet off. That I promise.'

Gérard climbed off the struggling girl, pulled her to her feet and led her out of the office. In the quiet, Abbadon's attention turned to the shadows behind his desk.

'What do you think?'

'I think you should have killed her,' replied Lilith from the shadows. 'I've said it before, there was a time when you would have.'

'And as the pure blood angelic say, times change.'

Abbadon removed a small leather bound book from his pocket and placed it on his desk. The antique brass clasp clicked against the polished hardwood surface drawing Lilith's attention to it. She stepped into the light.

'Another museum piece?'

'Probably, this could very well be the answer to dealing with Gabriel's soulcarriers.'

'And where did you pick it up from?'

'Aha!'

'So what is the importance of this little book?' Lilith stared at the leather bound antique.

'The Papal Rule. Its entirety, and before you say it, it didn't belong to Gérard.'

'How does this little book help us?'

'Gabriel is a being of tradition. He follows the rules and this,' Abbadon said tapping his finger on the cover. 'This Rule book. His soulcarriers follow this to the letter. Rules of engagement are listed along with rules on eating, sleeping, praying and how many weapons, squires etc, that each knight can have.'

'Didn't you just say, times change?'

'Yes, but Gabriel is a creature of habit. I know him.'

'What if he breaks the rules?' asked Lilith.

'I don't think he will. He has to tread very carefully; otherwise he'll get punished again. At the least, taken off Realm and return in a couple of hundred years again. For now, all we can do is get everything in place and wait. It's Gabriel's move now.'

XXIII

The First Realm.

KT Castle – 08.59hrs Tuesday 17th July AD 2001 GMT

Sir William passed the CD to Aston.

'Put it on the main screen Aston,' he instructed. 'This information involves all of us. It's only fair that we should see it for the first time together. This way it'll avoid rumours starting.'

Aston began to load the files into his terminal. The first file was a picture of a building, the headquarters of Apolyon Inc.

'Apolyon Incorporated,' announced Sir William, 'is where he lies.'

'And we are to attack it?' asked Aston.

'No not yet.'

'We don't know their strengths or their weaknesses,' added Sir Geoffrey. 'Observing the enemy can take time.'

'Through history we've known that every now again man has been forced into situations that were not his doing,' stated Sir William. 'I've believe that Abbadon, second only to Satan, has been behind it. Not all of it, just where it mattered.'

'So when are we to take on Satan?' asked one of the operators, laughter in her voice. 'Why not go to the top?'

'We don't, God willing,' Sir William replied. 'We have very

little writings on Satan. I think that scholars have mistaken Abbadon's work for his Master's. And I bet that pisses him off. He's out to prove himself. How far is he willing to take it and for what reasons? That's what we need to find out.'

Everyone in the C&C listened to every word. Since Sir William had become Grand Master, he had made many speeches in an attempt to make the members of the Order believe in the stories as much as he did. He wanted them to know he was right in what he was attempting to do. That was, to fight back. But to fight an invisible enemy with an army that could not entirely understand had been difficult at the best of times. It had been said before, they were only human and seeing is believing.

'You all know,' Sir William, continued, 'that I continued with my father's research after he died. And it was within the Chamber of Records that I found the puzzle and piece by piece, I began to put it together. Some of you have been sent on missions to the furthest places in the world and turfed up nothing. You might have thought it a waste of time, but I believe we had just missed opportunities. The pictures and data you see on the screen were provided by Henry, my son. He was instructed to gather this information by Gabriel.'

The hairs on the back of Henry's neck stood up. Was it just a CD of information that had brought father and son back together or the information that had begun to bind the Order together? Henry thought it was more than that. His father and grandfather had studied the books and sieved through the research. Now it was Henry's turn.

Sir William sat in his chair and with the rest of the operators, read the information as it scrolled up the main screen. Henry stood nearby chuffed with himself. If Henry's father had up dating his knowledge on the latest technologies, then maybe Sir William might have eventually found out that Apolyon Inc existed? But Henry, like his father, had a streak of 'old school' in him, and would rather spend time in a library, even if he wouldn't admit it.

The text on the screen listed the financial status of Abbadon's holdings from official records and the images showed the employee's. One employee would be the same as any other, but this was Apolyon Inc and these employees were demonic. The operators would have to memorise each and every face. This was the first time the Knights Templar were in a position were they could potentially get the upper hand.

The main screen flickered. Interference from somewhere was affecting the electronics. Sir William felt the tremor in the armrest of his chair and then a noise from behind, the grinding of stone. He stood up and passed a glance at the engraved wall behind. A small cloud of dust appeared from the ceiling and the whole wall began to move. The Templar were alert and prepared to avoid the possible threat. Sir William noticed his son had a smile on his face. The fear left him. Calm and collect, the Grand Master held his arms out motioning for everybody to stay calm.

'Is this what I've been waiting for, for the past sixty-seven years?'

The sound of grinding stone echoed through the great hall as the engraved wall slowly slid into a recess behind one of the freestanding pillars to the right of Sir William. Behind the other pillar, near to were Henry stood, a gap became visible, only an inch to start with, but it grew.

When the gap had widened to over three feet, it stopped. The dust settled. Sir William could see a flicker of light reflecting off the smooth surface of the stone doorway. The candle in the chamber was affected by the draft. Sir William knew what was to come, but what surprised him was that he did not know of the hidden chamber. Then how did his son? He was aware that a chamber existed in the old complex, but had no knowledge of one being built in the new one. The chamber itself; was almost the same in design to that of the original, only slightly larger. The shelves were empty as were the desk and drawers. The chamber had been made with Gabriel in mind, but no one had transferred his belongings. Over the years the secret was forgotten.

***

Iinnad was still waiting in the old chamber, annoyed, but dry. She had been listening to her music as requested until the batteries had run out. Now she was reading by candlelight, but her patience was wearing very thin.

***

Gabriel had to leave her there. This was to be his moment and the Knights Templar didn't need distractions. The Archangel transformed back into human form and brushed the stone dust off his hands as he stepped through the opening. The first person he saw was Henry, standing to his left at the bottom of the steps. He didn't acknowledge him. Gabriel was there to recognise Sir William and the position he held, not Henry and their friendship.

'Hello William,' he said, 'you have grown old.'

William said nothing. For sixty-seven years he had prepared numerous speeches for this moment, but now that moment was upon him, he chose to stay silent. Gabriel had not changed; he was just as he had remembered.

'The last time I saw you, you looked different,' Sir William said quietly.

Gabriel took a quick breath. 'Yes,' Gabriel remembered he had his wings.

The Archangel approached Sir William with an open hand. The Grand Master didn't accept it; the situation was beginning to sink in. His astonishment began to turn to anger. The angelic embarrassingly retracted his hand.

'It's been sixty-seven years!' Sir William said loudly. 'Have you any idea what has happened in that time? Have you any idea what we have achieved without you?'

'I'm sorry William, I should not have left it so long.'

'It was Gabriel who told me to gather the information on Abbadon,' interrupted Henry. 'I wouldn't….'

'Because he needed it,' snapped Sir William. 'I know! You told me.'

'That is not true.'

'We are *born* to serve,' replied Sir William sarcastically. 'You're the angel and… we mere humans do what *you* say.'

'No, I disagree,' Gabriel argued.

'You're right, we don't.'

Gabriel looked a tad confused by the reply.

'How can we do what you say when you're not here?' Sir William elaborated. 'You'd be surprised what we have become in your absence.'

'I believe I would be,' replied Gabriel attempting to calm the Grand Master. 'I used my old chamber, but damaged the platform wall when I opened the door. Sorry.'

'I have already been informed of the damage.'

'Do you want me to pay for the repair?' Gabriel asked.

'Don't play games with me,' Sir William retorted. 'Just tell me what you want.'

'Ok I will,' Gabriel said, changing to a more positive tone and taking centre stage. 'You have all briefly seen the data that Henry provided. That is Abbadon's headquarters.'

'We know,' Sir William remarked.

'But you are not going anywhere near it,' Gabriel explained. 'That is because I will. This is not your fight.'

'I'll join you,' Cole called out from the far back of the hall. He was still wet and had missed most of what was said, except 'Abbadon' and 'HQ'.

'Agent Cole, I will do this alone,' replied Gabriel.

'No you won't,' Cole protested as he walked the length of the hall.

'Why not attack?' Aston asked a little sheepish.

'Abbadon says he knows everything about me. That would therefore include all of you.'

'He does know,' Sir William expressed. 'He knows about the

hotel and the complex beneath. He probably doesn't know everything, but he knows enough to do damage; real physical damage.'

'How do you know?' Cole injected.

'Commonsense. In the short time that I've been researching this *Destroyer*, I have found out a few things. He has had several life times to gather all manner of information. He was around when the hotel complex was built.'

'I did not sense him,' Gabriel added.

'I take it, you were there too?' Sir William questioned.

'Was he here when *this* place was built?' Cole blurted out. 'Because if he was… we're in the shit!'

'I do not know,' Gabriel pondered.

'You weren't here, when *we* built the Castle?' Aston asked.

'No. I did not know about this place. If I had I would not have damaged the station. I would have come straight here.'

'Well I doubt that Abbadon would have missed out on that one,' Sir William said with a hint of disappointment. 'Another problem that crops up more often, thanks to man's ability to increase the power of a computer every six months, is keeping our anonymity. We are an organisation in hiding, not an individual. Not only that, for some of us in our other lines of work, it is not easy to stay out of the public eye. With Abbadon, we don't even know what he looks like.'

'You will know when you see him,' Gabriel admitted.

'I'll vouch for that,' Cole added.

'There is something else; the Rossal family highlighted that,' Sir William announced. 'Abbadon seems to know who we are, every damn one of us. We have always been very careful, but when we bump into one Abbadon's people in the street, they aren't discreet. They open up on us straight away; without regard for themselves or anyone else. It's as though it were instinct.'

The damp agent joined Henry at the foot of the steps. He noticed the large parcel addressed to Gabriel behind him, as the one the concierge had to deal with. 'Attention of Gabriel c/o Henry Sinclair' read the label. Cole could also see that the tension between the angelic and the Grand Master was not subsiding.

'Gabriel, why don't you want these people to attack Abbadon?' asked Cole believing he already knew the answer. 'These guys are trained.'

'Because it is my fight, not that of the Templar,' he replied. 'I will not have any one risk their life for mine. Abbadon wants me. That is why he tried to get my attention in Washington.'

'Washington! That reminds me,' Sir Geoffrey piped up, who had stayed completely out of the way until now. 'Naomi Chevalier was removed from her hospital bed by force yesterday. Ugly creatures, power cuts and two dead police officers are the few pieces of description from eyewitness reports. I can only guess that she would be in Europe now. The report said she stepped through the floor.'

'What!' A chill went down Cole's spine.

He remembered the black slime kitchen wall in the Chevalier's home. The eyes in the hall were now staring at the American.

'When were you going to tell us about Naomi?' Henry urged. 'Or did it slip your mind?'

'I didn't know about her,' Cole came clean. 'I've only spoken to my wife. Can we get back to Abbadon please, because I have another question. Does the Castle have any forms of defence?'

'We have a few tricks,' Aston answered. 'But then we don't need many, we're a couple of hundred feet underground.'

'A few tricks. These people don't seem to care anymore,' Cole responded. 'You're gonna need more than a few tricks. Your best defence is stealth. What about the hotel complex?'

Aston stepped forward. 'Like I said, we have a few tricks.'

Cole shook his head. 'They can't find you here, but they know where you are in London, you said so yourself. Which means you have no defence. Even the blast doors at the station are nothing to them.'

'Although I disagree with a lot of what Agent Cole has just said, he has got one thing right. Abbadon could just walk into the hotel,' said Henry.

The older section of the complex was built with metal sheets inserted into the ground on the out sides of the walls,' explained Gabriel. 'If anything starts to come through electrify the sheets. That should slow them down.'

'Slow them down?' inquired Sir William.

'Excuse me,' Aston butted in with a raised hand. 'A lot people here are going to be putting their lives on the line. You've got *some* convinced, but for the rest of us, we have just words, and words aren't enough – I'm sorry.'

'I haven't been here for you in sixty-seven years. In that time there have been five or six wars. In each case man fought and died because of a few words.'

'But we are bloodline,' replied Aston. 'If I die, my line ends with me. I apologise to the Grand Master for my rudeness, but I need more than that.'

Several of the lower ranking Templar nodded and muttered in agreement. Sir William was on the side of the majority.

'I am not asking *any* you to die for me,' Gabriel pleaded.

'Maybe not,' Aston answered. 'You're asking us to die for our Order and for our future. We'll choose if we wish to die.'

The Knight Commander, Troy Lavarda burst into the C&C like a thunderclap, breaking the silence and prolonging the challenge against the angelic.

'What I miss?' he snapped.

'Gabriel is to prove who he is,' Aston explained to his friend. 'It's that or we go to war on words.'

Troy waved at Gabriel. 'If it's all the same to you, lets see some wings.'

'I'd go along with that,' Cole supported. 'I maybe the outsider here, but… lets see some feathers.'

The room went silent; partly in anticipation and also because they knew that if Gabriel was really to change, they would see more than they would expect.

'From what I have seen, some of the intrusions and operations that the Order has carried out without my knowledge…'

'Without your knowledge!' blasted Aston. 'You weren't here!'

'Aston, let Gabriel speak,' ordered Sir William.

'You are right, I was not here,' Gabriel began to explain himself. 'If I was I might have said something. I might have stopped you from involving yourselves in the affairs of the angelic. To Abbadon, this Realm, your lives and deaths are just a part of a game. Like a game of chess, some games you win and some you lose. And yes,' Gabriel nodded. 'Some of you may die, but I do not want to see a single wasted death. Mankind over the years has learnt so much, but those of the bloodline have learnt the most. Knowledge is precious and should be treated as such. I have already said, that this is my fight, not yours. Nobody here has to die. I have seen this place and through conversations with Henry, I realised that the Order had grown. I did not come here to order anyone about. I did not come here to take command. I came here because of all the places on this Realm, what is behind this stone wall, is what I call home. Not the Castle, just the twelve square feet in there,' Gabriel pointed to the gap in the stone. 'If you do not want me here, then I will return to my room and close the door.'

'We still have much to learn,' Sir William said calming the situation further. 'Don't close the door. If need be, we will be wherever you need us to be, but seeing is believing.'

'Seeing is believing; indeed,' Gabriel whispered to the Grand Master.

Gabriel's body shuddered as the pain of the transformation began to travel through his veins. The Knights Templar took a few steps back. The Archangel hid the agony, as the tips of his wings broke free from their scars on his back. The angelic managed to stay on his two feet, but steadied himself with the help of the back of one the high chairs. When the transformation was completed, Gabriel paused for a moment to get his breath back. He stood tall; his wings raised high, the skin membrane stretched from bone to bone, from joint to joint.

‘I am Gabriel,’ he broadcast to the great hall. ‘Archangel, one of seven on the Council of the Seventh Realm and I stand as Guardian of this Realm. Is there one within these walls who does not believe? Is this how you remember me, William?’

‘It’s an improvement my Lord,’ Sir William joked bowing his head.

‘You don’t serve Gabriel,’ Henry whispered to his father.

‘So do not bow William,’ the angelic finished the sentence. ‘Speak to me as you have done. If you feel anger or disappointment, then express yourself, as you have done.’ Gabriel grabbed the old man’s shoulders with both hands. ‘It is good to see you William. I remember when you were eight years old and fell of that wall. You saw me, but you were not afraid. Now…’

‘Now!’ Sir William interrupted. ‘Now I’m a tired old man.’

‘Let us talk William,’ Gabriel said leading the Grand Master into his new room.

With less effort Gabriel transformed back into human form. He gave Henry a reassuring wink before disappearing. Sir William peered into the dimly lit room. The candle gave enough light for Sir William to find a place to sit. The ever-observant man glanced around the empty chamber, impressed with the private place.

‘A nice collection, but no videos,’ joked Sir William.

‘No electricity either,’ Gabriel returned the jest.

‘We can fix that.’

‘Thank you, but I like the candle light.’

‘I’m sorry for the entrance like that. I heard your voice and I needed to meet you first. I knew you would recognise me.’

'I heard you tell my father what you are probably going to tell me,' Sir William began. 'When you came outside the house that day, I ran, but fell. I thought you were there to kill my father. I wasn't afraid of you; I was just too young to fight you. I thought you were the evil my father had spoken of. He came out of the house after you had gone and the smile… the smile on his face, I still see it in my dreams. He knew he was on the right side. Whatever war, whatever battle was to come, we would prevail. I wanted to be just like my father and take the Order to a new level.' Sir William climbed out of the chair to finish his story. 'When he died and I was elected Grand Master I thought you would come, but you didn't. For 56 years I have used my judgement and my training to hold the Order together. Technology has changed the world and we have had to change with it. My goal has always been to build the Order back up to the size that it once was. We have our fingers in so many pies, so many companies. The Order makes money… sometimes lose it, but we grow. All this we've done without you. We've realised that our potential with those of the bloodline is far greater than those that are not.'

The Archangel's smirk was apparent. Sir William was right as Gabriel had observed, maybe more so than he realised. They had grown faster than Gabriel had expected. This was good news, but at a price. The Knights Templar had become totally independent. They had no need to listen to what Gabriel had to say.

'And everyday you learn,' the angelic suspected.

'Yes.'

'Then learn,' Gabriel emphasised quietly. 'Thousands of years ago I was in a battle with the dark forces on Sagun, which is the Third

Realm. We won, but the price was high. Abbadon was Guardian of that Realm and I took it from him. Not only did I take it from him, but I did so, right in front of Sataniel.'

'Satan? You're kidding?'

'No. In fear or disgraced, probably the latter, Abbadon disappeared. In Carcassonne, I discovered he was on the First Realm.'

'You're saying a couple of days ago?'

'He has been playing me… and I have been stupid. No more. My eyes are open and I am listening. I told Henry that I had neglected some of my duties and I have, I admit it. You and the Order are one of those duties and I am sorry. As I have said all along, Abbadon is not your fight, he is mine and I alone will deal with him. I will need information and your support, but not your blood. You are few, chosen at birth. Abbadon's army can be anyone, anyone with evil intent. If Abbadon could get away with losing a thousand souls to take one of yours, he would do it. He could easily win a war by attrition. The numbers are on his side. But Abbadon with all his might has a major flaw, self-preservation. Open conflict in view of the eyes of the world *and* God, would put his existence at risk, and therefore, he will not risk it. We need, *I need* to force his hand; to force him out into the open. But I cannot do that alone.'

'You put it like that, you only had to ask,' the old man jested.

'Thank you,' Gabriel replied holding out his hand once again.

The two shook, but Sir William still had his suspicions. It would take more than one little chat to gain total, unquestioning support.

'Action speaks louder than words,' Sir William whispered.

'Ye of little faith,' Gabriel nodded. 'But I do understand.'

The Archangel stepped out into the great hall followed by Sir William. He stood by Sir William's chair, recognising his authority as head of his army, only it wasn't quite *his* army anymore. Gabriel noticed the package at the bottom of the steps.

'Is that for me?' he asked.

'Yeah, I saw it arrive,' Cole answered. 'It's heavy, if you want a hand?'

'No thank you.'

'What's in it?'

'Memories,' Gabriel cryptically replied. 'Just memories.'

'Does this mean you're moving back in?' asked Sir Geoffrey.

'I do not know,' the angelic said looking over to Sir William. 'I have no fixed address and I have been dragging that box around with me for decades. Could I at least, leave it here?'

The Grand Master accepted Gabriel's request. The angelic was right; he didn't have to stay. Henry and Cole lifted the box up the few steps to the gap in the wall. It was heavy.

'Do you still use the COR?' questioned Gabriel.

'Yes we do,' Sir Geoffrey replied motioning with his head to Henry.

'Why?' asked Sir William.

'Would it be acceptable if Henry could teach Agent Cole about the history of the Order?'

'I've tolerated *his* being here,' Sir William muttered with Cole still in earshot.

'Thanks!' Cole replied.

Sir William exhaled heavily. 'He is an outsider and not

bloodline.'

'A tree has many branches,' Gabriel objected. 'Your history cannot harm.'

'Henry will teach him,' Sir William instructed. 'But security around him…'

'I've had free access,' Cole laughed. 'I've even been outside?'

'Only to what we allow,' added Sir Geoffrey. 'You must have realised that by now? What? We didn't follow you?'

'That's because you haven't opened your eyes yet,' barked Troy taking a cigarette out of a packet from his top shirt pocket.

'TROY!' Sir William shouted. 'There is NO smoking in C&C.'

Troy waved the cancer stick. 'It's not alight.' He placed it behind his ear.

'Access to your history is all he requires,' Gabriel got back to the request. 'And I am glad we finally met again, properly; and thank you.'

Gabriel stepped back away from the chair and picked up the package with ease and disappeared back into his secret room. The thoughts of the Knights Templar would have filled a hundred books and their questions at least another hundred. Were they really going to be working around an angelic? Why now? What had Gabriel foreseen? Sir William had as many questions as any one else. Henry was the only person visibly undeterred by the whole situation. He truly *had* been working with the Archangel Gabriel for sometime. However, like his father, he had wanted visual proof, although it didn't come as a surprise. Cole could not get his head around what he had seen. He was raised a Catholic and regularly attended mass when he was young. This was…

This was not what he expected. He glanced around. The expressions on the others faces matched his own. Like a schoolboy, he wanted to raise his hand and ask a question. Only one question.

'Why hadn't Gabriel got feathers?' Cole spoke under his breath. 'Do angels moult?'

Maybe two questions.

XXIV

The First Realm.

KT Hotel – 10.13hrs Tuesday 17th July AD 2001 GMT

'Welcome to the COR,' announced Henry, arms in the air. 'This is the Chamber of Records, COR for short. We haven't moved it to the Castle yet.'

The floor plan was that of an equilateral triangle with the main wooden double doors covered by a steel blast door at one corner. Opposite the main entrance, on the plastered wall was a painted family tree, starting with eight names a foot from the ceiling, too far to read, ending the list at the floor. The walls were made of large blocks of stone and encroached inward with each layer, until they met at the ceiling. This gave the impression of inverted steps on each side, as though the Chamber of Records had been built in the middle of a three-sided pyramid. The lower walls were lined with glass-covered bookshelves. Reading tables and glass cases that housed ancient artefacts were dotted about on stone plinths or raised sections of wooden floor. At first glance, the majority of what was on show was Egyptian, but on closer inspection; the artefacts were clearly from all over the world. It was the oldest looking museum Cole had ever seen, and that included the stuff of fiction from the silver screen; only this was real, very real.

The agent stepped through the doorway under the plaque, which read: We the Strong and the Few of the Island of the Mighty Will Find Knowledge to be Our Key.

'Interesting design,' he said looking up at the ceiling.

'It serves a purpose,' Henry replied. 'This section of the complex is the oldest. It's the deepest, making it the first part to be built. Without modern materials, what you see in the ceiling is the only method to support the city above.'

'And if the Thames flooded?'

'The complex started to leak a couple of hundred years ago, but it wasn't too serious. Since then, the entire complex has been waterproofed and the surrounding stone injected with water resistant agents. Hopefully that won't happen again.'

Cole walked up to one of the desks and sat down as a pupil would to await his first lesson, fidgeting and allowing his eyes to wander. The covers of all the books on the shelves were leather bound, fraying or cracked. The artwork of the genealogy, the lineage of the Templar was exquisite; as were the paintings of knights in combat on the walls of a city called Acre. On another wall, surround by books, were pages in an ancient text framed, entitled 'I. Maccabees.' Cole could have spent half a day in the chamber, just being nosy.

'To be honest, I don't know where to start,' Henry said.

'In that case Q and A,' replied Cole.

'Okay, but…' Henry raised a finger. 'There is one thing I used to say at the beginning. If I may?'

Cole opened his palms to the ceiling. 'You're the teacher.'

'In simple terms why are we, as in the Templar, here. I use a quote by the film director Alfred Hitchcock.' Henry cleared his throat and then began. 'We seem to have a compulsion these days to bury time capsules in order to give those people living in the next century or so, some idea of what we are like. I have prepared one of my own. I have placed in mine, some rather large samples of dynamite, gunpowder and nitro glycerine. My time capsule is set to go off in the year 3000. It will show them what we are really like. End quote. *We* are here to prove him wrong.'

'Understood,' Cole replied.

Henry calmly nodded. 'Then let us begin with some questions and answers.'

'First,' Cole felt a little embarrassed. 'Why doesn't Gabriel have feathers?'

'I don't know, ask him.'

'You knew what he was?'

'Yeah, but I'd never seen him change. When you spend time around him you notice weird things. It's almost as though time does not move as it should, I can't explain it.'

'Yeah, and the rain.'

'I don't know why either,' replied Henry before Cole could ask. 'I admit, I've notice that. You can't miss it.' Henry laughed.

'Have you any idea why Gabriel's brought me here? I don't just mean physically here, I mean to allow an outsider into so secret an organisation?'

Henry shook his head. 'No.'

Cole climbed out of his chair, the volume of his voice increased. 'Why me? I don't know the first thing about the Bible, about ancient history, about shit! I don't know anything. I know Gabriel doesn't want me for my investigative abilities – he has you for that. OK, I know I can be relentless and stubborn and my bosses think I'm a pain in the ass, but as an outsider in this world… that wouldn't be seen as good qualities. Do you agree?'

'That and you're also married,' said Henry. 'And faithful. You show devotion to your work and to your wife. Within the Order, devotion is expected without question; devotion to one another, to the Order and its goals. You only see what you want to see and not what you should see.' Henry wandered over to a drawer of photographs as he spoke. 'I'll give you an example. You were recently in Carcassonne. In the main town, not the citadel, there is a church, L' Eglise St. Vincent, which has some very ornate carvings in stone over the southern entrance. The carvings are hollow and lined with fine stone. They resemble flowers, possibly poppies. But when you look at the whole picture and join each line to each line through angles of 72 degrees, it creates a whole new picture; a pentagram over seven feet in diameter. A pentagram hidden in plain sight, built into the stonework of a church that was built for Christian worship. The feature is visible in the windows – The Star of David. Six pointed stars in the windows and a five pointed star over the door. If you can see with better eyes, then you will learn how *we* in the Order learn.'

'I take it that also means asking the right questions?'

'Yes it does.'

'Who and what is the bloodline?'

'Who – is the easy part. Every member of the Knights Templar is blood line; originally one of eight of nine families. It doesn't matter whether it was father to son or daughter or both. The bloodline are the family lines, which stem from those original eight families.'

'Why eight?' Cole questioned.

'The ninth knight had no bloodline,' Henry explained. 'The bloodline itself, some call Le Serpent Rouge.'

'Which is French for?'

'The Red Snake.'

'Wait a minute,' Cole said deep in thought. 'In Washington, the Chevalier home had a red snake on the plaque by the door.'

'It was their subtle way of saying that they were bloodline. It is said that there is more to it than the original eight families, but only Gabriel would know that.'

'Why call it the Le Serpent Rouge?'

'Look at the family tree on the wall behind me. You can see it goes back thirty-one generations. If the first family was the head of the tree and the genetic blood line flows down to an individual at the bottom, in red, the colour of blood, then the image would be that of a red snake; Le Serpent Rouge.'

'How is it that the NSA doesn't know who you are?'

'Because they're stupid. I'm kidding. To be honest, it won't be long before they do.'

'Why da'ya say that?'

'Technology, like Gabriel said. It won't be long before you can't take a piss on the way home from the pub, without it being caught on camera. Sooner or later everyone will know. We have bloodline in high positions of power, but not to rule the world like the conspiracy nuts think.'

'They're there to keep the Knights Templar out of the public eye,' added Cole.

'Exactly!'

'So Gabriel is trying to recruit me?'

'Yes.'

'I go back to the US knowing that you exist and if anyone at the NSA learns about the Knights Templar, kill the information. Is that the idea?'

'Yeah. I would think so.'

'One problem, I'm not bloodline, so how are you going to trust me?'

'I don't know. Can we?' Henry smiled.

'Completely off track here, but I need to ask, what is it with the museum?'

'I'm surprised you didn't ask earlier.'

'Everywhere you turn there is something; every watch; every beer bottle; everything.'

'In the Castle, you will find the museum of your dreams. You'll find *everything* that you haven't seen here.

'I know,' Cole came clean. 'I had a wander this morning.'

'Well, you probably didn't see everything. We have… everything you forgot was ever made.'

'What do you mean *everything*?' asked Cole. 'You keep saying everything.'

'Every issue of every newspaper; every publication; weekly and monthly. Every book and as many foreign language copies as we can store. We have most models of most cars and bikes. We have seeds in cryo-form of as many plants as we can find. Everything we have is catalogued and identified mainly using pictograms.'

'Pictograms?'

'Yes, because it doesn't matter what language you speak you can read a pictogram. In fact you don't even have to read to read a pictogram.'

'Why go to all the trouble?'

'All we have achieved is to gather the knowledge and achievements of man. This place and the Castle, holds the key to our future, but more importantly, houses our entire past.'

'But the real world will never see it. They will never know,' Cole added still not understanding why.

'We might all die,' said Henry. 'Another ice age or a major natural disaster...'

'Or a meteor strike?'

'Yes, a meteor strike,' repeated Henry. 'It happened once...'

'It'll happen again, I saw the movie,' Cole said sarcastically.

'It's actually a quote from a book,' Henry corrected. 'We probably wouldn't survive a meteor, but our museum would.'

Henry stood up and motioned with his arms to everything around them.

'All of this. Do you understand?' he asked the agent, praying that he might.

'Knowledge is more important to you than anything else, isn't it?'

'Yes it is,' Henry confirmed.

Cole got up and walked around the library closely staring into each glass case.

'Is something wrong?'

'I still don't understand why I'm doing this,' Cole replied. 'I understand what you're saying, but why does Gabriel require me to learn this? I was trained by the US government; you... you were born to all of this. This history, the knowledge, this entire museum is part of your heritage.'

'My father as you know is the Grand Master of the Holy Order of the Poor Knights of the Temple of King Solomon in Jerusalem. He didn't tell me until I was twenty-two. I didn't realise that subjects my private tutors were teaching me would be so important,' Henry explained. 'I left school, I rebelled and got a job on my own local engineering company. Underpaid and treated like crap, I realised that I was wasting time, working for people that didn't care for my well-being, making components for cars which in turn damage the ozone layer of our planet. I got into an argument with my father and during the disillusioned disagreement, he made me aware of my heritage. There was more to my life than my hand in destroying our world. My bloodline dictated my destiny of dedicating my life to this Realm.'

'My father was NSA, so I followed suit.'

'Generations of my family have spent a lot of time in this room, reading and studying these very old books. One in particular is of great importance. We call it the Twenty First Codex.'

'The twenty first? What about the others?'

'The biblical codex are numerous and spread around the world. National libraries and museums house many of them, a few are privately owned. They were written in the ancient languages and given names like the Codex Sinaiticus or Alexandrinus. For us, we numbered them, not in order of age, more like the order of discovery; it makes it easier when discussing them. Plus, many are numbered anyway. We have copies of the codex that we don't possess and…'

'And you keep the others safe?'

'Yes. There are thirty or forty ancient codex, but the Twenty First Codex is unique.'

'Only one copy exists.'

'The Book of Gabriel, his life and trials and allegedly, his death; is contained within its pages.'

'And you have been compiling this book for Gabriel?'

'Gabriel doesn't know I have been trying to collect it. He knows it exists, he was there when it was written by Enoch almost 10,000 years ago.'

'I'm waiting for you to hit me with the catch.'

'The catch is that Abbadon has also been collecting the pages. Since I'm now finding it so hard to obtain any pages these days; it gives the impression that Abbadon has more of them than I do.'

'Does he know that you have them?'

'We buy them. Abbadon doesn't, but you found that out yourself. There are 144 pages. I know that because I have the last two. In total I have managed to get sixteen of them. I have possible addresses of a few privately owned pages and I believe the Vatican may have a few. Abbadon must have around a hundred of them.'

'They prophesise?'

'It gives that impression.'

'So you and me are in this 'Book of Gabriel'?'

'I don't have those, but I think I have the pages that Abbadon really wants.'

'Obviously,' said Cole sarcastically.

'You miss the point. The book contains prophesies, but only in the latter chapters. Abbadon has been collecting them all, but he has been concentrating on the pages related to the future. And as I said, I have the last two.'

'And the pages that were taken from the Chevalier's in Washington?'

'Old ones I think.'

'Does this book tell you anything?'

Henry didn't answer. Instead, he briskly walked over to a small wooden cabinet and opened it to reveal a concealed safe. Unlocking it, he took out a couple of pages encased in glass. He held the first sheet in front of him and cleared his throat.

'Man has no future without a belief in himself. Why would anyone who can think for themselves, not think of the future?' the teacher continued. 'After hundreds of millennia man has been pushing himself forward to reach a point in his development, in his evolution, where a great step forward is required; a leap of faith, as it were. Not a faith in the form of religion, but a belief in himself. With that alone, can mankind survive?'

'And this was written when?' interrupted the agent.

Henry ignored the interruption and continued. 'There's a section missing. Here we go. We are born; we live; and we die. Life is not hard; life is simple. It is us, mankind, that makes life hard.'

Cole's jaw dropped. He had heard that before.

'There are three parts to our lives married with three aims: We are born, with the aim to survive. We live, with the aim to bare offspring. We die, with the aim of passing on the knowledge. Simple! What is so hard in that? Why, for thousands of years, has mankind struggled to follow this simple principle? Does this, basic of all rules need to be dictated to one and all for mankind to understand?'

Henry then placed the glass sheets by his side and continued with the next sheet. 'Dictating to the peoples of the world has never worked. Mankind is like a child. Tell it that fire will cause pain and they will put their hand in it to confirm that it hurts. Mankind is very similar in this manner. You cannot dictate the basic principles of mankind's evolution, for mankind will not listen.'

'Why are you reading this to me?' Cole interrupted again.

'Listen to the words,' replied Henry. 'Its not an exact translation, but let me finish, because some of this might sink in.'

The agent leant back in his chair and raised his hands, palms up, in a gesture to carry on.

'Subtlety is required in the approach of teaching mankind how he should live and why. The need to hold back and feed the knowledge in a gentle flow is needed to nurture mankind in its growth. The knowledge in this form of wisdom that we speak; is the great secret of our own legacy as human-beings. Secrets, in their own right must stay secret until the time is right. But as with time; a secret can become lost forever.'

Cole, the schoolboy, raised his hand.

'I've finished,' Henry said feeling as though he had wasted his time.

'People are dying for those words?' Cole said quietly.

'Yes. I have no prophesy within the pages as far as I see it, but there is a train of thought that we follow. There is also more to the COR than just prophesy.'

Cole raised his hand again, only this time to pause Henry. The American's brain needed a moment to absorb what he had said.

'So what else can this chamber tell us?'

'We study mankind's evolution as he migrated around the world,' Henry began again with spring in his voice. 'Say, a civilisation crops up in ancient Egypt.'

'We're talking pyramids?'

'No,' said Henry. 'The Egyptians as we know them, called these people 'the First Ones'. In the region of the Upper Euphrates another group prospered and they began to trade with the First Ones in Egypt.'

'What timeframe are we talking about here?'

'8000 to 5000 BC.'

'Where does Gabriel fit into all of this?'

'He doesn't. Gabriel is only one angelic. He doesn't talk about his past except through lectures in universities. I get the impression that he just blended into the civilisations that happened to be there at the time and wandered from place to place. It is very difficult to see what Gabriel has done or where he has been. I know from talking with him and piecing together bits of my own research, that he was in Egypt around 1500 BC, maybe slightly later in the 18th dynasty.'

'The Heretic Pharaoh. I saw that one on the History Channel. He preached of only one God. Gabriel?'

'I don't think Gabriel is what you think he is.'

'Henry, I get the impression, you think Gabriel is trying to correct some wrong from his past.'

'Yes I do and I'm willing to help him do it.'

'So that mankind gets back on track as it were.'

'Whatever back on track maybe, yes. I'm glad you understand.'

'I understand, but I disagree. Gabriel is a soldier, like I was. Soldiers follow orders. A little bit of interference maybe, but I think he's being played in the same way you or I get played; just on a grander scale. I think the player is Abbadon, so what's his story?'

'Abbadon is not one angelic. When we research him and go back through history; we're not looking at one person; he has followers, thousands of them. However, it does make him easier to track. According to scriptures, hundreds of thousands of angelic fell from the grace of God.'

Cole climbed back out of his chair. 'We're fighting an army!' he hinted.

'They took the daughters of man.'

'So they fancied human women. I can get that,' Cole said cheering himself up a little. 'We do have some hotties down here. But saying that, I wouldn't leave Heaven for Iinnad.'

'Yeah, well, Abbadon did.'

'There has to be more to them than that?'

'Mankind was given a soul.'

'Hence, soulcarrier's!' Cole understood.

'Resentment,' Henry continued. 'Abbadon left relevant evidence; angelic offspring; beings living for hundreds of years, and God's hatred of them. So around 3500 BC another comet hit the Mediterranean,' Henry paused in thought. 'A comet… new evidence suggests that possibly a volcanic island exploded, whichever it was, it caused a flood that wiped out the angelic offspring, the Nephilim.'

'Noah's flood?'

'Very probably. From that point on, Abbadon appeared to have fewer followers, but no more offspring.'

'You think the offspring were all wiped out?

'The Nephilim were, according to some ancient manuscripts, the downfall of the fallen angelic was at that time. Many may have died, we just don't know. What we do know is that when you look at the geography of historical events, we find that Abbadon was monitoring Gabriel's travels.'

'How do you know that?'

'There are many books on the subject of the ancients, Watchers and the Grigori. Some of these books are pure guesswork; others are based on oral traditions and translations of ancient scrolls. You find them in bookshops and libraries under the subjects 'New Age' or 'Mind, Body & Spirit.' Some are completely wrong…'

'I always skipped that section, anyway I got the impression it was for the hippies and flower power people from the Sixties.'

'There is ignorance even the highest places of learning; tunnel vision in its truest form. The learned fail to open their eyes. I am saying you're wrong.'

'So looking at the bigger picture...' Cole said, making a mental note to watch his mouth.

'I'll give you an example,' said Henry as he pulled a map out from his desk drawer and placed it on the table between them. 'Let's say Gabriel was in Egypt around 1350 BC. During that period the

Egyptians began to worship one God. Because of this, Egypt reduced its trade due to internal strife amongst its people over the new religion. Basically, Egypt became weaker as a nation, causing it to have difficulty protecting its distant borders, modern day Syria. In the north came the invaders, the Hittites, from Turkey. The eastern region of their empire was once inhabited by the Sumerians and Akkadians, a warrior race and a stone's throw from the Upper Euphrates.'

'I did see this on the History Channel, but I thought this happened thousands of years apart?'

'It did, but for Abbadon, what is a few thousand years? From our research, the fallen made a home in the Upper Euphrates. Then they migrated to the Cappadocia region of Turkey. Then they dug in, literally; thirty-six subterranean cities that could house two hundred thousand people; right in the centre of the Hittites' empire.'

'You're kidding? Then what?'

'Egypt's internal strife meant they invaded, taking back most of Syria. Not long after that, Ramases II came to power and took it back. Then a one God believing man called Moses leaves Egypt with all the Jewish labourers. 1300 years later, and the Christians and Jews are in Jerusalem the heart of one God religions. Jump forward to AD 600 and the religion's power base has already been relocated and split between Rome and Constantinople. Gabriel, according to the Koran is in Medina and speaks to Mohammed. The Muslims eventually take the city of Jerusalem.'

'And where was Abbadon?'

'Probably in Europe. 400 years after Mohammed in AD 1096, we have the First Crusade from Europe that takes back Jerusalem.'

'You're saying, we're just pawns in a chess game?'

'I don't know what we are?'

'You've just covered 8,000 years in five minutes. Have you told Gabriel this?'

Henry put the map away. 'Around 7400 BC a comet, I name Wormwood, from Revelations, broke into seven pieces and collided with this planet. 'Seven mountains of fire,' according to Enoch.'

Cole surrendered, his hands up. 'I thought you said a comet hit around 3500 BC? I'm lost here! Enoch?'

'I said *another* comet. You think there's only been one? Let me finish. Seventy-one percent of the earth's surface is water. Four pieces impacted into the seas and oceans. Two, crashed into the Pacific, with a force so great that they embedded themselves on the ocean floor. The waves, and am talking several miles high, radiated out from the points of impact in every direction travelling at tremendous speed. For the primitive civilisations that lived along the shorelines there was no escape. The wooden villages, the livestock, and even the wildlife, on the eastern and western continents, were all washed into the caverns and canyons to the north. The seawater settled into the low-lying pockets of land on the great landmasses, creating salt lakes miles from the oceans. Great Plains were formed when the force of the waves removed all the trees. 200,000 years of mankind's evolution was destroyed, washed away.'

'End of the world stuff, Revelations,' Cole whispered.

'The other three parts crashed into the landmass throwing hundreds of thousands of tons of earth and scorched vegetation skyward. The ash and dust particles were thrown so high that they floated in the troposphere, creating dust clouds that blocked out the sun. And that is what we call?'

'A nuclear winter and everything dies,' Cole answered, he knew this bit.

'And on that day Heaven stood by and watched, as they always had, as the power of destruction, the punishment and the judgment came and fell upon man,' Henry said. 'Revelations. Now,' Henry raised a finger. 'Be open minded…'

Cole smiled, he could be nothing but, considering what he had already seen.

'Mankind is resilient and does survive. But he has to survive the waters and then the darkness, and with the darkness comes the cold. As you said, a nuclear winter. In time, the dust particles in the atmosphere begin to settle and God said, 'Let there be light:' and there was light. The sun's rays finally break through the dust clouds to warm the surface of the earth. With herb yielding seed, and the fruit tree yielding fruit, nature had regained its foothold in the soil. The creatures of the earth, although small in number, began to multiply and the seas began to fill with life. Does any of this sound familiar?'

'The Discovery Channel?'

'You said I covered 8000 years of history in five minutes. So what about the Book of Genesis? First there was nothing but the word of God.'

'And God said let there be light,' Cole's eyes were open.

'And there was light and warmth.'

'And God separated the land and the sea,' Cole continued.

'When the lights are on, Richard. Mankind can see the land and the sea. And then the planet begins to grow.'

'In the Book of Revelations and the Book of Enoch, it happened once it will happen again.'

'Charlton Heston said that,' Cole added.

'Everything we need to know has already happened once before,' Henry stressed. 'We just need to make people…' Henry stopped and stared at the tiles.

'The Chevalier killings are irrelevant aren't they?' Cole asked.

'The Templar are just trying to make mankind listen to a world that can't hear.'

Cole's thoughts were beginning to wander back to some of the recent things that had been said. One point that kept coming up on the tip of his lips, *why me?*

'Can we cut this short I need to do something?' the agent said abruptly.

'Do you need a hand?' asked Henry a little surprised.

'No, I'm sorry. I'll see you back at the Castle,' said Cole as he left the Chamber of Records as fast as he could.

He stopped in the corridor and quickly returned, popping his head around the corner.

'Henry!' Cole snapped making him jump. 'Thank you. I needed that.'

***

KT Station – 12.18hrs Tuesday 17th July AD 2001 GMT

The two Templar didn't notice Agent Cole enter the station via the open blast door. Stopping at the gap in the wall by the broken tiles; he raised a fist to knock on the door. Being stone his knuckles had little effect. He looked at his hand poised to tap the stone slab again and shook his head.

'You idiot,' he said to himself and walked straight through.

Gabriel was standing in the middle of the dusty room with his back to him. The agent paused for a moment, not sure whether to venture further or ask his question. Gabriel glanced down to his right, aware that someone was there.

'Am I bloodline?'

He knew it was Cole. He heard him; he could smell him and as Cole surmised, he could sense him.

'You are bloodline,' Gabriel confirmed without turning around.

'Which line?'

'I do not know,' replied Gabriel as he faced the agent.

'What do you mean, you don't know?'

'All those of the Serpent Rouge have a *presence*. We call it the presence of being. You have it also, but... you are not of the Knights Templar. You are something else.'

'Something else? Is that why you led me around and brought me here?'

'Yes.'

'You were testing me? Is that why you wanted me to play your little games?' Cole said in a raised voice. 'The Templar follow rules laid down thousands of years ago, was that your doing?'

Cole had clearly followed what Henry had been telling him. He had followed it and understood it, but now he was confused and out of his depth again.

'There were eight families of the Serpent Rouge,' Cole continued. 'They grew into the bloodline we see today.'

'Correct.'

'Henry said there were some questions that he didn't know and I would have to ask you. Henry is subtle and waits for the right time. That time may never come and luckily for him, I'm as subtle as a brick.'

'Then ask your questions... but if you ask a wrong one, I will answer no more.'

'More games?'

'Your question.'

'If all eight families had the presence of being, then did they come from one source?'

'The answer is yes, and to your next question the answer is no.'

'My third question; these bloodline created the Knights Templar because you asked them to?'

'Yes.'

Why? Was it just to fight Abbadon or to hold the knowledge?'

'I have told you, I did not know that Abbadon was on the First Realm. Knowledge is more important than my battle with Abbadon. The combined knowledge of the people of the world will save it from destruction.'

'Is time running out?'

Gabriel looked away from the agent and sat down at his desk. He tapped his fingers on the table, the wooden panels warped and twisted with age, a sign that it was made before the wood had time to season.

'I made this table,' Gabriel said in a whisper. 'I was so busy that I made it from a freshly cut oak. Time has proved that I should wait for the right time.'

'You said you were busy.'

'I did not have the time,' Gabriel replied.

'The world has little time. That's what you're telling me?'

'Yes.'

'About ten years?' said Cole abruptly.

Gabriel's head turned around his body steadfast in the chair. There was a look of amazement on his face.

'What do'ya know?' Cole added.

'It is not for me to say.'

'It's not for you to say? You're trying to manipulate mankind so that we can see, so that we can learn how to save ourselves. *Now* it's not your place to say?'

'The first rule of the First Realm is not to interfere.'

'So what have you been doing?'

'Just that, but I have been doing it as subtly as possible, so as not to be seen.'

'Why? By whom?'

'I am a Watcher of Man. However, I am also watched. Why? Because I should not break the rules!'

'Abbadon doesn't follow any rules,' replied Cole.

'He follows the same rules as I,' Gabriel said calmly. 'He just breaks more of them than I. He gets away with it more because... in human terms, his side did not make the rules.'

'What happens if you break the rules?'

'I would be summoned to the Council on the Seventh Realm, I would never see you again and time would run out.'

'You've lost me.'

'Sixty seconds equals a minute. Sixty minutes equal an hour. That is the case on this realm. On the other realms time travels at different speeds.'

'Does it go back?'

'No,' Gabriel replied with a grin. 'A nice idea though. Time on the Seventh Realm moves at 247.7 times faster than the First Realm. If I were to spend thirty minutes on the Seventh Realm, over five days would pass here. If I were there for a week or even a day, that would be too long. Luckily, the council do not waste much time on such matters as this realm.'

'They don't care for the humans?'

'In a word, no.'

'So why d'you care?'

'I have been here quite a while. I have grown fond of this realm and I believe it is worth saving.'

'So why does the council hate us?'

'*You... have... souls!*' Gabriel hammered it home.

'But wasn't that resolved?'

'It will never be resolved.'

'So you're going to deal with Abbadon?' Cole asked, not waiting for an answer. 'Then, I'm going to Paris with you.'

'What for? Closure of your case?'

'Don't be so bloody patronising,' Cole jumped. 'I'm not your puppet!'

'I never said you were.'

The agent left Gabriel's sanctuary, but was followed.

'Close your door like a good boy,' called out Cole gaining the attention of the Templar at the other end of the platform.

Gabriel backed away into his sanctuary. Iinnad appeared from the shadows.

'Richard seems pissed. You could have asked him for some batteries?' she complained. 'I've waited here a day and now you're leaving.'

'I have to,' Gabriel replied. 'Sorry, go sightseeing or something. Stay close though and I will call for you.'

'You're kidding? Go sightseeing?'

'Go and buy some batteries,' Gabriel whispered. 'I have to close the door.'

'You're not locking me in here? There's no way I'm going in that water again.'

'You have too. I am sorry.'

'Wait!' Iinnad demanded as she transformed. 'No one will see me unless I allow it. I'll walk out of here. I'm not fucking swimming in that!'

'Okay,' Gabriel agreed. 'Now get out of here,' he whispered to the air.

The Archangel then closed the door with Iinnad's help, before transforming back into human form. Cole was already in the carriage. Gabriel stood on the platform in front of the open doors.

'Where are we going?' he asked.

'This train only has one other stop. Where d'you think? And then, you and I are gonna go over the plans of Abbadon's place, before we hit it.'

'No,' Gabriel shook his head. 'No, I have told Sir William and the others that this is my fight. That also applies to you.'

'I'm sorry,' Cole stepped up to the door, both hands holding the rail above his head. 'I got the impression we were becoming a team on this. You wanted me here and I'm here. So lets do this.'

'No,' Gabriel signalled to the security camera.

The doors closed trapping the American inside. Cole screamed through the glass as the carriage slowly began to move out of the station. The Archangel then turned to face the camera and mouthed the words, 'thank you'.

'YOUR WELCOME!' screamed the speaker on the station.

The angelic laughed aloud as he wandered towards the blast doors. 'Next stop the Chamber of Records.'

***

KT Castle – 14.38hrs Tuesday 17th July AD 2001 GMT

Cole stormed into the quiet C&C.

'Shit! Shit! Shit! Ssshhh…'

The agent then noticed the observing crowd.

'Is there anyone who can give me the address to Abbadon's HQ?' he demanded.

'We were told Gabriel would deal with Abbadon,' replied one of the operators.

'Fuck him! I'm going, not one of you.'

Sir Geoffrey, always in the background, stepped forward. The operator turned to her superior for guidance and his nod and slow blink was enough for her to hand Cole the address on a piece of a paper.

'Thank you,' Cole said quietly and ran out of the hall.

Aston counted the seconds. 'One, two, three!'

Cole casually walked back into the hall with a smile on his face. Ignoring everyone except Sir Geoffrey.

'Can I borrow some money, cause if I use my credit card I'm screwed?'

'By the time you reach the hotel foyer, there will be your money and a new passport, Mr Cole,' Sir Geoffrey informed him.

'Thank you again,' replied Cole. 'Since I've been here, I've spent most of my time on that damn train.'

The American left for the second time.

XXV

The First Realm.

KT Hotel – 16.38hrs Tuesday 17th July AD 2001 GMT

The lift door rattled open as the impatient agent squeezed out into the hotel foyer. Standing by the entrance of the glass door was the young female chauffeur who had ferried him from the police station. She was out of uniform; tucking her blouse into her trousers. Cole admired her slim midriff and noticed a seven-inch scar, which she quickly covered. Her appearance gave the impression that she was about to go home.

'Mr Cole I'll have the car for you in a moment,' she said.

'Give me a minute,' Cole raised a finger. 'I have something to pick up...'

'I have that too,' she replied waving an envelope.

The agent followed the pretty woman outside to a dilapidated rusty silver Fiat that had just pulled up. The driver climbed out being careful not to dirty his hotel uniform and handed the woman the keys.

'Shall we?' she grinned at Cole.

Cole's mouth opened, but he was at a loss for words.

'Are you okay? Mr Cole?'

'Yeah! No Aston Martin?'

'Listen to you!' his driver laughed.

Cole kept quiet as his chauffeur got behind the wheel and motioned to the, still stunned, agent to get in the car. The car pulled away just as Cole sat down, even though his door was not shut. It wouldn't shut.

'Seatbelt!' the driver snapped.

'I intend to!' Cole panicked. 'I'm surprised this works.'

'It'll get you from A to B, so don't knock it. This was short notice, so your in my car, and I'm not going to apologise about that, because this is my baby,' she patted the dashboard. 'She's never let me down.'

'I take it you've finished for the day,' Cole surmised.

'Yep, but your going my way, so I offered. Not only that; but my little baby's better in the London traffic.'

'The airport it is then.'

'Airport?' the Fiat negotiated a sharp bend violently, to avoid the pedestrians and some road works. 'International flights have one hour check-in; it would take me at least 40 minutes to get to Stansted or Heathrow; Charles de Gaul Airport is outside Paris and no use to you. You're going by train, Mr Cole.'

'Train? That'll take hours.'

'Twenty minute check-in; the station is five minutes away and trains leave every half an hour. Then I can do my shopping, pick up a few things and get back.'

'The name's Richard.'

'I know.'

'And you are?'

'Lucy.'

'I thought you had finished for the day, Lucy.'

'I have.'

'You live there?'

'No, nearby, but I socialise there.'

'Socialise where you work?'

'Yeah, they have a cinema, a restaurant and night club attached to the hotel. Also in an emergency; we're close by.'

The tiny car shot across the Thames and screeched around the Imax cinema roundabout; then up the small road past the front of Waterloo International train station. The car found a space under the curved rusty iron and dirty glass structure before stopping. Cole relaxed to allow his intestines to settle. He pulled his fingers out of the seat fabric and slowing clambered out of the death trap.

'You're here aren't you?' Lucy said, walking off towards the main entrance. 'You coming?'

'Aren't you goin' to lock it?' Cole called.

'Who's going to steal that? Come on!' she waved the envelope above her head.

Cole crossed the car park secretly praying that someone would steal Lucy's baby. As he entered the main entrance he took one last look to see if it had already gone, but it was still there. Lucy was right, *who would be stupid enough to steal it?*

The American followed the tight jeans across the polished white floor of the station and down the escalators to the International Terminal. Lucy ran to an empty ticket counter before someone else nabbed it. She began to talk to the cashier and beckoned the agent over. The tickets had already been ordered in his name. Lucy took out Cole's new passport from the envelope and showed the ticket assistant his new photo. The man shook his head.

'Shit, isn't it?' Lucy added.

'Nobody looks good in a passport photo Mr Crawford,' said the man.

'Tell me about it,' replied Cole accepting his tickets and taking his passport. They stepped away from the counter. 'How did you get my photo?'

'We have our ways,' Lucy tapped his shoulder leading him out of the ticket office. 'Come on, I've got shopping to do.'

Lucy led Cole to the automatic gate system and snatching Cole's ticket from him and then activated the gate. Cole needed a nudge to step through.

'There's money in the envelope.'

'And that's it?' Cole asked.

'That's it. You're already checked in, when you go through the gate. You've got the x-ray machine and that's it. You're not carrying are you?'

'No.'

'Because if you are, you'd better give it to me.'

'What are you, my mother? I'm not carrying.'

Lucy looked at her watch. An elderly couple passed by so Cole politely edged along the barrier. Lucy glanced up at the departure board then back at her package.

'You've got plenty of time.'

'Why do you do this?' Cole asked.

'I had a choice of jobs. I chose driving. Most of the time I drive

Sir William or Sir Geoffrey, now I seem to be driving Henry about. He's very knowledgeable and we talk.'

'You talk? So you learn.'

'I've learnt a lot from Henry in the short time I've known him.'

'So you want to teach?'

'No! I wanted to help people, you know?' Lucy answered. 'All I ever wanted to do was be a doctor.'

'But for now you're a taxi service.'

'Everybody makes sacrifices; even you.'

'Sacrifices? Oh, I'm in enough trouble as it is. I haven't got time for sacrifices.'

'Well, for now, I'm helping people in a different way, but my dream is still to be a doctor. Until then, I follow orders and learn as much as I can.'

'With no regrets.'

'I regret not becoming a doctor before starting a family. I think both *will* happen, but in the opposite order.'

'So you have a boyfriend?'

'Yes.'

'Is he in the Order?'

'Yeah, strange isn't it? We know we're very *very* distantly related, which is fine by me, but the Order does prefer us to marry outside. I can't, I don't think I could live the lie like everybody else does. I would've been a doctor if my brother hadn't have died. That's what pulled me in.'

'How can you sacrifice so much at your age?' asked Cole.

'Because I'm bloodline.'

Cole placed his hand on the thick glass barrier. 'I… I couldn't but notice, your scar,' Cole causally pointed to her mid-rift.

'An accident, when I was in the army.'

'You were in the army too?'

'All of us were. We're vast and capable, but we don't have resources to train everyone to the utmost abilities of the everyday soldier. So; every member has to serve a minimum, of three years service, in their respective countries military. Some countries have national service, but like America, we don't. So in their infinite wisdom, the powers that be, decided that every one put their life on hold and be a soldier for three years. I've just finished. As I said before, I *wanted* to be a doctor. My brother was a lot older than me and stayed in longer than he had to, he loved it. That's how he died. I was just about to leave school, and then I was told about the Order; so I signed up.'

'But you avoided the action?'

'Bloody hell no! Upstairs has connections everywhere. If there's action, we go. Depending on their age, everyone has seen action somewhere, from Korea, Aden, Oman, Vietnam, yeah be surprised; the Falklands, Chad and the Sudan to the Gulf and tours in Northern Ireland, obviously. My brother died in Afghanistan in 97.'

'You people love war?'

'No! We hate the wasted conflict between men, because it serves no purpose. We do it to hone our skill, basically it's training. We know we're different. We don't know why or how, but I was the fastest, the fittest and the smartest in my unit. We all were.'

'Funny, so was I.'

'What?'

'Faster, fitter, smarter; I was in the Gulf in 91. I didn't even know we had coalition forces in Afghanistan in 97.'

'Yeah, well, British Special Forces have a habit of sending troopers all over the world for training; even to countries we're not supposed to be in.'

'You knew I was in the Gulf?'

'We know a lot about you Mr Cole; and your fear for flying. That's the other reason for you going by train. We also know about your pregnant wife Rebecca. Congratulations, boy or girl?'

'We don't know. We've had the scans, but we decided that it would be a nice surprise. The doctor's know, but then again they would.'

'So do we!' Lucy smiled checking the station clock over Cole's shoulder. 'A bit of short notice all of this; so there'll be no one to meet you at the other end. You be careful and I'll probably pick you up when you get back. Bye!'

Lucy then turned and quickly left Cole to his journey. The agent approached the x-ray machine, cautious of the fact that the security might recognise him. He opened the envelope that Lucy had given him. There were several sheets of printed information neatly wrapped around 10,000 French francs. *I have nothing to declare? Yeah, right!* He put the envelope away and turned around to say thank you to his mad driver. She gave him the thumbs up from the escalator.

'How can you sacrifice so much at your age?' he said, knowing she could not hear.

'Because I'm bloodline,' Lucy mouthed the words.

Cole understood exactly what she meant.

***

KT Hotel – 17.26hrs Tuesday 17th July AD 2001 GMT

Gabriel knocked on the dark oak doorframe to gain Henry's attention. He almost jumped out of his skin. Spinning around expecting to snap at the American, he unclenched his fist when he saw Gabriel and hurried to lock the safe.

'Nervous?' Gabriel asked as he entered the library.

Henry nodded as he relaxed greeting the angelic in the middle of the chamber.

'Well, someone brought Agent Cole up to speed a little sharpish?' Gabriel provoked. 'We… we had words.'

'I fear he took little in,' Henry replied. 'But we have…'

'I fear he took too much in,' the angelic interrupted. 'From the questions he asked; and the way he spoke, I would not put it past him being bloodline.'

'If he were, you'd sense him. And that is why you brought him to us, because you do. I explained that Abbadon was playing games. I didn't tell him that you were.'

'I…' Gabriel paused. 'I was playing with words, not games. As I said last night; I will go to Paris. Sir William and the rest of you understand that. Agent Cole on the other hand…'

'Doesn't?'

'Exactly!'

There was another knock on the doorframe. The conversation stopped. James, Henry's son, was cautiously entering the library to join them.

'Sorry for the interruption,' James bowed. 'I thought I'd say hello to my father, since I was about to return to barracks.'

'I think this is where I excuse myself,' Gabriel admitted. 'Henry, I will see you when I get back. We have much to discuss. I sense there are things you want to tell me, but another time.' As Gabriel walked to the door, he acknowledged James.

'Yes Gabriel!'

'I am sorry that I am responsible for keeping your father from you. He has been a great asset to me,' Gabriel explained. 'However, sometimes one's children are more important and I, having none, forgot that. I am sorry.'

'To be honest Gabriel,' James addressed. 'If I'd heard that from my father, I wouldn't have believed him. They say… they say angelic don't lie; is that true?' Before Gabriel could answer James continued. 'Who am I kidding? If it's the truth, you say yes. If you're lying, you'd say yes. Forget the question.'

'A smart boy you have here,' Gabriel commented to Henry. 'I will answer your question. 'The fallen angelic will lie. The demonic will lie. Soulcarriers lie. Angelic of the lowest level of the hierarchy, do not lie. It is forbidden. Although, they have been known to withhold information. Whether that is lying depends on your point of view.'

'You mean whether you're on the receiving end or not?'

'Henry, he is a smart boy.'

'That answers my second question,' James injected.

'Which is?' Gabriel inquired.

'Are angelic sarcastic? Do they think that mankind is below them?'

Gabriel gave a nasal laugh. 'James you definitely have both your father's and your grandfather's blood in your veins. Now I shall leave you two. I have to get to Paris.'

'Yeah, before the American!'

Henry and Gabriel both stared at James.

'Sir Geoffrey gave him money and a passport,' James elaborated. 'He left, what, an hour ago… I take it from that look, you didn't know?'

'Henry!' Gabriel snapped. 'James, it was nice to meet you.'

With Gabriel gone, Father and Son faced up to each other. Neither was sure who should start, so both finding a distraction in the chamber began to wander around.

'My training's going well,' James volunteered. 'I know that the Order let their first- born know the secret at twenty-one, but with granddad, I found out a little early. I've already finished basic training and I'm returning from leave.'

'That's good,' Henry replied, not sure what else to say. 'Which regiment?'

'The Guards!'

'It's a good regiment.'

'How would you know?'

Henry couldn't verbally fight back on that one.

'The Order needs soldiers. I want to follow Troy.'

'TROY!' Henry gasped. 'Troy is a nutter. He's uncontrollable. He also joined the Order late.'

'And he's the best bloody soldier we have, eight years in the army; five of them with the SAS. You can't get better than that.'

'And you want to follow in his footsteps?'

'Yeah! Damn right! It'll make up for what you didn't,' James stood up to his father.

Henry placed his hand on his son's shoulder and smiled. 'Son, you follow in Troy's footsteps. You have the strength, the stamina and the speed. In three years, I want to see that sandy beret on that stubborn head of yours. And who knows, maybe you'll come back to us a better soldier than Troy. In fact you *will*, because you're a Sinclair.'

'You *really* mean that?' James questioned.

'Yes I do,' Henry nodded. 'I haven't been around to be a father to you. I can't just come back into your life and tell you what to do. Not only that; you're intelligent enough to know what's at stake and you're old enough to make your own decisions. What were you expecting me to say?'

'I don't know. Let's read a book?'

Henry laughed. 'Gabriel was wrong. You have your grandfather's blood, not mine. When do you leave?'

'A couple of hours.'

'That's not long to catch up.'

XXVI

The First Realm.

London 21.13hrs Tuesday 17th July AD 2001AD GMT

Dusk came early for the summer night. The rain clouds saw to that. The light from the silver moon fought hard to break through them. The sky was darkening except for the pale white area, which highlighted the moons struggle, still low on the horizon. The rain was light, mist like, but there was no breeze so it fell gently.

Iinnad wiped away the film of water from the convex glass between her legs and looked down into the capsule she was riding. The blue light shone through her tunic and outlined the capsule. Due to the late hour it was empty; with nothing to see she looked elsewhere, bored. Her straight blonde matted hair wrapped around her face as a breeze suddenly pick up from behind her. She could smell Gabriel's presence.

'Hi Gabe,' she said without turning around.

The beats of his wings became clear as he landed on the roof of the capsule to her right, twenty feet away and slightly lower. Iinnad ignored her friend; she armed her brace and searched the city below. An audio bleep informed Iinnad that her brace was charged and she looked down into the river in front of her.

'What are you doing?' Gabriel asked like a parent to a child.

'Looking for driftwood,' Iinnad answered without taking her

eyes off the river below.

'You fire that and everybody will know we are up here. You stand out in a crowd anyway and up here… That would not be a smart move.'

'Why?' Iinnad innocently asked.

'Because we are trespassing.'

'Trespassing? You're the Guardian of this realm, and you're worried about the soulcarrier's laws?'

'I live here Iinnad,' claimed Gabriel. 'Therefore, I follow their rules.'

'Well I don't,' Iinnad pointed out as she stood up. 'You're here for a reason, and I've already done my sightseeing. This apparently was the only place I could get a good view.'

'Iinnad, it's called the London Eye,' Gabriel told her. 'And we should not be up here.'

'Okay, so what are we doing next?'

'I am going to Paris.'

'Abbadon?' she questioned.

'Do you want to come?'

'You need looking after?'

'I may need another set of eyes.'

'As long as it beats shooting driftwood,' Iinnad replied.

She looked down at Gabriel standing on his blue-lit capsule and smiled. The angelic disengaged her brace, winced a little as she opened her wings. At the back of her mind was the promise she made to Abbadon; the promise she could not break. Gabriel stepped from his capsule gracefully, as would be expected of an Archangel and with a few beats of his wings soared into the darkening sky. In contrast, Iinnad ran off the capsule into the air, as a child would into a swimming pool, and frantically flapped to catch up with her favourite angelic.

'Gabriel, why are you in such a hurry,' called Iinnad after him.

'Because Abbadon is going to make a move, I can feel it.'

'Is that it? I got the impression there was more.'

'Agent Cole has a death wish.'

'But I thought you were gonna let him into your army or whatever it is?'

'I have opened the gates, I think, but Agent Cole wants to catch a killer.'

'You mean Lilith?'

'Yes.'

'I think you need to think about this, before jumping into the unknown,' shouted Iinnad over the sound of her beating wings.

'No, I do not!' Gabriel shouted his reply.

The Archangel sped ahead of Iinnad like a darting swallow over the chalk North Downs and over the low-lying countryside of Kent, before crossing the South Downs and out across the waves of the English Channel. The beautiful angelic flew high watching Gabriel's silhouette against the white crests of the waves. She dipped her left wing sharply, a signal to any pilot and she was about to dive. Out of the sky she fell, building up speed as she approached Gabriel. With all her strength, for a moment, Iinnad pulled out of her dive, clipping Gabriel on the back as she came from behind. The powerful knock was enough to send him crashing into the waves. Iinnad knew that Gabriel could not swim with wings, but at the same time, an angelic cannot take off if its wings are held down. Gabriel was helpless as Iinnad circles above waiting for him to transform, so that he could swim. Only then would she be able to pluck him from the sea and after quickly reaching land dumped the Archangel in a field, on the continent mainland, to dry off and calm down.

***

KT Castle – 21.40hrs Tuesday 17th July AD 2001 GMT

Sir William announced to the hall. 'Let's have a birds eye view of Apolyon Incorporated's headquarters, shall we?'

Aston moved from operator to operator confirming the information that was being received from the US satellites they were borrowing. The main screen lit up with a photograph of Paris taken by a KH 11 from 135 miles above the earth's surface.

'Sir William,' Aston called out. 'Give us a few minutes and we'll have Abbadon's HQ on the screen.'

'Take your time Aston. I have a feeling Gabriel will wait for Agent Cole. That'll give you a couple of hours to get set up.'

Aston was working on a computer with Sarah, one of the female operators. He had heard the Grand Master, but was still working as fast as he could. He wanted to be ready. The main screen began to zoom in on the northeast corner of the French capital. Then the image changed. The dark streets became green and littered with thousands of tiny red dots.

'We have thermal imagery,' broadcast Sarah.

'All we need to do now is increase the data stream so we can view it in real time,' Aston added. 'We're getting there Sir William.'

***

Northern France – 21.54hrs Tuesday 17th July AD 2001 GMT

Iinnad set Gabriel down in a freshly harvested maize field. The hard stumps of the cut crop tripped up the Archangel in the dark. The two carefully negotiated their footsteps to the edge of the field and sat in the long lush grass between the tractor tracks. The Archangel was as mad as he was wet. For Iinnad, it wasn't the cleverest thing she had ever done.

'You did that on purpose!' Gabriel said loudly.

'Yeah I did.'

'Why? To slow me down?'

'Yeah, give Richard a chance.'

Gabriel didn't answer while he got his breath back and calmed down. He thought about the potential situation that was approaching and could see no reason at all for Cole to be there. He could easily get himself killed. Agent Cole was headstrong, and determined, but he was also blind to the ultimate possibilities that lay before him. Not only that, but was Agent Cole, now in trouble with his superiors, willing to risk his life to prove his point? Jesuel died to prove a point.

'Gabriel, for Cole to avoid even more disciplinary action from his superiors, he would need to provide evidence to explain the situation that he has become aware of. As far as I can see the only evidence that Agent Cole could provide would be to reveal the existence of the Knights Templar. Weren't you the one that always told me to look with better eyes?' Iinnad pointed out. 'Richard could try and provide evidence of Abbadon's existence and that Lilith killed all those people. For him to do that though, he needs the evidence, and he is not going to find any of that stuck in London. He needs to go to Paris. He needs to see Abbadon's headquarters and what goes on there. Anyway, why do you want Richard to join the Templar?'

'Because he has the presence of being.'

'I know that,' replied Iinnad. 'I sensed it as well, but Richard's not the same as the others.'

'No, he is not. He is American.'

'Was that a joke? I've never known you to make jokes. Maybe you've been on this realm too long,' Iinnad paused. 'Don't you want him to help? Don't you want him to learn?'

'He will learn, but learning takes time. I wish I could say I do not want him to jump in the deep end...'

'It's a bit late for that.'

'I said, I wish I could say. He has the presence of being and has never had it explained to him.'

'Neither have the Templar,' added Iinnad.

'No, but as a group, they are aware. The difference with Cole is that he has no idea. No idea of how important he is, but more importantly, no idea of his potential.'

'So it's time for Richard to learn. When we get to Paris, we'll wait for him.'

'OK Iinnad. What do you have in mind?'

'You and I are going to split up as we always do. Richard will come with me; and before you say anything, I'll make sure he doesn't die. I asked you if you wanted Richard to help. You didn't give me an answer. This venture might help him with his superiors; at the very least, if Richard is seen helping in this situation there is more likelihood that he would be accepted into the brotherhood of the Templar. Agreed?'

'Agreed,' Gabriel sighed.

'Gabriel, what I'm going to say, I want you to listen to me,' Iinnad spoke very slowly and quietly. 'Two ears and better listen and all that stuff.'

'You surprise me sometimes,' Gabriel gave a little chuckle. 'I was listening.'

'Abbadon is clouding your mind. Open your eyes.'

XXVII

The First Realm.

Paris – 22.26hrs Wednesday 18th July AD 2001 GMT+1

The taxi rank at the Gare du Nord had plenty of Mercedes for rides; it was the way in Europe, like the Toyota pick-up for the third world militia. With his extremely poor French, he wasted considerable time finding a driver that knew of his destination.

Cole sat quietly on the back seat listening to the Algerian immigrant driver complaining about the debate on the radio. The agent stared out of the window. Without realising the distance travelled, the taxi came to a stop. Cole handed over the francs and climbed out. The driver U-turned quickly and left the agent alone in the dark in a country that didn't like him with a language he couldn't understand. He thought Sir Geoffrey's planning had been productive. Within the last few hours he had managed to catch a train to Paris; changed the Americans name and job description and provided all the documentation to boot. Agent Richard Lawton Cole was impressed; he also wasn't Richard Lawton Cole anymore, now he was Andrew Blake Crawford.

'My initials are ABC,' Cole quietly chuckled to himself, knowing the joke was on him. 'Nice one Sir Geoffrey.'

The American walked up the shiny black tarmac road to the main gates.

'Only light rain… that's strange.'

The main gates didn't have a gate as such, just a gap in the wall and a sentry box that was empty. The building itself had lights on and movement could be seen in several of the windows. Somebody was home. Cole entered the grounds and walked along the edge of the driveway following the low branches of the young pine trees that bordered the property. His eyes were fixed on the building and the guards that he could see in silhouette in the main entrance. He stopped in the shadows and listened. He heard nothing but the night.

'What are you doing?' Iinnad asked from behind.

Cole jumped out of his skin. When he came back to earth, he spun and dived into the undergrowth.

'Shit!' he said confronting the two angelic. 'Crap! What are you doing here?'

'We were waiting for you,' Gabriel said, stepping forward to get a better view. 'They have demonic for guards.'

'They have demons for guards?' Cole questioned. 'I thought the silhouettes looked a little funny.'

'We cannot kill them,' informed Gabriel. 'If we do, the fire alarms will sound.'

'What?' Cole tried to comprehend in a loud whisper. 'Pop quiz, what's the difference between an angel and a demon?'

Iinnad glared at Cole her eyes beginning to turn a cherry red.

'I'm sorry,' Cole quickly added, after noticing her eyes. 'It's only a question.'

'Angelic are pure,' she replied.

'No shit, so how come we have souls?'

'Don't even go there,' Iinnad responded sharply. 'That's a sore point.'

'OK, on a sliding scale,' said Cole. 'Angels, fallen and demons.'

'Yeah! Get to the point Richard.'

'In the grand scheme of things, where do humans fit in?'

'That's a sore point too.'

'Iinnad! You were the one that wanted him here,' injected Gabriel.

'Okay… I'll explain...' Iinnad began.

'The easiest way to look at it, is to imagine two boxes,' Gabriel interrupted. 'Angelic above humans in one box and the fallen above demonic in the other. The fallen are bad angelic and the demonic are...'

'Demonics are bad humans,' Cole concluded.

'You have it, only we do not call them demonics. It is demonic singular or plural, like sheep; one sheep or ten sheep, not sheeps.'

'Got it! So how come they catch fire when they die?' asked Cole moving on.

'Who told you that?' replied Gabriel.

'You did. 'We can't kill them, they'll set off the fire alarms.'

'Nice to see he's learning,' added Iinnad.

'If we talk, we will be here all night. Can we go?' Gabriel asked as he walked to a gap in the undergrowth to view the building.

'And how we gonna get in there?' the human questioned.

'The roof,' Gabriel replied as he backed away from the car park to a patch dry grass by the perimeter wall.

The angelic bowed his head to hide his face from Cole as he

began to transform. Iinnad did the same.

'You'll be with me,' Iinnad said.

'Wait for the guards to look the other way,' whispered Gabriel.

'What about the cameras?' Cole asked.

'You should have thought of that when you strolled into the car park.'

'OK point taken, but you the didn't answer my question.'

'Only those that we wish to see us can,' said Iinnad. 'It takes a lot more energy to be invisible to those with the presence of being.'

'The presence of being?'

'Bloodline,' added Gabriel. 'I thought you were learning?'

'Sorry. So, what happened to the feathers?'

Iinnad sniggered. 'Don't you have creatures on your realm that have the ability of flight without the aid of feathers?'

'Yeah, they're called bats! Nasty little buggers!'

'So am I!' she purred.

'Gabriel,' called Cole in a whisper, 'Have you noticed how sexy she can get?'

Gabriel ignored the agent as he searched the building for a roof access.

'Cute,' replied Iinnad.

'*I'm* cute?' Cole responded. 'You should look in the mirror sometime.'

'I thought you were married?'

'I thought you were an angel?'

'Will you two shut up!' Gabriel muttered. 'Flirt all you like another time. An angelic and married soulcarrier; it will not happen.'

'He called me a soulcarrier,' whispered Cole to Iinnad.

'That's because you are. It's Gabriel's way of saying he's pissed with you.'

'Gabriel,' insisted Iinnad. 'There is another way. We just leave Richard behind.'

'Like hell you do,' Cole protested. 'I thought you waited for me?'

'In time you will learn some of the things that we do, only to a lesser degree,' said Gabriel. 'It is the way of things.'

'Like flying?' Cole joked.

'Like moving within the blink of an eye,' Iinnad said.

Iinnad had disappeared from Cole's field of vision.

'You see we don't just fly,' elaborated Iinnad, from behind the agent. 'We have been given gifts as it were; gifts that aid us to do the jobs we were created to do.'

'And weapons?'

'The weapons are used for the same reason, but not for soulcarriers. Our technology was not meant for you.'

'The guards are not looking,' announced Gabriel as he took flight.

Iinnad gripped Cole tightly as she leapt into the air. As the elegant angelic cleared the treetops she glanced down at the human; his eyes tight shut. Gabriel flew up in a sharp arc and then landed on his tiptoes, on the roof. He turned to receive Cole allowing Iinnad a speedy descent. The agent hung underneath, dangling in her hands, like the prey in the talons of an eagle waiting to be planted firmly on a solid surface. Gabriel snatched the human from the angelic as she came into land. She did so as quietly as Gabriel. Cole however, did not. His legs dragged through the small pebbles that covered the flat rooftop; the sound echoed against the small perimeter wall. The first thing Cole saw when he opened his eyes was Gabriel holding his index finger to his lips. He acknowledged the signal and stayed quiet.

'I don't like flying,' Cole whispered as quietly as he could. 'Sorry.'

Gabriel shook his head implying not to worry. 'You've heard the saying; face your demons?'

'Face my demons?' Cole sharply replied. 'I'll beat the hell out of the demons!'

'That's not quite what he meant,' Iinnad commented. 'But that's good too.'

Then all eyes were trained on the rooftop door; focused and zoomed in on the handle. Even with the low visibility, if the handle were to move, it could still be seen. Cole could hear his heartbeat; he had been under these circumstances far too often for comfort. Gabriel's brace was armed and charged, but to fire it at such close range would be stupid, since the objective had not been reached. Iinnad had yet to charge her brace due to the distraction created by Cole when he landed. As for Cole, he wasn't even packing. The x-ray machine at Waterloo and the incident at the airport meant he had learnt his lesson. His only weapon was a razor sharp combat knife made from a composite, developed by the CIA decades ago, covertly sewn into his tie. Still in the prime position, closest to the door, Cole took hold of the wider end of his tie and gripped the handle within. He slowly turned the knife away from his body, the material pulling on the back of his neck and then against the blade cutting free. The agent then positioned his feet gently so as to stand, making sure the pebbles would not make a sound as he redistributed his weight. The three of them stood and faced the door as Cole stepped forward and raised the knife above his head, his tie still attached.

'Relax Richard,' Gabriel whispered. 'Allow them to come to you.'

'How long do you want to wait?'

Cole lowered the knife, concealing the blade against his wrist. He took a deep breath and continued to creep towards the door. Before he could turn the handle himself it moved. Cole froze. The heavy fire door swung open and a Hercules of a man stepped out. The guard raised a P90 Belgian made machine-gun to his eye and pointed it at the agent. His eyes darted from side to side, across the sights, scanning the rooftop.

'Vous étés seul!' the guard asked.

Cole gave the impression of being confused, which he was. He looked over his shoulder at Gabriel and Iinnad standing side by side, wings still out-stretched.

'English?' the guard asked.

'American,' replied Cole.

The guard stepped back away from the door, the P90 still trained on him. He attempted to check the rest of the roof and at the same time radioed for help. Cole shuffled his feet in the pebbles causing the already jumpy guard to react. He leapt forward and pushed Cole against the doorframe. Cole raised his hands in response.

'You're the American. Where are your friends?' the guard very quickly scanned the rooftop again. 'Open your jacket,' he ordered.

Cole opened his jacket to show he wasn't carrying a firearm or holster being careful to keep the knife concealed.

'Where is the rest of your tie?' the guard inquired.

'Here!' Cole replied as he thrust the blade into the guard's neck, knocking the P90 free as he did so.

The guard fell to the ground with his jugular severed; a pool of blood promptly appeared beneath the body. Cole stood over his victim, blood on his hand.

'Why doesn't he catch fire?'

'Because he's human,' Iinnad answered as she contorted, hiding her wings.

'He's human? Not a demonic?'

'No,' said Gabriel as he stepped over the body and entered the stairwell. 'Why do you think he could not see us?'

'I didn't think.'

'No, you did not. He probably had bad tendencies, that is why Abbadon would have hired him.'

'Oh, that makes me feel a lot better,' Cole shrugged.

'On the other hand,' Iinnad offered. 'He could've been completely innocent with a wife and three offspring, just to put us off.'

'How will I know the difference?' Cole inquired using his severed tie to clean his hand. 'There's no way of telling. How will I know?'

'You won't!' Gabriel's response was harsh. 'Now you have to fear what you don't see. Soon there will be so much to fear that it might cause you to freeze.'

'I won't freeze!'

'Look on the bright side,' Iinnad butted in. 'At least you killed him. If it had been one of us…'

'…A sentinel would have appeared and it would have all been over,' Gabriel finished. 'I have no time to explain now. Shall we?'

The American and the angelic followed Gabriel down the stairwell, all the time listening for the ever-expected security guards. Gabriel blatantly sniffed the air.

'All clear,' he whispered.

'How come he didn't see you?' the fidgety agent asked.

'And you said he was learning,' Gabriel jested. 'Well done, Iinnad.'

'So Gabriel chose to be seen back in London?' Cole questioned.

'No,' Gabriel replied. 'Bloodline have the...'

'Presence of being,' completed Cole. 'And that changes everything.'

Gabriel jumped ahead to the bottom of the stairs.

'Yeah, you're right,' Iinnad whispered in Cole's ear. 'They're part our kind.'

Cole stopped as Iinnad passed the agent to catch up with Gabriel. The agent began to compound the questions in his head, one after the other, queuing up waiting to be asked. *How could he be part angelic? And if he was, why didn't he know sooner like the Knights Templar? Maybe they didn't know?*

At the bottom of the staircase, out of Cole's earshot, the angelic discussed their plans of attack. He descended the remaining steps to join them aware that something was not quite right.

'We are splitting up,' announced Gabriel. 'I will be honest with you, I can hold my own, but Iinnad is a better fighter, so you are going with her.'

'You don't need to protect me,' Cole protested. 'I can look after myself and I know I've a lot to see.'

'Yes, you have,' replied Gabriel honestly.

'Okay, now shut up, you're with me,' snapped Iinnad as she checked her brace.

'What's the plan?' Cole demanded.

'I will deal with the demonic guards,' Gabriel announced.

'All of them?' the human joked.

'You two save Naomi and find out what Abbadon's up to.'

'Is she here? And what are you doing again? Because I…' Cole stopped.

Gabriel had already gone.

'Question!' Cole stated catching a sign on the wall. 'What is 'WRM'?'

'No idea, why?'

'It's a warning sign,' Cole stated.

'Don't know,' replied Iinnad.

'I think this is going to be easy.'

'Why do you say that?' Iinnad was surprised by the comment.

'Because there are no fallen here, just demonic. Well, may be one or two.'

'How do you know?'

'Because when I first got here there was only light rain and it had just started. Whenever Gabriel's around it pisses down. Hadn't you noticed?'

***

On the ground floor by the elevators was a junction of corridors out of view of the reception area where two demonic and one human guard stood nattering to a fourth guard, who sat behind the security desk.

'I've heard nothing from the roof,' stated the seated guard.

'Parler Français!' replied the demonic leaning against the polished wall.

'Abbadon said English and I don't want to be overheard by him, do you?'

'I'll check the roof on my round,' replied the guard closest to the stairwell door. 'If he's not on the radio, I'll make the roof my first stop.'

For some reason the guard's eyes glazed over, with the expression of someone who had eaten something sour. He lowered his head, looking down to the pain in his stomach; a dark patch of red began to grow in the centre of his blue shirt. The material, wet with blood tore easily as the tip of the blade passed through it. The guard stumbled forward, sliding off Cole's knife and collapsed on the floor. Iinnad raised her brace before any of the others had could react and fired continuously. As the angelic moved from across the corridor, her motion meant the blades from her brace were spinning on all axis to devastating effect. The closest demonic was hit first as he drew his side arm. The blade hit his left shoulder, square on, spinning him around to face his colleagues, minus an arm and a hole in his body the size of a dinner-plate. The firepower that Iinnad produced in a matter of seconds could be compared to that of a water hose at point-blank range against a sand castle.

Without a chance of survival the seated guard witnessed his colleagues skewered; dismembered and literally cut in half within seconds. He turned to raise the alarm. His hand needed a command from his brain to press the switch. There was none; the P90 Cole acquired had removed his brain. Iinnad recharged her brace and proceeded to pick up any intact blades from the scene, shaking them sharply to remove the blood and placed them where they belonged. Cole peered around the corner attempting his best to hold down the meal he had on the train.

'Reusable ammo?' asked Cole.

'Yes.'

'With that sort of firepower, a frontal assault would have been easy.'

'Yeah and the rest of the building would have known. Also, I did promise I wouldn't get involved.'

'You have now!'

'Not exactly, but if you say so.'

Iinnad checked the area for any sign that she had been there, apart from the obvious dismembered bodies. Fire extinguishers were on hand for the demonic, preventing the alarms to sound. Iinnad then call for an elevator. Ping! The doors opened. Discarding his extinguisher and P90, the agent grabbed the nearest automatic weapon with the least amount of blood on it and joined Iinnad in the lift.

***

Gabriel was still darting about the building, doing his utmost not to clash with anyone. Apparently and inadvertently, Iinnad and Gabriel's role in their plan had been reversed. On sub-level two, all that stopped. He entered a narrow corridor, which led towards a vault, watched over by two uniformed demonic guards. Without question or request for identification the two men, on spotting him, instantly opened fire. Gabriel leapt back into the corridor he had just come from; as he watched the lead projectiles re-decorate the walls. He managed to hear one of the guards attempt to radio in the whereabouts of the intruder. The angelic brashly poked his head out into the narrow corridor again only to be met by more lead. He ducked back and brought his brace to bear. His arm was aimed at the opposite wall, slightly below head height. He visualised the course the blades would take, bouncing off the walls to their target. Then he fired continuously for a few seconds moving his arms slowly in a circular fashion. Every blade fired, took a different path, whether it be high or low; slightly to the left or to the right; each ricocheting off the walls and propelled themselves down the narrow corridor. The blades bounced off the walls and the ceilings until they had run out a momentum or had found a soft target. Gabriel crouched down poised like a compressed spring, his back against the wall and waited for quiet. The broken glass settled, as did the crashes of masonry from the walls. Gabriel rested his head back and stared up at the plain ceiling.

'Plain ceiling, no sprinklers,' Gabriel spoke quietly. 'No

sprinklers?'

He then leant out of his hiding place to view the mayhem. One of the guards was dead and on fire, the other critically wounded. The victor walked down the passage to the creature lying on the ground, he picked up all the spent blades and cleaned them before reloading his brace. He kicked the weapon from the injured demonic. It slid through the shards of glass and cylindrical bits of metal to rest several feet away. Gabriel then knelt down beside him. The Archangel surveyed the damaged corridor; all the cabinets built into the walls were broken, their contents, the cylindrical bits of metal, all scattered over the floor. The walls were scarred with cuts and burns, caused by the blades. Thick black smoke filled the roof of the corridor from the burning corpse.

'Sorry about that,' Gabriel said. 'May I ask what is in a vault?'

'You know!' stuttered the injured creature. 'Or you wouldn't be here.'

'I do not,' said Gabriel surveying the shiny parcels through the view hole. 'Are there books in here?'

'Books?' painfully replied the guard. 'Money! You idiot! Just money.'

Gabriel shook his head and started back up the passageway.

'You died for *money*?' Gabriel shouted.

The guard didn't answer. Unimpressed, the angelic left the dying demonic struggling to reach for his weapon. His blood soaked fingers picked up one of the small silver cylindrical bits from the floor and popped it in his mouth. The guard did not ignite; he exploded. However, Gabriel had reached the safety of the next corridor before the shockwave knocked him off his feet. Picking himself up, he returned to the vault brushing the dust from his clothes as he did so. Several ceiling panels had collapsed and bricks and mortar lay about making it difficult under foot. As the smoke diminished Gabriel could see the destruction left by the explosion. A depression a foot deep had been left in the concrete floor. Gabriel gazed down at the broken glass and shiny pieces of metal. Hanging on the wall, lopsided, attached by only one screw was a sign. It read: Caution WRM. Gabriel had no idea what it meant, but knew it related to the explosion and the silver pieces of metal. He was also surprised that no other guards had arrived. The angelic quickly drew his sword and removed the cap from the hilt, placing five of the cylindrical metal pieces into the secret compartment, then he sealed it. Gabriel then had a flash back; realising what he had just done. He scanned the destructive area, but saw no water.

'Cherubs?' he questioned himself.

***

Back on the top floor Iinnad and Cole were nipping from room to room searching for anything that would help them in their quest.

'There aren't any demons… demonic here,' stated Cole, disappointed.

'No demonic means no Abbadon,' responded Iinnad with considerable concern. 'This doesn't make sense.'

'Why are you so worried?'

'Because he likes to play games, and he's good at it.'

Iinnad sniffed the air, but shook her head in disappointment. The entire building had continually been used by the fallen, making it impossible for her sense any one individual. She crossed the hallway to the first set of doors she came to. The doors were locked and she wasn't going to force them, not yet. Cole passed her and carefully walked to the end of the corridor where the tiled floor turned to carpet.

He read the written notice on the door aloud. 'Boardroom.'

'Wait,' Iinnad quietly called. 'Something...'

She sniffed at the air once again, then turned direction and sniffed again.

'I don't know,' she said. 'I sense them everywhere.'

Cole was ready. He pushed one of the doors open and stepped back, viewing the inside in a wide arc. Without warning, he entered. Placing his back against the other door and raised his weapon at arm length swiftly swinging it from side to side. In the darkness he tried to find a target. Iinnad impatiently waited in the hallway. She was supposed to be keeping an eye on him, but the task was not as easy as she had hoped.

There was no sound from within the boardroom, so Iinnad crept towards the double doors attempting to get an advantage point to look in from a safe distance. The scent was stronger now, recognisable; some being she had met was inside.

Iinnad's silhouette stretched the length of the table, the only light source being behind her.

'Come in Iinnad, and join us,' came an unfamiliar voice from the shadows.

'Crap.' Iinnad said, knowing it was a set up.

There was nothing she could do, except what was requested.

'I'm losing patience,' said the voice from within the dark.

Iinnad patiently waited. Impatience in an enemy can cause mistakes. Once in the room, she would need to identify each and every target. The calm in her mind slowed her heart rate. She took three bold strides towards the doors and opened the other one as wide as the first. The lights came on. In one sweeping glance she scanned the room; four demonic, but no Richard. She took three more steps into the room. The doors slammed shut. Behind the right door was the fifth demonic. Behind the left was the sixth, holding a blade to Cole's throat, tightly forcing his six-foot frame onto tiptoes to avoid being cut. The automatic Cole had so easily obtained lay by his feet, not a shot fired. Six to one were not the best odds. What Iinnad needed was a distraction.

'Oops,' the American struggled to say.

'Too easy,' replied Iinnad as she positioned herself between the two demonic furthest from the door.

The demonic were confident, with blades and swords in hand, and above all, transformed. Their strength was greater and their awareness heightened. Iinnad made mental notes of the enemy's position in relationship to her own as she glanced around the boardroom. Two more demonic stepped out from their hiding places; one from behind a statue on a plinth, by another set of doors behind her, to the right. The other appeared from behind some curtains to her left on the far side of the boardroom table.

'A lot can be said for round rooms,' she said.

'Why?' uttered Cole ignoring the predicament.

'Evil can't lurk in the shadows; because there are none. Now is everybody present and accounted for?'

***

Gabriel had found no one on any other sub-levels. Using the stairs, he came across Iinnad and Cole's work in the reception area. Killing the guards in the control centre also cut off their communications. Iinnad was only doing what was required to get the job done quickly and efficiently. He knew the potential repercussions of her assistance.

The demonic he came across on the second floor stairwell entrance only had time to see his attacker. The automatic pistol he was carrying clattered its way down the stairs followed by the hand that held it. Gabriel was still swift with his sword. He removed it from the demonic's torso as the flames began to appear. The smoke triggered the sprinklers. The water dousing the corpse as the dusty remains were washed down the concrete steps. The alarms activated, but much quieter than expected.

The artificial rain filled the stairwell with mist as Gabriel reached the top floor. There, the door, already opened by yet another guard, assisted in his silent approach from behind. The jittery guard in demonic form had left a wet trail on the polished floor. He heard nothing but the sprinklers in the stairwell as he felt a piercing pain rip through his body. The demonic raised his hand to fire a warning shot, but the gun fell from his carbonated hand taking several fingers with it as his whole body ignited. Gabriel walked around the flames as the sprinklers in the corridor engaged. Before the water had washed the scent from the air, he could sense something. He couldn't put a name to the scent he had briefly smelt as he neared the boardroom. He had already felt the presence of the demonic, but like Iinnad he was distracted by the familiarity within the lair of evil. He tried the door to Abbadon's office; it was unlocked.

***

Unbeknown to Gabriel, only metres away down the corridor, in the boardroom stood Iinnad. She stepped closer to the nearest and the largest of the demonic.

'I surrender,' she said raising her forearms, bent at the elbows meant her hands only just ran level with her shoulders, palms open and fingers stretched.

'No, you don't,' replied a demonic behind her. 'You're just looking for an angle, your reputation precedes you, Iinnad.'

Cole couldn't move; his demonic friend had restrained the agent to the point of suffocation. As for the outspoken demonic, he was right; Iinnad was working an angle.

Iinnad dropped her arms to her front and undid her belt. It hung loose around her waist, held only by three loops on her tunic. She unfastened the clasp on her brace. In one swift move she raised her hands again to the surrender position and in doing so the weapon slid from her forearm, flew through the air to land a short distance away on the boardroom table, scratching the surface as it landed.

'I surrender,' she repeated. 'I don't understand what you're waiting for.'

Iinnad carried her sword across her back, just as all Gabriel's tower did, the hilt visible just over her right shoulder. She still needed that distraction and with demonic only being human, she had one. She allowed her right hand to drift near the hilt of her sword. Distracted by the motion, the demonic did not notice her slip her left thumb through the eye of the tie on her shoulder pad.

'Hands away from the sword, Iinnad!' demanded the head demonic.

Iinnad stuck her arms out from her side, straight away from her body, palms faced skyward. As she extended her left arm out, the cord slid through the stitching in the upper section of her tunic. The single thread bound together her clothing across the shoulders. Once her arms were fully extended, the thread was removed and then gravity took hold. The material peeled away slowly at first, then with the momentum fell to Iinnad's waist revealing her slender torso. The weight of the metal linked belt assisted the tunic and under garments in its fall to the floor. Naked, Iinnad spun around to face Richard and exposed herself to the enemy, literally. Her smooth skin, athletic physique and feminine features; chosen when she was created, were visible to all those present. All eyes followed her form, heartbeats increased and imaginations flowed. No one blinked.

The lead demonic's hand relaxed, as did his grasp. The glistening metal blade hit the carpet followed by a splatter of blood and then his head. As his body keeled over, the skin began to dry and ignite before it reached the fabric floor. Iinnad's sword had already passed through the first victim and swiftly entered her second. Cole blinked. The second demonic fell backwards into the arms of the third before catching fire. The third, with his arms ablaze, dropped his fallen comrade and attempted to aim his weapon. Iinnad's drawn sword was at arms length as she pirouetted through 360 degrees to face Cole again. In doing so, she took the heads of number three and number four from behind her and embedded the sword into a fifth, severing his arm just below the elbow and cutting into his side.

With the element of surprise gone, the demonic on the other side of the room fired a blade, but Iinnad was too quick. She threw her sword directly at the assailant standing to the left of the double doors, diving towards him at the same time avoiding the incoming blade from her left. Her weapon of war flew straight and true, embedding itself in the creature's chest and the mahogany behind. Then she leapt into the air, naked in body and weapons and cart wheeled across the boardroom table taking up her brace as she went. She landed feet firm and with a sharp jerk backwards, elbowed the armed demonic standing nearby, in the face, knocking him to the ground. She then fired her brace twice into the body on the floor.

'Bitch! You broke my nose,' screamed the burning corpse completely out of context with the situation.

The third blade sliced the demonic's raised fingers before entering his head just above his top lip. The other blade found no soft target, bouncing off the burning floor, it shattered the smoke glassed window behind. Flames appeared from behind the boardroom table, the only confirmation of a target acquired. Cole blinked again.

Iinnad quickly glanced over her shoulder. Swinging through ninety degrees to her left she raised her brace once more, and stopped. The sprinklers had kicked in and the odds had now changed. In the boardroom stood one demonic, one angelic and the American in between. Iinnad calmly walked around the far end of the huge table.

The effort exerted had brought about a little sweat, but it was hidden from the water that glistened on her naked body in the light of the seven small fires in the room. The smoke rose in its own battle against the water, trying to reach the ceiling. The demonic glanced up at the spray. It was the last thing he ever did. Cole stepped away from the burning body behind, checking that the blade had not clipped him. He then picked up his automatic. Blinking, the water falling from his eyelids, he stared at the still naked Iinnad as she picked up her soaked tunic.

'I thought you were gonna help?' she asked.

Cole said nothing. All he could do was stare.

'I thought, that if my body has an effect on you, it's bound to have an effect on them,' Iinnad said as she strolled passed Cole to retrieve her sword. 'The demonic are just human. And the fallen aren't fallen just because they fell from grace.'

'They're not?'

'It's what they did, to fall from grace. They fell for the daughters of man. Don't you read anything?'

'I didn't realise I was supposed to take it literary.'

'Some of it,' Iinnad replied holding up her tunic to inspect it for fire damage.

Cole could not help but stare at the still naked angelic.

'Have you finished gawking?'

Cole snapped out of it and closed his eyes. Iinnad climbed into her clothes, but struggled to straighten the wet material against her skin. She checked her brace, and then with Cole's help began to retrieve the blades she had fired. The sprinklers stopped.

***

The Archangel cautiously forced open Abbadon's office doors to what appeared to be yet another empty room. The only light source was that of the display cases lining the walls. Gabriel's disadvantage was that he was positioned in the doorway and his silhouette darkened the view. The angelic double checked the corridor behind him and entered the office. Immediately, he stepped aside out of the light. Once the door was closed, he sniffed the air. He definitely knew that scent. Gabriel squinted as he looked around the office waiting for his eyes to become accustomed to the low level of light. The only other light source was coming from under the doors to his right, but still providing not enough to see clearly. The angelic slowly walked around the illuminated display, his outline clearly visible from anywhere within the office.

'This is all my life,' Gabriel said to himself as he peered through the glass and glanced over each page. In an anti-clockwise direction Gabriel followed the pages back to the first sheet that Enoch ever wrote. 'Eayah would awake. Who is Eayah?' he questioned before continuing. 'Before sunrise to the shadows created by the poles from her window and read the message from her distant lover. I do not remember this.'

Gabriel stepped away from the display. He ignored the grotesque statues in the centre of the room and turned his attention to Abbadon's desk. The desk was tidy with two board games, Othello and Chess, situated in the corners furthest from the leather chair. They had both been left in a state of play. A small leather bound book with a brass clasp was situated just off centre.

'You're taking a chance entering the enemy domain alone,' came the voice of Abbadon from the shadows.

Gabriel spun around and drew his sword. He saw no one.

'I am not alone,' he answered.

'Taking a chance on a soulcarrier… bringing him here.'

Concern leapt into his mind. *Was Cole ok?* But Gabriel's mind drifted again, back to the scent.

'Leaving things to *chance* is not something I strive to do,' replied Gabriel. 'I have learnt that from the mistakes of others.'

'Whose mistakes?' snapped the hidden voice angered by the comment.

'My enemies. My friends.'

'Speaking of which, how are they?'

The look of concern flashed across Gabriel's face. He sniffed the air once more. Cole and Iinnad were close, but he could also sense the demonic. He sniffed again. Something was not right. He knew the scent of Abbadon clearly, since his recent encounter, but this was different, yet familiar.

***

Iinnad recharged her brace, suddenly turning to face the office doors.

'Movement,' she whispered beneath the noise of the sprinklers.

'But the door in corridor was locked,' Cole whispered.

'Maybe it was a good thing, you not helping and all,' she said as she turned the handles. 'Grab a weapon!'

The agent held up his automatic with a sarcastic smile.

'I meant a blade.'

The doors swung open and a drenched Iinnad stood in silhouette in the doorway; the fires behind her were dying down to an ember. She was not in the best of moods.

'We were just talking about you,' Gabriel stated.

'We?' Iinnad inquired.

'And the mistakes that individuals make,' Gabriel added.

'You say *I* made a mistake? Iinnad questioned.

'No.'

'Are you suggesting I made one?' came the voice from the shadows, its tone changed mid-sentence from that of Abbadon to another.

The hairs on the back of Gabriel's neck stood to attention. That eerie feeling ran down his spine as Barakiel stepped into the light.

'Yeah! One bloody big mistake,' continued Iinnad showing no surprise. Her sense of smell was more acute than Gabriel's. 'And you've obviously paid the price.'

'Iinnad, this has nothing to do with you. Let it go,' Barakiel instructed.

In an instant, she stood between the two old friends.

'I'm sick and tired of being told that things have nothing to do with me, when I'm smack bang in the middle of it. What do you think I was doing? Filing my nails?'

'Do you realise you have all the traits of one of us?' Barakiel stated.

Iinnad immediately gave him the finger and a false smile. Gabriel stepped aside the arguing pair and noticed Cole appear in the doorway at the far end of the office. In his peripheral vision, the finger of one of the statues moved. They were alive! Iinnad sensed something was wrong. The forceful shove from Gabriel confirmed her suspicions. A blade passed between them as Iinnad re-drew her bloodied sword. Gabriel instantly prepared. However, he was completely thrown off guard when Barakiel threw him his own sword. Gabriel instinctively caught it by the handle. In the subtle light of Abbadon's office the Guardian of the First Realm's present world froze.

XXVIII

The Seventh Realm.

27th Sunrise 4th Cycle (Before Time)

And the angelic had forged metals to create weapons. Blades that were sharp and carried with them the spirit of the heavens. Each angelic was given his armour; a brace that was also a shield to protect them, but each angelic was also given a sword; a sword of memories. Barakiel took hold of his sword and held it up high. He held it with pride as all angelic did. Although pride was not a trait of the angelic, yet on this one occasion it was forgiven. Gabriel remembered doing the same. Sophia was happy as she handed each angelic their weapons of war. Surrounded by crystal walls and walking on clouds; the best of friends practised together. Gabriel relived their duels in the Seventh Heaven. He relived the practical jokes, the teachings and the wars. As the ages passed and the battles were re-visited, Gabriel saw through Barakiel's eyes the conflicts they had fought and the enjoyment they had shared in each other's company. He saw Bethany cuddle up next to himself by the fire next to the Temple of Icea as though it were yesterday and not thousands years ago. Then he saw the fallen die as Barakiel killed them. The eons past by in moments.

***

The First Realm. 65th Sunrise – 1st Cycle (26th May) 7436 BC

Suddenly Sariel appeared before him on the drop-ship War.

'Barakiel! Don't argue with me!' he shouted. 'I want you on the First Realm! I don't trust Michael and I think Gabriel will need back up. He is your friend, isn't he?'

'What unit shall I take?' Gabriel found himself asking with Barakiel's voice. 'I don't have a tower of my own at the moment!'

'What do you expect when you've been demoted? Ask for volunteers and if no one steps forward; pick them!'

To Gabriel's surprise, Barakiel's old tower all volunteered to support him. It was a little late for Gabriel to feel anything now, but knowing that he was respected within the other towers put a knot in his stomach. Standing before him were six angelic; Balberith, Asbeel, Tabaet, Lauviah, Islesen and Douis. Gabriel made a conscious effort to remember their faces. He would never forget those that risk everything to support him, unbeknown that it was a game to others.

Being the Angelic of Chance scared Gabriel as Barakiel's tower fell through the clouds as he had, only Barakiel opened his wings very late and only just managed to land safely. He found himself gazing at the body of Islesen, who had followed Barakiel and failed to open in time.

'Gabriel needs us!' he shouted at the others. 'We'll mourn Islesen later.'

As they rushed through the trees and undergrowth to Gabriel's position, Naes – Barakiel's *eyes*, screamed into his ear.

'Barakiel it's a set up! Sariel's playing you. Get out of there! I repeat get out of there now!'

Gabriel tried to confirm the message but there was no response.

'Barakiel!' called Sariel over his link. 'Naes is no longer with us, on this mission. Proceed as ordered. Protect Gabriel!'

The Angelic of Chance stopped dead in his muddy tracks. Naes is no longer with us? Douis overtook Barakiel, taking point and venturing further into the trees. They could hear the CEL weapon fire and see the flashes of fire a short distance ahead. Douis received the first shot fired in their direction. He collapsed into the undergrowth just like Serael in Gabriel's tower. Gabriel could now see the two rows of fallen that were firing on his own position around the wooden structure.

He could see from Barakiel's perspective how dangerous his situation had actually been and that if Barakiel hadn't come to his aid, how the mission could easily have ended in failure. Something was not right about Sariel blatantly disobeying orders though. The way he spoke unnerved him.

'I have to be quick with these,' Gabriel explained to himself. 'Find me a target Gabe cause these little Cherubs don't like water.'

The silver metallic cubes exploded just as Gabriel remembered. He was back in the thick of battle. He looked down at the sword in his hand; it was Barakiel's. In the distance, he could see himself leaving his friend. He now knew how Barakiel had felt.

The dust cloud that was generated by the engines of Pestilence reduced the visibility as Gabriel saw himself and his tower climb aboard as the dropship took off leaving the body of Ubaviel in the sand. The events played out just as Gabriel had remembered it, only this time *he* felt the betrayal.

Over the com-link Michael spoke. 'Barakiel! You are on your own!'

Sariel spoke on the private channel. 'Good luck Barakiel! As Michael said, you're on your own. Say hello to Abbadon for me!'

Gabriel was stunned. He tried to repeat the line, but could not. The words that came out were not the words that he wanted to say. 'What?' he screamed. 'Gabriel! Gabriel! Don't leave me Gabe!'

Barakiel's tower continued to fire their brace weapons. However, in the sky above seven mountains of fire could be seen hurtling to earth.

A blooded hand grabbed his shoulder, one of Barakiel's team, Lauviah was injured and unintelligibly screaming, at him. Gabriel tried to focus, to clarify in his mind what he was seeing.

'They're leaving us to die!' Lauviah panted almost out of breath.

'They'll get the target to safety and return,' Gabriel found himself say.

Over the com-link Michael could be heard. Gabriel did not know that Michael had made contact again.

'Get back to your drop-ship Barakiel!'

Gabriel found himself calling his own name over the com.

'Tell him about the drop-ship,' screamed Lauviah. 'Tell him it's gone.'

'Get back to your drop-ship Barakiel!' Michael repeated. 'And good luck!'

'We… we have no drop-ship,' Gabriel's heart sank with his own words.

The brace weapon fire subsided as the fallen appeared out of the undergrowth surrounding Barakiel's tower. Abbadon was beaming from ear to ear. He had failed to capture the seer, but he was happy with an angelic tower. Barakiel lowered his brace arm and sheathed his sword.

'The Angel of Chance,' Abbadon announced. 'You can't win all the time.'

This was a dark day, but for the skies above, the gloom was to worsen. In the far distance to the west, the cloud line glistened with light for a few moments, catching the eyes of all those present, but then the gloom took back the sky.

'No fight left in you?' asked the Dark Prince.

'I'm too tired,' Barakiel replied. 'I've lost too much this day already.'

'And the day is not yet over.'

The sky grew darker, as though a shadow had been cast over the land. From the west the source of that shadow could be seen approaching, fast. A wave from the seas a few days travel from their location was heading straight for them, covering the horizon as far as the eye could see.

'God in Heaven help us,' Gabriel muttered Barakiel's words in astonishment.

'I think we're on our own on this one,' Abbadon replied.

'Who in the Hell are you?'

'Open your eyes and lift up your horns Barakiel, if ye are able to recognise the one they call Abbadon,' the destroyer replied. 'You have no where to go and judgement is coming. You and these angels that have descended; we will reveal what has been hidden from the children of men and seduce their daughters. You have no choice Angel of Chance.'

Barakiel paused for a moment – no time.

'Those that can take flight, do so,' Abbadon shouted out his orders. 'Those that can't, seek cover behind the ridges in the land and… pray.'

Balberith and Asbeel were already in the dark sky before Barakiel could open his wings. Transformed he took hold of the injured Lauviah. It was hopeless; the wave was too high and travelling to fast. He would not clear the crest. Abbadon, always one to spot an opportunity, opened his wings and caught the gust of wind lifting him up as he snatched the two angelic. Not gaining enough altitude, Abbadon landed near Enoch's small outcrop of rock. Gabriel suddenly realised the strength in this fallen Seraphim as he dragged the two of them to relative safety.

First, the wind came; growing louder, whistling passed the outcrop. Debris began to fall round about, stones, branches and then trees. Then the water came. The deafening sound of millions upon millions of tonnes of the destructive liquid filled their ears as the waves ripped through the wooden structure on the plain and crashed over the tiny outcrop. Being the stronger, Abbadon held fast with Barakiel locked under his arm. The angelic managed, with seconds to spare, to close his wings on the off chance he would have to swim to the surface. The weaker angelic was not so quick as the torrent crashed down filling his wings and dragged him away to his death. Barakiel dug his hands into the ground to gain a firmer hold. Abbadon was steadfast.

It only took a few moments for the wave to pass. Like all forms of destruction, whether man-made or natural, the event takes moments, but the recovery takes a lifetime. The wall of destruction had continued on its path leaving the residual waters behind only fifty to sixty paces deep. Abbadon loosened his hold and allowed his enemy to float to the surface and wait for the waters to subside. Gabriel could see the sadness on Abbadon's face as he drifted on the surface. This destruction had not been his doing, but it had resulted in his losing many of his army.

Gabriel had witnessed the devastation from the air several thousand years previous. Now he had seen it from the ground and much closer to home. The landscape that Abbadon and Barakiel set foot on was a different place, void of life. The rain clouds had gone, but the sky still had an eerie gloom about it. The millions of tonnes of dust particles that had been thrown into the atmosphere and now it was changing the climate. This was a new land of destruction. Soulcarriers would not have survived. Abbadon had wanted the First Realm for himself. How could he rule a dead realm?

As for Barakiel, he owed his existence to Abbadon; the enemy had become his friend. In the face of danger, his long time friend had left him to an uncertain fate. His enemy, although in the same position had stood by and not let him die. Through the eyes of his friend, his brother, Gabriel was witnessed his friend's betrayal, anger and survival. The Archangel now knew why, when and where Barakiel had come to be at his present position in existence. But Gabriel's ordeal was not over yet.

Centuries passed by in seconds as Gabriel saw *his* hand kill hundreds in battles from Hiberland to the 18th Dynasty in Egypt; from the Temples of Apollo in Greece to the judgement of Jesuel in

Jerusalem. Every place that Gabriel had visited since his arrival on the First Realm was being re-lived through Barakiel's eyes. It was no coincidence that Abbadon had been present in these places at those times. Abbadon said he knew everything about him, Gabriel now knew why. It was Gabriel that interfered; Abbadon had only responded to his actions.

As Barakiel's vision of time approached the middle ages, the images began to flicker. Unable to concentrate, Gabriel looked down at Barakiel's sword as it fell from his hand.

XXIX

The First Realm.

01.28hrs Wednesday 18th July AD 2001 GMT+1

Back in Abbadon's office, Iinnad shouted as she knocked the sword away from Gabriel. 'Gabe! Behind you!'

Dazed, Gabriel turned to confront a fallen, his hands up high bringing his sword down hard to meet Gabriel's forehead. A flash of light and a gunshot rang out. The fallen hesitated, Gabriel grabbed the fallen's hands, making sure he didn't hold the sword this time. In rapid succession ten shots rang out and the fallen fell, dropping his weapon at Barakiel's feet. Barakiel picked up his dying comrade's sword and left the scene smiling. Gabriel, still disorientated, did nothing to stop him.

Iinnad was now in full battle mode. She immediately took on the other two fallen. To Cole, chuffed as he was for saving Gabriel's life, the speed at which the angelic fought was literarily a blur.

'Gabe!' Iinnad called out of the indefinable blur. 'You ok?'

'Yes,' he replied as he came to.

'You sure you're alright?' shouted Cole.

'Where's Barakiel?' he replied.

'He left,' replied Cole. 'If you're going after him, then I'm with you.'

'No! Stay with Iinnad,' Gabriel ordered as he left the office after Barakiel.

The Archangel sprinted down the flooded corridor, an inch deep courtesy of the sprinklers. Like a speedboat, Gabriel's feet forced a plume of water behind him. Gabriel's attention instantly turned to the stairwell. With the sprinklers still on and the amount of water in the corridor the elevators would not work. He opened the door releasing the water from the corridor.

'Up or down?' Gabriel asked himself.

The fallen still had their wings, but they could only use them to glide. If Barakiel were to escape he would need altitude to launch from.

'The roof!'

***

Considering the circumstances, Agent Cole was quite calm. He took it in his stride, the blur of bodies to his right, the grunts and clashes of swords. In front of him, lay the shot fallen angelic, which just moved. Ten shots and it wasn't dead? Cole stared at the automatic in his hand.

'It didn't die,' he shouted.

'If they don't burn, they're not fucking dead!' screamed Iinnad from the blur.

Cole waited for the fallen to get to his feet, straightening his body; he stood up facing the door. Cole raised the automatic in line with the back of his head. One shot. The unknown angelic that had once fallen from grace fell to the floor once again, only this time in flames. Cole realised he would have to get used to this.

'Everyone finds a sword the decisive way to finish these guy's off,' Cole said to himself as he bent down and picked up Barakiel's weapon.

'NO!' screamed Iinnad's voice in the back of his head as a searing pain, like a lightening bolt shot between his temples. He dropped to the floor, his body twitching as though in shock. Then he stopped moving altogether. As Gabriel had forgotten and Cole was unaware, an angelic's sword records its own existence. This meant that other angelic could witness a battle or series of events by holding the hilt. The sword began to down load its entire history straight into Cole. All its history; right from the beginning, eons before.

***

The combating blur moved towards the centre of the office. Then without warning one of the fallen ungracefully crashed into the dark carpet and burst into flames. The blur immediately reduced in size. A second pyre ignited on the carpet. Then there was Iinnad, exhausted, breathing heavily her chest rising and falling almost taking her off balance. She sheathed her sword and armed her brace.

'Where's Gabriel?' she panted not realising the state Cole was in.

Cole was still learning from Barakiel's sword.

The sprinklers in the ceiling had just about given their all. The two remaining corpses burnt quickly as Iinnad very slowly walked over to Cole.

'Oh shit!'

Gracefully, Iinnad knelt down beside Cole's lifeless body and attempted to remove Barakiel's sword from his vice gripped hand. Being careful not to touch the hilt, her hand slipped cutting her palm on the blade. She placed her hand on the side of the agent's neck and felt a pulse. Agent Cole was still alive.

'If you were human, you'd be dead right now,' she whispered in his deaf ear.

***

Washington DC – 19.40hrs 17th August AD 1941 EST

Cole stood in front of a bright red door. He remembered the door from his childhood. This was his grandmother's house. He entered the building and was confronted by his grandfather; only he looked really young, like he had in the army photographs that Cole still kept in a tin box in the bedroom.

'Annalise, go in the kitchen,' his grandfather instructed. 'I need to speak with Mr. Kiel alone.'

Cole's grandmother waddled down the hallway, maneuvering her pregnant belly with care. The gentlemen wandered into the living room. It had the same carpet; the one he remembered; the one he burnt when he knocked a log from the open place, when he eight. Only now the carpet appeared new.

'Abbadon has been in touch with you,' Cole found himself saying in the voice of the fallen that had just fled the fight in the office. 'You didn't reply. This is worrying for all concerned.'

'And why is that?'

'Because Orlando… you're special. You work for the newly

formed intelligence agency. This world is changing. It wouldn't surprise us if the US was to enter this world war. We need someone on the inside; that someone will be you.'

'You're gravely mistaken Mr. Kiel,' Orlando replied. 'I will not betray my country.'

'We're not asking you to betray anyone. We might need information from time to time. That's all, nothing more.'

'I told Abbadon,' Orlando raised a finger. 'I told your boss and now am telling you. The answer is no.'

'That's unfortunate.'

'Why, because now you have to kill me?' Orlando surmised. 'I'm a lot faster and stronger than you think.'

'So am I,' Cole found himself saying as he drew his sword from beneath his raincoat and thrust it through the heart of Orlando, before his victim could move. 'Listen carefully Orlando Lawton Cole. We will find another. It might even be your unborn son.'

Cole's grandfather slid off the sword and Cole found himself not even waiting to see him fall.

***

Washington DC – 14.22hrs 10th November AD 1964 EST

Next, Cole found himself sitting in a café down a side street near the old NSA office building. He listened to the Beatles on the jukebox and watched the mini skirts pass by; a tall young black gentleman in a dark suit stood in the doorway surveying each table. It was the first time Cole had ever seen his father. Barakiel raised his hand to get his father's attention.

'Jonathan!' Cole called.

Cole's father approached. Barakiel stood up and shook his hand. The two men took their seats and Barakiel ordered two coffees.

'May I start,' Barakiel requested.

'By all means.'

'You are faster and stronger than anyone else in your division. Do you know why?'

'No,' Jonathan answered then sipped the coffee that had just been placed in front of him. 'Was I a government experiment?' he smiled.

'Funny,' Barakiel laughed. 'You have your abilities because you're one of us and now we need you to work for us.'

'You're kidding? So what do I get out of it?'

'For starters, we can tell you how your father died. I believe you failed to get any information on Orlando Cole's death.'

'Do you work for the Russians?' Jonathan whispered, hoping the answer would be no. 'I will not betray my country. The US is having a difficult time with the Russians right now. So if you want me to spy; you can forget it!'

'What is it with your family? The answer is no. I'm not Russian and we don't want you to spy. Every now and then we may require information. You'll provide it for us. We will not sell the information on to a third party or to any foreign country. So are you with us?'

Jonathan put his coffee down and stood up. 'Mr. Kiel, the problem is, I don't trust you. I don't know how you found out who I work for. I don't understand what you want from me. On those grounds alone, I'm going to have to say no to your offer.'

'You don't want to do that.'

'Are you threatening me?'

'If you don't want to join then I'm afraid that makes you a threat. Maybe your unborn son will be easier to turn.'

'Mr. Kiel, now you've threatened my family. Touch them and I'll kill you. Enjoy your coffee,' Jonathan left the café.

Richard found himself cursing his father as he left.

***

Jonathan straightened his suit as he briskly walked down the street towards his office. He stopped by the entrance of a tiny side alley, to calm himself since the threat to his pregnant wife had riled him somewhat. A vice-like grip and a jolt of his arm pulled him into the alley. The jerk of his body threw him off his feet. He instinctively rolled over and grabbed for his revolver in his shoulder holster. Through Barakiel's eyes Richard stood over his father the sword in his hand. Jonathan Cole was defenseless.

The sword continued it journey through Barakiel's life, right up until the point that he threw it at Gabriel

XXX

The First Realm.

Abbadon's Office – 01.29hrs Wednesday 18th July AD 2001 GMT+1

Iinnad peeled Cole's fingers off the hilt one by one until the steel fell free. The agent's body jolted, his eyes only half opened as he tried to focus on the familiar voice.

'Shit! Shit! Shit! I saw my father,' whispered Richard, as he looked passed Iinnad. 'I saw my grandfather.'

'Richard, listen to me,' Iinnad instructed. 'Listen to me, you're in shock! Okay? Are you listening? You're gonna be fine.'

'My father! I saw how my father died! I saw how my father died.'

'Richard! What was the last thing you remember?'

'I threw Gabriel my sword. No, Barakiel threw…'

'What was the first thing you can remember?'

'Clouds, crystal, transparent floor and someone giving me my sword, a pretty woman with blue eyes, only it's not my sword.'

***

Gabriel stepped out onto the pea-beach rooftop. Barakiel had already transformed and was about to step off the ledge of the building.

'I will find you,' Gabriel called.

'That you would, brother.'

'I followed orders, Barakiel.'

'You left me to die, Gabriel,' Barakiel said stepping back onto the roof.

'I do not want to fight you,' Gabriel admitted.

'Then let me kill you.'

'Why Barakiel?' Gabriel asked. 'I have seen what happened through *your* eyes. I did not know that your own drop-ship was gone. I doubt Michael even heard your last transmission.'

'He knew!'

Barakiel raised his forearm, armed his brace and activated the shield. Then kicking the pea-beach at Gabriel, he launched his attack. Gabriel raised his sword, prepared for the clash of metal and instead was showered by tiny pebbles. He stepped back. The pebbles were followed by the steel.

'I told you I did not want this,' Gabriel said, as they broke free.

'I missed you for a long time, but now, you're better off dead!' Barakiel finished his sentence with a downward blow of his newly acquired sword.

***

Iinnad grabbed Cole's shoulder and pulled him to his feet.

'Can you stand?' Iinnad asked, her voice showing signs of distress. This was something else Cole had not seen in Iinnad, nor ever thought he would. 'Talk to me Richard! Can you stand?'

'No,' he replied. 'No I can't!'

'Try!'

'No! JUST… give me a minute!'

Iinnad ignored Cole's request and manhandle him into a chair next to Abbadon's desk. The exhausted agent slumped down into the padded leather and with eyes lids almost closed, watched Iinnad as she began to check the office and the boardroom for any more hostiles. With the blonde angelic now out of sight, Cole's attention wandered to his close surroundings.

'Board games,' he said to himself. 'Everything's a game.'

Iinnad returned from the boardroom, closed the doors behind her and began to check the windows.

'Find anything?' Cole asked, tired.

'The other room and secretary's place are clean,' she replied. 'I don't think there's anybody else here. I still have this feeling that something's not right.'

'What?'

'I don't know,' Iinnad replied. 'Just a feeling.'

'It would be risky for the guards to call in the local police, wouldn't it?'

'Abbadon wouldn't do that unless he'd turned them,' Iinnad answered as she checked the last window.

All that remained to be checked were the main doors to the corridor that were still open. The sprinklers had finally stopped, but the flood was clearly visible outside the office. Although, there was water in the office, the floor was about two centimetres higher than the corridor and the water was flowing out.

'What you got there?' Iinnad inquired as Cole studied the board games.

Othello and Chess and… a book.'

'What's Othello?'

'Apart from a Shakespearian play…'

'A what?'

'It's a… I *thought* you read my mind.'

'I did,' she panted. 'I just skipped bits,' she added raising hand her to Cole's forehead.

'Oh no!' Cole knocked her hand away. 'Othello is a game of strategy,' he continued. 'We used to play it at the agency between lessons. Two players; one black; one white; the objective…'

'To take the opponent's pieces… I remember that bit,' she said staring at the glass display.

'That's the point. The objective is to turn them, convert your opponent's pieces to your side. The winner is the one with the most when the boards full.'

'Okay, I didn't take much notice of your game playing. Interesting though. In reality that's what Abbadon does; turn people. He has soulcarriers join his ranks and…' Iinnad was distracted.

'What is it?' Cole asked.

Iinnad was carefully working her way around the display cases. She would read a few lines to herself; skip a page or two as though trying to find her place in a book.

'Here we have angelic script in the form of a book about Gabriel,' she stated.

'The Book of Gabriel,' Cole injected.

'I just said that.'

'He should have a hundred pages of it. Does it tell you anything?'

Iinnad stopped at a page near the boardroom doors.

'Yeah, I'm in this… And I *die*,' she said quietly.

'I didn't think you could die. Are you sure that's what it says?'

'It says I fall in battle,' Iinnad sombrely replied.

'Am I in there?' called Cole from the other end of the room.

'Yeah, you die too. Well, I think its you.'

'Well, everybody dies,' joked Cole attempting to hide his thoughts. 'What do you mean you think its me?'

'It speaks of *a Firestone*,' replied Iinnad totally detached.

Suddenly the building shook; followed by a flicker of the desk light. The room then shook again and muffled explosions could be heard.

'What the hell was that?'

'Gabriel probably,' Iinnad snapped to it. 'I think we should go.'

The angelic helped the agent to his feet. Cole had to lean on the desk for support since his legs still weren't working as they should. The building shook a third time, but now the sounds changed to that of mechanical grinding of gears and motors. Cole struggled to stand.

'Is this normal?' he asked out of breath.

'What d'you mean by normal? You or the building?'

'What do *you* think?'

'I don't know,' replied Iinnad. 'It can be painful for an angelic, but you're a soulcarrier, albeit… you know, which is probably why it didn't kill you. You were holding the sword for a long time. You should be dead.'

'How long?' Cole panted.

'About fifteen seconds.'

There was another explosion.

'I didn't mean the sword. I meant the windows.'

Iinnad turned her attention to the windows of the office. The panes of glass were intact, but the mechanical noise that could be heard was a shield of shuttered metal being wound down and locked into place. One window was already covered; the second and third were almost closed.

The agent took a couple of deep breaths and took the pain as he stood firm, touching the table with his fingertips.

'Richard we have to go!'

Cole stared at the desktop as he gathered his thoughts and strength. He stared at the board games still in play.

'Have you tried to finish a game that's half in play?'

'No! Hate the games,' Iinnad snapped. 'Never listened when they were explained to me. Now lets get you out.'

'I want my sword,' Cole said quickly.

'Your sword?'

'After what I've just been through, that's my fucking sword.'

Iinnad pick up Barakiel's sword by the blade and Cole took it in his left hand. There was no pain, no jolt, and no trance. The agent had seen all there was to see. He reached for the book; Iinnad beat him to it and stuffed it into his inner jacket pocket.

'You said I don't read enough,' he joked.

'Do all soulcarriers joke at times of danger?'

The blast shield closed over the third window as the building shook again. Next, the boardroom doors began to shake as the blast shield began to cover them.

'The shields are protecting this room,' Iinnad stated. 'We have *got* to go.'

'You ever play chess?' Cole shouted over the noise.

'No! I told you. Michael used it as a form of tactics instruction, but I didn't pay attention,' she replied pulling Cole away from the desk.

'Wait!' he screamed. 'You get me through that door in two seconds. Throw me if you have to, but wait. I play chess.'

'Meaning?'

From his jacket pocket he quickly removed his mini travel chess set and placed it on the desk. 'You said Abbadon plays games,' snapped Cole, while he studied the layout of the Othello board Cole began to copy the chessboard onto his pocket set. 'Give me 30 seconds!'

The boardroom door broke free from their hinges and crashed to the sodden carpet. The steel shutters were now closing on their only exit.

'Hurry up! Couldn't you have done this when you were sitting down?'

Cole carefully checked all the remaining pieces positions on the board.

'That's it,' Iinnad screamed. 'Now we're leaving.'

Cole felt a surge flow through his body as the chessboard disappeared from view, as did the desk, chair and office. The bright strip lights of the corridor replaced the dark subdued light of Abbadon's chamber. He checked his hand; the chess set was still there. He put it back in his pocket and relaxed for a moment. The splashes of water on his face were refreshing as Iinnad rushed down the passageway to the fire escape hauling Cole with her. She opened the door to the stairwell, releasing more water down stairs into the sub-levels.

'I think I know what the explosions are,' Cole panted.

'How?'

'I have what's his name's sword, it's seen a lot.'

Cole pointed to the sign on the back of the door.

'Caution WRM beyond this point. Water Reactive Material. We keep metals like that under oil.'

'Angelic weaponry?' Iinnad pondered. 'We keep it warm.'

The both of them looked down at the stream passing their feet and cascading down the stairs.

'Oops,' Cole commented.

'Gabriel must be on the roof,' replied Iinnad as she steadied Cole on her shoulder. An explosion knocked her off balance, but she steadied herself without comment or complaint. The sound of the chemical reactions wasn't muffled in the stairwell, below them the railings rattled and the smell of carbon from all manner of substances on fire filled their nostrils.

***

Metal clashed with metal as Gabriel attempted to subdue Barakiel. The Archangel was tired. He could not sustain the amount of punishment that Barakiel was delivering for much longer. Gabriel had to concentrate on his position just to stay on his feet. The problem was he was distracted by the fact that it was his brother in arms he was fighting. Barakiel knew this; it was his advantage. The other advantage was strength, since he had yet to give Gabriel the chance to transform. Another spin and clash of blades, and this time Gabriel dropped his sword. Breathing heavily Gabriel made no attempt to pick it up, opting to step back away further and waited for the moment he needed to transform. The fallen bent down slightly still keeping an eye on the Archangel. Barakiel's hand hovered over the sword he couldn't decide whether to hold the blade or the hilt.

'Take a chance Barakiel,' Gabriel urged. 'You might learn something.'

'And you might change.'

'Oh I will,' Gabriel promised.

That distinctive pain shot through Gabriel's shoulder blades, up his neck and proceeded to give him an almighty headache as he began to transform once again. Barakiel, in turn, grabbed hold of the angelic's sword and braced himself. He closed his eyes. Nothing. He looked down at the sword in his hand, it didn't make sense, unless Gabriel hadn't seen combat since that fateful day. Barakiel straightened his back and stood in a corner of the rooftop, the city lights of Paris behind him a sword in each hand. Gabriel re-emerged from behind the roof access fully transformed; his wings open wide crisp and clean. In contrast, Barakiel, the once proud warrior of God looked shabby, a dirty a remnant of the past. His wings were torn; cuts and stitches were still visible. As for Gabriel, not even a scar could be seen as he approached the fallen unarmed, his hands by his side, palms facing forward.

'I did not want this,' he repeated.

'Then let's leave it here,' Barakiel suggested throwing Gabriel his sword. 'You could let me leave, no one would know.'

'I could, but I have my sword, I thank you for that, and I am stronger now.'

'But you lack experience, Gabriel. Your sword tells me you haven't used it since you left me to die. Did you feel that bad about that?'

'No!' Gabriel replied sharply changing his tone. 'I did not think about it at all. Why would I have? You were stupid you should have followed orders. But you do not follow those orders. Barakiel is the *Angel of Chance*, there has to be that element of risk with you; with *everything* you do. Why did Islesen die? Because of you!'

With each sentence Gabriel carefully and subtly took a step closer to his prey. His mind was made up. He had a job to do, for he was the Guardian of the First Realm.

'You think I would rise to that?' Barakiel challenged.

'Not at all! It is the truth and you know it.'

The door to the roof swung open with a crash, bending back its hinges. Iinnad struggled out carrying Richard and gently placed him in the pea-beach against the brick wall of the roof exit. The refreshing night air and the cool rain was a pleasant change to the acidic smoke and chlorinated sprinklers.

'Don't mind me. Didn't mean to interrupt,' she said casually. 'You carry on!'

Barakiel brought his arm back and swung it over his head bringing his sword down to bare on the momentarily distracted Gabriel. The Archangel raised his brace arm to deflect the blade; the telescopic shield extended taking the full force of the blow.

'That's new,' calmed Cole.

The impact was still enough to knock Gabriel back a few steps. Unsteady, physically and mentally, Gabriel knew that Iinnad had been right about his lack of ability. However, the best form of defence was to attack.

He disengaged his force shield and lunged forward with his sword. Barakiel startled by the sudden change of stance retreated momentarily. It gave Gabriel time to unclip his brace and throw it over to the collapsed agent. A sign that he was not going to give up just yet, if anything, he was to see it through. Had Barakiel forgotten? Gabriel had always hated this part of his existence, having to show his rank. After all, Gabriel was not just an angelic; he was Archangel, one of the seven angelic on the Council of the Seventh Realm. Gabriel knew that it was practically in name only, but Barakiel wasn't to know that.

The fallen tried in vain to conceal the doubt that appeared in the lines on his forehead, but there was no escaping the fact that he was no longer one of God's soldiers. That element wasn't on his side any more.

Gabriel began to sidestep to his right towards the edge of the building. Barakiel matched his every move and it was he who reached the ledge first, delicately stepping up onto it without taking his eyes of his combatant. Gabriel followed suit. The two angelic faced up to one another about forty feet apart. Eye contact was made without blinking, to move within the blink was one of those unfortunate abilities. Gabriel knew he had to strike, but a blow that only wounded would be sufficient. For Barakiel, he had to beat an Archangel.

Without warning, controlled and balanced, the two warriors ran the ledge towards each other; swords raised. Neither would waver, neither would stop. As the two passed on the narrow ledge, neither gave way as steel struck steel and blood was drawn. Gabriel stopped almost immediately and turned on a dime.

'Damn you Gabriel,' cursed Barakiel.

It took him a moment to face his opponent.

Gabriel stared at the sixteen-inch gash up Barakiel's left side ending near his collarbone. The wound was bleeding, streaming and staining his clothes down to his shoes. The deep cut from his collarbone led straight into his chest where Barakiel's own sword was located. In the clash, Gabriel had managed to deflect Barakiel's sword back into him. Gabriel also noticed that one of Barakiel's wings, the left one, was slightly lower than the other. The fallen was breathing heavily.

'You know,' he said battling to breathe. 'You know the soulcarriers wrote a book? We're in it.'

'Yes I do,' Gabriel said.

'You read it?'

Gabriel's lips moved, but no words came out, so he just nodded, yes. The Archangel then winced in sympathy for Barakiel, as did Cole and Iinnad as he withdrew the sword from his chest and dropped it over the ledge.

'Psalms. Chapter 42 Verse 10. As with a sword…' he mumbled as his skin began to dry.

'Forgive me,' Gabriel quietly requested as he stepped forward to help his dying friend.

Barakiel's left wing fell from his body, cut too badly it tore from his back. It was Gabriel's intentional cut. The wing burst into flames on the pea-beach. Now off balance, the fallen angelic toppled over the side of the building a ball of flame before he hit the car park below. Gabriel didn't move. To lose a friend suddenly is hard to come to terms with, but this was the second time he had lost his friend, both by his doing. The moment didn't appear to end and then the building shook. Another explosion. Gabriel was alert and his attention turned to the other members of his team. He approached Iinnad, crouched beside the slumped agent both wet through. Gabriel made a closer inspection as he used his wings to shelter the breathless man from the rain.

'I'm sorry Gabe,' comforted Iinnad.

'He chose his path,' replied Gabriel.

'He killed my father,' said Cole. 'I wanted to finish him.'

'Well, technically…'

Gabriel's glare silenced Iinnad.

'What?' demanded the vengeful agent.

'He is where he belongs,' Gabriel lamented.

'And Psalms 42.10?'

'As with a sword in my bones, mine enemies reproach me; while they say daily unto me, Where is thy God?' Gabriel quoted.

'So now he has to be judged?' Cole asked.

'Gabriel, you know as well as I do, this isn't the end,' Iinnad stated.

'I know,' Gabriel replied.

Another muffled explosion shook the building. This time cracks started to appear in the roof and smoke managed to escape.

'Lets get Cole on the ground, it will be safer there,' the Archangel instructed as flames began to flicker through the gaps in the pebbles. Iinnad automatically began to transform again as she stood, still holding Cole. The flames began to grow, creating bright orange and red walls of intense heat. The quantity of flames was eliminating all forms of shadow on the rooftop. Gabriel gracefully stepped off the ledge.

'Hold onto me and don't let go of the sword,' Iinnad ordered.

Cole held tight as Iinnad lifted him into the air and glided across the car park to the tree line where they had initiated their assault. Gabriel joined them.

***

The building was now completely engulfed in flames. The windows on the upper floors began to shatter and flickering heat lapped the framework. On the roof the remaining shadows diminished completely as Lilith stepped into the light. The ability to move within shadows had many advantages, but only at night. The burnt demonic; sprinklers and the explosions had kept her scent cloaked from the angelic. With her invisibility she was able to observe, which was all she was ordered to do, even though it was accepted with the greatest of objections.

'This was not meant to be,' she said to herself as she appeared over the edge of collapsing roof. 'Who attacked first, Iinnad?'

The panels on the roof began to drop into the furnace of the building beneath. The heat liquefied the pitch, the pea-beach sinking into the black viscous surface. Lilith ran with lightning pace through the flames to the far side of the melting roof, out of view of the car park.

She leapt high into the air and transformed as she did so. With her wings outstretched she silently glided into the dark to the chorus of fire engine and ambulance sirens.

***

Iinnad set Cole down on the wet grass, his back against a tree.

'The chess game,' he said as he rested his head against the bark.

'What chess game?' Gabriel asked, his attention still sharp and focused.

'On Abbadon's desk!' added Iinnad. 'Which realm have you been on?'

'Why did you not tell me?' Gabriel snapped.

'We only just escaped a burning fucking building!' Iinnad stated.

'Iinnad, do you remember the layout?' Gabriel inquired.

Iinnad raised her eyebrows; Gabriel should have known she never paid much attention to Michael and his board games. The Archangel, frustrated, turned to the still exhausted agent.

'Do you remember the layout of the board?' he said calmly.

'I can do better than that,' Cole replied revealing his chess set. 'It's a setup; a trap. The layout of the pieces; at first glance you think white will win, but in two moves black could take out the rear line.'

'Well we *know* that,' Iinnad sarcastically added.

Gabriel's stern stare immediately quietened the loud angelic.

'If I had the next move it would have been obvious to attack on black's rear line with the most powerful pieces.'

'We just did that,' Iinnad stated.

'Yes, we did,' Gabriel thoughtfully confirmed.

'But black would ignore the attack,' Cole continued. 'And… allow the damage to continue, because it was in a position to take the white knight and checkmate.'

'We were lured away from London,' Iinnad said stating the obvious.

'This is only half of it,' Cole hadn't finished. 'You have said over and over that Abbadon plays games. You were in the room Gabriel, you must have seen the other board game?'

'I saw them both, but I was distracted by the scent of Barakiel. I saw Othello. I take it that he has turned members of the Templar, or he has informers on the inside?'

'Normally I would agree, but they're a pretty dedicated bunch,' admitted Cole. 'But it goes further than that. I can't remember the complete layout, but if I was black…'

'You are!' Iinnad joked.

'Iinnad!' Gabriel snapped. 'Shut up!'

'Same as the chess set, only faster,' Cole peered into the dark to find the game in his head. 'One move by black and over half the board changes; black wins. He plays games; you keep telling me that. I should have seen this.'

'Well, it is done now,' said Gabriel. 'You cannot turn back the clock.'

'And now what?' Cole asked.

'Are you well enough to travel?'

'He should be,' Iinnad answered.

'I thought you were going to keep him alive?' Gabriel said sharply.

'He is! How was I to know he'd pick up Barakiel's sword.'

'And for how long?'

'I was busy!' replied Iinnad.

Gabriel turned back to Cole. 'Luckily you should be fine, a human would not have been.'

'I am human,' replied Cole. 'But, yeah, yeah, I know what you're getting at.'

'No you don't,' Gabriel pushed. 'You are bloodline.'

'I'm aware of that!'

Gabriel's attention turned to Iinnad. 'Did you get the Codex?'

'What?'

'The 21st Codex,' whispered Cole under his breath.

'What are you taking about?' Iinnad insisted.

'You should read more,' Cole sarcastically smiled.

'Iinnad,' Gabriel flicked his fingers in front of her face. 'I was talking about the display in Abbadon's office. He would have collected it for a reason.'

'So was I,' Cole opened his eyes wide, his strength was coming back. 'Henry told me. The Templar know of the Book of Gabriel, they call it the 21st Codex.'

'I knew Henry's teaching would do you some good,' Gabriel said turning back to Iinnad. 'So did you get it?'

'No, I had enough trouble getting Richard out *alive*.'

'Why d'you need it so much?' asked Cole. 'Is it because Abbadon has it?'

'The whole objective of Abbadon's existence now appears to be my demise,' explained Gabriel. 'But we also have some similar goals; even though the reasons may vary. I require the truth, which he wants to expose. Exposure would be damaging to the majority of the populace. My main enemy is not Abbadon; it has always been 'lies' and those who spread them. From a historical point of view that would be...'

'The church?' Cole interrupted.

'I was going to say, mankind itself.'

'So you want the control?'

'Is that what you think?' replied Gabriel. 'No, I do not want the control. I need people to open their eyes, to see this realm the way I see it; to see its future; to see its beauty. The problem is, there is a conspiracy of ignorance that has built up over the centuries, and I cannot stop it... So, I use the Templar to insert pieces of information here and there, hoping that it will be found.'

'You said you didn't use them,' Cole argued.

'Not in the context of risking alliances, but when the information is found, mankind studies it, publishes papers, but now we have documentaries about it as well. The information spreads.'

'So if you don't want control, then to what end?'

'The pages from the crime scene in Washington…'

'The Chevalier house?' Cole butted in.

'The Codex that Henry has been searching for; pages from Washington are part of the same. It was written by a soulcarrier called Enoch. We lost it a long time ago.'

'You never read it,' Cole gasped. 'You never read it!'

'No,' Gabriel was cautious. 'Why are you surprised?'

'Enoch? Henry mentioned him. Wasn't that with Bara... kiel?' Cole inquired.

'The memory of that sword could serve you well, I'd keep it,' Iinnad advised.

'The Codex contains...' Gabriel said thoughtfully. 'It is a biography. No, it is more than a biography; like the Bible, it deals with the past, but it also influences the present and gives insight to the future.'

'Your future? This whole fight is about you, right?' Cole indicated.

'No... It is about man. I am the Guardian of the First Realm. This is the First Realm of Heaven. Soulcarriers live here and so do I. The Codex of Gabriel, *me*, is about the future of the First Realm as well as its past. Now do you understand?'

'If this book, Codex, could mess things up that much then why doesn't Abbadon use it?'

'I do not know. Maybe it is his way; maybe it is another one of his games, who knows?' Gabriel turned to Iinnad. 'You knew the codex was important?'

'Yeah!'

'Then why did you not bring it with you?'

'WHY?' Iinnad barked, then remembering to keep her voice down. 'How could I take out half the bloody room? The codex was bolted to the walls.'

'Children!' Cole verbally got between them. 'This isn't the time!'

The agent then slid his feet under his rear and then wriggled up the side of the tree using his newly acquired sword for stability to stand. He stooped forward to keep his balance. The little leather bound book from Abbadon's desk fell to the ground. The clasp broke open and the pages turned in the damp breeze.

'Any more surprises?' Gabriel asked as he picked up the leather bound pages. 'I have not seen this in over... 680 years,' his eyes glowed red with the anger filling his veins once again.

XXXI

The First Realm.

Paris – Morning – Monday 18th March AD 1314

Six and half years after his arrest, Jacques de Molay had spent the entire time in prison under the care and supervision of the Dominican monks of the Inquisition. What would Dominic have thought if he had seen what the Pope had done to the Order that he had founded? Originally established during the bloodletting days of the Albigensian Crusades almost a hundred years previous, the Inquisition had been authorised to use *any means*, stopping short of spilling blood or breaking bones, to gather a guilty verdict. However, as it had already been witnessed in the heretic crusade in the Roussillon Languedoc, this rule was not often adhered too.

That morning, the Archbishop of Sens took his seat alongside the other three papal commissioners behind the long table covered with fine linen that was situated on a specially erected stage in front of the Cathedral of Our Lady, Notre Dame, in the centre of the River Seine, Paris.

The scruffy crowd pushed and shoved in the cobbled square to get a better view of the proceedings. The Regal commissioners sat with pride, with their backs to the Notre Dame before the Knights Templar.

The last of the now dissolved Order were brought up onto the stage for all to see. Jacques de Molay stood out from the others; Hughes de Piraud, Geoffroi de Gonneville and Geoffroi de Charney. After years of imprisonment, torture and confession he still stood proud and the crowd, his witness.

The papal commissioners should have suspected something was not quite right, but the four men had, according to testimony, openly and publicly confessed to all crimes listed before them. The Bishop of Alba stepped forward and the crowd quietened to hear his words. He looked down at the people of Paris, in the shadow of the bell towers of the cathedral, and then proceeded to read out the charges that had been made against the four leading men of the most powerful military Order the known world had ever seen. From the back of the silent crowd, Gabriel watched the proceedings. If imprisonment was all they were to receive, it would be no hardship to spring them free. However, he also knew that Jacques de Molay was a good man and a man of honour with a steadfast faith, stubborn, almost pigheaded. Unfortunately, at this point in time, all the decisions would be Jacques' alone. All Gabriel could do, like the crowd, was watch.

The sun climbed into the cold spring sky creating a silver lining around the ornate outline of the cathedral bell towers. Below the Bishop continued.

'These are your public confessions,' he said as he waved the papers high above his head. 'In the year of our Lord 1311 you all admitted your guilt, in court.'

Gabriel translated the words in his head as the bishop spoke. The Archbishop of Sens then stood up and raised a small leather bound book with a brass clasp in his hand. He turned slightly from left to right to allow the crowd to see.

'Your *Holy* Order was issued with this Rule by the Pope himself,' the Archbishop stated. 'But it didn't take long for you to change it to suit yourselves.'

All present were well aware of the incident that had occurred a century before, but the four men said nothing. As for Gabriel, he recognised the book. It was one he gave Molay on the night of Friday the 13th October 1307, before he left him to his fate.

'But you failed to even follow your *own* rule,' the Archbishop declared.

'Your sentence,' continued the Bishop of Alba, 'will be perpetual imprisonment for the grossest of crimes, the unspeakable acts.'

The ageing Grand Master took centre stage.

'The commission is right,' bellowed Molay across the square to an astonished crowd. 'They have heard my pleas, and so here I stand, to be sentenced, before Heaven and Earth and with all of you present to bear witness. I say to you all, this day, that I am guilty of the grossest of crimes. Not only am I guilty, but I knowingly did so, as did so many Knights of the Order before me.'

The seated commissioners nodded their heads in agreement with the beguiling Grand Master's statement.

'I am an old man,' Molay continued. 'An old man approaching the end of my days and as I age, I should not shy away from what is right. So I declare, the truth obliges me to do so, that I am guilty… of admitting to the false accusations brought against me. I stand here an innocent man!'

The crowd erupted into a roar of support for the old man, possibly the last of his kind. The commissioners tried, but failed to quell the crowd. Molay raised his hand.

'Like all those before me who have admitted to these lies, and did so under torture,' he shouted over the cheering mob. 'I confessed to those inflicting such plain, only to appease them and reduce my own suffering.'

Jacques then pulled at his habit, which gave way, falling from his shoulders and settled around his waist. The evidence of his pain was only too apparent. The crowd fell silent, as did the commission. The Dominican monks had done an exquisite job of torturing the aged leader.

'I reject the falsehood against the purity of the Order, knowing it to be as innocent as I. I retract my original confession in the presence of you all as witness, knowing fully, in this doing, I shorten my life more so. But I cannot live a lie; compounding the lies of others. My life has been offered to me, but at a price I cannot afford. I say again, here and now that the Order is innocent, its saintliness has been stained by these allegations and that I willingly give up my life an innocent man.'

The last Grand Master of the Knights Templar bowed his head as he finished his speech to the jubilation of the crowd. The people of Paris punched the air and jumped with joy at the sight of blatant defiance against the regal, rich, pompous commission. Geoffroi de Charney stepped forward and stood beside his Grand Master and friend, a sign of total agreement. The simple gesture had sealed his fate also. Jacques de Molay viewed the crowd from the stage unaware that

Gabriel, from his advantage point watched with admiration, a tear in his eye as he had translated all that was spoken. The two men had now set in motion a chain of events that Gabriel could not covertly stop, as he would have wished.

The face of disgust appeared on the Archbishop of Sens' face, he motioned to the members of the papal commission to join him within the sanctuary of the cathedral, away from the baying crowd. As the four men of the cloth left the raised platform they could not help but notice Hughes de Piraud and Geoffroi de Gonneville cowering at the edge of the stage, doing their utmost to distance themselves from the farce that presented itself centre stage.

Within the thick walls of Notre Dame, the air was chilled, colder than the spring morning outside. The atmosphere mirrored that of the climate as the Archbishop instructed the Bishop and cardinals as to what to do.

The guards of the Inquisition climbed the steps to four condemned men. Piraud and Gonneville were led away immediately to carry out their sentence; harsh and perpetual imprisonment, as was promised. As for Jacques de Molay and Geoffroi de Charney, the Archbishop of Sens was to debate further over the fate of these thorns in the backside of the Church. A meeting was quickly arranged that afternoon with men of the Church and theology to determine what should be done.

On hearing the news, the King of France was outraged by the revised confession. He saw it as a defiant stand against the crown as well as the Church. He was right to think so, considering it was he who had brought about their downfall in the first place. Before the King's reply had reached the ears of the Archbishop, a pyre had already been constructed on the nearby island of Ile-des-Javiaux. The Biblical scholars and theologians would not be required, for it was to be Jacques de Molay's last day.

The two Templar Knights were led through the square and down to the shore of the River Seine beneath the ramparts of the cathedral where they boarded a boat for the short journey to Ile-des-Javiaux. Gabriel was helpless, perched amongst the gargoyles on the towering buttress at the western tip of Notre Dame. A short distance below, the two old men were tied to stakes at the centre of the pyre.

Before the flickering torch sealed their fate the Grand Master made a request, for his bonds to be cut so he could face 'Our Lady' before he died. The request was granted and the two highest-ranking Knights Templar stood side-by-side in flames. As the heat increased and scorched his skin, Molay cried out so all could hear.

'For your punishment of the innocent,' he called. 'I demand that both the King of France and my Pope stand in front of the supreme judge before the year's end.'

The searing heat then scorched his lungs and the old man slumped into the flames and died aside his dear friend.

Gabriel turned away tears of pride on his cheeks. To fulfil Molay's promise was the least he could do. From the bell tower of the cathedral, the angelic stared down at the empty square, the wooden stage still in place. A solitary figure, a tall man with a long stride marched across the cobblestones and up the wooden steps to the Archbishop's seat. On the table lay the leather bound book of the Templar Rule, forgotten in the excitement. Beneath the dark robes extended the long fingers of a hand that snatched the book removing it from view. The figure marched away as quickly as it had arrived. The smell of burning flesh had subdued the scent of the figure below.

***

Paris – France – 00.51hrs Wednesday 18th July AD 2001 GMT+1

'Abbadon,' Gabriel said to himself reassuringly, as he opened his eyes.

'I take it - the book means something?' Cole asked. 'Something bad?'

'Abbadon knew all along.'

The Archangel's eyes turned red. Gabriel could not control his feelings anymore. He turned sharply away and disappeared into the low branches of the fir trees by the perimeter wall.

'Don't worry Richard, he won't do anything stupid,' Iinnad reassured Cole. 'Well, I hope he won't.'

'You can't blame him, it's a lot to take in.'

'But it's been a lot for you too, you're human.'

'Yeah, but us humans have a way out – it's called denial,' Cole chuckled.

'You refuse to believe?'

'No. In a few weeks, back in DC, at home with the wife, I'll probably breakdown and cry. But right now, I don't have the time. It's a human thing.'

'What about feelings?'

'Highly overrated. Now are you gonna help me up or what?'

Cole asked, arms outstretched, implying assistance to his feet.

Iinnad ignored the request. 'We need to get back to London, but you need rest.'

'Henry explained some of the *human* angle; Barakiel's sword explained a lot.' Cole's thoughts changed direction. 'I should have killed that bastard.'

'You want revenge?'

'Didn't you see? Gabriel got there first.'

XXXII

The First Realm.

KT Castle – 00.10hrs Wednesday 18th July AD 2001 GMT

Sir William Sinclair wasn't sitting in his chair. He stood at the other end of the C&C a couple of feet from the main screen. So close that the image had lost definition and the pixelated view was just a wall of rapidly changing colour.

'What am I looking at?' he bellowed. 'Are we still looking at Apolyon Inc?'

'Yes sir!' replied Sarah. 'We have managed to get real time on thermal imaging. There seems to be a…'

'So what am I looking at?' his repeat was louder.

'A fire,' Aston added. 'And a large one at that.'

'Elaborate!'

'It looks like the whole complex,' Aston surmised.

Sir William took a few paces back into the rows of computer stations. He continued to stare at what was a plain dark colour with patches of the warm colour spectrum, the largest and brightest of which was the building itself.

'How did they manage that?' Sir William said on his breath.

The large bright mass flicked as it grew in the centre of the screen working its way outward. To the bottom of the screen were two small yellow dots slowly moving away from the scene.

'The emergency services have arrived,' Aston announced.

'And the two dots at the bottom?'

'I don't know,' Aston replied. 'A moment ago, there were three, but now we have a constant two. Gabriel, Agent Cole and the third a prisoner maybe?'

'Abbadon?' suggested one of the operators.

'There is presently no way of telling,' Aston admitted.

'What about the building? It looks like the fire is spreading, but it's going out in the middle,' Sir William observed.

The screen's image enhanced the building, zooming into twice its original size. The dark area became a clear image, oval in shape, but definitely colder than the rest of the structure. Had it caught fire at all?

'I am open to any opinion at this point,' the Grand Master announced at the top of his voice. 'If you have idea, I want to hear it!'

'Could it be possible that...' quickly spoke a female operator, but then stopped.

'Speak up!' snapped Sir William.

'Nothing Sir!'

'You said something. That was more than anyone else here. That means you have something that no one else has.'

'No Sir!'

'An idea! I want to hear it!'

The operator took a deep breath and glanced over at Aston, her unit leader. He nodded for her to continue. The Grand Master surveyed the room; as his eyes fell upon an individual they would look down and then he moved on to the next. Not used to the attention the operator nervously began.

'Could it be possible with the technology that they… possess…'

'Go on,' Sir William ordered. 'Anna isn't it?'

'Yes Sir!'

'Well?'

'Is it possible that – that that section of the complex is shielded against... well, anything, including fire?'

'Like the safes within the Castle?' suggested Sir William.

'No, Sir. I was thinking larger. The chamber *or* safe is round, well more oval. It could be sealed top and bottom. In fact, hypothetically, the building could be totally destroyed and that section survive. A human might not be able to get in, but I bet Abbadon could. I mean, didn't Gabriel move that wall?' Anna pointed to the other end of the hall. 'I mean…' Anna calmed down and continued in a more confident manner. 'Sir, we are dealing with angels and demons. We have to think outside the box. What if what we're looking at is Abbadon's office or like you said a safe? He has thousands of years on us. God!' she laughed to herself. 'Imagine, if Abbadon kept a diary, he would have enough to fill this hall. Then again, it could be a life pod.'

'You're suggesting somebody could be in there? The oval chamber could be a panic room as such?'

'I hadn't thought of that Sir. But one thing is for certain, something important is in there,' Anna replied.

'It's a valid point!' snapped Sir William. 'My research on Abbadon shows that he cares little for life other than his own. Thank you for your input, we will go with your theory.'

'But it's only a theory Sir,' Anna insisted. 'I wouldn't want the

Order to waste money on my account sir.'

'Yes, it's only a theory, but it's the only one we have,' Sir William said as he turned to Aston. 'Find out who legally owns that property; which company and what they are. If Anna is correct, breaking into that pod will take time. It would be best that we own it. That way it will not raise suspicion.'

'I guess, Abbadon owns it,' Aston answered. 'Apolyon Inc.'

'I know that he might, but legally, I want to know who owns it – is it a subsidiary company? Abbadon has been around for hundreds of years. He can't openly own it. Somebody else does, even if it's in shares; find out who! Also find out who has the insurance on it and if there's any possible way that *we* can acquire it. In the meantime, see if we can get there and find out what that oval thing is.'

Aston moved into the role he was born for, immediately distributing his instructions and delegating to his unit the tasks at hand.

Meanwhile, Sir William continued to stare at the two yellow dots.

***

KT Hotel – 02.25hrs Thursday 19th July AD 2001 GMT

There are some capital cities around the world that have activity 24 hours a day. The City of London is not one of them. That doesn't mean the City is dead, just that after the clubs have turfed out the last of the hangers on, it's not long before the streets are quiet. The delivery drivers increase their speed; the doormen of the swish apartment blocks and hotels managed to catch a few minutes shut eye. The façade of the hotel used by the Templars was no exception. The doorman behind the reception desk dosed, his eyes half open. From his advantage point he could watch Lucy struggling to move a couple of large cardboard boxes into the concierge.

'You could've offered to help me?' she panted.

'You were doin' fine and it's a beautiful view.'

'Sexist!'

'It's the night shift, nothing ever happens on the night shift.'

'Is that the best you can come up with?' she shouted from behind the concierge.

'Wait up. Stay there!'

'Mark! I'm not even in uniform,' Lucy complained.

'I know, and you've been drinking, that's why I want you to stay there. I've got another delivery.'

'At two in the morning,' Lucy said to herself.

Only the thick glass security door separated the doormen and the deliverymen One pushed a trolley with two more boxes the size of televisions and the other with a clipboard. The lorry was parked directly in front of the hotel entrance obstructing the view of the rest of the street. Lucy stayed in the concierge and watched the security monitor, which had a camera just outside the entrance filming the doormat. She could see the two deliverymen patiently waiting for Mark to let them in. The man with the clipboard distributed his weight from foot to foot while he waited. He was nervous.

'Don't open the door just yet,' called Lucy.

'Give me a reason...'

The key chain extended from Mark's belt to the first lock. The dead bolts made an echo, as metal churned against metal and the lock was undone. The second lock followed as noisily as the first. Once open, the two men stepped in pushing the trolley as Mark helped by holding the door.

'So, what you got for me?' he asked.

'No idea,' replied the man with the clipboard. 'We're just here to deliver.'

'Where do you want it?' asked the second man.

'By the concierge will be fine.'

'Damn! I left my pen in the van,' muttered the clipboard man.

'No problem, I have plenty,' Mark offered heading to his desk.

Behind him, the two men followed, watched by the concealed Lucy. Mark bent over his desk reaching for a spare ballpoint, when he heard the cocked silenced automatic behind his head. His brain recognised the sound; remembered Lucy's concern and deduced the future events before the silenced 9 mm bullet entered his skull. His body slumped over the desk, the pen hitting the tiled floor. The blotting paper soaked up his spilt blood. Lucy, shaking with shock, quickly ducked out of sight and reached for the concierge phone above on the desk. She muffled the speaker with her hand to dial the in-house number. She licked her dry lips impatiently waiting for someone, anyone, to answer. The ring stopped.

'We have a breach, hotel lobby,' she whispered not waiting for the courtesy greeting. 'We have a breach in the hotel lobby.'

***

KT Castle – 02.28hrs Wednesday 18th July AD 2001 GMT

In the C&C Sir William, coffee cup in hand, watched Lucy on the main screen. He did not take his eyes off her as he was handed the phone.

'Hold your position,' he said calmly. 'The backup units are on their way.'

'What do I do?' Lucy whispered. 'What do I do?'

'Stay calm,' Sir William quietly spoke, then placed his palm over the receiver. He turned to Aston. 'Get me every bloody monitor up in the foyer. I want see their every move and hear every word.' His tone then changed as he removed his hand. 'Lucy, hold on. We'll stay on the line.'

Every angle of the hotel foyer began to pop up in separate squares on the chequered screen. One of the screens had the view of the rear of the van as the retractable door rolled up and the giant figure of Abbadon stepped to the ground. He was followed by a fidgeting mass of demonic. In the hotel foyer, the two men checked the stairwell and halted the elevators. Behind them, their Lord approached. The glass door had already begun to close. Out of the corner of his eye, the man with the clipboard caught it shutting on the boss. He grabbed it, but was abruptly pulled forward. The door *was* closing under power.

'Shit! The door! The door!' he shouted.

Abbadon quickened his pace. The other deliveryman rushed to the ever-reducing gap and positioned the metal trolley with its contents to prevent the door from closing. There was a crunch and a humming sound as the motor overheated. An indistinguishable breaking sound was heard from within the first crate. The cardboard crates collapsed, but the trolley jammed it solid. Slowly, the door increased its pressure and continued to close destroying, not only the crate, but was now working on the trolley. Abbadon stepped over the debris observing the glass crushing metal and calmly entered the domain of his enemy. A dozen demonic quickly filed through the gap. Abbadon sniffed the air.

'How sweet,' he remarked, his chilling voice was clear over the speaker.

'What does he mean?' Sarah blurted out.

'Where's the backup?' screamed Sir William his eyes still glued to the screens as he then placed Lucy on the loud speaker. 'Lucy, just wait.'

'You want me to sit here?' questioned Lucy over the speaker, her body language pleading to the camera, visible on the wall of moving images.

'Lucy, can you clear the trolley obstructing the door? We can't close it from here, the motors are overheating,' Sir William asked. 'We'll release the pressure.'

'Thanks, now I'm a janitor. And I wanted to be a doctor.'

'Do your best, it's all you can do.'

The line went dead. On-screen, a very careful and calculating young lady was about to risk everything she had and everything she would be on one objective – to move a metal trolley from a closing door. Lucy helped herself to a letter opener from the concierge's desk and snatched one large breath. The foyer was now full of demonic. On screen, the Templar watched as she sprang from behind the desk and darted the five yards to the door as fast as she could. With the letter opener still in her hand, she steadied herself, and bent down to lift the trolley out of harm's way. As she bent her knees, a grossly deformed foot made its presence known resting on the crushed metal. Lucy missed the demonic that was on watch outside. She peered up to meet his bloodshot eyes.

'Ten to one are not good odds and you're just a girl,' he sneered.

'It's seventeen to one, moron,' she snapped her grip tightened on the weapon.

Lucy then calmly stood up. She knew her fate before the other demonic were even aware of her presence. A faint hiss was her signal that the pressure was off. A sharp kick sent the trolley and a crate sliding out onto the pavement; knocking the demonic off balance. He attempted to grab the *girl*, but the door closed too quickly trapping his arm with him still outside. He began to thump the glass entrance, the sound muffled. Inside, the nearest the demonic turned and grabbed her shoulder. Instinctively she kicked his feet from beneath him and he fell to the ground. The letter opener quickly chased his head to the floor.

'Trapped between a blade and a hard place springs to mind,' she confidently said to herself. 'Fifteen to one and this is my battlefield.'

Lucy then face the combatants – and Gabriel's nemesis. In comparison, Abbadon was four times her size. One of his demonic was in flames, another was trapped, but Abbadon saw the situation in a light that Lucy would not comprehend. With the glass entrance closed, the second door, that of a set of ornately carved wooden shutters began to automatically close concealing the trapped demonic from public view. Whatever the outcome, it would now be played out behind closed doors; the world need not know.

Abbadon laughed. 'And the brave stood before the baying hordes!'

'What's that from?' Lucy boldly asked.

'Nothing, but if you want a quote, I'll give you one. You might understand.'

'Understand?'

'If any man have an ear, let him hear,' Abbadon addressed. 'He that killeth with the sword must be killed with the sword.'

Lucy's throat went dry. She licked her lips and tried to swallow, but she couldn't. Even an idiot could understand that quote, if not from where it came.

'It's a letter opener you idiot,' she snarled, trying to hide her fear.

***

On the monitors and the video wall, Lucy's fate was only moments away. Without access to the elevators, backup units were struggling to assist. The eight-man team raced across the monitors – passing security camera after security camera – climbing the stairs to ground level. In the foyer the figures froze. The C&C fell silent. All eyes were fixed to the flickering screens. Lucy stood there in the entrance to the building she had known since she was a child. She could remember marking the marble with crayons. Trying to fill in the cracks to make the stone better again. The definition of the monitors did not reveal the tear that rolled down her cheek.

'Why haven't you killed her?' Sir William said to himself.

'What are you thinking Abbadon? What are you waiting for?'

With each question, the Grand Master's voice grew louder. His eyes transfixed on the screens, darting from one image to another, trying to see what could not be seen; trying to read what could not be read.

'The backup team is on sub-level four,' called out one of the operators.

'Inform Troy… …its Lucy!' barked Aston. 'That'll speed him up.'

'We're almost there Lucy,' Sir William spoke knowing she could not hear him. 'Don't do anything stupid, girl.'

***

'Fifteen to one,' Abbadon sniggered. 'Fifteen to one. A hundred to one, even a thousand to one; I still have the prize.'

'The prize?'

Abbadon spoke by syllable. 'I have the *one*.'

'Ha! Am I really that important to you?' Lucy laughed.

'Yes,' Abbadon said as though it were obvious. 'Each and every one of you. You are so few, and so hard to kill… yes, you are that important.'

Lucy's eyes began to glaze as another tear ran down her cheek. Only now had a member of the bloodline *finally* understood; realised what Abbadon had been doing all these years. It had been said, that their entire existence was a game. However, to the members of bloodline the existence of all men was precious, but theirs more so, because it was *they* that possessed the knowledge that would allow mankind's existence to survive. The knowledge, all knowledge was precious. Now Lucy had in her possession a piece of that knowledge that the bloodline may have overlooked or were not aware of. What she had could be shared, if only she could reach the stairwell, just a few paces to her left. A few paces; two deliverymen; twelve demonic and Abbadon, the fallen angelic.

'Make your move.'

Unlike a trapped animal, Lucy was calm and calculated. She darted right towards the elevators and the demonic standing on the pew by the wall. Her initial actions lead most of the demonic to follow suit; although the deliverymen were too slow and Abbadon awaited her true intentions. As she approached the first demonic, it drew a blade. The female human was faster and the scaly creature spontaneously combust. Out of the corner of her eye, Abbadon was still, but the deliverymen had drawn their handguns and taken aim. The nearest demonic was ready to fight, but not to be used as a shield. Lucy pulled him forward to block the line of fire. At the same time as the shots rang out, she stretched out her right leg to kick the legs from under the demonic standing on the pew. Losing his balance, gravity immediately brought him down on to the spiked armrest and then he too, burst into flames. Holding her demonic shield, she ran at the two deliverymen as they continued to fire. The young bloodline ran across the foyer lifting the demonic cleanly off the ground. He scratched at her arms as the bullets repeatedly entered his back and his skin began to dry. She discarded the burning corpse onto the nearest of the two men, who fell to the tiles fighting the flames. She ignored the pain of her burnt hand as she leapt at the only other human that stood between her and the stairwell. The material of his breast pocket ripped open as a three round burst of machine-gun fire rang out. The deliveryman dropped his gun and slumped to the ground. Behind him, in the stairwell, Lucy's backup had arrived. Troy smiled and picked his second target. Behind him, in two lines, the unit kept low and picked their targets. The short bursts of fire made Lucy jump, as did a glowing spinning disk, which shot past her ear, hitting the curved roof of the stone stairwell and ricocheting down on her eight saviours. She froze. Now there were seven saviours. Around her she felt the heat from the dying demonic as the bullets rained down on them. Abbadon returned fire with his brace, the blades bouncing off all the stone surfaces and being channelled into the stairwell as though it were a funnel.

Another of the blades found a target, then another. The second died instantly, caught by the razor sharp steel across the back of his neck. The third embedded itself in one of the men's arms.

'Run!' screamed Lucy standing with her arms in the air and her legs apart creating the largest target possible to block the entrance to the stairwell. 'Run! Don't risk your life for me. It's what he wants.'

Troy ignored her and fired three clear bursts directly at Abbadon. The projectiles knocked him back, but as he fell he returned fire twice. The first blade hit Lucy like a sharp punch in the back shattering her ninth vertebrae; severing the spinal cord; cutting through her lungs and imbedding itself on the inside of her ribcage. The second blade cut clean through ripping the eyelets of her crimson blouse as it exited her flesh. She fell to the cold tiled floor, her heart pumping blood into her lungs. As the light began to fade all she could see was her killer's feet beside her. Abbadon was already back on his feet.

'What you thought was a sacrifice,' he whispered, 'in reality was a waste.'

Lucy tried to talk.

'And now you think you're going to a better place. Even the innocent go to jail.'

The light had gone.

***

'I want to know what he said!' shouted Sir William dropping his cup. 'All this technology and we don't have decent microphones on our security cameras.'

'Troy has withdrawn to sub-level two,' informed Aston. 'They have three casualties, two fatal. Your orders?'

'Lock that place down. He's there; we'll keep him there. Remind all personnel to stay on their guard and not to engage unless they have a clear kill. I don't want to lose anyone else.'

'Yes sir!'

'I need someone here that can tell me what weapons they're using.'

'I'll see who I can find,' Aston responded.

'Would I be sufficient?' offered Sir Geoffrey from the back of the hall.

'I thought you were asleep – at home *old man*,' replied Sir William.

'*This* is my home and how can I sleep when you sound the

general alarm?'

'Aston! Lock that place down.'

Aston's team of computer operators began to shut down the hotel complex. Each and every internal door began to close, from fire doors and service doors to reinforce steel blasted doors in ever corridor and major junction of the entire network of tunnels beneath the hotel. Each operator then proceeded to check that they were closed. As the blast door to the station began to close, two armed Templar, one injured, were seen on the screens, carrying two more as they squeezed through. The uninjured Templar returned before the blast door slammed shut.

'Sorry Sir William, we couldn't get through to the infirmary,' panted the wounded man over the speaker. 'Can you bring us in?'

'Don't apologise. Where are the others?'

'Playing cat and mouse, Sir,' the Templar replied as he dragged the bodies aboard the train. 'Troy's pissed. He said he was staying.'

Sir William turned to Sir Geoffrey. 'Get the boys home!'

The old man nodded his response.

'As for the others!' Sir William broadcast to the hall. 'Find them! Find them and give them any support they need. I can't stress how much I don't want to lose anyone else.'

Sir Geoffrey proceeded to help get the train to the Castle as fast as possible. He wanted to see the men in hospital as quickly as possible. His true interest in the bladed weapon was only too apparent. The Grand Master caught Aston's concern in his eyes as he glanced over the operator's shoulders at the monitors.

'You have a problem?'

‘Yes sir! We have a few doors that won’t shut.’

‘A few?’

Aston gave forced smile.

‘How many, is more than a few?’

‘Five, and one of them is the C.O.R.’

Sir William glanced around the communication room. ‘Where’s Henry?’

‘He returned to the C.O.R.’

‘Is he safe?’

‘For the time being. But there are no blast doors between him and Abbadon.’

***

KT Hotel – 02.38hrs Wednesday 18th July AD 2001

The antique two-piece phone was perched an old oak pedestal design solely for the purpose. The ringing echo filled the library. Henry rushed to pick up the earpiece in one hand and with a firm grip held the stem of the phone in the other.

‘Hello,’ he spoke panting.

‘Get the hell outa there!’ screamed his father.

Henry’s head jerked away from the earpiece, distancing himself from the scream.

‘The door won’t close!’ Henry replied.

‘I know it won’t close!’ screamed the phone. ‘Leave it!’

‘I can’t do that. I’ve got to get the door shut, there’s far too much to lose.’

‘Listen to me son...’

‘I don’t have time! I’ve got to get the door shut!’

Henry put the phone back on the pedestal, then rushed back to the door and continued to clear the area of piles of books in a frantic search for something beneath. It was not long before the area was clear. What he was looking wasn’t there. Henry’s attention then turned to the other side of the door.

‘Forgive me, I am truly sorry,’ he said to himself in a vain hope that the books could hear as he slid the piles away from the base of the bookcase and the edge of the door. He then brushed the tiles with his fingers in order to find the loose ones. The rattle of ceramic signalled the spot and Henry pushed down on one of the corners to tilt the tile, so he could remove it. But it wouldn’t tilt enough. He tried to get his fingertips under it; around it, but there just wasn’t enough to grasp. Half the tiles were covered by the bookcase bolted to the wall, built decades ago by the then librarian who never knew about the internal manual release. Frantically, Henry found the antique crank, and using both hands brought it down hard on the tile. The clash echoed down the corridors and tiny chips of hardened clay flew through the air. Again and again the crank came down on the stubborn tile.

‘Shit!’ screamed Henry out of breath.

The phone rang again, but Henry ignored it, consciously staring in the opposite direction, out into the corridor. The tile outside the door tilted without any obstruction. Henry removed it with ease to unveil the socket that the crank slipped into. He began the circular clockwise motion to lower the door. Inch by inch the present librarian built up a sweat in a manic attempt to protect the knowledge within his sanctuary.

***

Abbadon stood with his back to the Aztec sun calendar pondering which direction to take. The signposts - Quarry Hill, Castle Hill and The Ridge, meant nothing to him. He was correct in assuming the names were more sentiment than directional. The remaining demonic impatiently stood fidgeting behind their Lord as they awaited their orders.

Power within the complex had been reduced to secure the already closed doors. The added bonus was that the lower light level could heed the demonic a little, but was advantageous for concealment for the remaining members of the backup team. Three shots rang out in rapid succession from the far right tunnel. Abbadon, quick with his senses, had already moved on hearing the first shot; his back hard against the entrance wall of the tunnel to his left. His minions had taken cover also, except for one; the flaming corpse remained in the centre of the reception area.

'And then there were nine,' Abbadon said to himself. 'Two of you! Find the shooter and kill him, whatever the cost.'

The demonic did not move. They all understood the instruction and although they feared Abbadon, they equally feared death.

'If I have to choose two of you, you will die where you stand,' Abbadon barked without even facing them.

The two demonic closest the tunnel glanced at each other and volunteered knowing that the odds would be in their favour in doing so. The creatures cautiously entered the dimly lit corridor and disappeared into the shadows.

'The rest of you, follow me!'

The Destroyer sprinted down the left corridor chased by the six grotesque figures. He reduced speed only to check his directions within the labyrinth that unfolded before him. The layout of the complex was coming back to him. It had been a long time, four hundred years, since he had sat on the spire of St Clement's Church and watched from afar, the construction of the maze.

A distance from the blast door, another two members of the Templar backup lay in wait for their quarry to arrive. Hidden from view in the dark and unaware that Abbadon would possibly see them, their only ally could have been Abbadon's overconfidence, but at what price? As children, they had been told the stories, like so many children before, the stories of beasts in the night. They will come and get you if you are not a good boy. On this night the beasts were coming.

The emergency lighting produced an eerie effect to the shadows of the demonic against the blast door. Abbadon surveyed the barrier preventing his access. He smiled at the closed circuit camera, but chose not to destroy it.

'Let the caged prey see their hurt,' he said to himself.

From his pocket he produced a small silver sphere the size of a golf ball and tapped it against steel door, cracking the seal around the sphere's circumference. It separated into two perfect halves, and these, he placed against the barrier, one as high as he could reach and the other near to the floor. The tacky and magnetic internal surface fixed them firmly to the steel and then they quietly began to hum. The low vibrating sound filled the surrounding area. The two Templar could feel their lungs match the rhythm.

'And the walls of Jericho were filled by the sound of trumpets,' bellowed the Dark Lord. 'Do they truly believe that they can keep *me* out?'

Just then his attention was diverted, he sensed something, he could smell a familiar scent. Sensing the danger, Abbadon instantly took cover behind a pillar on the opposite side of corridor. A shot rang out. Another demonic fell, his entrails splattered over the steel before the echo was heard. Through the darkness he could see the Templar take aim. The burning corpse illuminated their second target, but the vibration within their chests prevented a perfect shot. Bang! Another shot and another, then a third. Finally, another intruder self-combusted, but the prize in the form of Abbadon had still eluded the bullets. The yellow flickering flames brightened the end of corridor, revealing an opportunity for the ancient warrior of a thousand battles. Leaning against Abbadon's pillar was a mop protruding from a steel bucket of water on wheels. From his other pocket he removed two small cylindrical objects and dropped them into the pail. He grabbed the mop and with one sharp but firm jab; he shoved the pail down the corridor. The wheeled container disappeared into the dark towards the two snipers. The clatter of its wheels could be heard as it rolled from stone slab to stone slab. Both Templar continued to fire at the demonic, not quite sure what to make of the pail of water. The bucket came to rest several feet from where the snipers lay. Without warning an ear piercing explosion followed. No screams of pain, just silence. Out of the ball of incinerating light flew the curved projectile of the bucket handle. Abbadon swerved to avoid it as the boomerang shaped piece of metal embedded itself into the skull of one of his minions.

'You win some, you lose some,' Abbadon said turning his attention back to the vibrating blast door.

***

KT Castle – 02.46hrs Wednesday 18th July AD 2001 GMT

The entire control room was in panic. Several of the screens were blank.

'How many cameras have we got working in the hotel complex?' Sir William screamed. 'I know we haven't used them in a while.'

'Not many,' Anna replied. 'And the explosion might have severed the feeds.'

'We are also picking up interference from some sort of low sonic resonance,' added Sarah. 'We've got no idea what it is.'

'Put what we have on the main screen!' the Grand Master requested.

The images of empty rooms and corridors began to re-appear. Each square depicted a static view of the aged complex, some in monochrome and others, with updated cameras, in colour.

'Flood the complex!' came the order.

Silence fell on the control room. The view screens flickered. No one moved.

'Didn't you hear me?' Sir William snapped. 'I said flood the complex.' Sir William lowered his tone and placed a hand on the shoulder of the computer operator nearest to him. 'Trust me. Flood the complex.'

XXXIII

The First Realm.

KT Hotel – 02:48hrs Wednesday 18th July AD 2001 GMT

In the subterranean complex beneath the City of London the warning lights flashed and the sirens announced the impending doom. The sound of water could be heard, but for the dark, not seen. The vibrating spheres grew louder still to a near pitch, the demonic expecting some climactic result; and then suddenly the noise stopped. Abbadon raised a clenched fist and struck the door in the centre between the two silver spheres now darkened, their energy spent. The steel fractured and began to crack and then crumble. A hole appeared, large enough for a demonic, but not the Dark Prince. The giant struck the fractured steel again and the hole grew. Mercilessly, Abbadon snatched the arm of the nearest demonic and placed him in front of the hole and firmly held him there for a moment. To his immense surprise, there was no retaliatory fire. Abbadon cautiously peered over the shoulder of his shaking minion. His red eyes then widened with curiosity.

'I see trains boss,' stated the demonic gratefully. 'Two underground trains.'

The Destroyer, his hand on the back of the demonic's neck, forced the creature through the hole headfirst and held him there. The minion struggled to turn his head and then smiled with relief.

'Just trains boss, just trains.'

Abbadon stepped through the hole still using the grotesque figure as a shield. Under the fluorescent lights, the fallen Seraphim stood on the platform and shook his head slowly.

'Well, well, well.'

The sound of rushing water increased in volume, as it flooded the far end of the platform and finding the lowest point, cascaded onto the track. The level had already reached the top of the wheels of the carriages, but the rest of the platform was still dry.

'I am surprised,' Abbadon said to himself. 'When did they manage this without my knowledge?'

Back in the corridor, the demonic were beginning to flap, in panic. Instantly, in a blur, Abbadon was back in the corridor. He took three steps up the stairs to return to the Aztec Sun disk, but stopped. He changed his mind and vigilantly wandered over to the remains of the two Templar snipers. The remaining demonic warily followed.

'The back up team!' he announced. 'There were eight; now four. Find them! Kill them! And then meet me in the hotel! Understood?'

The demonic understood and left their master to his curiosity. Abbadon then took several more steps down the stone corridor past the damage and the burnt bodies. The water level had risen and was now pouring through the fractured blast door. The Destroyer was already ankle deep when he stopped again. He sensed something, another bloodline.

***

The emergency lights were also flashing in the Chamber of Records. The phone was continuously ringing, but Henry ignored his surroundings as he franticly wound the handle. The door to his sanctuary inched its way down. Ripples of murky water appeared from both directions, filling the hole that the crank was secured in. He could no longer see the fixture, but the torque told him to keep turning. Each rotation sapped a little more strength from his wearisome arms, but he had no choice; he could not stop. As he tired, splashing footsteps could be heard in the darkness further up the corridor. With less than a foot to go, the Thames water began to flow under the door and into Henry's library. Using every last bit of strength, Henry tugged on the handle and the door splashed into place, the handle snapping in his hands.

Henry hoped the door would protect his precious books. Flooding the complex had never been tested. The water level had now reached his knees, but there was no current so Henry could not determine which direction to escape. His decision was made for him. Abbadon stood patiently facing his prey.

'You can't out run me!' Abbadon stated the obvious.

'So now what?' Henry replied, still holding the broken handle.

'I want information.'

'No! You want the missing pages to the Codex.'

Abbadon gave a sarcastic smile and then looked down at the rising water.

'I take it, the pages are behind that door,' nodding to the library entrance.

'Yeah! If you break the door, the water could destroy the precious knowledge you seek,' Henry replied surveying the flood.

'I have another plan.'

'Tell me Abbadon. I take it you're Abbadon?'

The Destroyer said nothing.

'Tell me Abbadon, why are those few pages so important to you? Why lure Gabriel away?'

'You don't know what's written on those pages, do you?'

'I've spent half my life trying to translate them...'

'Gabriel could have. I could do it for you, if you like?' Abbadon offered.

'I've managed to translate a couple. I haven't translated the last two. *Yes*, I have the last two,' Henry emphasised.

'And Gabriel doesn't know you have them. All these years and you still don't know why you are fighting. You don't know what's at stake or what's to come.' Abbadon laughed. 'And all these years I thought your little organisation was more of a threat to me then Gabriel. Today has been full of surprises.'

'The complex is still flooding,' Henry stated as the water lapped at his belt.

'Sir William would risk your life, the life of his son, just to stop me?'

The look of surprise appeared on Henry's face. How did Abbadon know who he was? Abbadon knew more about the Templar than they had realised.

'I have my sources,' Abbadon said, answering Henry's confused expression. 'As for the knowledge you withhold from me; you are also willing to destroy it.'

'I'm sorry; we know not what we do.'

'Funny, soulcarriers always quote from old books in times of trouble.'

'How about a more modern approach? Fuck you?'

'We are very much alike, your father and I,' Abbadon ignored Henry's comment. 'So much alike. It's ironic. I would sacrifice my people when necessary, just as your father does. I also lost my sons to a flood. Not by my hand I might add,' Abbadon enlightened the Templar knight. 'I came here for information. I have it. Not exactly what I was expecting; maybe I don't have to deal with Gabriel right now after all. I only need to wait a few more years.'

Abbadon then turned to leave.

'That's it?' Henry said instinctively.

'No! Thank you for reminding me.'

Abbadon raised his arm, engaged his brace and fired. The blade skimmed the water and ripped through Henry's chest sending him beneath the surface. The murky Thames water turned crimson. Abbadon left the scene before Henry resurfaced. The flooded corridor prevented him pursuing the knowledge he required, since the water could easily destroy the contents within. Abbadon had no choice, but to leave

.

***

KT Castle – 02.54hrs Wednesday 18th July AD 2001 GMT

On the screens the Knights Templar had watched the evil presence kill another of their own. Now, he was leaving their hide.

'Turn off the water,' Sir William calmly asked.

The Grand Master slowly walked over to his chair and paused. He decided to sit on the stone blocks in front. He had witnessed the simplistic strength of the ultimate enemy. He had also witnessed the death of his son, which had made him realise the importance of what Henry had been studying. The study of knowledge that both sides, good and evil, were aware could be found within the Chamber of Records, but only Henry knew where. In Sir William's ignorance, he had failed to listen to his son, realising that only Henry knew the secret. What also grieved the Grand Master was Lucy's sacrifice. Before she died, she could see the battle could be lost and through her death, so had Sir William. Abbadon's exploratory insertion into the complex had been foiled by the removal of all that was important to the Castle, within the sandstone ridge of southern England, without his knowing. The old base was nothing more than a shell and although Abbadon had always seen Gabriel as his true enemy, now it was the Knights Templar that were the threat. Lucy died and in doing so she carried the banner of the Knights Templar. She did them proud, but it was not enough. She was gone.

It would take a lifetime to train another Templar, whereas, Abbadon need only find a murderer, a thief, any form of criminal he chose; anyone with bad intentions and turn them. In the simplest form of war by attrition, Abbadon would win; it was basic mathematics. If it took him one hundred demonic to kill one Templar, then he would do it.

And now, the saddened Grand Master also understood at considerable cost. *How could the Templar win?* Sir William Henry Sinclair needed to know what Abbadon was looking for, even if it meant his life. The future of the Order of the Knights Templar would depend on it.

Aston approached the seated old man, deep in thought.

'Sir William,' he said. 'Sir William!'

'Sorry Aston,' Sir William replied quietly. 'I was miles away.'

'We didn't release as much water as it looked on the monitors. I have a team standing by. The complex will be drained by the time they get there.'

'Have them wait for me in the car.'

'Yes Sir! Is it wise that you go?'

'I wish to see my son.'

'Yes Sir!' Aston replied as he backed away.

'Aston!'

'Sir!'

'I need a small discreet radio. Have it activated and monitored from here. I want you to have someone you trust to monitor the link. Can you do that?'

'Someone I trust?'

'I'm sorry Aston, you're right, I shouldn't have said that.'

'I understand Sir. May I ask why?'

'There are questions that need to be answered.'

XXXIV

The First Realm.

KT Hotel – 04.01hrs Wednesday 18th July AD 2001 GMT

The Archangel crouched on the ledge of the hotel a hundred feet or so above the rainy streets of London. His wings were open and raised over his head shielding him from the downpour. A glint beneath him on the top balcony caught his eye. The broken shards of glass flickered in the lightening as the water ran across their surface. He stepped off the ledge and landed silently on the tiled floor facing the broken door. Opening it, he stepped inside. The light was off, but the smell of death told him what he didn't need to see. The angelic passed the bodies of the innocent on the bed. The tourists had nothing to do with the clash between the good and the evil, but were victims all the same. The door to the hallway was ajar, the lock shattered with its pieces thrown about. Gabriel opened it with a wet finger and sniffed the air. He then put his wings away. The coast was clear.

In the hallway the lights were on. Gabriel closed the door on the crime scene and bent down to pick up the 'Do Not Disturb' sign that Abbadon had ignored, and placed it over the bent handle.

'Why did Abbadon not use the front door?' the angelic asked himself.

***

In the foyer, Gabriel got his answer. Did Abbadon kill the tourists as punishment being locked in? Or did Abbadon do it to expose the hotel? The Archangel could only guess. He shook his head in sorrow at the loss of Lucy as he quickened his pace down the stairs to the lower levels.

In front of the Aztec sun calendar, a well-armed Templar confronted Gabriel. His heavy breathing gave away his nerves, but he recognised Gabriel and held his fire.

'Are you alright?' Gabriel asked.

'Yeah, I'm fine. Where the hell were you?'

'In Paris. It was a mistake.'

'No shit!'

'Do you have customers in the hotel?' Gabriel inquired.

'Yeah. What's that got to do with anything? I was sent here to kill demonic.'

'Can we have a clean up operation put in place in the hotel right away? Room 712. We would not want this to get out. Do we?'

'Yeah!' the knight replied. 'I take it Abbadon's gone?'

'You expect to take him on your own?' Gabriel questioned quite surprised.

'I would, if he stopped running away.'

'Are you suicidal?'

'No, I'm Troy,' the Templar held out a hand. 'It's nice to meet you.'

'Did you volunteer to be here alone?'

'I wasn't alone! The demonic hit us. One injured, another fatal. They all died.'

The shock flashed across Gabriel's face. 'How many you?'

'Seven!' Troy sharply answered. 'Eight including Henry.'

'Henry?' Gabriel's voice trembled. 'Henry Sinclair?'

Troy lowered his eyes. 'I think Sir William is already with him. At the C.O.R.'

Gabriel left Troy to radio in his request and headed for the library.

***

The pitter patter of wet footsteps slowed as Sir William approached the sodden body of his son.

'Sir!' came a voice from behind him. 'We haven't cleared any of this section yet.'

'Then clear it!' screamed the grief stricken father. 'And find Troy! I doubt if he was killed! Report to Aston! Now leave me!'

The two armed men continued down the corridor, leaving the Grand Master with his son. He knelt down by the body of Henry.

'I'm sorry. I'm so sorry,' he said quietly. 'Only now do I realise that you understood what I have been trying to do here.'

In the shallow water that remained, Sir William sat beside his son and cradled him in his arms.

'I wish I knew what you knew. I should have spent more time with you.'

The old man could not hold back the tears.

***

Gabriel's brisk walk broke into a run through the dimly lit damp maze until he arrived at the library's entrance. He found Sir William unceremoniously sitting with his son, like a statue, frozen in the wet corridor. The Grand Master briefly glanced up at the angelic, but stayed silent. The silence lasted an age.

'This is my fault,' Gabriel accepted.

'This day was inevitable. Sooner or later… we knew Abbadon would come.' Sir William didn't take his eyes off his son. 'Right now, I don't care if you blame yourself. We expected this. We prepared for this without your help.'

'I am sorry.'

'You believe we have a gift. It's not a gift; it's a curse. We are born to the bloodline, to help man and we die doing so. I will bury my son *because* I am bloodline; *because* he was bloodline. How many men have you seen die, Gabriel?'

'I have seen many good men die horrible deaths; too many good men have died because of what I believe is right.'

'That's just it. Isn't it? It's what you believe. I don't believe in God. You know why?… because I *know* he exists. It's not a faith or religion to us. The other six and half billion people in this world have a choice; a choice of whether to believe or not. We don't believe, we *know* and its not faith, but its not our choice either. We know, because of you and the likes of Abbadon.'

'But does not the knowing clear your mind to concentrate on other things?'

'No!' replied Sir William as he stared at the Archangel. 'It scares the hell out of us. My father told me that you said that the angelic have waged war on every Realm and that one day that war would be fought here.'

'He was right.'

'...and the war has started! In the beginning you trained us. After the Crusades you taught us how to grow, to hide and to advance ourselves. We did that and now we are ready for your war!'

'No!'

'Well! We're all going to die then!' Sir William admitted, defeated.

'This is not your war! William, the wars on the other Realms are like your wars, with man and machine. The angelic and the Council, do not want to fight here. They do not want to fight for you.'

'Why not, if it's God's will?'

Gabriel joined William on the floor.

'Because He gave you a soul, William. That is something even I can *never* have. Henry understood that.'

'My son understood that. My son understood you and your knowledge. My son understood it was so important he was willing to die to protect it. Only when I lose my son do I understand,' Sir William almost whispered.

Gabriel looked over his shoulder at the library door. His head did not move, but his eyes followed the edges of the seal all the way around.

'Abbadon does not have the knowledge.'

'What?'

Gabriel turned back to William. 'I said, Abbadon does not have the knowledge. He still does not know the future.'

'Who does?'

'Enoch!' Gabriel replied.

'Enoch? As in the Book of Enoch, Book of Noah, Enoch?'

The Archangel stood up and faced the door. Gabriel then slowly and gently began to laugh, trying not to upset the grieving father.

'You laugh in the presence of my dead son?'

'I laugh because of Henry. Abbadon took a great risk. He tricked me into going to Paris. We destroyed his base of operations.'

'He probably has another.'

'It is irrelevant! He lost a number of his followers. He failed in his mission,' Gabriel stated. 'He opened his hand, all because he wanted the knowledge that Henry had… and Abbadon failed.'

'Because he didn't get it?'

'Your son… William, Henry beat Abbadon. Right here!' Gabriel pointed at the ground. 'A soulcarrier beat a prince of hell. And I need to know what Abbadon was looking for.'

Sir William squeezed Henry. 'I never told you how proud I have been of you, but believe me I am. Goodbye my son.'

The Grand Master took the broken handle from his son's hand and kissed him on the forehead. He then gently rested Henry's head on the floor and stood. The angelic took the handle and placed it in the socket in the hole in the floor, still full of water. He tried to turn it, but could not. Due to the crack in the stem, Gabriel could not obtain a secure grip to raise the door. The Archangel sarcastically smiled at Sir William and then transformed. With his newfound strength, he wrapped one hand around the stem and with the other spun the handle as fast as he could, lifting the door faster than Henry had lowered it.

'The books!' Sir William gasped jumping through the door.

The Grand Master frantically began to snatch the books, that were on the floor near the entrance and stack them on the desks and chairs. Luckily, only the bottom two books of each pile contained saturated knowledge. He carefully placed them on a raised wooden step; the books open in an upturned 'V' so the pages would hang from the spine and ventilate. The Archangel was motionless.

'Are you gonna help me?' Sir William barked.

Gabriel was belittled by the countless bindings of knowledge that lay within Henry's sanctuary. He had seen them before, but only with Henry's death had the their importance opened his eyes. In awe, Gabriel walked along the rows of knowledge and speculation, his finger running the length of the ancient oak shelves, leaving a light trail in the fine dust. Sir William ceased what he was doing and stood in the doorway and watched. For all he had achieved as Grand Master, the creation of the Castle, the expansion of the Templar and the insurgence of knowledge into the public domain; the angelic had been impressed. But to witness an Archangel in awe of what his son had achieved in his short time among the secretive few, became William's proudest moment. Father and son were alike; fighting the same war from different angles.

Sir William broke the silence. 'This was Henry's doing.'

Gabriel continued to wander amongst the volumes as though looking for something. Sir William got back to creating tents out of wet books.

'We used to argue about the amount of time he spent in here, when he should have kept to the routine and training,' Sir William divulged. 'I guess I was wrong.'

'There are many ways to fight a battle William; you should know that?'

'This chamber was one of the first to be built.'

'I remember,' replied Gabriel. 'I was there… after the great fire.'

'You were probably there when they converted this place into a library then?'

'No, but I did suggest that after devastation, construction always follows.'

'Henry always said this place had character. It has its own history. When we moved, which took several years, Henry refused. It was tradition, he said.'

'But when he left the Order, you kept the library here?'

'Partly in ignorance I guess. Partly because I wanted him to know it was here when he came back.'

'Ignorance William?' Gabriel smiled. 'You?'

'I didn't realise until I saw Henry die, the importance of what must be in here. That was also confirmed by you… just now. Your response.'

'The other day I spoke to Henry here. James distracted me. I did not notice the books. The last time, before that, there were only five books here… and they were mine,' Gabriel said as he looked at the ceiling. 'Only one library in the world comes close to this one William;

and that is the Secret Archive of the Vatican. They have some wonders in there. Henry would have loved to have seen that place.'

'I guess we'll move the library to its new home now?'

Gabriel was not listening.

'There is no computer here,' he stated.

'The main library has computers. It's not that Henry was technologically phobic; it's just computers speed things up and he didn't want to overlook anything. So, he wrote everything down first. He loved to write. I didn't always encourage that.'

'Never stop a child doing what it believes it must do.'

'Well, I did,' Sir William admitted.

'I take it, you knew that I had known Henry for quite a while?'

'I got that impression.'

'He never mentioned his writing or his work here. We used to talk about all sorts of things and I admit that it would puzzle me sometimes as to why I did not have to explain points I felt needed explaining.'

'That was Henry.'

'Was it just the knowledge he was working on or something more?' Gabriel asked his tone changed.

'There was a codex he was working on, but I don't know any more than that. Henry was more than willing to teach the American.'

'Henry would talk to those that would listen and *that* American is bloodline and willing to listen.'

Gabriel began to move swiftly around the books trying to catch what he may have missed. Sir William matched his movement on the opposite side of the room, although he had disappeared from view.

'If you put those wings away you might avoid knocking the books.'

The angelic stopped and popped his head over a shelf. 'In this form my senses are heightened and I am stronger.'

'I noticed that!'

'I am out of practice as it were. I neglected my training and spent too much time in books.'

Sir William laughed out loud; then stopped suddenly, remembering Henry. 'Just like my son.'

The Archangel's nostrils widened. 'Just like Henry.'

Gabriel then took a sharp deep intake of air through his nose. His eyes turned a deep crimson.

Sir William stepped back. 'I was wondering if…'

Gabriel was beside him in the blink of an eye. He sniffed the air again. His head moved quickly in a different direction as he scanned the wall of books the old man was standing in front of.

'Something is wrong!' Gabriel sharply admitted.

'No shit!' replied Sir William catching a glimpse of Gabriel's red eyes.

'What is behind these books?'

'A wall?' stated Sir William as he attempted to move one book to prove it. However, he moved several plus the shelf. The Grand Master let go. 'It's false!'

Gabriel snatched at it, moving a panel three feet square. There, embedded in the wall was a grate lined with water proofing, obscuring a tunnel.

'Where does his this lead?' he asked the Grand Master.

'Why? What do you…'

'Where does this lead?' Gabriel raised his voice.

'I think it's a vent from the…' Sir William thought for a moment. 'It's a vent leading from the old… crypt, I think!'

'The temple crypt?' replied Gabriel already at the door.

'Yeah! Why?'

'Naomi! This is not going to happen again,' Gabriel said disappearing in a blur.

The anger within Gabriel was still growing. He passed the bodies of the snipers, their faces charred beyond recognition. The burnt remains, although wet, filled his nostrils. The smell of burnt flesh took the angelic back to the bell tower of Notre Dame.

'This is not going to happen again!' he demanded to the empty corridor.

***

Sir William removed the radio, Aston had given him, from his pocket and checked it. It was still broadcasting.

'Could whoever's listening tell Aston to get a maintenance crew down to the C.O.R. and have this door fixed. Make sure they're armed,' he spoke as he glanced at his watch. '04.36 hours! Shit!'

The antique phone rang. Once Sir William had gathered his nerves after the sudden ring, he answered it.

'Sir, Aston here! I have got teams collecting the bodies. Sir Hugh is dealing with the police regards the tourists that died in the hotel…'

‘How many?’ Sir William interrupted.

‘Only two. Japanese nationality!’

‘Thank God they’re a country we can deal with. Get in touch with our contacts… they should still be in the country and see if they can deal with it.’

‘Yes Sir! Anything else?’

‘Just clean up the hotel and get the bodies back to the Castle. It’s getting light and we can’t do anything right now. Gabriel’s angry. His eyes went red and he disappeared. I’m just going to have a look at the damage in the hotel for myself.’

‘Okay Sir.’

The line went dead. Sir William paused by the body of Henry for a moment.

‘I am sorry son, I’ll get the son of bitch.’ Sir William kissed two of his fingers and touched his son’s forehead. ‘See you on the battlefield.’

XXXV

The First Realm.

Northern France – 05.42hrs Wednesday 18th July AD 2001 GMT+1

Iinnad gently landed in the lush grass of a meadow, some distance from any habitation. She lay Cole down in the refreshing gathering dew. The blades of grass glistened in the early morning sun as Iinnad listened to the silence and the light rain.

'I hate the bloody rain!' she stropped.

'I noticed it always rains when you guys are around,' stated Cole.

'It always has,' she replied. 'It always will.'

'Everywhere you go?'

'No,' Iinnad answered. 'Not the Third Realm.'

'I wasn't talking of other worlds.'

'Yeah! Everywhere we go,' she said. 'The more of us there are… you know.'

'And hurricanes and twisters?'

'Don't blame everything on us!' Iinnad snapped. 'Just the rain!'

'So your kind caused this?' Cole motioned up to the darkened sky.

'You don't see us unless we choose it. But when we're in flight our wings block out the sun and that's why the clouds form,' the angelic explained.

'But at night?'

'Hey, I don't know everything.'

'Thunderstorms,' Cole thought. 'You control the weather?'

'No,' laughed Iinnad. 'Atmospheric high and low pressure cause the weather, but if there is an unexpected storm at the wrong time of the year, then... then maybe.'

'Washington DC is having a heat emergency, they're handing out free water,' Cole stated. 'It's even in the papers. The night of the killings in D.C. it rained, hard.'

'Gabriel wasn't alone.'

'It's the middle of the summer and it's raining all over Europe. Are your kind here now?'

'I guess the fallen have been busy,' Iinnad replied. 'Looks like Gabriel has got his work cut out.'

'Do the angelic go to America much?'

'Gabriel normally stays on the east coast. Why do you ask?' Iinnad inquired.

'I was wondering if you could explain Seattle?'

'Is that another one of your poor jokes?' Iinnad replied gazing skyward.

The angelic was still staring up into the dark sky and then over to the east to the coming day. Something passed overhead, she sensed it, but could not see it.

'Birds don't fly at night,' she said.

'Bats do,' coughed Cole. 'What is it?'

'Nothing.'

'Why are you really here Iinnad?' the agent asked changing the subject.

'The Council of the Archangels have become aware that Gabriel may have in his possession, a key,' she sat cross-legged in front of him, unashamed of her short tunic.

'A key?' Cole asked trying not to stare.

'The key opens the gate to the Abyss. Your books tell of a battle with Sataniel, Satan and he's cast down into the Abyss, which he's trapped in for a thousand years.'

'I take it, times up?'

'Time moves at different speeds on different realms, but even on the Third Realm of Sagun; you're right, the thousand years are up.'

'So Satan's real and now he's out.'

'Of course he's real. We are real, so he has to be. And he's pretty pissed off because he can't get out.'

'Because Gabriel has the key,' Cole added. 'So what's the Council gonna do with it?'

'Destroy it, that way it keeps Sataniel incarcerated.'

'How d'you know?' Cole was thoughtful. 'Maybe that will release him.'

'I like the way you think Agent Cole.'

'But Gabriel wouldn't let Satan out, would he?'

'The day that Gabriel fought Sataniel was the day he lost his heart to fight.'

Cole glanced down at the dewdrops forming, deep in thought. The agent, once the soldier, knew what war could do. He knew how it could change a man, so why not an angelic?

'He lost someone?' he deduced.

'Gabriel had a mate. Her name was Bethany and she entered the Abyss with Sataniel. That's all I know, I wasn't there. Gabriel has never mentioned her since or even uttered her name. If the gate is opened, Sataniel will be released...'

'And so will Bethany.'

'I've known Gabriel for so long, but I don't know if he would use the key.'

'But Abbadon knows, because he has the Codex.'

'Maybe, maybe not? Abbadon doesn't have all the pages. We don't know what Abbadon knows. He might not even know about the key.'

'Henry probably knows.'

'What?' Iinnad screamed. 'How do you know?'

'He showed me.'

'Showed you? What? The Codex? Why did he show *you*?'

'Because I was willing to listen. This is all new to me. I was willing to learn.'

Iinnad stared straight into the soulcarrier's eyes.

'What?' Cole barked. 'Don't look at me like that! I didn't realise the bloody thing was that important until tonight. A week ago I was happy in D.C. knowing I'm going to be a father. Now, I know God exists, Satan's banged up and whenever you lot turn up, it pisses down with rain.'

'You now know more than you realise. You alone could turn the tables.'

'Bullshit! I'm one man, nothing more. I can't change anything.

The old saying 'don't shoot the messenger;' I'm no one, in a war between the angels. I'm not even the messenger.'

'You're wrong Richard. Come on!' Iinnad jumped to her feet. 'We need to get you back to the island of… England.'

Cole got up. As he did so he dropped Barakiel's sword in the process. Instinctively, Iinnad grabbed it and froze.

'Shit!' snapped Cole as he fell back into the wet grass.

Eyes closed, Iinnad stood there frozen in a different time. Travelling through the history of her old friends weapon. Seconds later and without warning, the beautiful angelic opened her eyes and offered her hand to Cole and pulled him to his feet. She firmly placed the sword in his hand.

'Don't ever lose this. This is your sword now.'

'You ok?'

'Yes! We need to go!'

'No! You explain to me what you saw, what I saw. Why did I see my father?'

'Later! We don't have the time.'

'Make time!' the soulcarrier screamed.

Iinnad paused and took a deep breath. She shook her head.

'Why are you primitives so stubborn?' she asked.

'It's the way God made us.'

Iinnad turned away in disbelief and threw her hands out, then allowed them to fall, slapping her thighs in unison. She laughed and faced the primitive.

She gave a heavy exhale. 'Barakiel has been working for Abbadon for almost ten thousand years; since the day he saved his life.

Abbadon passed himself off as your grandfather and Barakiel was the assassin.'

'My grandfather?'

'Your grandfather was in the American intelligence services during your Second World War. Abbadon thought he could use that. He passed himself off as your grandfather.'

'I don't understand.'

'Abbadon has the ability to change his appearance, as we all do. Your father was one of Abbadon's many sons. When your father grew up and followed in your grandfather's footsteps into the intelligence service, Abbadon tried to turn him, but he refused and fought back. Your mother became pregnant and Barakiel killed your father, because that left you wide open, to be manipulated.'

Cole looked down at the sword in his hand. He opened his fingers and allowed the weapon to fall into the dew. Iinnad step forward and picked up the sword and offered it back to its new owner. Richard Lawton Cole refused to accept it.

'That sword killed my grandfather and my father and I...'

'...will do good with it,' Iinnad continued. 'It has had millennia of good use. Now, it's back in good hands, once again.'

'Did the sword really tell you all that?'

'Not all, I filled in the blanks. Take it. This is a piece of the armour of God and you are probably the only soulcarrier who possesses one. Use it, use it for the reason it was forged. The last fifty years of this sword infinite history is also your history; you're past. If this sword belongs to anybody, it belongs to you.'

The soulcarrier nervously took the sword. He watched the

droplets of dew run the length of its glistening blade in the sunrise.

'I think you're meeting Gabriel, was pure chance,' Iinnad continued, smiling. 'Ironic, considering Barakiel was the Angel of Chance.'

'I guess.'

'So, when Gabriel said I was bloodline, he meant, mixed heritage with an angelic. But I don't carry Abbadon's traits.'

'Good and evil, that's your choice. As bloodline, it's the only choice you have left. Use it well.'

'So I am bloodline?'

'Yes, only your bloodline is different from that of the Templar, but you are still the same as they.'

'That's why I move so fast and everything?'

'Yes,' Iinnad confirmed.

'I am Nephilim!'

Iinnad's permanent smile vanished. 'Yes,' she replied cautiously. 'You know what that means?'

'Yeah, God hates me... angelic father born of a daughter of man. And the Templar are Nephilim?'

'Yes they are.'

'But a watered down version?'

'Watered down? No, I understand…' Iinnad thought for a moment. 'No, the angelic line doesn't diminish through each generation.'

'But they don't know what they are, do they? Only Henry knows.'

'And Gabriel, Abbadon and the other fallen angelic,' Iinnad

added.

'You can sense us, can't you?'

Iinnad nodded in agreement. 'I asked you if you knew what all this means?'

'Yeah! The fallen angels are coming. It's gonna rain. I've got to build a boat... and learn to swim.'

'Funny,' the angelic smirked.

'I was joking about the swimming. Shit! I wish I'd killed that son of a bitch.'

'Barakiel?' Iinnad questioned.

'You'll get your chance. Now we have to go!'

'OK,' Cole was trying to get his head around Iinnad's last comment.

Iinnad placed her hands just below Richard's shoulders and looked at him.

'Close your eyes... *close* your eyes.'

'Why?'

'Trust me. This will hurt a little, but you're Nephilim.'

Cole stood helpless in front of Iinnad in the morning glow.

'What are you gonna do?'

'Travel within the blink of an eye,' she whispered.

***

Southern England – 04.47hrs Wednesday 18th July AD 2001 GMT

Cole opened his eyes and stamped his foot on the ground. It was hard; not soft like soil. He glanced up and around. The morning rays created a shimmer on the still water like liquid silver. The black shadows of the trees in their foliage, like tentacles, reached out from the far side of the narrow, but deep cut valley. The American sat on the granite by the water's edge, still disorientated from the trip. The gentle sound of the waterfall a short distance upstream was relaxing to his ears in the stillness of the morning. Iinnad stood by, her eyes adjusting to her surroundings as she kept a cautious eye on the soulcarrier. He *was* bloodline and so the effects of the trip were not as severe as she first suspected.

'I could quite happily stay here till morning,' he said.

'It is morning and I thought you were a man of action?' replied the angelic.

Cole continued to sit and watch liquid silver, contemplating his next line.

'The eye of the storm,' he said to himself as he turned to Iinnad. 'You must be the only angel around.'

'Why do you say that?'

'Because it's not bloody raining!'

'I think it's trying.'

One raindrop broke the stillness of the pool, its ripples radiated out to the edge by Cole's feet. Iinnad turned away and faced the large wooden door in the face of the rock wall. She broke the silence with two sharp knocks, and then stepped back and awaited a reply. Nothing.

'Hanging around with you is bringing in bad habits,' Cole commented.

'Like what?'

'For a start, I have lost out on my air miles,' Cole realised Iinnad might not understand. 'It was joke.'

'Oh! I'm glad you told me.'

The clouds gave the sun some space to brighten the area. The agent could now see the size of the pool, the size of a tennis court. To his left and right were two stone pillars, at least six feet in diameter. Behind him, beneath the canopy of trees, was a door, which Iinnad was knocking on. It reminded him of an ancient Egyptian temple without the desert or the heat.

'Where the hell are we?' Cole asked.

'Eleven years from the destruction of your realm,' Iinnad shrugged.

'What?'

'We are in the southeast of the Island of the Mighty, as Gabriel would say.'

'The Templar Castle?'

'Well, it doesn't look like a castle, but if you say so – yes!'

'How did you know it was here? And how come Abbadon doesn't?'

'My senses are more acute than Gabriel's or Abbadon's. It's in a steep valley with the overhanging trees to obscure the entrance and the falling water obscures the scent, well almost. It reminded me of something. I acted on instinct and when I saw the entrance I just knew.'

Cole, still slightly disorientated, struggled to get up and walk towards the door.

'Are you in pain?' Iinnad asked.

'No, a little headache and a bit stiff, apart from that I feel fine.'

'Maybe you're stronger than I thought.'

'Why don't you always travel like that?'

'It's tiring and it can draw the Council's attention,' Iinnad replied as she hammered at the door once again. A bolt latch was suddenly heard before the wooden covered steel door opened. 'Success!'

'Agent Cole?' asked the woman looking straight passed Iinnad.

'Yes.'

'This way.'

The American unsteadily walk through the door followed by the angelic.

'I'm impressed,' she stated as she stopped in her tracks to admire the great hall.

Cole admired the door. From the outside, it appeared old, wooden and weathered. On the inside, four hydraulic pistons, each the size of a man, forced the door closed. A second door, several feet from the first, in the form of a shutter from the ceiling, also closed behind them. He observed as the second door locked itself into the floor. In the roof, Cole could see a third door still suspended.

'Why three doors, if it's not stupid to ask?'

'In an emergency these doors close and the cavity is filled with wet sand. It's protection against conventional military firepower,' explained the woman.

'What about unconventional fire power?'

The woman smiled.

'Forget the door!' replied Iinnad. 'I *love* this hall.'

The three of them stood at the top of the seven steps leading down onto the marble polished floor, chequered like a chessboard in black and white squares each about a yard in size, sixty across and a hundred long. The ornately carved roof was twenty-five feet above them and added to the echo in their voices.

'I never saw this on the tour,' said Cole. 'What's it used for?'

'Nothing,' said the guide as she began down the steps.

'Nothing?'

'Nothing is good enough for me,' said Iinnad with a radiant smile.

'When the Castle was first built, we knew we would expand. We didn't know by how much and you can never have too much space. Please, you are required in C&C,' she said as she pointed to a side corridor off to right.

'Good! I have some things to sort out,' Cole replied.

Iinnad was still wandering around the hall. She really did like it.

'Iinnad! You coming?'

***

KT Castle – 04.55hrs Wednesday 18th July AD 2001 GMT

'Play it again!' Aston shouted across the control room. 'And keep playing it. Every time Sue or Fiona wants it played, you play it! I need to...' Aston paused on seeing the American at the back room. 'I need to know what he's saying.'

Aston briskly walked over to Cole, but before he could say anything the American opened his mouth.

'What the hell is going on?'

'The hotel was hit!'

'Abbadon!' Iinnad announced looking at the main screen on the far wall.

'You know him?' Aston asked turning back to Cole before Iinnad could answer. 'I was about to ask why you brought her here...'

'She brought me.'

'Young lady,' Aston addressed, 'you are?'

'Impressed! Gabriel's done well.'

The Templar turned his back on the angelic. '*Gabriel* had nothing to do it.'

'There's hope for you yet.'

'Thank you,' Aston replied sarcastically. 'I take it, you were the third blip on the monitors in Paris?'

Iinnad initially looked puzzled.

'Yes she was,' answered Cole as he wandered towards the main screen.

'Where's Henry?'

'His sword rests in the cave,' Aston softly responded.

Cole dropped his head. He was not quite sure of Aston's metaphor, but he understood tone. In the short time he had spent with Henry, he had grown to like the man. He had so much to teach, so much that Cole could have learnt. All that knowledge was now gone and Cole's urgency was now pointless.

'And what's she doing?' Iinnad asked pointing directly at Sue, unabashed.

'Sue and Fiona can lip read. We have no audio on the security cameras in that area. Abbadon spoke to Henry for several minutes before killing him. We...'

'That's because Henry knew. Is the library safe?' Cole was back with the conversation. 'Is the C.O.R. safe?' the agent raised his voice.

'Yes, the C.O.R.'s safe. What do you mean, Henry knew?' asked Aston. 'Why would Abbadon kill Henry if he knew, and knew what?'

'That's not important right now,' Iinnad interrupted.

'Yes it is!' disagreed Cole.

'No, because I think Henry lied.'

'She might be right,' announced Sue. 'Henry denies knowing anything.'

'We have an advantage,' stated Iinnad. 'Abbadon doesn't think you know.'

'Know what?' Aston demanded. 'We don't know!'

'Abbadon could turn anyone of evil intent to create his army. You are what you are by birth; all of YOU,' she announced. 'Abbadon doesn't care if he loses fifty of his soldiers for one of yours. He knew that Henry knew. He knows that you do not understand and he knows you won't go after him. Henry knew this,' Iinnad explained. 'That's why Abbadon killed him.'

'Who are you?' Aston asked as he tried to make sense of what was just said.

Cole's attention was diverted back to the screens. The repeated images had stopped. Henry's body could clearly be seen by the open door of the library.

'Abbadon believes Henry had some of the information that he required,' stated Fiona. 'He thought we were a threat, now he doesn't.

He thought he was out of time, but now he believes he has plenty.'

'Overconfidence, as per usual,' added Iinnad. 'That's Abbadon.'

'Well, were not planning on going after him anyway. From the satellite images, you caused one hell of a fire in Paris. That will be enough to hurt him for now,' stated Aston as he sat down.

'Where's Sir William?' asked Cole.

'Where's Gabriel?' asked Iinnad.

XXXVI

The First Realm.

KT Hotel – 05.17hrs Wednesday 18th July AD 2001 GMT

The hotel foyer was full of activity. An extractor system was whining away in a corner, sucking the smoke and burnt particles from the air. Two cleaners, a male and a female, both armed with machine guns and sword, were washing the bloodstains off the reception desk and marble floor. Lucy had already been placed in a body bag and was about to be carried into the lift. The weapons of the demonic were gone; they were to end up on Sir Geoffrey's desk. Sir William silently watched Lucy's body be removed and once the lift doors closed he turned his attention to the demonic trapped between the glass and the steel shutter.

With a blank expression, Sir William approached the painfully twisted creature. He scanned the doorframe, his eyes moving in an ever-decreasing circle until they fell upon his enemy.

'You break into my house,' he stated.

Everybody else in the foyer stopped what they were doing and listened.

'You break into my house and you kill my people; you kill my family.'

The Grand Master addressed one of the cleaners behind the

reception desk.

'Close the portcullis!'

'To crush him?' the man verified.

'Into dust,' Sir William quietly replied.

The cleaner felt under the desk and pressed a button and then slowly tried to get back to his work, all the time watching the portcullis lower, as did everyone else; everyone except Sir William. The saddened old man followed the stone steps down to the Aztec calendar and headed back to the train; leaving behind a demonic that knew his time was over. As the interlinking iron grid, with its spiked base pierced his scales and crushed him into the ground, the flames began to appear.

***

KT Castle – 07.32hrs Wednesday 18th July AD 2001 GMT

The entire combatant Templar had been called upon. In the C&C, there had been a shift change. Those that had worked a double shift, working through Abbadon's visit had been given the chance to get some rest. Above ground, the sun was climbing into the murky British summer sky and with the light upon them, for now; there was nothing the Templar could do, except clean up the mess.

The bodies of their fallen comrades in arms were at rest in the chilled cubicles of the Templar morgue. Sir William was in his quarters, pen in hand, his mind searching for the right words to start the letters that he dreaded to write. He had yet to inform James, his grandson, of his father's death. As he sat slumped over his desk, the Grand Master stared at the clock in front of him and wondered whether his grandson would have left on time and be back at his barracks. If he called James on his mobile, he would return to the Castle. It was better he stayed out of harms way. Thoughtfully, Sir William put pen to paper.

***

KT Castle – 08.37hrs Wednesday 18th July AD 2001 GMT

Iinnad had been vouched by Cole; allowing her to wander the Castle at will, not that anyone could stop her. She had found the new library and it was immense. As with the rest of the Castle, the library was not just a library. Putting the books aside, it also contained almost every known newspaper in the western world. On a daily basis, one set of the papers arrived and was catalogued, scanned and transferred to the computers and then boxed away for storage. The shelves were also filled with all manner of magazines, from knitting to shipbuilding; from Star Wars to Playboy. As she entered the next hall, her permanent smile became a broad grin. She was in the music department. Before her, stood row after row of tape, eight track, vinyl 33, 45 and even 78, none of which, meant anything to her. Beyond the old music she found the CDs; every album from every artist. She was at home. She unclipped her personal stereo from her belt and asked the solitary assistant for some help. As with librarians the world over, the proud old man read the CD that she had removed from her player. The old Templar shook his head.

'The youth of today,' he said. 'It's called Trance.'

'I like it,' Iinnad replied. 'It's better than what I heard last time I was here.'

***

KT Castle – 09.11hrs Wednesday 18th July AD 2001 GMT

Cole had been granted a secure outside line in his dormitory. It was untraceable. He paused with the receiver in his hand. Ever since he had meet Rebecca he had never hesitated to contact her, until now. The other end of the line started to ring.

'What?' answered a tired Rebecca.

'Did I wake you?'

'Of course you woke me,' she yawned.

'I'm sorry darling.'

'That's alright. I forgive you.'

'Because you love me?'

'No, because you're a man. Call me in the morning.'

The line went dead. Cole glanced at his watch.

'Crap! It is morning,' he gave a deep sigh and felt totally alone. 'Where are you Gabriel?'

***

KT Hotel – 09.49hrs Wednesday 18th July AD 2001 GMT

Cole arrived beneath the hotel on the secret railway line, along with several Templar, maintenance crews and security personnel. As the doors opened to his carriage he stepped out onto the tiles directly in front of Gabriel's private chamber. The stone doorway was ajar and you could hear the presence of someone inside. He stood, motionless and silent waiting for the platform to clear. The doors to the carriage closed, and covered by the noise the agent drew his sword. As the train pulled out of the station Cole cautiously approached the gap in the tiled wall. Then Gabriel appeared.

'Blast!' he cursed. 'Now I will have to get the next one.' Noticing the American, his tone changed. 'Are you practising with that?' he motioned to Barakiel's sword, held firmly in Cole's hand.

'No,' Cole replied, somewhat embarrassed. 'I thought... In fact, I don't know what I thought.'

'Well, since you are here, you can give me a hand.'

The American entered Gabriel's tiny museum of memories of events long since past. He realised that he had entered a bizarre curiosity shop of ancient artefacts from this world and many others. While Gabriel quickly, but carefully packed away his few possessions, Cole, his feet fixed to the stone floor, stood in the centre of the chamber and gazed in amazement at the age of everything that surrounded him. Though it was the simplest of things that amazed him the most. The wax from the three burning candles had cascaded off the bookshelf and on to his desk and united the two, not only to each other, but also to the wall.

'How long have you been coming here?' he asked.

'A few centuries,' Gabriel calmly replied as he continued packing.

'And now you're going to leave?'

'No,' Gabriel bitterly answered. 'Of course I am not going to leave. I am going to move all this to the Castle.'

'Why now?'

'Why now? Because Abbadon knows that this place exists. If he attacks again, he may find all of this. Do you not think it wise to move?'

'I guess,' Cole replied, not quite sure what to say at all. 'I was actually looking for you.'

'Why? You are now a part of something greater than you could possibly have believed. I think that the Templar have all the answers you require.'

'No. Henry had the answers I require,' Cole corrected. 'Now I believe that I'm… lost. That probably means nothing to you.'

'What is on your mind, Richard?' Gabriel asked, sitting down.

The agent cleared his throat. 'There are what? Six billion people on this planet and probably over seventy-five percent believe there is a God. And there are a few, just a few that know he exists. Me! I was never sure, but now I know. I don't believe, I know. Like I know that's a chair you're sitting on. I don't believe it's a chair, I know.'

'This is the second time this morning that I have had this conversation.'

'Well, I'm sorry if I'm boring you,' Cole continued. 'If I pray to him tonight, I know he's listening, right?'

'Why do you say that?' Gabriel asked.

'What? Are you saying He doesn't or are you just pissed off with Him?'

Gabriel jumped from his chair. 'It is not important! Eight bloodline died last night! This is not their war! It is mine! They should still be alive! I know where Abbadon is, but I cannot tell anyone because more bloodline will die!'

'How do you know?' Cole immediately raised his arms in surrender. 'I didn't ask where… I asked how you knew?'

'I sensed Naomi in the C.O.R.' Gabriel calmed down.

'So what's your problem?'

Gabriel turned away before he lost his temper. 'I cannot go and sniff Abbadon out. He cares nothing for open war. *That* is my problem. I have to wait until it is dark. That is when I will fight him, *alone*!'

'Maybe it's time for the world to…'

'To what?' Gabriel piped up. 'You want to know why I do not reveal myself to the world?'

'Basically, yeah!'

'Do you believe in aliens? Do you believe in top-secret government projects?'

'Considering what I have seen?'

'No, think back to before we ever met,' Gabriel pointed a finger. 'Saying that, think back to the police officer and the dinky toy!'

'To be honest, I've investigated some really weird shit. I've never given it much thought. If you showed the world what you are, it could at least stop a few wars.'

'Do you think the governments of the world should reveal all?'

'No,' Cole replied.

'Why not?'

'Because the people aren't ready for that.'

Gabriel slowly turned and smiled. Agent Cole had answered his own question.

'But if the world knew for certain God did existed, they could get on with more important things,' Cole suggested.

‘Are you saying, that God is not important?’

‘No! No! I didn’t mean it like that.’

‘I know you did not,’ Gabriel smirked.

‘I mean, like the Templar, advancing the knowledge of mankind and...’

‘And what about fear?’

‘What fear? Fear of God?’

‘To know that God exists means that Satan exists, hell exists and hence, fear. People will know that when they die they will go to hell to be judged.’

‘Stop! What did you say?’ Cole questioned. ‘Everybody goes to hell?’

‘Everybody.’

‘To be judged?’

‘Yes.’

‘Gabriel, everyone knows you go to heaven to be judged.’

‘Who told you that?’ Gabriel inquired.

‘Everybody knows that.’

‘In the history of mankind, I know of only two people that ever come back from the dead and they did not really speak of it.’

‘That can’t be right,’ Cole shook his head in disbelief. ‘No.’

‘Why not? If the authorities on the First Realm believe you have done something wrong, where do they take you?’

‘Jail.’

‘If you are guilty you stay there; and if you are innocent you are released.’

Cole stood there, dumbfounded, completely speechless.

'Why do you find it so difficult to understand?' Gabriel urged.

'Because? Because...'

'I will clarify your mind with one line,' Gabriel enlightened. 'There is a saying, as it is on earth… it is in heaven.'

Cole remembered the plaque over the entrance to the Templar complex in London.

'As it is above, it is below,' he said quietly. 'Everything that I see around me is testament to that fact; the underground stream, the secret knowledge; everything beneath mirrors everything above.'

'Now you understand,' Gabriel stated.

'There's one thing I don't understand, why don't you have feathers?'

Gabriel stayed silent. Cole was patient, but not that patient. His response was not to stay and help. It was a simple question?

***

KT Castle – 12.45hrs Wednesday 18th July AD 2001 GMT

Back in his dormitory, Cole sat on his bunk, the laptop on his knees. He had almost completed his email to Rebecca. He yawned as he tried to concentrate.

'I can't send this,' he complained to himself.

Send to:

Time Sent: 12.46 07.18.01

Hi Rebecca,

What have I got myself into?

There is a war going on between good and evil, angels and demons. I am smack bang in the middle of it and I don't know how to escape. To be honest with you my darling, I don't even know if I want to.

The killer is a woman. Her name is Lilith. Doesn't anyone have surnames any more? She killed the Chevalier and Rossal families. She also killed Sean Grayson and I believe Agent Soames. She's fast, faster than me. I needed help and I found it. Gabriel is here and he has an army. These soldier's - men and woman as strong and as fast as me, hundreds of them.

Don't bother checking up on Gabriel or linnad. You won't find them on the usual data bases. You will find them, right where you would have thought of looking in the first place.

I am right up to my neck in all manner of weird crap and I can't wait to see you. Garrett has left me in the cold and put the British police onto me. Luckily, the people I'm with are phenomenally well connected. I can't send you this email.

I love…

'What are you doing?'

Cole slammed the laptop shut and jumped off the bed.

'You scared the crap out of me!' the American snapped.

'Yeah, I do that with most people,' the Templar replied.

Cole re-opened his computer. 'Shit! Shit! Shit!'

The agent pressed a couple of keys. Select all and delete.

'Problems?' the Templar inquired.

'Yeah, and I think things are going to get worse.'

It was only then that Cole noticed Aston in the doorway. Cole nodded at the Command of the House, beckoning him into the dormitory.

'Are you okay Richard?' he asked.

'I don't know. I might have sent my wife an email I shouldn't have,' Cole replied switching off the computer and stuffing it into his cabinet. 'Luckily it will go to her private email. Work doesn't know she has it.'

'How do you know? You're NSA,' the Templar stated.

'Because… I'm NSA,' Cole sarcastically answered.

'The name's Troy,' the Templar announced, hand out. 'I'm a bit like you, I joined the Order late. I've always been a late developer. A good swimmer though.'

'I see!' Cole replied attempting to work out what Troy wanted.

'That was a biological joke!'

'I… got the joke.'

'You look familiar… wait!' Troy jumped and pointed at his face. 'I recognise you. Iraq… 91!'

'You were in Iraq?' Cole glanced over at Aston. 'The Templar were in Iraq?'

Aston gave Troy a stern glare.

'Why would we be in Iraq?' Troy inquired. 'There's something I have to do. I'll erm… see you later.'

Cole stood up towering over Aston, as Troy left the two to argue it out. Aston patiently waited for Cole's next move. There wasn't one. The American was beginning to understand the way the Templar operated.

'Troy… is a little… Troy is Troy. He's a good soldier and he lost Lucy last night.'

'Lucy was going out with Troy?'

'No,' Aston tried to explain. 'Troy and Lucy were like… the closest friends can get without... Lucy's boyfriend is out of the country at the moment. He hasn't been informed yet.'

'You were the guys I bumped into in Iraq?'

Aston exhaled. 'Three of us were Templar. Troy was not. He was on leave, about to start active duty. He was helping us out for a day or two.'

Aston sat down on a bunk two away from Cole and began to take his shoes off.

Cole did the same. 'Who were you looking for?'

'Guess! I'm going to get some sleep. I suggest you do the same. I'll get woken in four and half hours, so I'll wake you.'

***

KT Castle – 17.50hrs Wednesday 18th July AD 2001 GMT

The corridors were buzzing with activity. New faces were appearing around every corner. Not only that, but the languages were not always English. Cole and Aston had been awake for some time and had just finished their late breakfast in the mess hall and were now heading towards the C&C. Cole felt like a fifth wheel, following Aston around. The American wanted to help and knew he was quite capable of doing so; but at the back of his mind he knew it was not his place.

Aston pointed right. 'This way! We have incoming from the farm!'

Cole followed Aston down a very narrow corridor where the lights did not appear to be working. They passed a small sandstone arched doorway, completely out of character with the rest of his tour. On each side, surround by candle light, stood a pair of gold coloured statues about three feet tall.

'Aston!' Cole barked. 'Those are statues of Apollo!'

'Yes they are,' he whispered.

'Why are you whispering?'

'Have a look,' Aston offered. 'C&C is through the door at the end; turn left and to the right. I'll see you in a while.'

Aston briskly marched off leaving Cole examining one of the statues to confirm it was gold. After concluding that they were, he entered the arch and followed the tiny crumbling passage down towards yet another glimmer of candlelight. The passage opened up into a cavern fifty feet high. The stone slab path continued in a straight line down the middle with the loose dirt ground on either side slightly climbing to the sides seventy feet away. In the low candle lit cavern, Cole could not see the end. All he could see was the glimmer of steel blades, miscellaneously placed throughout, some shiny, some rusted as they reflected the candlelight. The swords protruded from the dirt on either side in every direction.

'His sword rests in the cave,' Cole quietly said to himself. He had understood the meaning, but now he could see. 'A cave of swords.'

In what appeared to be the centre, the path divided as it curved around a circular granite plinth. It was not ornate in any way, its vertical sides smooth and the top flat, about four feet from the ground, covered in a thin layer of sand. Embedded in the sand were a circle of crystal stones, not valuable, and placed about two inches apart. In the centre was a small candle that gave the impression that it was emitting more light than another in the cave.

As he walked around the plinth, he noticed two swords resting against its far side. One was a Crusader sword, the sort knights used in movies. The other was of Japanese design, a katana, a Samurai sword. The agent reached out…

'Don't!' echoed a voice. 'Don't touch the swords.'

Cole spun around, but saw no one. The edges of the cavern were almost black; therefore concealment would be easy. However, to Cole's surprise, less than ten yards away a seated individual lit up a cigarette. His lighter and the prolonged drag illuminated his face.

'Hello Troy,' Cole said calming down.

Troy exhaled the smoke and stood in the dirt surround by swords. 'Hello Richard, can I call you Richard?'

'Yeah.'

'What do think of our shrine to the dead?' Troy slowly surveyed the swords. 'They found this cave when they were excavating for the Castle. That was in the Great War. Those Templar that died had their belongings stored here for safekeeping. When their belongings were sent on to their families, someone – no one knows who, had stuck their swords in the ground. The tradition started.'

'All these people have died since the First World War?'

'No,' Troy admitted. 'Some families thought it nice to have a place to remember the fallen Templar. Tombs and graves were opened; swords were removed and brought here.'

'There are no names.'

'That's because we die in secret. Nobody above knows we're fighting. We die for one another and mankind. We are nameless soldiers, hence, no names.'

'I've got to tell you; I have seen so much in the last couple of days. The power that your organisation has; its connections and the way you work, but this place… This place… shows me how you die for what you believe. This place is the heart of what you truly are.'

Troy leapt onto the path and walked up to Cole. He picked up the two swords, one in each hand and offered the knight's sword to the American. Cole hesitated at first but then took it with a nod of acceptance.

'You fight pure evil,' Cole continued. 'You fight the fallen angelic and the demonic.'

'In a nutshell, yeah.'

'But what about the others?

'What others?' Troy was confused.

'In the subway, when you caught me. Who were the others?'

'Don't worry yourself about them,' Troy shrugged off the question. 'We don't. They're our… thorn in the backside.'

'What about the Yakuza and the Triads?'

'Yakuza and Triads? We don't deal with criminal organisations.'

'That's what Henry said…'

'…and he'd be right. You listened to him. Believe want he told you.'

'Not everything is as it appears.'

'Yep! You've changed,' Troy claimed. 'The last time I saw you, you were a magnet to Iraqi artillery. Now look at you.'

'That's a compliment?'

'Yeah, sort of,' Troy replied looking around. 'Now, let us plant these swords.' Troy raised a finger before Cole's mouth could open. 'Before you say it; there's no ceremony. The sword you got there; is Henry's. Why aren't his father and son here? I was coming to that! You place the sword. When Sir William or James come here to remember; they remember everyone. No names, you see?'

'You break the rules often?' Cole asked motioning to the katana.

'Actually, it was Sir William's suggestion,' Troy explained as he stabbed the dirt with the Samurai sword. 'I would recognise Lucy's sword, since I was the one that gave it to her.'

'You place Lucy closest to the light.'

'That is because she was one of the brightest.'

'Then so shall I with Henry,' Cole announced, using both hands he pierced the earth. 'Goodbye, Henry it was a pleasure to know you.'

The two men stepped back from the protruding metal for a moment and remembered. A few seconds later and Troy was already walking up the path. The agent hurried to follow. After a few paces he glanced over his shoulder, but he could not see Henry's blade. It was already one of a multitude of steel stems on the cave floor.

'How long had you been sitting there?' Cole called after Troy.

'All day.'

'And I thought you were just a British Forces trained killing machine. There's more to you than meets the eyes.'

'And as you've already commented, you've been getting a lot that recently?'

'Yeah.'

'I'm also an outrageous flirt, but you're not my type.'

***

KT Castle – 20.23hrs Wednesday 18th July AD 2001 GMT

Cole had been sitting on the stone in front of Sir William's chair for over an hour. He was watching the Templar gathering information and communicating with operatives around the world. Every now and again his ears would prick up, when he heard the name of place that he had been or never even heard of. There was an archaeological deep-sea dive off the southern coast of Spain. Why? All he heard was that they were having trouble with the weather. He discovered that the Templar were in contact with other organisations that, like the Templar, he never knew existed and probably no other government agency did. Most of the time the operators referred to them as the Japanese, or the Chinese, or the Africans; never giving away their true name. Maybe that was because he was there, but he got the impression it had nothing to do with him. It was standard operational procedure to name the country, rather than the group. It reminded him of the NSA; only, and he hated to admit it, they worked better together. At Fort Mead, the American government had put together an incredible team of people within the

NSA, but the way these people worked was fascinating. There was no barrier in communication, country or religion; everyone had one goal – mankind.

Sir William brushed passed him. 'Still here?' he commented as he entered Gabriel's new chamber.

Cole glanced over his shoulder, but a coat of arms blocked his view. He turned back to watch the main screen, but Troy stood before him.

'How you doing?' he asked.

'I'm okay, watching, learning.'

'That never stops around here,' Troy replied.

'What's the farm?'

'The farm,' Troy exhaled. 'The farm is a farm, just east of Tunbridge Wells. The barn is a car park and the house has a lift to here. We don't have to use the train all the time and…'

'NO!' shouted Sir William from the chamber. 'You listen to me!'

The hall fell silent. Cole got to his feet.

'This is not your fight!' Gabriel enforced. 'I have told you that!'

'I've lost eight members of this organisation, so don't stand there and tell me, this is not our fight. We are all in this; you and everyone outside this room,' Sir William pointed at the gap in the wall. 'You do what you want – *we* are going to war.'

'Is that the Grand Master speaking or a grieving father?' Gabriel shook his head and lowered his voice. 'Eight bloodline have died. I do not want to see one more die. Not now, the time will come, but that time is not now!'

The old man calmed down. He knew Gabriel was right, but he was a proud man and the death of Henry had made him want to take the offensive.

'You have called the Templar to arms, say it was a training exercise. Just, do not put them in the line of fire; please, I beg you!'

Sir William stormed out into the hall, almost colliding with the American.

'Aston!' he snapped. 'Inform everyone it was a training exercise. Cover their expenses and if there are any problems… Sir Geoffrey will deal with them.'

'Yes Sir!'

Sir William paused in thought. 'As they say in the British army, tell them we train to fight the first day of the next war, not as though we were to fight the last day of the last. The recall was training. Train hard, fight easy.'

'Sir!' Aston snapped.

'We made mistakes last night!' Sir William broadcast to the hall. 'It happens, accept it. Man has always learnt by making mistakes; but in this day and age, mistakes are seen as a weakness, a form of failure. But remember, without mistakes we wouldn't grow. So why fear it? We learn, we move on! Tonight will be different,' the Grand Master glanced over at Gabriel's chamber. 'Maybe tonight?'

The Templar present acknowledged what their leader had said with nods and grins and got back to work.

'Aston! I'll be in the C.O.R.' Sir William then faced Cole. 'Did you put Henry's sword in a good place?'

'Yes Sir! Yes, I did Sir William,' Cole replied immediately, recognising his authority. 'Surrounded in darkness, but where it can see the light.'

Sir William took a deep breath through his nose and smiled the cracks on his deep. 'As I would have. I thank you,' he said as he began to leave the hall. 'We'll make a Templar of you yet,' he called out.

Cole patted Troy's shoulder and entered Gabriel's chamber. The angelic had one box left to unpack.

'I thought you offered to help me?'

'Sorry, I needed some sleep,' Cole answered staring into the box and carefully removing a small clay bowl. 'What's this?'

Gabriel, on seeing what Cole had picked up, froze, his arms still in the air.

'Please be very careful with that,' the angelic spoke calmly and pronouncing each and every syllable. 'What you are holding is very old.'

The agent, understandably realising he had touched what he should not have, delicately handed the bowl to Gabriel.

'What is it? The cup of Christ,' the agent jested.

'No,' Gabriel replied. 'It is mine. Now help me get these empty boxes out of here. I can handle the last one.'

'I apologise,' Cole said staring at the heavy brown parcel, partially opened.

He could see an incomplete wooden carved tree trunk of a temple of some kind. The chisel still embedded into its base. He took hold of the handle and tried to remove it, but it was stuck fast with age.

'This was one of your memories?'

Gabriel said nothing, but he didn't have too.

'Thought so,' replied Cole answering the silence. 'What is that?'

The answer was along time coming. 'A carving to take my mind off things.'

'What's it of? A temple?'

Gabriel stopped what he was doing. Annoyed, he confronted Cole, much to his surprise. The agent took a step back as the angelic approached.

'I only asked. You don't have to tell me.'

'It is the Temple of Icea. It is on the Third Realm, on the journey to hell. You will see it one day; every being does.'

'Iinnad told me about Bethany.'

The pause was also painfully long. In the silence Cole felt he should not have mentioned it. Then again neither should Iinnad.

'Iinnad had no right to tell you!'

'I'm sorry.'

'The last night I ever spent with Bethany was by the Temple of Icea. It is a reminder of what can be lost in this war.'

'No one wins in war, Gabriel. You more than any one knows that.'

'That is why I must fight alone. For I have nothing to lose.'

'Does He know what's going on down here?' Cole asked.

'Probably, somebody probably keeps the information flowing.'

'Not you?'

'No, I do not talk to Him as much as I should.'

'Why?'

'He does not seem to listen to me.'

'Shit! That's the excuse everybody on this planet gives.'

'The Council make the decisions,' Gabriel said.

'Yeah! He's just pissed with you.'

'We are very much alike, you and I.'

'I'm not Batman,' Cole stated with a smile. 'I was referring to the…'

'We are soldiers. We take orders and we follow them.'

'I don't always do that,' Cole admitted.

'Neither do I and we have both been punished for it.'

'That's true.'

'They're not going to help are they?' Cole inquired.

'No,' Gabriel replied softly.

'Before, you said the world has little time. That's what you're telling me?'

'Yes.'

'About eleven years,' said Cole abruptly.

Gabriel's head slowly turned to face Cole.

'I maybe as subtle as a brick, but I'm not stupid,' Cole added. 'You mentioned earlier and I did not pick up on it.'

'You did not pull that figure out of a hat.'

'No, the Mayan Calendar in reception. It counts down every one knows that. Oh, and Iinnad mentioned something.'

'Iinnad,' Gabriel huffed. 'Iinnad is the only angelic I know that could match Abbadon.'

'In combat?'

'No, in combat she *would* win.'

'*Iinnad*?' Cole questioned the comment.

'I meant in playing the game,' Gabriel elaborated. 'To Iinnad everything is a game. Had you not noticed her smile? When is she without it?'

Gabriel stood and placed both hands on Cole's shoulders.

'This is not your fight either. One day you will do something that will change the course that mankind has taken. Until that day, watch and learn. Now I must leave.'

***

KT Hotel – 23.58hrs Wednesday 18th July AD 2001 GMT

Gabriel was going to fight alone. However, Sir William had already decided that the angelic might require some help. On the platform, two members of the advanced team stood awaiting the train's arrival. In the quiet, they could both here some mutterings from further up the platform. As they cautiously approached the gap in the tiled wall, Gabriel stepped through it, mumbling to himself. He looked up at them, startled. With his wings outstretched, the Archangel closed the entrance to his hide. He turned to face the members of the bloodline.

'This is not your fight, do not waste your lives.'

Gabriel disappeared upstairs through the hotel and out into the late hour. It was still raining in London. The scent of the demonic was in the air, but Gabriel had been on the First Realm far too long and he could not determine which direction it was coming. Perched high on the hotel's roof next to a gargoyle, he watched the few soulcarriers heading home after a long night. For the mortals, it was time to sleep. For

Gabriel, it was time to hunt. Like a bird of prey, he carefully searched the nearby streets below, his wings opened above his head, sheltering himself from the rain.

'The first rule of the First Realm, is not to interfere,' he reminded himself.

But the Archangel was not interfering now. The angelic was hunting the fallen angelic. This was very personal.

XXXVII

The First Realm.

KT Hotel – 00.22hrs Thursday 19th July AD 2001 GMT

Sir William had spent hours sitting in his son's library. As a boy he had done the same. The atmosphere took on a different feel. He had stared at the false bookshelf for a while. It was time to act. Gabriel had made it look so easy to move. However, Sir William built up a little sweat in doing it himself. He stepped back from the vent and tried to peer through the holes. Then he confidently strode over to the aged grid in the crumbly stonework and gave it a brutal kick. The rusted bolts snapped like dry sticks as the grid fell flat in the tunnel. His right hand dug deep into his trouser pocket producing a small bunch of keys with a tiny torch attached to the ring. He grinned with satisfaction having carried it for years and never once used it. Would the battery work? It did. He could now see the floor and the sides of the vent. Even with the flooding they appeared dry.

'Don't figure,' the old man said to himself as he climbed in.

The last time Sir William had struggled as hard in a confined space, it was to escape his mother's womb, he chuckled to himself. He continued to wriggle. As the minutes passed by and the sweat began to pour, the Grand Master could now see a light at the end of the tunnel. No really, he could. He quickened his crawl to arrive at an obstruction that covered his exit, another grate matching the one in the library.

***

KT Castle – 00.36hrs Thursday 19th July AD 2001 GMT

Cole and Iinnad stood quietly beside Sir Geoffrey as he patiently waited for Aston to acknowledge his presence as he watched the young man issue instructions and give out orders in an efficient and speedy manner, showing all the signs of a leader with the respect of his troops. Sir Geoffrey allowed it to pass. Aston had been on top of the situation from the start and was therefore aware of the majority of Sir William's plans even if he was not. The young man spun around to face his senior.

'Sir!' Aston snapped breaking Sir Geoffrey's train of thought. 'I apologised for overstepping my mark. It's just... I am aware of the full situation and...'

'If!' Sir Geoffrey interrupted, '...I had any reservations about your abilities, young Aston, don't you think I would have said something a little earlier?'

'Yes Sir,' Aston humbly replied.

'Then carry on.'

'Yes Sir,' Aston piped up now knowing he had Sir Geoffrey's full support.

He turned to Sue, his lip reader.

'Leave the rest of that and listen to the com-link on Channel 359, maybe you'll get something. Start at the beginning and fast forward through. I want anything that will tell us what's going on.'

‘Aston!’ called an operator.

‘Well, speak Martin!’

‘Smith and Greenwood are on the platform, they’ve reported that they saw Gabriel suited and booted.’

‘Gabriel in a suit?’ Iinnad whispered to Cole.

‘It means armed and ready for battle,’ he explained.

‘Right!’ Aston turned to Iinnad. ‘And what’s your role here?’

‘Observer!’

‘Observer?’ the Templar repeated looking straight at the American.

Cole shrugged his shoulders.

‘Martin!’ Aston snapped without taking his eyes of Cole. ‘Did they say where Gabriel was going?’

‘No, but he was in a hurry. He also said not to interfere.’

‘Of course he would. On any camera, could someone please find Sir William. He said he was going to the C.O.R. but that was hours ago.’

‘He’s in a tunnel,’ Sue replied trying hard to listen to her earpiece over the noise of the control room. ‘A vent, leading to... the crypt.’

The hierarchy of the control room was surprised at the information that Sue had given them. If Sir William should have been anywhere, it should have been in the C&C watching over the operation.

‘Sir William is talking to himself,’ she explained.

‘The crypt?’ Cole requested confirmation.

‘Yes,’ Sue replied. ‘Definitely the crypt. That’s where Gabriel is heading.’

'Any idea why?'

Sue shrugged her shoulders. For a few seconds, everyone in the control room tried to fathom why.

'If Abbadon's still playing games,' Iinnad interrupted, 'then the answer is Naomi. He knows your past. Where else would he hide his army in London? Unless he has his own place.'

'All his properties that we've found, are abroad,' said Sir Geoffrey.

Aston piped up again. 'I thought you were an observer?'

'I am,' Iinnad replied. 'An observer that can talk.'

'Question, who is Naomi?' Aston inquired.

'Naomi Chevalier,' Cole enlightened. 'Sole survivor of the reason why I'm here. Where's the crypt?'

Aston paused, knowing he did not have the authority to take the situation to the next level. Guidance from Sir Geoffrey was required.

'Sir Geoffrey,' he said calmly. 'If we are to go after Abbadon, I don't have the authority to place bloodline in harm's way.'

'Neither do I Aston. Only Sir William, the council or an angel have that right.'

'The rest of the council have already been alerted to the situation and are presently on their way,' Aston stated. 'But with one of them in Turkey and another in China; it'll take time.'

'We don't have time for this,' Iinnad replied

'I *thought* you were an observer?' Sir Geoffrey reminded Iinnad.

Iinnad casually glanced at Cole, who shrugged his shoulders the way you do when it has nothing to do with you.

'Shit!' was the only word to come out of Iinnad's beautiful lips as she began to transform. 'Crap! Crap! Crap!'

The control room fell silent.

'What?' she barked. 'I thought you'd all seen an angelic before.'

Sir Geoffrey shook his head. 'No,' he said quietly. 'Not everyone.'

'Just a suggestion,' Iinnad responded. 'Gabriel has risked his existence for you for hundreds of years, but it's only a suggestion.' She then whispered in Cole's ear, 'He's gonna kill me for this.'

Aston received the nod of acceptance from Sir Geoffrey.

'I want twenty six units! Thirteen units to create a perimeter around Temple.'

Troy entered the hall dressed in black combat gear, machine gun, side arm, two of them, and his sword.

'Glad you could make it Troy!' Aston snapped.

'I thought I'd swing by.'

'TROY!' Sir Geoffrey shouted.

'Sorry Sir!'

Aston continued. 'The other thirteen units are to follow through to the crypt!' He then turned to the late knight. 'Troy!' he barked.

'Aston!' came the joking reply.

'You've got blue team!'

'Who's the blonde?'

'Did you hear me?'

'Yeah! I got blue team. Who's the blonde?'

'Can you *please* concentrate on the job at hand!' Aston raised his voice.

'Yeah! No problem! Is she with me?'

'NO!'

'Can she be with…' Troy stopped. He noticed Cole. 'Blimey! Sorry Cole didn't see you there. Artillery magnet,' Troy pointed.

'You were in the desert,' Iinnad joined in.

Troy caught Aston's glare once more. 'Don't know what you're talking about!'

'You were there!' Iinnad insisted. 'What *were* you doing there?'

'Hunting! Safari!'

'Who?' Iinnad demanded.

Troy blew air out the side of his mouth instead of answering. He had already said too much to an individual he didn't know.

'Abbadon!' Iinnad answered or him.

'You know him? Aston! She's gotta be with me!' Troy begged.

Iinnad faced up to Aston. 'Do you have a map of the area?'

He turned to the nearest operator. 'Sarah, could you call up a map of Temple?'

The layout of Temple Church London appeared on the main screen.

'Stop!' Iinnad demanded. 'What's that?' she pointed.

Sarah checked her monitor. 'It's the ground floor of the Temple Church. If you give us a sec, the crypt's beneath. I'll…'

'We need to find an access point,' Aston interrupted. 'The crypt hasn't been used in years.'

Iinnad motioned with her head. 'The circle has fifty-two alcoves.'

'Damn! You can count quick!' Troy added. 'I only got as far as three.'

Iinnad ignored his comment. 'Is there a disk in the centre?'

'A plaque? Yes,' Aston curiously replied. 'Why?'

'That's how you gain access to the crypt,' Iinnad explained.

'Most of what is directly under the Church was filled with concrete after the war,' Aston declared. 'We won't get through that way.'

'If Abbadon has sentries covering the entrance, then you know you can!'

'She's not just a pretty face… great body… beautiful…'

'Troy! Focus!' Sir Geoffrey snapped.

'Yes Sir!' the jovial Templar lowered his head. 'I'll split my team and come in from the west. My team can also clear The Strand.'

'I'll take Red Team and clear the Embankment and enter from the southeast,' Aston added. 'Let's do this! Get the units suited, the train leaves in five. And that was yesterday people! This is NOT an exercise!'

The additional personnel in the C&C were beginning to edge towards the exits; when Sir Geoffrey stepped up and took command.

'Listen up!' Sir Geoffrey announced. 'Ladies and gentlemen, we have a job to do. We have to covertly insert one hundred and four armed personnel into the centre of London. The night clubs are still open and there are civilians on the streets.' With a smile on his face he added. 'So let's shut the city down.'

***

Aston led the outsiders down the corridor towards the armoury where the unit members were already preparing for the operation ahead.

'Aston, listen to me,' Cole requested. 'Naomi Chevalier is bloodline. And if I'm right, that is why Gabriel's going after Abbadon.'

'And Sir William?'

'I know what I would do, if someone had just killed my son,' Cole replied.

'So how do you know this, Naomi is bloodline?'

'Because Gabriel told me,' Cole lied. 'That's probably how he knew she was there, because the angelic can sense bloodline. That is our weakness.'

Troy handed Aston his body armour, which he proceeded to put on.

'You said *our* weakness?' Troy questioned.

'I'm also bloodline,' Cole admitted.

'He told you that too?' Aston added.

'No, I did,' Iinnad butted in.

'I'm in on this,' Cole demanded.

'Then you have three minutes to suit up Mr Cole,' Aston stated.

The agent was given a uniform, including body armour and magazines for his automatic pistol and an MP5 submachine gun with a laser sight, scope and silencer.

'The angelic can sense us,' Aston continued. 'Is that true, angelic?'

'Yep,' Iinnad replied. 'You stink.'

'Iinnad's telling the truth,' Cole supported her.

'Iinnad is it?' Aston inquired.

'Yes, and you do stink.'

Several of the Templar laughed as they continued to make ready.

'An angelic with a sense of humour. So tell me, how are we going to fight them if they know we're coming?'

'With the element of surprise,' Iinnad answered. 'I will make my own way there. I'll meet you at the hotel.'

Troy butted in, his face half painted black. 'I'm out of camo-paint! You guys ain't gonna need it.'

'Are you really a soldier?' Iinnad asked Troy.

'Are you really an angel? Stupid question!'

'So you didn't see?'

Troy's eyes followed the contours of Iinnad's body, hovering around her chest. 'I didn't see what?'

'Your eyes wander. You can't stay still.'

'It's a human trait,' Troy replied. 'I won't apologise.'

'No, it's not! Males of the species, they all do it. Look at any animal, always checking out the females.'

'We're not talking animals. Were talking humans.'

Iinnad leaned over and whispers in Troy's ear. 'But I'm not human.'

Cole straightened his clothes; Iinnad found herself copying him. Then she froze. She quickly rubbed her hands around her belt.

'What have you lost?' Troy asked concerned.

'My…' Iinnad tried to remember the name. 'My music!'

'Your walkman,' Cole corrected.

'I left it in the music library.'

'Is that where you've been all day?' Cole inquired.

'Yeah! Why?'

Troy had finished painting his face. 'I love a girl with priorities.'

'Can I have that?' Iinnad said snatching the black paint from Troy. 'Aston, I'll meet you at the hotel.'

She left the Templar in a blur as they finished suiting up.

'Isn't the library locked?' Troy asked.

'Like that's going to stop her,' Cole added.

Aston was immediately on the radio to C&C.

'This is Aston! Open the library now! And then allow the angelic to leave.'

Troy then handed Aston his sword, which he placed in a sheath across his back. He already noticed that Cole had his own.

'You'll need that,' Aston grinned.

'I know,' he smiled.

'See you on the battlefield,' said Aston as he slapped Cole's shoulder.

***

The doors to the library opened just as Iinnad arrived. She rushed in ducking her head as she did so to avoid the opening door. In the music section she found her walkman and strapped it to her belt.

Satisfied that it was secure she was about to leave when she spotted the large golden Eye of Horus on the wall.

'Well, well, well! How many slaves died for you?' she said with a smile. 'Music's improved. So how did you end up here?'

She could not believe she had not noticed it before. Then again she had spent most of the time with her eyes closed as she discovered her favourite tunes. The angelic was mesmerised by the shimmering gold. As she slowly approached she could see her reflection in the curved yellowy surface. From her only pocket, she removed Troy's camo-paint stick, smearing some on her middle finger. Peering at her golden image, she then drew a line in black down her pale face, from the corner of her right eye, down the side of her nose and stopping just above her lip. The second line covered her eyebrow and continued another inch horizontally towards her right ear. The third went under her eye and stopped short of touching the second line. Finally, the last line started where first had started and diagonally branched down onto her check ending in an upward curl. It was the first time an angelic had worn make-up and she hadn't applied it very well. But Iinnad didn't care. She had re-created the Eye of Horus on her face.

***

Temple – London – 00.51hrs Thursday 19th July AD 2001 GMT

For anyone who has visited the city of Greater London, like all European cities steeped in history, it is the size of the older buildings that the visitors see. For those that have worked and lived there, like life itself, they are taken for granted. A large area of land around the Tube station of Holborn was once the centre for the Knights Templar, but by the 1150's the Knights had outgrown it and acquired the land on the north bank of the Thames known now simply as Temple. Within the grounds of the Inner Temple, now privately owned by lawyers and the law firms of England; lay Temple Church a stone's throw from the Old Bailey, the Crown Court of England. The Church was built in AD 1185 and although damaged during the Second World War, it still stands to this day. Beneath, lay the crypt, dark and unbeknown to many, its original entrance and tunnel, just inside the southern door, crumbled away due to bomb damage and was therefore filled with concrete, as was the crypt, so some say, to save the rest of the building.

Through the darkness and obstructed by the pillars of the cloisters to the west of the southern entrance, Gabriel could see the two demonic standing just inside the open doorway. He dared not attempt to cross the expanse of the paved courtyard between them, so he retreated, and stepped back into the darkness and down the stone steps into the garden overlooking the river. Once in the garden, he took flight over the red tiled buildings to the south of the Church. Then gently, he glided down into the car park to the east, facing the courtyard, which he could see through the archway of a house, beneath a white painted window with its curtains drawn. Through the archway, the cool breeze flowed into the Archangel's face as he entered the shadow of the Church in front of the vicarage garden to his right. Now downwind, he could smell the demonic in the porch, but could not see them. By the small black iron gate to the vicarage, was an old stone alcove, a former well, with the garden above. The rusty gates to the alcove were closed, but not locked. Gabriel entered the stone shelter, the remnants of the well still visible in the moonlight, and quietly closed the gates behind him. In front, was a stone wall of crumbling mortar. Gabriel gave it an effortless shove, moving it several feet further back beneath the garden. He squeezed through the gap into the concealed passage that was now revealed, and headed down the damp slimy covered stone steps towards the crypt deep beneath the Church.

***

Beneath London – 00.57hrs Thursday 19th July AD 2001 GMT

Lying on his belly, in the tunnel, peering through the slots in the grate, Sir William saw nothing. It was as though he had missed the crypt and found himself in a form of antechamber, empty for the most part with only a few stone pillars to support the roof. His ears could almost hear his heart racing as it pumped the adrenalin filled blood through his veins. He curled up into a ball and turned his body, so he was feet first and lay on his back. With his arms braced against the sides of the tunnel, torch in mouth, his boots struck the grate. Dust fell from the framework. His boots struck the grate again. The rusty metal gave way and only made a quiet thud as it landed in the sand that covered the floor much to Sir William's relief. He rolled forward, his feet landing in the sand and sat on the ledge of the vent a foot or so from the floor. He surveyed the chamber by moving his head, the torch still locked between his teeth.

'Hmmm,' he muttered to himself removing the torch. 'I don't remember it being this big a place.'

The subterranean secret chamber resembled an excavated

ancient Egyptian tomb or one of any eastern Mediterranean archaeological digs. The chamber had pale yellow sandstone walls and a blackened ceiling, from years of cumulative soot from the flaming torches that protruded from the giant pillars. Sir William took a paraffin cigarette lighter from his jacket pocket, with the torch back in his mouth; he removed the closest pole from its pillar and ignited the lighter. The tiny blue flame illuminated his hand as the smell of fuel reached Sir William's nostrils. The old man lit the dry wadding tightly bound around the end of the two-foot long pole. Uncontrollably, it burst into flame. Realising that the wadding was too dry and that the torch would not last, Sir William held it at arms length and quickly rotated 360 degrees on the spot. At one end of the chamber was an oak door with rusty iron bolts and brackets and a small keyhole in the centre, clearly visible in the flickering flame light. On either side of the door, pinned to the stone were two displays of battledress. The right, medieval, from the Crusades and the other Sir William had not seen before. In the yellow-orange light the armour gave the appearance of sentries guarding his only exit. The right displayed had a sword and chain mail with shield and on the left, a fine linen tunic, with a belt and sword. On what should have been the left arm was an ornate bracelet, which Sir William unhooked from the wall and slipped on to his arm. It covered his entire forearm from wrist to elbow and felt comfortable and light. The Grand Master clenched his fist; the muscles in his forearm expanded to trigger the bracelet that fired a razor-sharp blade into the sand by his feet. Startled, he jumped, his feet left the sand as the burning torch crashed into it. A humming sound filled the chamber. The brace was warming up.

'Christ Almighty!'

The nervous Grand Master stooped down to pick up the torch, but stopped. Through the keyhole in the centre of the door he caught a glimpse of light, electric light. He left the torch where it fell and instead, took the sword from the medieval guard.

'Now that explains why the power output has been high for the past few days,' Sir William said to himself.

With the slightest effort he pushed the oak panels. The latch was up and the stiffness eased as the door began to open. The old man's exit from the chamber was more of an arched tunnel with a corridor of the yellow stone, like those found beneath the hotel, only neglected for centuries. It was only three feet wide, not even wide enough for Sir William to draw the sword he had just acquired. However, the bracelet weapon could protect him. The roof began to curve at shoulder height, leaving little headroom, forcing the old man to walk down the centre of the sand packed path.

At the far end, the tunnel veered to the right slightly obscuring the exit about forty feet ahead. The far left wall danced with the silhouettes of unknown persons passing the exit. Nervously, with knees bent, and his brace arm poised, Sir William edged on. Each stone block gave way to reveal the next as the old Templar followed the curvature of the wall until the junction of the tunnel was visible. In the quiet, Sir William crouched as he peered further around the corner. His quick assessment did not look promising. He stepped back, stood up and pulling his left sleeve down over his hand, he clenched his fist to hold it. Then with a sharp jab, he struck the nearest light bulb with the back of his hand. Surprisingly, the bulb only cracked around the neck, and dropped to the floor. The gas released created a muffled pop. The fixture then slid from the stone roof and dropped 10 inches until the twisted electrical cable caught it.

Pop. Pop. Pop.

'Shit!' Sir William gasped as he dropped to the sand.

He lay there, as the seconds ticked by, he could feel the dust settle on his arms in the darkness. His actions had created a chain reaction, which had taken out every light in the tunnel. Only a few of the fixtures had remained in place, the rest suspended only by the brown twisted cable. The figures *were* the enemy, clearly visible now and none the wiser to Sir William's darkened hide.

'Well! That wasn't so bad,' he smugly said to himself.

***

KT Castle – 01.06hrs Thursday 19th July AD 2001 GMT

The train sped towards London. Row upon row of warriors stood in the carriages as it raced through the secret tunnel towards the now familiar platform. Apprehensive, the men and women poised to meet the enemy that they had trained to fight for generations. Cole blended into the mass of black uniforms, identified, by only one characteristic; the stars and stripes flag of the United States of America, which he proudly wore on his shoulder. One stars and stripes amongst a sea of Union Flags, crosses of Saint George, St Andrew, the Red Dragon of Wales, French and Portuguese flags; the agent made sure he did not slump his shoulders.

***

Iinnad was on her own mission. She would make sure that the hotel was as clear as the monitors and the security cameras appeared, before the arrival of the Templar.

***

The three carriages ground to a halt in the still wet station. The moment the doors opened, the Templar disembarked, checked their weapons and made sure their swords slid free from their sheaths. The ranks of units moved quickly and silently towards the subterranean reception area beneath the Aztec calendar. Cole, however, stayed behind. With his torch on, he could see down the corridor from the damaged blast door to the percussion-damaged area, where the snipers had died. He knew his way to the library and moved swiftly through the damp passages arriving at the entrance in no time. The hole in the floor marked the spot where Henry had left this realm. The words of sorrow and gratitude for what Henry had taught Richard slowly went through the agent's mind, but not one managed to reach his lips. He closed his eyes for a moment to focus; remembering Henry's sword and what Troy had said.

'No names,' he whispered to himself in the quiet corridor.

Once focused, he entered the Chamber of Records and checked the cabinet for the pages of the Codex. The safe was dry and untouched. On closing the cabinet, he noticed the removed panel on the far wall. The agent switched his mind to military mode. His adrenalin and his memories increased his awareness as he switched off his laser sight on his MP5 and locked his torch to the barrel all in one swift move, as he crossed the tiles to the opening in the wall. He ducked to avoid the stone rim and clambered into the vent. Without hesitation, due to the size of calibre and rate of fire of the weapon in his hand, the agent crawled as fast as was humanly possible along the tunnel, until he practically fell into the antechamber. Surprised by his sudden change in surroundings, Cole spun the torchlight around the chamber. He sighed with relief that he was alone. His nose twitched. The air was filled with carbon and by the door the American could see Sir William's discarded burnt torch. The door was ajar, so Cole continued to pursue the old man. The tunnel had a gloomy yellow tone to it, but there was something in the distant dark. Around the curve, Cole could see the silhouette of a man. He switched off the torch and engaged the laser and placed the red dot between the shoulder blades of the silhouette. He switched the safety off, but the shadowy figure moved into the warm light of the main corridor and the agent lost his shot.

'Please be Sir William,' he said to himself.

The agent ran to the silhouette's position and re-aimed the laser across the sandstone corridor to an alcove where his target stood. In the old tungsten light he could see it was Sir William and instantly lowered his machine-gun. The red dot passed Sir William's line of sight. Instinctively, the Grand Master raised his arm and accidentally fired a blade into the tunnel just missing the agent. The deadly projectile ricocheted its way down the tunnel walls several times until it came to rest in the sand.

'Keep the noise down,' Cole whispered loudly.

'Agent Cole?'

'Yes it's me,' the agent answered and then joined the old man in the alcove.

'I could have killed you!'

'I had you in my sights first! Tell me, where did you get the brace weapon?'

'The what?'

'That!' Cole pointed with his free hand. 'The brace, where did you get it?'

'This?' Sir William asked as he held up his arm.

The agent nodded and with his free hand lowered Sir William's arm. 'Be careful! You could take someone's eye out with that.'

'I nearly took my own out with it. I'm too old for this.'

'It's angelic weaponry. If it's not Gabriel's, then where did you find it?'

'In the chamber, off a piece of armour. How do you know what it is?'

'It's a long story,' said Cole as he checked the rear of the tunnel.

'Shorten it.'

'Even the short version's long,' Cole laughed.

'Americans. Never a straight answer.'

'I could show you, but at your age, it would probably kill you!'

'I'll give you my age…' Sir William complained.

'Where are we going?'

'Straight, turn right into that dimly lit part of the tunnels. Can you see?'

The agent appeared out of the alcove over the old man's shoulder to get the better view. The coast was clear so he began to move covering every angle as he did so with the old man covering his back. At the junction with the dark passage Cole checked each route. For some reason there was not a demonic to be seen. The agent followed the instructions and turned to the right. The arched corridor he stood in was wide enough to take a car and at the end, ten yards away, was a set of closed wooden doors.

'The crypt is behind those,' whispered Sir William as he pointed.

Light could be seen flickering through the gaps in the wooden panels. It was accompanied by faint voices, but neither of the men could make out the words.

'There is a less obvious approach down the steps to the left.'

'How do you know all this?'

'I used to play down here as a kid, but everything was a lot bigger back then.'

The Grand Master headed for the steps, which via a small room led back up to the crypt. The American paused for a second in the corridor before retracing his steps back to the junction and swiped the butt of his machine-gun at the naked light bulb on the ceiling. It just clipped the glass, cracking it and the light went out. To his surprise, all the wiring failed and he stood in darkness. Sir William's torchlight guided him down the steps to the old man.

'You weren't expecting that were you?' Sir William grinned.

***

KT Hotel – 01.26hrs Thursday 19th July AD 2001 GMT

Iinnad patiently sat on the foyer reception desk of the hotel and waited for the arrival of the bloodline. She sniffed the air and could sense a faint presence, but could hear nothing. Elegantly, she slipped off the marble surface and cautiously wandered down the steps to the first sub-level car park. The angelic opened the door and saw nothing, but rows of expensive vehicles. The angelic did not see their value, just how shiny they were. As she arrived at the second sub-level car park she could hear the Templar assembling. The engines were running and one by one, the polished black 4x4s, each seat occupied were leaving their spaces and heading for the surface. Troy leant out of a window.

'Hey sexy! You seen Cole?'

She shook her head, no.

Iinnad left the hotel in a hurry; crossed the wet street and began to run as she entered the alleyway opposite. As she picked up speed she began to transform and then soared into the night sky. High above the lights and cityscape of London, Iinnad glided towards the area of Temple. Iinnad settled on the highest advantage point she could find near Temple Church, making sure she was downwind of the entrance and waited for the arrival of the warriors she had incited.

***

From the depths of the hotel car park the column of 4x4s, like ants from a nest, fanned out into the sparsely populated streets, each taking a different route to the same destination, Temple Church.

***

Temple – London – 01.32hrs Thursday 19th July AD 2001 GMT

Gabriel calmly walked down the wide corridor, lit only by the occasional bulb. Unbeknown to him, Agent Cole had already seen to the others. At the crossroads, he turned right and faced the dark. Beyond the wooden doors was the Destroyer, Abbadon. He knew it; he could sense it. He could also sense the American and the Grand Master were nearby. The Archangel approached his destiny; with sword in hand and his brace charged.

'You can never force children, it causes friction,' he muttered to himself.

He undid the latch on the main door and pulled the heavy wood towards him. The candles and lights illuminated his wings, but did not manage to reach much further down the corridor.

Sataniel's first Prince stood in the centre of the crypt surrounded by tombs with effigies of cross-legged knights, their swords resting on their chests. The polished stone walls were lined with his minions, demonic and a few fallen, forty or fifty of them in all. Gabriel chose not to count. Lilith was at his side as she had always been.

'You came!' the Dark Lord barked. 'Great!'

Gabriel closed the doors behind him. It was an air of confidence on his part; to show strength in the eyes of Abbadon's followers. It worked. As the angelic stepped further into the crypt, those that could step back, did so. For most of the demonic, this was the first time that they had seen a Warrior of Light.

XXXVIII

The First Realm.

South Bank – London – 01.36hrs Thursday 19th July AD 2001 GMT

Stamford Street was quiet. Most of the nightlife in London was on the north bank in the centre of the city. The neat rows of residential houses on either side of the street that led from the Imax cinema were silent, being a weekday. A police car was park on the street. The rear occupant tried his radio.

'I've got a problem with my radio,' he said.

'My God John! Our radios are being jammed!' the front passenger sarcastically joked. 'Nigel, I'm serious!'

His sarcasm turned to concern, when Nigel also failed to get a response.

'They can't be,' he said. 'I thought they were digitally encoded.'

'They are,' the driver confirmed. 'To the station it is then!'

Guy, the driver, checked his wing mirror before pulling away from the kerb. Just as the patrol car began to move, the wing mirror was filled with the radiator grill of a large black 4x4.

'Christ!' Guy slammed on the breaks. 'Where the hell did he come from?'

John looked through the rear window. 'You mean *they*?'

The police officers watched as four black 4x4's rushed by.

'They haven't got lights on,' Guy pointed out.

'Suspicious, don't you think?' Nigel added. 'Even if they *did* have the lights on. Did you catch the plates?'

'Yeah!' John said. 'Nothing. I've a bad feeling about this.'

As the black unidentified vehicles drove into the distance, Guy revved the engine, and accelerated after them. Five hundred yards ahead, the column of vehicles turned left and began to cross Blackfriars Bridge. Guy controlled the car around the sharp bend and then increased speed further to overtake.

'We could just pull them over?' Guy suggested. 'Driving at night, no lights?'

'Four vehicles and three of us,' John reminded the others. 'I think we should leave it.'

'Why? Bad vibes?' Nigel commented.

'Something like that!'

'Hang on!' Guy ordered.

He manoeuvred the patrol car, swerving out from behind the rear vehicle and accelerated to over sixty mph to the front of the column and then made a handbrake turn; bringing the car to a halt across the path of the lead vehicle. Guy had managed to block both northbound lanes of the bridge. The 4x4's stopped.

'I have a bad feeling about this,' John repeated.

'Wimp!' replied Nigel as he switched on the blue lights and opened his door.

***

In the lead vehicle, Margaret – Templar Knight, patiently sat, her hands resting on the wheel. Using the hands-free radio she had open communications with the Castle.

'Sir Geoffrey! Units Five, Seven, Eight and Nine have just come up with a problem.'

'We don't have time for problems!' bellowed Sir Geoffrey's voice through the vehicle. 'Deal with it!'

The electronic window on the driver's side lowered into the framework as the Templar in the passenger seat cocked his tranquilliser gun. The police officer cautiously approached the driver's side, keeping a distance between himself and the vehicle. He could see that the driver was female and his nerves calmed a little, although, she could not see his scared eyes beneath his peaked cap. Margaret smiled to calm his nerves further as the officer noticed a coat of arms on her shoulder patch. What he didn't notice was that on the opposite side at the rear of the vehicle, a military clad man with a tranquillising sniper rifle had now positioned himself behind the 4x4.

'Excuse me Miss!'

Margaret greeted the police officer. 'It's a little wet out.'

Then the passenger, without hesitation, raised his gun and fired. The tranquilliser dart made contact with Nigel's neck. The power of the sleeping projectile was not enough to knock him to the ground, but the shock of the weapon and the pain in his neck caused the police officer to fall anyway. The chemical in his veins acted swiftly; for the police officer was to sleep for the rest of his shift.

***

From the patrol car, it appeared that Nigel had been shot dead. John lay flat on back seat trying his best to stay out of view and also using the car door as protection against any more projectiles. Guy grabbed the steering wheel and accelerated. In the panic, he had forgotten that he had not taken the handbrake off. From behind the lead vehicle appeared the sniper. He fired the high-powered weapon through the open passenger door and Guy dosed off.

Margaret was already out of her vehicle and running towards the patrol car. The sniper had slung his weapon over his back and was now dragging Nigel, by the scruff of the neck, onto the pavement, resting him against the low white and burgundy painted wall. Two Templar leapt from the rear vehicle, leaving their doors open, and ran down the column to the first 4x4. One jumped into the driver's seat, the other occupied the sniper's space. Instinctively, Margaret slammed the passenger door of the patrol car and dived over the bonnet in one swift move, landing with both feet firmly on the ground. She opened the driver's door and climbed in practically sitting on Guy. She then put the vehicle into reverse and took the handbrake off as she glanced through the rear window. Only then, did she spot the third policeman.

'I'm not going to kill you,' she calmly said, seeing the officer was no threat.

'From what I've seen...'

'You've seen nothing,' Margaret ordered. 'You've heard nothing. Your friends are asleep. Our fight isn't with you.'

'You're saying the Metropolitan police are just in your *way*?'

'Yeah! Sort of!' Margaret replied as she reversed the patrol car up the curb and parked it on the central reservation between the street lamps.

'Who are you people?'

'Do you believe in angels?' Margaret asked as she took the keys out that the ignition.

'No!' John stammered. 'My wife does!'

'Then you can tell her, you met the next best thing,' Margaret explained as she climbed out of the vehicle and slammed the door.

The police officer sat in the rear of the car shaking. Due to the security measures on the rear doors, he could not get out. He watched as the column moved on and the unidentified female and sniper climbed into the last vehicle. Before doing so, the female threw the car keys over the bridge and into the Thames.

***

The ring of keys caused a splash in the black water, one of millions, because of the downpour. Beneath the bridge, roared four small speedboats cutting through the water, heading upstream towards Temple. Aston had full radio contact with all the active units as he knelt on the bow of the third boat. With no obstructions or river police, the Templar assault craft had sped up the Thames with no interruptions. Few lights shine across the Thames at night, so the assault teams went completely unnoticed.

As the assault craft approached Temple, identified from the river by the three large battleships that were moored on the north bank, they reduced speed. The lead boat touched shore at Temple Pier, the second between the bank and the battleship HMS Wellington. The other two came to a halt beside the HMS Chrysanthemum. The well-trained amphibious teams carefully climbed ashore, tying their best to avoid the slippery stones. Their respective pilots then began the return journey, taking the craft back to their secluded base, somewhere on south bank.

Even at 01.45hrs in the morning the Embankment had too much traffic for their liking. It was one of the fastest roads to bypass the centre of London and was presently full of black cabs. The amphibious assault teams waited behind the low walls of the river walk, for the signal from Sir Geoffrey to proceed.

***

North Bank – London – 01.44hrs Thursday 19th July AD 2001 GMT

From Iinnad's position, she had seen Aston's units arrive; Margaret's column of vehicles approached Temple from the east and now, she was observing Troy's units from the west. They had approached, in a convoy, down The Strand. Just beyond the Church of St. Clements, the five vehicles had pulled over and parked up on either side of the street. Using his headset, Troy instructed the two units nearest the entrance to Inner Temple to proceed to their objective. The old black painted wooden doors that fill the arch opposite the Old Bailey, the Royal Court of Justice, were unlocked and the armed men and women disappeared. Blue Team were now in position, ready and waiting.

***

Temple Crypt – 01.48hrs Thursday 19th July AD 2001 GMT

'In all the years that I have been here Abbadon, have I hunted you down? Have I sought to find you or kill your followers?' Gabriel asked.

'No, I can't say you have. In all the years I have been here, have I tried to make you look like an idiot in front of your superior? We can both play the game.'

Gabriel was lost with the statement. His face revealed that to his nemesis.

'On Sagun, the Third Realm,' Abbadon continued. '*Our* Realm! You attacked us, you tried to destroy Amente...'

'That was war, Abbadon.'

'So is this Gabriel.'

'War on the First Realm?'

'Why not? There is war on the other realms, why not here?'

A fallen angelic appeared in the corner of Abbadon's vision. He bowed low.

'Speak!' Abbadon bellowed.

'There was movement in the streets,' the fallen announced.

'It's a city! Are you stupid? Were they police?' Abbadon asked, not waiting for a reply. 'Not that it matters.'

'Something bothering you Abbadon?' Gabriel inquired.

'I don't know if it was the police,' the fallen admitted.

'Have the look-outs reported any problems?'

'No problems!' the fallen replied.

'Where's Iinnad?' Lilith broke the futile discussions.

'I understand Iinnad is under instructions not to get involved,' Gabriel replied.

'But where is she?' Lilith demanded.

'France probably. No! I believe, she is in England, but not in London,' Gabriel said thoughtfully. 'I assure you, she is not in London.'

'In Paris, she fought alongside the American,' Lilith injected. 'She promised she wouldn't get involved.'

'If Iinnad promised, then she would have kept her promise,' Gabriel stressed. 'If she was attacked then she would fight. But, Iinnad has nothing to do with this.'

'Why is she here?' Abbadon demanded.

'I told you, she is probably still in France…' Gabriel realised that Cole was in England and therefore. '…or England! Still worried about Iinnad?'

'You underestimate her. Why is she on the First Realm?'

'Council business!'

'Council business to do with a key?' Abbadon quipped.

Gabriel was stunned. He nervously began to look around the crypt for any more surprises. He blatantly sniffed the air, but too many scents were in the area to make anything out. As with the Caves of Enlightenment, Gabriel had entered the crypt with the odds stacked against him.

'You're getting paranoid in your old age Gabe,' Abbadon laughed. 'You think I have spies in your little army? I have spies yes, but not in your army.'

'How did you know about the layout of this complex?'

‘Oh, that’s a hard one,’ Abbadon said sarcastically. ‘A big fire 400 years ago. London’s gutted. Some soldiers did a big hole. Build this place then fill the hole in and I watch. That’s what we do, isn’t it? Gabriel, we watch. We don’t interfere.’

‘You are telling me you do not interfere?’

‘Compared to what you and Jesuel have got up to, I’m a bloody Saint.’

‘You turned Barakiel!’ Gabriel raised his voice.

‘I wouldn’t have been able to if you hadn’t left him behind.’

‘In 1307 you destroyed my army!’

‘No I didn’t, actually.’

‘I left that in the message to get your attention,’ Lilith added.

‘The greed of a king and the weakness of a Pope destroyed your army,’ Abbadon explained. ‘I didn’t do it. I’m innocent.’

‘You were there!’

‘I didn’t say I wasn’t there,’ Abbadon added, his hands raised inoffensively. ‘I said I didn’t do it.’

‘But, you have been following me, watching me.’

‘That’s true, but isn’t that what we are? Watchers! I have dabbled in a little bit of this and that. I’ve made money… made lots of money, but I haven’t interfered to the extent that you have. Now, why would someone like you break such a rule? Why would you teach these primitives how to fight? Don’t you think help from above will come when you ask for it?’

‘You have no idea!’ Gabriel bluffed.

‘Apparently, no more than you. Don’t you think I know of the bloodline? Who did the dirty deed? Was it you?’

Gabriel increased the grip on the hilt of his sword.

'It couldn't be Jesuel?' Abbadon added.

'You do not know what you are talking about Abbadon.'

'I've been there Gabriel, but I was punished for interfering. I was punished for taking the daughters of men. I witnessed my entire bloodline drowned in the deluge.'

'I was there!' Gabriel snapped.

'No you weren't!'

Gabriel look puzzled.

'Five and half thousand years ago another comet fell. It hit the Mediterranean, that flood destroyed *my* family. The Council knew. Then you came along. This is *my* realm Gabriel.'

'No. This realm belongs to the soulcarriers.'

Frustrated, Abbadon walked around the crypt.

Gabriel's eyes follow him. 'You say you don't interfere, but you kill soulcarriers? You talk of destruction of your family... and yet killed an entire family.'

'They were bloodline! Nephilim, Gabriel. Nephilim!'

'They did not know that,' Gabriel emphasised.

'And that makes it all right. None of them know Gabriel. None of them!'

'Then why kill them?'

'They had something I needed,' Abbadon admitted.

'Pages from the Codex...'

'And anyway... I didn't kill them all.'

To Gabriel's right, the demonic begin to part as Naomi was pushed forward. Ridefort marched the bound girl passed Gabriel to one of the pillars by the Destroyer. The Archangel stared at his old Grand Master from the Levant as Gérard De Ridefort chained Naomi's left-hand around the carved stone.

'Don't you look so surprised Gabriel,' Lilith taunted.

'Are you all right?' Gabriel asked Abbadon's captive.

'For a guardian angel, you have a funny way of watching over me,' she joked trying her best to laugh off the moment.

'Archangel Gabriel's entire life on this realm has been a failure,' Abbadon encouraged aiming his comments at Naomi. 'You've just been added to the very long list. Don't take it too hard.'

'Abbadon! She has nothing to do with this. Please… let her go.'

'She's bloodline Gabriel!' Abbadon let rip as he grabbed Naomi's hair. 'She has *everything* to do with this. I don't know what shocks you more, this pretty little thing or your old Grand Master?'

The Destroyer placed his firm hand on Ridefort's shoulder. Gabriel glanced over to the knight. Abbadon could not see the sorrow in his eyes, but the angelic could see the forgiveness he was yearning. Abbadon then drew his sword and in response Gabriel tensed.

'If you win, the girl lives. That's fair! Isn't it?'

'Abbadon, you have me. I am surrounded. Let the girl go.'

'Always the hero,' Abbadon commented. 'It'll be the death of you Gabriel.'

'That is what you want, is it not? My death?'

'A little fun wouldn't go a miss.'

'Then have your fun, but let the girl go.'

'But Gabriel – she is *my* fun!'

Gabriel began to look nervous as he quickly scanned the crypt and the positions of the enemy around him. Somehow, he had to save Naomi.

'Look around all you want,' Abbadon barked. 'Iinnad's not here to save you.'

'I am not expecting Iinnad!' Gabriel stressed.

'No? I am!'

After so many years the two enemies clashed swords once again. Only this time there was nowhere to run. As Abbadon's sword came down a second time Gabriel dived from the oncoming blow. The Destroyer spun around as Gabriel engaged his shield. The evil mighty sword struck the emblem of Pestilence as the Archangel thrust forward; his blade was deflected down into the sand, the dust rose from the floor. Steadying himself, Gabriel attacked Abbadon forcing him back against one of the tombs. In a blur Abbadon leapt over the stone effigy as the angelic pursued.

XXXIX

The First Realm.

London – 01.54hrs Thursday 19th July AD 2001 GMT

A couple sat in their blue Ford Mondeo and waited for the traffic lights to change. The driver noticed that all the cars along the Embankment had stopped *and* that all the lights were red.

'What the hell is going on?' he said.

'Don't worry, we'll be home soon,' his wife replied.

Then one by one the street lamps began to go out. The illuminations of the battleships followed. Sir Geoffrey's voice came over loud and clear on Aston's headset. The low stone wall of the river walk was nothing for the assault teams to negotiate as thirty-two shadows darted across the pavement and quickly snaked their way through the stationary traffic. On the other side of the road, the wrought iron fence appeared as easy to climb as the stone wall, in the eyes of those sitting in their cars. Within seconds, the shadows were gone and the streetlights began to flicker back on. The traffic lights were green and the cars slowly began to move.

***

Temple Crypt – 01.55hrs Thursday 19th July AD 2001 GMT

The minions and demonic stepped back as the fighting blur began to move around the crypt more rapidly. The two angelic warriors collided into the wall catching a disfigured creature in their path. The sorry figure burst into flames. Their master cared nothing for their lives; for Gabriel it was one less demonic. Suddenly, the blur froze and Abbadon stood over Gabriel, his foot firmly pinning the angelic's sword into the sand. The Guardian of the First Realm was motionless. Abbadon had raised his sword in his right hand. Naomi was close enough to grab his wrist and did so. For a split second, Abbadon tugged to free his arm and lowered his blade to Gabriel's throat.

'You give lectures. I enlisted in every war I could find. You've lost your ability to fight Gabriel, you...'

'You what?' Sir William butted in, his strong Scottish accent echoing through the crypt. 'You what?'

The Templar knight stood in the tiny archway. Cole over his shoulder, fired two shots into the nearest demonic, just to make some space as the flaming corpse fell.

'Hi there, I believe we've met,' Cole added.

'Oh yes, we have Agent Cole,' Abbadon answered.

'Now this is interesting,' Lilith announced.

'Move away from Gabriel!' Cole ordered, his laser dot in the centre of Abbadon's chest. 'I won't ask again.'

'Or what? A bullet or two won't hurt me.'

'How about 32 in 3 seconds?'

'I could move faster than you could pull the trigger.'

'You wanna try that?' Cole challenged.

Abbadon stepped back. Gabriel got to his feet, the disappointment clearly visible to the two soulcarriers. Sir William moved to the centre of the crypt as Cole stayed put covering the Grand Master. The Templar and Guardian of the First Realm stood up to the dark angelic, but Abbadon's confidence did not waver.

'Three for the price of one... Or is it two?' the Destroyer perplexed as he looked over to Cole.

The agent looked amazed by the comment. Sir William was poised to use his brace, when Gabriel grabbed hold of his arm and very slightly tapped it with his index finger.

'Agent Cole, we had met before. I'll do anything, if you get me out of this alive. Remember? Ten years ago – 91, in the Gulf. You were alone...'

'I needed help,' Cole continued. 'I pleaded for help.'

'To be saved? Well, I saved you.'

'U.S. Search and Rescue saved me.'

'I guided them to you. I was watching you because you are of *my* bloodline. That's why you have...'

'Speed! Strength! Yeah, I've heard it! You were being hunted in that desert, Abbadon. Sir William's boys were after you. They knew you were there. How could they possibly know?'

Abbadon began to lose his composure. The Destroyer's eyes checked the crypt. This was not what he had expected.

'Surprised?' Cole questioned. 'You had Barakiel kill my father because he wouldn't turn.'

Abbadon's planned surprise had backfired.

'You thought this shock revelation would catch someone off

guard,' Cole continued as he stepped into the crypt. 'You couldn't turn my father, my grandfather or me. You're not very good at this evil thing, are you?'

'Turn one or turn many? My army is vast,' Abbadon claimed. 'Hell! Even I don't know how big it is. Every human who turns to dishonesty is mine… every drug lord, pusher, pimp and thief are already mine… most of them don't even know it yet. And that's why you can't win… I don't know how large my army is, because my troops are ten a penny. I could lose a hundred…'

'It would take more than a hundred,' Sir William stated.

'You! Old man… are just like Gabriel. You believe soulcarriers will save their own existence. They can't stop fighting amongst themselves, let alone fight me.'

'Never underestimate us!' Sir William stood proud.

'Sir William, mankind's predictability is the only thing that bores me on this Realm. Although saying that, I was surprised to find how much you and Gabriel had in common… I was going to divide you, then conquer…'

'Would never happen!'

'No! Maybe not this time,' Abbadon replied.

'Glad that's settled then!' Sir William chimed as he raised his arm and fired two blades straight at Ridefort.

The two demonic closest to Sir William sensed something in his voice and had already begun to move closer. The medieval master moved just as fast as the nearby demonic. The spinning metal blades clipped Ridefort's hair before ricocheting off the wall towards the curved roof and sharply diving harmlessly into the sandy floor.

'Too slow old man,' Ridefort taunted.

Cole opened fire. The silence shattered as each round was released and the ear-piercing echo chased each bullet to its target. Each three round burst hit a different creature. Determined to punish the traitor, Sir William released two more blades at Ridefort. Both missed only this time the trajectory was different. Bouncing off the wall they entered Ridefort's back. With a curious smile of gratitude he died breathing his own blood and Sir William's steel.

Without hesitation, Gabriel resumed his steel disagreement with Abbadon as Cole emptied his first magazine into the heads of as many willing demonic that he could. Once empty, he used the butt of the MP5 for a moment only to position himself as to draw his sword. Cole's head shots killed several as had Sir William's blades, but the two mighty warriors ignored the death around them and disappeared into a blur once again. Lilith drew her sword and faced the American. The smoke from the burning corpses began to blacken the ceiling of the crypt as good fought evil. The Grand Master, wary of his lack of firepower, kept his back to the nearest wall. He continued to fend off the demonic as he slowly worked his way around the chamber to Naomi. When he reached the chained girl he had no means to free her. Frustrated, tired and old, he didn't see the blade from the demonic behind him as it pierced his chest. Defeated, he fell into the spare arm of Naomi as she tried to lower him to the ground gently.

'I'm sorry,' he gasped as he stared into her brown eyes. 'I have done all that can. I have nothing more to give Lord.'

'You have done well, William,' Naomi whispered as the Grand Master died.

***

Inner Temple – 02.00hrs Thursday 19th July AD 2001 GMT

The guttering of Temple Church was overflowing and cascading into the small stone paved square to the south of the church, lit only by two turn-of-the-century cast iron lamp posts. From her rooftop vantage point, Iinnad, sheltered by her wings, was doing her utmost to keep her walkman dry. Below, the Templar had surround the square via the only access points, east, north and south and the back up teams had already secured the perimeter of the whole of Middle Temple.

The ugly creatures on guard duty could sense something through the downpour. It wasn't the sweet musty smell that you always get with summer rain, but something else. Both were considering contacting their Lord when they were hit, dead centre, by a burst of silenced machine gun fire.

From Iinnad's view, the Templar, like ants, swamped the entrances, plashing through the square puddles made by the sunken paving slabs to the dry inside of the church. She gracefully glided into the doorway behind them and followed the black clad soldiers inside. The knights spread out, walking quickly with their knees bent and weapons steady, checking every corner and pew within the confines of the structure.

Once out of the rain, Iinnad transformed back into human form, turned left and marched to the centre of the rounded end of the church between the four effigies of the Crusader knights of old that lay at rest. For hundreds of years they lay in perfect condition, until the blitz damaged them beyond repair. She stood in front of the plaque in the tiles with her back to the large door. She raised her head towards the altar at the far end of the church. The red velvet cloth of the altar, had a gold crown with Greek symbols embroidered on it.

'Alpha et Omega,' she read. 'The beginning and the end. And so it begins.'

Fluttering circles of torch light filled the building, each sphere of white a target area for a MP5.

'Vestry clear!' shouted an armed knight.

'Tower clear!' shouted another.

'Everything clear,' she said to herself, knowing it to be true. She had sniffed the air on entering the building. 'At least we're out of the wet.'

'Hope you know what you're doing?' Troy asked Iinnad as he entered the circle, his MP5 resting in the nook of his elbow pointing at the wooden roof. 'There's no other way out of here; and there's no way into the crypt.'

'Ye of little faith!' Iinnad replied.

'Impress me!'

'I thought I already had,' the angelic gave a cheeky smirk. 'Remove the cushions from the stone benches. I need fifty-two to sit, one in each alcove.'

'You heard her!' snapped Aston. 'Do it!'

The brown heavy weave padding wiped the dusty floor as they came to rest by the stone knights that lay within the circle. The Templar made him or herself comfortable, one soldier to each alcove; framed by pillars embedded in the wall supporting a sharp arch. Iinnad spun around staring at each knight being individually watched over by a twisted face of a lost soul in purgatory carved in stone. She armed her brace, clicked her neck and gazed upon the disk in the centre of the circle.

'Remember in your prayers those who died in the Second World War 1939-1945,' she said reading the plaque. 'You do like your wars, don't you?'

Iinnad stepped onto the plaque and pressed the button on her brace. What should have happened didn't.

'Bugger!' she cursed stepping back off the plaque and with the heel of her boot struck the edge of the disk as hard as she could. The plaque flipped on a central axis, replacing the words with a glowing disk. The angelic grinned and stepped into the light.

'Now that's better!'

She pressed the button on her brace again; this time all the alcoves filled with light, illuminating the entire church. Then the disk disappeared and Iinnad fell through the floor followed by the fifty-two seated Templar. For the knights that remained, the plaque and stone bench reappeared and the circle was in darkness once more.

The angelic now stood underneath the church surrounded by the seated soldiers each illuminating the sealed ceiling above by torchlight. Amazed, they stood and checked each other to make sure they were okay. Troy approached Iinnad as he glanced at the stone roof.

'Now, I'm impressed!'

'Good! Shall we?'

Iinnad faced the only way out; an arched tunnel ten feet wide that headed into the black labyrinth below the city. The knights gathered in a group behind her. She sniffed the stale air and began to walk down the passage.

'Two lines,' Troy spoke into his headset. 'Blue team on me! Red team on Aston! Remember, they are stronger than us. As the saying goes, only use great force against itself.'

'You believe that?' Iinnad questioned.

'I need a motion detector,' Aston called. 'Front and centre!'

One of the knights leapt to the front and held out a small electronic device, the size of a household brick. The green illuminated screen was static. Iinnad glanced down at it.

'What's that for?'

'Checking for movement via a heat register,' Aston explained. 'Anything down here that's moving; other than us and we shoot.'

'I have a nose for this sort of thing,' Iinnad replied. 'Put it away!'

'No speech before we go,' Troy asked.

'Three words,' Iinnad replied. 'Let's do it!'

'See you on the battlefield, Aston.'

'And I you, Troy.'

Iinnad sniffed the air once more. She switched on her walkman and began to briskly walk down the passage. The Templar followed, torch lights pointing at the sand. The angelic's walk became a jog and then, as she began to transform, she began to run. With her wings open, Iinnad then began to glide, her feet hardly touching the ground.

'Ten o'clock,' she pointed as she passed a junction.

Aston opened fire and as the Templar passed by a demonic burst into flames. Iinnad began to beat her wings as the knight sprinted after her.

'Three o'clock!' she pointed right. 'Nine o'clock!' she pointed left.

On each direction, silenced gunfire followed and as the Templar ran the length of the passage fires were all that remained in their wake.

***

Temple Crypt – 02.06hrs Thursday 19th July AD 2001 GMT

Lilith's sword rained down on Cole. Blow after blow was intercepted by Barakiel's blade. The agent's speed and bloodline instinct was just enough to protect himself from the experienced fallen angelic, but not enough to engage in any form of attack. The leather-clad woman darted from side to side only to be met by Cole's defence. Lilith became more artistic in her attacks in an attempt to catch the soulcarrier off guard. However, Cole's training prepared for just about anything. The fallen's blade clipped his arm, drawing blood. He could not persevere much longer.

As for Gabriel and Abbadon, their speed was incomprehensible to the human and demonic eye alike. The clashes of steel filled the eardrums of everyone present. Out of the blur a sword hit the sand in a cloud of dust. Gabriel appeared on the ground Abbadon towered over him again. The fallen angelic raised his sword, but hesitated. His eyes darted around the crypt, then back down to Gabriel. There was an unusual melody in the air catching his attention. It unnerved him.

'What is that sound?' he asked all those present.

The unusual, but now familiar sound of digital beats and harmonious melody grew louder as the battle ceased.

'Trance!' Cole smiled.

'Music to my ears,' Gabriel added with relief.

'You call that music?' Naomi tried to joke.

A loud clunk echoed through the chamber as the latch moved between the large wooden doors behind the Archangel. The oak panels parted as the doors brushed the sandy floor, opening fully. There stood Iinnad, wings out-stretched, headphones resting on her shoulders, with a grin of surprise and nodding to the beat. She took a step into the light; the corridor behind still black in shadow. She stood alone; one angelic fully transformed in appearance, stronger than all that stood before her. Her matted hair clung to her war painted face as her wet tunic did to her body.

'Interrupting anything?'

'Iinnad!' Cole called.

On hearing the name, several of Abbadon's followers stepped back. In the ten thousand years of battle on Raquie, the Second Realm Iinnad had made quite a name for herself.

'HELLO!' she shouted above the music. 'Richard! Abbadon! Gabriel! Don't know you!' she nodded at Naomi. 'Lilith! Still here?'

'What did you do to your face?' Lilith asked in disgust.

'Eye of Horus!' Iinnad snapped. 'Read a book! You can read… can't you?'

'You look a mess,' Lilith replied. 'First attempt at make-up? No… wait… you look like one of us.'

'Iinnad, this is not your fight,' Abbadon stated.

'We are Watchers on this Realm,' Iinnad answered.

'Then watch! Remember you gave your word!'

'Yes, I did!'

'Then you don't mind if I finish what I started?' Abbadon boyishly asked.

Iinnad moved her eyes to focus on Gabriel and Abbadon's foot firmly placed on his sword. Iinnad reluctantly *had* given her word. Her expression changed to that of a broad smile. That smile that never left her face.

'*Mind*? I don't mind – but *they* will!'

Iinnad folded her wings as fifty-two red lasers shot out of the darkness from behind her, placing dots that covered Abbadon's chest. The flashes of light, the crack of gunfire told Abbadon that each dot would be met by a lead projectile. In a blur he moved. Gabriel dived deeper into the sand grabbing his sword as the Templar entered the crypt. Naomi sat, her back to the pillar, her arm still chained high above her head. As the bullets flew, the warriors in black fanned out taking on demonic and fallen alike. Lilith lost her concentration on Cole; her attention was now fully focused on Iinnad. She fired her brace at the stationary target still standing in the doorway. The blade drew blood as it clipped Iinnad's left wing, slicing a vein.

'That's what I was waiting for,' Iinnad announced as she turned towards the leather-clad fallen and briefly glanced skyward. 'Thank you!'

For Lilith, this was the fight she wanted. Abbadon couldn't stop her now. He was occupied with Gabriel on the other side of the stone effigies. Cole was grateful for the break to catch his breath as both Aston and Troy's teams rained fire down on every grotesque figure that came into view. Lilith needed a clear spot for her battle and realising that the chamber was too crowded; darted down the nearest side tunnel with Iinnad closely on her tail, if she had one, which Iinnad believed she deserved.

Within moments the two were alone and the sound of the battle, faint down the corridor behind. Iinnad waited for Lilith to make the first move. She wanted to give her at least a slight chance, but Lilith stood still.

'You wish to fight as you are?' Iinnad inquired.

'Why should I change? Heaven and Amente will know if you beat me the way you are.'

'Heaven and Hell, you idiot!' Iinnad corrected. 'I wanted this to be fair. If you're not going to change, then I shall.'

'As you wish, it makes no odds to me,' Lilith challenged.

Iinnad began to regress as her wings closed back into body. To her horror, Lilith's blue eyes flashed red as she charged at Iinnad, kicking the transforming angelic against the stone wall. Lilith's battle scarred wings flexed behind her as she grabbed Iinnad by the neck, her nails extending to cut her flesh.

'That was too easy,' she gloated.

Iinnad struggled to punch the creature, the bitch that had cheated her. Every strike had little effect. She felt her feet leave the ground, but she couldn't break free. Try as she might, neither could she draw her sword nor get the right angle to use her brace. Sophia's words flashed through Iinnad's mind.

'Soulcarrier and angelic alike will do whatever it takes to win,' Iinnad repeated Sophia's line in her head as the grip around her neck tightened. *'You may fight, but not like an angelic. You will do this to*

win!'

Everything became clear. Iinnad resorted to something *very* un-angelic. Through the leather, with all her might, she pinched Lilith's nipple and twisted hard. The fallen cried out in excruciating pain, dropping the bleeding Iinnad. She drew her blade and clipped Lilith's wing; a little payback.

'Sophia!' Iinnad called out. 'You were right. By any means.'

'What?'

'Private joke, never mind!'

The claw marks on Iinnad's neck oozed red as she clicked it and straightened her shoulders. Lilith was astounded by Iinnad's actions as she turned to face her, still rubbing her chest. However, she knew her opponent would not have time to transform again.

'With your war markings you look more like one of us,' Lilith repeated.

'I will *never* be one of you!'

'Now you fight like one of us.'

The fallen angelic leapt forward bringing her sword down, only to be met by Iinnad's hand catching hers. Iinnad countered the move, her blade thrust towards Lilith's chest, but she gripped the steel. The tip nudged against the leather, Iinnad pushed, but the blade didn't move.

'I'm stronger than you,' Lilith taunted.

'And Heaven and Hell will know I beat you like this,' Iinnad snarled.

'*You* beat me?'

Iinnad smiled and bent her knees. Leaning backwards she moved her centre of gravity and fell, her back crashing into the sand.

Lilith, still in the embrace, couldn't help but follow, landing on Iinnad's blade. The tip ripped through her internal organs and exited between her shoulder blades. Iinnad rolled clear of the corpse as Lilith's skin dried and began to ignite. She snatched her sword from the flames.

'Only use greater force against itself,' she spoke to the flickering light. 'Bitch!'

***

In the crypt, the demonic and fallen ran from the bloodline as their headshots became more effective. If a Templar got too close or ran out of ammunition, he drew his sword, beheading or cutting the injured enemy in two. Either way the crypt was to fill with flames in a very short space of time. Amongst the demonic were a few fallen, their brace weapons continuously firing their deadly blades. Only a couple of minutes into the battle and those that had stayed in the crypt were now on fire. The Templar had two mortally wounded and six with severe lacerations, their valuable blood uncontrollably rushing from their wounds.

Cole dropped behind the pillar by Naomi to release her as several of the warriors attempted to watch the blur of Abbadon and Gabriel moving around the centre of the crypt.

'Leave them!' Cole shouted. 'It's their fight! Find the others!'

Troy immediately reacted to the instructions. 'Blue team! On me!'

He disappeared down the left passage, situated behind Cole as several of the black clad knights followed suit. Aston led Red Team down the passages to the right. As the Templar disappeared, Cole continued to struggle with the chain that incarcerated his fellow American. He tried to ignore the blur of clashing swords as he frustratingly pulled at the iron links. Naomi calmly watched the fight between good and evil. Her intense concentration gave the impression that it was as though she could see it unfold before her eyes. Shaking his head, Cole took out his Berretta firing one shot at the lock on the calm girl's wrist. She jumped to her feet from the sudden sound. However, the iron had cracked and she was free.

'Let's go!' Cole instructed.

'No!'

'We have to get you to safety!'

'No! I'm staying!' Naomi insisted.

'If Gabriel doesn't win; Abbadon will kill us!'

Calmly, Naomi spoke. 'Then Gabriel *must* win. We stay.'

***

Red Team switched to night-vision as they spread out into the unlit passages. Knowing that the demonic had better eyes put them on edge. Although, being on edge was to be the demonic's undoing. With adrenalin, the Templar's ability to fight became even more effective. Screams of burning demonic echoed from the tunnels. One by one, the grotesque fell to the skill and training of the knights; their bodies illuminating the labyrinth with flame.

***

Troy entered the chamber where a charred corpse with wings lay. Iinnad sat leaning against the opposite wall. Blue Team fanned out and explored the remaining exits. Troy crouched down in front of the tired beauty.

'You Okay?' he asked with genuine concern.

'Yep!' Iinnad gave the thumbs up.

'Can you stand?'

'Of course I can stand!'

Iinnad jumped to her feet and brushed herself down.

'You're bleeding.'

It'll pass,' Iinnad replied. 'Thank you.'

'For what?'

'I never thought a primitive would be able to teach me anything.'

'There's a lot I could teach you,' Troy flirted with a sweaty grin.

Iinnad ignored him. 'Where's Gabriel?'

***

Naomi and Cole, hand in hand did their best to avoid the blur as it darted about the crypt. Momentarily, the blur would stop. The out of breath angelic would be visible. A cut wing or a grazed arm was the only indication of injury. As they both tired, the blur became a more recognisable motion as the two slowed in their defences and attacks. Gabriel had very quickly realised he had not only neglected his duties, but his training as well. Abbadon however, had neglected much, but centuries of fighting in the primitive's wars hadn't honed his skills as he had thought. Gabriel could do nothing, but defend. Their swords clashed again and again.

Troy appeared in the small entrance followed by Iinnad. The Templar raised his weapon. Cole caught the action in the corner of his eye and did the same. Abbadon could not win. Iinnad placed her hand over the barrel of Troy's MP5, gently pushing the nozzle to the ground.

'This is their fight,' she said. 'It's personal. No bullets.'

The Destroyer's blows came down one after the other as Gabriel could only parry the blows. As he dropped to the ground the Dark Prince caught a glimpse of something he had not seen in thousands of years. The key to the Abyss swung free from the angelic's cord. Abbadon paused by Naomi's pillar, on the other side stood the two Americans. Cole could see Gabriel's position was defenceless. Abbadon could strike at will. Without thought, Cole stepped forward his sword drawn. Unexpectedly, the Abbadon attacked Cole; his sword met him square in the stomach. He yanked the blade upward through the human, but it gave Gabriel that moment he needed to get close for the killing blow. With his free hand Abbadon swiped the key and allowed Gabriel's blade to pierce his black heart.

'Like grandfather, like father and son,' he muttered as he hit the sand. 'You lose Gabriel. The First Realm…'

The Destroyer, Abbadon, the Dark Prince of Amente's life was at an end. His last action to embed the key deep within the mortal wound and then his body engulfed in the cleansing red haze of flames as his essence returned to Sagun along with Gabriel's lucky charm.

Cole fell off Abbadon's sword as the Destroyer died. Templar and angelic alike gathered around him. Gabriel knelt beside his new friend as Richard tried to keep his eyes open.

'Rebecca, shit! Did you kill him?' Cole's dying breath.

'He has gone,' Gabriel replied.

His answer fell on deaf ears. The crypt was silent. The remainder of Red team returned with Aston leading. Gabriel checked the other two Templar by the main door, but both had passed on. The able Templar began to head back to the surface, clearing weapons, checking safeties; the wounded waited in the darkened corridor. Transport was required to get them to hospital without bringing attention to themselves. Gabriel crouched beside Sir William's body.

'I should have opened my eyes. I am proud of what you have accomplished William,' he whispered touching his forehead. 'I am so very proud old man.'

'Why didn't Abbadon finish you?' Iinnad broke the quiet.

Gabriel turned his attention back to Cole. 'I do not know.'

'Why kill the American? Why's he so special?' Troy added.

'I do not know,' Gabriel replied placing his hands over Cole's bloody chest.

'What d'you think you're doing?' Iinnad barked.

'What does it look like?' Gabriel answered as his hands began to glow.

The light from the Archangel's hands was emitting a shimmering haze that blended into Cole's body. Gabriel closed his eyes to focus all his energy into what he was doing.

'Gabriel!' Iinnad snapped. 'I know you don't listen to me, but listen to me now. What you're doing will have repercussions. Believe me, this is not what you want to do! Let him go, Gabriel! Please… let him go!'

By now Gabriel's whole body was emitting the same hazy white light, as was Cole's lifeless shell. Once the haze had reached full strength it began to jump to the others in the crypt. Soon every being beneath the City of London was bathed in light and then suddenly it stopped. Gabriel sat back in the dust and took a deep breath, then sniffed the air.

'Aston!' Gabriel called looking around a little dazed.

'I'm here Gabriel,' he said stepping from behind him.

'Do not let the authorities know Richard died.'

'It's a bit late for that. It's already been radioed in.'

'You're way too efficient!' Troy butted in.

'Why?' Aston asked Gabriel.

The angelic hesitated and climbed to his feet, somewhat unsteady.

'Because he's not dead!' Iinnad explained. 'Well… he is dead! But he won't be. It takes time.'

'They will take him to a morgue. You must retrieve the body in three days. Promise me. Promise me!' Gabriel barked.

'I promise,' Aston was little confused. 'Where will you be?'

'Not here!'

'Oh crap!' Iinnad blurted out. 'They're coming, aren't they?'

The blonde, now centre of attention, ran to the main corridor. Facing everyone Iinnad transformed faster than she had ever done before. She stared at each in turn.

'Gabriel repercussions! Troy! Thank you. Aston, good music! What's your name! I can't be here. I'm in enough trouble as it is!'

'Iinnad! GO!' Gabriel ordered.

And she did. *Like the wind…*

'Gabriel, who's coming?' Aston inquired.

'The Sentinels.'

Troy grinned. 'Isn't that a comic book?'

Before Troy's echo had ceased, two cracks of light appeared in the roof. The light created two columns of mist that reached the sand floor in which a human figure stood in each. Six and half feet tall and wearing plain white robes, one of the Sentinels, his eyes closed pointed at Gabriel.

'You are required before the Council,' said his solemn voice and mouth shut.

'Remember, three days,' Gabriel repeated and stepped between the two figures.

A third circle of misty light engulfed the Archangel and then all three began to climb back into the roof until only a tiny crack of light remained. Finally that also vanished, taking with it, the three heavenly beings. Troy was about to speak.

'Troy!' Aston snapped. 'Don't even mention Scotty or I'll thump you.' He wiped the grin from his face as he stared at the sand. 'Take Naomi and clear the surface units! London's going to be a mess after the blackout we caused. I'll deal with the clean up down here.'

XL

Sagun – The Third Realm.

28th Sunrise 2nd Cycle AD 2001 (First Realm Time)

Everything is dark when one dies. However, there is a light at the end of the tunnel. It was just not the light that Richard Lawton Cole was expecting.

As the light grew brighter Cole realised he was coming to, in a place alien to him. He sat upright; surprised that he could still feel sand between his fingers. Above, was the sky and the glaring sun. He stood and found himself in the middle of a vast plain surrounded by a circle of rocks made of crystal. He wasn't the only one. Several hundred other people, beings, from a few children to the many old, were standing in the crystal circle with him. Some were following the line of the worn path that led off the plain and into the mountains. As it did so, it pasted the ruins of a temple that Cole recognised, Gabriel's carving, the Temple of Icea. Cole knew where he was. With nowhere else to go, Cole began to walk with the others along the path towards the burnt out shell of the Temple.

'Cole!' shouted a familiar strong Scottish accent. 'Cole! Is that you?'

Out of the crowd of faceless dead emerged eleven Templar.

'They got you too?' Sir William gasped. 'We put our heads together and came up with the fact that we're dead and this is hell.' The Grand Master looked around. 'Not bad considering. But we don't know where *they're* all going?'

'This isn't hell,' Cole replied.

'Bit of a let down, if this is heaven,' jested Mark, one of the sniper team.

The group gathered around the American, curious as to how he knew, especially Henry. Cole stared at each one in turn. Physically everyone looked fine, but their clothing told a different story. Henry appeared bloodied and wet, even in the sun. Sir William's jacket was sliced across the chest; the snipers were burnt and the rest of the Templar were cut and slashed. Lucy had a hole in the back of her blouse and was tied in a knot at the front. The eleven of them stood in a circle around Cole.

'I'll tell you what Gabriel told me. This…' Cole proceeded to explain. The Templar silently listened, until he had finished. 'In those mountains is hell. Abbadon's true place of residence.'

'Oh, he's dead too,' Lucy piped up still holding her clothes.

'So Gabriel got him?' Cole smiled.

'And I thought we were really in trouble,' joked Garry, the other sniper.

'Why are you so damn cheerful? We're dead! We have just left everything, everyone we love behind. There is nothing for us here!'

No one spoke.

After a long pause Cole suggested. 'We should follow the others to hell. There we'll be judged. Good or bad is not up to us. That's basically how it works.'

'Why can't we stay here?' Lucy asked.

'What are we going to live on?' Henry pointed out.

'Maybe we don't have to eat because we're dead,' added one of the other Templar. 'We could explore the entire realm?'

'Cole's right!' Sir William announced. 'We follow the path. Come on son, walk with me.'

The Grand Master took Henry by the shoulder and began the long walk to Amente, blending into the line of beings that walked the path.

Except for William and Henry the soulcarriers walked in single file along the trail of a million footprints as it climbed into the foothills to the east of the Great Plain.

'Hey Lucy!' called Mark. 'You into necrophilia?'

'You weren't that funny when you were alive. Trust me on this; your poor humour died when you did!' she answered.

The others laughed; it helped to hide how they really felt. Cole was right; they had left everything behind them forever.

***

Finally, the group stood in front of the Caves of Enlightenment. Cole walked ahead of the others, but winced in pain. He grabbed his stomach in a vain attempt to stop the hurt. Lucy was immediately at his side.

'Are you alright?' she asked, her hand on his back as he bent over.

'No!' he panted. 'Don't any of you feel that?'

'Feel what?' Henry questioned.

Cole took another step. 'The closer I get to the cave; the more… it hurts!'

The Templar moved forward, but none experienced what Cole was going through as they cautiously entered the caves. Cole huddled at the back trying his hardest to keep his mumbles of pain down, so as not to draw attention to himself.

'Who art thou? State you name and prepare to be judged,' rang the voice through their ears. 'Cross the threshold of this cave and there is no return. Return and you *will* be no more. You are here to be judged!'

Sir William stepped forward, but did not cross the line of stones embedded in the dirt. He adjusted his eyes to the gloom until he could see the figure seated opposite.

'Do you say that to every one who enters?' he questioned.

'Only those that should be here. Many beings from the realms come here; some to be judged; some for enlightenment. Some rest before judgement, because the journey has been hard on them; for others not so. Each being is different, but there is one amongst you who I feel is truly different. Allow me to see him.'

The group banded together hiding the American from view. Lucy could do nothing to comfort Cole as he dropped to his knees. To their right appeared a fallen angelic, his tunic black and burnt. The judge jumped from his seat.

'Barakiel!' he confronted. 'You cannot harm these beings!'

'Mithra, *these beings* are soulcarriers. I just wanted to see the new arrivals,' he said as he strolled across the cave and entered a downward tunnel. 'I'll let Abbadon know the Templar are here. I think he'll be interested.'

The fallen angelic disappeared into the dark. Cole staggered to his feet on hearing Barakiel's voice. He pushed through the black clad obstacles and crossed the line of stones. The pain in his stomach suddenly vanished.

'Cross the threshold; state your name,' Cole stated. 'Then what?'

'Thought it was the other way around?' whispered Garry with a chuckle.

'Richard Lawton Cole; an American from the First Realm! Now judge me!'

'I cannot!' replied the figure. 'You should not be here!'

'Yeah! I get that a lot! Where did Barakiel go?'

Mithra tried to block Cole's path, but as the soulcarrier got closer he backed away.

'You're scared of me?' Cole deduced.

'Sir William Henry Sinclair!' boomed the Grand Master's voice behind him.

'Henry James Sinclair!'

'Lucy… Vera Sheriff!'

Mark sniggered. 'Vera?'

Each in turn followed suit, stating their names out loud and then taking the fateful step over the sunken stones.

'You may rest now or be judged,' spoke the fearful figure.

'You didn't answer my question. Why are you scared of me?' Cole pushed.

'In time, in a moment. As I said, you should not be here. You must return!'

'I can't return. If I do, I am no more. But… I'm dead… so how can I die?'

Mithra shook his head. For eons, he had sat at the threshold of the Caves of Enlightenment and on only two other occasions had beings arrived that had to return. A young boy and a middle aged man, but neither had been as difficult as the one that stood before him. The others had accepted what was to be, without question.

'Do you judge us?' Sir William calmly asked breaking Cole's line of questioning and reminding him that they were all present in hell.

'No! Do you wish to rest?'

'No thank you. I believe we would all like to get this over with.'

'To your left is the Chamber of Light,' explained the judge. 'On the far side of the chamber is a passage that leads back to this place. Walk through to the passage. If you are true of heart then the stairway will ascend you. If not, you will reach the passage and return to this place and stay.'

'That's it?' Cole expressed.

'Not you. You must return,' insisted Mithra.

'I shouldn't be here! I can't go in,' Cole continued. 'You said if I leave…'

Sir William stood in front of the Chamber of Light. He glanced over to Cole.

'I should really thank you,' he interrupted.

'For starting a war?'

'For bringing us out of the shadows. For bringing my son back to me,' Sir William replied turning to Henry and smiling. 'If I don't get the chance; I wanted to say, I'm sorry I doubted you. I am truly proud. You have lived up to the family name.'

The Templar said their farewells to the American and then each entered the Chamber of Light heading for the passage as instructed.

'I envy you Richard,' Henry said. 'You know all this and your future is still uncertain. I know all this and now it ends.'

'You don't know that!'

'I know there are more secrets out there to learn; and you are going to learn them without me.'

'Just think of the secrets that *you* are going to learn. Goodbye Henry. You taught me more than you know.'

Henry smiled and stepped into the chamber. Only Lucy remained.

'What a sacrifice, hey?' she said with a shrug of her shoulders.

Cole nodded. Lucy was right.

'Say hi… and sorry to Troy for me; if you *do* see him again? Bye Richard.'

Cole smiled, a tear on his cheek as Lucy entered the chamber.

The remaining soulcarrier faced Mithra, edging closer, but without touching him, forcing him against the side of the cave.

'Where did Barakiel go?' he demanded.

'He went to the Abyss. Please! Please! Please don't touch me!'

'Why not?'

'Because… it burns,' was the cryptic reply. Then he pointed. 'The Abyss is that way, down. Each turning only has one path that leads down. Keep going down.'

***

Cole headed deep within the heart of the Malam Grigori Mountains. Stumbling in the dark and occasionally being blinded by flaming torch light; it wasn't long before he could hear voices. Abbadon and Barakiel he recognised, but there was a third voice; a low deep sound that vibrated in his lungs and raised the hairs on the back of his neck. He arrived at the edge of a large cavern. The voices were clear now. Barakiel had already informed Abbadon of their arrival, but he was only angry that his conversation with Sataniel had been interrupted. Cole thought for a moment. *Satan?* He wanted to kill Barakiel, but that wasn't going to happen. Since he was there, he might as well take a peek at the Devil himself. Then the pain in his stomach returned, although gradually this time. He had an unexplainable urge to return to the surface.

A sharp jab, from a stiletto, in his backside pushed him forward. He scrambled to gain a footing, but ended up in the dust. Something pulled him to his feet as the pain in his stomach began to intensify. He was a long way from the surface and if he didn't get there soon the hurt was going to be unbearable.

'Look what I found!' broadcast Lilith as she strutted in behind Cole. 'My Lord! This soulcarrier followed me half way around the First

Realm and he's managed to get here. Persistent aren't you? I bet it was painful?'

Lilith lifted Cole up off the ground, the tips of his boots just scraping the dust. With both hands holding him, she ran across the cavern punching the American into the soft clay wall.

'Agent Cole – the National Security Agency has no jurisdiction in hell, even if your superiors think they might have,' Lilith jested.

'You killed two whole families,' Cole said, out of breath. 'Some laws… are the same the world over; any world. For that, you deserve to die.'

'I'm already dead. So are you!'

'Lilith! Hold him there!' Abbadon called out. 'I want him to see this. If it wasn't for his distraction, I wouldn't have *this*!'

Abbadon held the key up high. Then he jumped into the Bottomless Pit, landing on the gates with a crash. He bent down and placed the key in the lock.

'Richard!' Abbadon laughed. 'You made all this possible. I thank you. You definitely are my offspring.'

The soulcarrier fought his jailer, but Lilith held him firm. Abbadon turned the key. Nothing happened. He tried it again. The frustration grew in his eyes. Barakiel backed away seeing the anger overflow in his master. Sataniel's laughter filled the air.

'Did you think it would be that easy?' he asked his prince. 'You should never make a deal with me. Only the one that locked me in here can release me. Only Gabriel can release me. Get Gabriel to free me and the First Realm is yours, you fool.'

Abbadon screamed with rage, throwing the key at the wall. The polished piece of metal buried itself into the clay. Abbadon continued to let out his anger; only now it was on the rusty gate. Beneath Sataniel continued to laugh.

Lilith, to her surprise, was now having trouble holding the soulcarrier. She intensely stared at his body, but the effort that Cole was exerting didn't match what she was feeling. She forced her pursuer back into the clay; it wasn't just him she was fighting, there was something else. She tried to see what Abbadon was doing with all the shouting behind her.

'Your hands are burning, Lilith,' Cole noticed, since she had not.

The fallen glanced back at her hands. The human was right; slight columns of faint smoke were drifting from her extremities.

'You son of a bitch!' she cursed.

'My *mother* was a good woman,' replied Cole. 'She raised me well enough to turn Abbadon down.'

'You have no idea what is happening to you, do you?

'Nope! And I don't care. I've lost my wife; my baby. I've lost my whole life because of you.'

'Your wrong Agent Cole,' Lilith whispered. 'You're being resurrected. Gabriel's a clever son of bitch; *and* I do know his mother.'

'What are you…'

'Shut up and listen!' she kept her voice down as Abbadon crashed about on the gate behind her. 'You are being drawn back. You *will* leave this place and *we* can't follow.'

'You mean you can't stop me,' Cole smiled.

'No! When you see Iinnad, tell her this isn't over. She could have been a great fallen. She could have had her own army and been the leader of legions. She is *nothing,* until next time.'

'What do I get in return?'

'You're in no position…'

'What do I get in return?' Cole calmly pushed with nothing to lose.

'What do you want?' Lilith hushed.

'I could take you with me. I could grab Abbadon. I cross the threshold and he is no more. He dies. As in dead! But you wouldn't let me.'

'No I wouldn't.'

'Barakiel is by Abbadon's side. He killed my father. Do you want to regain your place by your master's side?'

Lilith was now having trouble holding onto the soulcarrier; her feet were slipping in the dust. Her high heels were ploughing the dirt; her attractive face changed to ugly expressions of effort as she tried to pin Cole back against the clay.

'Lilith, I'm not even struggling and you can't hold me. I *want* Barakiel. The enemy of my enemy is my friend, but the next time we meet, it will be different.'

'Agreed!' Lilith nodded out of breath. 'Pretend to fight and cover my burning… cover my hands. Hurry…' Lilith whispered in pain, a lot of pain.

Cole took his time. Lilith deserved to burn for what she had done on the First Realm, but Cole was also in pain and so he did not take as long as he would have liked. It was Catch 22. How much pain could he endure? Not much, so reluctantly, he did as he was asked.

'Barakiel!' Lilith beckoned. 'Help me with this piece of waste.'

Barakiel casually crossed the cavern, kicking at the dust and smiling at the struggling woman. He stood beside Lilith as Cole hid her hands from view. The agent pretended to kick Lilith, occasionally doing so for good measure.

'Don't stand there smiling; help me!' Lilith shouted.

Barakiel leant forward and the two fallen held Cole back into the wall. Lilith hid her hands under the folds in Cole's clothing giving the resurrected time to firmly grabbed hold of Barakiel.

'I killed your father,' the fallen angelic gloated.

'I know!' Cole replied kicking himself away from the wall as Lilith let go.

The agent's eyes met Lilith's. The thank you had been said. Cole kept hold of the killer he wanted. The other had escaped. There would be another time for Lilith he hoped. She watched the two roll through the dust towards the tunnel that they had come.

'What's happening?' Barakiel shouted. 'What in the hell!'

Abbadon stopped his rant and jumped from the pit. Lilith was by his side as they stared at the two struggle, all the time being pulled back up the tunnel. Abbadon was prepared to follow, but Lilith grabbed his arm shaking her head.

'I don't think you want to touch him my Lord,' Lilith calming informed him. 'Gabriel has just broken another rule.'

'I can't stop him!' Barakiel screamed.

'Gabriel resurrected him,' Lilith shouted after the frantic dirty angelic.

'No!' the fallen screamed. 'Let go of me! Get off me!'

His voice echoed through the labyrinth as the indescribable force pulled Cole back up the passages to the surface. Panicking, Barakiel frantically fired his brace, trying to get the correct angle so as not to injure himself. A jabbing pain shot through Cole's right foot, but he held on. He could feel the wound was bad, bleeding heavily, but he was struggling to determine how far he had to go before he reached the threshold and the death of the fallen angelic that had killed his father. Barakiel stuck his arms out, his fingers snatching at the rock; the rough surface cut his hands, breaking his nails and a finger. Barakiel then forced his hands harder against the rock and stopped just paces from where the tunnel opened into the cave entrance, and the threshold. Cole abruptly slid down his body to his waist. He wrapped his arms around Barakiel's belt and then locked his fingers together. He wasn't going anywhere and if he was; Barakiel was coming with him. The force that was pulling the soulcarrier was now so strong, that neither were touching the ground; like two people hanging off a cliff, one holding the other, only horizontally. Barakiel couldn't shake the human free. He tried, but risked losing his grip. He couldn't undo his belt without losing his grip. Cole was determined to hold on, locking his body, so that if Barakiel killed him, the force would still pull them both across the threshold.

'Help me!' Barakiel shouted at the figure. 'Mithra! Get over here! Help me!'

Cole entwined his bloody foot up and around Barakiel's legs shaking and jolting his body with all his might.

The agent glanced down the length of his body and noticed the sniper Garry. He had not ascended. His field of vision was then blocked by another familiar face. Lucy had stepped from the chamber; she had yet to enter the light.

'You must be judged!' Mithra snapped, ignoring the commotion to his left. 'You must enter the Chamber of Light!'

'In a second,' Lucy calmly replied.

She grabbed Cole's bloodied leg and pulled. Barakiel began to loose his grip. Mithra darted across the entrance shoving Lucy into the light. She was gone; ascended. Cole continued to jolt his body.

The agent screamed with each jolt. 'You!' Jolt. 'Are!' Jolt. 'Coming!' Jolt. 'With!' Jolt. 'ME!' Jolt, jolt.

The rock broke free. Barakiel lost his grip.

'Die! You bastard!' Cole shouted as he pulled the exhausted murderer across the line of embedded stones.

The American's hands began to blister wherever he made contact with Barakiel. The blistering became a burning and Cole had to let go of the fallen angelic allowing him to fall into the swallow stream that covered the floor of the gorge. Barakiel crashed into the water, but the wet didn't prevent his skin from drying. He staggered to his feet and stared up at Cole as he was lifted into the blue sky. The skin of the fallen began to flake and burn, setting in motion the process of death. All Cole could see before he was pulled out of view was the being that killed his father scream as he burst into flames. Barakiel was dead; his essence destroyed; cleansed in fire, but Cole had failed in his promise to bring Lilith to justice. He cursed himself in his moment of success; he had chosen revenge over the justice that he sought.

He retraced the path through the Malam Grigori Mountains, passed The Temple of Icea and The Great plain as the brightness engulfed him. Suddenly all went dark.

XLI

The Fifth Realm.

28th Sunrise 5th Cycle AD 2001 (First Realm Time)

The Sentinels left Gabriel to walk down the long Grand hallway towards the golden doors of the Celestial Court. He paused when he noticed the old man, Enoch, sitting on a marble bench, scribbling. The image before him took him back to Pestilence.

***

65th Sunrise – 1st Cycle 7436 BC

The mission was over. Uriel tended to Enoch, who sat in one of the alcoves near the exit to the deployment bay. The silence was broken when Iinnad burst in.

'Where's Bara... Barakiel?' she panted.

Nobody answered the question.

'What happened down there?'

She looked around the bay for an answer, but stopped when she spotted Enoch.

'Why did you bring a primitive on board?' using the only insulting description she could think of. 'He was the target? I thought it was the book!'

There was still silence.

'[illegible]?' she repeated her insult.

'He sees things,' replied a tired and breathless Jesuel.

'He's a soulcarrier! How many had to die for a soulcarrier?'

Iinnad was still looking around the bay for an answer *from anyone*, when Michael appeared.

'We have a rough ride ahead,' he revealed calmly. 'That comet has been pulled too close to the moon. It could break up as it passes the gravitational pull of this realm, hence the change in the time frame. It was not expected. Phul, when you have rested I would like you to look at this *moon*. We took no notice since its trajectory would have been on its far side, but its strong gravity pulled it into the realm's own gravity. Not what we expected at all.'

'I don't believe that for a wing beat,' Iinnad snapped.

'Seven mountains of fire...' repeated Enoch.

'There is your answer. It will break into seven pieces,' Jesuel emphasised.

'How does he know?' asked Iinnad pointing at the primitive.

'He sees things,' said the chorus within the bay.

'He sees things? *He sees things?* Well, if he saw us coming, he could have waited on the beach and saved us a hell of a lot of trouble.'

Iinnad, as always, blunt and to the point. This time, as with many other occasions, she was right.

'Come Enoch,' said Michael calmly. 'Have faith, come with me. I promise you; you will not see death.'

And Michael took Enoch by his right hand and led him away to show him the secrets of the angels, for his time on the First Realm was over. Uriel began to follow, but Iinnad blocked his path.

'You withheld too much information for a mission like this,' Iinnad stated.

'Deep are all thy secrets and innumerable,' Uriel replied.

'I care as much for your quotes as a block of ice in hell.'

'You are just an angelic. I am Archangel.'

'And Barakiel was Prince of the Second Heaven and once of the Order of Confessors.'

'*Once*, he was demoted,' Uriel calmly replied. 'Remember?'

Jesuel was about to speak, but Gabriel shook his head.

'Balberith was Cherubim. How many ranks higher than you is *that*?' Iinnad continued. 'Lauviah was also Cherubim *and* of the Order of Thrones. How many ranks higher than you is *that*?'

'They both volunteered and dropped their rank, Iinnad. Do you wish to drop yours?'

'I'm an angel. I'm as low as you can get.'

'Yes you are,' Uriel sarcastically replied as he pushed Iinnad's arm aside.

Iinnad grabbed the Archangel by the scruff of the neck and pulled him back into the bay. Uriel flew across the floor and crashed up against the opposite wall. He began to climb back to his feet.

'I haven't finished yet,' she continued. 'So don't bother getting up.'

'Iinnad!' Gabriel stood up, his uniform now clean, as was the way with garments that do not grow old, provided by the Lord of Spirits.

'Shut it Gabe! Nine angelic for one soulcarrier! Who came up with that plan? That was clever! Nine for one, you calculate the numeric, because as far as I can see it, that's plain *stupid*!'

'Iinnad!' Gabriel barked.

'*Now* we've got a comet to deal with!' Iinnad continued to ignore Gabriel.

'Seven Mountains of Fire,' repeated Phul.

'The comet is not our concern,' Uriel added calmly, although he was now pinned to the floor with Iinnad's foot on his shoulder.

'Not our concern?' she barked. 'We *all* know what destruction a comet will bring; the floods, the dust clouds that will block out the sun for years. And we snatched a primitive from the jaws of death… and you're telling me… *you* didn't know? How many soulcarriers are going to die because of *that* chain of events?'

'A moment ago you did not care,' Uriel stated. '*He was just a primitive!*'

'That was until I realised that no one else did. How many primitives are going to die, Uriel? How many?'

'A million,' Uriel answered in a calculated tone. 'Maybe more.'

Iinnad, surprised at Uriel's honest answer, released him.

'Who made you God?' she asked.

'Ouch!' Phul mimed looking at a wincing Gmial.

Everything stopped in the circular chamber. The Archangel jumped to his feet and stood tall, staring straight into Iinnad eyes. 'Do not cross swords with me Iinnad!'

'Why? Too scared you'll lose?'

'I have warned you.'

'You save one soulcarrier,' Iinnad continued in a lower decibel, knowing she had crossed the line. 'You could have saved thousands.'

'She's right Uriel,' Gabriel inserted.

'You are right, Iinnad,' Uriel agreed. '200,000 years of learning, of growing into the beings that they have become, wiped out, washed away…' Uriel paused, his fist clenched in front of her. 'But Iinnad, I have watched these beings. I have watched them grow.' He opened his hand like a rose bud to the sun. 'You are right! The destruction will be followed by the darkness. The darkness will be followed by the long winter, but in a mountain cave or a great plain far from the sea a few, just a few will survive. They will survive and mate and start again. Watch! That is what *we* do!'

'We didn't do that today! We *died* today.'

Uriel said nothing. Iinnad, knowing her battle was lost, marched out.

Gabriel approached Uriel blocking his path.

'Iinnad's heart is in the right place,' he apologised for her.

'And you jump in to protect your her,' Uriel sharply replied. 'You forget that you are Archangel. You are one of us now.'

'Uriel,' Gabriel spoke calmly, 'I *wasn't* there when Sataniel fell from grace. I wasn't *there* – when the first battle of the angelic began. *And...* I wasn't there when the angelic stopped being angelic, and became *them and us*. Some of us have different opinions, but we are all on the same side.'

'You have a lot to learn Gabriel.'

'Yes, I probably do. That's the difference between you and I. I know and accept that there are things I need to learn.'

Uriel slowly walked around the obstruction and exited the bay.

***

The Fifth Realm – 28th Sunrise 5th Cycle AD 2001

Why had the Council chosen to move the court to the Fifth Realm? He prepared himself for what lay before him. Before he even reached the entrance to the court, the doors began to open. Gabriel entered and stood in the centre of the round hall. It was a splendid court, but did not have the power of excellence of the Court of the Seventh Realm. Beneath him, through the crystal floor, Gabriel could see the clouds drifting by. While above, the roof was clear and legions of angelic gazed down upon the proceedings. He faced the other Archangels, but to his horror there were seven of them. He said nothing. Iinnad had tried to warn him, but he had not listened.

Michael stepped forward. 'Do you understand why you have been summoned?'

'To be condemned!' Gabriel replied sharply.

'That awaits to be seen,' Remiel added.

'From where I stand, I would say not! Judgement has been made! Sarael now stands in the place that I once held.'

'It was Sarael's suggestion that the Council be complete for such an important judgement. The Council agreed,' Michael explained.

'And I am not of the Council and therefore not to be informed?'

'We are informing you now, Gabriel,' Uriel retorted.

'Do you understand why you have been summoned?' Michael repeated.

'No!'

'Rules are not to be broken,' Raguel began. 'The first rule of the First Realm, laid down by the most High, is not to interfere. You have done just that. You have purposely interfered in the development of mankind.'

'I disagree!'

'You disagree?' blurted Uriel. 'You interfered!'

'I only followed your lead. You interfered when you took... removed Enoch from the First Realm, just prior to its destruction.'

'That decision was made by the Council,' Uriel raised his voice.

'Uriel, am I not Archangel?' Gabriel calmly questioned.

Uriel stepped back, his lips sealed.

'You made decisions that were not your own,' Zerachiel elaborated.

'As did the Council. As I said, I followed your lead. I did what I believed was best.'

Uriel leapt forward again. 'You did what you thought was best? What makes you think you know what is best? I have studied mankind for millennia...'

'But you have not lived amongst them as I have! You have studied mankind for millennia and yet you stay with them for no more than a few days. I have spent *thousands* of years with these people. I have *watched* them. I have *listened* to them. I have *learnt*. I stand by my decision with regards to my actions.'

'You stand by your actions?' Sarael stepped up.

'Yes Sarael, as I hope you would.'

'You believe in your actions?' Sarael pushed.

'Would you not believe in yours?'

'You say your actions are just?'

Gabriel paused for a moment. 'As just as yours, yes!'

Michael intently listened to each question that answered the next. Gabriel was getting at something, but he knew that it was Gabriel who was on trial, not Sarael. This was not the time or place to continue with this line. It would have to wait.

'Then… let us begin with these such actions,' Michael announced glancing across to Raguel.

Archangel Raguel accepted the lead and began. 'Three thousand three hundred years ago on the First Realm you spoke with a human. You may have thought one Pharaoh the same as the next. However, *actions* or should I say the *conversation* with Amenophis IV subsequently changed the First Realm to this date. As you are well aware Amenophis IV changed his country, his peoples beliefs, by *force* I might add. All this because of a conversation with *you*?'

'You have been watching me?' Gabriel interrupted.

'Listening, would be a better a way of putting it,' Sarael divulged.

'I ask you,' Raguel continued. 'Why would one conversation change so much? Why would his wife Nefertiti stand by him with such vigour? Or is that… there was more than a conversation?' The pause was long. 'Gabriel, did you reveal yourself to Amenophis IV?'

'Yes,' Gabriel could not lie.

'And where was Jesuel at this time?' Sarael intervened.

'You know that Jesuel has nothing to do with my actions.'

'Did you fight alongside the soulcarriers during the Crusades?' Remiel inquired.

'Only the First Crusade as did many of the fallen. I had learnt what I needed to know and fought no more, in any of the campaigns.'

'Were you the Ninth Knight?' Raguel suggested.

'The Ninth Knight?' Gabriel gently smiled.

'Gabriel, you know where this is leading. Were you the Ninth Knight?' Raguel pushed.

'Yes.'

'And you followed their progress until their demise?'

'I did not interfere with their affairs, but yes, I did follow their progress. I was not a part of their demise.'

A door behind the condemned slammed shut and Sophia clicked her heels across the crystal to stand at Gabriel's side.

'Sophia, you are not required,' Michael told her.

'I wish it,' she firmly replied. 'And I will stay!'

'Mother!' Gabriel spoke firmly. 'You should not be here.'

'Shut up Gabriel,' she whispered. 'You rarely listen to anyone, so listen to your mother for once.'

'Sophia, this is not your fight,' announced Uriel.

'Are we to fight amongst ourselves now?'

'You turn my words, Sophia.'

'But they are *your* words, Uriel!' she smiled.

'Now we come to one of the two main reasons as to why we are here,' Raguel continued. 'King Phillip IV of France and Pope Clement

V were, in the eyes of history, responsible for the demise of the Templars. They died by your hand, did they not?'

Gabriel cleared his throat. 'Yes.'

'You murdered two soulcarriers in cold blood!' Uriel snapped.

Gabriel would not stand to his accusers a moment longer. He took several paces towards them.

'I passed judgement on those two individuals! On their orders hundreds, if not thousands of innocent people had been tortured, burnt alive or just plain killed! They burnt two innocent men at the stake in front of my own eyes, and in the name of what? Those innocent men claimed to believe in the truth, which they did. They made a promise, which was witnessed by thousands and I fulfilled it. Why? To make people believe in the truth. If that was wrong then I am guilty. Maybe I should have saved them?'

'No,' Uriel calmly said. 'The only thing that you did right was to let them die.'

'Like *you* did with Enoch?'

Sophia smiled; maybe Gabriel didn't require her help after all.

'Enoch was prophesied,' Uriel defended himself.

'Who is to say that my actions are not?'

'Do not think yourself that important!' Michael interrupted before the voices of the argument raised the crystal roof. 'The heavens felt your energy flow through the soulcarrier Cole. This is not acceptable.'

'There is something about the American.'

'There is now,' Sarael chipped in. 'You designate a soulcarrier by region? You have been amongst them far too long.'

'Yes I have, and I have learnt from that. Uriel said they would persevere. I believe they will, but why not help. *You* did with the Enoch mission.'

'The Enoch situation is none of your concern,' Uriel warned the condemned. 'That was an individual incident and cannot be compared with your actions.'

'You are right,' Gabriel admitted. 'I agree! It cannot be compared. At the end of the day my actions have caused *no* angelic death! Can you say the same?'

'Rules have been broken,' Michael reminded all concerned. 'That is why you are here.'

'I accept that I have broke certain rules, with no angelic death and I am guilty of that. So punish me! Remembering that no angelic died.'

'You have nothing else to say?' Michael asked, pushing for more.

Gabriel stared at Sarael. 'No! I was condemned before I entered this court. Iinnad warned me of that!'

'And where is Iinnad?' Zerachiel piped up.

'On an errand for myself,' Sophia stepped up to the Council. 'She informed me that she had found Gabriel and passed on your message.'

'So what of the key?' Remiel asked.

Gabriel rested his hand to his side, but felt nothing.

'The key!' Uriel barked.

'I believe it is safe,' Sophia answered.

'So this is what it was all about?' Gabriel added.

'You could redeem yourself, if you were to hand over the key,' Sarael suggested. 'I believe we could over look some of your actions.'

Sophia stepped forward to emphasise her point. 'You could, could you?'

'How did you know?' Gabriel asked the Council.

'That was me,' Sophia admitted. 'It was my job to detail the Battle of Sagun and inform the Council. I was there and I had to report the knowledge of the key.'

'Why? The Council believe in withholding information. The key has been safe for thousands of years. Why ask for it now?'

'The Council has its reasons,' Uriel divulged nothing. 'However, the key was useless, until a thousand years had passed on Sagun.'

'I was brought up through the ranks, Uriel. I was *made* Archangel and now you knock me back down. I was never *chosen*, I was never one of you and now I am glad that I am not.'

Michael nodded and could see Gabriel had nothing more to add. 'A punishment had been discussed prior to this court. It appears that you were expecting punishment. So it shall be granted. You are to remain on the First Realm, indefinitely. You are not permitted to travel to any other Realm. The Realm you love will be your jail.'

'And my rank?'

'Your rank stays with you…'

'I object!' Sarael bellowed. 'I admit, I was not a part of this decision, but…'

'You are only temporarily a part of *this* court,' Michael sharply warned the complaining Archangel. Diverting his attention back to Gabriel. 'You will not have a ruling part on this Council.'

'I did not know I had,' Gabriel quipped.

'The whole situation will be reviewed when the key to the Abyss is in our possession.'

'Is that wise?' Sarael asked Michael.

'You foresee a problem, Sarael?'

'I am just saying that punishment should *mean* punishment; with no conditions.'

'I would not worry, Sarael,' Gabriel interrupted. 'Your place on the Council is secure. The power you have gained will remain. I have no intention of returning the key. It will be in safer if the Council has no idea where it is. I accept my punishment.'

'Do you have anything else to add?' Michael urged Gabriel.

'No!'

'Are you sure that there is nothing you wish to reveal to us?'

Gabriel paused. Michael was getting at something.

'I am sure,' Gabriel insisted to his teacher.

Disappointed that Gabriel would not speak up, Michael continued. 'You will relive those moments as a reminder and return to the First Realm where you will stay.' Michael had passed judgement. 'So be it!'

Michael had known Gabriel since the beginning. He had trained him. He knew Gabriel, almost like a son. He could feel that Gabriel was holding back. Now, Gabriel was withholding information, which was unlike him. Why the verbal attacks against Sarael? What Gabriel did not know was that Michael was the only Archangel of the Council who stood against Sarael's appointment and he could not stand by the warrior he admired so much. The decision had been made. Archangel Michael turned his back on Gabriel. He was followed by Uriel. One by one the Council turned away. Gabriel had been judged, guilty. He was becoming too human. The clear roof became solid and the legions had gone. The clouds beneath his feet were not visible, only the cracks in the marble. Even though Sophia stood at his side, Gabriel felt alone.

XLII

The First Realm.

Roquemaure – France – Afternoon – 20th April AD 1314

Pope Clement V's entire fifty years had been filled with ill health. Now a weak man, he lay in his bed, frail and tired. Gabriel entered the tiny room via the open leaded lattice window. The interior was dark, like inside a polished mahogany box with a small four-poster bed in the middle, a cupboard in the far wall, one chair and a bedside cabinet. The angelic tiptoed to the door and locked it. As he dragged a small chair, its seat of woven straw, across the uneven floorboards, the noise woke the man in slumber. Gabriel sat down, his index finger to his lips.

'Ecouter!' Gabriel said. 'I want you to listen. I have questions. Do you understand?'

The Pope nodded. He had a grasp of the English language after many dealings with the English king, Edward.

'Who are you?' he spluttered. 'How did you get in here?'

'I am Gabriel – a servant of God. I used the window to get in.'

'But we are so high up?'

Gabriel ignored the comment. 'Why did you destroy my army?'

'I destroyed no army,' the Pope coughed.

'Pauperes commilitones Christi Templique Solomonici,' Gabriel answered in Latin. 'The Poor Fellow-soldiers of Christ and of the Temple of Solomon in Jerusalem. The Knights Templar are no more.'

'That was Philippe! He wanted their gold; their land. They had too much power. It was Philippe, not me. He is King, I am just Pope,' the pontiff blurted out.

'I was under the impression that the Kingdom of Heaven and the Pope made kings?' Gabriel replied.

' I am weak and tired. He is strong. I wrote a letter to the King's court after the arrests and complained,' muttered the pontiff. 'I protested about the treatment, but he ignored me, *me*! So, I annulled the entire trial.'

'Was it six Papal Bull's that you issued against the Templar?' Gabriel asked ignoring the Pope's pleas. 'You ordered their arrest throughout Christendom.'

Pope Clement bowed his head in shame. 'I suspended the Inquisition. I ordered a commission to investigate… I absolved them!'

'Then you reinstated the Inquisition that found them guilty!' Gabriel snapped.

'The charges would not stand, but they had a poor defence…'

'Which collapsed when you burned fifty-four of them alive. They admitted to lies to avoid the flames as you would have?'

'Yes,' the Pope whispered. 'I would have done as they did.'

'I only have two more questions for you Pope Clement,' Gabriel spoke sternly. 'Do you believe that the people of France should see justice and that God is watching them?'

'Oui! Yes. Oh yes I do.'

'Then we agree,' Gabriel said as he stood and placed the chair back where he had found it. 'The people of France must believe.'

'Oui!'

Gabriel placed his hand over the mouth of the bedridden man and pinched his nose. The Pope struggled, but was to weak to remove the angelic hand that had taken his breath and was taking his life. His limb fell limp and the Pope died as Jacques de Molay had said he would. Gabriel quickly checked the bedchamber and removed from his pocket a tiny tanned leather bound copy of the Rule of the Templar, similar to the one he had given Molay seven years earlier. With its iron clasp locked, he neatly placed it on the bedside cabinet. Unlocking the door, Gabriel left by his means of entrance.

History recorded that the one hundred and ninety sixth pontiff, Pope Clement V died of ill health. A curiosity for academics was the fact that the Rule of the Templar was found by his bedside.

***

Fontainebleau – France – Late Morning – 29th November AD 1314

Royal hunts are always a prestigious affair. The colours of the banners of the King's entourage were clearly seen across the French autumn fields around the town that Philippe le Bel was born forty-six years earlier. The sturdy and well-groomed horses carried the huntsmen as the kestrels cut through the chilled sky; no manner of creature with flight or without was safe that day. In the nearby woodland, the wild boar ran from the hunt through ditch and bush desperately trying to find somewhere hide. Philippe, an accomplished rider, sped ahead of the pack, reins in his left hand and crossbow in his right, turning and weaving his way through the trees; old even when his was a boy. The hunt was on. The boar had been spotted, dark brown with patches of black, one of its tusks broken. The King would easily be able to identify his quarry.

The boar darted across an open stretch of field and through a high hedgerow. Philippe followed, his horse nervous on the approach, but managed to climb into the air, clearing the thorns with ease. However, unseen, on the other side was a ditch, and the royal horse stumbled, throwing the King of France to the ground.

Gabriel was stood near a tree and watched as the king struggled, his leg in severe pain. Philippe noticed Gabriel watching him.

'Vous!' he called.

'Me?' replied Gabriel.

'Come here and help your King.'

'You are not my king,' the angelic answered. 'You formally condemn a man of God. You only seek power.'

'I condemn no man!' Philippe barked. 'Now, help your *King*!'

Gabriel stepped closer as the regal garments became dirtier in the mud. He picked up the crossbow and checked that it was still armed.

'Pope Clement V is dead,' Gabriel said.

'He was weak,' the Philippe claimed.

'You placed, Guillaume de Nogaret, an excommunicated man, in charge of your investigation. You ordered the torture of the Knights Templar.'

'Who speaks to his king this way?' Philippe asked.

'*You are not my king*,' Gabriel replied raising his voice and the crossbow to his shoulder. 'I am Archangel Gabriel.'

'I am the King of France!' Philippe demanded.

'What is a king without a kingdom?' Gabriel inquired as he took aim.

His finger pulled the trigger and the twine snapped taut. The goose feathered flights kept the bolt on its true course as the iron tip entered the king beneath his chin, entering his skull, killing him instantly. Gabriel then dropped the crossbow where he had found it and left. He had no need to look back. His promise had been kept.

History recorded that Philippe Le Bel, King Philip IV of France died in a hunting accident.

In ancient times, was it not the angels that were the bearers of bad news? Gabriel was a soldier of God; now he was a Watcher, but before then, all he knew was death. Archangel Michael's punishment had the reverse effect. It had opened Gabriel's eyes.

XLIII

The First Realm.

London – 03.00hrs Sunday 22nd July AD 2001 GMT

Agent Richard Lawton I was cold. It was dark, wherever he was. He was also naked and that un-nerved him. He slowly moved his arms until they touched the sides of the steel casket that he was entombed.

'I'm buried alive,' he said to himself, his throat sore.

Above his head, a door opened and the tray he was lying on slid from his tomb. I stood beside him. I tried to focus, but I's grinning face was too close. Every second or two I kept glancing up, as though to see if anyone was coming.

'Richard!' he mumbled. 'Are you okay? I was right. You're alive!'

'What?'

'Why's your foot bleeding?' I asked a little confused.

'What?'

'Do you know who I am?'

'What?'

'Let's get him out of here so he can rest,' whispered a female voice.

***

Scotland – 11.50hrs Tuesday 24th July AD 2001 GMT

Cole's ears alerted him to the familiar drone of a helicopter engine behind him. He opened his eyes. He was seated between Aston and another Templar that he didn't recognise. Still dazed, he leant forward and peered over the pilot's shoulder, but his seat belt restricted his movement. The motion also made him light headed. The varying shades of green passed beneath lined with all manner of trees as the mechanical bird followed the contours of the landscape. In the distance Cole could see a city and two large rock outcrops to its right. The landscape didn't look English.

'Where are we?' he managed to ask, his throat still sore for some reason.

'Scotland!' the pilot shouted.

Aston pointed to the city ahead; the castle clearly visible perched on top of a rocky outcrop in the centre of his field of vision. 'That's Edinburgh!' Aston replied, his finger dropped to a corrugated iron and scaffolding structure in a walled enclosure on the side of a steep valley in the foreground. 'We're going there, to Rosslyn! But we have to land at the airport first!'

'That hunk of iron?' Cole questioned as he sat back in the seat; rested his head and waited for the pilot to land and the noise to stop.

***

Within twenty-five minutes, Cole arrived in the quiet Chapel Lane leading towards Rosslyn Chapel. Peering between the driver and passenger in front he could see the straight tarmac lane lined with hedges leading to the Old Rosslyn Inn, the four hundred year old building now painted in an eerie pale orange wash. Poking up behind its tiled roof was the west wall of the chapel, capped with a corrugated iron roof.

Eight miles south of the city of Edinburgh was the land of the Templar of old. Unbeknown to Cole, he had entered the last piece of history of the Order, the history that had begun with Hugues de Payens, the first Grand Master, who married Katherine St. Clair and ended with the Templar going underground to avoid persecution. The story had continued even after the dissolving of the Order in AD 1312. Nearby, was the village of Temple and the ruined eight hundred years old church of the Order.

The tiny parking area by the chapel wall was full as was the car park next to the Inn and so the driver pulled up next to the small green door in the wall next to the gift shop.

'Are you ok to move?' Aston asked unclipping the seat belts.

'It's a bit late now,' Cole sarcastically replied. 'Couldn't you get an air ambulance and land in the field here?'

'The doctors said you were well enough to travel. We suited you up and brought you here. Thought it best you show your face.'

'Why? How long have I been out?'

'What's the last thing you remember?'

'Aston, that's not as easy a question as you might think, but I'll say Abbadon stuck a sword in my gut.'

'It's Tuesday! Five days to be precise. We're here to pay our respects.'

Cole understood and nodded so. 'Five days? Has Rebecca been informed? I need to tell her…'

'Rebecca's been informed.' Aston climbed out followed by a delicate Cole. 'All in good time Richard. We have a service to attend.'

On the gravel by the parked cars stood four Templar in dark suits. They were also there for the funeral, but their appearance and build gave the impression of bodyguards for a VIP than men in mourning. One of them offered a hand to the American.

'Watch your head!' he said. 'It's a low door.'

Cole steadied his walk and entered the shade of the trees that lined the north wall of the enclosure of the chapel. He felt an energy that he could not explain. What made Rosslyn Chapel so special?

It was a beautiful sunny day and all the mourners present welcomed the shade of the trees around the perimeter wall. As the members of the Order gathered in groups on the short bright green grass around the tree trunks and benches, they nattered and greeted old friends and family that they had not seen in years. Cole recognised many of their faces. Aston motioned that he would be back in a moment as he left Cole with the unknown Templar to greet several acquaintances he had not seen in a while. Cole watched and realised that all funerals were the same; sometimes it was the only time in years you get to meet distant relatives. So many to say hello to and not enough time to catch up; Cole had been there before as everyone had.

He carefully sat down on the nearest bench and surveyed the chapel. Even with the concrete blocks that were piled up around the bases of each steel pylon that supported the metal roof, the agent could see the beauty of the carved stone.

Sir William's namesake, Sir William St Clair, third and the last St Clair of Orkney, founded the chapel in AD 1446. The original plan was in the form of a cross, unfortunately, after forty years of construction Sir William St. Clair died and he was buried within the unfinished structure. Still, what Cole saw before him gave him a sense of awe.

The metal roof that had caught Cole's eye as they had approached from the air was there to protect the stone-carved roof. Carved stone is what the chapel was. Every square foot of the chapel, inside and out was fascinatingly carved with images that related to Christianity, pagan religion, the Templar, Jerusalem and so much more.

'Hello,' came the only American voice in the crowd breaking Cole's concentration. 'It's nice to see you.'

Cole spun around, then stopped in pain. 'Naomi!' He was pleased to see her. 'How are you?'

'Better than you,' she offered a hand of support.

'That would be appreciated,' Cole replied turning to the Templar. 'No offence!'

'None taken, I'd rather have a pretty girl by my side than me,' the knight answered with a grin and a nod. 'If you need me, just holler.'

The quiet Templar left his side; his duties fulfilled. The two Americans then began to slowly walk anti-clockwise around the chapel admiring the ornately carved stonework, left alone by the rest of the crowd in black.

Beneath the west wall of the chapel lay eleven coffins in a row, each draped with the countries flag of the occupant; three crosses of St. Andrew, one Welsh Dragon, one French and seven crosses of St. George. In the centre of each lay the small shoulder shield that many of the Templar wore into battle with their family coat of arms engraved and painted on them. On the grass were rows of wooden collapsible chairs facing the draped flags and slowly, one by one, they were filled by the mourners.

'Look at them!' Cole stopped. 'Two Americans in a crowd of English! Aren't we out of place?'

'English, French, Portuguese, Welsh and Scottish,' Naomi replied as her eyes covered each person of nationality. 'Sir William was well respected. It's a big family.'

'I liked him,' the agent admitted. 'Honesty, I like that in anyone.' They continued to walk arm in arm. 'So tell me; French, Portuguese, Welsh? You've been doing the rounds.'

'I got here a couple of days ago. You know, trying to get a feel for the people. I've met quite a lot of them. They're nice. The hotel's nice too. We're in the Royal.'

'I'm in the Royal?'

'Yes,' Naomi replied. 'There is one other thing – some of the family members don't know about the Order, so don't mention it!'

'Ok, I wouldn't want to put my foot in it,' Cole said.

'And what did you do to your foot?'

'You know, I can't remember everything, just bits and pieces,' Cole came clean. 'It'll come back to me.' On the south side of the chapel Cole spotted a domestic rabbit free and eating by the wall. 'So you've been milling around and getting to know the people… when are you planning to return to the States?'

Naomi cleared her throat. 'I'm not. I have thought about it and I've decided to stay. There's nothing for me back there.'

'What about your family?'

Naomi's dark eyes glared at Cole. '*My* family are dead!'

'I'm sorry, I meant uncles and aunts.'

'No uncles or aunts. My grandparents are also dead. The Order has arranged to sell the house and transfer the funds here. I'm bloodline. This is the only family I have now. Same as you!'

'Oh no!' Cole sharply responded, stopping by the low wall that over looked the forest filled valley below. 'I have a wife and a baby on the way.'

Naomi watched her feet shuffle the pebbles in the gravel. 'They haven't told you then?'

'Haven't told me what?'

Her eyes didn't look up. 'Richard, you died!'

'I'm aware of that. I didn't know it was common knowledge? I died; I was revived. So?'

'After three days.'

'*Three days*!' Cole gasped glancing north and west checking that no one had noticed his outburst. 'You're fucking kidding? That's impossible!'

'Garrett was going to fly over to identify your body, but DNA was taken to compare with your NSA file and Rebecca was informed; she wasn't fit to travel.'

'Aston said she was informed. He just didn't clarify… So Rebecca was told I died? Then how come I'm still here?' he raised his voice in frustration.

A couple of the mourners near the grave of an old St. Clair looked in his direction, but turned back to their conversations. Cole lowered his head.

'How come I'm still…' the dead man remembered something. 'Lilith said… resurrection.'

The two stood motionless for a moment until Cole received a sharp slap on his shoulder, which made him jump.

'How's the second Messiah?' Troy jested from behind. 'If the rest of the world knew about you, we'd have another national holiday. Maybe I'll tell 'em!'

Cole brushed Troy's hand off his jacket in disgust. 'I wish you would. At least my wife would know.'

'Can't do that; sorry. I take it you have a long story to tell?'

'I died! I came back!' Cole replied hoping Troy would leave.

'That's the short version!'

'Troy, not now,' Naomi intervened. 'This is not the time or place.'

'Sorry, but Lucy wouldn't want me to be sad at her funeral.'

'Lucy?' Cole queried.

'Yeah, Lucy. You met her.'

'Yeah I did. She wanted me to say that she's ok. She said sorry,' Cole said.

Troy was thoughtful. 'Forte est vinum. Fortior est rex. Fortiores sunt mulieres.' He watched Cole's astonishment. 'Yes, it's Latin.' Then he quietly returned to the mingling groups in black.

The vicar appeared from the tiny southern door as Naomi followed Cole around to the entrance of the enclosure. The two of them could hear the vicar begin his sermon once everyone was seated.

'Are you going to join them?' Naomi asked.

'You go,' Cole urged. 'I'll be along in a minute.'

Naomi joined the mourners on the back row of seats as Cole watched from the bench that he sat on when he first arrived. Over the sound of the vicar's sermon the summer air was filled with birdsong. The American's eyes followed the stone slab path from the gift shop to the chapel entrance. He stared at the north wall and the intricate carvings and noticed the angels that protruded from the stonework. Each looked out in a different direction as though covering every possible angle of approach. It was as though they were guarding the chapel. He had heard of this place. Rebecca had mentioned it in her studies. The most amazing carvings lay within, but this wasn't the time to sightsee. He felt out of place, so he left.

***

Bar stools must have a wire mechanism built in, thought Cole. As he sat down, like a trigger, the barman Chris appeared smartly dressed in his grey shirt and black pressed trousers.

'What can I get you?' he asked in a strong Scottish accent that Cole took a moment to work out what he had just said.

Cole checked his pockets. 'I don't have any money.'

'From the way your dressed; I take it you're with the service,' he motioned through the bay windows in the direction of the chapel. 'It's paid for.'

Cole understood the motion, but couldn't understand the words that came from Chris' mouth. He had heard stories that the further north you travel; the harder it is to understand the locals. He guessed it was true.

The American smiled. 'A bottle of Beck's please,' he instinctively replied. 'And can I keep the bottle cap?'

'The cap?' Chris inquired. 'You can't take the bottle out of the pub!'

'No, it's a habit! I want to drink the beer.'

'I can think of worse,' he placed the cool green bottle next to the cap on the bar. 'Did you know them?'

Cole paused. 'Yes… I knew all of them.'

'A sad thing; a mighty sad thing,' Chris replied. 'You would think holidays were to be enjoyed and then you have a coach accident.'

Cole realised that the Templar had produced a cover story as he sipped his beer. The slender built barman left the foreigner to his drink and approached a local that was seated nearby.

'Gary you'll have to make that the last one mate,' Chris apologised. 'We've got a private function today.'

'Nor problem,' he replied finishing his drink and lighting a cigarette. 'I'll be out of here in a mo…'

Gary followed Chris out of the bar leaving Cole all alone except for Geronimo, a large solitary and ugly looking fish, motionless in the tank by the door. It looked dead, or at least old.

'I'm sorry we have a private function today,' spoke a gentle female voice.

Cole turned and viewed a very slender blonde girl in black trousers, flat shoes and a white skin tight t-shirt with her hair in a ponytail, standing at the door.

'Iinnad?' he inquired.

'I'm sorry,' she turned round to face Cole. 'What did you say?'

Cole raised a hand to apologise. 'I thought you were some one I knew, but I do know him,' Cole pointed at Aston. The waitress' smile let him pass.

'You're a part of this Richard,' Aston stated.

'I don't feel it.'

'I… was going to tell you,' Aston spoke slowly, then waved the barman away as he sat down. 'But I thought I'd wait until you were a little more clear headed.'

'Too late!' Cole raised his beer.

'Gabriel told us what to do, but we had already radioed C&C and informed the authorities of your… you know?'

'Now what?'

'You can't go back!'

'What do you mean? Of course I can go back!'

'Richard! You're…' Aston lowered his voice. 'Richard you're dead.'

'Damn, I feel fine; a little back pain; foot hurts like hell, but a part from that...'

'As for as the rest of the world is concerned, Richard Lawton Cole died last week. Rebecca gets the insurance policy, you get honoured at work, but you can't go back. If you did, how would you explain what happened to you?'

'One! I don't care about the rest of the world. Two! Rebecca would rather have me than an insurance policy. Three! I *never* did my job for any honour. I did it because it was the right thing to do.'

Aston smiled.

'Four!' Cole continued. 'Somebody else can explain it. *You* want me to *forget* my wife?' Cole's voice broke. 'Well, I'm sorry I can't do that.' His eyes glazed. '*She is my world.*'

'We make sacrifices.'

'Yeah! Lucy said that.'

'What?'

'Lucy said that I would make a sacrifice and I wouldn't have a choice about it.'

'She was smart; she would've made a good doctor. And you're smart. You realise the complications if your wife found out you were still alive.'

'Yeah! Troy called me the second Messiah.'

'Well… that's Troy. His brain doesn't quite function the way yours or mine does. In fact it doesn't function…'

Both men laughed and Cole wiped his eyes.

'I hate to sound materialistic, but I don't have a job or an income.'

'Technically, I don't either. We'll sort you out with a job,' Aston patted him on the back getting up from his seat.

'In the meantime, could you lend me five pounds?'

'As long as you don't phone the ex-wife.'

'I won't call Rebecca. You have my word.'

Aston delved into his pocket and produced a crumpled fiver and placed it on the bar.

'I keep getting flashes,' Cole explained. 'I wanted to get a notepad and pen to jot things down; hence the money. Thanks.'

'That's okay,' the Templar patted his shoulder. 'I'll see you out there. You're bloodline remember! That makes you a part of all this,' Aston had said his piece.

Cole finished his beer and grabbed the cap and a book of matches from a nearby empty ashtray. As he left the bar he noticed the pretty blonde in the reception area.

'Iinn…' Cole paused his finger raised.

'Amy,' she replied.

'Amy I was wondering if… there was a post office in the town?'

'Yes,' she smiled. 'Out of the hotel, turn left,' she motioned with her hand. 'Follow the road round and up the main street. It's on this side, painted blue. You can't miss it.'

'Thank you.'

The American left the hotel and watched Aston head back down Chapel Lane. Following Amy's instructions Cole found the post office.

It was late and the post office counter was closed. In the stationary section Cole managed to buy an envelope and a couple of stamps to the USA. He complained of pain in his hand and was unable to write the address. The elderly man behind the till was happy to oblige; writing Cole's home address on the envelope and sealing the bottle top and the book of matches inside with some tape.

'Is that it?' he asked curiously.

'That's it!'

The stamp sealed the message and the American happily paid for it almost forgetting the notepad and pen before leaving the shop. Directly outside the shop door was a red cast iron letterbox situated on the curb. The American posted his message and patted the curved red surface with the palm of his hand. Slowly, he headed back to the chapel.

As he approached the grounds he could hear the vicar finishing his sermon.

'But if they obey not, they shall perish by the sword, and they shall die without knowledge. Book of Job 36:12.'

***

Along with all the mourners Cole paid his respects. As he touched each coffin, he said goodbye and wished them a good journey; naming each of them to the surprise of everyone present. Aston knew that Cole had not met the backup team or the snipers, but his curiosity would wait. Naomi had joined him.

'It looks like I'm staying too,' he told her.

'I'm sorry, but it's good! I didn't want to be the only American here.'

Aston joined them after over-hearing their exchange.

'Well Aston, it looks like you've got me,' Cole admitted defeated.

'Glad to here it. I am sorry Richard, but it's for the best.'

'What happened to Iinnad?'

'Nobody has seen her,' Aston replied. 'I know Troy misses her.'

'That's because she's female and got legs,' Naomi piped up.

'So have you,' Cole grinned.

'Don't remind me!'

'And Gabriel?' Cole added.

'He felt bad about what happened,' Naomi explained. 'Personally I think it is more embarrassment than anything else. I was reading up on Gabriel. Did you know that all those that have met him have died?'

'So where is he, because I really need to talk to him?'

'That's brave,' Naomi gently nudged. 'Paris! I think!'

***

Paris – France – 17.56hrs Tuesday 24th July AD 2001 GMT+1

Punished by the Council and abandoned by Heaven; Gabriel was alone. He was Guardian of a Realm that he would not conquer, of a people he would not rule. He could only watch. The angelic rested on a bench opposite the Notre Dame and stared at the cobbled square in front of him. Seven centuries ago, the River Seine was full of little islands, now there were three.

Gabriel then began to stroll down the south side of what was now, the Ile de Paris. He passed the Palais de Justice and on the opposite side of the square where the Pont Neuf crossed the island, he descended the steps into the shadows of the trees. At the base of the steps he turned around and faced the stone of the bridge. There, about two metres off the ground, was a brass plaque. He read the words.

'A cet endroit
Jacques de Molay
Dernier Grand Maître De l'Ordre Du Temple
a été brûle le 18 Mars 1314'

***

As the night approached, the Archangel found himself wandering the cobbled side streets, heading in a north-easterly direction. Realising how close he actually was, Gabriel headed straight for the site that was once the headquarters of Apolyon Incorporated. Now it was a pile of black smouldering rubble. It had been days since the fire, but the ashes deep within, still smouldered. Gabriel stood amongst the ash of the ruined building; the smell of charcoal filled his nostrils. He was beyond the police line, but there was no one present to send him on his way. Below lay the sealed chamber of Abbadon's office with the pages of the Codex. What would become of them now?

The memory of Iinnad's voice was clear in his head. 'Why did you bring a primitive on board? He was the target? I thought it was the book! I thought it was the book!'

Gabriel shook his head. 'I hear you, Iinnad. I am sorry it has taken me 10,000 years. Now, I understand.'

On the distant hill overlooking Paris, the outcast Archangel Gabriel stood and glared at the remaining embers, knowing that within the ashes were the words that could tell him of his fate. He stood there for what appeared an age, until the sunrise…

Here endeth Book I of The 21st Codex Trilogy –
'The First Realm'.

I

Rome – 15.01hrs – Tuesday 11th September AD 2001 GMT +1.

A kilometre outside the city limits to the north of the capital of Italy was a quaint farmhouse that had been converted into a hotel. Seated at the tables on the patio beneath the shading vine was Troy bellowing in laughter at his own joke. Aston wasn't amused, but he could not stop the others from encouraging the leader of Blue Team from his wild and crude comments. Luckily for all concerned, the wife of the landlord, who was presently serving them, did not speak English, since the joke was about her.

Bleep! Bleep! Bleep!

Troy's pager instantly stopped his laughter.

Bleep! Bleep! Bleep!

Aston unclipped his from his belt. Troy had already done the same. He jumped to his feet, his chair flying across the terracotta tiles.

'We're good to go!' he snapped as all the Templar pagers began to ring. 'Let's do this!' Troy then removed a small remote control from his pocket, switched it on and pressed the red button in the centre of the black pad. There was a low audio bleep. He turned to Aston. 'We'll be ready for you. Good luck.'

'Let's suit up people!' Aston ordered, a little pensive. 'We've a long day ahead of us, so keep focused.'

'Blue Team on me!' Troy barked, leaving the patio. '*Aston!*'

'See you on the battlefield,' Aston replied.

Troy stopped. Then turning to his colleague, he smiled. 'See you on the battlefield, my friend.'

***

KT Castle – 14.14hrs Tuesday 11th September AD 2001 GMT

'Control, this is Aston!' the speaker awoke. 'Red Team have entered the zone. Now moving in for a pizza.'

'Control, Blue Team here! Objective achieved,' Troy's voice was perfectly clear. 'Whatever that distraction was, it really worked!'

One by one the news channels changed to video links with Templar on the ground. As each screen changed, Cole's eyes moved to the next image of the horror in New York. He couldn't take his eyes away from the flickering pictures of the dust cloud. When the last of the images from New York disappeared, Cole spun around to Sir Geoffrey.

'Put it back on!' he demanded.

'Right now Mr Cole, it's not our priority!'

'What d'you mean? Not a priority! People are dying!' Cole screamed. 'They're jumping out of the fucking buildings!' The American was panting. 'Don't tell me it's not a priority!'

'Sue,' Sir Geoffrey calmly called to one of the translators. 'Give Mr Cole a monitor so he can watch the death on television.'

'Forget it! I'll watch it in the rec-room.'

As Cole stormed out, Sir Geoffrey addressed the rest of C&C. 'Ladies and gentlemen we have operation to complete!'

***

to be continued…..

The 21st Codex Trilogy – Book II

Between Heaven and Hell

Printed in Great Britain
by Amazon

44762762R00401